MW00752541

LARTEN

THE SAGA OF LARTEN CREPSLEY

OCEAN OF BLOOD

DARREN SHAN

LITTLE, BROWN AND COMPANY

New York   Boston

Little, Brown and Company

Hachette Book Group
237 Park Avenue, New York, NY 10017
Visit our website at www.lb-teens.com

Little, Brown and Company is a division of Hachette Book Group, Inc.
The Little, Brown name and logo are trademarks of Hachette Book Group, Inc.

The publisher is not responsible for websites (or their content) that are not owned by the publisher.

First U.S. Edition: April 2011
Simultaneously published in Great Britain by Collins in 2011

The characters and events portrayed in this book are fictitious. Any similarity to real persons, living or dead, is coincidental and not intended by the author.

Library of Congress Cataloging-in-Publication Data

Shan, Darren.
  Ocean of blood / by Darren Shan. — 1st U.S. ed.
    p. cm. — (The saga of Larten Crepsley ; 2)
  Prequel to Cirque Du Freak series.
  Summary: As young vampires, Larten Crepsley and his blood brother Wester travel widely, trying to experience fully the violent, hedonistic pleasures of the human world before fully committing to the vampire life.
  ISBN 978-0-316-07866-5
  [1. Vampires—Fiction. 2. Horror stories.] —I. Title.
  PZ7.S52823Oc 2011
  [Fic]—dc22

2010043180

10 9 8 7 6 5 4 3 2 1

RRD-C

Printed in the United States of America

ALSO BY
DARREN SHAN

The Thin Executioner

THE DEMONATA SERIES
Lord Loss
Demon Thief
Slawter
Bec
Blood Beast
Demon Apocalypse
Wolf Island
Dark Calling
Hell's Heroes

THE CIRQUE DU FREAK SERIES
A Living Nightmare
The Vampire's Assistant
Tunnels of Blood
Vampire Mountain
Trials of Death
The Vampire Prince
Hunters of the Dusk
Allies of the Night
Killers of the Dawn
The Lake of Souls
Lord of the Shadows
Sons of Destiny

Part One

*"A howling, hungry creature
of dark delights."*

Chapter One

The vampire known as Quicksilver threw a knife high
into the smoke-clogged air of the tavern. Those around
him watched with beady-eyed, bloodthirsty fascina-
tion as he held his head back, opened his mouth wide
and waited for the knife to drop. A few people shrieked
but Quicksilver didn't flinch, expertly tracking the
flight of the dagger. At precisely the right moment he
clenched his teeth together and caught the blade two
inches past the tip. As the handle quivered, he turned
slowly, so that everyone in the room could see. Pulling
out the knife, he threw it into the wood of the table – it
drove in all the way to the hilt – and took a bow.

As the crowd went wild with applause, Quicksilver

grinned and slumped into a chair close to another vampire and a gaggle of admiring young ladies.

"There," he beamed. "I told you I could do it."

"One of these nights," the other bloodsucker said, "you'll time that wrong and end up with a knife through the back of your throat."

"Don't be such an old woman, Wester," Quicksilver laughed. "You'll scare these lovely creatures and I would hate to send them to bed with nightmares."

"It will take more than your dull tales to scare *us*," one of the ladies snorted, but they were undeniably impressed.

"What's your real name?" another lady asked, cuddling up to the man with the odd orange hair, immaculate gray suit and dazzling smile.

"I only reveal that to my *very* special friends," Quicksilver murmured. Then, as she blushed, he whispered in her ear, "Larten Crepsley." After that he called for more wine and the rest of the night passed most pleasantly.

A groggy Wester rose before Larten and stumbled to the window of the inn where they had bedded for the day. He peered through the curtains at the sunlight, hissed and let them swish shut. It would be another couple of hours before they could go out. The sun wouldn't kill the vampires instantly, but they'd start to redden within minutes and would be in agony in less than an hour. If they were exposed to its rays for two or three hours, there would be nothing left of them except for charred bones.

Wester washed in a basin of water and studied his beard in the mirror above it. Shaving was a complicated business for vampires. Normal razors were useless on their tough hair. He and Larten had picked up specially hardened blades a couple of years ago, but Wester had lost his in the course of their travels. He'd asked to borrow Larten's, but the slightly older vampire had said it was time Wester learned to take better care of his possessions. Larten had just been teasing him, but Wester didn't want to give his friend the satisfaction of seeing him plead, so he'd grown a beard since then.

"My head," Larten groaned, sitting up, then flopping back again. "What time is it?"

"Too early to be getting up," Wester grunted.

"How much did we drink last night?"

"I don't want to think about it."

Vampires could consume a lot more alcohol than humans and it was difficult for them to get drunk.

But Wester and Larten had been managing to defy the physical odds most nights.

"They were nice ladies," Larten chuckled. "They loved my knife trick."

"You should try it at the Cirque Du Freak," Wester said drily. "It would go over well there."

The pair had bumped into their old ally, Mr. Tall, a while ago. They'd spent a fun few nights with the circus crew and Larten had performed some of his old magic routines in the show. He had been rusty to begin with, but adjusted swiftly. He had an incredibly fast hand, even for a vampire. It was how he'd earned his nickname—one of their friends had once said his fingers moved as if made of quicksilver.

Larten and Wester had been traveling the world for almost twenty years since their first time at Council. Both had learned a lot, not just about the ways of vampires, but about ladies too. Larten had been a slow starter but was making up for lost time, dazzling maidens with his smile, confidence and agility wherever he went.

The pair occasionally met with their master, Seba Nile, but spent most of the time by themselves or with others their age, vampires in their thirties, forties, fifties or sixties. They were youths by vampire standards and had been cut loose by their masters to explore the world of humans one final time before pledging themselves to the demands of the clan.

The door to their room crashed open. Wester whirled defensively, then relaxed as a large vampire with long blond hair staggered in. It was Yebba. He had been traveling with them for the past month, though it had been a few nights since they'd last seen him.

"I'm thirsty," Yebba roared, kicking Larten's bed. "Up, cur, and come keep me company."

"Wester says the sun hasn't set yet," Larten yawned.

"I don't give a damn," the massive vampire said, then collapsed like a bear and sat on the floor, blinking dumbly.

"A heavy night's drinking?" Wester smiled.

"Aye," Yebba said morosely. "A woman broke my heart. What else could I do but drown my sorrows in ale?"

"Another broken heart?" Wester tsked. "That must be the fourth this year."

"Aye." Tears welled in Yebba's eyes. "Vampires weren't made for love."

"What happened this time?" Wester asked slyly. "Did you bite her?"

"That only happened once," Yebba scowled. "And it was an accident."

"It has happened to us all," Larten said, propping himself on an elbow.

"I don't remember you biting any of your lady friends," Wester frowned.

"No, but there was one time..." He coughed and blushed. "Never mind."

"Tell us," Wester hooted. "Come on, *Quicksilver,* you can't leave Yebba to bare his soul alone."

"Well, do you recall a night a couple of years ago when I didn't return to our inn?"

"That happens at least once a month," Wester said.

"This was different," Larten snapped. "I'd been out with a lady and drank more than was good for me. I felt hungry on the way home, so I popped into a room to feed. But I made too much noise and woke the woman up. She screamed bloody murder and I tumbled out of her room without silencing her."

"Why didn't you breathe on her and knock her out?" Wester asked.

Larten shrugged. "I was drunk. I forgot about my vampiric breath. Before I knew it, a mob had formed and I was chased out of town. I was almost trapped in the open and burned alive."

When Wester and Yebba had stopped laughing, Yebba said, "Why didn't you flit? They couldn't have troubled you once you hit top speed and vanished from sight."

Larten's blush deepened and Wester had to answer for him. "He can't flit when he's drunk—he loses his sense of coordination and can't run that fast."

The pair fell apart with laughter. Larten sniffed angrily, but his lips were twitching at the corners. Eventually he burst out laughing too. When their fit had passed, Wester trudged down to order food and ale, then the three of them waited for the sun to set, so that they could again seek excitement in the inns, taverns and gaming halls of the humans they had once been.

Chapter Two

After a few drinks downstairs, the three young vampires went in search of whatever pleasures they could find. They were adept at sniffing out all of the hidden delights of a town.

The trio gained admittance to a boxing match that they enjoyed greatly, wagering heavily on the outcome. Vampires usually didn't bother with money, but Cubs often stole from sleeping humans when they fed. Superstitious people thought that vampires were fanged beasts who ripped open the throats of their targets. In reality they normally slipped into a bedroom, made a small cut on the arm or leg of a sleeping human, drank just enough blood to sate their hunger, then used their spit to close the wound.

Larten studied the scars on his fingertips during a rest between rounds. He had been blooded the traditional way. Seba sliced the tips of Larten's fingers with his hard, sharp nails, then cut his own and pumped blood into his assistant. Larten was proud of the scars, though sometimes when he studied them he felt a stab of guilt. They reminded him of Seba and he wondered what his master would think of his student's recent behavior.

Larten and Seba had parted on bad terms, but had made their peace since then. Larten worried that by gambling, drinking and stealing, he and Wester were soiling their master's good name. Wester often had to remind him (especially when Larten had too much to drink and was in a maudlin mood) that Seba had told them to work their human interests out of their system. There were lots of other vampires going through the same thing. They were called Cubs by the older members of the clan.

The fight recommenced and the burly men closed in on one another. Larten looked up from his fingers and focused on the boxers. This was the thirty-second round, and it had been a long time since he'd seen so engaging a battle. He cheered on the stout-hearted warriors as they clashed, weary and unsteady on their feet, but determined to keep going.

The flesh of their bare fists had been torn to pieces and blood splattered every time one of them landed a blow. The ruby-red drops made Larten's mouth water – Wester and Yebba were staring hungrily too – and he had to warn himself to stay by the side, not dart forward and latch on to the delicious wounds.

All around, men were betting and roaring encouragement or abuse. They all had the same greedy, heated look in their eyes.

"My one's winning," Yebba whooped as one of the brutes landed a blow.

"You didn't bet on him," Wester retorted. "You bet on the other one."

"Did not!" Yebba shouted.

"Yes you did. He has that mark on his left arm, remember?"

Yebba squinted at the boxers, then cursed. "These humans all look the same to me," he growled. Larten and Wester laughed and passed the disgruntled vampire another mug of ale—that was guaranteed to settle him down.

After the fight, Larten and Wester collected their

winnings and took Yebba to a tavern where they found ladies to dance with. Small towns lacked the dance halls of big cities, but you could always sort out something if you splashed enough money around. They joined a card game later. All three were drunk and they lost heavily, even Larten, who rarely tasted defeat at the gambling tables. But they didn't mind. Money was easy to come by if you were a creature of the night.

Larten wanted to do his knife-catching trick again, but Wester wouldn't let him. He took his friend's knife away and held it out of reach as Larten tried to snatch it back. If they had been sober, Wester couldn't have kept it from the faster, stronger vampire. But Larten was woozy and helpless. Wester had a knack for knowing when Larten was going to drink more than he could handle, and he stayed relatively clear-headed on those nights so that he could keep an eye on his reckless friend.

"Ish not fair," Larten complained to a man with a monocle. "I'm Qui-*hic*! I'm Quick-*hic*!" He gulped ale until the hiccups went away. "I'm Quicksilver," he growled majestically.

"Aye?" the man said, passing Larten a pinch of snuff. "I'm in the leather trade myself."

"Not my bizzzness," Larten slurred. "Ish my...
ish my..." He pulled a face and forgot what he was
trying to say, then fell facedown on the table and
knew no more until morning.

Larten awoke to savage pain. He was outside in the
sun and his skin was a nasty shade of red. As he
blinked sleep from his eyes and tried to raise a hand
to protect his face from the rays, he found that his
arms were tied behind his back and he was hanging
upside down. His shirt has been ripped away, expos-
ing his torso, which had been burned as deeply as his
face.

Fear flared in his heart, but he thrust it from his
thoughts. He didn't know what was going on – perhaps
he had been caught feeding drunkenly – but that
didn't matter. He had to escape quickly or he would
burn like a pig on a spit.

Larten set to work on the knots around his wrists.
He was hanging from a thick length of rope, swinging and turning in a soft breeze, but he ignored that
and kept as still as possible, except for his fingers,
which danced over the knots. The long, hardened
nails of the vampires were invaluable when it came to
picking knots and locks, but Larten would have been

13

able to make short work of these regardless. He had learned well from Merletta all those years ago.

Once his hands were free, he wriggled loose of the ropes binding his arms and chest. Bending upwards, he grabbed the supporting rope with one hand, tore apart the ropes around his legs with the other, hung in the air a moment, then dropped to his feet and landed in a crouch. His first instinct was to dart for the safety of the shadows, but he forced himself to scan the doorways of the sheds around him – he was in a courtyard – looking for the enemies who had strung him up.

For long, anxious seconds, Larten searched for his foes and readied himself for battle. Then he caught a scent and his nose crinkled with disgust. He rose and brushed dirt from his trousers. He dug out his watch and checked the time – it was for show, as Seba had taught him to read the time based on the position of the sun and stars – then coolly glanced at the sky and sniffed.

"My watch has stopped, Tanish," he called. "If it's broken, I'll have the price of a new one out of you."

Laughter greeted this statement and four vampires lurched out of a shed. One was a sheepish-looking Wester Flack. The others were Yebba, Zula Pone and

Tanish Eul, the vampire who had originally given Larten his nickname.

"The same old Quicksilver," Tanish snorted admiringly, then hurried forward to throw a cloak over the head and shoulders of his friend and bundle him into the shadows of the shed, where a barrel of ale was waiting.

Chapter Three

Tanish Eul was tall and thin, with a stunning smile and carefully groomed hair and nails. He was always stylishly dressed, and spoke in the smooth tones of a silver-tongued rogue. If Larten was a Romeo, Tanish was a full-blown Casanova—his success with the ladies was legendary.

Zula Pone, on the other hand, was one of the shortest people Larten had ever met. He was stout and ugly. Many vampires were rough by human standards, their faces laced with scars and patches from old wounds, but they were considered fair among their own. Poor Zula was ugly by any reckoning. Fortunately he didn't care, and even wore shabby clothes and cut his hair crookedly to prove he was immune to what others thought of his looks. Despite this, Zula was a surprise hit with those of the fairer sex. He generally repulsed them to begin with, but after ten minutes in his company virtually any woman found herself won over by his charm.

Tanish had run into Zula a few years ago and instantly recognized a kindred spirit. They'd become fast friends and it wasn't long before Larten and Wester were introduced to the newest member of their rowdy pack.

"You've got fairer skin than a baby," Tanish hooted as Larten rested in the shed and tried not to move—his burned flesh sent needles shooting through him every time he shifted. "You were only up there half an hour. I'd be a mild pink color if it had been me."

"You'll be red with your own blood if you ever try that again," Larten said angrily. "What if I hadn't been able to undo the knots?"

"We were keeping a close watch on you," Wester said. "We would have seen if you were in trouble."

"And left you there to burn!" Zula exploded.

Larten found himself laughing along with the others. It had been a good joke, even though he was the butt of it. Wester was the only one who couldn't see the funny side. He smiled along with the rest of them, but his smile was strained. Larten would be tender for the coming week, his flesh would peel and some of the sores might fester. Wester saw nothing humorous in that.

The vampires drank and chatted for a few hours, telling tall and bawdy tales. Tanish and Zula had been involved in a number of near scrapes as usual and had been run out of the last three towns they'd visited.

"The problem with humans is that they take life too seriously," Tanish sneered. "Admittedly, we burned down a storehouse with a winter's supply of grain in it, so a few children will go hungry this year. So what? It will sort out the strong from the weak. Humans are too attached to their young. The vampaneze have the right idea—humans are only fit for killing."

Tanish winked at Larten as he said that, then looked as innocent as he could when Wester flared up. "That's a horrible thing to say! We were the same as them before we were blooded. They have shorter lives than us and are much weaker. If we kill humans, we disgrace ourselves. The vampaneze are soulless scum who will never find Paradise, and you're a fool if you can't see that."

Wester ranted for another fifteen minutes. His

hatred of the vampaneze had set in him like a disease, and though he spoke little of the matter most of the time, those close to him knew of his true feelings. Seba had tried reasoning with him – just because a vampaneze had killed his family, it didn't mean he should hate all of them – but Wester refused to listen.

Wester's hatred of the breakaway group of night-walkers troubled Larten more than it worried Seba. Their master had seen this dark bent in Wester many decades before and was convinced the young vampire would meet an early end at the hands of one purple-skinned vampaneze or another. But Larten had always hoped that Wester would come to terms with his loss and put his hatred behind him.

Larten had urged his dearest friend to track down Murlough – the one who had slain Wester's family – and kill him. He thought that would finally help Wester to put that dark night behind him. But Wester was reluctant to do that. He had come to hate the entire vampaneze clan. He sometimes swore that he would finish off Murlough only when he was done with the rest of the scum, that he wanted his foe to suffer the same kind of loss that Wester had been forced to endure.

Tanish shrugged when Wester finally lapsed into a fuming silence. "The vampaneze mean nothing to me," he said. "If war breaks out between us, I'll fight them and be glad of the challenge. But as long as the truce is in place, what do they matter?"

"Desmond Tiny would beg to differ," Wester growled. "He said the vampaneze would unite behind a mighty leader one night, that their Lord would lead them into war with us and wipe us from the face of the Earth."

"I've never seen the legendary Mr. Tiny and I don't believe he's as powerful as certain old fools claim," Tanish said dismissively.

"Seba saw him," Larten said softly. "He was at Vampire Mountain when Tiny visited after the vampaneze split from the clan. Seba heard him make his prophecy. *He* takes it seriously."

Desmond Tiny was a being of immense magical power, who had predicted the downfall of the clan at the hands of the vampaneze. Lots of younger vampires thought he was a mythical creature. Larten might have too if his master hadn't told him of the night when Mr. Tiny visited the vampire base. He had seen the fear in Seba's eyes, even all these centuries later.

"When I was blooded," Larten continued, "Seba made me hold on to the Stone of Blood for longer than necessary. He said that the Stone was our only hope of thwarting destiny. Mr. Tiny gave us the Stone to give us hope. Tiny craves chaos. He doesn't want the vampaneze to eliminate us too easily. He'd rather we get dragged into a long war full of suffering and torment."

Larten stared again at the marks on his fingers, remembering the night when he had embraced the Stone of Blood and surrendered himself forever to the rule of the clan.

"I didn't mean to belittle Seba Nile," Tanish said, choosing his words with care. He wasn't close to his own master, but he knew Larten respected Seba. "If he says he saw Desmond Tiny, I believe him and apologize if I offended you."

Larten made light of Tanish's apology, though secretly it made him uneasy. He could feel himself starting to drift away from Tanish and the Cubs. Larten was growing tired of the endless drinking, gambling and womanizing. He wasn't yet ready to turn his back on the human world and its many delights, but he was sure he would return to Seba in a few more years to resume his studies.

He doubted Tanish would abandon the easy life so willingly. Some Cubs ended up rejecting the ways of the clan. They grew attached to human comforts and chose to remain in that soft, safe world. The Generals allowed them their freedom so long as they obeyed certain laws. Larten thought that Tanish would be one of those who never returned to Vampire Mountain, but wandered forever among humans.

"Enough of the damn vampaneze," Zula scowled. "A pox on their purple skin. We have more important matters to discuss."

"Such as?" Larten asked, a twinkle in his eyes, anticipating the answer.

"A war pack has formed." Zula licked his lips and grinned. "They're no more than a night's march from here."

"We thought we'd swing by for you two in case you were interested," Tanish said.

"You thought right," Larten chuckled. "We'll set off at dusk."

"With your skin as red as a lobster's?" Wester asked.

"A minor irritation," Larten said, wincing as he leaned back on his bed of straw.

Without any further discussion he closed his eyes.

The others lay down and also prepared for sleep, though it would be a long time before any of them dozed. They rested in the shade for much of the morning, eyes closed but awake, thinking of the war pack, stomachs rumbling with excitement...and hunger.

Chapter Four

War was the great addiction of humans. Vampires loved to fight and got involved in bloody, brutal challenges all the time. But they had only been involved in a war once, when seventy of their clan broke away to become the vampaneze. Although various vampires had clashed with human forces in the past, they had never engaged in all-out conflict. As an old pun put it, war was not in their blood.

Humans, on the other hand, seemed to be interested in nothing else. Larten had seen much of the globe in the last twenty years. He had explored the continents of Europe, Africa, America and Asia. Wars raged everywhere as men found new, inventive ways to kill even more of their race. It was like a contest, the many tribes of mankind competing to see who could commit the worst atrocities.

Although mature vampires were not drawn to war, the Cubs were fascinated by it. To them it was a spectator sport, the same as boxing or wrestling. Many met at battlefields and cheered on the soldiers, laughed at the innocents trying to escape the crossfire, gambled on who would claim victory.

And of course they fed. By the gods, how they fed!

The war that Larten and his associates traveled to observe that night was a minor skirmish. Scholars might recall it in later decades, but it would not be marked as one of the important battles of its time. No vast chunks of land were at stake. History didn't hang in the balance. There were no real profits to be made. It was just one more clash of men who felt driven to kill each other for reasons only their leaders knew. And sometimes not even their kings and generals could explain why they were fighting. They often went to war simply because they could think of nothing else to do.

The vampires arrived a few hours before dawn. Signs of fighting were everywhere—bloodstained fields, discarded swords and muskets, limbs that had been left to rot, even a few whole bodies. There was a foul stench and the animals and birds of the night were gorging themselves, picking flesh from bones and nibbling on guts, making the most of the unexpected feast.

Tanish studied a field of trampled crops. His sharp eyes picked out the corpse of a child among the broken stalks. The head of a soldier was half-submerged in a rabbit hole. A bare foot was sticking up into the air—the four small toes had been chewed off, leaving only the big toe pointing oddly at the sky. Tanish ran his gaze over the blood and entrails, taking it all in.

Then he laughed.

"These look like an especially vicious lot," Tanish said enthusiastically. "We should have an interesting day."

"You don't think we've missed all the fighting?" Zula asked.

"Not by a long shot," Yebba said. "I smell human fear in the air. That way." He pointed west. "And there." East. "They mean to clash again and they know many more will die when they do."

Although Larten could smell the soldiers, he wasn't able to pinpoint the scent of fear. But Yebba was fifteen years older and had been blooded when he was only thirteen. A vampire's senses improved for most of their first hundred years.

The sharp-nosed Yebba led the way as they homed in on their kin. Vampires were harder to track than humans. If Larten hadn't known there were others present, he probably wouldn't have noted the subtle traces of their smell in the air.

They found the war pack resting beneath a massive, leafy tree. There were eight of them, a couple younger than Larten, the rest the same age as him or older. Tanish was the eldest and immediately acted as if he was the ranking vampire.

"On your feet, you lazy, good-for-nothing Cubs," he snarled, standing just beyond the limbs of the tree, glaring like a General. "Is this any way to behave in front of your betters?"

"You're no better than the pimples on my backside, Tanish," a vampire drawled. Larten recognized him—Jordan Egin, one of three in the pack that he'd met before.

Jordan rose, slouched towards Tanish, sneered in his face, then laughed and hugged him hard. "Good to see you again, old friend."

"And you," Tanish beamed. "You'll remember these two."

"Larten and Wester," Jordan nodded. "We feasted heartily last time, aye?"

The pair chuckled at the memory, although Wester looked somewhat ashamed. He had overindulged on that occasion and been violently sick afterwards.

"These are Yebba and Zula Pone," Tanish said. "Yebba has a nose like a hound and Zula is a villain of the highest order. You'll get along well."

The vampires shook hands, then moved forward to greet the rest of the pack. It wasn't long before they were guzzling ale and swapping tales of their adventures.

War packs were a relatively new phenomenon. Vampires had tended to stay out of the way of warring humans in the past, not drawing attention to themselves. But there were so many wars being fought now, on such a massive scale, that the night-walkers could mingle freely with human troops in most places. The Cubs had started frequenting battlefields several decades earlier and now it was a common part of their lives. A lone vampire could nearly always be assured of finding company in a war zone.

Larten listened happily to the stories of Jordan and the others, and told some of his own in return. There was much laughter when Tanish told them of the trick he had played the previous night, and Larten had to take off his jacket and shirt to show his sun-burned back. He had already recovered from the worst of the burning, but his skin was still sore to the touch and a few of the vampires slapped him and hooted when he screeched. He had to knock a couple of heads together before they left him alone, but it was all done in good spirits.

The next bout between the armies wasn't due to start until late in the morning — both sides were waiting for fresh recruits. So the pack turned in when the sun rose and caught some sleep. When they were awakened by the sound of gunfire, they groaned, stretched, took umbrellas from a large sack and set off to find the battle.

Larten had felt foolish the first time he'd stood by a group of soldiers hell-bent on killing one another, sheltered from the sun beneath an umbrella that would have suited a lady far better. But he had grown accustomed to it. He now felt the same way a huntsman must when he pulled on ridiculous-looking clothes before mounting his horse and riding out behind his hounds.

The Cubs found the soldiers massed in a large field. They were fighting hand to hand. Most were armed with swords or knives, which the vampires preferred. They disliked guns for a number of reasons, firstly because the clan frowned on the use of them — guns were the choice of cowards. There was also the fact that guns could be turned against the Cubs. Vampires were tougher than humans and much harder to kill, but a well-placed bullet could account for even the best of them. It was an embarrassing way to die, your brains blown out from a distance.

But mostly the Cubs disapproved of long-range warfare because it was boring. There wasn't much fun in watching humans shoot each other. The delight came in observing them struggle to stay alive. In dirty scraps like this, dozens of duels were being fought, life-or-death dramas that the vampires could follow with ghoulish glee, then turn away from at the end and discuss like a play.

Some of the soldiers noticed the curious men with the umbrellas, but most were too focused on the business of staying alive. If they caught sight of the scarred, pale-skinned figures walking among them, they paused to assess whether or not the strangers posed a threat. When the soldiers saw that the observers meant them no harm, their attention returned to those who did.

The vampires were almost never challenged. Humans who spotted them didn't always know who the spectators were – many had never heard the vampire myths – but they could tell that the guests were not of their own kind. They would watch the wanskinned creatures gliding through their ranks, neatly stepping out of danger's way whenever they got too close to the action. Sometimes the soldiers would cross themselves and mutter prayers. But the majority chose not to confront the spectral visitors and did their best to forget about them if they survived. There were things in the world that most people didn't want to dwell on at any great length.

Larten had a fine time that day. As Tanish had predicted, the armies fought with a vengeance. Whatever they were warring over, the troops clearly hated their opponents and were determined to shed as much blood as possible before a truce was declared. They didn't just stab one another and move on. When a soldier knocked down a foe, he paused to strike again, gutting his opponent, smashing his face to pieces, often maiming him even after he was dead. It was a savage, bloodthirsty display, very much to Larten's liking.

Occasionally, when straddling corpses and wading through puddles of blood, Larten would remember that he had once been human. If his life hadn't taken the turn it did, he might have wound up on a field like this, fighting to the death, killing because he had to. He'd wonder how he would have felt in that position if he had looked up and seen a vampire studying him like an insect.

Larten always pushed such thoughts swiftly from his head. One of the hardest things about being a vampire was separating yourself from your origins. You had to leave behind your old ways to truly fit into the clan. There was no room for pity if you wanted to become a vampire of good standing. You had to force yourself to see humans as a different, lesser species.

A young man was shot in the shoulder and spun around from the force of it. He fell against Larten, who steadied him with one hand, keeping his umbrella straight with the other. The man's eyes widened with fear and wonder. Then the pain kicked in and he doubled over. Larten nearly bent to help him, but if he showed favoritism the soldiers of the other army might fire on him. Both sets ignored the vampires because they were neutral. If they interfered, they risked drawing fire. So Larten left the young man to writhe in the dirt, lonely and untended, and strolled along.

The battle lasted most of the afternoon. The war pack withdrew in the evening to rest. They debated the highlights, each reporting on what he had witnessed. A few had been cut or struck, and Jordan had been shot in his left arm. But the wounds weren't serious and they laughed about them as they relaxed beneath a tree, comparing scratches.

The vampires dozed, letting the sun drop. When darkness had settled on the world, they returned to the killing zone. There were no smiles this time, or if there were, they were tight, vicious, inhuman sneers. No banter either. They proceeded smoothly and silently. The umbrellas were left behind and when they reached the edge of the battlefield they shed their coats, cloaks and boots. A couple even stripped naked, baring all beneath the moon.

For a minute they stood on the flanks, drinking in the sight of the corpses and mouthwatering pools of blood. No humans moved. Even those who'd never heard of vampires had sensed menace in the night air and withdrawn to the safety of camp. In the morning they would return to bury the bodies of their fallen allies and pick weapons, shoes and other items from the dead. But the night belonged to the Cubs.

When the vampires were satisfied that the field

was theirs, they closed in. They trod softly, barely trampling the grass as they advanced on the corpses. Their nostrils and eyes were wide. Drool dripped from the lips of many. Some trembled with expectation. Others growled softly.

They held as a pack until they were in the middle of the slaughter. Then all eyes settled on Tanish. Though they had scorned his claims of leadership earlier, in this situation they acknowledged his right to command. If he hesitated, they would ignore him and press on, but they gave him the chance to unleash them, as was the vampire way.

Tanish beamed wolfishly, then snapped his teeth and threw himself to all fours. Around him the others did the same. Breaking away from one another, they dug into the bodies of the slain, slicing flesh from bone, gulping blood as it gushed into the air, wallowing in the thick red liquid.

After a while they started to howl and beat the ground with bones that they had snapped loose. Some fought with each other, wrestling clumsily, but the fights didn't last long. They could challenge one another for real anytime. These ripe nights were reserved for pleasures more savage than battle.

Like the rest of his pack, Larten soon lost himself

in the feeding frenzy. For an hour or more he was neither human nor vampire, just a howling, hungry creature of dark delights. At times he slithered across the cool, sticky bodies like a ravenous worm, cutting, chewing, drinking. And all he knew...all any of them knew...all that their world consisted of in that intense, vicious, darkly delicious time...was *blood*.

Chapter Five

The vampires slept late the following day. A couple rose to observe the fighting in the afternoon, but most had seen enough and preferred to rest, digest their feast and dream of future feeding frenzies.

"Wake up," Tanish grunted in the evening, digging Larten in the ribs.

"Leave me alone," Larten growled.

"You've slept enough," Tanish said. "I'm bored. I want you to teach me some new tricks."

"Have you mastered the ones I taught you last time?"

"Some of them." Tanish laughed. "I'm quite good at those that I can use when playing poker."

"You cheat when you gamble?" Larten frowned, sitting up.

"If I need money." Tanish shrugged. "I don't like to steal. I'd rather work for my ill-gotten gains."

"You think cheating is work?"

"We're only talking about humans," Tanish said. "I'd never scheme against one of our own. Come on, Quicksilver, you love to show off. You have the fastest hands I've ever seen. Teach me, O wise and nimble-fingered one."

Larten smiled and took a pack of cards from a small leather bag. He shuffled for a couple of minutes to limber up, then taught Tanish a few new ways to make the cards do whatever he wished. He had to slow down his movements so that his friend could follow.

"You're unnatural," Tanish said admiringly. "Are you this fast in a fight?"

"You've seen me fight many times," Larten said.

"Drunken skirmishes, yes, but never in a real battle. Have you ever fought to the death?"

Larten shook his head. "Not since I was blooded."

"You mean you killed before?"

"I don't want to talk about it."

"Oh-ho! Quicksilver's hiding a secret. Tell me. I won't leave you in peace until you do."

"This is not a topic for discussion," Larten said softly, and although there was no menace in his tone, Tanish knew immediately that the orange-haired vampire was serious. He snorted as if he didn't care, then focused on the cards.

As they played and the others stirred around them, a man approached across one of the fields of carnage. He was moving faster than a human and was sheltered beneath a heavy cloak. Larten assumed it was another Cub coming to join the pack. The newcomer would be disappointed—by the diminished sounds of battle, it seemed that the soldiers had spent the worst of their anger. The war was winding down.

The man slowed when he spotted the vampires under the tree. He studied them, his face masked by the shadows cast by his cloak. Then he came forward. When he was at the edge of the tree's reach, he let his cloak drop.

"By the black blood of Harnon Oan!" Wester roared, leaping to his feet, gaping at the stranger with disbelief.

The newcomer was no human, but he wasn't a vampire either. He had light red hair and fingernails and a pair of burning red eyes, and his skin was a purplish shade.

"I am Randel Chayne of the vampaneze," he said as the rest of the Cubs leapt up like the shocked Wester. "I come to seek a challenge."

Nobody spoke. They were astonished. Challenges between the two tribes of the night were nothing new, but Cubs were normally ignored in favor of Generals. This was the first time most of them had seen one of their estranged blood-cousins.

Randel studied the dumbstruck vampires, his eyebrows arching. "If this is how vampires react in the face of a challenge, perhaps you are not worth fighting."

"We'll teach you about *worth,* you scum!" Wester screamed, lunging at the vampaneze, hands twisted into claws, hatred darkening his features.

Larten grabbed his friend and held him back. "No," he snapped. "You're not ready for this. He'll kill you."

"Let me go," Wester snarled as Randel laughed cruelly. "You have no right to get in my way. I'll rip his throat open, and if you try to stop me, I'll –"

"He'll break your neck before you can lay a hand on him," Larten said coldly. "He's not an assistant, you can tell by the dark color of his skin. He's a full vampaneze. He must be a vampire-hater or he wouldn't

40

have bothered with Cubs like us. He's not looking for a challenge—he just wants to rack up an easy kill.

"That's it, isn't it?" Larten shouted at the vampaneze. "You don't dare face one of our Generals, so you hunt among the inexperienced Cubs. You're a coward."

Randel sneered. "I've fought and killed Generals, and one night I will fight and kill a Prince if the gods are good to me. I have nothing to prove and I don't react to the insults of curs like you. But today, to pass the time, I want to face a Cub. I've been told you're slow and soft. Can any of you prove me wrong?"

Wester's eyes flashed and again he tried to strike. Larten blocked him and said without emotion, "If you fight, he'll slay you and you'll never be able to take revenge on the one who murdered your family." Then he stood aside, letting Wester make the final decision, as was his right.

As Wester agonized – he wanted more than anything to kill the stranger, but he knew Larten spoke truly – Randel gazed with disgust at the war pack. "Surely you have a leader," he teased. "Vampires love to be led. Will not even the mighty pack leader meet my challenge?"

All eyes turned to Tanish. He had demanded the

right to rule and they'd granted it. If he didn't meet this challenge, he would be disgraced. Any vampire of good standing in his position must step forward. Even the wayward Cubs had standards to uphold. The members of the pack expected Tanish to face this purple-skinned villain, put up a good fight and die with honor.

But Tanish didn't move. His cheeks were burning and he stared at the ground as if he could never look up again. When they realized he wasn't going to react, their faces hardened. Several puffed themselves up for battle – even the wounded Jordan struggled to his feet – but Zula Pone was the first to step forward.

"I will face you, Randel of the vampaneze," Zula said, taking off the overcoat in which he had been sleeping. "And when I kill you, I will honor your corpse and say a prayer to the vampire gods to accept your wayward soul."

Randel laughed, but the sneering tone was gone from his voice when he said, "I accept your challenge. But I'll not ask for your name or make pleas on your behalf to the gods when this is over. That's not our way. We simply kill or die. The glory lies in the battle, not what is said or done afterwards."

Randel edged away from the shelter of the tree,

into the deadly sunlight. Like vampires, he couldn't comfortably stand exposure to the sun. But fights between children of the night seldom lasted more than a minute or two. One way or the other, he wouldn't have to tolerate the irritation for long.

The squat, ugly Zula followed Randel into the clearing. He went calmly, eyes clear and steady, ready to accept whatever came his way. In that moment he was a true vampire, nobler than any of the Cubs watching him, and all of them felt humbled.

"What is your choice of weapon?" Zula asked as they squared up to each other.

"Hands are fine by me," Randel said, flexing his fingers.

"As you wish."

Zula lashed out, five sharp nails guaranteed to cut through almost any material on Earth, including the flesh of a vampaneze's throat. But Randel blocked Zula's arm and kicked him in the stomach. Zula grunted and fell back. Randel could have pressed after him, but he held his ground and waited for the vampire to attack again.

Flushed, Zula darted at his foe, then stopped and took a deep breath, regaining his composure. When he was in control of himself, he advanced slowly, studying

Randel's eyes for warning signs of what his intentions might be. Larten had thought that Zula was doomed when he accepted the challenge, but watching him now, he believed that maybe the Cub had a chance.

When Zula was within reach, Randel swung a fist at him. Zula blocked it and kicked at Randel's shin. He connected and Randel went down. The vampires roared with excitement, but their cheers were short-lived. As Randel fell, he caught Zula and twisted him around and down. Zula realized too late that his opponent had anticipated his strike. Before he could adjust, he landed heavily on his back — and on the outstretched fingers of one of Randel's hands, which the vampaneze had slyly slid beneath him.

Zula cried out as the vampaneze's nails ripped into his lungs. Then he stiffened, his breath catching in his throat. His legs spasmed, but his arms were strangely still by his sides. He gulped a few times, blood exploding from his mouth, eyes widening, staring at the sun. He had always thought that he would die by the light of the moon. It seemed unfair that a child of the night should perish this way, before the sun had set. He wished Randel had come a few hours later, so he could at least have counted the stars one last time.

And then he wished no more.

Randel shoved the dead vampire away, wiped his hand clean on the grass and stood. He didn't even glance at Zula, but he did cast an eye over the pale-faced vampires sheltering beneath the tree.

"You're a disgrace to your masters," Randel growled, then picked up his cloak, settled it over his head and moved on.

The Cubs stared after the departing vampaneze and watched in silence until he flitted out of sight. Then Larten and Jordan went to fetch the body of Zula Pone. They would burn it later or launch it down a river, depending on what the majority thought the ugly vampire would have preferred.

Tanish was sitting by himself when Larten returned. He had his back to the rest of the Cubs and nobody went near him. They ignored their fallen leader, treating him with the scorn he deserved. Larten felt sorry for his friend, but it couldn't be helped. One of the first things Seba had taught him was that every man made his own decisions in life, and each must stand by the consequences of those choices.

As the sun set, Tanish stood and set off. He didn't say good-bye and nobody asked where he was going. He took nothing, even dropping his expensive coat and discarding his silk shirt. Larten knew, as he watched the disgraced Tanish leave, that this was probably the last they'd see of him. Tanish Eul was no longer part of the clan. He wasn't a traitor, but the Cubs would never mention his name again, and if anyone ever asked about him, they would respond with a simple, damning, "He walks with the humans now."

Part Two

"If the entire clan stood against her, we would fall."

Chapter Six

The American Civil War was the bloodiest waste of life Larten had yet to witness. Vampires had known about America long before Europeans *discovered* it. One of the clan had sailed with Leif Ericson and thirty-four others early in the second millennium, and before Paris Skyle became a Prince he stayed Columbus's hand when the human had lost hope and was on the verge of turning back. The elderly vampire would have been saddened to see what had become of the country, but not surprised. Why should these tribes be any different from those they had left behind? People might speak of it being a New World, but they were the same old humans.

Larten watched from a distance as thousands of

young men clashed and went to an early grave. He, Wester and Seba had made camp on a hill out of the way of the fighting a few nights earlier. Since then they'd kept vigil, leaving only to hunt and stretch their legs.

The pair of Cubs had abandoned the war packs and returned to their master a few years after Tanish's fall. They had never been able to lose themselves in warfare and other petty pursuits in quite the same way after that dark day. They felt shamed, and the Cubs they cavorted with were a constant reminder of what had happened.

Seba never asked his assistants why they had returned. He was surprised to see them come back to him so early – he hadn't expected them for another decade – but a master didn't need to know everything about his students. He let them keep their secrets and focused on their training.

Seba didn't humiliate them as he had before, or give them tasks they couldn't complete. The pair had changed, Larten in particular, and Seba now deemed them worthy of respect. He believed they were ready to undertake the testing trials that would decide whether or not they were capable of playing an active role in the affairs of the clan.

As Larten studied the warring American factions,

he wondered again why Seba had brought them to this place. Their master had never shown an interest in the affairs of humans and hadn't even glanced at the soldiers since they'd arrived. What could have lured him to this maelstrom of slaughter?

Wester stepped up beside the man he thought of as a brother and watched for a while with him. Both were thinking of Tanish Eul.

"How much longer do you think we'll be here?" Wester asked, but Larten only grunted in response. "Did you smell the war pack last night?"

"Aye."

Larten's senses had improved greatly in recent years. He'd been aware of the other vampires for the past two nights but had avoided them, staying by Seba's side, ready to obey his master's orders.

"I miss being part of a pack," Wester sighed. "Feeding on the battlefields was barbaric but exquisite."

"I am sure reformed opium addicts miss their pipes," Larten said drily. "It does not mean they should return to their old ways."

"It wasn't *that* bad," Wester said.

"No?" Larten shrugged. "I have often told myself that there was nothing wrong in what we did, since so many other vampires were reveling in the bloodshed.

But that is no excuse. Humans might not deserve our respect, but they do not merit our contempt either."

Wester smiled. "You sound just like Seba."

Larten winced and scratched his nose, then his ears. He had tried to copy Seba's way of speaking in the past, and Seba had simply corrected him when he made a mistake. But since he'd returned from his time with the Cubs, Seba had taken it more seriously. He had asked Larten if he truly wished to master his vocabulary. When the unsuspecting assistant confirmed that he did, it was the beginning of a new phase, one he had come to despise. He had often begged Seba to stop, but the ancient vampire wouldn't relent.

Under the new regime, when Larten said "don't" or "can't," Seba plucked hairs from his student's nostrils, which was far more painful than Larten would have imagined. After a year of that, he'd tried to outfox his master by burning the hairs from his nose, but Seba set his sights on the hairs in Larten's ears instead, and that was even worse! The orange-haired assistant had learned swiftly in the face of such punishing lessons. He suffered an occasional lapse, but only rarely. It had been weeks since Seba had felt obliged to pluck any hairs.

As Larten and Wester stood watch, Seba joined them and stretched, enjoying the weak evening sun.

It had been nearly half a century since he'd met a scared boy in a gloomy crypt and taken him on as an assistant. Seba had aged a lot in that time. His long hair was mostly gray now. He'd shaved his beard and the skin around his throat was dry and wrinkled, covered with old scars and blotches. He looked battered and weary, and groaned if he moved too quickly.

Yet he could set a pace his assistants struggled to match, and he was as light of foot and fast of hand as ever. He often spoke of being near to his end, but Larten suspected his old master might see out this century and perhaps a couple more. Not that he ever said such a thing—he didn't want to invite bad luck.

"Wester thinks I sound like you," Larten said.

"He must be going deaf," Seba huffed. Shading his eyes, he studied the soldiers. They had concluded their killing for the day and were limping back to camp, dragging the wounded, leaving the dead for the creatures of the night that they could sense circling them. "Such noble fools," Seba sighed. "One war should be enough for any race. Why do they go on and on?"

Neither Larten nor Wester tried to answer. They hadn't been vampires anywhere near as long as their master, but as young as they were, both found it hard to recall the time when they had walked as humans, or how their thoughts had functioned in those less blood-riddled days.

"We will move on tonight," Seba said. "Just a few miles. I would be obliged if you carried my coffin."

Larten and Wester fetched Seba's coffin from the rough shelter they had made, then followed him down the hill and around a field of corpses. The younger vampires had not yet developed a taste for coffins. They'd slept in many while traveling with Seba, holed up in crypts or tombs, but when given a choice they preferred beds. Their master, however, only felt snug with pine walls encaging him and a lid overhead. He had tried several coffins since they'd landed in America. When he finally found one to his liking, he claimed it for his own and begged pardon of the skeleton he'd evicted. His assistants had been carting it around after him ever since.

As the trio followed the course of a small stream, someone called out abruptly from a tree on the other side. "Same old Seba Nile, always has to have the modern conveniences. Can't settle for a stone floor and a roof of sky."

Larten and Wester set the coffin down and squinted. Larten knew the voice, but couldn't place it. As he tried to put a face to it, a shabby vampire dropped from the branches. He was dressed in animal hides and had a couple of belts strapped around his chest, throwing stars hanging loosely from them. He had long green hair. He spat into the stream as he crossed and Larten was fairly sure he heard the General break wind, though it *might* have been the creaking of the trees.

"Vancha March," Seba smiled. "I wondered where the foul stench was coming from."

"I don't know what you're talking about," Vancha scowled. "I bathed last spring, even though I didn't need to." He frowned. "Or was it the spring before?" With a laugh, he tossed a salute to Larten and Wester. "Still hanging around with this old vulture?"

"Someone has to look after him," Larten said.

"He's too weak to carry his own coffin," Wester added.

Larten and Wester hadn't seen the filthy General since their first meeting in Vampire Mountain, so there was much to catch up on. But before they could ask questions, Seba pointed to his coffin and coughed purposefully. Groaning, they picked it up and followed behind at a respectable distance as their master strolled with Vancha and the pair discussed business that was not for the ears of the young.

In time they turned a bend and Larten caught

sight of a tent. He might have dismissed it as the camp of a human officer, but Seba and Vancha were heading for it, so he adjusted the coffin on his shoulder and stole a closer look.

The tent was like none he'd seen so far. It was circular, tall and wide, adorned with beautiful, stitched patterns of water flowers and frogs. It looked a bit like the tent in which the Cirque Du Freak performed, but nowhere near the same size. There were three smaller tents around it and a clothesline stood behind them, hung with a variety of dresses and women's undergarments.

A confused Wester nudged Larten, who frowned at the feminine clothes and said, "What sort of a woman would pitch her tent at the edge of a battlefield?"

The answer came to both of them at the same time, but Wester was the one who exclaimed, "A woman of the wilds!"

Sharing a thrilled look, they bustled after their master and his foul-smelling ally, heading for the tent of the woman who – if they had guessed right – was as powerful and as crucial to the fate of the vampire clan as any goddess of legend.

Chapter Seven

Seba paused at the entrance to the tent and asked Larten and Wester to set aside his coffin. He tugged at his red shirt and cloak, straightened some creases, then examined the material for dirt.

"How do I look?" Vancha asked, spitting into his palm and using it to brush back his green hair.

"Like a cherub," Seba murmured.

"Do you think –"

The flap over the entrance swished back, cutting short his question, and a woman stepped forward. She was short and ugly – she reminded Larten of Zula Pone in some respects – and even filthier than Vancha. She wore no shoes or clothes. Instead there were ropes wrapped around her body. She had pointed ears, a tiny nose, one brown eye and one green. She was as muscular as a man and hairier than most, from a thin beard and mustache down to ten furry toes. Her fingers were stubby and the nails cut short on all of them except the two little fingers, where they grew long and sharp.

Larten thought this was a strange choice of servant for a witch as powerful as the Lady Evanna (if that was indeed who they were coming to meet). He had assumed that Evanna would have pretty, finely dressed maids to wait on her. Maybe she had taken pity on this unfortunate creature and given her a home because nobody else would.

Then, to Larten's astonishment, the short, ugly woman squealed, darted forward and cried, "My little Vancha!" As the General tried to back away in a panic, she hoisted him off the ground and shook him in the air as if he was a large doll.

"Let me down!" Vancha yelled furiously.

"Not until you give me a kiss, you naughty boy," she chortled.

"I'll give you a kick up the –"

"Language, Vancha," she stopped him, squeezing his ribs so hard that his eyes almost popped.

"Apologies...Lady," he wheezed, then pecked her cheek before he suffocated.

The woman smiled and let him drop, then curtsied gracefully to Seba. "You are welcome as always, Master Nile," she said in a soft, melodic voice.

"And grateful for that privilege, my Lady," Seba said, bowing as he would have before a Prince.

"You've brought a couple of assistants," she noted, turning her brown eye on Larten and her green eye on Wester. Both were gaping at her.

"This is Lar –" Seba began to introduce them.

"I know their names," the woman interrupted. "And I believe they know mine. Don't you, gentlemen?"

"*Evanna?*" Wester gasped, barely able to believe it.

"They expected someone more glamorous," she said to Vancha.

"Many do," he grinned.

"Perhaps this is more what they had in mind." She shimmered and changed shape. She was now tall and lithe, with long blond hair and an angel's features, clad in a flowing white dress. Larten stared at her, enamored. He reached out a hand to caress her, then let it drop. He didn't feel he had the right to touch anyone this beautiful.

"Too easily impressed," Evanna tutted, resuming her former appearance. "You shouldn't judge by what's on the outside. Only a fool falls for a pretty face. Are you fools?"

Larten was first to speak this time. "For you, Lady, I would be anything," he said softly, the words springing to his lips.

Evanna raised an eyebrow and glared at him. But as he blinked, confused by her icy look, she realized he wasn't being impudent. "I like this one, Seba," she cooed. "Not the brightest vampire I've ever met, but he has a good heart."

"Both my assistants have good hearts," Seba said. "But is Larten's a heart you might wish to win?"

Evanna laughed at the eagerness of the question. "You're here just a couple of minutes and already you want to pair me off with the nearest vampire at hand." She brushed his cheek fondly and shook her head. "Ask no favors of me yet, old friend. Let us simply enjoy each other's company for a while. I would know all that you have been up to and how things go with the rest of the clan."

Taking his arm, she led the gray-haired vampire inside. After a pause, Larten and Wester followed. Vancha came last, having run another palmful of spit through his hair to make it *extra* stiff and shiny. "If that doesn't impress her," he said smugly to himself, "I don't know what will!"

Evanna was Desmond Tiny's daughter. He had created her a thousand years ago, mixing the blood of a vampire with that of a pregnant wolf. She was a powerful enchantress who could work many magical charms. But the night-walkers were most interested in one particular ability of hers.

Vampires couldn't have children. That was the way it had always been. To keep the race alive, they needed to blood humans. The clan used to think that would always be the case, but Evanna had the power to bear a vampire's child. If she chose, she could breed with a vampire and her offspring would be able to reproduce too.

Vampires had been wooing Evanna for hundreds of years. Mr. Tiny had warned that she and her young would have the power to wipe out the clan, but they cared nothing about the risks. The possibility of being able to rear children of their own was intoxicating.

But Evanna had so far shunned their advances. She had never taken a vampire as a mate, or given any hint that she intended to. Still they sought her out and tried to win her heart, fighting in her name, offering her gifts, doing all that they could to make her theirs. To no avail.

Larten secretly hoped to captivate the legendary Lady of the Wilds. He had a way with ladies – few had been able to resist his charms when he was a Cub – and he was confident that she would fall for him as many others had. If Evanna mated with him, he'd become the founding father of a new generation of vampires and his power and fame would be assured.

"I would have worn finer clothes if I had known we were coming here," he whispered to Wester as they sat on a couch laden with feather pillows.

"Don't worry," Wester grinned. "If Vancha is your only opposition, you can't fail."

Though Wester had also dreamed of winning the hand of the famed Lady, now that he'd seen the intent in Larten's eyes, he put such thoughts from his mind. He always gave way to his best friend. They had never fought over a woman or anything else that Larten set his sights on. Wester thought of Larten as his brother and he loved the orange-haired vampire totally. He never tried to take the things that Larten desired, even if he craved them himself.

The tent seemed larger inside than out. There was

a plush bed in the center, paintings hanging from beams, statues set around the sides. Huge candles burned steadily, while bowls and jugs overflowed with fruit, vegetables, water and wine. There was no meat or fish, which surprised Larten until he recalled a rumor that Evanna didn't eat anything that couldn't be grown.

Three young women brought the bowls and jugs to the vampires once they were seated. All were dressed in plain white shirts and beige trousers. Larten had only rarely seen a woman in trousers and his gaze kept flicking over the servants. One of them – she had long dark hair and sharp gray eyes – caught him looking and glared challengingly. He tried his infamous smile on her – it set most women's legs wobbling – but her glare only deepened. Surprised and unsettled, Larten coughed and turned his head aside. Wester saw this and hid a smile.

"First things first," Evanna said, lying on a chaise longue and plucking a grape from a tray. "How has my little Vancha been? Tell Mommy all."

"*Mommy?*" Larten gasped.

"I wish you wouldn't say things like that," Vancha grimaced. "I don't call you a witch, do I?"

"With good reason," Evanna snapped, eyes flashing.

"I'll cut out the tongue of anyone who calls me that. I'm the world's most powerful sorceress, a priestess of dark arts, mother of the future and Lady of the Wilds. You, on the other hand, will always be my sweet, cuddly Vancha. I still remember feeding you and the way you used to burp when you were done." She giggled. "That much hasn't changed."

"Evanna found me when I was a baby," Vancha muttered to Larten and Wester. "My parents had been killed and I'd been left to die. She rescued me and carried me with her for a few years before handing me over to...someone else," he finished vaguely.

Evanna's smile faded. "You make it sound as if I carried you alone," she said softly.

"As *I* remember it, Lady, you did," Vancha said, and there was an edge to his tone now that surprised the younger pair of vampires.

Evanna held Vancha's gaze for a few seconds, then shook her head and sighed. "A man should never turn his back on his—"

"Please!" Vancha snapped. "Let the past lie."

"The past never lies buried forever," Evanna muttered. "We cannot hide from those to whom we are bound by nature. But if you wish to keep your silly secrets, so be it. You know that I only ever wished the best for you."

"And I'm grateful to you for that," Vancha said, his features softening. Then he spat and winked. "I just wish you didn't treat me like a damn child."

Evanna laughed. "When you have a few more centuries under your belt, I will consider you an adult. Until then . . ." She pinched his cheek.

"Charna's guts!" Vancha roared. "You go too far!" He threw himself at her and they rolled across the floor of the tent. He was punching and kicking at the witch, but she only laughed and tossed him clear. As he landed, he whipped a star from his belt and launched it at her head.

Evanna plucked the deadly throwing star from the air and calmly picked her teeth with one of the prongs. "Still playing with your shurikens?" she mumbled. "I thought you would have found a new toy by now."

Vancha looked like he would attack again, but in the end he threw back his head and laughed. "By the gods of the vampires, you're a piece of work! Come, let's drink toasts to absent friends and sing songs of the old nights."

"I will drink with you anytime, my dear," Evanna said. "And with your companions too." She clicked her fingers at the servants. "Milk for Master March." Then she looked at the others. "Ale, I suppose?"

"Aye!" Larten and Wester exclaimed.

"Why not?" Seba added with a smile.

Barrels of the finest ale Larten had ever tasted were brought, and the rest of the night was a blur for him from that moment on.

Chapter Eight

Larten woke in the afternoon with a pounding head. He was in a hammock, though he had no recollection of getting into it. As he rose, he saw that someone had painted a series of tattoos on his hand with a piece of charcoal or some similar marker. He frowned, thought about making investigations, then decided he was better not knowing. Groaning, he made his way to a barrel of rainwater outside and dunked his head.

When he came up for air, one of Evanna's assistants – the one with the dark hair and gray eyes – was standing beside him, holding out a mug of something hot and steaming.

"Drink this," she said.

"It's not ale, is it?" Larten asked, his face whitening at the thought.

The assistant smiled briefly – she looked quite pretty when she smiled – then shook her head. "A cure of my mistress's. You will feel better after you drink it."

Larten had tried a number of hangover cures in the past, none of which had done much for him. But to be polite he took the mug from the woman – not much more than a girl when seen by daylight – and downed half of it. He finished off the rest a few moments later and almost immediately his headache began to lift.

"This is amazing," he gasped. "What is in it?"

"You'd feel sick again if I told you," the girl laughed. She had crooked teeth, Larten noted, but a man could easily ignore a flaw like that.

"I do not think you told me your name," Larten said smoothly.

"You think wrong," she answered. "In fact you made up a song about it. *Lovely Arra Sails, nectar to all males, how I'd like to spear you like a whaler spears a whale!* There was more, but that, sadly, was the best line."

Larten winced. "I have a habit of making up insulting rhymes when drunk. My apologies."

"No need. Your songs about my two sisters were worse. But they were nearly as drunk as you, so I doubt they'll remember."

"Three sisters working for the same mistress? That is unusual."

"They're not my real sisters," Arra sighed, as if explaining something obvious to an idiot. "That's just how Evanna refers to us." She shrugged. "They're pleasant enough, though I don't think of them as friends." Arra squinted at Larten and pursed her lips. "You're a vampire, aren't you?"

"Aye," Larten said proudly.

"Don't vampires perish in direct sunlight?"

"Not immediately. I would start to burn if I stayed out, but it would not kill me for a couple of hours. A lot of the myths are false or distortions of the truth."

"Evanna doesn't talk much about vampires, except to complain about how you follow her around like dogs."

Larten scowled at that but said nothing. He headed back inside but Arra blocked his way. "That's my tent over there." She nodded at one of the three small tents that stood next to Evanna's. "If you have no pressing business, I'd like to talk with you and learn more about vampires."

Larten arched a merry eyebrow.

"When I say talk, I *mean* talk," Arra growled, reading his mind. "You tried to kiss me last night."

"How did you respond?" Larten asked.

Arra smiled. "Let's just say the next verse of your song began with, *Nasty Arra Sails, she has a vicious tongue.*"

Larten managed a laugh, then followed Arra into her tent. Like Evanna's, it was larger than it looked from the outside, though it was plainly decorated and Arra didn't have many personal belongings. The pair sat on her bed – Arra making sure there was a discreet distance between them – and Larten spoke for a long time about his life, the clan and Vampire Mountain. Arra listened with silent interest to everything. It was only when he spoke about flitting that she interrupted.

"My mistress can flit too. And she can breathe out a gas to make people faint, although she rarely needs to. Do you think the vampires inherited their magic from Evanna or her father?"

"Have you met Desmond Tiny?" Larten asked.

"No. But I have heard of him through visitors like yourself."

Larten had always taken the magical talents of the clan for granted, such as their longevity, strength and speed. But now that he thought about it, he realized that such gifts were mysterious. Had their supernatural talents developed naturally, or were they the work of a meddler with more power? Larten made a mental note to ask Seba later, though he had a feeling his master wouldn't be able to answer the question either.

"Tell me about yourself," Larten said, changing the subject. "How did you come to work for Evanna? Are you the age you look or are you old like your mistress?"

"*Old?*" Arra screeched, chucking a pillow at him. "Manners, vampire, or I'll stake you to the ground outside and leave you to burn."

As Larten smiled, she relaxed and told him a bit about where she'd come from, how she'd run away from home in search of adventure and found Evanna. "Or was found by her," Arra added suspiciously. "I've a feeling she sends for apprentices. We don't just wander into her life, even if we seem to."

Evanna had taught Arra a few spells, but mostly the girl was employed as a servant, to cater to her mistress's guests and clean up after them. She wasn't happy about that. She wanted to learn the secrets of Evanna's world and become a mighty sorceress.

"It's not as if she even needs us," Arra complained. "I've seen her snap her fingers and conjure up a full meal, or wave a hand at a dirty room and suddenly it's clean. She just likes having servants to boss around."

"Why don't you leave?" Larten asked.

"I will," Arra said. "But I don't want to move on until I have somewhere else to go. I fled without direction once, when I left home, but I'd rather not leave everything to chance a second time."

Her eyes narrowed. She started to ask Larten something, but then somebody whistled in the distance and she grimaced. "My mistress wants me."

"She whistles for you like a dog?" Larten grinned.

"If you laugh, I'll poison your next drink," Arra growled, then hurried to see what Evanna wanted. Larten followed, still smiling. It had been nice, chatting with Arra. She was a sharp little thing, and scowls came easier to her than smiles, but Larten liked her. He hoped they could be friends, at least for a while, before he moved on with Seba and Wester. After that he figured it was unlikely that he would ever see the surly-looking girl again.

Chapter Nine

They spent two more nights with the Lady of the Wilds. Other vampires came to see her while they were present. Most were from the war pack shadowing the warring humans, but some had come from farther away, crossing oceans as Seba and his assistants had.

A few of the Cubs recognized Larten and Wester, and greeted Larten by his nickname. It had been some years since he'd been called Quicksilver and he found it oddly unsettling. That part of his life was behind him and he wished to move on. Though he was polite to the Cubs who had once been his friends, he made no effort to renew any of those friendships.

Evanna hosted most of her visitors openly, but

sometimes she sent Seba and his assistants away so that she could greet a newcomer in private. She seemed to know what each of her guests would prefer, and did what she could to satisfy their requirements—except agree to their pleas to accept them as her partner.

"We came to this country just to meet Evanna, didn't we?" Wester asked Seba on the third night as they were resting on a nearby hill after they had slipped into one of the soldiers' camps to feed.

Seba nodded. "You are as sharp as ever, Master Flack. Evanna would rather the clan left her alone. She tires of our endless proposals. But she knows how highly we regard her, so she sets aside several nights every now and then for us to court her. A favored few are welcome at her home too, but most have to settle for meetings like this."

"Where does she live?" Wester asked.

Seba shook his head. "If she wants you to know, she will tell you."

"So you brought us here for her to have a look at us, in case she liked our faces?" Larten asked.

"Aye." Seba rubbed the back of his neck and sighed. "We believe Evanna will choose a mate one night, either a vampire or a vampaneze, but –"

"A vampaneze?" Wester barked. "She consorts with them too?"

"She meets with all creatures of the night," Seba said calmly. "Evanna makes no distinction between us. The vampaneze are as dear to her as we are. She tries to keep us apart – she will move to a new site soon, I think, where she will meet with our blood-cousins – but if a vampaneze came here we would have to treat him with respect."

"I wouldn't," Wester snarled. "If I spot any of those scum, I'll –"

"– do nothing but bid him a good night," Seba said bluntly and there was an edge to his voice that his assistants rarely heard. "If you anger Evanna, she will crush you. Never let her charm blind you to the fact that she is Desmond Tiny's daughter. Respect her wishes when in her presence, Wester, or no words of mine will be enough to save you."

Wester glowered at his master. To ease the tension, Larten asked how Seba had known that Evanna would be here.

"She led me here," Seba answered vaguely. "Those who seek Evanna simply follow their feet. I did not know this was where we would end up when we set out. All I knew was that we would find her wherever she wanted to be found."

"And you really hoped that one of us would seduce her?" Larten pressed.

Seba chuckled. "I doubt if anyone will ever *seduce* Evanna. But you made a good attempt, Larten. I did not know you were so smooth with the ladies."

"I am usually more successful," Larten grunted sourly. All of his flattering words, sideways looks and tricks had fallen flat on the witch. She had been kind to him and laughed at his jokes, but never gave the least hint that she might consider him as a mate.

"Do not be too hard on yourself," Seba said. "Many fine vampires have been rejected before you, and many will be in the future too, I am sure. As I was about to say before Wester interrupted, we believe she will choose a mate eventually, but we do not know which qualities she is looking for, or even if she *is* looking—maybe she is waiting for a certain time or event.

"Since we know so little of her heart, many of us come to see her from time to time, and bring our assistants when they are ready for such a meeting. We continue to hope that one night she will claim one of us as her own. But so far, no luck."

"What if she takes a vampaneze?" Wester growled.
"We fear that more than anything," Seba said.
"Evanna has the power to destroy the clan. If she chooses
to mate with a vampaneze, their children will certainly
gain some of her magical powers. Maybe the dreaded
Lord of the Vampaneze will be a child of Evanna's."

"Then why don't we strike?" Wester hissed. "Kill
her or abduct her and make her do as we wish?"

"If this foolishness continues, I will whip you until
the flesh of your back peels from your spine like a
snake's shedded skin," Seba rumbled.

Wester blinked with shock. The old vampire had
never threatened either of them like this before. There
had been many cuffs and kicks over the years, but
never a savage, brutal vow.

Seba saw the hurt in his assistant's eyes and softened. "Understand me," he said gently. "She is much
stronger than any of us — than *all* of us. If the entire
clan stood against her, we would fall."

"Surely no one is that powerful," Larten said
dubiously.

"I do not exaggerate," Seba insisted. "Her power
is not of this world. There are myths of gods raising
countries, leveling mountains, making the seas churn.
I do not know if those stories are true, but I believe

Evanna could do all that and more. So let me never hear either of you plotting against her. She would be an enemy far greater than any other, with the exception of her meddling father."

Seba looked into the eyes of his assistants, trying to make sure his words had sunk in. He saw that he had made an impact and hoped it would be enough to prevent future follies.

"Now," he said, forcing a smile. "Let us return and say nothing more about this. Only, if she *should* at any time bat her eyelids at you, do not bother with a long courtship!"

Larten and Wester laughed weakly, then trailed Seba back to the tent, all three silent and immersed in thought.

The tent had been dismantled when they returned. Evanna's apprentices were standing behind a cart, glumly preparing to push. There was no way everything from inside the tent could fit onto the cart – the canvas itself would have required a wagon – but Larten wasn't surprised. The Lady of the Wilds could work many wonders.

"Time to be off," Evanna said cheerfully. "I've

had fewer visitors than normal. The clan must be losing interest in me."

"Have you far to travel, Lady?" Seba asked, kissing her cheeks.

"You know very well that I go to greet my other admirers nearby," Evanna said.

Seba smiled. "Aye, but I would rather not admit it."

"Foolish children," Evanna snapped. "Why don't you put your squabbles behind you and reunite? Life would be much easier if you did."

"It is not that simple," Seba sighed. "We are bound by strings of destiny."

"We're all bound by those," Evanna said hollowly, a sad look crossing her face. Then she shook her head and picked up Vancha, who had stayed behind while the others hunted. "Farewell, my little baby."

"Let me go!" he roared, clubbing her ears.

She laughed and kissed his nose. As he struggled and swore, she kissed his lips. His arms and legs relaxed and he was smiling shyly when she set him down again.

Evanna turned to Wester and Larten. The witch was no fairer than she had been when he first saw her, but Larten no longer noticed her ugliness.

"It was a pleasure to meet you," she said.

"It was our honor, my Lady," Wester replied, bowing.

"An honor," Larten echoed, then knelt on one knee and took her dirty hand. "I would like to visit you again sometime, if you can find it in your heart to grant me permission."

"He's bold, this one," Evanna chuckled. She slipped her hand out of Larten's and gripped his chin. Tilting his head back, she gazed down at him. He thought for a moment that her eyes had traded places – hadn't the blue one been on the right before? – but then she spoke and he lost interest in such trivialities.

"My home is my refuge from the world. I invite only a select handful of my closest friends to visit me there. Why should I welcome a snip of a vampire like you?"

He had the feeling that if he gave the wrong answer, he would never see the Lady of the Wilds again. Trying not to worry about that, he grinned shakily and said, "I am good with a flannel. If you ever cared to take a bath, I could scrub your back."

Evanna blinked slowly. Larten could see her pondering whether to laugh or rip his head off. Fortunately for the young vampire, she chose to see the funny side of his proposition.

"Bold as a monkey," Evanna chortled, releasing

Larten's chin and thumbing his nose. "A strange choice of assistant, Seba, but I like him. Aye, Larten Crepsley, you may visit anytime the fancy takes you." She pressed a finger to his forehead and he felt something buzz deep inside his brain. "You will be able to find me whenever you wish."

Evanna nodded at Wester politely, and although he couldn't suppress a stab of jealousy, he managed a genuine smile. This confirmed what he had always thought—Larten was in some way superior to him, destined for greater things. Wester would have liked to be a vampire of import, but the world needed its secondary players too. There was no point wishing he could be more than he was. He was happy to make the most of whatever life had set aside for him.

Then the witch was off, slouching away, looking like a crazy woman who had escaped from bedlam. Arra Sails and the other apprentices shuffled after her, groaning as they pushed the cart. Arra rolled her eyes at Larten and he smiled sympathetically.

"Very well, gentlemen," Seba exclaimed before the women had moved out of sight. "We have wasted enough years. It is time to return to more pressing matters. Grab your belongings and prepare for a hard trek. We make for Vampire Mountain immediately."

Part Three

"It means respect."

Chapter Ten

It was time for another Council at Vampire Mountain. Vampires traveled from all over the world to meet old friends, challenge one another, debate laws, tell tall tales and have a grand time. Larten and Wester were kept busy in advance, helping out in the gaming halls, preparing the rooms for the chaos of the Festival of the Undead.

The pair had been permanent fixtures in the mountain for the past few years. Both had passed their Trials of Initiation – five perilous tasks that all vampires had to overcome – not long after they'd returned with Seba. Larten took his Trials several months before Wester and sailed through, but Wester almost failed. In his second trial he'd faced two wild boars that had been driven insane with vampire blood. He managed to kill them, but one speared him with its tusks before it died and he had struggled to complete his last three trials.

Seba had visited Wester before his third trial and asked if he'd made peace with the vampire gods. Death was nothing to be afraid of as long as one was ready for it. Wester had nodded soberly and said he could die with no regrets if that was his fate.

Wester had summoned Larten a while later and told him what their master had said. Then, in a soft voice, he'd said, "I lied. I want you to make me a promise. It's a lot to ask, and I'll understand if you refuse, but if I die, I want you to track down and kill Murlough for me."

Larten had almost made the promise – even though the vampaneze had spared their lives when they were his to take – but something in Wester's expression stopped him. The Trials of Initiation were as much a mental as a physical obstacle. If you lost belief in yourself, it could prove as fatal as losing an arm or leg.

"Murlough is your nemesis, not mine," Larten had said icily. "If you die, I will not pursue him on your behalf. I would not ask you to take my enemies as your own, and you should not ask it of me."

Wester had been surprised and hurt, but he'd

accepted Larten's decision and grimly battled through the rest of his Trials, spurred on by his desire to survive and gain revenge for the slaughter of his family.

The pair had been studying hard under Seba and others since then, taking the first steps on the long road to becoming vampire Generals. Much of their time was spent learning the intricacies of combat. They would often pass entire nights in a gaming hall, sparring with each other, overseen by a tutor.

One of their tutors now bellowed at them to empty a chest full of axes. "What are you waiting for? The last vampire arrived three hours ago. The Festival starts at sunset. Perhaps you want them to hunt for the axes, to make a game of it?"

"Sorry, Vanez!" they roared, speeding up even though they had been working fast already.

Vanez Blane glared at the assistants, then moved on. He was in a foul mood. This was his first time working in the gaming Halls ahead of Council. The guards normally took care of such matters, but they'd been understaffed this year and he had volunteered to help. He regretted his offer now. So much to think about and take care of. He was determined not to fall into this trap again. As soon as Council finished he'd be off, and he would make sure he never got caught for duty like this a second time. He belonged in the wilds, not cooped up inside a mountain!

As busy and stressed as he was, Larten was looking forward to Council. The last few years had been dull and strenuous. While he didn't regret his choice to join Seba again and devote himself to his studies, he missed the outside world, the travel, the nights spent drinking, gambling and flattering ladies, the thrill of warfare.

Larten was pleased with how he was developing. He learned swiftly and improved quickly. He wasn't the biggest of vampires, but his speed and skills helped him get the better of most opponents. The nights of Larten being a punching bag for others were long gone.

Yet he wasn't truly happy. He couldn't put his finger on the reason for his discontent. He just felt as if he'd come here before he was finished with the world. He had no desire to be a Cub again or to run with a war pack, but he felt like he was missing out on *something*.

He often thought about Vur Horston and the plans they had made as children to explore every last inch of the world. Even though Larten had traveled the globe widely, he wanted to see more of it, to honor the memory of his lost cousin. Of course he would be able to do that once he became a General – he could spend the rest of his life roaming if he wished – but Larten was impatient. He wanted to do it all and see it all *now*.

Still, he wouldn't have to endure life inside the mountain much longer. Every vampire was forced to undergo a degree of training here if they wished to become a General, but the majority of their lessons could be learned on the road. Seba would take Larten and Wester away from here soon, perhaps at the end of Council, and they could study at a more relaxed pace while traveling far and wide as they had in the past.

When they'd finished setting out the axes, Larten and Wester reported to Vanez for further instructions. He kept them darting around the Halls and tunnels for the next few hours, yelling at them even when they worked speedily and efficiently. Larten was on the point of snapping back when Vanez suddenly smiled at the pair.

"You've done well," he said. "Go get ready for the Festival. And please forgive me if I vented my frustrations on you."

"Nothing to forgive," Larten grinned, then shared

an excited look with Wester. They hurried down to the Hall of Perta Vin-Grahl for a quick wash, then to the cave they shared with Seba and five others, to pull on their finest clothes and make sure they looked their best for the opening ceremony.

The first few hours of the Festival were crazy as usual, vampires fighting as if the clan was on the point of extinction and there would be nobody left for them to battle the following night. Bones were shattered, limbs were severed and four vampires made a premature journey to Paradise, their friends cheering them on — dying in combat was a noble way to perish.

Larten let himself be washed along with the tide of warring vampires – there was no point trying to fight it – but as soon as things calmed down a little he went in search of a particular opponent. He didn't know the vampire's name, only that he was tall and burly, with a nose that had been broken many times. The General had mocked Larten when easily defeating him in a challenge the first time he'd come to Council. Larten had been looking forward to facing him again ever since.

Larten was challenged a few times while searching for the General and he had to respond to each –

you weren't supposed to avoid a contest during the Festival – but finally he found his man standing by the bars in the Hall of Oceen Pird, watching two vampires with round-ended staffs trying to knock each other flying.

"You!" Larten shouted, pounding the vampire's back.

The General looked around and scowled. He didn't remember this young pup, but something about the orange hair struck a chord.

"Wrestle with me," Larten growled.

The vampire smiled bitterly and turned. Larten's heart sank—the General's right arm was missing from just beneath the shoulder.

"Why the long face?" the General snapped, then glanced at the space where his arm should be. "Surely *this* won't deter you? It's just a flesh wound."

"I…" Larten hesitated.

"…don't want to fight a cripple?" the General asked softly, fire burning in his eyes.

Larten stiffened. "I have no intention of offending you with pity. I was merely going to say that I did not want to have an unfair advantage. So…" He pulled his right arm inside his shirt, tucking it in tight.

The General gaped at Larten, then laughed. "That's

a first! Have at me, then, youngster, and may the luck of the vampires be with you."

Larten moved in on the General and tried to get a grip with his left arm. But he wasn't used to fighting one-handed. The General, who'd had years to adapt, threw the younger vampire to the floor and pinned him with his legs.

"One to me," he grinned as Larten rose and dusted himself off, then went on to throw his challenger two more times in quick succession.

Larten hadn't imagined the fight going this way, but then again he'd planned to use both arms. As he picked himself up for a third time, all he could do was laugh at the unexpected direction the bout had taken.

Many years ago the General had mocked Larten and walked off contemptuously after defeating him. But this time he helped the orange-haired vampire to his feet and embraced him warmly.

"I might have beaten you with ease, but you've earned my respect, young one. It's not easy fighting one-handed. You didn't have to challenge me on my own terms. By doing so, you proved you have courage and dignity, as well as something even more elusive—style! We'll fight again sometime, when you've had more practice with a single arm, aye?"

"Aye," Larten chuckled.

They drank much and spoke of many things that night. The General told Larten about some of the times his nose had been broken and the great vampires he had faced in challenges over the years. But he never mentioned his name, or if he did, Larten failed to note it.

Over the coming years Larten often trained with an arm tied behind his back. But he never got to test himself against the broken-nosed General again, for he died soon after Council in a fight with a panther. He was alone and his passage went unmarked, but if anyone had been present, they would have seen him smile just before his throat was ripped open. They wouldn't have known what he was grinning about, but he was fondly remembering the night when a young orange-haired assistant had challenged him to a one-armed wrestling match in the Hall of Oceen Pird.

Chapter Eleven

Night gave way to day and most of the vampires went to rest for a few hours, or tend to their injuries. At sunset they gathered in the huge Hall of Stahrvos Glen for the traditional howling contest. At the signal, every vampire howled loudly and tried to sustain it. The one who held his howl the longest would be afforded the title "of the Howl" for the next twelve years.

Larten didn't have a particularly impressive howl and faded from the contest early. But two vampires he knew well were among the last three. One was his old Cub ally, Yebba, who seemed to have grown even larger since Larten last saw him. The other was a less familiar acquaintance, Mika Ver Leth.

Larten was surprised to see Mika – dressed in black, as always – among the final trio. Normally the successful howlers were bulky and large-lunged, like Yebba, but Mika was of average height, and slender. Yet he was holding his own against the others. Larten cheered on Yebba because of their friendship, but secretly he hoped Mika would take the honors—he had always had a soft spot for an underdog.

Yebba came to a sudden, choking stop and scowled, disgusted with himself. Mika and the other General carried on for another minute, the cords in their throats strained to the breaking point, tears coursing from their eyes. Mika was in trouble – his voice was wavering – but then the other vampire fainted without warning and it was over.

A huge cheer went up and Mika was engulfed by Generals eager to toast his name and be the first to challenge him to a fight. Larten bumped into him later that night and hailed him as Mika of the Howl.

"It sounds strange," Mika said, managing a rare, thin smile.

"Were you surprised to win?" Larten asked.

"No," Mika said. "I practiced for the last decade. I took singing lessons from a human tenor and he taught me how to extend a note."

Larten frowned. "Why? It surely cannot mean that much to you."

"It means respect," Mika said seriously. "I hope to be a Prince one night and I want to be invested sooner rather than later. As trivial as this contest was, it got me noticed, and that's important."

Larten was amused by the ambitious General. Most vampires weren't political—they didn't care about power games and moving up the ranks. Mika was more like a human in that respect. But the clan was changing. The world was becoming hostile as mankind bred in ever greater numbers and claimed more territory. Vampires would have to keep an even lower profile than before if they were to survive. That meant taking the clan in a new direction. They would need youthful, imaginative leaders. A hundred years ago Mika wouldn't have gotten far in his quest to be a Prince, but Larten believed he might prosper in the current climate. He wished Mika luck in his princely pursuit, even though it wasn't a goal he personally aspired to.

But Mika wasn't the only one earning respect at that Council. Although he was unaware of it, Larten had caught the eyes of many of his peers and was beginning to make a name for himself. The clan approved of the way he had faced the one-armed

General, and although he'd lost that challenge, he had won most of his subsequent contests, defeating a host of older, more experienced vampires.

Paris Skyle heard of the youngster's success and sought out his friend Seba to congratulate him.

"The credit is not mine," Seba said with a smile, watching from the sides as Wester struggled with a vampire who had only been blooded within the last couple of years. "Larten is driven by an inner passion. I have helped him, I hope, but he cannot be molded, merely guided."

"He could go far, according to the rumors," Paris murmured.

Seba sighed. "Is that so important? If he lives a good life and is true to himself, should that not be enough?"

"My words stung you," Paris said, surprised. "Forgive me."

"You do not need to apologize, Sire," Seba said. "I have heard others talk highly of Larten, but they have noticed no merits that I had not already seen many years ago, even when I first met him as a child. I have always known that he will climb high, if he chooses to climb."

Paris frowned. "You hope that he won't."

Seba pulled a face. "Larten could be a great General, maybe even a Prince. I will be delighted if that is his aim and he achieves it. But I will be just as pleased if he merely wants to lead a clean, honest life. I have no desire to be a mentor of Princes. I simply hope that those I care about are content."

"Do you worry about what power will do to him?" Paris asked, recalling a time when he had offered Seba the chance to become a Prince. "Do you think he is not suited to a position of authority?"

Seba shrugged. "Think it? No. *Fear* it? Aye. Whether my fears are well founded or not, I cannot say. He is much like I was at that age. Perhaps I see flaws that are not there, reflections of my own weaknesses. Only time will tell. Either way, there is no point worrying about the future. He could break his back tonight and that would be the end of the matter."

"The gods give and the gods take away," Paris agreed.

Across from them, Wester finally got the better of his opponent and the pair went to drink to each other's health. Wester was beaming—he didn't enjoy many victories. Seba was pleased for him. He worried about Wester too, but felt his weaker assistant might find his path sooner than Larten, and take to it with more ease. He suspected Larten didn't yet understand his true desires, and there was nothing harder than chasing a dream if you didn't know what it was.

As if reading his friend's thoughts, Paris said, "Have you told them your good news?"

"No. I will wait until after the Ceremony of Conclusion."

"Do you think that they will stay with you?"

"Wester, aye. Larten...I do not know." Quietly he added, "I hope not."

"Come!" Paris boomed, taking his friend's arm. "I've darkened your mood. Let me lighten it again with a glass of wine."

"Wine?" Seba smiled. "I thought we only drank ale at Council."

Paris winked. "Ale is fine for younger, less sophisticated palates, but it's the juice of the grape for veterans like us, aye?"

"Aye," Seba chuckled and went to try to drown his worries with the Prince.

The children of the clan began departing Vampire Mountain a few nights after the Ceremony of Conclusion, once their heads had cleared and they could stand without wobbling. It was an undramatic exodus. Most didn't even bother to bid their friends farewell, especially the older vampires, since that wasn't their custom. They simply slipped away, some heading off in specific directions, others wandering wherever their feet took them.

Larten and Wester helped clear up inside the Halls and tunnels. It was a mammoth task, even more involved than the preparations beforehand. But it was a calmer time and they went about their work in a merry mood. Even Vanez Blane was relaxed now, often stopping to joke with the pair and tell them not to work too hard. He had already forgotten the stressful lead-up to Council and was thinking about offering his services again in the future.

Seba let the dust settle before summoning his assistants to a meeting in the Hall of Khledon Lurt. Over a bowl of bat broth he told them of his exciting offer.

"The Princes have asked me to become the quartermaster of Vampire Mountain. I have accepted."

Wester had expected the announcement – he had heard rumors during the Festival – but Larten was taken by complete surprise.

"Quartermaster?" he frowned, pushing his bowl aside. "I thought you did not yearn for power."

"I do not want to become a Prince," Seba corrected him. "Quartermaster is a very different proposition. I will wield no actual authority. In theory I will be responsible only for taking care of supplies and keeping the Halls tidy. But as you know, in reality the quartermaster has a huge say on everything that happens in Vampire Mountain, not just at Council but the rest of the time. Princes and Generals come and go as needs dictate, but the quartermaster is ever present. I will have the task of approving tutors and guards, determining how and what students are taught. I will have the ears of the Princes – the *ear* in Paris Skyle's case – and they will listen carefully to my opinions."

"They do that anyway," Larten said.

"Perhaps," Seba smiled. "But it is a different situation now. I cannot command as I could if I became a Prince. But if I live a long time – and the gods seem unwilling to take my soul, even though I am old and weary – I will be able to exert a strong influence for many decades to come. I can be a link between the old ways and the new. I think the clan needs someone like that right now."

Seba studied his assistants, awaiting their reactions. As he had suspected, Wester responded enthusiastically. "Congratulations, master. You deserve this and I know you'll be a credit to the clan."

Larten wasn't sure what to say. He already had an idea what this would mean for him and he was struggling with which path to take now that he had come to an unexpected fork in the road.

"Aye," Larten muttered. "Congratulations. May the luck of the vampires be with you."

Seba nodded, then said as lightly as he could, "What will the pair of you do now? I do not expect you to stay. I imagine you will want to leave and –"

"No!" Wester exclaimed. "I'll stay. I still have much to learn and nobody can teach me better than you."

"Are you certain?" Seba asked, ignoring the flattery. "It will be twenty or thirty years before you can become a General. That is a long time for a young vampire to spend caged inside a mountain."

"I don't care," Wester said stubbornly. "I'm staying. You will too, won't you, Larten?" There was a faint, desperate edge to Wester's voice. He was trying to sound casual, but he knew Larten was eager to leave. He didn't want to be forced to choose between his best friend and his mentor.

Larten didn't reply immediately. His brow furrowed as he considered his options. Seba longed to advise

Larten to leave, but thought it would be wrong of him to try to influence his uncertain assistant, so he held his tongue.

"Stay," Wester hissed. "This place isn't so bad. You'd have to look for a new master if you left."

"There are many who would accept you," Seba murmured, interceding only to counter the pressure that Wester was exerting. "You made a fine impression at Council and would have your choice of tutors, perhaps even Paris Skyle or another Prince."

Larten's eyes narrowed. The Princes trained only those with great potential, the vampires who might become powerful Generals and replace them further down the line. This was the first indication he'd had that the path to the Hall of Princes might open up to him in the future. Mika Ver Leth would have jumped at such an opportunity, but Larten wasn't Mika and he didn't hunger for power. Yet it was tempting. . . .

Larten glanced at Wester and saw both hope and fear in his blood brother's eyes. It was ridiculous. The pair were in their sixties. They would have been great-grandfathers with at least one foot in the grave if they hadn't been blooded. Men of their age should have long outgrown the need for a best friend.

But they were young as vampires measured such

things, and hadn't been apart since facing Murlough in the ruins of the old house. The pair had gone through much together, blooding, training, running with war packs. Larten would be lonely if they parted, but it would be harder on Wester. In the long run it might be better for him—Wester thought of himself too much as a lesser brother and maybe he needed some time apart from Larten to grow. But in the short term it would hurt.

Larten tried to distance himself from Wester's feelings, to decide what *he* wanted. But it was difficult. He felt – wrongly – that Seba would be disappointed if he left. The old vampire might think that Larten hoped to learn more from another master. He should have known better – Seba had made it clear on many occasions that the time would come when his assistants would need to establish their own lives – but his thoughts were jumbled up.

Finally Larten sighed and went with the easiest option. "I will stay," he said glumly.

Wester cheered and hugged him. Seba smiled, but inside he was troubled. When he retired to his coffin the following morning he lay awake for a long time, plagued by an uneasy feeling, wondering if he should have spoken up rather than let Larten make what he believed to be a potentially damaging call.

Chapter Twelve

The next few years were difficult for Larten. Training to be a General was a hard time for any vampire. To start with, he had to master a variety of weapons, even though he would never use most of them. Larten looked forward to his knife and ax lessons but there were others – like the throwing stars Vancha favored, and a spiked, four-headed club – that he loathed. There was no such thing as an easy lesson. He was thrown in at the deep end every time and forced to defend himself in the face of a very real attack by his tutor. Larten spent many weeks nursing broken bones, and was concussed so often that he regularly couldn't get to sleep because of the ringing in his ears.

What particularly depressed him was that Wester was making relatively smooth progress. His younger friend suffered a vast array of injuries, the same as every trainee, but nowhere near anything like Larten's. And it didn't seem to matter how hard the orange-haired assistant worked—he always came to more grief in his lessons than Wester or the others in their group.

What Larten didn't know was that his tutors were working him harder than the rest. It wasn't a conspiracy but simply the way they operated. When the taskmasters of Vampire Mountain trained someone with above-average ability, they gave him especially grueling tasks.

Vampires were ruthless. They had no time for weakness and weeded out those who would be of no benefit to the clan. This was widely known. But many of the trainees were unaware that their masters were as harsh with those who had the potential to become leaders. If a tutor thought a student had talent, he pushed the youth to his limit, to either exploit or exhaust his potential. If Larten stayed the course and proved himself worthy of the challenges he was given, he would find himself on the road to success. But if his tutors broke his spirit and he failed, they'd consider the clan well rid of him. More was always asked of those with more to offer.

Seba had no time to comfort or reassure his struggling assistant. The job of quartermaster was more demanding than he had imagined and his first few years were a hectic period of adjustment. There were so many details he had to stay on top of, from cultivating luminous lichen in tunnels where the glowing moss had died out, to maintaining the stocks of live animals, to ensuring coffins were kept clean for visitors, to dealing with the eerie Guardians of the Blood.

When Larten was injured and unable to train, he sometimes assisted Seba. It was while helping his master that he came to learn about the Guardians. He had always assumed that the blood in Vampire Mountain was shipped in and stored in vats, but now he found that most of it came from a tribe of humans living in the bowels of the mountain.

The Guardians were pale, strange creatures. In exchange for their blood, they took care of certain burial details when a vampire died, extracting each corpse's inner organs and brains, draining its body dry. Many vampires chose to be sent down a mountain stream when they died. If their corpses weren't fully cleaned out in advance, animals would feast on their poisonous organs and go insane.

Larten didn't like the Guardians – they had an aloof air and seldom answered if spoken to – but he wanted to learn as much as he could about the clan and its workings, so he studied them as dispassionately as possible.

Memorizing facts about the clan was also part of his training. Vampires were expected to familiarize themselves with their history, learn the names of their past leaders, be able to recite the many legends of their gods. Most vampires were illiterate. Books were for humans, not children of the night. Their history was recorded in tales and legends, passed on by word of mouth, and all had to help sustain it. If a disease or war ever wiped out the majority of the clan, the few who were left could at least keep their origins, achievements and myths alive.

Larten learned much about his race. Those were the nights he looked forward to most, when he and the other trainees sat around and listened to their elders wax lyrical about the past or chant ancient songs. He had a keen memory and was able to recount most of what he heard. Wester was even smarter and stored away details that Larten couldn't retain, but his friend had always been mentally sharper, so Larten didn't mind lagging behind in that department.

Wester was most interested in stories about the vampaneze. Many Generals would have happily made no mention of the breakaway group, but the war that had erupted subsequently was a crucial part of their heritage, so they reluctantly discussed the reasons behind the split and what the other night creatures had been doing since then.

Wester wanted to find out everything he could about the vampaneze, and he never seemed satisfied with what the Generals told him. He began sidetracking vampires in the Halls and tunnels, asking questions and learning more about their foes. He fell in with a group of vampaneze haters. Each of them thought that the purple-skinned traitors should be hunted to extinction. They respected the rule of the Princes – that went without question – but schemed on the sly, keeping abreast of vampaneze movements and activities, in case their leaders ever decided to sanction another war.

Wester tried to involve Larten with his new network of friends. He invited Larten to meetings and urged him to listen to their tales of vampaneze atrocities. Because Larten thought of Wester as a brother, he met with the disgruntled vampires and listened quietly as they spun wild stories of vampaneze drinking the blood of babies and targeting royals and politicians in human society. According to the rumors, they were establishing contacts around the globe, gathering an army of humans to support them in a strike on Vampire Mountain.

"They'll kill us all if we don't hit them first!" was the common rallying cry.

Larten dismissed the speculation and urged Wester to do the same. "They are mad, the lot of them," he argued. Then, before Wester could refute that, he said, "No, not all. Some speak truly, those who simply report on what the vampaneze do and where they travel. But these tales of armies and master plans..." He snorted. "The vampaneze have nothing but scorn for humans. They see mankind as cattle to drain and discard. One of the reasons they broke away from us was because of our leniency. They mock us for not killing when we feed. To suggest that they are working in league with humans is a lie and one that can easily be exposed. Question the *conspirators*. Vampaneze always tell the truth. Ask them if they plot against us. They will answer honestly—and answer nay."

"Don't tell me you believe that old tale," Wester

sneered. "Of course they lie. They just want us to think that they don't."

Larten realized he and Wester would never see eye to eye on this matter. To avoid arguments – and maybe a fight, since Wester felt that strongly about it – he stopped mingling with the dissidents. Whenever Wester invited him to a meeting, Larten made an excuse not to go. Wester soon acknowledged his friend's wishes and cut Larten out of that part of his life. He cut out his master too, knowing in his heart that although Seba disliked those who had split from the clan, he would never urge war against them. The old vampire might welcome a war if it came to pass, but he wouldn't try to provoke one or approve of those who did.

Seba would have been worried if he'd seen the vampires Wester was involved with. Maybe he would have urged his hotheaded ward to stay out of such complex, dangerous affairs. But the quartermaster was still adjusting to his new position and had little time to focus on his assistants. He kept up with reports of their development, but other than that he trusted them to the guiding hands of their tutors. By the time Seba settled into his job and was able to pay closer attention to his charges, Wester had learned not to discuss his feelings except with those who felt the same way he did.

Larten could have told Seba what was happening, but he didn't think it was important. Wester and his allies respected the rule of the Princes, there was no doubt about that, so he saw no real threat in their angry mutterings. As long as the vampire leaders maintained the truce, dissenters like Wester could do nothing to cause trouble. They were bound by their sense of duty, the way every vampire was. At worst they could march off to perish in the wilderness, as Perta Vin-Grahl and his supporters once had.

But Larten was sure it wouldn't come to that. They were just letting off steam, all talk and bluster. Nothing would come of their scaremongering. They'd need the backing of a Prince to move forward with their plans of war, but what vampire of high standing would ever support a crazy, bloodthirsty cause like theirs?

Chapter Thirteen

Larten's mood had darkened steadily. He was growing more disillusioned with every passing night and had come to hate his training, Vampire Mountain, the hierarchy of Generals and Princes. It all seemed pointless. What could they achieve, cut off from the world, never interfering in the ways of humans, settling for the shadows instead of controlling the night?

He had been looking forward to Council – he'd spent long hours practicing one-armed combat in the months leading up to it, anticipating his rematch with the broken-nosed General – but even that proved disappointing. He enjoyed the fighting and games, but every vampire seemed full of disquieting tales.

Mankind was making massive industrial advances. Cities were growing at a dizzying rate. Men were dominating the planet more than ever before. Vampires were having to withdraw deep into the wilds to roam freely.

There was an air of crisis about that Council. Two new Princes had been elected, but the clan felt as if they were at a crossroads and didn't know which way to turn. There was no sense of direction from their leaders — the Princes were divided on the issue of how to respond to the changing world. Seba had seen indecision like this before, so he took little notice of the alarm, confident that time would iron out the creases, that vampires would adapt as they always had. But to Larten it seemed like the clan was unraveling, that he was wasting his time training to be a member of an outdated order.

While Larten flailed, Wester had found a new calling and was fully focused on it. After a long talk with Seba, he had realized the life of a General wasn't for him. What he relished was life in Vampire Mountain. Abandoning his training, he instead started studying to become a guard. While they weren't as highly respected as Generals – no guard had ever become a Prince – it was an important position and

Larten was happy for his friend. He suspected Wester would make a fine guard and might one night replace Seba as quartermaster. He was pleased that Wester had chosen a suitable path and was forging ahead.

But it also made him more unsure of his own route. He couldn't say with all honesty that he still wanted to be a General. He'd had doubts before Council, and they increased afterwards. Was he pursuing this course simply because it would make Seba happy? He had no idea what he would do if he quit — was uncertainty about his future the only reason he continued to study?

In the months and years after Council his unhappiness festered. Joy seeped from his life and he went about his training halfheartedly, taking no joy from his successes, learning nothing from his failures. Seba saw the gloom that the young vampire had succumbed to. He had more time for his assistants now, but Larten was distant around his master. Seba tried getting him to talk about his depression but Larten rebuffed all advances.

Seba desperately wanted to help his troubled charge. He would have done anything to bring a smile to Larten's face. But he was helpless. Larten had to make the first move. Change was essential, but only the trainee General had the power to take his life by the scruff of the neck and shake it up.

Then, one night, thanks to a cluster of dead vampires, he did.

The Guardians of the Blood informed Seba of the problem, sending one of their pale members to track him down. Seba had been aware of the stench – most of the vampires in the mountain had caught a whiff of it – but there had been similar cases in the past and each time the issue had resolved itself. But the Guardian said that this was different. They needed to sort it out.

Seba summoned a team and had them meet him in the Hall of Final Voyage, a small cave with a stream flowing through it. This was where many vampires over the centuries had chosen to be cast off when they died. The stream would carry their bodies down through the hidden tunnels of the mountain, then wash them out into the world and far away. The custom was dying out – cremation was the current popular trend – but some of the elder vampires still preferred the more traditional method.

"I trust you can all smell that," Seba said cheerfully once his crew was in place. He took a deep breath of the putrid air and smiled as if sniffing perfume.

"I thought it was Goulder," someone laughed.

"Shut your mouth or I'll shut it for you," a vampire named Patrick Goulder snapped. Larten and the others covered their smiles. Patrick did have a problem with his odor, but it was nowhere near as bad as this.

"Bodies are stuck in the tunnel," Seba said. "This is not the first time it has happened. Usually, when the water rises in winter, it washes them away. But the Guardians have told me that will not happen on this occasion. We have to go down there and free them."

The vampires frowned, then a few looked to Larten with their eyebrows raised. Since he was Seba's assistant, it was his place to ask the question going through all of their minds.

"Surely this is a job for the Guardians," Larten muttered. "They are in charge of burials."

"No," Seba said. "*We* are in charge. We let them take control of certain details because it suits our needs. But this is our problem, not theirs.

"Come now," he chortled, trying to raise their spirits. "It is not that bad. I have brought pegs for your noses and you will be tied to one another with ropes to ensure that none of you gets washed away.

The water is no colder than in the Hall of Perta Vin-Grahl. Our chefs have prepared a fine broth for when you return. It will be an adventure!"

"Are you going down the tunnel, Seba?" one of the team asked.

"I would love to," Seba sighed. "But my back..." He winced and held his sides like an old woman.

The vampires laughed and started roping themselves together. Some would stay with Seba, to hold the ropes and pull back the others if the current proved too strong. But Larten was one of those charged with wading down the tunnel.

Larten shivered as he lowered himself into the fast-flowing water. Partly it was the chill, but mostly it was the eerie feeling of staring directly into the mouth of the funereal tunnel. Larten had never expected to pass through this opening alive. It was a journey only the dead were meant to take. It felt wrong, as if he and the others were trespassing, going where the living weren't welcome.

"I know this is difficult," Seba said seriously, "but you have nothing to fear. There are no ghosts. All of the vampires who passed through here were of good standing. Their souls flew directly to Paradise when they died."

The team in the water hesitated despite Seba's reassurances, staring down that awful hole at the blackness. Then Larten, since he knew that Seba would expect it of him, clapped loudly. "Move on, there!" he shouted at the vampires ahead of him. "The sooner we finish this, the sooner we can be back in the Hall of Khledon Lurt, warming up with a bowl of broth and a mug of ale."

Cheers greeted that and the vampires in the lead – there were two teams, set side by side – released their grip on the bank and let the current carry them out of the cave and into darkness.

Each team had a torch-carrier, but they came at the rear. So, when Larten entered the tunnel, he had to endure a minute of near-total gloom. He imagined lonely spirits drifting around him and was almost afraid of what the light of the torches would reveal. But, as Seba had said, there were no ghosts here. When the torch-bearers finally lit up the area, Larten saw nothing except rock and water. Offering up a quick prayer to the gods, he moved on in search of the blockage.

The stench worsened as they advanced and the pegs on their noses didn't help much. It seemed to thicken in the air around them and soak into their pores. A couple of the vampires choked and were sick.

The teams paused to let the vomit float ahead of them. Larten could feel his own insides rumbling, but he managed to keep his food down.

They inched their way along the tunnel, the team in the cave keeping a tight rein on them. Nobody knew what lay ahead. If the floor suddenly dropped into an underground waterfall, those on the ropes didn't want the others being swept away. As impatient as the vampires in the tunnel were, Seba made sure that the team in the cave kept a firm grip on the rope and fed it out at a slow, steady rate. Larten had no idea if he'd been in the water ten minutes or an hour. All he knew was that it seemed like an age.

Eventually they came to where the bodies had stacked up, and it was far worse than anyone had imagined. Larten tried to count the corpses, but it was impossible. They were rammed tight, a wall of bones and rotting flesh. Some were skeletons – this had been building for a number of years – but most were dotted with scraps of skin and hair. Larten could probably have recognized some of the dead if he'd looked closely.

He didn't.

Gagging and pale-faced, they closed in on the wall of the dead. One of the vampires near the front screamed and had to be released. Clinging to the rope, he scuttled back to the safety of the cave. Larten should have felt contempt, but all he could muster was envy. He wanted to follow the coward and it took all of his willpower not to.

Larten watched sickly as the two vampires at the head of the team reached out and tugged at the obstruction. If luck was with the group, the pair at the front would shake the corpses free and the rest of them need never touch the remains of the dead.

But the luck of the vampires was in scarce supply that night. The wall of bones rattled but didn't give. Sighing, Larten and the others edged forward until all were within touching distance of the stinking corpses.

Patrick Goulder raised a fist and threw a punch at the bones nearest him, trying to smash a way through.

"Stop!" Larten roared. When Patrick looked at him, Larten growled, "They might be dead, but they are still children of the clan, Generals who fought bravely and deserve our respect. We will not shatter their bones unless all else fails. We will try to pry them apart gently, to keep each corpse intact."

Patrick snorted. "Do you think it makes a difference? They'll be torn to pieces by animals on the outside anyway."

"What happens outside is not our business," Larten said. "What happens within this mountain *is*."

Patrick rolled his eyes but didn't argue. Since Larten had spoken up and taken charge, it fell on him to make the first stab at the mound of bodies. Gulping, he reached up, ran his fingers over a few of the skeletons, located the shoulders of one and pulled softly. When nothing happened, he tugged harder. Finally the upper half came free, but so did a mess of rotting bat corpses that had lodged in the network of bones. They shot out of a hole that Larten hadn't seen, propelled by a snapping bone, and splattered his face.

Larten shrieked, fell backwards and went under, pulling the skeleton with him. For a moment of pure panic he thrashed beneath the water, the bones of the dead pushing him down. In his fear he thought the vampire had come back to life and was trying to kill him. He lashed out at the skeleton, tasting the foul guts of the dead bats. He tried to spit them out, but water drove bits of disgusting organs down his throat. As Larten retched, hands gripped his arms and pulled him up.

He cried out as he broke the surface, eyes wild. The peg had been knocked from his nose and the stench hit him harder than ever. He retched again, vomiting up the contents of his stomach.

"Do you want to go back?" Patrick Goulder asked.

Larten wanted to retreat more than anything. But it would have been a sign of weakness and he didn't want to lose face in front of the others.

"Just give me a minute," he gasped, wiping his lips clean and letting his heart settle. When the tremble in his hands subsided slightly, he joined the rest of the team and went to work on the bodies again.

They spent most of the next hour in the cold, wet confines of the tunnel, freeing bones and limbs, picking intertwined skeletons apart, carefully loosening the knot of bodies. It was hard, horrible work, and they did it in silence. Each of them knew that they would never discuss this afterwards. This wasn't a dirty job that they'd make light of later. It was an awful task and it would haunt them for many weeks and months to come. No amount of ale would erode this unpleasant memory. Larten had a nasty suspicion that he might even take it with him to the grave.

Chapter Fourteen

When the crew in the tunnel returned solemn and grim, nobody tried to lighten the atmosphere. Seba and the vampires on the ropes could see the horror in the eyes of those they dragged back. Without saying anything they covered the sodden team in blankets and led them to where broth, bread and ale were waiting in abundance.

Larten ate mechanically, filling the emptiness of his stomach, his eyes unfocused. He was thinking about the corpses, imagining himself as one of them. Vampires could live for hundreds of years. Most rarely thought about time the way humans did, since they had so much of it to play with. Death was a far-off, distant thing for the average child of the night.

But the bodies in the tunnel had reminded Larten of his mortality. There was no guarantee that he would live to be as old as Seba. Maybe destiny would strike him down young. If it did, he wanted to be able to say that he had truly lived, that he had experienced all of the pleasures of the world, that he hadn't just trudged along miserably like a turtle in the shell of Vampire Mountain.

Larten didn't even touch his mug of ale. In a corner of his mind he had already made his decision, and although he hadn't consciously realized that yet, part of him made sure that he kept a clear head. When he acted, that part wanted him to be sober, so there could be no doubt that he meant it.

He was halfway through a second bowl of broth when he stopped, pushed it aside and stood. The others glanced at him but said nothing. He wasn't the first to depart the table abruptly. They assumed he was leaving to be sick. But they were wrong.

Larten made a beeline for Seba's cave. The quartermaster had his own room in the mountain. He'd offered to share it with his assistants, but they had declined — Seba was now a vampire of great importance and he was entitled to his privacy.

Wester was with their master, discussing some matter to do with his training. Larten was relieved—it meant he'd just have to go through this once. It was only years later that he wondered if Seba had read the intention in his eyes when he was pulled out of the tunnel, even before he knew of it himself, and summoned Wester on a pretext to make things easier for Larten.

If Seba *did* know what Larten was going to say, he hid the knowledge well. There was nothing in his expression but mild curiosity when Larten entered. "Can I help you?" he asked politely.

"I am leaving," Larten said.

Wester stared at him oddly. He knew nothing of the pileup in the tunnel or what Larten had been through. But Seba knew what his assistant meant and he nodded softly. "Very well."

Larten frowned. "You do not understand. I am quitting my studies. I do not want to be a General. I am sick of this place. I am *leaving*."

"No!" Wester gasped. "You can't mean it. What's happened? Why are you –"

"I understand perfectly," Seba interrupted. "I never asked you to stay and I do not hold you against your will. You are no longer a Cub. You are a man of wisdom and experience. I am honored that you and

Wester still call me master, but in truth no one is your master now or ever will be again. If you wish to go, you can go with my blessings."

Larten hadn't expected this. In a strange way he felt cheated. He wanted Seba to be hurt, to try to convince him to stay. It was childish – *human* – but in his heart he craved attention. This was a momentous decision and he needed an argument to mark it.

Wester unwittingly gave Larten what he required.

"You can't leave," he huffed. "This is madness. Seba told me you've nearly completed your training."

"I also asked you to keep that information to yourself," Seba snapped, his eyes flashing with a rare spike of anger.

"Is that true?" Larten asked, momentarily flustered. He had thought he was five or ten years away from becoming a General, assuming he passed his tests at all.

"You have impressed some of your peers," Seba sniffed, still glaring at Wester. "There was talk of passing you in the near future. But after this display, I doubt it. A General must know his mind completely. On this evidence, you do not."

"I damn well do," Larten growled, finding his fury again. "I want out. I do not want to be a General. You are all old-fashioned and backwards."

132

"Larten!" Wester cried, alarmed by this vicious, uncharacteristic attack.

Larten laughed bitterly. "Every vampire should pursue his dreams, live life to its maximum, chase a glorious, savage death. We should not be imprisoned here, *training*. Are we students or men? Humans or vampires?"

Before Wester could answer, Larten pressed on. "I say to hell with Generals, Princes and the rest. Life is too short. I want to live, fight, love, die. Not waste my time studying."

"Who is stopping you?" Seba thundered. He had been sitting, but now he rose and faced Larten on his feet. His cheeks were flushed. "If we disgust you, leave immediately. Do not even pause to pack your belongings — you can do without them. I never intended to come between you and your *dreams*." He invested the word with as much sarcasm as he could.

"Very well," Larten snarled. "I will."

And with that he stormed out of the room. Wester gave a cry and darted after Larten, but Seba grabbed him as he tried to pass.

"No," Seba said quietly. "Leave him be."

"But we can't let him run off like that!" Wester exclaimed. "He wasn't thinking clearly. He'll be sorry when he calms down. He'll want to apologize. We have to let him know –"

"He was more himself in that outburst than he has been for many years," Seba said, then chuckled.

Wester was astonished to see his master smiling.

"Larten needs to go," Seba said, sitting again and narrowing his eyes. He was imagining the path the young vampire would take, the tunnels he'd hurry through, the thoughts that might be crashing around inside his head. He hoped Larten would stay true to his convictions— it would be disastrous if he turned back now.

"Master...I don't understand...don't you like Larten anymore?"

"Like him?" Seba's features softened. "I love him, you idiot, as I love you. You are sons to me, as I have told you before. But every son must put considerations of his father aside eventually. You did that when you chose to train to be a guard—you made a choice and became your own man. Larten is doing the same."

"But he left in such a foul temper. Perhaps I should call him back and –"

"By the gods, no!" Seba shouted. "You are wiser than that, Wester Flack, so do not act like a fool. I know you will miss Larten – I will too – but it is time for him to seek his own way. If you interfere now, you might destroy him. This has been a difficult decision for him to make. If he relented, returned and had to make the choice again later, I do not think that he could."

"But..." Wester stared at his master. "What if I went with him?"

"You have the same right to leave as he has," Seba said stiffly. Then he smiled. "But you will not. Your place is here and you know it. We must let him go. If the luck of the vampires is with him, he will return when he is ready. But for now he must walk his own path, or at least try to find it."

Wester nodded slowly, then looked at the gaping space of the doorway. "I fear for him. He doesn't know what he wants. He'll run into trouble."

"Probably," Seba said glumly. "But he is strong and I believe that he will find his way in the end. If I am wrong..." Seba sighed and pressed the middle finger of his left hand to his forehead. Keeping his eyes open, he covered them with his second and fourth fingers, spreading his thumb and smallest finger wide. "Even in death may he be triumphant."

Then Seba put all thoughts of his departing assistant from his mind and focused on his duties, leaving Larten Crepsley to the unknowable workings of whatever destiny held in store for him.

Part Four

"I can stitch you up if you wish."

Chapter Fifteen

The next few years of Larten Crepsley's life were his wildest and most carefree. Larten flitted to get away swiftly from all that he had come to loathe, even though vampires were not supposed to flit on the path to or from the mountain. The rebellious act was his way of showing how little he cared for the rules of the clan. He knew it was a petty gesture, but that didn't stop him.

He cut through the world at a frenetic pace, traveling freely, spending much of his time on boats, carriages, even trains. It was his first time trying one of the iron horses. The rocking motion made him feel sick to begin with, but he adjusted to it after a while, even though he never wavered from his opinion that it went far faster than any land vehicle had a need to.

For years he avoided contact with other vampires, moving from one town and city to another, mixing mostly with men of lax principles and ladies of easy virtue, since they were the ones who came out at night. He stole vast amounts of money and spent it lavishly. He gambled heavily, backed many foolish, high-risk ventures for sport, and at one stage ran his own stable of boxers and fighting cockerels.

Larten tried things he'd avoided even as a Cub, things no sane person should try. He treated his body with disrespect, interested only in how far he could push it. There were many nights when he couldn't rise, only lie in a dark room, shaking like a rabid rat, waiting for death to put him out of his misery.

If he had been a lesser vampire, he would have surely died. But his years of harsh lessons had toughened him. He could take more punishment than most, go further, last longer. No matter how many mad nights he subjected himself to, he always struggled back.

In time he calmed down and put the worst of the craziness behind him. He had tasted almost all the dark pleasures of the human world and was bored of them. He made no friends in those seedy years, but many cronies flocked to his side, men and women all too eager to spend the money he never seemed to run out of, to go on wild sprees with him and try to match his wild appetites. They praised Larten and spoke of their love and respect for him, but he knew they were lost, base creatures, wringing what profit they could from one in an even worse state than themselves.

One night he simply walked out on the hangers-on, the same way he had walked out on the clan. They were much easier to leave behind than Seba or Wester. These people didn't truly care for him, only for the wicked pleasures he brought into their lives. They were vermin and vultures. He didn't think he was any better than them, but he hoped that he could be. Out of pity, he threw what cash he had at them and left while they squabbled over it.

He tried running with the Cubs again. There was a gaping hole in his life that needed to be filled. He craved company and excitement. He didn't want to wake every evening by himself, bored, lonely, desperate to kill time. He yearned to find a purpose and he thought the Cubs might give him that, at least for a time.

But going back to the war packs was a mistake. All of the vampires he'd known had moved on or died. Their replacements welcomed Larten into the fold, but he felt awkward around them. He couldn't work up the same enthusiasm for drink, war, women and gambling. He found the young Cubs loud, ignorant and dull. He didn't like to believe he'd ever been so shallow, but was sure he must have been.

He fed with war packs a couple of times, then no more. Bidding the Cubs a not-so-fond farewell, he wandered again, keeping to himself, avoiding the larger towns and crowds. He spent many lonely nights in graveyards or caves, brooding, feeling as if he would never find his place in the world.

Returning to the Cirque Du Freak, he asked Mr. Tall if he could help out as he had before. Hibernius Tall wasn't one to turn away an old friend, but Larten soon realized this wasn't the life for him, certainly not in his current state. He loved the circus and would have been happy at another time to settle down there. But he was restless, so he moved on with no more idea of what he wanted than he had when he left Vampire Mountain.

A few years after that, Larten was hunting deer. He had been tracking a herd for hours. He could have moved in for the kill sooner, but he was in no rush. His clothes were filthy rags. He'd grown a beard – a light brown color, which must have been the original shade of his hair – and his nails were long and ragged. There were bloodstains around his mouth from previous feasts, and dried-in smears across his cheeks.

"Charna's guts! You look even rougher than me," someone laughed behind him, startling the vampire. He twirled so fast that he lost his balance and fell. As he landed on his backside, his gaze settled on a grinning Vancha March.

"What are you doing here?" Larten barked.

"Just happened to be passing," Vancha sniffed. "I caught your smell – couldn't really miss it – and thought I'd come see what you were up to."

Vancha spent the next couple of nights roaming with Larten, letting him tell his sorry story. The General made no comment, just listened quietly. When Larten finally ran out of words to express his miserable state, Vancha said that the younger vampire could travel with him if he wished.

"I'm going through a bit of an aimless period myself," he said. "I went on a quest to find the palace of Perta Vin-Grahl a few years ago." Vin-Grahl had led a group of vampires off into a frozen wilderness to die not long after the war with the vampaneze. According to legends, they'd built a castle of ice and turned it into a mass burial tomb. Many vampires had searched for the last resting place of the doomed group over the centuries.

"Any luck?" Larten asked.

"No," Vancha sighed. "I really thought I'd find it, but all I got in the end was frostbite. Almost lost a few toes. I've been too ashamed to report back to the clan. I can't avoid them indefinitely, but I'd like to wait a bit longer before subjecting myself to their laughter. Paris will be especially tickled—he bet me my favorite shuriken that I wouldn't find the palace."

The pair wandered purposelessly but pleasantly for the next year. They hunted and told each other stories. They regularly sparred to pass the time and Larten unwittingly found himself completing many of the tasks he would have had to pass to become a General. Vancha would always swear over the decades to come that he hadn't meant to play the part of a mentor, but Larten had his doubts. Like Seba, Vancha could be a sly operator when slyness was called for.

Most nights they slept beneath a tree or a bush. Vancha didn't believe in creature comforts like coffins. He was never happier than when sleeping on a cold, rocky floor, covered in nothing more than his purple animal hides. Larten didn't enjoy such lean living, but he got used to it. In any case, it was better to sleep rough with a friend than in the lap of luxury by himself.

One night, while resting, Vancha decided to show off his spitting prowess. He spat high into the air, kept his mouth open and caught the spit as it dropped back down. Gulping, he chortled and said, "I bet you can't do that."

"Why in the name of all the gods would I want to?" Larten muttered.

"It's a talent," Vancha said.

"So is picking your nose with your tongue."

"Can you?" Vancha asked eagerly.

"I have never tried and I do not intend to," Larten said.

Vancha stuck out his tongue and explored, but although he could touch the tip of his nose if he pushed it down with a finger, his tongue wouldn't reach as far as his nostril of its own accord. In the end he grunted and settled for spitting high and catching it again.

"Come on," he urged Larten. "Try it. It's fun."

"I have no intention of spitting on myself," Larten said stiffly, smothering a smile. "Now leave me alone or you will be swallowing one of your shurikens instead of a gobful of spit."

"Leave my shurikens alone," Vancha growled,

caressing the throwing stars that were attached to belts looped around his body. Vancha preferred to fight with his hands – he believed weapons were a sign of weakness – but the shurikens were an exception. "Some of these are hundreds of years old. They're historical."

Larten frowned. "I thought you made them yourself."

"Most of them, aye. But I've got a few from the Edo period, even one that I think goes back to the Kamakuras."

"What are you talking about?" Larten asked.

"The great Japanese dynasties. Don't you know anything of history?"

"Not a lot," Larten said. "I spent the last thirty or so years trying to memorize all of the vampire milestones. I had no time to research human history too."

"You should have made time," Vancha tutted. "Only a fool forgets where he comes from. I don't have much to do with the human world, but we all started off there and we can learn much about ourselves by studying the highs and lows of mankind over the centuries."

"Then tell me, good master," Larten simpered. Although he was being sarcastic, Vancha took the request seriously. For the next few nights Larten was treated to a full rundown of the Japanese dynasties from the Asuka up to the Edo, with special emphasis on the weapons each favored, particularly those of the small, pointed, throwing kind. By the end of his lessons, he almost wished he *had* followed through on his threat and rammed a shuriken down Vancha's throat. The shabby, smelly General was a fine friend but a truly boring historian!

Chapter Sixteen

Eventually Vancha had to resume his duties. As a General he had to sit in on various meetings, keep an eye on the Cubs, monitor the movements of the vampaneze, investigate rogue vampires. He invited Larten to join him on a few assignments. Since he had nothing better to do, Larten accepted.

Having checked on a few of the rowdier Cubs and admonished them – even the tearaway youngsters were expected to obey certain rules – Vancha and Larten set off in pursuit of a vampire called Arrow who had severed contact with the clan. The Princes wanted to know why he had cut himself off.

Vancha found their target by a process known as

triangulation. Like almost every vampire, Arrow had placed his hands on the Stone of Blood in Vampire Mountain when he'd pledged himself to the clan, allowing it to draw blood from him. One of the Princes in the mountain checked with the magical Stone and located Arrow's position. The Prince then communicated telepathically with Vancha and directed him.

Vancha followed his directions until they came to a house in a forest. They arrived late at night and made camp without approaching the house. After a short sleep, they lurked behind a couple of trees and kept watch throughout the day. They saw a red-haired woman at work within and around the house over the course of the day, but there was no sign of Arrow.

He appeared as the sun was setting. He came out, squinted at the sky, kissed the woman, then went to get water as she slipped inside the house. Arrow was a large, bald, thickly built man. There were tattoos of arrows on both sides of his head and down his forearms. He didn't look like someone who would walk away the worse for wear from most fights. His scowl as he drew a bucket of water from a well to the side of the house did nothing to soften his tough impression.

Arrow set the full bucket on the ground beside the

well, then growled without looking up. "Come forward if you're coming. I don't like peeping Thomases."

"Apologies," Vancha said airily, stepping out into sight. "I wasn't sure what the state of play was. Didn't want to barge in and create any difficulties."

Arrow nodded gruffly at Vancha, ran a cold eye over Larten, then sniffed. "Sarah will have dinner ready soon. You're welcome to share it with us."

Larten and Vancha exchanged a glance, then moved forward. Vancha looked relaxed, but Larten noted the way his fingers stayed by his shurikens. He made sure his knives were within easy reach and kept close to Vancha, ready to back him up if they were attacked.

The woman inside the house – Sarah – looked up with surprise when Arrow stomped in and said, "We have visitors." She started to smile curiously when the odd pair entered. Then Arrow said, "They're vampires." Her smile vanished in an instant and she set the table in silence.

Arrow laid the bucket close to the fire, kissed Sarah again, then sat and nodded for Vancha and Larten to join him. "Sarah's my wife," he said quietly, his hands clenched into fists. "Where does the clan stand on such issues these nights?"

"You married a human?" Vancha frowned.

"I married a beautiful, loving woman," Arrow corrected him. Larten saw a smile dart across Sarah's lips as she half-turned to look at her husband. "Now answer my question."

Vancha scratched an armpit. "You weren't this grumpy before. The soft life doesn't agree with you."

"It agreed with me nicely until you and your assistant turned up," Arrow said.

"Larten's not my assistant, just a friend."

"No matter. I've asked twice already, Vancha. Don't make me –"

"The Generals aren't interested," Vancha said. "We don't approve of vampires mating with humans, but it's been a long time since we banned such unions, so why are you worried?"

"Times change," Arrow noted. "I wasn't sure what the current mood was. When you turned up, after I'd asked to be left alone, I thought –"

"Slow down," Vancha interrupted. "Who did you *ask*? You dropped out of sight without a word to anyone. That's why I came."

Arrow frowned. "I told Azis Bendetta of my decision when I chose to abandon my studies and not become a General."

Vancha sighed. "Azis is dead."

"When?"

"Four years or more."

"Even in death may he be triumphant," Arrow muttered, making the death's touch sign. He looked sad as he lowered his hand, but relieved too. "He must have died before he delivered my message."

"Aye." Vancha was smiling now.

"So I'm not in any trouble?"

"No."

Arrow shook his head and chuckled, then boomed, "Sarah! Ale and warm milk for our guests."

"I'll take mine cold, thanks," Vancha laughed, then leaned forward and clapped Arrow's shoulder. When Larten saw that, he relaxed and smiled at Sarah as she passed him a mug of ale. When no one was looking, he shifted his knives around to the side. This wasn't to be a night for fighting after all.

Arrow's story was short and simple. He had met Sarah and fallen in love. He'd told her the truth about himself early in their relationship, that he was a barren, bloodsucking night creature who would live for hundreds of years.

"His sterility was the hardest thing to accept," Sarah said. She had a soft voice and a shy smile. "I wasn't worried about the vampire part – I could tell he wasn't evil – and I'm glad he'll live so long. But not being able to have children..."

"We'll probably take in some orphans one day," Arrow said, rubbing a finger down Sarah's arm. "But at the moment we're still enjoying being a couple. The novelty hasn't worn off yet. We'll start a family in a few years, aye?"

"Aye," Sarah giggled.

It wasn't unheard of for a vampire to take a human mate, but usually only Cubs crossed that divide.

"Five years ago I'd have said you were crazy if you'd told me this would happen," Arrow insisted. "I didn't approve of those who mated outside the –"

"Arrow..." Sarah said warningly.

"Sorry. Those who *married* outside the clan."

"What's wrong with mating?" Vancha asked.

"Animals mate," Sarah said frostily. "Humans marry."

"But we're neither," Vancha noted.

"You're more human than animal," Sarah said. "At least Arrow and Larten are." She cocked an eyebrow at the odd-looking, green-haired General and he hooted with delight. To Vancha, an insult from a beautiful woman counted as a twisted compliment.

"Anyway," Arrow went on, "I was content as a vampire. I never meant to look for a human mate—wife," he corrected himself quickly as Sarah narrowed her eyes. "But we met while I was recovering from a wound and..." He shrugged.

"...you lived happily ever after," Vancha finished with a smile. Then his smile faded. "Except you won't, will you? Forgive me for speaking bluntly, Sarah, but human lives are short compared to ours. Do you plan to let Arrow blood you?"

"No," Sarah said with conviction. "I love the sun too much to hide from it. I'd rather have a short life of days than centuries of nights."

"So what happens when your heart gives out and Arrow has to stick you in a hole to rot?" Vancha asked.

"As diplomatic as ever," Arrow said drily, sharing a sad look with his wife.

"That worries me," Sarah whispered, grasping Arrow's hand. "I almost didn't marry him because I don't want to leave him like that, but..."

"The future will bring what it brings," Arrow grunted. "There are no guarantees in life. I might die before her, of disease or an accident. If I don't, I will grieve as any husband grieves when his wife dies.

Then...I'm not sure. If we have children, I'll finish rearing them. If we have grandchildren, I might stay and watch them grow. If not, or after that...who knows?"

"The clan will welcome you back if you choose to return," Vancha said. "We won't cut you off just because you fell in love. You can finish your training — you were only months away from your final test, and you know we all thought highly of you."

"That's kind of you, but I can't see myself ever becoming a General now. Maybe that will change, but I doubt it. Perhaps, if I outlive her, I'll just sit by Sarah's grave, drink no blood and wait to join her."

"You'll do no such thing!" Sarah barked. "If you do, and there's a Paradise, I'll make your life a misery for the rest of eternity."

Arrow leaned forward and kissed her flushed forehead. "Whatever you say, my dear," he murmured.

They stayed up late, eating, drinking, chatting. Sarah went to bed a few hours before sunrise and then it was just the vampires. When they were alone, they spoke of the clan. Vancha told Arrow about Azis Bendetta's death and brought him up to date with all the latest intrigues and happenings.

"The anti-vampaneze brigade is going strong," he

said at one point. "The fools are spoiling for a war. As if one wasn't enough."

"Do you really think it might come to that?" Arrow asked, alarmed.

"No," Vancha said. "The Princes know that war would be catastrophic. One or two might be swayed if the situation was different, but as long as there are the likes of Paris and Chok Yamada to talk sense to them, the truce will hold."

They slept in Arrow's house that day – Vancha reluctantly made his bed on the soft (by his standards) wooden floor, not wanting to offend his host by sleeping outside – and ate with him and Sarah the following night. After their meal, Vancha wished the pair the luck of the vampires, then he and Larten took their leave.

Larten was thoughtful as they slipped through the forest. He'd never considered returning to the human fold as Arrow had. Part of him liked the idea of finding a mate, marrying, adopting children. He'd thought that he had left that world behind forever, but now he saw that it could be his again if he truly wanted it.

"That's a waste of a good vampire," Vancha sighed, disturbing Larten's train of thought. "Arrow was a great fighter. He could have gone far."

"But he is happy where he is," Larten noted.

Vancha shrugged. "Since when did vampires care about happiness? A creature of the night feels satisfied when all is well with his world. That's nature's way. Happiness is a human folly. Vampires who seek it usually come to no good."

"That is a cynical way of looking at life," Larten said.

"I call it like I see it," Vancha huffed. "If Arrow had taken a vampiress for a mate, that would be different. But marrying a human..." He shook his head, then chuckled. "Mind you, having cast my eye over the vampiresses at the last Council, I can't blame him. They're a grim lot, aren't they? Fine fighters, but you wouldn't want to kiss any of them!"

"I do not think that someone in your position can be too particular," Larten said.

"What are you talking about?" Vancha frowned. "I'd be a first-rate catch. No woman could go wrong with a specimen like me." To prove his point, he spat into his palm and wiped phlegm into his scalp. "I mean, seriously, what lady of taste could resist a shiny green head of hair like mine?"

Chapter Seventeen

Soon after their meeting with Arrow, Vancha was summoned to Vampire Mountain on business. Larten chose not to travel with him. They made vague plans to meet up again, but their paths took them elsewhere and several years passed without any contact.

Larten spent those years falling back into the dark pit from which Vancha had briefly rescued him. His time with the General had refired his love for the clan, reminding him why he'd agreed to become Seba's assistant in the first place. But he still didn't want to return to Vampire Mountain and complete his training. Not yet. He had a sense that he wasn't finished with the human world, that until he worked whatever was troubling him out of his system, he would never know peace.

One night as he glumly considered his options – trying to pick a country or city he hadn't visited before – he found himself thinking about Lady Evanna. He hadn't thought of the witch in a long time. He'd meant to take advantage of her offer to visit her at home, but it had slipped his mind.

He knew instantly that this was what he craved. Something different, a place part of neither the human nor vampire world. He had no idea where Evanna lived, but he was sure he could find her. She'd given him that ability. All he had to do was set off and his feet would lead him.

It was a long trek. He had meant to use trains and carriages, but whenever he got on one he lost track of where he was going. Flitting disoriented him too. Evanna's directions only revealed themselves when he was on foot, so he had to abandon the easy alternatives and walk. But the path wasn't difficult and it was a pleasant time of year. He enjoyed the journey more than any he had undertaken recently.

Finally, months after setting out, he arrived at a small hill in a clearing. There was a cave near the base of the hill and a pond farther down. Larten didn't see the mouth of the cave the first time he looked. If he hadn't felt certain that this was the place, he would have walked by. But when he forced himself to peer harder, he saw the cave clearly and went towards it.

There were lots of frogs by the rim of the pond, croaking noisily. Some were oddly colored and a few had strange inklike markings on their heads and backs. Larten decided to investigate further and set out to catch one of the frogs.

"I wouldn't do that," someone said as he crept towards the pond. Larten looked up and spotted a girl no more than twelve or thirteen years old. She was carrying a bucket and staring at him seriously. "They're poisonous."

"Poisonous frogs?" Larten asked dubiously.

"Sacs along their tongues," the girl said. "If they hit your skin, they'll break and poison will seep in. Death within minutes, even if you're a vampire."

"You know what I am?"

The girl nodded. "My Lady has been expecting you." She pulled a face and shook the bucket. "That's why I'm dragging this. Evanna said you'd want a hot bath when you arrived, so I've been fetching water for the last couple of hours."

"My apologies," Larten said. "I can carry that for you if you like."

The girl smiled shyly. "That's all right. I can manage."

They chatted as they walked to the cave. The girl was called Malora. She couldn't remember her surname—Evanna had taken her as an apprentice when she was five or six and much of her early life was a mystery.

"Did your parents let Evanna take you, or did they sell you to her?" Larten asked.

"They didn't *sell* me," Malora huffed. "I'm not a slave, even if my Lady treats me like one much of the time."

Larten smiled. "I have heard such tales of woe before. Does Arra Sails still serve here?"

"Never heard of her," Malora said. "Was she one of Evanna's apprentices?"

"Aye. She did not like her mistress any more than you seem to."

"Nobody does," Malora snorted. "She had four other girls when I came. I'm the only one left, and I don't think I'll hang around much longer either. As soon as I find someone to escort me safely back to the normal world, I'm gone!"

Larten chuckled. The girl was young but feisty, like Arra had been. It was a pity she wasn't older — maybe he would have had more success wooing her than he'd had with the fiery Miss Sails.

As they neared the cave, Evanna appeared. She looked exactly as she had the last time he'd seen her. She hadn't changed or aged. Her hair was long and dirty, she still wore ropes, and her nails were cut in the same unusual fashion.

"Welcome, wanderer." She curtsied before Larten, then hugged him hard. She didn't pick him off the ground, but she did pinch his cheek. "I thought you were never going to pay me a visit," she chided him. "Come — the bath is ready."

Larten frowned. "What makes you think I am desperate to have a bath?"

"It's not for you, fool," she snorted. "Don't you remember what you said when we last parted?" He stared at her blankly. "You promised to scrub my back," she reminded him, and as he recalled that brash boast, his face dropped and his cheeks turned several shades redder than they had when she'd pinched him.

Larten spent the next few nights with the Lady of the Wilds, Malora always in close attendance, although the apprentice didn't say much, so he often forgot she was there. The vampire and witch sparred – she enjoyed testing herself in battle against him, although he was sure she could have flattened him with a flick of a wrist if she'd wished – and she treated him to a variety of vegetarian dishes. He had been skeptical of the food at first, but Evanna had surprised him with a variety of extraordinary concoctions. It wasn't enough to sway Larten away from meat, even though she kept urging him to put his carnivorous side behind him, but he wouldn't turn up his nose at vegetables and fruit again.

Evanna had some news of Seba and Wester, which she shared. It was all minor – reports of changes Seba had made in his role as quartermaster, news that Wester was close to becoming a guard – but Larten lapped up the tidbits.

In return Larten told Evanna of his indecision. It was good to get the doubts and regrets off his chest, to admit how sorry he felt about the way he'd spoken to Seba, bemoan the years he had wasted and wonder aloud at what the future held. He asked her for advice, but she was reluctant to give any.

"When it comes to the future, I have to be careful," she said. "I have the gift of foresight – I see things that have not yet happened – so I can't interfere."

"Have you seen *my* future?" Larten asked eagerly.

"Parts of it," she said cagily. "I try not to learn too much about the destinies of those I like. It's not nice knowing how much time a friend has left, the hardships they'll face, the pain they'll suffer."

"You see hardship and suffering in my future?" Larten asked quietly.

"I was speaking in general terms," she corrected him. "We all suffer one way or another. In your case..." She seemed set to reveal something and he leaned forward eagerly. Then she paused and cocked her head. Larten thought he heard a faint ticking noise – a watch perhaps – but he couldn't place it.

"Destiny watches over all of us," she said softly. "But some catch its eye more than others." She gazed at Malora and her expression was troubled. Then her head swung towards the mouth of the cave. By the way her face creased, Larten thought that somebody must be lurking there. But he could see no one, and moments later the witch waved away her worries.

"This is not the time to worry about what the future might bring," she said. "Let us drink and be merry. Your fate will reveal itself in due course, as it always does. But muse on this the next time you fret about your path—we always travel the way we must.

You might think that you have strayed, but no one ever steps from the path of destiny. Your doubts have always been waiting for you. Accept them, deal with them, and you will find your way to that which destiny requires of you.

"For better or for worse," she finished glumly and would say no more about it, leaving Larten to puzzle over her strange mutterings for a long time to come.

That night Larten took Evanna's advice to drink and be merry a little too closely to heart. Ale was his tipple of choice, but he had tried most alcoholic brews in his time. Since Evanna preferred wine, he drank it with her, even though she warned him that it was stronger than the wines he was familiar with.

"I can drink any man under the table," Larten laughed. "And any vampire too."

"What about a sorceress?" Evanna asked.

"I will give it a good try," he winked, toasting her health and asking Malora to refill his glass.

In a light mood, Evanna drank more than usual, and although she could never get drunk – it was physically impossible for one of her kind – she relaxed to the point where she wasn't thinking clearly. She laughed at Larten's jokes and smiled when he flattered her. The flattery was nothing new, but her response was different. Larten began to think that she might be warming to his advances. The more he drank, the surer he became that the Lady of the Wilds was falling for his charms. She would become his mate and they'd have many powerful children. He wouldn't have to worry about his future then — every vampire would idolize him, regardless of whether he'd completed his training or not.

"Evanna," he murmured late in the night. His voice was only slightly slurred, but inside his head was spinning. "Do you remember the form you took before? The beautiful lady you became?"

"Are you saying I'm not beautiful now?" she snorted.

"Of course you are!" he cried. "You are always a delight to behold. But that other form...you know the one I mean...that was *nice*. Could you change again?"

"Don't be impudent," Evanna snarled, but she was smirking at the same time.

"Please, Lady, I beg you, give me a vision to send me to bed mesmerized and dreamy."

Evanna usually rejected such pleas – she only changed form to suit herself – but Malora saw her mistress smile in an odd way and sensed trouble brewing. The girl topped up the glasses for Evanna and Larten, then slipped away. They thought she was going to bed, but Malora had other plans. If things worked out the way she suspected, this would be an eventful night not just for the witch and vampire, but for her too.

Evanna didn't notice her apprentice pick up a bag from beside her bed and slip outside. She was still considering Larten's request. Seeing this, he pressed harder.

"It was a most fair form, Lady. Please let me worship before it again."

"Save your worship for the gods," Evanna sniffed, but she decided to oblige him. Her body shimmered and moments later she was slim and tall, her hair long and blond, her eyes soft and deep. Larten had never heard of a fairy-tale princess more beautiful than this. His heart leapt as it had on that previous occasion and the laughter drained from him.

"This pleases you, young monkey?" Evanna purred, twirling for him, letting the hem of her dress swish around her like a mist.

"It pleases me a lot," Larten said weakly. He'd meant to come out with some lavish compliment, but that was the best he could manage.

168

"Vampires are simple creatures," Evanna giggled. "So easy to please. I wish I was like you. Life would be so straightforward if I could be content with shining like an angel, winning the heart of every man who saw me. I think I would..."

Evanna kept talking but Larten was no longer focused on her words. His heart was pounding and he had only one thought in his head. Not even a tiny part of him cried caution. He yearned for Evanna totally, as he had never longed for a woman before.

He rose shakily as Evanna prattled on, steadied himself, wiped his lips dry, then took hold of the heavenly maiden in the long white dress. Evanna thought he wanted to dance and she laughed. But then he leaned forward and kissed her, and everything suddenly, drastically changed.

"You cur!" Evanna yelled, more shocked than outraged. She pulled back from him and he tried to follow. Snarling, she lashed out with her right hand. The long nail on her little finger caught the flesh high up his left cheek, dug in deep and ripped a channel down to the side of his lip, where it tore free.

Larten shrieked and fell backwards, blood oozing from the wound, his eyes wide with fright and pain. For a moment he thought Evanna was going to finish him off and he cowered as she fixed him with a glare and her hands rose into claws.

Then the Lady of the Wilds caught herself and took a step back. "Get out!" she barked.

Larten didn't wait to be told a second time. Stumbling to his feet, he ran for his life, trying to stem the flow of blood by tearing a strip of material from his shirt and pressing it to his cheek.

Evanna only meant for him to leave her sight and come back once she'd calmed down. But as he ran, she realized he had taken her order the wrong way. He thought she was banishing him. She started to call after him, to say that he could stay and she would repair the flesh of his face so that he didn't get a scar. But as the words formed on her lips, she heard a soft ticking sound. Her chest tightened and she almost called to him anyway. But she knew that she couldn't. This was destiny, and it wasn't her place to interfere in such workings.

"It most certainly isn't," someone said in a pleasant yet chilling voice. "You did well to hold your tongue. I might have had to cut it out if you hadn't."

Evanna saw a pair of green boots coming across the floor towards her. The man inside them must have been standing almost directly in Larten's way when

170

he fled, but she wasn't surprised that the vampire hadn't seen the uninvited guest. The tiny meddler only revealed himself when he wanted to be noticed, and only when such sightings were guaranteed to lead to conflict and mayhem.

"I didn't know that you were watching him," Evanna said softly.

"Oh, yes," her visitor smirked. "I have been keeping a close eye on Master Crepsley for a long time now. He's heading down a deliciously dangerous path and I plan to be there when he comes to the drop at the end. In his darkest hour I will be at hand to reach out to him and offer him hope. What a lucky man he is to have a friend such as myself watching out for him. Don't you agree, daughter?"

Closing her eyes, Evanna sighed and offered up a short prayer for Larten and Malora, even though she knew, as an agent of destiny with the power of foresight, that her prayer wouldn't help the poor, doomed pair in the slightest.

Chapter Eighteen

Larten staggered down the hill from the cave, his cheek stinging, blood dripping from the sodden rag covering his wound. The pain and night air sobered him up briskly. How could he have been such a fool? Evanna had killed vampires for less. He didn't blame her for cutting his cheek. He was just surprised he'd gotten out of the cave alive. In a way he was sorry that he had—at least he wouldn't have had to live with his shame if she'd killed him.

On unsteady legs he weaved his way to the edge of the pond. Making sure he wasn't in range of any poisonous frogs, he knelt and peeled the rag from his cheek. Fresh blood cascaded down his chin. Moaning softly – more from guilt than pain – he cupped a handful of water and splashed it over his face. It stung, but not as much as he'd thought it would.

Lowering his head, he drove it deep beneath the water and held it there until he ran out of breath. When he came up gasping, he heard footsteps. He guessed that the witch had come after him. Instead of fleeing, he held his position, staring into the water as the ripples cleared, hoping to die honorably when she attacked.

But when he glimpsed her reflection as the person came closer, he realized it wasn't Evanna. It was her apprentice, Malora.

"Does it hurt terribly?" she asked, kneeling beside him.

"I have known worse," Larten sighed. He had suffered many more serious injuries while training inside Vampire Mountain. But his pride had only taken this severe a beating on that initial night of fighting at his first Council.

Malora passed him a clean handkerchief. He thanked her with a short smile, then winced as he pressed it to his wound. "I have a needle and thread," she said, patting a bag by her knees. "I can stitch you up if you wish. If I sew cleanly, the scar shouldn't be too noticeable."

Larten considered her offer, then dismissed it. "I

will bear the scar openly," he said. "It will remind me what a fool I was and hopefully help me never repeat the mistake that I made tonight."

Malora smirked. "You tried to kiss her, didn't you?"

Larten nodded. "She struck me, then chased me off. I am shocked that she did not kill me."

"It was the wine. If you'd been sober, I'd be wrapping your severed head in a cloth now. You're not the first to try to take advantage of her," Malora said in answer to his raised eyebrow. "I've had to pick up the pieces of a couple of overly amorous suitors in the past. But Evanna knows the effect wine has on mortals. You angered her, obviously, but she realized your pass was more clumsy and innocent than cynical and insulting."

"Will you give her my apologies in the morning?" Larten asked.

"No," Malora surprised him. "I'm leaving with you."

"What are you talking about?" Larten frowned and the gesture brought a fresh torrent of blood from the cut.

"I told you I was unhappy," Malora said. "I've been waiting for an escort to lead me out of here. You'll do."

"Wait a minute," Larten said, alarmed. "I am no escort. You do not know where I am going. I might not see another human for months."

She shrugged. "That doesn't bother me. I might not even go back to my human life. I'm interested in vampires. I want to learn about your ways, maybe become one of you."

"No!" Larten barked. "I do not want an assistant. I am not a General. You heard me talking with Evanna. I am confused, lost. I do not know what I want for myself, so I can hardly make decisions for *you*."

"I'm not asking you to make any decisions for me," Malora said coolly. "I've already made them. I'm coming with you. Where you lead doesn't matter. I don't care that you're not part of the clan, that you might never be again. I just want to travel with you awhile. When I've had enough of your company, I'll move on."

Larten stared at the girl, not sure what to say. "You are too young," he tried. "A vampire's life is hard and testing. I could not make allowances for a child."

"If I'm old enough to be a witch's apprentice, I'm old enough to serve a vampire," Malora huffed. "As for making allowances, that won't be a problem. I need your help to get out of here, but once we reach civilization I'll look after myself. If I can't keep up, you have my permission to cut me loose."

Larten tried one last tactic. "You might not be

safe traveling with me," he said darkly. "What if I try to kiss you like I kissed Evanna?"

"Nonsense," Malora snorted. "You're not the type of man to make an advance on a girl like me. Even if you were...well, I have sharp nails too, only I'd slit your throat, not your cheek."

Larten laughed, then grimaced as his wound flared. "Very well," he muttered. "As long as you understand that you are not my assistant, just a companion, aye?"

"Of course," Malora said meekly, then added wickedly, "*master.*"

Larten pushed himself up. He offered Malora a hand, but she waved it aside and hopped to her feet. Smiling brightly, she asked, "Which way?"

Larten blinked, then looked around and pointed to his right.

Malora shook her head.

"Left?" he tried weakly.

"An excellent choice," she beamed and started down the path ahead of him. Larten thought about fleeing in the opposite direction – she couldn't catch him if he flitted – but he didn't want to leave the girl alone in the dark. Wringing blood from the handkerchief, he reapplied it to his cheek, rolled his eyes at the heavens, then followed after Malora like a lamb.

Part Five

"And like a sliver of deadly mercury, he attacked."

Chapter Nineteen

Larten blew his nose, doubled over and coughed. His face was red when he came up for air and he had to spit a mouthful of thick, horrible phlegm into an already laden handkerchief.

"Give me that," Malora said, taking the snot-riddled rag and handing him a fresh replacement. Her nose wrinkled as she dropped the handkerchief into a tub of hot water. This was the fifth he'd gone through since sunset.

"I didn't think vampires could catch the flu," Malora muttered.

"It is rare," Larten groaned. "We are immune to

most sicknesses. But when the strain of vampire flu strikes, it strikes hard."

He shivered and pulled his blanket tighter around himself, even though it did no good. He had come down with the symptoms a couple of weeks earlier. He'd worsened steadily for ten nights, but then seemed to recover. He was surprised by his rapid comeback — vampire flu often killed those it struck, or stayed in their system for months on end.

Malora pressed the back of her hand to the vampire's forehead, checking his temperature. She hadn't learned much in her years with Evanna, but she'd picked up some helpful healing tips.

"Drink more broth," she grunted.

"What about ale?" Larten asked hopefully.

"If I catch you anywhere near a mug of ale, you'll be sleeping in the street," she snapped. It was a familiar threat and he knew better than to dismiss it lightly. She had driven him from his room more than once in the past when he'd drunk too much and irritated her.

Larten blew his nose again and studied Malora over the top of his handkerchief. She had grown into a beautiful young woman. She kept her hair short and wore trousers more often than skirts, since they were easier to travel in, but nobody could have mistaken her for a boy. She caught the eyes of gentlemen wherever they went. But even though she'd celebrated her sixteenth birthday earlier in the year – an age at which, in Larten's youth, many girls had already married and given birth – she had never shown any interest in the men who wished to woo her.

"Are there no spells you could use to clear this up?" Larten asked.

"Evanna probably knows a few," Malora said with fake sincerity. "We could visit her if you like."

Larten blanched and his fingers went automatically to his scar, which he traced from top to bottom. The prominent scar would have been considered disfiguring by humans, but he carried it with pride. It reminded him of his foolishness, but also his daring and good fortune—there were few vampires who could say they had invoked the wrath of the Lady of the Wilds and lived to tell the tale.

He shuffled to the window and stared at the street outside. There weren't many lamps, but he could see clearly, albeit through watery eyes. He wasn't sure where they were staying. Malora had guided him for the last fortnight. They usually slept in crypts or caves, but she had insisted on inns while he was sick. He'd resisted at first – he thought clear air would be better for him – but he was so ill by the third night that he would have slept on top of a giant needle if she'd ordered it.

As he was staring out the window, he saw an elderly gentleman approach. The man had long, white hair and a flowing, silver beard. His right ear had been cut off long ago and his face was lined with wrinkles. Although he looked ancient, and was even older than he appeared, he walked with a spring in his step that many younger men lacked.

"I do not believe it," Larten gasped. "Paris Skyle!"

"The Prince?" Malora asked.

"Aye. You know him?"

"Only by reputation." She stuck out an arm as an excited Larten tried to dart past her. "Where do you think you're going?"

"To catch him," Larten said impatiently. "I have not seen Paris in ages. I must stop him before he –"

"It *could* be coincidence that of all the inns in the world, he happens to pass by this one," Malora said witheringly. "But what are the odds of that?"

"You think he has come to see me?" Larten asked, delight giving way to nervousness.

"Have another look—has he moved on or is he coming in?"

Larten returned to the window and watched as Paris paused, studied the sign outside the inn, then entered.

"You are as canny as Evanna," he muttered.

"Nowhere near," Malora sniffed. "But even the dumbest woman has more sense than the average man. Wait!" she shouted as Larten tried to push past her again.

"What now?" he scowled.

"You're not meeting a Prince dressed like that," she said firmly. He hadn't changed his clothes recently. They were filthy and smelly, spattered with dry – and some fresh – flecks of spit and snot.

"Paris is a *vampire* Prince," Larten said. "They do not care about looks."

"Be that as it may, I'm not letting you leave in such a state. I'm going to call for a hot bath. Once you've bathed, dressed in clean clothes and blown your nose a few more times, you can present yourself to him."

"But if he is waiting for me –" Larten exploded.

"– he will have to be patient," Malora finished calmly. "I'll take him a glass of wine to keep him quiet – they don't have a great selection here, but there are a few nice bottles tucked away in the back – and say that you'll be with him presently."

"How do you know what wine they have?" Larten asked as she let herself out.

"I'm your assistant," Malora said. "It's my job to know things like that. Now make sure you're undressed by the time I get back, and don't be shy, you don't have anything I haven't seen before."

"*Malora!*" Larten gasped, but she was already gone.

Paris was amused and impressed by Malora, and when Larten was finally allowed to present himself to his elderly friend, they spent the early part of the night discussing her. He told the Prince how they'd met and grinned sheepishly as Paris howled with laughter when he heard how Larten had acquired his scar.

"Don't tell anyone else that story," Paris chuckled. "Let them think you got it fighting a lion or a vampaneze."

"Evanna is far more dangerous than that," Larten said.

"Aye, but she's still a woman. Trust me, if you want to keep your reputation, be mysterious about this."

"I did not think that I had a reputation," Larten said glumly.

"In some quarters you do," Paris replied kindly. "You're not the first vampire to lose his way. We understand how difficult it can be to choose the path of the Generals. If you return to the fold, you'll find us more welcoming than you imagine. We'll even accept your strange choice of assistant."

"Malora is not a real assistant," Larten said. "She does not show any interest in being blooded. I think she just likes having someone to boss around."

"Show me a woman who doesn't," Paris chortled and called for another glass of the interesting wine Malora had found for them.

The pair chatted the night away, retiring to a cozy back room when all the other customers had gone to bed, where they drank by the light of a single fat candle. Paris sipped wine and Larten quaffed ale. (He would get into trouble for defying Malora, but he didn't care. This was an occasion for ale.) Paris relayed the latest news from Vampire Mountain. Seba and Wester were well. Wester had become a guard and was proud as a peacock.

"Seba is just as proud," Paris said.

Larten was too, though it reminded him of his own failures and he had to strain to keep his smile in place.

Paris gave Larten some advice on the best way to fight off the flu. The Prince had endured a few bad cases himself over the centuries and he recommended herbs that were no longer fashionable but that had eased the worst of his suffering in the past.

"But to be honest, you just have to ride it out as best you can," he added. "It will plague you for at least another month. It comes and goes in waves, so don't think you've beaten it. Wrap up warm, heed Malora's advice, and pray to the gods to let you live if that's their will."

Shortly before dawn, when they both had a rosy glow from the wine and ale, Paris spoke of his real reason for tracking down the stray vampire.

"Seba is in poor spirits," he said.

"Sick?" Larten yelped with alarm.

"No—upset. He misses you, but there's more to it than that. Seba doesn't care whether or not you become a General, live among humans or take some other path. He just wants you to be happy. But from reports he's received over the years, you're not. He senses you struggling and wandering blindly. That troubles him."

"I never wanted to disappoint Seba," Larten said miserably. "I wanted him to be proud of me, like he is of Wester."

"Then give him something to be proud of," Paris said softly but pointedly. "In the name of the gods, Larten, *choose*. You're not a new-blood. You've enjoyed your wild years and had time to reflect since distancing yourself from the clan. Surely by now you must have some idea of what you want to do with your life."

Larten sighed. "It is complicated. I yearn to be a General, but I feel there is more I must do before I return and complete my training. I do not know what, but at the moment the thought of coming back..." He shook his head.

"What if you could train outside of Vampire Mountain?" Paris asked. "I could be your tutor and teach you as we travel."

Larten was stunned by the offer. Seba had said that the Princes were interested in him, but he hadn't believed it—he'd thought his old master was merely trying to flatter him. This was an amazing opportunity. Only a fool would turn it down. The chance to train under a Prince would probably never come his way again. And yet...

For some reason Larten recalled the ticking sound he'd heard in Evanna's cave. That noise disturbed his dreams occasionally, though he had no idea why, just as he didn't know why he should think of it now.

"Sleep on it," Paris said, seeing the flicker of temptation in Larten's bloodshot eyes. He rose and stretched. "There's no rush. I don't have to leave for a few more nights. Think it over. Discuss it with Malora. I won't press you for an answer."

"You are too good to me, Sire," Larten mumbled, bowing his head respectfully.

"I know," Paris laughed, then went upstairs to the room that Malora had prepared for him, where he was stunned to find a coffin lying on a couple of tables. "Now this is what I call first-class service," he murmured as he lay inside and happily pulled the lid closed over himself.

Chapter Twenty

As soon as Larten rose in the afternoon, Malora scolded him for drinking the night before. He tried to defend his actions and said he thought the ale had done him some good, but she made him take a cold bath to purge himself of the evils of alcohol. Afterwards he told her of Paris's offer and asked her opinion. She thought about it a long time before answering.

"It's not a question of *if* you become a General but *when*."

Larten was surprised by her certainty. "You think so?"

"You were born to be a General. It's just a matter

of whether you think this is the right time to complete your training or if you'd rather roam the world a few more years, moping about what a hard choice you have to face."

"That is a cruel way to put it," Larten muttered.

"But true," she smirked. "I don't know why you've strayed for so long. I doubt you even know that yourself. If you feel this is the wrong time to commit, say no to Paris. But you should consider the possibility that the *right* time might never come. Maybe you'll feel indecisive all your life and you just have to pick a moment to say, *I am going to become a General, damn the consequences*." She did an accurate impression of him and he found himself smiling.

"What about you?" Larten asked. "If I return to the clan, you will have to study hard before I can blood you."

"Don't be ridiculous," Malora snorted. "I've no intention of letting you blood me. Vampirism doesn't interest me in the slightest."

Larten gaped at her. "Then why, by the black blood of Harnon Oan, have you been following me around the world?" he thundered.

"You really thought I wanted to become a vampire?" she asked. When he nodded, she sighed. "I knew you were naive but I didn't think you were *that* dense." As he puffed himself up to bellow at her, she reached out and gently caressed his scar. Her touch calmed him.

"I never wanted to join the clan," Malora said softly. "I said I did because that was what you needed to hear. I don't care about returning to the human world either. I only want to be with you for all the nights and days that I have left. I knew you were the man for me the moment I saw you."

"Wait a minute!" Larten gulped. He hadn't been expecting a declaration of love. "You're a child," he wheezed.

"A young lady," she corrected him. "And getting older. I'm patient. I can wait until you decide I'm old enough."

"But –"

"If you're about to say that I'll always be a girl in your eyes," she interrupted sharply, "*don't*. You might reject me, but don't insult me. I won't stand for that, not from any man, even the love of my life."

"The love of..." Larten echoed weakly.

"You don't need to do anything now," Malora said sweetly. "You're slow, like most men, but you'll catch up soon and realize you love me as much as I love you. I just want you to know that, in the meantime, I'll follow you no matter where you go. Your path is mine because my heart is yours.

"Now go enjoy yourself with Paris. I'll be waiting for you when you get back. I'll always wait for you, my love."

With that she shooed him out of the room and left him to stare at the closed door in bewilderment. After he'd scratched his head for the sixth time, he turned and trudged down the steps to get a drink and mull things over.

Paris was nowhere to be found – Larten assumed the elderly Prince was still asleep – but a middle-aged man with a beard was sitting at one of the tables, writing in a notebook. He hailed Larten and invited him over. As Larten cautiously sat, the man said, "You're Master Skyle's friend, aren't you?"

Larten relaxed. "You know Paris?"

"Oh, yes," the man beamed. "My name's Abraham, but please call me Bram."

Larten gave his own name, shook hands and accepted the mug of ale he was offered.

"What are you writing?" Larten asked.

"Just a few ideas for a story I'm researching."

"You write stories?" Larten was interested. He had met several authors over the decades and found them a curious bunch.

"Novels, mostly. You might have heard of *The Snake's Pass,* perhaps?"

Larten shook his head. "I am not a reader. I never learned." He expected the man to look surprised, maybe even sneer at him, but Bram only shrugged.

"You might be better off. Writing is my life – on top of running a theater – but I often think I'd have been more successful and a lot happier if I'd never taken up a pen. The muse is a cruel mistress."

Larten pressed Bram for details of his books and the theater. He learned that the writer was from Ireland but now lived in London, "when I'm not trotting around Europe trying to finish this dratted novel!"

When Larten asked about his new book, Bram waved aside the question. "I never discuss a work in progress. I don't want to jinx myself. Tell me about your life instead. You're a vampire like Paris, aren't you?"

"A vampire, aye, but hardly like Paris," Larten chuckled.

"He's something of a legend, isn't he?" Bram smiled.

"Among vampires, certainly," Larten agreed. Over

the next few hours he told Bram some of his favorite Paris Skyle stories, becoming more eloquent the more he drank. After a while Bram asked if he could take notes, "just for fun," and Larten said that of course he could.

Bram was interested in the rest of the clan, as well as the vampaneze. He wanted to know when vampires had stopped killing when they fed, and if any ever overstepped the mark now.

"Never," Larten said. "The punishment is severe if you break that law."

"A stake through the heart?" Bram guessed.

"Or something similarly fatal," Larten nodded.

"The stake tradition started with Vlad, I suppose," Bram murmured, trying to disguise his interest in the answer.

"Vlad?" Larten blinked.

"Vlad the Impaler? Also known as Vlad Tepes or Vlad Dracula? He was one of the clan, wasn't he?"

"No, you interfering busybody," somebody growled behind them. "He was not."

Larten stared up at a glowering Paris Skyle, who had appeared behind Bram's chair. Bram choked back a gulp and turned, smiling shakily. "Good evening, Paris, I'm glad to see –"

"What have you been telling this *scribe*?" Paris snarled.

"Nothing much," Larten said hesitantly, beginning to realize that he had been speaking freely with someone he didn't know. "He asked about you and the clan."

"And you told him what he wanted to hear?" Paris snapped.

Larten flushed. "Yes. I was open with him. He said that he knew you and I did not think I needed to be wary in his company."

"Think a bit harder next time," Paris said coldly, then placed a hand on Bram's shoulder and squeezed. Bram winced, but didn't try to escape. "You're persistent, Master Stoker. I assume *you* sent me the message requesting my presence across town. You wanted my friend to yourself for a while, aye?"

"I need more facts for my story," Bram said quietly.

"*Facts*? I thought it was going to be a work of fiction."

"It is. I gave you my word that I wouldn't do anything to expose or harm the clan. But the more I know about you, the more steps I can take to ensure I don't write something that accidentally leads people to investigate your movements."

"If you didn't write about us at all, you could be even surer," Paris said icily.

"Someone's going to write about vampires sooner or later," Bram said. "Would you prefer a work of fiction, where I blur the truth and give the world something fantastical, or a tome that mentions Vampire Mountain, Generals and the rest?"

Paris thought about that, then removed his hand. "Perhaps you're correct. If your story tricks people into thinking that vampires are mythical beasts, it may do some good. Not that I think many will read it—people want uplifting tales, not morbid stories of bloodsucking creatures of the night."

"You might be surprised," Bram said, picking up his pen again. "You'll answer my questions?"

"Aye," Paris nodded, "but not tonight. I'm entertaining a friend. Remain a few nights and I will let you have your...how did you put it last time...your interview with a vampire."

"Can we shake on that?" Bram asked, extending a hand.

"No," Paris said flatly. "A vampire doesn't need to shake hands once he has given his word. Go from here, Abraham Stoker, and give me the space I asked for. I will speak with you shortly."

Bram nodded and gathered his belongings. "Sorry if I got you into trouble," he said to Larten.

"Move along," Paris barked. "We haven't dined yet and that neck of yours looks ripe for the biting."

Bram flashed Paris a dark look, then backed away from the table, tossed some coins to the innkeeper and let himself out. Paris watched him leave, then sat and called for a glass of wine.

"Sire, I'm sorry if I –" Larten began.

"It matters not," Paris said curtly. "That man has been dogging my footsteps for three years. He would have forced a confrontation eventually. I'm not worried. I'm sure his book won't amount to much even if it's published, which I doubt. Let us speak of more important issues. Have you considered what we spoke of?"

Larten nodded.

"And?"

If Paris had asked the question a few hours earlier, Larten would have accepted the Prince's offer to train him. But his careless conversation with Bram Stoker had disturbed him. Paris had made light of it, but Larten knew he should have been more circumspect. Even new-bloods didn't discuss the clan with anyone they couldn't trust completely. Larten's self-confidence had been shaken. He could have taken more time to answer – Paris wasn't rushing him – but his head was sore from the flu, which seemed to be returning with a vengeance, and the ale was sitting heavily in his stomach. All he wanted was to slink back to his room to brood.

"I thank you for offering to take me under your wing, but I do not think that I am ready to resume my lessons," he said.

Paris sighed. "I had hoped for a different answer."

"I am sorry to disappoint you, Sire. I mean no disrespect."

"You must do as your heart dictates, of course, but..." Paris hesitated, then pressed on. "Wander if you must, Larten, but the longer you live in exile, the more risks you run."

"Risks, Sire?" Larten frowned.

"You risk losing yourself forever," Paris said. "You might never find your path, and end up becoming something bitter and adrift. This world can corrupt a lone vampire. We are beings of the night, but the darkness is a dangerous place for one without friends."

"I have Malora," Larten said softly.

"She might face even worse dangers," Paris retorted, then grimaced. "But I'm doing what I said I wouldn't,

200

trying to persuade you. Ignore my last comments. I am old and addled. Like all old men, I see pitfalls where none exist. You are eager to return to your room, I know, but pray have one last drink with me. I promise not to speak of this matter again."

Larten had a final drink with Paris, but he couldn't enjoy it. He kept thinking about what the Prince had said. Talk of dangers in the darkness had unsettled him. He had survived this long by himself and never felt under threat. And no harm could befall Malora while she had Larten to protect her. Yet he sensed truth – almost a prediction – in Paris's warning.

Coughing heavily, wiping phlegm from his lips with one of the handkerchiefs that Malora had washed clean for him that morning, Larten struggled to pinpoint the source of his unease, but he couldn't. He decided in the end that the flu had simply sapped him of his strength. That was why he felt so gloomy. It would pass when he got better. Everything would be fine then, he was sure of it. After all, in this world of humans, he was little better than a monster, and what did a monster have to be afraid of in the dark?

Chapter Twenty-one

"Going to sea!" Larten snarled, dragging himself towards the docks.

"This is a bad idea," Malora gasped, trying to tug him back, but having as much luck as a dog would have with an elephant.

"Want to sail...the seven seas." Larten laughed. "Sick of these towns and...cities. Got to keep... going. Don't trust land."

He stopped in the middle of the street and glared at the people who were looking at him oddly. He was dressed in a smart pair of trousers and a dirty white sweater that he'd bought from a sailor the night before, with a shoe on his right foot and an old boot on his left. He was holding a lady's umbrella over his head to protect him from the sun.

Malora thought that the sweater had put the idea into his head. The flu was ultimately to blame – it had ebbed and flared in him over the last six weeks, and was now worse than ever – but he'd been content to stay inside and follow her lead until he bought that stupid sweater. As soon as he pulled it on, he began ranting about going to sea—he had smelled the salt air a couple of nights before when they'd come to this town. She'd managed to calm him and get him to sleep, but he had woken with the notion fresh in his head. Without pausing to eat, he had dressed and hobbled down to the docks, Malora hurrying to keep up, trying to make him change his mind.

"Larten!" she snapped as he stared around. "This isn't a good idea. We'll go on a long cruise when you feel better. You're sick. We should stay somewhere warm and dry, so that you can –"

"No!" he bellowed, taking off again. "Vampire hunters...on land. They'll stick a stake through... my heart. Have to get to sea. Life on the waves. Aye!"

Malora argued with him all the way, but he ignored her. At the docks he strode around like a madman, checking all the ships. He stopped several sailors and asked if they knew which boat was making the longest journey. Some shrugged him off and didn't answer. Those who responded gave conflicting reports. But when a third man mentioned the *Pearly Tornado,* Larten's mind was decided.

Malora was almost crying. When Larten found the gangplank, she darted ahead of him and set herself in his way. "No farther," she croaked. "This is madness. If you go on, you'll go without me. I'll leave you here, Larten, I swear I will."

"Then leave," he said coldly and leapt over her. As he stormed up the plank, Malora cursed, looked longingly at the dry land of the docks, then followed him. She tried to put on a brave face – "Very well. I've always wanted to see more of the world." – but she was dreadfully worried. The flu was playing havoc with Larten. If it worsened at sea, he was a dead man.

A boy was swabbing the deck when Larten boarded. The boy glanced at the shoddily dressed stranger, shrugged and spat on the boards, then wiped them clean.

"You!" Larten yelled. "Where's your captain?"

"In his cabin," the boy said.

"Get him for me."

The boy was going to tell the man to run his own

errands, but then he spotted Malora and straightened. "Afternoon, ma'am," he saluted, smiling in what he hoped was a rakish way. "Can I help ye at all?"

"Larten," Malora tried one last time, but he shook his head aggressively. She gave up and sighed. "I am Malora. This is my master, Larten Crepsley. He seeks travel onboard this ship."

"This ain't a passenger ship, ma'am," the boy said. "We sometimes take a few paying customers when there's space, but mostly it's crew and cargo. I don't think there's any cabins left on this trip."

"Did you hear that?" Malora said brightly.

"Nonsense," Larten sniffed, tossing a coin to the boy. He caught it midair and pocketed it immediately. "What is your name?"

"Daniel Abrams," the boy said smartly.

"You will get another coin when you bring your captain to me."

"Yes, sir, Master Crepsley, sir!" Daniel yapped, then raced off.

The captain was a gruff, thickset man. He eyed Larten dubiously, but like Daniel, his face lit up when he spotted the pretty Malora. "Sir. Ma'am. Can I be of help?"

"We seek a cabin," Larten said.

"Alas, this isn't a passenger ship. We have a handful o' passengers, but we've already squeezed in as many as we can fer this journey. If it's America ye're looking fer, I can recommend –"

"I do not care where you are going," Larten snapped, then paused. "America?"

"Ultimately," the captain nodded. "Got a few stops t' make first, and we're going by way o' Greenland, but –"

"Greenland!" Larten yelled with excitement. "That is where I want to go."

"A strange place t' want t' get off, sir," the captain said. "But I can recommend a couple o' ships fer there too."

"I do not want any other ship," Larten growled. "This is the ship for me. The *Pearly Tornado* — a fine name, a fine ship and a fine captain."

"Very nice o' ye t' say, sir, but I'm afraid I really can't –"

Larten dug into his pockets, pulled out all of his money and thrust it at the astonished captain. "Is that enough? Malora, give him more if he wants."

"I don't think he needs any more," Malora said quietly. She shared a look with the captain and took back a couple of notes. He didn't object — in fact he seemed relieved. "Will that cover the cost of our voyage and help you persuade some of your other passengers to make way for us?"

"It will," the captain said weakly. "But ye'll have t' share a cabin."

"No," Malora said firmly. "We need a cabin of our own."

"But –" the captain began to protest. Malora handed him one of the notes she had retrieved and the captain glumly pocketed the money. "Give me fifteen minutes. I'll have it sorted fer ye by then."

"And, captain," Malora called him back. "Fresh linen if you please."

He grinned thinly and tipped his hat to her. "Aye, ma'am."

The *Pearly Tornado* set sail on the next tide. Larten missed the launch. He was asleep in their cabin, tossing and turning from the fever. Malora had washed him down once already, after he had vomited all over himself and the sheets. The next few days or weeks were going to be hard, until the flu passed. (*Or until he dies,* part of her whispered, but she preferred not to consider that grim possibility.)

When she felt the ship get under way, Malora left

Larten and went on deck. This was her first time sailing and she was fascinated by all the activity going on around her. She had never guessed that the running of a ship would be such a complex process.

The other passengers were on deck too, looking at the shore with sad longing as they pulled away. There were four men, two women and a baby that clung to its mother and cried shrilly. Malora assumed they were going to start a new life in America, and were so poor that they hadn't been able to afford passage on any of the regular ships.

Daniel Abrams – the boy who'd first greeted them – edged up to Malora, spat over the railing and nodded pleasantly. "Yer master's asleep?" he guessed.

"Resting," Malora said.

"He looked right sick when he came aboard," Daniel noted.

"Influenza," Malora said. "He's over the worst of it, but will probably lie low for most of the journey. His eyes are weak from the illness. He can't bear to be out in the sun at the moment—that's why he had the umbrella."

"Ah." Daniel nodded again, this time like a doctor. "If ye need anything, liquor, medicine or hot food, let me know. We don't have much, but I can fetch the best of what there is...fer a price." He coughed uncomfortably, unaccustomed to such bargaining.

Malora smiled at the boy. "My master is a generous man. You will be well rewarded for any services rendered. And you already have my gratitude for making such a kind offer."

Daniel blushed. "Anything ye want, ma'am, just ask fer Master Abrams. I'm a right little jackdaw, me."

Malora remained on deck a couple of hours, adjusting to the swell of the waves, breathing deeply of the salty air. Before returning to her cabin, she asked Daniel to arrange some supplies for them, drink, food and a burner—she said she would cook in their cabin while her master was sick. As he was doing that, she went to check on Larten.

The vampire was awake but ill. He didn't recognize Malora when she came in—he thought she was Evanna, come to scar the other side of his face. He tried to hide beneath his blankets, but as she whispered his name over and over, his eyes half cleared and he sat up.

"Malora?" he whined.

"Who else?"

"Where are we?"

"On a ship." When he stared at her, she said, "You wanted to see Greenland."

He tried to work out why he might have said such a thing, but his head hurt when he thought too much. "I'm hungry," he whimpered instead.

"Food is on its way."

"No," he said. "The other kind of hunger."

Malora frowned. She had already considered this – it was one of the reasons she'd been reluctant to set sail in the first place – but hadn't thought he'd need to feed so soon.

"Can you wait?" she asked. "We dock at our first port in less than a week. We can slip ashore then and…"

He was already shaking his head. "Can't," he wheezed. "The hunger…I have to feed when it comes. Dangerous not to. Might drink recklessly if I do not sip regularly."

"Very well," she sighed and sat beside him. She rolled up a sleeve, took a knife from her belt and made a small cut beneath her elbow. She didn't wince as the blade bit into her flesh—it would take more than that to make her cry. "Not too much," she murmured as Larten leaned forward eagerly. "We have to make it last."

He nodded, then fixed his lips around the cut. Malora smiled and stroked his hair as he fed, her expression and gestures very much like those of the mother's on deck had been as she'd tried to soothe her wailing baby.

Chapter Twenty-two

Malora hoped that Larten would disembark when they docked. His condition was worsening and he needed rest and warmth. But he wouldn't hear of it. When the fever made him feisty, he insisted on going to Greenland to search for the palace of Perta Vin-Grahl. (Malora had no idea who that was.) In his lower moments he moaned that he wanted to die onboard and be buried at sea. Either way, he had no intention of setting foot ashore at any of their early stops.

Malora never lost her temper, even when he was at his most pitiful and demanding. This was the man she had chosen and she loved him as completely as any sixteen-year-old had ever loved. Nothing he did tested her patience, whether he yelled abuse, wept and asked her to kill him, threw up over her or spat in her face. It was the flu that made him do these things and she refused to blame him for his addle-headed actions.

The captain, Daniel and the rest of the crew were enamored with Malora. She spent a lot of time making friends, joking with the sailors, stitching clothes for them, helping out in the kitchen. Daniel was especially fond of her, even though he knew he couldn't win her heart, being younger than she was and just starting out in life. He trailed her like a faithful dog whenever he could. He even asked her to teach him how to cook, so that he could spend more time with her in the kitchen. He was a terrible chef, but he stuck with it to be close to Malora.

Because they liked the girl so much, they said nothing critical of her bedridden master. When he roared abusively, they turned a deaf ear to his insults. On the rare occasions when he staggered out of his cabin and caused a disturbance on deck, they veered around him and waited for Malora to usher him back inside. They would have put ashore any other passenger who proved so disruptive, no matter how much he had paid, but for Malora's sake they tolerated the orange-haired nuisance.

Looking after Larten was exhausting, but Malora

was up for the challenge. She worked hard, guarded him fiercely, and let him feed from her when he needed blood. The only problem was that her blood was not going to be enough. He was drinking more than usual because of the fever and she would not be able to supply him indefinitely from her own veins.

When they made their final dock before embarking on the long, uninterrupted stretch to Greenland, Malora tried to convince him to go ashore with her, to feed on another person's blood and restock the vials he carried in case of emergencies. But Larten thought she was trying to trick him, that the ship would sail without them if he got off, so he refused to budge.

Out of desperation, Malora took the vials and went ashore by herself. Scouring dark, unpleasant alleys, she found a number of sailors sleeping off hangovers. Taking care not to hurt them, she made small cuts on their arms and legs and tried to fill the vials. It was a messy job, but she returned with something to show for her efforts, pleased with what she had brought back.

Malora would have been far less pleased if she had spotted Daniel Abrams trailing her through the alleys from one victim to another.

The boy hadn't set out to spy. At first he'd followed

after her like he did on the ship, simply wanting to be close to the girl. When she started exploring the alleys, he figured he should watch out for her in case she ran into trouble—he had vague notions of saving her life and winning her heart. But when he saw her bleeding the snoring sailors...

Daniel was deeply troubled when he returned. His first instinct was to report it, but he was certain the captain would throw them off if he knew what the sweet-looking girl had been up to. Daniel couldn't care less about Larten Crepsley, but he would miss Malora. In the end he kept his own counsel, but decided to monitor the girl and her mysterious master. He wasn't sure what Malora wanted with the blood. It might have been for some strange medical purpose. But he thought there was something more diabolical going on. He wasn't sure what, but he was certain he'd find out. Daniel was sharp. He would uncover their dark, crimson secret in the end, no matter what it was.

The ship sailed on, one day blurring into another. The waters were calm for that time of year, but they still had to endure a few rough nights when Malora was sure the vessel would capsize. The other passengers were as scared as she was on those occasions, but the crew never looked worried. Malora didn't know if that was because they felt safe, or because as sailors they'd accepted the fact that they were going to die at sea eventually. She never asked—it was better not knowing, in case the answer was the latter.

Larten's spirits improved temporarily, then darkened again. She had never known a fever like this. She was sure it couldn't be natural, even in a vampire. Paris Skyle could have told her otherwise, and there were herbs and treatments he could have recommended. But as the Prince had tried to tell Larten in the inn, there was only so much a human could understand about the creatures of the night. Larten had cut himself off from the clan, and Malora had to deal with the crisis as best she could.

She changed his clothes regularly, bathed him, wiped sweat from his face when the shakes took hold. She made sure he ate and drank enough, and kept the small window open to let in fresh air. He had stopped asking for blood, and though she forced a few drops into his mouth – from another of her cuts, having long since worked through the vials – he spat out most of it. She wasn't sure if he was trying to die or just couldn't digest blood in his weakened condition.

Larten looked like a man on the verge of death.

He had aged several years. His skin was saggy and gray, his nails broke off easily, his eyes were red and lifeless. Only his orange hair looked the same as ever—Traz would have been proud to note that his dye could withstand even the ravages of vampire flu.

The last couple of days and nights had been particularly difficult. Larten had thrashed and moaned nonstop, denying Malora sleep. She'd been awake for sixty hours. This was the closest she had come to breaking, but even at her weakest, exhausted and irritable, she kept her wits about her and saw to Larten's needs before her own.

"He'd better appreciate this when he pulls through," she grumbled, refusing to consider the likelihood that he might not recover. "I'll expect presents, fine meals and the grandest hotels. I won't settle for Greenland. He can forget about his palace of ice. I'll insist he treat me to the best New York has to offer."

Malora had heard much about the marvels of New York, mostly from Daniel—he'd never been there, but had picked up tales from other sailors. As Larten snored and lay peacefully for a change – he seemed to be recovering from his latest setback – she thought of the famous city, the delights it could offer, shops full of incredible trinkets and dresses, bustling streets, bright lights that lit up the sky at night. Smiling at the prospect of being able to relax in such a wonderland, she nodded off and was soundly asleep when Larten stirred, rose from his bed and let himself out, moving like a man in a trance.

Screams woke Malora. For a moment she thought it was a nightmare – she'd had plenty of those recently – but then her head cleared and she realized the screams were real.

Malora grabbed the covers on the bed and whipped them away — no sign of Larten. They were in trouble. She knew it instantly. It was now simply a case of if she could fix the situation before it got any worse.

She hurried out of their cabin and tracked the screams. They were coming from a cabin lower than theirs, where the other passengers were staying. The women were shrieking and the men were shouting. When Malora arrived, some of the crew were already there, gathered around the open door, staring at something inside.

Malora pushed her way through, knowing what she'd find, trying to think of a way to make light of it, to dismiss it as a moment of madness brought on by the fever. As she reached the door, she saw that her fears were well founded. Larten was inside and he had latched on to Yasmin's left arm. Yasmin was the mother of the baby, and Larten was feeding from her as her child did every day. But he wasn't interested in milk. He had made a cut, either with his nails or his teeth, and was gulping blood from a wound far bigger than any a sane vampire would have ever made.

"Larten!" Malora screeched, trying to fake shock. "What are you doing?"

He didn't respond. His eyes were closed and he was drinking happily, ignorant of the screams, the way Yasmin and the other woman were striking him, the men trying to tug him off. He only knew blood.

As the sailors gaped, Malora looked around, spotted a bucket of water, picked it up and doused Larten. The shock of the cold water made him fall away. He tried to get up and grab the bucket, but he toppled and fell in a heap on the floor.

Yasmin ran to her husband and her baby and they barged through the sailors, wanting to get as far away from the madman as possible.

Malora knew she had to act quickly. "Help me," she snapped at two of the crew. "He's had some kind of fit. We have to take him back to his cabin."

The sailors were dubious – a fit couldn't explain

the blood smeared around his lips and chin – but they liked Malora, so they picked up the almost unconscious Larten and hauled him back to his bed. Malora followed, talking rapidly, telling the others trailing behind of the medicine she'd need, asking them to apologize to Yasmin, hoping they wouldn't stop to ask questions if she kept them busy.

As the sailors maneuvered Larten through the doorway of their cabin and into bed, Malora paused outside and offered up a silent prayer to the gods. It seemed as if they'd gotten away with it. The captain was arriving and he looked like thunder, but she was sure she could laugh her way out of this. She'd blame it on the flu, let them strap Larten down if they wished to stop him straying again. No real harm had been done. All things considered, it could have been a lot worse.

And then, as the captain roared at his crew and demanded to know what the hell was going on, it *did* get worse.

"He drinks blood!" someone yelled.

The captain and the others fell quiet. The sailors who'd dropped off Larten joined the rest of the crew outside and stared with them at the person who had spoken. It was, of course, young Daniel Abrams.

"He's a bloodsucker," Daniel said, relishing the

221

attention. He hadn't meant to speak up, but the drama in the cabin had excited him and he wanted to see more fireworks. "He's some sort of demon."

"Don't be ridiculous," Malora snapped. "It's the flu. He didn't know what he was doing. Captain, you must believe me."

And maybe he would have, except that was when a chaos-craving Daniel played his ace.

"If he's not a bloodsucker, why was you cutting open sailors and bottling their blood the last place we docked? It was t' feed yer bloodthirsty beast of a master! There's vials in the cabin," he said triumphantly to the shocked captain. "Search. You'll find 'em, still bloodstained I bet, unless he's licked 'em clean."

"Daniel!" Malora cried. "Why are you doing this? I thought you were my friend."

But Daniel had forgotten about his crush on Malora. He craved bloodshed. The scene with Yasmin had whet his appetite and he couldn't stop now, any more than Larten could have when the hunger overwhelmed him.

The captain studied Daniel soberly, then turned his gaze on Malora. "Step out of the way, please, ma'am." He nodded at a few of his sailors.

Malora shook her head. "Captain, no, don't listen to him, it was just –"

"Ma'am!" the captain barked. "Ye're not listening t' me. Ye have t' move *now*. This is bad fer yer master and if ye don't get away from there immediately it'll be bad fer you and all. If ye give him to us, I'll settle fer that and spare ye. But if ye stand up fer him... fer what he did..." His features hardened. "It's time t' choose."

The young woman looked from one stern-faced sailor to another. There was a vicious gleam to their eyes — they had caught the same dark lust as Daniel. Her friends had disappeared and she knew better than to beg for mercy. It didn't exist here now.

Malora nodded slowly, accepting what destiny had unleashed upon her. Unlike Larten, she had no problem choosing her path. No problem at all.

"So be it," she said, softly closing the door so as not to disturb the unconscious vampire. As the sailors bunched around her, silent as a pack of sharks, she laid the palm of one hand on the door and bid a silent farewell to the lover she would never get a chance to truly love. Then, turning calmly, she faced the mob closing in on her, sneered at their savage, bestial hunger, drew a knife and made her stand.

Chapter Twenty-three

If the crew had stormed the cabin, Larten would not have been able to resist. He had passed out on top of his bed. It would have been a simple matter for them to turn him over, bare his left breast and drive a sharpened stake through his heart.

But superstition and fear swept through the sailors once they had dealt with Malora. Instead of rushing to finish the cruel business, they paused to debate the situation. And in that pause their doubts exploded.

"He's a vampire," one hissed, and explained what vampires were for those who didn't know. It was a maelstrom of myths, theories and hysteria after that.

"He can turn into a bat."

"He can turn into smoke and slip away."

"He's powerful at night, but weak in the day. We should wait for the sun."

"A stake through the heart will destroy him."

"So will sunlight."

"And holy water, but we ain't got any of that."

"If we attack now and he wakes, he'll be stronger than us."

"Wait."

"Daylight turns them to ash."

"Aye, wait."

"He can't hide from the sun."

"Wait."

"Aye."

"*Wait.*"

Larten was groggy when he awoke. He could have happily slept much longer, but something had disturbed him. Creaking noises, sharper and louder than the normal twangs of the ship, coming from directly overhead. As he listened, the sounds came again. It was as if the room was trying to rip itself apart.

As Larten sat up, confused, a couple of planks were torn loose from the ceiling and sunlight pierced the cabin. He flinched and drew back from the beams. There was laughter outside.

"There! He's frightened o' the light. Hurry, lads. Once we pull the rest o' that ceiling away, he's finished. He'll be ash by breakfast."

Larten stared with astonishment as a crowd of sailors hacked through the thin roof of his cabin. They were working like a team of ants. They'd tear all of the planks away in a matter of minutes and Larten would have nowhere to shelter.

He couldn't remember much of the night before, but he swiftly worked out what had happened. They had discovered his true identity and were coming to kill him. This was serious. The sunlight wouldn't destroy him instantly, but he couldn't stay exposed to it for long. He would have to retreat and seek shelter in the bowels of the ship. He could barricade himself in somewhere, but it was going to be nigh impossible to keep them out. Still, he had to try.

"Malora?" he croaked, although he already knew she wasn't there. He looked for her, to be sure, then sighed with relief. They'd either captured her or she had gone over to their side to save her own neck. He didn't mind which, just as long as she wasn't sucked down into the pit with him. If this was to be his end, so be it, but there was no reason why the innocent girl should suffer too.

The vampire grinned bleakly as the sailors tore the ceiling to shreds. He felt better than he had in ages, stomach still warm with Yasmin's blood, head clearer than it had been for several days. Ironically, it seemed that he had gotten the better of the flu at last, so at least he could die in good health.

Larten washed his hands in a finger bowl, gargled from a glass of water, then drank the rest. He dusted off his clothes, brushed his hair back and blew his nose several times for good measure. Vampires didn't fear death. Larten had already lived longer than most humans. This would be a good way to die, hunted and staked by a mob. Seba would chuckle proudly if word ever reached him in Vampire Mountain. "When you have to go," he had often said to Larten and Wester, "try to go in style!"

As the last of the ceiling was pried away with crowbars, Larten crouched, then sprang through the gap that had been created, landing on the deck like a cat. The sailors cried out with alarm and reeled away from the freed vampire. As they scrambled over one another, shrieking with terror, Larten stood to his full height and glared at his tormentors, looking majestic despite his dirty clothes, red eyes and scraggly beard.

"Come then, humans!" he bellowed. "I am Larten Crepsley of the vampire clan and I fear no man."

The sailors paused and gaped. They hadn't expected a response like this. They thought he'd howl and screech and fight like a cornered rat to the bitter, bloody end. But here he stood, tall and straight, unafraid of his foes, challenging them to do their worst.

The captain recovered and pointed at Larten with a hook he'd kept over his bed for many years in case he ever faced a mutiny. "Crosses!" he barked, and six sailors pressed forward holding crucifixes.

Larten laughed. Perhaps the clan didn't require Bram Stoker to spread silly myths about the creatures of the night. These humans had accepted the old, crazy legends without any need of a novel.

The captain scowled. He didn't like the way the monster was laughing. The beast should be cowering, begging them to spare his worthless life. The captain was eager to finish off the vampire, but first he wanted to see that smirk wiped from the villain's face.

"Ye think this is funny?" the captain snarled.

"I think it is pathetic," Larten retorted.

"Ye're a monster. A vampire. A servant o' the devil himself."

"You know far more about the devil than I do, sir," Larten replied. He wouldn't normally have played for time – it would have made more sense to make his break and seek shelter from the sun – but he was scanning the crowd for Malora. He wanted to be sure she was safe before he fled. Maybe curse her as a traitor or act as if he'd fooled her along with the rest, to make them think she hadn't been working in league with him.

The captain saw Larten looking and realized what he was searching for. A dark flicker of a smile danced across his lips. "Are ye worried about yer wench?" he asked innocently.

Larten felt a chill form inside his stomach. "She knows nothing about me," he said, trying to distance himself from Malora to help her as much as he could — if that was still possible. "She is just a girl I picked up and used. I do not care what you do with her."

"That's good," the captain purred. "Then ye won't be too upset when ye look up and see *that*." He pointed to the rigging with his hook.

The last thing Larten wanted to do was raise his gaze. He knew what was waiting for him if he did. But a vampire of good standing never tries to hide from the truth, and Larten had been trained to always face his fears and losses.

It was a bright day and his eyes were narrow slits against the painful rays of the sun. But he could see the sails clearly enough, and the wooden rigging to which they were attached. And he could also see poor Malora hanging from one of the poles, a length of rope looped around her neck, swaying lifelessly in the breeze and from the ever-constant rise and fall of the ship.

A cold calm washed through Larten Crepsley. Many years earlier, as a boy, he had experienced a similar calmness just before he'd killed the brute of a man who had murdered his best friend. It was as if he withdrew emotionally from the world. He forgot every rule he'd lived by and every moral restraint he had ever placed upon himself.

In that moment he was neither man nor vampire, but a force, one that would not stop until it had been spent. In the factory he'd only had one man to direct his fury against. Here he had dozens. And for that he was glad.

"They used to call me Quicksilver," he whispered, smiling hollowly. "Fastest hands in the world."

Then the smile vanished. His eyes flashed. And like a sliver of deadly mercury, he attacked.

Chapter Twenty-four

Larten sat near the prow of the ship. He was holding the baby and absentmindedly bouncing it up and down. The baby was cooing happily. Larten's hands were soaked with blood and the red, sticky liquid had seeped through the baby's shawl, but neither seemed to notice or care.

He would never recall the slaughter in detail. Fragments would haunt him, both awake and sleeping, for the rest of his life. Faces would flash in front of him or shimmer in the theater of his dreams. He'd see his nails, jagged and deadly, slicing open a throat as if it was a slab of butter. His fingers gripping a man's skull, digging deep, crushing bone, sinking into brain.

Sometimes he'd get a strange taste in his mouth. It always puzzled him for a few seconds. Then he would remember biting off a sailor's salty toes while the man was alive, leaving him awhile, then returning to finish the job like a butcher who had been momentarily sidetracked.

He had saved the captain for last, letting him bear witness to the destruction. The seasoned sailor wept and begged for his men's lives, then for his own. Larten only grinned and pointed to the girl dangling above their heads.

In his dreams he often chased sailors into the rigging. In reality only three had tried to climb to safety, but in Larten's nightmares there were hundreds and the poles stretched to the sky and beyond. But no matter how many fled ahead of him, he always killed every last one of them before he stirred and woke.

The baby gurgled, then started to cry hungrily. Larten bounced him a few more times, hoping to shush him, but the infant boy wasn't to be distracted. With a sigh, Larten reluctantly turned from the prow and surveyed the deck of corpses.

He knew it would be bad, but this was even worse than he'd feared. So many hacked (*bitten, chewed, torn*) to pieces. Blood everywhere. Guts hanging from the ropes in the rigging. Heads set on spikes and hooks. The eyes of one were missing, two crosses rammed deep into the bloody sockets.

Larten had seen much in his time on the battle-fields of the world, but nothing as vicious as this. He wanted to weep, but he could find no tears within himself. It would have been hypocritical to cry. He didn't deserve that release.

Steeling himself, Larten stared long and hard at the bodies. This was *his* work. He could blame it on the flu, but that would be a lie. He had chosen to do this. Malora had been murdered and he had let himself go wild and wreak a terrible revenge. He felt shame and disgust, more than he could ever express. There was no justification and no hiding. *He* did this. He had become the monster these people feared. Paris had warned him of the dangers of inde-cision and isolation, but he had ignored the Prince's advice. This was the result. This was what happened when vampires went bad.

Larten picked his way through the mess, holding the baby high above it, glad that the child was too young to understand any of this. Entering the boy's cabin, he found a small bottle half full of milk. Sitting on the bed, he perched the baby on his lap and let him feed.

It was only as the baby greedily gulped the milk that Larten wondered what had happened to the boy's mother.

When the child had his fill, Larten scoured the ship from top to bottom, praying he'd find the pretty Yasmin alive, cowering in a corner. If he could hand her baby back to her, he would have done at least that much right on this awful, notorious day.

But Yasmin was nowhere onboard. He found the body of the other woman, along with the corpses of the male passengers, mixed in with the remains of the sailors, but Yasmin must have leapt overboard, preferring the sea to death at the vampire's wretched hands.

Or else he had thrown her off.

Until the night he died, Larten would pray a few times a week, begging the gods to reveal Yasmin's end to him. It seemed important, a crucial missing piece of the puzzle. Until he put it in place he could never draw a line under the calamity. But as hard as he prayed, that memory would always be a mystery to him.

What he did find during his search was a sealed door. It had been locked from the outside. The key was missing, but to Larten – *Quicksilver,* he'd told them, as if by using a different name he could distance himself from the guilt – it was a simple thing to pick. Moments later he pushed the door open, and four terrified pairs of eyes stared out at him.

One of the four was a high-ranking mate. Larten immediately understood why he had spared this man — even in his murderous rage, he'd known that he would need someone to steer the ship. Right now Larten didn't care if he lived or died, but a part of him had been thinking about life, even while he was dealing out death to all in sight.

But what of the others? There were two men, and the boy, Daniel Abrams. Why had he let these live? It couldn't have been mercy or because he needed them for the ship — he would have spared another mate, not a worthless boy, if that was the case. So why...?

The answer came to him and he chuckled drily.

He'd had to keep a few alive. The deck was awash with blood, but it would soon spoil and be of no use to him. He had to assume that they were a long way from land. He might be on this ship a good while yet.

He would need to feed.

Still chuckling – edgily now, the laughter threatening to turn into a scream – he shut the door on the moaning, weeping humans, locked it, then retired to the deck with the baby, to wet his whistle before the pools of blood thickened and soured in the sun.

Having drunk his fill on deck, Larten retreated from the daylight before it burned him. He didn't care what happened to him now, but if he gave in to bloodthirsty insanity or let himself die, the baby would perish too.

Larten cradled the boy in the shelter of the captain's cabin, holding him gently as if he was something precious. Nothing would ever set right this dreadful wrong, but if he could protect this innocent child, that would be one less dark mark against his name when he passed from this world of hurt and shame. He felt as far from the gates of Paradise as it was possible to get, so it wasn't redemption that he sought. He simply didn't want to add to his crimes, even though in the greater scheme of things one more wouldn't make any real difference.

He changed the baby's undergarments when he realized why the boy had started crying again. Then he went below deck to find more milk and look for other food.

They slept in the cabin that night, the baby tucked between Larten and the wall. But although the boy snoozed sweetly, Larten spent most of the night staring at the ceiling. It wasn't because he had become accustomed to sleeping in the day or because of the baby's surprisingly deep snoring, but because after what he'd done, he couldn't face the nightmares that were certain to be lying in wait for him.

Shortly before dawn, after feeding the baby again, Larten returned to the room with the four captives and opened the door. They thought he'd come to kill them, and they cowered against the wall. But he only pointed a finger at the senior mate and said, "You."

The sailor crossed himself, muttered a quick prayer, then staggered out of the cabin. He was sweating and trembling, but otherwise carried himself with dignity.

Larten locked the door and led the way to the deck. The mate's face blanched when he cast his eye around, but he didn't try to run.

"You can sail this ship?" Larten asked wearily. If not for the baby, he'd have lowered himself over the side and gone for a swim with the sharks. But if the boy was to live, this had to be done.

"I'm no captain," the mate said quietly.

"If we are to live, you will have to be," Larten retorted.

"If I had a crew..."

"You do not. Can you steer it anyway?"

The mate checked the rigging and shrugged. "We're not so far from land—a week's sailing, I reckon. I can get us there if the weather holds. We'll struggle t' dock, but we can get close enough t' set one o' the scows down and row ashore. *If* the weather holds. If we hit a storm, we're finished."

Larten nodded. "Do your best. I will be taking care of the child. If you need me, shout. Do not try to release the others, and do not try to kill me—I will hear you coming, even in my sleep. If you can drop us ashore, I will set you free."

"What about them?" the mate called as Larten left. He pointed a shaking finger at the corpses. "They'll fester if we leave 'em. The stench..."

"I will dispose of them later," Larten promised. "When the sun goes down. That is when I am most powerful, is it not?" Smiling thinly, he went inside to play with the baby, leaving the mate to steer the ship of corpses through the waves of the ever-hungry sea that would soon receive their lifeless, bloodied hulks.

Chapter Twenty-Five

Feeding the baby and prisoners became the focus of Larten's time. Daniel and the sailors were easy to care for – he just threw them food and water a couple of times a day – but the baby was a different matter. Larten had no experience with babies and was astonished by how often the child wanted to feed. Keeping the boy content was a full-time job.

The mate in charge of the ship reported to Larten regularly. Larten had no interest in their course – he wouldn't have cared if they'd sailed in circles forever – but it was easier to let the mate deliver his reports and nod thoughtfully while pretending to listen.

Larten was ravenous – he needed blood – but he

waited until the mate said they were a day from shore. Tucking in the baby, he went below to the locked room and opened the door. Daniel and the sailors thought that he was coming to feed them, and they shuffled forward eagerly. They still feared the vampire, but had come to believe that he meant them no harm.

Not wishing to alarm them, Larten moved quickly, as he had when he'd embarked on his killing spree. Darting from one to another, he blew a sharp breath of gas in their faces, the gas of the vampires that sent humans to sleep. Once they were unconscious he drank from each of them, then refilled the vials that, unknown to him, had cost Malora her life.

Daniel stirred as Larten was leaving. The vampire had breathed on the boy last, so Daniel hadn't been dealt as strong a blast of the gas as the others. Larten took no notice as the boy's eyes flickered open, only closed the door and locked it, then went to feed the baby.

Larten spent most of that last night on deck, watching by the light of the stars as they drew closer to land, thinking of what he'd done, numbly considering what he must do next. He didn't know much about Greenland, but he knew it was an ice-covered, sparsely populated country. Many cold, lonely, unforgiving places where a vampire could pass quietly from this world. He would find a suitably desolate spot and let the snow and ice finish him off. A fittingly meek finale for a vampire who had lost the right to die a noble death.

The mate approached late the following evening, as Larten was feeding the baby. "We're almost there," he noted.

"Aye," Larten murmured.

"We should make port not long after sunset, if the wind's fair."

"I will disembark before that," Larten said.

The mate frowned. "Disembark?"

"I will take a scow and sail ashore by myself."

"Are ye sure?" the mate asked. "There's nothing much along this stretch and the weather's fierce inhospitable."

"Good," Larten said shortly.

A wave of joy swept through the sailor. He had tried not to think about what would happen when they docked, but whenever he did, he saw no way that the vampire would let them live. They were witnesses to the massacre. He surely could not spare them if he wanted to escape.

But now the mate saw that Larten didn't care. He was going ashore to die. For the first time in a week, the sailor faced the future with real hope. He almost cried, he was so relieved.

"You will take care of the child when I go?" Larten asked.

"Of course. I'll take him home with me. I have six already, so one more won't make much difference."

"Thank you," Larten said softly. "And," he added as the mate returned to the wheel, "you will keep him away from vampires?"

The sailor nodded grimly. "Aye, sir. That I most definitely will."

The mate helped Larten ready and lower the scow. Before he departed, Larten went down to the locked room one last time, to release the prisoners. He could have left that job to the mate, but he wanted to do it himself, so they could come up, see him leave and know for certain that they had nothing to fear from this night on.

"Come, gentlemen," Larten said as he opened the door. "Your time of captivity is over. You are free to..."

He came to a stunned, horrified stop.

Daniel Abrams was sitting on the floor, hands and lips as red with blood as Larten's had been a week before. The boy had torn open the throats of the two men while they were unconscious and drank as much of their blood as he could stomach. He'd even bitten chunks out of their flesh and eaten it. He was chewing a sliver of cheek, pausing every so often to spit out blood, when Larten entered.

Daniel's face lit up crazily when he spotted the vampire, and he staggered to his feet. "I'm one o' yer lot now," he cackled, waving the strip of flesh at Larten as if it was a flag. "Ye don't have t' kill me. Ye can take me with ye. I'm a bloodsucker too, see? We're the same."

Larten stared at the boy, first with shock, then disgust. "You think that you are the same as me?" he snarled.

"Aye," the boy hooted. "We both kill and drink blood. What's the difference?"

And the awful thing was, he was right. When you put the two of them side by side, there was no real difference at all. A pair of well-matched monsters.

Larten backed out of the room, away from the blinking, spitting, blood-smeared boy. He glanced at the murdered sailors, then bolted for the deck, where he raced to the side and threw up over the railing. Before Daniel Abrams could climb the steps and ask again to travel with him, Larten ducked into the captain's cabin and picked up the baby.

He had meant to bid the child farewell, but as he stared at the chubby babe, he decided he couldn't leave the boy behind. Not with a beast like Daniel Abrams on the prowl. Maybe they *were* cut from the same cloth, but at least Larten wouldn't feed on the innocent baby. If Larten took him from the ship, the boy was doomed, but death in the wilds was preferable to what might happen to the infant if he remained.

Larten never considered the possibility of simply killing Daniel. In a mindless panic, he thought that there were only two options—take the baby or leave him to be bled and devoured.

Larten wrapped the child up warmly and staggered across the deck to the scow. The mate was bewildered when he saw the wild-eyed vampire climb in with the baby. "What are you doing?" he shouted. "I thought you were leaving him."

But Larten would neither listen nor respond. Before the mate could stop him, he cast off and rowed madly towards the icy shore. Understanding would come to the sailor later, when he discovered the young cannibal below, but for the time being he could only stand on deck and stare dumbly at the swiftly receding boat.

*   *   *

Larten thrust ahead without pause, muscles aching, neck bent stiffly, never looking up. If he'd gone in the wrong direction and missed land, perhaps he would have rowed until he weakened and died. But the mate had pointed the scow true, and before long he struck shore and ground to a halt.

Larten stood in a daze and gazed at a giant sheet of ice that seemed to stretch from one end of the horizon to the other. For a moment he was overwhelmed and thought about returning to the ship. Then he grinned darkly, seeing the obstacle for what any true vampire would have judged it—a challenge to be met.

Picking up the baby, Larten strapped the silent, shivering boy to his back and made sure he was secure. Then, with a cry of total abandon, he leapt from the boat and cut a path towards the glittering wall of ice. Dragging his way through mounds of thigh-high snow, Larten laughed manically at the moon and stars as he pushed on in delirious pursuit of his place in that other, eternal, always freezing night.

To be continued...

MW00754849

SLICKROCK

Also by Laura Crum

Roped
Roughstock
Hoofprints
Cutter

SLICKROCK

LAURA CRUM

THOMAS DUNNE BOOKS
ST. MARTIN'S MINOTAUR
NEW YORK

THOMAS DUNNE BOOKS.
An imprint of St. Martin's Press.

Library of Congress Cataloging-in-Publication Data

Crum, Laura.
    Slickrock : a Gail McCarthy mystery / Laura Crum.—1st St. Martin's Minotaur ed.
        p.   cm.
    "Thomas Dunne Books."
    ISBN 0-312-20910-X
    I. Title
PS3553.R76S55   1999
813'.54—dc21   99-15948
                                                     CIP

First Edition: November 1999

10 9 8 7 6 5 4 3 2 1

For Andy Snow, allways.

Thanks to Wally Evans, Carl Dobler, and Bill Crum, who helped organize many mountain pack trips, and to Willie Ritts, Matt Bloom, and all the crew at Kennedy Meadows—a constant inspiration.

Thanks also to Dr. Craig Evans, D.V.M.

And especially, thanks to my mother, Joan Awbrey Brown, who encouraged me to write this story.

AUTHOR'S NOTE

The Sierra Nevada Mountains of California are very real, as are the lakes, rivers, and peaks of the area around Sonora Pass, where this book is set. I have visited most of the places described in the story, but they have been rearranged and sometimes changed to fit the purposes of the plot, and the descriptions and locations of various lakes and passes, etc., are not always accurate. Though the pack station described in this book may resemble a real pack station in many respects, it—and its crew and visitors—is entirely a figment of my imagination. Happy trails!

"Jack, as far as I can see
mistakes are only horses in disguise
ain't no need to ride 'em over
'cause we could not ride them different if we tried."

—Guy Clark, quoting bronc rider Larry Mahan,
in the song "Ramblin' Jack & Mahan"

SLICKROCK

PROLOGUE

It all started with the dead man in Deadman Meadow. Not the original dead man, of course. An unfortunate emigrant who came west in the 1800s, the first victim met his unspecified end in one particular meadow along Crazy Horse Creek in the Sierra Nevada Mountains of California. The place thereafter recalled his fate; I always wondered if the naming of the creek and the meadow were related.

But it was the second dead man who changed my world. Or rather, the events that followed in his wake. Until I came upon him, I thought I knew the direction my life would take; afterwards, I found that the only thing I knew was that I did not know. Knowing is much more comfortable than not knowing, and I can't exactly say I'm happy about that eventful summer and the upheaval it caused. Yet I can't really regret it either. Who would not move closer to the truth?

ONE

The roan colt rocketed around the bullpen, making every jump high, wide, and handsome. Stirrups swung wildly, latigos popped and slapped, leather squeaked with strain. The colt grunted, head down between his knees, and put all his effort into stiffening his front legs and kicking his back feet as high as possible. I stood outside the bullpen and watched Ted Reiter watch the colt.

Ted was in the middle of the pen, a short, stocky figure wearing dirty jeans and a white straw cowboy hat. He watched the colt buck with the empty saddle on his back and spat out some tobacco juice. Ted didn't look like the boss of a big outfit; he looked like another dirt-poor ranch cowboy. But appearances were misleading in his case.

The colt was getting mad. He was determined to rid himself of the saddle that had been cinched so uncomfortably around his belly, he had made every effort to do so, and the saddle was still there. He bucked harder and began to squeal—grunting squeals, like a pig. His eyes had a blind look. Ted dodged out of the horse's way when the roan bucked in his direction. Not exactly an easygoing colt, was my thought. Oh well, he wasn't my business. My business was finding a vodka tonic. I'd had a long day, and I was ready for a drink. I waved a casual hand at Ted and headed down the hill toward the bar.

It was six o'clock on a July evening in the Sierra Nevada Mountains of California. This time of year Deadman Meadow was brilliantly green. It stretched out in front of the Crazy Horse Creek Pack Station like a patch of the Emerald Isle itself. The little bar sat facing the meadow, a small shack of a place with a porch all along the front. I pushed open the door and went inside.

Six o'clock on a Friday evening in July meant the Crazy Horse Creek Bar was fairly crowded. I found a gap and ordered my drink from the bartender.

Talk rose around me like bubbles through tonic.

"Did you see the bay son of a bitch Charley was riding?"

"I swear to God he caught a fifteen-inch brookie out of Kennedy Lake."

Horse talk, fisherman talk. I sipped slowly and let the talk and laughter swirl and fizz around me. Like Ted's roan colt, it wasn't my business.

This turned out to be a mistake. When you're sitting in a bar full of drunks it pays to stay alert. But I was absorbed in my own thoughts and didn't see it coming.

The first clue I got was when the stranger on my left pushed me hard against the bar and shoved his body in front of me. My angry "What the hell" was swallowed up in a jolt of surprise as I felt the secondhand impact of the drunk on my right, who catapulted into my benefactor (as I now realized), who in turn launched the drunk into the open area in the middle of the bar. Scuffling and shouting rattled around me.

In a minute I pieced it together. Two of the fairly drunken fishermen in the group to my right had gotten in an argument and were now engaged in the sort of shoving match of a fight that drunks usually pursue. The original attack had thrown the one guy in my direction, and the solitary man on my left had seen him coming and fended him off. At this point my rescuer stepped away from me and resumed his place at the bar; the fight, if you wanted to call it that, was moving out into the parking lot.

"Thanks," I said, looking up at him.

"No problem. I didn't want to see you get run over."

This man was big. I'm five-foot-seven and he looked to be about a foot taller. Wide shoulders, too, although he was fairly lean. I could see why he wouldn't have a problem defending strange women from drunks. Some sort of further politeness seemed to be called for.

"I'm Gail McCarthy." I held out my hand.

"Blue. Blue Winter," he said, a little sheepishly. His hand felt surprisingly fine-boned and slender.

"Do you know those guys?" I asked, gesturing in the direction of the shoving group at the doorway.

"No."

Polite conversation was proving difficult. Blue Winter (could that possibly be his real name?) stared at his drink. Not only was he roughly six-and-a-half feet tall, he had red hair and wore a gray felt hat somewhere between a cowboy hat and a fedora. Regulation Wrangler jeans, a faded denim shirt, and cowboy boots completed the effect. He looked exactly like the "tall red-headed stranger" in Willie Nelson's song.

I tried again. "Are you here for a pack trip?"

"Yes, I am."

"The pack station taking you in?" I asked.

"No, I'm packing myself."

My ears pricked up. "So am I."

He looked directly at me for the first time. "Are you with a group?"

4

"No, I'm going alone."

"So am I."

We looked at each other with mutual curiosity. The bar fight still seemed to be going full swing in the parking lot; at least, there was a fair amount of shouting outside. The bar, however, was relatively empty, most everyone having dashed out the door, either to participate or to spectate. Blue Winter and I were surrounded by vacant bar stools.

"So have you packed in the mountains much?" Blue Winter's shyness or reticence or whatever it was seemed to have been swallowed up by his curiosity. Gray eyes regarded me steadily from under the brim of his hat.

"Well, no, I haven't," I admitted. Knowing what was going through his mind, I added, "I'm pretty well prepared for this trip, though."

He watched me quietly, and I had the sense he was wondering what to say. I decided to help him. "Have you done a lot of packing?"

"Yes, ma'am."

"Any advice for a novice?"

He smiled. Immediately I liked him. He had crooked teeth and kind eyes, and when he smiled his somewhat somber expression became shy and friendly.

The smile receded and his face was once again reserved. "Sometimes you need to doctor a horse," he said.

My turn to smile. "I'm a vet," I said.

As I expected, a brief flicker of surprise in his eyes. Women vets aren't uncommon anymore, but still, I often caught that look. "A horse vet," I added. "I'm from Santa Cruz."

At this, he looked startled. Then that charming, unaffected smile. "You must be Jim Leonard's lady vet."

"That's me," I agreed. Jim was my boss. "How did you know?"

"I'm from Watsonville."

5

Watsonville was maybe thirty minutes from Santa Cruz. The same neck of the woods, in other words.

"So if you're from Watsonville, and I take it you have horses, you must use Bob Barton."

"That's right."

"Bob's a good guy." This was professional courtesy; in my opinion Jim was a vastly superior horse vet. Bob Barton was mainly a small-animal practitioner who did horses on the side. He *was* a nice guy, though.

"So, what are you doing here at Crazy Horse Creek, about to take off in the mountains on your own?" It was the most forthcoming question Blue Winter had asked yet, and I couldn't think of a simple answer.

Crazy Horse Creek Pack Station was five hours from my home on the coast of California. I had never taken my two horses on a pack trip before, though I had done some solitary backpacking up in these mountains during my college years. However, I hadn't been camping in any way, shape, or form for many seasons; the three-week vacation I was currently indulging in was the first time off of any length I'd had since I started working as a veterinarian five years ago. So, what exactly was I doing here, preparing to take my two flatland horses over the granite of four High Sierra passes on a two-week expedition?

I decided to cut to the chase. "Well, the reason I'm here, specifically, is my boyfriend used to own this pack station, and the people who run it were willing to put me and my horses up for a few days while we got acclimated."

He took that in. "Your boyfriend must be Lonny Peterson."

"That's right."

"I know Lonny a little."

I changed the subject. "So, how about a few tips for a beginner."

He was quiet, considering. "Well, you obviously know how

to take care of your horses, and I guess you must have some idea about camping, or you wouldn't be going.''

I didn't respond to this, and I could sense him sizing me up, looking me over the way a man will size up a horse. I tried to imagine what he was seeing.

A tallish woman in her mid-thirties, with dark hair in a braid, olive skin, wide shoulders and hips, long legs. I wore a T-shirt, jeans and boots, hoop earrings in my ears, no other jewelry. I weigh about 140—not fat, but not thin either.

"You look strong enough," he said.

I laughed. "Why, thanks."

He smiled. "To deal with the packing. That's hard, when you're alone."

I nodded. "Uh-huh."

It had been my main problem. I was packing Plumber, my younger horse, and he and I had learned the routine of putting on the pack rig fairly easily. Plumber hadn't minded the back cinch, or the crupper under his tail, or the wooden forks strad-dling his back. But he hadn't been crazy about my lifting the heavily loaded panniers up onto him.

Docile as always, his only expression of objection had been to sidestep away, but since I had a hard time lifting the pack bags up at all, it had proven virtually impossible to get the straps over the forks that were to hold them unless Plumber stood perfectly still. Thus, we had practiced the routine of pack-ing over and over again, with many reprimands for moving.

Plumber had learned. His name wasn't Plumb Smart for nothing.

"I had to work at that," I told Blue Winter. "My pack horse is only about fifteen hands," I added. "That helps."

"What kind of horses are you taking in?" he asked.

"Well, they're Quarter Horses."

He nodded. Many, if not most, western riding horses in Cal-ifornia were American Quarter Horses.

7

"I've used the saddle horse as a team roping horse, mostly. The pack horse used to be a bridle horse, a show horse, before I got him."

Another abbreviated story. Gunner and Plumber, my two horses, with their complex histories and equally intricate personalities, had been a big part of what my life was about for many years.

"So, how about you?" I asked. "How do you come to be here?"

"Oh, I come here every year." His face looked withdrawn.

"You take your own horses?"

"Yes, ma'am." No further information forthcoming.

I half shrugged. If he didn't want to answer questions, that was no skin off my back. The conversation had gone on long enough for politeness. Trouble was, I was in this bar waiting for Lonny, and he still hadn't shown up. Oh well. I could look for him later.

"Speaking of horses, I guess I'll go check on mine." I held out my hand. "Nice to meet you."

Blue Winter took my hand in his oddly long, slender one. "Likewise," he said.

Nice man, I thought, as I left the bar. Quiet, though.

Stepping out the door I took a deep breath of the cold-water, pine-tree scent. It was a sunny summer evening, and I happen to think that such evenings in a Sierra meadow are perhaps the prettiest things on earth. I don't know what it is—the generous gold of the light, the contrast of soft green meadow grass against hard silver-gray granite ridges, the smell of the mountains, the lively voice of the creeks. It filled me right up with happiness, just being there.

Taking another deep breath, I strolled toward the horse corrals, reviewing with pleasure the proposed events of the next couple of weeks. I had arrived here this afternoon, horse trailer in tow, prepared to meet Lonny and spend the weekend with him here at the pack station. Tomorrow we had plans to take a short ride, Sunday I would rest, and on Monday ride in on my solitary two-week excursion. This trip was the result of a year of planning on my part, and I felt a deep sense of anticipation and excitement that it was happening at last.

As for where Lonny was at the moment—"out for a ride," the bartender had said. Ernie, the bartender, tended to use as few words as possible; I hadn't pressed him. Lonny and I had agreed to meet in the bar Friday evening before dinner—no doubt he would show up eventually.

A familiar nicker rang out as I neared the corrals. Plumber. My younger horse was a talker. He constantly nickered at me—when he was tied to the rail waiting, while I saddled him, whenever I approached his corral, even occasionally when he saw me in the midst of a group of people.

Walking toward him now, I smiled. His head was thrust out between the bars of the corral where I had put him and Gunner, his eyes bright and inquiring. "So there you are," he seemed to say. "What's up, what are we going to do?"

Gunner, in contrast, had his head down, munching on the hay I had put in the corral. He glanced up and over his shoulder at me, snorted softly, and went back to eating. I had been using Gunner as my main saddle horse for several years now, and he knew the score. We were here to work, no doubt in his mind. Best for him to eat while he could.

I leaned on the fence for a moment, watching them. Gunner, at 15.3 hands, was fairly tall and leggy for a Quarter Horse. He had a bright bay coat, three high white socks, a big blaze, and one blue eye. Plain-headed and big-boned, his friendly, clownish expression made him appealing.

Plumber, on the other hand, was almost cute. Smaller than Gunner, he was finer-boned, with rounder muscling, and he had a little breedy head. Cocoa-brown in color, with a small white spot right between his bright, mischievous eyes, and the sort

of personality that caused him to thrust his head into your lap—
Plumber was a real puppy dog of a horse.

I rubbed his forehead for a minute, told him to go back to
his dinner, and turned away. The horses were fine.

Next stop—the pickup. It was parked nearby, my brand new
acquisition—the very first new truck I'd ever purchased. A gray
Dodge, it had four-wheel drive, an automatic transmission
(good for hauling horses), and an extended cab (good for piling
junk in). It also had a camper on the bed. For Roey.

A short, excited yip emanated from the camper as I approached. I'd been spotted.

Sharply pricked red ears pointed at me through the screened
windows of the camper. Heavy-duty metal screen, I might add.
Roey had destroyed the light nylon screens that had come with
the shell months before.

I had hopes that at a year old my young dog's destructive
impulses were diminishing. It was debatable, though. I had
taken the pup last summer; she was a purebred Queensland
heeler, bred by a friend of mine. I liked both the parent dogs,
I missed my old dog, Blue, who was also a Queensland, and I
thought I was ready to raise a pup. I'd simply forgotten just
what that entailed.

Blue had died a couple of years ago at the age of fifteen, so
it had been many years indeed since I'd dealt with a puppy. I
was accustomed to a dog who understood what I was saying
to him, who knew my ways (and human ways in general),
and who obeyed me (albeit with a lot of grumbling). I was
now faced with a fluffy bundle of energy who had no clue
what I wanted in the way of behavior, and who had a strong
desire to tear things up with her teeth. Any things. Not to
mention, she saw no reason why she should not defecate
wherever the impulse took her, or why she should follow my
arbitrary orders. She was, like most Queenslands, smart, stubborn, and endearing.

I opened the door of the camper and rubbed the wide, wedge-shaped head that was thrust over the tailgate at me. Roey wagged her tail frantically and wiggled all over. I ran my hand down her back. Roey was a red heeler, like her mother, Rita, and with her small size and her pricked ears, I often thought she looked just like a little red fox.

She reminded me of my old dog, Blue, in being very intelligent and incredibly hard-headed, but unlike Blue, Roey was generally friendly. She liked people, and other dogs, and cats, and for that matter, the whole world, as far as I could tell. Lonny teased me that she'd never make a watchdog; she'd probably try to inveigle potential burglars into throwing a stick for her. This was true. After Blue's protective tendencies I found Roey's amiable nature somewhat of a relief. No more worrying that my dog would nip (and mortally offend) a client.

A few more pats, a check to see that her water and food bowls were full, and I shut Roey back in the camper. I'd taken her for a run when I first got here; she should be fine for the night.

So where the hell was Lonny? Out for a ride. But the sun was sitting right on top of the western ridge at this point, and nobody had come riding in down the trail for the last hour.

Lonny knew he was meeting me tonight. So why wasn't he here? Annoyance and worry struggled for dominance in my brain.

Well, neither of those emotions was going to help anything. I stared off across Deadman Meadow, already in shade. Crazy Horse Creek ran along its far side, as I knew. And right where the creek emerged from the canyon and rushed out into the meadow was a pretty little waterfall. I'd just walk quietly up and check out the waterfall. Spend a moment enjoying the mountains. If Lonny rode in, he'd know I was here—horses in the corral, rig parked nearby. We'd find each other.

Resolved, I headed off down the trail that crossed the

meadow, looking around with a deep sigh of relief. I was here, at last, about to achieve a goal I'd held all my life. I was going to spend a sizable chunk of time in these mountains all alone, with just my horses and my dog for company.

The farther I walked into Deadman Meadow, the more the busy bustle of the pack station receded and I could feel the presence of the mountains around me. Granite and pine tree–clad ridges rose up all about me; the meadow was springy under my feet. Ahead of me the chatter of Crazy Horse Creek grew louder. In another few strides the bright water was visible, jumping and chasing between boulders.

I followed a faint trail that led upstream, worn by the feet of many fishermen over many seasons. The creek got noisier and noisier as I neared the canyon from which it emerged.

It was dusk now. The air was soft and still and dim—with every moment that passed, the shapes around me dissolved further. I could see the lights of the pack station across the meadow. Wondered if Lonny had come in yet. Don't worry, I told myself, Lonny's had more experience in the mountains than anyone you know.

Still, I peered hopefully through the gathering darkness at the big barn, although it was impossible to see anything as small as an individual horse and rider from here. And even less possible along the unlighted main trail, though I traced its course along the far side of the meadow. I could see a white horse, maybe.

In point of fact, I saw nothing. I scanned the meadow one more time, started to turn away, and stopped. There was something out there. Something shiny. A car.

The car was behind a clump of willows that screened it completely from the pack station and the main trail. It was partially obscured, but visible from where I stood on the banks of the creek. Small and low and dark, some sort of sports car, it had only caught my eye due to the sheen of light reflecting off its metal surface. It was pretty damn well hidden.

This, I supposed, was because it shouldn't be there. The Forest Service did not allow cars to be driven out into the meadow. However, the big gate that blocked such vehicles from the main trail was often left open so that various ranger Jeeps, or pack station trucks, could go up to the ranger station at Bright Water Flat, a couple of miles up the trail. The gate had been open this afternoon, I recalled. But duly posted with many signs declaring it off-limits to cars.

Well, this car had clearly ignored them. I guessed it belonged to a particularly lazy fisherman, and wondered briefly if it was now stuck. The meadow was damp in spots and the car didn't look the sort to have four-wheel drive.

It was possible. And the light was dying fast. If I wanted to reach my destination, a mere hundred yards away up this canyon, I'd better go.

I turned and headed for the waterfall.

TWO

Twenty minutes later, when I got back to the meadow, it was almost dark and the car was still there. Knowing where to look was the only thing that made it visible.

I stopped and studied it in mild consternation. What in the world was it doing here? Was it, in fact, stuck?

I had a small penlight in my pocket (as well as a Swiss Army knife and a waterproof container of matches). Perhaps I should go and see.

Ten steps in the direction of the car and I stopped. Was this smart? I was a woman alone; I had no idea what the car was here for. On the other hand, I argued, I was perfectly safe skulking out here in the dark willows. No one who was in the car would be able to see me without a light.

Cautiously I approached the vehicle from the rear, out of headlight range, my hand on my own small flashlight. No humans seemed to be about; the car looked deserted. But it also looked too expensive to be cavalierly abandoned.

From twenty feet away, I stared. It was some kind of two-seater sports car; I couldn't put a name to it. No movement in it, or around it. My eyes tracked along the ground nearby. A patch of white. Not large. Bigger than a paper bag, smaller than a picnic blanket. Next to the car, about ten feet from the front bumper. I stared. The white thing didn't move.

Cautiously I brought the flashlight out of my pocket. Wiggling gently behind a sheltering screen of willow branches, I aimed it at the white shape and clicked it on.

For a second I still couldn't figure it out. White cloth, it looked like; I moved the light. And something darker. A face. Shit.

The white was a shirt, a shirt that was on a man lying flat on his back in the meadow.

I clicked the flashlight off. This was weird.

Peering through the near-dark, I ascertained that the man hadn't moved. I mentally replayed what I'd seen. A man lying flat on his back—I'd had a brief glimpse of his face, staring upward. No one I recognized.

Was he hurt? Dead? Asleep? Drunk?

I clicked the light on again. The grass and willow branches obscured him somewhat, but there was no doubt of what I was seeing.

Pointing the flashlight right at his face, I looked for signs of life. For a second, nothing. Then the face turned slowly toward my light. I couldn't read his expression.

I hesitated. Before I could make up my mind what to do, the man sat up.

Big, dark blotches all over the front of his white shirt. What? No. Yes. Blood. Dark red blotches. Blood, or something like it.

"Leave me alone," he said.

My mind spun.

He lay back down.

Now what the hell was I supposed to do? Could it really have been blood on his shirt front?

I kept the flashlight on his face. Thought about it. Then I shouted, "Do you need help?"

No response. And then, slowly, he sat up again, looking in my direction. "Leave me alone," he said again. And then quite distinctly, "I'm trying to kill myself."

Once again, he lay back. Shit, shit, shit. This time I was sure the dark red blotches were blood. "I'm trying to kill myself," he had said. I played the flashlight on the ground around him. In a moment, I caught the dull flash of reflected light off the blued barrel.

A gun. Lying on the ground near his right hand. Within reach of his hand. If I approached him, he could shoot at me.

I trained the flashlight back on his face. "I'll get help," I shouted.

This time he spoke without moving, and I had a harder time making out his words. "No, no help. Don't want help."

"Just hang in there," I said, using my strongest reassuring-veterinarian tone. "I'll help you."

"No. Leave me alone. No help. Let me die."

I tried to decide what to do. If I went near this guy, he could potentially shoot me, though he had made no move toward the gun so far. I had no idea if he was dying, or if there was anything I could do immediately that would help him. Get some help, I thought. Don't get yourself shot for no good reason.

"Listen," I yelled at him, "I'm going to get help. Just hang in there. You'll be okay."

"No, please." He didn't move; I thought his voice was weaker. "Don't try to help me. I'm dying. I want to die. Like the horses."

"Like the horses?" I repeated, startled.

"Dying." He stared straight up at the night sky. "Green fire in their bellies. I couldn't save them. Dying."

This made no sense to me. "I'll be back," I yelled. "Please. Just hang in there." Then I turned and ran.

16

Running through the dark, to the jouncy, jerking beam of the flashlight, running down the trail. I could see the pack station lights ahead of me, across the meadow; they seemed a long way away. I stuck to the trail; I could run faster on the trail than I could through the meadow.

All I could hear was the thump of my feet, the panting of my breath. Hurry, hurry.

The lights across the meadow flickered and bounced to the rhythm of my feet, the bob of my head. Faster, a little faster, I urged my body. I kept my eyes on the trail as it flared and faded before me in the flashlight's lurching beam.

Even as I ran, I planned. I would go straight to the bar; someone would be there, there was a phone there. God, what in hell was that man doing out in the meadow? Why shoot himself there, of all places?

Hurry, hurry. I was tiring; my breath came in gasps. Find the rhythm, keep breathing, keep running, I chanted to myself. Keep your eyes on the trail, keep moving, keep running.

I looked up. The pack station was closer. Eyes back on the trail, I forced myself to put one foot in front of the other in a steady rhythm.

A man with blood all over his shirt front, lying on his back in Deadman Meadow, wanting to die. Had he picked this spot to shoot himself because of the damn name?

Come on, Gail, I urged myself. Move it a little. Save this guy's life for him.

I could see the bar, with the long porch across the front of it. Not so far now. God, I was out of breath, though. I was really out of shape.

Closer, closer, almost there. The meadow was soggy, almost boggy, here; my feet squished and stuck a little. I could feel moisture seeping through my boots.

No matter. The lights were in front of me, the parking lot, the cars. Gasping for air, I pounded across the dark road—

empty of tourists, for once—up the wooden steps, across the porch, and through the open door of the bar.

Lights, noise, faces, confusion. My eyes struggled to adjust to the bright light; all faces looked my way. And then I saw Lonny.

Standing at the bar with Ted, I registered. Turning toward me with a look of welcome changing to concern.

"Gail, what's wrong?"

He took three fast steps toward me, put his hand on my arm.

"A man . . . shot himself . . . still alive . . . in the upper meadow." I said it between pants.

Lonny had never been slow. "Damn. Go get the Jeep," he ordered one of the boys. "Pick us up along the trail. Bring the first-aid kit. We're headed up there." He turned to Ted. "Better call the ambulance, and the sheriff."

"I think," I gasped, "he's going to need a chopper."

Ted nodded. "Okay." Then he headed for the phone.

"Come on, Gail, show me where." Lonny had hold of my arm.

"He's got a gun," I said.

"Ernie." Lonny held out his left hand.

Without a word Ernie produced a short shotgun from under the bar and handed it over the counter to Lonny.

"Okay. Let's go," Lonny said.

"Okay."

I started out of the bar, still panting, but a little better for the rest. I could keep going until the Jeep picked us up.

Lonny had the long stride of a six-foot-plus man, and despite the fact that he walked rather than ran across the parking lot and down the main trail, I had to jog every few steps to keep up.

Before he'd had time to ask me more than, "So just where is this guy?" we could hear the noise of the Jeep behind us. Headlight glow lit the trail as Jake, one of Ted's crew, pulled the vehicle up beside us.

As we climbed in, I told Lonny, "Behind some willows at the far end of the upper meadow. His car's out there. Some sort of black sports car."

I could barely see Lonny's face in the peripheral glow of the headlights; he looked strained and tired. And old, I thought.

Well, he was fifty-one. Considerably older than I was. But until recently I'd always thought he looked young for his age.

"So, did you recognize this guy?" he asked.

"No." I thought about it. "He had dark hair, sort of an aquiline nose. He'd be about your age."

We were bouncing along the trail now. Lonny asked Jake, "Did you bring the first-aid kit?"

"Yeah. And three flashlights." Jake was all of sixteen, but, like most of the crew, he had already picked up Ted's laconic way of speaking. He said nothing more, just kept manhandling the Jeep over and around boulders, jolting up the trail.

When I judged we'd gone far enough, I said, "Stop."

Jake stopped.

"See if you can get the headlights pointed out into the meadow."

Jake began jockeying the car; Lonny and I were already scanning with the flashlights.

In a second I saw the sharp reflected gleam. "There."

"Take it as far as you can without getting stuck," Lonny told Jake.

Then he was out of the Jeep, with me scrambling to follow him, and we were both half walking, half running through the meadow grass and low willow scrub toward the car.

"He has a gun," I reminded Lonny.

"Did he threaten you with it?"

"No, but that doesn't mean he won't."

Lonny grunted. We both kept moving. Until, about twenty feet from the car, he stopped. "You wait here," he told me.

"What are you talking about? I'm not going to stand back here watching while somebody shoots you."

"Gail, will you for once in your life do what you're told? Especially when it makes sense. Why should we both get shot? Now stay here." And he walked off.

I stayed. What the hell. He was right, more or less. I kept my flashlight on the car. From this angle I couldn't see the man, but I knew about where he was.

Lonny moved cautiously forward; I could see him sweeping the ground with his flashlight beam. In the other hand he held the shotgun loosely. He stepped quietly around the front of the car, stopped, stepped forward again, and stopped.

"My God," he said. "It's Bill."

THREE

Do you know him?"

"Yeah, yeah I do. It's Bill Evans. He was my vet."

"Your vet?" I walked toward Lonny.

He bent down; I saw him come up holding the pistol.

"While I was running this pack station; he's Ted's vet now. Or was."

Lonny handed the pistol and the shotgun to me and bent down again, pressing his fingers under the man's jaw. No response from the recumbent figure. He was either unconscious or dead.

"He's got a pulse," Lonny said.

We both stared at the big, dark blotches on the white shirt front, the still face. Bill Evans didn't appear to be bleeding heavily.

"Is there a blanket in the Jeep?" I asked.

"Should be."

I could hear Jake slowly piloting the Jeep toward us around scrub, boulders, and wet spots.

"I guess all I know to do is keep him warm, maybe try to put some pressure on the wound if it's still actively bleeding."

"Yeah." Lonny looked stunned; he stared down at the man as if he couldn't believe what he was seeing. "Jesus," he said quietly. "Bill."

"So why would try he to kill himself?" I asked.

"I don't know. But he has been acting real strange. He was up here last night, got drunk and obnoxious, and Ted threw him out of the bar. Jesus."

The Jeep was behind us now; Lonny yelled, "Bring a blanket."

In a minute Jake stood beside me, staring down at Bill Evans. I handed him the guns and took the wool blanket out of his hands. Jake didn't say a word. Bending down, I covered the man's legs with the blanket. Gingerly, I explored with my fingers the wet red spot in the center of the chest. Seeping. Not much of a hole. The pistol had been a .22, I recalled. The bullet appeared to have gone right into the sternum. Whether it had hit the heart or lungs I had no idea. Probably not the heart, or the guy would be dead by now.

"Get the first-aid kit," I told Jake.

He headed back toward the Jeep; I looked up to see Lonny still staring blankly downward. "What's the matter?" I asked.

He shook his head. "I just can't believe it," he said slowly. And then, "My father killed himself."

"He did?" I hadn't known this.

"He shot himself. In the head. I found him." Lonny recited these facts quietly enough, but I sensed that the emotions behind them were roiling wildly through his mind.

"It's okay," I said soothingly. "This guy's alive. I can see Ted coming," I added.

Sure enough, headlights were bouncing along the main trail— Ted or somebody.

Jake handed me the first-aid kit; I opened it and began making a pad with gauze and cotton. This I pressed firmly against the wound. Lonny and Jake stood over me, wordless.

After a few minutes two others joined them. I looked up. Ted and Jake's older brother, Luke.

"My God." Ted's voice. Pain and shock were plain.

I had never heard Ted Reiter express so much raw emotion. About my age, Ted was short, stocky and stout, with a round face, guileless blue eyes, a boyish manner. Lonny had taken him on as a hired hand when Ted was seventeen, then, later, as a business partner. Now Ted was sole owner of the pack station. But you'd never know it to look at him. Wearing dirty jeans and denim jacket, usually messing with a horse or flirting with a girl—that was Ted. And despite his unlikely looks, quite the lady-killer.

But now, in this moment, he looked as devastated as Lonny looked stunned.

"Not Bill," he said. "He couldn't."

Luke and Jake were silent. Lonny put a hand on Ted's shoulder.

Some dark emotion seemed to twine through the little group of men. Not grief, not shock, though they were present, too. Something blacker. I could feel it, but I didn't understand it. I wasn't part of it. I hadn't known this man.

After a minute Ted said quietly, "Chopper's coming. Is he still alive?"

"Yeah," I said.

"Better get out in the meadow with the flashlights," Lonny said to Luke and Jake.

"Come on." Ted turned abruptly. "That chopper will be here soon."

The three of them hurried away; setting up guide points for a helicopter to land in the dark was familiar to them. All serious medical emergencies had to be carried out of these mountains by the medevac helicopter. Other methods were prohibitively time-consuming.

"So, what's the deal here?" I asked Lonny. "You all knew this guy, I take it."

"Everybody knew him. He was up here all the time. I'm surprised you never met him."

"I've only been up here on the occasional weekend in the summer." I pressed the pad gently against the man's chest.

"Bill was virtually part of the crew," Lonny said. "He's been the vet for us up here ever since I owned the place. We all knew him real well."

"So, what was going on with him that he would shoot himself?"

"I'm not sure," Lonny said. "Bill would get depressed. He had these bouts of depression every few years. And he tended to drink when he was in one. It made for problems."

"I can see that."

"His wife left him a few years ago, I think because of his drinking. He's been worse ever since. But I had no idea he was thinking of killing himself."

"No," I said.

"Damn, Gail, I wish I'd known." Lonny sounded sad and ashamed; I thought I could guess what it was that had been in the air as the men looked down at their friend. Guilt. They all felt guilty that he had come to this and that they hadn't known, hadn't helped him.

"Ted threw him out of the bar last night because he was trying to pick fights with the customers. Told him to go sleep it off. Damn."

"Where did he stay?"

"In the lodge."

Faintly, in the distance, I heard a steady *thump, thump, thump*. Lonny heard it, too.

"Here they come."

I pressed my fingers to the man's carotid artery. The pulse was there, thin but steady.

"He's still alive," I said.

The thumping grew louder; I could see the lights of the helicopter in the western sky. Ted and the boys were out in the meadow, waving their flashlights. Steadily the chopper approached, seeming to know where it was headed.

In a minute the noise was overwhelming—*whump, whump, whump.* Floodlights came on in the undercarriage as it hovered over the meadow, and the night receded instantly. The mountains seemed to disappear in harsh white light and the gigantic pounding heartbeat of the blades.

No point in talking; we couldn't have heard each other. Lonny and I stood in silence, watching the odd scene. Slowly the chopper lowered itself in a blaze of light and loud, whirling wind. Willows and grass bent away in waves as the machine touched down on the ground.

The intense noise diminished to an idle; the blades rotated gently; two men in white coats jumped out the door and ran toward Ted, who waved them on and turned in our direction. Help had arrived.

Twenty minutes later, Bill Evans was on a stretcher in the belly of the helicopter as the beast lifted off in the same flurry of noise with which it had arrived. Bill was still alive, they said. When asked if he would make it, they shrugged.

Ted and Lonny and I stood together watching the chopper disappear into the night sky. Luke approached and tapped Ted on the shoulder.

"The sheriffs are here," he said. "They want to ask you some questions."

FOUR

Two sheriff's deputies, as it turned out, a man and a woman. We all trooped back to the lodge, and over cups of coffee in the lobby, they questioned the five of us who had gone up to the meadow.

It wasn't terribly formal. They listened carefully to my recitation of how I had found the man, and the female deputy asked me, "He definitely said he was trying to kill himself?"

"Yes, several times. He said he wanted to be let alone to die." I didn't look at Lonny or Ted as I said this.

"Did he say anything else?"

"He talked about dying horses. At the time, it didn't make any sense to me, but now that I know he was a vet, I wonder if he wasn't talking about treating some colicked horses that died."

Both deputies nodded, apparently familiar enough with horses to understand this statement. This wasn't entirely surprising. They were from Sonora, which has the notion that it's a cowboy town; many people from that part of the world have some understanding of horses, and usually pretend to more.

"Did you see him shoot himself?" the woman deputy asked me. She was apparently the leader of the team, or at least the talker.

"No. Nor did I hear it. When I first saw the car, I didn't see the man. He could have shot himself before I ever got up there, or later, when I was off looking at the waterfall. It's noisy enough there that I might have missed the sound of a twenty-two pistol."

Both deputies nodded again. They had confiscated the pistol earlier, ascertaining that Lonny, Jake, and I had all handled it. We were duly fingerprinted; the pistol was sealed in an evidence bag.

"Did you know this man?" Once again the question was addressed to me by the female deputy. She was a big woman, tall and broad, with black hair, hazel eyes, even features, and a forthright manner. I was getting used to looking at her face.

"No." I left it at that.

"I take it the rest of you did." She glanced around the room as she spoke, but her gaze ended up on Ted.

"Yeah, we knew him. He was our vet." Ted sounded terse, his business manner. His playful streak only showed after a few drinks, or when faced with what he considered a pretty woman.

"So, do you have any idea why he would shoot himself?"

There it was—the big question. The female deputy was looking right at Ted; he kept his round blue eyes candidly on hers, another typical Ted ploy. He always looked customers candidly in the eye while he talked to them.

I glanced around the room. Lonny was seated next to me on the couch; he was staring at his boots, stuck out in front of him. Luke and Jake sat in a couple of battered armchairs off to the side—both of them looking down.

"I think Bill was depressed," Ted said. "He was up here

last night and he got drunk, tried to pick a fight in the bar. I told him to go to bed.''

The deputies took this in. ''Does anybody know why he was depressed?'' the woman asked.

''Oh, Bill's like that. He's a damn good vet, though,'' Ted said.

The woman made a note on the pad in her lap. ''Any other possible reasons?''

''Not that I know.'' Ted kept meeting the deputy's eyes. ''He was staying in the lodge here, room number seven,'' he added.

''We'll check it out. And we'll take the car back down to the department, have a look at it.'' She stood up. ''If you'll give me his room key?''

''Sure.''

Ted went to the main desk, found a duplicate key, and handed it to the woman. She headed for the stairs, her quiet partner in tow, and turned back to give us a look.

''This seems pretty straightforward; however, I'd like to ask you all to stay here and be available for questioning tomorrow, in case there's a problem.''

''Okay if I go out for a ride during the day?'' I asked.

''As long as you come back.'' She smiled.

The two of them turned and creaked their way up the stairs. We all stared at each other.

''I wonder if he made it?'' Ted looked directly at me as he spoke.

''I don't know,'' I said. ''It would depend on whether that bullet hit something vital.''

''I'll call the hospital in Sacramento in the morning.'' Ted said it with decision—another Ted trait. I'd noticed before that he tended to deal with difficult situations in a black-and-white fashion.

Now, having settled the matter of Bill Evans, he stood up. ''I'm going to bed.''

28

He looked at Luke and Jake as he spoke; the two brothers stood up with him. Both tall and lean with light brown hair, brown eyes, fair skin, unremarkable faces, they were hard to tell apart from a distance. Closer up, Luke had a squarer jaw and looked older. Jake's hair was curlier, his expression shyer. They followed Ted up the stairs now; we all knew that they would be up at 4:00 A.M. Saturday was a big day at Crazy Horse Creek—lots of pack parties going in. Feeding and saddling began early.

Once they were gone, I looked at Lonny. He still stared at his boots, his face withdrawn. Tracing his familiar features with my eyes, I felt a disturbing sense of frustration.

I'd been with this man for five years. Like all long-term relationships, ours had its ups and downs, but we'd survived them well, or so I thought. Until this last six months.

Lonny had finally gotten a divorce from the wife he'd been separated from for seven years. The divorce had entailed a fair amount of financial dickering; by the time all was said and done, Lonny had sold his home in Santa Cruz County and his interest in this pack station. True to his announced intention, he'd purchased sixty acres in the Sierra Nevada foothills and moved. Two months ago, to be exact. He'd packed up his furniture and his cats, put his three horses in the stock trailer, and gone.

Not without asking me to marry him, though. Which had caused me a lot of grief.

Lonny's idea was that I would marry him and move with him to the foothills, giving up my job and my home, in order to make a new life with him. Although the offer was flattering, it didn't fit into any of my plans, and therein began to lie a problem.

For Lonny was determined to pursue his plan, with me or without me, as I came to see; no amount of lobbying on my part for a compromise had much effect on him. Going back to the mountains was his goal, and back he was going.

I'd adjusted, in a sense. I'd acknowledged that it was my choice not to go with him. I'd agreed that we would continue to have a relationship. But as anyone who's ever been in one knows, a long-distance relationship is not the same as having a boyfriend a few miles down the road.

Lonny and I had never lived together, but we'd lived near each other, and we'd always spent most of our nights together. Suddenly I was sleeping alone. And Lonny lived three hours away.

I didn't like it. And I didn't know what to do about it. I loved Lonny, but I did not love the direction our relationship had taken.

"So," I said to him, "how's it going?"

He stared at his boots. "All right, I guess. Until this."

"How are things on the ranch?"

"Okay. The barn's getting built. Feels like I don't have a lot of time for anything else."

I studied him, mingled exasperation and affection welling up inside of me. I'd been with this big, untidy, rough-featured man for long enough to understand him pretty well.

He still stared at his feet; I was quite aware that he felt the estrangement between us and was as uncomfortable with it as I was, but there was no way in hell he was going to bring it up. Ignore it out of existence—that was Lonny's way. Pretend everything was all right.

What do you want out of him, I asked myself, looking at the lines framing his eyes, the strong, thick, callused hands that had touched me so often. An answer jumped into my mind: that he make some space for me in this relationship.

Lonny loved me, of that I was sure. But he loved me in much the same way he loved his horses. He'd do what he could to take care of me; he thought I was great. But I was supposed to be part of his life.

What I wanted, what I needed, was to have my feelings, my ideas, my agenda acknowledged. Especially when it was different from his. I needed to have him take my goals as seriously as he took his own.

I sighed. This dialogue was rattling around only in my head; Lonny and I still sat in silence, sipping our cooling coffee. And that was just the trouble. I'd spoken these thoughts aloud before, too many times, always with the same results.

Lonny gave lip service to the notion that my feelings and needs were important, but when it counted he followed his own road, as he always had. And I had to admit, I did the same. As I told him once, neither of us was really a team player.

Trying to distract myself from the direction my thoughts were leading me, I stared around the lobby. The Crazy Horse Creek Lodge had been built in the late 1800s and still looked the part of the stage stop it had once been. No one had ever remodeled, or ''cuted up,'' the rugged post-and-beam construction or the utilitarian pine plank floors and siding. From earlier owners through Lonny and on to Ted, the proprietors had all been satisfied to repair what broke and leave what still functioned alone.

I smiled as I looked at the room. The armchairs and couches were threadbare and battered, the photos and prints tacked on the rough walls were torn and dusty, the floor was scuffed and none too clean. Crazy Horse Creek was no multi-star resort. But the fire chugged away in the woodstove, making the lobby warm on chilly mountain nights, feet were welcome on the furniture (as were dogs), and nobody had to take their boots off to come inside.

''So, is it good to be back up here again?'' I asked Lonny.

''I guess. If this hadn't happened with Bill. I have a hard time getting it out of my mind.''

''You said your father shot himself.'' I scooted closer to him on the couch. "I never knew that. It must have been hard on you."

"I was in my early thirties. My mom had died a few years earlier and my dad came to live with me. We lived here in the summers." He gestured in a general way at the lodge; I knew what he meant.

Lonny had owned a small ranch near Sonora where he kept the pack station horses and mules in the winter. But from May till October he and his family and his crew had lived here. The Crazy Horse Creek Pack Station opened every year on Memorial Day weekend and closed when the snow drove them out of the mountains.

"He seemed okay," Lonny went on. "I knew he drank too much; I knew he missed my mom. But he didn't complain. He wasn't really well a lot of the time, but he tended bar when he felt up to it. I thought he liked being here.

"And then one Monday morning he didn't show up at breakfast. It got later and later, and finally I went to check on him. He was living in the log cabin; you know where I mean?"

"I know." The log cabin, one of the many cabins scattered around the pack station grounds, was the oldest structure. The story ran that it had been built by one Justin Roberts, who lived in it while he built the lodge. The log cabin was just that—a genuine log cabin, with all the logs neatly notched and fitted, big squared beams for a floor, and no milled wood anywhere.

"So, anyway," Lonny said, "I went out there and banged on the door, and when he didn't answer I went in. And there he was, in his chair, with a hole in his head. He left me a note. 'Doctor says I have cancer.' That was it."

I leaned my shoulder into his. "That must have been really hard for you."

"It was. I kept wondering what I'd done wrong. How I'd failed him."

"Maybe he just didn't want to go through it all."

Lonny was about to answer when we both heard feet clomping on the creaky stairs. The deputies were returning.

They stopped at the bottom of the stairs and looked at us. The male deputy was about the same height as his partner, a thick, square fireplug of a man. He looked strong as hell, with a heavy neck and a quietly pugnacious face. I revised my opinion that she was the dominant one of the pair.

"Did you find anything?" Lonny asked them.

"Not really." She spoke; he watched us. "Some paperwork that suggests he was doing some work for," she looked down at her notepad, "Dan Jacobi."

"That's right," Lonny said affirmatively. "Bill did a lot of work for Dan Jacobi."

"Do you know him?" she asked.

"Sure. He's a horse trader. A big one. He's got a ranch in Oakdale. I'd guess he buys and sells more horses than anyone in California. Bill was his vet. Dan comes up here a fair amount," Lonny added. "Ted buys quite a few horses from him."

The deputy nodded. I nodded. Her partner watched.

I'd heard of Dan Jacobi. He was well known as a supplier of horses, particularly western-style horses. Lonny's two older team roping horses, Burt and Pistol, had come from him.

We all waited. I watched the male deputy study Lonny and me in turn. He didn't seem inclined to speak.

The woman said, "Well, we're headed back down the hill. We'll be in touch if there's a problem."

She nodded at us both; the two of them tramped across the floor and dragged the heavy wooden door open and shut behind them.

I looked over at Lonny. He was staring down again; it struck me that he was genuinely distressed. This silent contemplation of his feet was his way of saying that he hurt.

Snuggling my body closer to his, I asked him gently, "Does

Bill Evans's shooting himself remind you of your dad?''

"Yeah, it does. I didn't know my dad was thinking of killing himself. I didn't know he had cancer. I thought he was doing all right. But I never asked him. And it turned out he wasn't.

"Same with Bill. I've known him for years. He was a friend, in the way people you've known for a dog's age become friends.

"I would have helped him if I'd known he needed help. But just like my dad, I didn't know. I watched him get drunk last night, watched Ted throw him out of the bar, and I never said a word. I thought he was a silly ass.''

I sighed. Wondered what to say.

"It bothers me,'' Lonny went on, "how completely ignorant I was of what those people were feeling.''

Here it was, the perfect opening. I could say, once again, that maybe Lonny needed to try and be more aware of other people, more responsive to their needs. That if he weren't so wrapped up in getting done what he wanted to get done, he might notice how someone else felt. Like me, I added to myself.

But I didn't say it. Instead I said, "No one can do everything right.'' Trite and not very helpful, I guess. I put my hand in his. "What do you say we go to bed?''

Lonny stood up. "Let's go,'' he said.

FIVE

I awoke the next morning to the familiar sound of Lonny snoring. Lying on my side, head propped on my hand, I watched him sleep. He'd made love to me last night with enthusiasm, and I'd responded with pleasure; we'd fallen asleep relaxed and sated. Still, this morning, studying his face, vulnerable with unknowing, I felt not only tender and protective but also stymied.

Lonny snored on, oblivious. What is it about snoring that causes a person to look so pathetically ridiculous? Suddenly I wanted to get up, get out, be on my own.

I dressed quickly—jeans, a tank top, another denim shirt—and pulled my boots on, all without waking Lonny. Then I was out the door, stepping quietly on the creaky floor as I headed down the hall.

The second floor of the lodge was arranged along the lines of old-fashioned hotels—long, narrow halls with small rooms on either side, and a couple of communal bathrooms near the stairway. Stopping at one of these, I performed brief morning ablutions and then creaked on down the stairs and out the back door of the lobby.

The mountain air met me, cold and fresh, tingling in my nose like the icy water of a high lake. Everything sparkled. I shut my eyes for a moment, dazzled by the brilliance of the sunlight. The whole world—pine trees, meadow, granite ridges—was sharp and clear and pure. So different from the soft atmosphere of the coastal hills I called home.

I walked out into the morning, half-startled, as I always was, by the intensity of these mountains. Yips greeted me as I approached my pickup. Roey leaped out when I opened the tailgate, bounding around me with shrill, excited squeaks.

"Don't bark," I admonished her firmly.

Grabbing her tail in her mouth, she spun in frantic circles, her usual response to this command. I had the notion she felt she needed something in her mouth to stop herself from talking.

Exuberance overcame caution and she leapt around me, barking happily.

"Knock it off," I warned, about as amused as I was deafened.

In this noisy fashion we approached the corrals. Plumber and Gunner neighed at me, their "Hey, where's breakfast?" neigh. I broke a couple of flakes of alfalfa hay off the bale I had brought and threw them into the corral. Both horses turned to eagerly.

I was watching them eat, making sure they both looked healthy and unscathed, when more excited yips from Roey got my attention. I looked in her direction; she was sniffing noses with a dog.

I laughed out loud. This had to be the funniest-looking dog I'd ever seen. About Roey's size, it had short white fur extravagantly speckled and blotched with red-brown spots, a long whiskery muzzle, perky ears, and blue eyes, with a big blotch over one of them. It wagged its tail furiously as it nuzzled

Roey, who was wagging hers equally furiously back.

In a second the two dogs were leaping and running happily together in a game of chase. The stranger dog looked to me to be female and still a pup.

I was watching them play with a grin on my face when a voice said, "Hello, Stormy."

I turned around. A man on a dun horse, leading a pack horse. Tall man, with red hair and a gray fedora-style hat. Blue Winter.

"Stormy?" I said.

He smiled at me. "I spent a few years in Australia. Every woman named Gail gets nicknamed Stormy in those parts. I thought you might have heard it."

I shook my head, smiling.

"That's where they started calling me Blue. All redheads get that. Blue or Bluey." He smiled again. "Nobody thought about how it would sound with my last name."

I smiled back at him, thinking that he seemed much friendlier out here on horseback than he had in the bar last night.

"I had a dog named Blue once," I said.

He laughed. "Don't tell me, he was a blue heeler."

"That's right."

"Is she yours?" He gestured toward Roey, who was racing madly after her new playmate.

"Yeah," I agreed.

"The other's mine."

"You're kidding," I said.

He laughed again. "Why would you say that?"

I smiled at him. "I don't know. You don't seem the type to have such a, let's see, different-looking dog."

"You mean funny-looking. She's half Australian shepherd, half Jack Russell terrier. She's just a pup." He snapped his fingers. "Come here, Freckles."

The spotted dog raised her ears in his direction and veered

away from Roey. Still going full blast, she dashed up to the big dun horse and stopped by his left foreleg, waving her tail at her owner.

The dun horse didn't flinch. Blue Winter said, "Good dog."

I studied his horses. The saddle horse was a gelding and had to be sixteen hands tall. Big-boned and heavy-muscled, he looked like a Quarter Horse type. He was a medium dun, a soft dusty gold all over, with a white blaze and a faint dorsal stripe down his back. An easy horse to pick out of a crowd.

The pack horse was less conspicuous. A small sorrel mare with a little white on her face and a couple of socks, she had no obvious distinguishing characteristics.

"Are you on your way in?" I asked him.

"Yeah, we're headed to Snow Lake tonight."

I looked at him curiously; Snow Lake was my chosen destination for my first day's ride in. "Staying there long?"

He shrugged. Once again his face seemed withdrawn. Whatever. I waved a dismissive hand.

"Well, have a good trip."

"I hope to. You, too."

"Thanks."

He clucked to his horses, said, "Come on" to the dog, and the small entourage moved off, the pack horse dragging a little on the lead rope. I smiled. Plumber had a tendency to do that, too.

I watched them head down the main trail, small puffs of dust rising around the horses' feet, the dog running in a big curving circle through the meadow. Ahead of them Relief Peak glowed in the early sunlight. Snow Lake was quite a ways on the other side of that mountain, over Brown Bear Pass. A twenty-plus-mile ride.

Blue Winter and his horses were a small vignette now. A cowboy riding down the trail. I couldn't see the dog.

Turning, I headed toward the pack station barn. The crew

was busily saddling horses and loading packs; it looked as though they had several parties getting ready to go out. Ted stood by the loading dock, talking to a strongly built man with a white straw cowboy hat.

Both men turned to look at me as I approached; the stranger had a square bulldog jaw and high cheekbones and seemed vaguely familiar. He said something affirmative to Ted and turned away, nodding civilly in my direction. Now where do I know him from, I wondered.

His back gave no clue; a long-sleeved blue shirt, pressed Wrangler jeans, and dusty boots were so typical as to be almost a uniform. But I'd seen him before, somewhere.

"Morning, Gail," Ted said.

"Hi, Ted. Did you call the hospital?"

"Not yet." His blue eyes looked candidly into mine. "I'll do it when I go in for breakfast." The eyes traveled over me a little, then moved back to my face. "I saw you down there talking to old Blue Winter."

I smiled. "I'm sure you did."

Crazy Horse Creek Pack Station was familiarly known as Peyton Pines by everyone who visited it often. New romances, one-night stands, illicit affairs . . . the place was known for these, and the whole crew, Ted in particular, loved to gossip.

"So, do you know Blue?" Ted prodded. "He comes from your part of the country."

"That's what he said. No, I never met him until yesterday in the bar. Do you guys know him?"

"Sure. He comes up here every year. Brings his horses, stays a few days, and rides in on a trip. Lonny knows him." Ted laid a little extra emphasis on Lonny's name.

"Is that right?" For some reason this conversation was annoying me. "Who was that guy you were talking to?" I asked. "I'm sure I know him from somewhere."

"Dan Jacobi."

"The horse trader."

"That's him."

"He was here last night?" I asked curiously.

"Nah. He drove up this morning from Oakdale. He comes up here a lot. Takes a pack trip every summer. He was pretty shook up when he heard about old Bill."

"I'll bet."

Ted and I stared at each other a moment. The same thought must have been chasing through both our minds, because he dropped his eyes and said, "I'd better go call. Find out how he is."

"Yeah," I said. "Let me know."

"Okay."

Ted headed for the lodge; I called Roey and wandered around the meadow for a while, letting the dog run. Eventually I felt a cup of coffee calling me.

Going into the lobby, I walked past the small cafe, where paying customers could get meals, and through the kitchen door. Here, amongst an odd, old-fashioned collection of stoves, refrigerators, cupboards, counters, sinks, and shelves, Harvey the cook had his domain.

A big, stout barrel of a man, as befit a cook, Harvey was autocratic in tone and mercurial in temperament, in the time-honored tradition of camp cooks. He grunted at me as I poured myself a cup of coffee. Apparently Harvey was not in a talking mood this morning.

Carrying my coffee, I walked through the open doorway that led to the cowboy room, a large dining room with one big table in the middle where the crew and friends ate. Lonny was seated alone near the end of the table, working his way through a plate of pancakes, sausage, and fried eggs. I sat down next to him and sipped my coffee.

Besides a brief and muffled "Morning," Lonny's attention remained on breakfast. He ate neatly and steadily, in a workmanlike fashion, until all food items had been dispatched. Then, cradling a coffee cup in his hands, he leaned back in his chair, with the air of one who had just completed a pleasant chore, and smiled at me.

I took a sip of weak but very hot coffee and smiled briefly. "Have you heard anything about that guy . . . Bill?" I asked.

Lonny's smile faded, but his green eyes looked clear and untroubled as they rested on mine. Apparently last night's distress had gone.

"I heard Ted went to call the hospital," he said. "I don't know any more."

We looked at each other; after a moment his eyes crinkled slightly at the corners. "So, are we going for a ride?"

"I guess so."

True to form, Lonny was now focused on the day's possibilities. He didn't carry pain around much; a night's sleep usually restored him to his typical optimistic good humor. A nice trait, I had always thought; it was only lately that I'd begun questioning its implications.

"What do you say we ride to the cow camp at Wheat's Meadow and have a look at Ted's cattle. It's only a few miles; it ought to be a good warm-up for your horses."

"All right." I'd made the short ride to Wheat's Meadow before, using Ted's horses. The trail was good and there wasn't too much rock. About what Gunner and Plumber needed.

"And you get to ride over the bridge."

"Yeah."

A mile out of the pack station, the main trail crossed Crazy Horse Creek in the middle of a steep canyon, via a stout wooden bridge. In Lonny's packing days, the trail had taken a lengthy detour to reach a spot where the creek could be forded. Ted had built and placed the bridge (via helicopter) in the early days of his tenure. The cowboys reckoned it saved them half an hour in each direction.

This was great, and of course, all Ted's horses were quite used to crossing the bridge. Mine, however, weren't. I'd taken them on numerous trail rides in the coastal hills around Santa Cruz in preparation for this trip, and a couple of these rides had included small bridges. Gunner and Plumber hadn't been crazy about them, but they'd agreed to walk across them, despite being nervous about the hollow echo their hooves made on the wooden planks. None of these bridges, though, bore much resemblance to the Crazy Horse Creek bridge, which spanned a hundred feet, with a drop of a couple of hundred to the crashing water.

"Better to go across it following me the first time," Lonny said.

"Yeah," I agreed. I had thought of this.

"So, what do you think? We'll saddle up in an hour or so, after you've had breakfast and the horses have finished theirs."

"All right." I was about to ask Lonny which horse he planned to take when Ted walked into the room.

Instantly our eyes swiveled to him.

Ted stood by the end of the table, his round face quiet. "Bill didn't make it," he said.

SIX

Damn." Lonny stood up. "Did he make it to the hospital?"

"They said he died there." Ted's voice was uninflected.

We were all quiet. I thought about the man lying under the night sky wanting to die. I hadn't saved him.

Lonny and Ted were still staring at each other. Aside from Lonny's angry "damn," neither man showed much recognizable emotion. And yet I was quite aware that both were very upset.

Bill Evans had been part of their world; he was one of the family. Such were not supposed to give up, give in, put a bullet into their heart. They were supposed to carry on.

I tried to think of something comforting to say. Nothing seemed possible. We all stood in silence.

Lonny turned abruptly toward me. "There isn't a thing we can do now," he said. "I'll go saddle the horses."

Without waiting for any response I might have made, he banged out the screen door at the back of the room; I watched his long, hasty stride as he headed toward the barn.

Ted looked at me questioningly. "We're going to ride up to Wheat's Meadow," I said. "Give my horses a chance to get used to the rock, and the bridge," I added.

Ted nodded, still not saying anything. For a moment he reminded me of a small boy, mute and sad.

"Do you want to come with us?" I asked.

He hesitated. His eyes were blank, all their playful sparks in abeyance. "I could have a look at those cattle," he said at last.

"Yeah, you could," I agreed. "Let me just go up and use the bathroom and I'll be right with you guys."

When I got to the barn ten minutes later, three horses were saddled and tied to the hitching rail, Gunner among them. Plumber stood next to him with the pack rig on his back, but no pack bags. I walked over and checked the cinches.

It was like Lonny to have saddled my horse as well as his. I couldn't decide whether I was mildly pissed off that he didn't let me deal with my own livestock, or mildly grateful that he had done one of my chores for me.

Tightening the cinch on Gunner, I looked at the other two saddle horses. The bay was Chester, Lonny's young horse. The buckskin I recognized as Hank, the horse Ted usually rode.

Ted and Lonny emerged from the barn, carrying bridles; I noticed Lonny had hung Gunner's bridle on the saddle horn. I got it off and offered my horse the bit. Opening his mouth obligingly, Gunner accepted the metal bar; I pulled the bridle on over the halter and fastened the lead rope around the saddle horn with a couple of half hitches. This would make the horse easy to tie up if need be.

Ted was tying saddlebags on Hank. "I brought us some lunch," he said.

Lonny carefully fastened a long case made of PVC pipe to Plumber's pack rig.

"You plan on doing some fishing?" I asked.

"Might as well," he said. He patted Plumber's neck. "Just about the right kind of a load, huh kid?" Plumber sniffed Lonny's elbow and then tucked his nose into the crook of his arm. Lonny rubbed the horse's forehead and smiled at me. "What a puppy dog he is."

"I know," I said. "I like him that way."

No need to justify my preference for friendly horses to Lonny; he felt the same as I did. Ted, however, was a different matter. Like many cowboys, he treated his horses standoffishly; a slap on the rump was about all they got in the way of affection.

Ted swung up on Hank. I called Roey. I had left her to wait on the pack station porch, something she was reasonably good about. In a minute she appeared from that direction, bounding through the grass. She ran up to the group of us and barked happily. She knew what the horses meant.

"Be quiet," I said, as I swung up on Gunner.

Lonny handed me Plumber's lead rope and climbed on Chester. The little bay started to move off as Lonny got on; Chester was a restless, lively horse who always wanted to do something. Lonny hung in one stirrup for a moment before he was able to get his right leg up and over the horse's back.

"You better teach him to stand still," I said. "You're getting a little stiff for that kind of a running mount."

Lonny grinned at me from Chester's back. "I know it. But it's so hard for him. He just wants to go so bad."

Ted grunted. "This so-and-so knows better than to walk off when I get on him."

Lonny and I said nothing. We were both familiar with Ted's ways.

Ted clucked to Hank and turned him up the trail; Lonny and I followed. I took a half turn around the saddle horn with

Plumber's lead rope, encouraging the little horse to come along. In a moment we were moving down the trail in a caravan, Roey frisking around us.

Deadman Meadow was a vivid, even green in the morning sunlight. The main trail ran along one edge of it, and Crazy Horse Creek ran along the other, with the exception of a narrow channel of water that the original owner of the pack station had created. This branched off the creek shortly after it emerged into the meadow and ran along the pack station side of the little valley. Eventually it fed into the horse corrals, through a couple of big stone troughs and a beautifully constructed granite-lined channel that provided an endless supply of fresh water for the horses.

I looked back at the pack station, seeing a picture right out of an old Western movie. The two-story shingled lodge building, with its long front porch and gray stone chimney, was outlined against a towering granite cliff. Scattered clumps of pines surrounded it, and the meadow spread out like a carpet in front of it. Add in the old barn and wooden corrals with their granite troughs, and picturesque was a mild description.

Turning, I gazed up the valley to where Relief Peak raised a snowy head in the sun, feeling a sense of amazement that I was actually here, riding down this trail on Gunner. I still couldn't quite take it in.

Lonny and Ted rode ahead of me, Roey scampered alongside, and Plumber plodded behind. I watched Gunner's black-tipped red ears, seeing them flick forward curiously, cock back toward me, and flick forward again. The old cowboys used to say that you could tell a good horse by the way he "works his ears."

Ted had fallen back beside me, and I glanced over at Hank. His ears moved forward and back, like Gunner's. I smiled at Ted. "How come you always ride him?" I asked.

"Oh, I like him," Ted said, a little sheepishly.

I studied the horse. He had some obvious faults; he carried his head too high on a neck that was too straight, and he had one front leg that was noticeably turned out. On top of which, he was jigging a little as we moved along the trail, and I'd noticed before that this habitual prancing was a trait of his—a trait most cowboys are not fond of. But he did, indeed, seem likable, with his bright gold buckskin color, kind eye, and good attitude.

"He's not too smart," Ted said, "but he's willing." He laughed. "He's a good son of a bitch. I tell the kids I keep him for my own riding horse 'cause he's got a smooth trot. But I just like him."

I smiled back at him, knowing what he meant. Liking a particular horse was a lot the same as liking a particular human. Often the feeling was inexplicable, as much because of as despite what others might regard as faults.

We were almost at the end of the meadow now. I glanced at the spot where Bill Evans's sports car had been, and noticed that Lonny turned his head away, keeping his eyes on Relief Peak. None of us said a word.

We started up the steep piece of trail that led out of the meadow. The horses were on granite now, but the trail had been blasted out by crews with dynamite and carefully built, and the footing was good. Gunner seemed confident, following Hank and Chester. I kept a careful eye on Plumber, but the sheer drop off one side to the boulder-strewn creek below didn't seem to intimidate him any more than it did the others. Like Gunner, he cocked an alert ear at the noisy water occasionally, but both horses picked their way over the rockier sections of the trail like good mountain ponies and seemed happy enough to be there. Gunner stopped dead when he saw the bridge, though.

I couldn't really blame him. It was a narrow one-horse-wide wooden ramp, and the railings only reached about to stirrup height. It looked insubstantial as hell, stretching from one rim of the canyon to the other, with the long drop beneath it to the cascading roar of the creek. At first sight most people tended to stop, as Gunner was doing now, and stare at it apprehensively.

Lonny smiled back over his shoulder at me. "He'll follow the other horses," he said reassuringly.

I nodded. Hank was on the bridge now, and Chester followed him. I clucked to Gunner and urged him forward. He obeyed, but I could feel his trepidation. Plumber was leaning back a little on the lead rope, but he was coming, too. No horse likes to be left behind.

The bridge was spooky enough, even for me. The horse's hooves banged hollowly on the wooden floor, the water far below crashed and echoed on the canyon walls, and the sense of being exposed and vulnerable, high above the railing, was extreme. If a horse did jump, and either he or you went off, you'd be dead for sure.

We made it across with no problems and began the mile of steep switchbacks on the other side to reach the top of Camelback Ridge.

"Are there many bridges like that in this part of the Sierras?" I asked Lonny, as we climbed.

"A few. You're liable to meet a couple of them, the way you're planning to go." Lonny knew my proposed itinerary; he'd helped me plan this trip last winter. I wanted to get to several of the high mountain lakes that I'd heard about for years but never seen. And I wanted the easiest possible route. After all his years of packing, Lonny was a veritable mine of information.

"Sure you don't want some company?" Lonny grinned at me; he knew what my answer would be. It had been somewhat of a sore spot initially, but as time had passed Lonny had accepted and understood my need to go on this trip alone. Goal-oriented himself, he had a lot of sympathy for my desire to achieve a dream I'd held for so many years.

I smiled back at him as the horses worked their way up the ridge. All the time, half my mind was on Gunner; I kept a light feel of him through the reins, guiding him to the easier side of the trail, checking him when he started to hurry. Lonny, in contrast, left Chester's reins completely slack, allowing the horse to pick his own course and speed. Chester had been up in these mountains several times in the last few months; he understood about rock.

But Gunner didn't. Nor did Plumber. All the intricacies that to a mountain horse like Hank were automatic reactions, were uncharted territory for my ponies. Avoiding V-shaped clefts, stepping slowly and cautiously through scree, being wary of loose rock, and above all, staying off the slickrock, were things they were learning as we proceeded up the ridge.

I tried to help, guiding Gunner toward better footfalls, making sure Plumber had plenty of slack in the lead rope and wasn't hurried when we crossed rough ground. And the horses did well, seeming, in my estimation, to gain a sense of how to move on rock as we went along.

We stopped twice to let the horses breathe before we reached the top of the ridge. The pass, such as it was, was inconspicuous, but the views as we started down the other side were wonderful. All around us the granite glowed with light. Pine trees lined the distant ridges, blue-green in the sunshine, stiff and erect like soldiers. The sky was an endless, clear Sierra blue. I smelled the sharp scent of pine resin and dust and felt completely happy.

Gunner picked his way down the ridge like a pro, following Chester. Plumber seemed to be doing fine. Roey was following the pack horse now, tongue hanging out, a grin on her face.

The wind made a rushing noise in the pine trees, like big

trucks on some distant highway. I thought of my friends in Santa Cruz County, perhaps driving to work right now on just such a highway. And here I was, I thought in amazement, here I was.

The trail forked when we reached the creek in the bottom of the canyon. The main trail continued on toward Relief Peak and Brown Bear Pass. Wheat's Meadow trail crossed the creek and headed over a different ridge.

We let the horses drink; Roey splashed about happily. Neither Gunner nor Plumber turned a hair when we waded across the creek. Fording creeks was a routine part of our trail rides back in the coastal hills. This was a good ford, shallow and not too rocky. No problem.

One more ridge, and then through a shadowy pine forest. A sudden dazzle of light and openness ahead, and we emerged from the trees into Wheat's Meadow, as from dark to daylight—the wide, sunny grassland was so vastly and dramatically different from the dim, shady silence under the pines.

Wheat's was a green jewel of a meadow in a setting of silver granite. There was an old cow camp at the north end—a log cabin and a barn—which was deserted. The uneven chiming of bells marked the presence of Ted's cattle in the trees behind the barn.

We reined our horses to a stop, standing in the bright, breezy openness of the meadow. Lonny smiled at me and I smiled back. "It's great, isn't it?" I said.

"It sure is."

Ted said nothing, just gazed out over the grassland. After a minute, he reined Hank toward the barn. "Let's go have a look at those cattle."

The cattle were in a little grove of willows on the other side of Wheat's Meadow Creek. We rode around and through them, while Ted counted heads and checked to make sure all were healthy. They looked good, their red and black backs sleek and shiny, and we could all see that there was plenty of feed left in the meadow. A Brahma cross heifer stepped toward Plumber and sniffed noses with him curiously. Plumber snorted and pinned his ears. I laughed.

"I love the bells," I told Lonny.

He nodded, a brief downward motion of his chin, his eyes on the cattle. The cowbells were hung around the necks of the older cows with leather straps like collars. They clanked and chimed with every step, helping the cowboys to locate strays that were holed up in the brush. Up close as we were, the noise could be cacophonous when the whole herd was moving, but from a distance it made a strange music, half-harmonious, half-discordant, almost eerie. Fairy music.

"Ready for lunch?" Ted asked.

"Sure," Lonny answered for both of us.

We tied the horses to some pine trees by the old barn and sat down by the banks of the creek to eat. Ted had packed us each a sandwich as well as a beer apiece, wrapped in a plastic garbage bag full of ice. The beers were icy cold and perfect. We ate and drank contentedly and watched the creek. When we were done, Lonny broke down his case and put two fishing poles together.

Ted declined fishing in favor of napping, so Lonny and I creek-stomped together for an hour. Wheat's Meadow Creek was full of trout, and they were quick and eager. I got at least one hit at every hole. Ten inches was a big fish, but they fought hard and were fun to catch. We hooked a dozen or so apiece, on lures, turned them all loose, and went back to the horses and Ted.

The ride out was pleasant and uneventful; I slouched a little on Gunner's back as we worked our way down Camelback Ridge, feeling confident in him. Plumber, too, looked sure and poised as he picked his way over the rock. It was all going to be fine, I told myself.

This trip, the trip of my dreams, was coming off just as I'd planned. Everything would be great.

In retrospect, I can't remember when I've ever been so spectacularly wrong.

SEVEN

Once we were back at the lodge and the horses were unsaddled, turned out, and fed, Lonny was keen to go to the bar and have a drink. I acquiesced, not altogether enthusiastically. I enjoy a cocktail in the evening as much as anyone, and mostly, I find bars pleasant. But the Crazy Horse Creek Bar on Saturday night was often a madhouse, and I wasn't sure I was up for it.

Stopping to put the dog in the camper and give her food and water, I arrived at the bar a few minutes after Lonny to find my fears confirmed. The place was a zoo—the tourists three-deep at the bar itself, the few tables full. Several couples were dancing—well, frugging in place—to Johnny Cash on the jukebox. I scanned the crowd for Lonny.

He was in the corner, talking with Ted and Luke. I made my way toward them, pushing gently through the throng. Chatter and laughter roiled around me; I heard the cowbell over the bar ring, a signal that somebody had bought the place a round. A rich somebody, I reflected.

Which wasn't surprising. Most of the folks who were up here

to be packed into the mountains by the pack station crew had plenty of dollars. Horses, mules, and packers did not come cheap; those who weren't long on money carried their gear in a backpack. Shoe buckaroos, as the cowboys called them.

There were probably a few shoe buckaroos in the bar tonight, and some who were just car camping in the Forest Service campsite at the other end of Deadman Meadow. But the majority would be what Ted called "customers," heavily emphasizing the first syllable. Most would be staying in the cabins that clustered around the lodge, eating in the cafe and drinking in the bar, en route to being packed into a mountain lake. These were the people who made Ted a lot of money, and he was always very happy to see them.

On the other hand, he didn't much like to talk to them, and usually avoided the bar. Lonny's presence had created the exception, I surmised.

I started to work my way as unobtrusively as I could between two men in cowboy hats in order to get to where Lonny was standing.

"Excuse me," I said, as one of the men turned around.

He was in his late twenties, blond and handsome, and arrogant with it. He was also, I realized a quick second later, very drunk.

He looked me up and down. I was pinned by the crowd behind me, and he was firmly blocking the route to Lonny.

"Excuse me," I said again.

"Well, you're a pretty thing." He drawled it out.

I sighed. "Thanks. I need to get through here, if you don't mind."

"I don't mind at all. Just you squeeze your pretty backside right in."

He shifted slightly to one side, leaving a six-inch gap between himself and his neighbor.

I shrugged and insinuated myself shoulder first; at the same time I felt him grab my ass—hard. It pissed me off.

I'm used to drunks and I'm used to cowboys; I'm used to drunk cowboys, for that matter. But I didn't like this guy. I kicked him in the kneecap with the pointed toe of my boot.

"Fuck off, asshole," I said clearly.

I wasn't prepared for his reaction. He yelped and grabbed me by the breasts. "You like this better?" His eyes were mean.

"You son of a bitch." I said it loudly enough for the people around us to hear.

The cowboy-hatted man next to us turned, took a look, and said, "Knock it off, Steve."

His voice was deep and hard and familiar. Dan Jacobi, I realized.

Steve let go of me.

Dan Jacobi gave me another glance, in which recognition dawned. "Apologize to her," he said to his companion.

Steve looked sulky. "The hell I will. I work for you; you don't own me."

"Apologize to her." Dan Jacobi enunciated each word clearly.

Steve shrugged and turned back to the bar. "The hell with it."

Dan Jacobi put a hand on his shoulder. Steve looked at him. Effortlessly as an ax splitting firewood Dan drove his fist into Steve's gut.

The blond gasped and grabbed his stomach and sat abruptly on the floor of the bar.

"I'll apologize for him," Dan Jacobi said. "He's busy."

Wheezing and retching, the unfortunate Steve half crawled and half walked to the door, doubled over with both hands holding himself. I had the impression he would be puking for a while.

"Sorry about that," Dan Jacobi said. "He's had too much to drink. Can I buy you something?"

"It's not necessary," I said.

Lonny had witnessed our little scene, along with the rest of the barroom crowd, and stood by my side.

"What did he do?" he asked me.

"Grabbed me." I grinned. "I kicked him; he didn't like it."

"Good for you." Dan Jacobi smiled briefly. "How about I buy you both a drink?"

"Sure." Lonny answered for both of us. "Gail, this is Dan Jacobi. Dan, Gail McCarthy."

"Nice to meet you, ma'am," Dan said. "What'll you have to drink?"

"A Stoly vodka tonic with an extra squeeze of lime," I said.

"Jack Daniel's and soda for me." Lonny grinned at Dan. "Gail's my horse vet."

"Is that right?" Dan Jacobi looked at me with mild curiosity.

I studied him back. He would be about the same age as Lonny—fifty or close to it. His thick, big-chested body looked powerful, an impression that was bolstered in my mind by his quick dispatch of a much younger man. Everything about his face, from the square, bulldog jaw to the hard, dark eyes, confirmed this sense of inner force. Dan Jacobi was clearly a man to be reckoned with.

He handed Lonny and me our drinks; we thanked him. I took the first cold, sharp sip and sighed.

Dan Jacobi addressed both of us. "That was a terrible thing about Bill Evans."

Lonny looked somber. I could feel Ted stepping up on the other side of me, a drink in his hand. Dan continued talking about Bill, saying what a nice guy he was, that he'd been his vet for years, that he, Dan, had never imagined that Bill would do such a thing.

I listened with half an ear, most of my attention focused on Lonny and Ted. Lonny still looked blank and sad; Ted's face was expressionless, but I could feel the tension in his body.

Dan Jacobi was talking to me now. "I heard you found him."

"Yeah, I did."

"And that he was still alive and talking."

"Yeah."

Ted's voice was high and sharp. "So what did he say?"

"Nothing that made any sense, really. That he was trying to kill himself. That he wanted to die. He said something about horses with fire in their bellies. I guess he was talking about colicked horses, since he was a vet."

"Did he say anything about any people?" Ted again.

"No, not that I recall."

Dan and Ted were both watching me; Lonny was looking at the floor. I took another swallow of my drink and felt it tingle all the way down to my stomach.

Around us the barroom crowd talked and laughed, oblivious to our strange, tense conversation. I ignored the men next to me for a second, feeling the eager, excitable ambience of the place—everybody here on vacation, ready to have a good time. The cowbell clanged again; I could see Ernie and Luke, who were both behind the bar tonight, hustling to make another round of drinks.

Next to me, Ted shifted, took the whiskey and water that Ernie handed him, and looked at Dan. "I heard you were looking for Blue Winter."

Dan's eyes moved to Ted. "That boy owes me some money."

Ted grinned; all the tension in his body dissolved. "You're too late. He rode in this morning. Nobody knows when he'll come back out." He took a long swallow of his fresh drink.

"Why does he owe you money?" I asked Dan.

"That big dun gelding he's riding. He bought the horse from me and he never paid for him."

"Oh." I took that in. "He didn't seem like that kind of person."

Dan shrugged one shoulder.

"Maybe you'll see him while you're in," Ted said to Dan.

"Do you know where he was headed?" Dan's voice was quiet.

"Snow Lake, I heard," Ted said. "That's where you're going, too, right, Gail?"

My turn to shrug. I wasn't real keen on the whole world knowing exactly which lakes I was headed for.

"Gail's going on a pack trip," Ted went on, seeming unaware of my discomfort. "All by herself."

"Is that right?" Once again, Dan Jacobi looked at me curiously. "Ted's packing us in next week. To Huckleberry Lake."

I nodded. Sounded like it would be a busy time in the backcountry. Well, mid-July, what did I expect? With any luck at all, though, I would still find myself alone at some of the high country lakes and meadows.

Taking another sip of my vodka tonic, I wished suddenly to be out of this bar, out of this crowd. I looked at Lonny.

"You ready to go?" he asked.

"Yeah."

"I'll buy you dinner," Dan Jacobi offered.

"I'll buy you all dinner," Ted said. He finished his drink and grinned at the group of us, seeming restored to good humor. "Steak on the house."

No use protesting. I was clearly in for a social evening. I followed the men out of the bar and down to the lodge, listening to Lonny and Dan talk about team roping horses. Ted added nothing to this conversation.

Ted didn't rope, or rather, he didn't team rope. He roped enough to catch and doctor his cattle when they needed attention and no chutes were handy. But, like many ranch cowboys, he disdained the competitive rodeo sport of team roping, con-

58

sidering it impractical, for dilettante cowboys with no real chores to do.

Lonny, on the other hand, had never been a rancher. Unlike Ted, when Lonny'd owned the pack station he'd kept only the horses and mules. Lonny roped for fun and was a keen competitor, although he was also perfectly capable of roping cattle out in the open, in order to help Ted or some other ranching friend.

We settled ourselves in the cowboy room and were served dinner and beers by a silent Harvey, to the accompaniment of a nonstop conversation about horses. I contributed the occasional question or story, but mostly I just listened.

Dan Jacobi had a knowledge of horses that was wide and deep and eclectic. Though he was primarily known for cowhorses, particularly team roping horses and ranch horses, he appeared willing to deal in any kind of horse, as long as he could make a profit. He talked of buying Thoroughbred horses off the track and selling them to be jumpers; he mentioned buying horses from the livestock auction, destined for the killers, and sorting through them to find which might be suitable pack string and dude horses for Ted.

"And you've been buying those gaited horses, what do you call them?" Ted asked him.

"Pasos. Peruvian Pasos. People with bad backs like 'em. They've got real smooth gaits."

"Where did you say you got them from?" Ted asked.

"South America."

Ted grinned at me. "Old Dan's a real wheeler and dealer."

Well, sure, I thought. Dan was a horse trader. Where you could make a dollar on a horse, there he would go.

Seeming to catch my thought, Dan Jacobi smiled at me. "I was raised by the gypsies, back in Oklahoma," he said. "I grew up buying and selling horses. Sometimes I like it; sometimes I hate it. But it's what I know how to do." He was quiet

59

a moment. "I sure am gonna miss Bill," he said reflectively. "He was a friend. And he knew a hell of a lot about horses."

I nodded sympathetically.

He smiled at me again. "Sure you wouldn't like to move to Oakdale?"

Before I could reply to this sally, Lonny asked Dan a question. "Do you have any idea what was on Bill's mind to make him do a thing like that? Was he sick?"

"Not that I know of," Dan said.

"Maybe it was seeing Blue," Ted interjected.

"Seeing Blue?" I asked.

There were a couple of seconds of quiet. Lonny looked uncomfortable; Dan Jacobi looked impassive. Ted's eyes were sharp with prurient interest. I had the distinct sense all three men knew something I didn't.

"Seeing Blue?" I asked Lonny. "You mean that guy, Blue Winter? What does he have to do with it?"

Lonny looked at the remains of his dinner, then at me. "When Bill's wife left him, she lived with Blue awhile."

"That's right," Ted said. "She left him for Blue. And then she left Blue and went back to Bill. And then she left Bill again."

"I thought you said Bill's wife left him because of his drinking." I was addressing my remarks to Lonny; Ted's gossipy tone got on my nerves.

"She did," Lonny said. "Blue just happened to be in the right place at the right time. I don't think Katie was ever very serious about him. She left him within a year and went back to Bill."

"Blue was pretty broke up about it," Ted said.

"But then she left her husband again?" I asked Lonny.

"That's right. He was drinking a lot."

"What happened to her?"

"She left the country," Dan Jacobi said. "Nobody knows where she went."

"Oh."

"Maybe Blue shot Bill," Ted said. "Over Katie."

I looked at Ted. "You don't like this guy Blue much, do you? And Bill Evans told me he was trying to kill himself."

"Maybe Bill was covering up." Ted said.

"Why would he do that?" I was feeling fairly annoyed at Ted. "And what is it you have against Blue Winter?"

Ted shrugged. "He thinks his shit don't stink."

Belatedly it occurred to me that Ted had had several drinks in the bar and a couple of beers with dinner. He was now more than a little drunk, his straw cowboy hat tipped back on his head, his eyes slightly unfocused, his voice sloppy. There was no way I was going to get a straight answer out of him.

Besides, I thought I could answer my own question. No doubt Ted disliked Blue Winter partly because Ted didn't make any money on him. Blue packed his own horses into the mountains; he didn't use Ted's stock or his crew. And more than that, I imagined that Blue Winter probably didn't kowtow to Ted the way most of the customers did. Ted was a czar in his little fiefdom; he didn't have much use for those who weren't interested in paying homage.

So what's the big deal, I asked myself. You know Ted's that way. What do you care about Blue Winter? You're getting to be a grouch in your old age, Gail.

It was true, kind of. Once again I was getting tired of the situation I was in. I was bored with Ted's gossip and posturing; I wanted out of here. When I was younger I was more patient, more enthralled with the lengthy business of cowboys talking about horses—and other cowboys.

I stood up. "I think I'll go check my horses. Nice to have met you," I said to Dan Jacobi.

61

He stood up. "Likewise, ma'am."

Lonny stood up, too. "I'll go with you, Gail."

Ted remained seated and didn't meet my eyes.

Turning, I walked out the back door, Lonny following me. I wished he weren't. I wanted to go into the Sierra night alone, check my horses in peace and solitude.

Well, you will, I told myself silently. You will. You'll be alone soon enough.

EIGHT

Sunday passed uneventfully. I spent it going over my gear, checking my lists, packing the last of my food items. My horses rested, the dog rested, I rested.

Monday morning I was up early. Dressing in the cool, sharp air, I went over my mental lists one more time. Had I forgotten anything? If I had, I would be doing without it. There were no convenience stores, no human habitations of any type, where I was headed.

I selected my clothes with a little more care than usual, thinking not about looks but comfort. Comfort and safety. I picked a soft cotton tank top in dusty brown, a faded sage-green shirt, and some old jeans. I wanted clothes that wouldn't restrict me at all, and in the unlikely event I needed to conceal my presence, would help me blend into the landscape.

The issues to do with being a woman alone had not escaped me when I planned this trip. Of things that were genuinely a threat to me, there were few: rattlesnakes and bears, in the way of animals; lighting and trail accidents, in the line of natural phenomena; and of course, other humans.

The likeliest danger was probably a slip on the slickrock, but I had tried to prepare for other possibilities as well. Were I, for instance, to be camped alone at a lake with a party of drunken men nearby, I wanted to be able to hide if need be. And if that didn't work, to defend myself.

So I had chosen the colors of my clothes with care, and my .357 pistol was at the bottom of my saddlebag, under my rain gear. It wasn't, strictly speaking, legal; however, the law wasn't going to be much help to me where I was going.

I zipped a shelled pile jacket (dark green) over my shirt, and pulled my boots on. Creaking down the stairs, I could feel my heart thumping away, adrenaline rushing into my system. I was getting ready to ride into the mountains alone. For two whole weeks I would be completely on my own, cut off from civilization, dependent on my own resources. I was excited and scared, both at once.

I let Roey out of the camper for a brief run, gave her food and water, and locked her back up, hoping she'd eat as much as possible before we left.

When I got up to the horse corrals, I found that Gunner and Plumber had already been fed. Lonny leaned on the corral fence, talking to Ted.

The pack station was much quieter this morning, most of the parties having gone in on the weekend. Ted's crew was saddling a few horses; I didn't see any pack rigs in evidence.

Ted himself looked wide awake as usual; I heard him tell Lonny that he would be packing Dan Jacobi in himself.

I made a mental note to stay away from Huckleberry Lake, and smiled at the two men. "Morning," I said.

Lonny grinned. "So, are you ready?"

"As ready as I'll ever be."

He slapped my shoulder. "You'll do just fine."

"The horses look good," I said, running my eyes over my two happily munching equines.

"You bet. You go on in and have some coffee and breakfast and I'll saddle and pack 'em for you."

I started to protest and shut my mouth. I would be leaving soon enough. Why argue with Lonny now?

"Come on in and have a cup of coffee with me first," I said instead. "Let these guys finish eating."

"All right."

We trooped down to the cowboy room, Ted in our wake. So much for a few romantic moments together before I left. Instead I had breakfast with virtually the whole crew; the cowboy room bubbled with laughter and jokes.

Ted was telling Lonny about the horses Dan Jacobi had brought with him. I listened with half an ear.

"Best-looking gray gelding you ever saw in your life. Big and strong and pretty-headed. I told him he was crazy to take that ten-thousand-dollar horse up here in the rocks. Take one of my horses, instead, I told him. But he just says, 'That's what I own 'em for.' " Ted snorted. "I'd say he owns 'em to sell 'em, and there's no use crippling 'em up. But him and those two boys of his are riding those three fancy geldings to Huckleberry Lake."

Lonny shrugged. Ted had made the same point to me—I ought to ride his horses and leave my flatland ponies at home. Lonny didn't agree.

"I like riding my own horses. Maybe Dan does, too." Lonny grinned at Ted. "So you make a little less money."

Ted's turn to shrug.

I worked my way through a plate of French toast, more or less forcing myself to eat despite my chattering nerves. My mind flipped constantly from item to item—had I brought enough dog food, would I wish I had a heavier jacket, did I have enough painkiller in the vet kit?

Horse talk drifted past me; I barely heard it. Soon now, I would be on my own.

Lonny got up and poured me another cup of coffee. "I'll go get your horses ready."

"I'll go with you."

I stood up, carrying my coffee, and followed him out the door. Cold, clean early-morning air washed over me; the ridge line glowed in the pale gold sunlight. The Sierra Nevada, the range of light.

Lonny was catching Gunner and Plumber; I began ferrying my gear up from my truck. I'd packed the panniers yesterday, weighed them to be sure they were even, and organized my top load. Packing Plumber up this morning would be a relatively simple process.

I lugged my saddle up to the corrals, wondering yet again if I was making a mistake. The heavy roping saddle was familiar and comfortable, both to me and Gunner, but it weighed much more than necessary. Built to tow six-hundred-pound steers around, the saddle was certainly nothing a long-distance endurance rider would choose. But I reckoned the comfort factor was most important, and I wasn't planning on any really long rides. Twenty miles was the most I intended to cover in a day.

Lonny put the pack rig on Plumber while I saddled Gunner. Working as a team, we lifted the pack bags onto the forks, set the top load in place, and covered the whole deal with a plastic tarp. Lonny watched as I lashed the tarp in place, using the diamond hitch and the trucker's knots he'd taught me.

Plumber pinned his ears crossly when I cinched everything tight; like most horses, he disliked that part.

Almost ready now. I tied my saddlebags to the back of my saddle, let the dog out of the camper, locked the truck, and handed my keys to Lonny.

"I should be back two weeks from today," I told him. "You know my route."

"That's right." Lonny was bridling Gunner, and didn't look at me as he spoke. "If you don't show up, I'll come looking for you."

"Okay." Watching his back, the long muscles strong despite the roll over his belt, I felt a surge of affection. "Give me a hug," I said.

He turned, holding Gunner's reins with one hand, and hugged me roughly. "Have fun," he said. Then he handed the horse to me. "You'd better get going."

I smiled at him, knowing from long experience that he disliked protracted farewells. Well, so did I.

Setting my foot in the stirrup, I swung up on Gunner. Lonny put Plumber's lead rope into my hand and our fingers touched. He met my eyes, and his own eyes crinkled at the corners. "I envy you," he said.

I smiled. "See you soon." Taking a half turn around the saddle horn with Plumber's lead rope, I clucked to Gunner and called Roey, feeling slightly light-headed. Here we go, I thought, here we go.

The sun shone in my eyes as I rode out from under the pine trees; I was headed east. I turned to wave good-bye to Lonny, saw him standing in front of the old corrals, waving to me, and my heart twisted. Why so many choices, I wondered, not for the first time. To fulfill my dream, I had to leave Lonny behind. Just as he'd had to leave me behind in order to fulfill his. Why did life have to be like this?

I didn't know. I only knew I was riding down the trail on a bright summer morning in the High Sierra, headed for Snow Lake. This was the here and now, the present moment. It was time to toe that line.

Relief Peak glowed ahead of me; the ridges rose around me. I was where I'd wanted to be for so many years.

I reached down and smoothed a strand of Gunner's heavy black mane over to the right side of his neck. He walked down the trail, looking alert. Roey swished through the meadow grass beside us, a wide grin on her face. I grinned back at her.

So here we were. I began, slowly, to lapse into the trail rider's mind-set. Part of my attention stayed on the horses; I guided Gunner to the safer, easier parts of the trail, looked over my shoulder every few moments to take note of how Plumber was doing. I admired the scenery meanwhile, watched the dog scampering through the rocks, enjoyed the sun on my face. At the same time my mind drifted, going over the route ahead, touching on Lonny, wondering briefly what was happening back at the veterinary clinic.

In this way we progressed uneventfully up Camelback Ridge. I felt some trepidation as we approached the bridge, but did my best to hide it, knowing my own attitude would influence my horses. I talked out loud to the dog as we neared the spot, speaking in a light, conversational tone as though I were talking to a companion about the weather. Nothing settles a spooky horse better than the sound of his rider's voice sounding happy and unconcerned.

So I told Roey what a nice day it was, and sat easy and relaxed in my saddle, and though Gunner hesitated briefly and snorted, at a gentle thump on his ribs, he stepped forward onto the bridge. Snorting again and cocking a watchful ear at the odd-sounding thunks his hooves made on the wood, he tiptoed forward, as if he were walking on eggs.

But he went. Plumber followed. They'd been over this bridge before. They knew it could be done.

Once we were on the other side I heaved a deep sigh of relief. There was nothing too scary ahead, as far as I knew.

Upwards, ever upwards we went. Then, topping the ridge, we came down to the trail fork that led to Wheat's Meadow. I let the horses and the dog drink at the creek and then continued on, headed over the next ridge.

I was starting to relax now. The horses' necks were slightly damp with sweat; they appeared to be handling rocky areas easily and confidently. We climbed a small area of switchbacks that had been dynamited into a solid granite face, and despite the rock and the exposure, neither horse hesitated or slipped once.

Good. Very good. I let my eyes wander over the rock-and-pine-tree country spread out around me. In some ways, the Sierras, through dramatic and beautiful, were repetitive; how many ways can gray stone, blue sky, green pines be arranged? The tumbling streams and startling lakes and meadows were a motif constantly repeated. Although I never grew used to the flicker and dazzle of the aspen, or the human-sounding voices in the white water, or the stark moonscapes of the granite passes, they became familiar.

We were approaching a small meadow called Saucer Meadow. Relief Creek ran along the far side of it, and the whole thing was a blaze of brilliant wildflowers. Bright red-orange, sharp yellow, deep blue-violet, brilliant magenta pink. As the trail dropped into the little basin and flowers were all around me, I could identify some.

Lupine and paintbrush and asters in impossible profusion, wild columbines and leopard lilies, penstemons, larkspur, and monkey flower—to name only the ones I recognized. Arranging themselves in perfect harmonies and rivulets of color along the stream, colonizing a fallen log, grouped around a solitary gray granite boulder. I stopped Gunner and stared in amazement and delight.

There were no more flowers than butterflies. Small brown ones and blue ones the color of forget-me-nots, slightly larger ones like bright orange mosaics, large black-and-yellow striped swallowtails, and lots of monarchs. In the mid-morning sunshine, the meadow was a blaze of green, slashed with colors and flashes of colors.

Roey was delighted. Despite the five miles or so she'd covered already, she gamboled about, showing me the proper way to appreciate a meadow. Rolling in the long grass, wading in the creek, chasing and bounding after the butterflies—I laughed out loud to see her.

Gunner gave an impatient tug on the reins. Either let me eat some grass or let's get moving, he said. I thought about it. Saucer Meadow was lovely, but we still had roughly fifteen miles to go. I had planned to stop for lunch at the aptly named Lunch Meadow, another five miles ahead. Better keep moving.

I clucked to the horses and rode on. The breeze brushed my face gently, as I tried to take it all in. The sunny expanse of green and flowers, with the wind blowing through the willows and cottonwoods that fringed the stream banks. Such warm, open, friendly greenness, so free and full of light. It was an amazing contrast to the hard stone country all around it; it seemed almost magical.

I looked over my shoulder as we entered the pine forest once again, saying good-bye.

Another rocky ridge ahead. Pine trees and granite. The wind moved, that clean, lonely Sierra wind that blows in the pines. Around me the rocks seemed to tumble in a frozen cascade, a jumbled silver granite landscape ever restless in its heart. The meadows and lakes were tiny flecks of stillness in a great, rough tapestry of hurled rock.

I rode on. Slowly the feeling of being alone in these mountains was coming back to me. Each mile that took me farther from the pack station, from civilization, from my real life, brought me closer to that old feeling, that elusive sense of place.

I'd been here alone before; I knew these mountains. They weren't a place of close, warm, familiar beauty, they won't cuddle up to you as some gentle hills and pretty valleys will. I felt dwarfed, always, by the roughness of this place, by its indifference.

And I felt honored to be here. To be tolerated by these bizarrely lovely mountains—this place not made for man. Only in the meadows, and in those little pockets of meadows on the shores of the lakes, did I ever feel briefly at home, as though perhaps I could really live here.

I clucked to the horses, called to the dog. For now, I was a sojourner; for the present moment, my home was on my back. Or, more literally, on Plumber's back.

I was getting hungry. By my reckoning, it was almost noon. Reckoning was all I had to go on; I hadn't brought a timepiece. By choice, not error. I'd learned from my solitary backpacking expeditions that I could tell time well enough for my own purposes by the sun, and it was an extraordinarily freeing feeling to do without a watch.

We should hit Lunch Meadow between noon and one, I thought. I would eat there and let the horses rest for half an hour, then push on and hope to reach Snow Lake in time to make camp before dark. Today's ride was the longest one I had planned for the entire trip. But I felt that the horses were fresh, and I wanted to get as far into the backcountry as possible right away.

The farther I went, the fewer people there would be. More or less. As a matter of fact, the way to avoid people was to avoid the lakes and the big meadows with good fishing creeks. The trouble was that like most of the other folks in the backcountry, I really liked the lakes. And I needed to camp where there was plenty of feed for my horses. So I was liable to run into a few other travelers.

Amazingly enough, I hadn't seen anyone yet. This was probably because it was Monday. Weekends in the mountains were a lot more crowded than weekdays.

The trail was following the banks of Relief Creek now, and the terrain was leveling off. I passed the old Sheep Camp, knowing Lunch Meadow wasn't far ahead.

It was getting warm. I'd shed my jacket several miles back; now I took off my overshirt and tied it around my waist. The sun felt good on my bare arms. Absently I brushed flies off Gunner's neck.

The landscape was opening up, and I could see the wide spaces of Lunch Meadow ahead. I rode until I was out of the forest and then sent the horses off the trail to a pocket-sized hollow along the creek. Here the water made bathtub-like pools in the rocks, perfect for soaking feet.

Dismounting stiffly, I tied Gunner and Plumber to trees, and hobbled around, taking saddlebags off and loosening cinches. Damn. I wasn't used to riding this many miles. God knew how stiff I would be when I got into camp this evening.

Settling myself by the banks of the creek, I cut hunks of dry salami and mozzarella cheese and rolled them in a flour tortilla. Humble but very satisfying. Long swallows from my water bottle washed it down. I eyed the icy cold water of the creek, but didn't drink it. *Giardia*, an intestinal parasite, was a problem in these mountains. I would only drink from springs that had not had a chance to become contaminated. Either that or pump my drinking water through the filter I'd brought.

Once my hunger was satisfied, I took off my boots and socks and soaked my feet in the creek. The water was so cold it hurt, but my skin tingled and I felt invigorated. I let my feet dry in the sun with my soles pressed against the warm, scratchy surface of the granite.

Time to go. I put my boots on, tied the saddlebags back on the saddle, and tightened Gunner's cinch. Plumber nickered at me. I looked him over carefully. The sweat had dried on his neck and flanks and his eye was bright. He was my chief concern on this trip. I had used Gunner a lot in the last couple of years, and knew him to be a trouper—a horse who traveled well and was tough. Plumber was more of an unknown quantity. Younger, smaller, and perhaps less tough-minded, he was also somewhat inexperienced. Although he'd been shown quite a bit as a youngster (by someone else), he'd spent his last few years turned out because of a lameness. Since he'd been sound, all I'd done with him was some gentle trail riding and the legging-up necessary for this trip. I wasn't sure how he would tolerate it all.

He looked okay, for the moment. I untied both horses, climbed on Gunner, and headed off across Lunch Meadow.

It was really more of a desert than a meadow. A big, open flat covered with low-growing, scrubby sagebrush, Lunch Meadow had been decimated many years ago by sheep. The four-footed locusts, who were both tended and decried by John Muir, had spent many summers here, while their shepherds relaxed and played cards at nearby Sheep Camp. Too many. Overgrazed and beaten down, the meadow had never recovered.

I rode across it, thinking about the ecological issues the sheep brought to mind. For the subject wasn't ancient history—far from it. Sheep were no longer pastured in Sierra meadows, but cattle, Ted's cattle, for instance, were. And there was a vociferous group of folks who thought that this should not be so.

An even more extreme contingent wanted to ban livestock altogether, including saddle horses and pack horses. Their thinking ran along the lines of preserving the meadows, and looking at the waste of Lunch Meadow, I couldn't help but feel some sympathy for their position. Trouble was, they didn't seem too long on facts.

I'll admit I'm prejudiced. I like horses; I like riding into the mountains. I've backpacked a fair amount, and I prefer taking my horses. These issues aside, I didn't see that the occasional use of livestock to travel through the mountains was likely to do any great and irreversible harm. Pasturing them in the meadows for the summer was another thing altogether.

Though Ted would hate to hear me say it, I'd several times wondered if his contented heifers were slowly turning Wheat's

Meadow into the desert that Lunch Meadow had become. I didn't know. I was pretty sure Ted didn't either.

I could see the steep slopes of Brown Bear Pass in front of me; my horses were on rock again. Red-brown lava rock now, rather than silvery granite. Brown Bear Pass was hot, dusty, exposed, and bare, the long slog up it a matter of plowing steadily through the scree. The trail was good, though.

Stopping to let the horses rest a number of times, I progressed steadily toward the ridge line. No trees up here. Several small, chattering creeks made green rivulets. Wildflowers clung to the dusty slopes—blue flax, white yarrow, bright red California fuchsia—all lovers of dry, well-drained places.

Everything was empty and quiet. A hawk circled in the blue. Gunner snorted. Roey trudged behind the horses, starting to look tired.

The jagged red-brown crags around us were peaceful with the peace of supreme unconcern. These constant, ever-changing, ever-similar vistas—stone in sunlight—seemed prehistoric in their inviolate purity.

Steel-shod hooves clicked sharply against rock; Plumber grunted as he struggled to haul the pack up the steepening trail. I could see the pass ahead of us—a curious collection of rosy pink, more-rounded boulders marking the spot.

Slowly, and then suddenly, we were there. Over the top, the wind in our faces, and all of Emigrant Meadow and Emigrant Lake spread out in front of us. I grinned in sheer delight.

Brown Bear Pass might have a steady slog of an ascent, but it also had a breathtaking view from the top. Looking over my shoulder, I could see the long vistas of granite and pine trees—the country I'd just ridden through. Relief Peak raised its head in the middle ground; in the distance were the shoulders of the mountains around Sonora Pass, where the pack station was.

And ahead of me was a vast, treeless meadow with a sheet of blue water in the middle. Beyond that the sharp outlines of the little ridge between Emigrant Meadow and Summit Meadow. And right next to Summit Meadow was Snow Lake. We were getting there.

I clucked to the horses and called the dog, who had plopped herself down in the shade of a boulder. She got up slowly, looking tired and a little footsore. Damn. I'd been afraid this long day might be hard on her paws.

Still, everybody seemed to be moving okay as we worked our way down the gradual slope to Emigrant Meadow. As I got closer, the meadow began to appear as blue as the lake—wide swathes of wild lupine carpeted it, the sweet, elusive fragrance as heady as the deep blue-violet color.

Riding through heaven, riding through the sky, I thought, as the lupine surrounded us. Flowery images, for sure. But what else could one say? How many people had ridden through fields of lupine, solitary on horseback, alone with the wind?

I sang. The dog pricked up her ears and lapped water from a stream. The horses drank; I took a long swallow from my water bottle.

"Not too far now," I told them all.

And it wasn't. Not too far, and not too steep. Just a gentle dirt trail, running through a series of small meadows and pothole lakes, climbing only briefly here and there. Until, an hour later, we reached the wide, grassy openness of Summit Meadow, with the peaks of Bonn Pass hovering above it.

I stopped to let the horses water one more time by the old stone cabin in Summit Meadow. Still plenty of daylight left. And Snow Lake was just ahead. No problem.

No problem at all. In fact, all my problems seemed to have dropped away as I'd ridden. I forgot about my job, I forgot about Lonny and our strained and tired relationship. As for the dead man in Deadman Meadow, he'd never crossed my mind, even once.

NINE

Snow Lake was a quarter of a mile from Summit Meadow. I rode over the little ridge that separated them, and was unprepared for the feeling of apprehension that hit me at my first sight of the lake.

I'd camped at Snow Lake before, with Lonny; I'd chosen it for my first camp on this trip because it was the right distance away, and there was a particular campsite I liked. I called it the lagoon camp. But I'd forgotten how dark and forbidding Snow Lake can seem.

Every mountain lake and meadow has its own particular character. I never wanted to camp by Emigrant Lake, for instance; it always felt too exposed to me. Snow Lake was sheltered enough, in a rocky hollow near the ridge line, but it seemed darkly opaque, mysterious, and even ominous. It never struck me as a pretty, sunny mountain lake.

This evening, already in the shadow of the ridge, riffled with little waves, Snow Lake looked more forbidding than welcoming. Oh well. We were here and we were staying, I told myself.

Just ride on to the lagoon camp; you've always liked that spot.

The lagoon camp was half a mile away; we skirted the lake, riding west. And sure enough, as we rounded the tip, where Forest Service workers had built a little stone dam in the forties, I saw the small lagoon below the main lake lit with evening sunshine. It was empty; I hadn't seen another soul so far.

Once again my heart lifted, my mood as mercurial as the light. There was a meadow next to the lagoon, and a campsite in some boulders near the meadow. This was all going to be just great.

I tied my livestock to trees near the campsite and unsaddled the saddle horse and unpacked the pack horse. Judging that both were tired and hungry enough not to wander, I left them turned loose while I strung a picket line out in the meadow between two pines.

Both horses lay down and rolled right away, choosing a sandy spot near the lake. I smiled, watching them. Once they'd gotten up, shaken off, and taken one more drink, I caught Gunner and tethered him to the picket line. He was tied long enough to reach the grass, and short enough that (I hoped) he wouldn't tangle himself up.

Methods of dealing with livestock while camping were as various as the people who went. Some hobbled their horses, some staked them out, some built rope corrals, some tied everything up, some left everything loose. The last method was a bit fatalistic in my opinion: the traveler trusting to his horse's loyalty and love of grain to stay in camp.

I didn't care for hobbles; many horses could move along at a fair pace in them. Nor did I like staking out; I'd seen too many horses get tangled up. Rope corrals were notoriously unreliable. My preferred method was to keep one horse on the picket line and one off, during the daylight hours, and tie both up at night. Generally speaking, a horse is very reluctant to go off on his own; I had no doubt that Plumber would stay within sight of Gunner.

Keeping half an eye on the horses as I worked, I unpacked and set up my small dome tent, unrolled and laid out my pad and sleeping bag, gathered firewood and built a fire. Then I tied Plumber up and turned Gunner loose.

Next I fetched a pot of water from the lake and pumped it through a filter, unfolded my collapsible chair, got out some salted peanuts and a bottle of Jack Daniel's, and made myself a drink.

The light slanted low and golden over the meadow and the lagoon, raising bright sparks on the surface of the water and gilding the feathery stems of ryegrass. In fifteen minutes or so, the sun would drop behind the rim of the canyon behind me. I leaned back in my chair, watching the fire flicker, and took a long swallow of bourbon and branch water. Ah, the cocktail hour.

The horses cropped grass peacefully; the dog lay sacked out flat on her side, taking a well-earned rest. I put my feet up on a boulder, ate a handful of peanuts, and sighed with contentment. I was here.

Content lasted until dark. I had two drinks, not because I'm so fond of Jack Daniel's, but because it was all I had. Wine and beer are prohibitively heavy to pack in, and nothing seems to mix as well with lake water as bourbon. So I drank my whiskey and water, ate peanuts, and watched the light die out of the sky.

When the air began to grow dim, I caught Gunner and tied him up, made myself another tortilla with salami and cheese, and gave the dog a bowl of dried dog food, which she disdained. All she seemed to want was to sleep.

I put another log on the fire and thought I'd do the same. This long day was trailing its way toward night, and I was tired. I'd brought some steak and cans of chili, and other more labor-intensive dinners, but I really didn't feel like cooking.

What I felt like, suddenly, was having somebody to talk to. Dusk gathered around me; smoke rose from my small fire and curled out over the lagoon. Flickers skimmed over the water, hunting flying insects. A fish jumped with a splash, making a ring on the still surface of the lake.

I could go fishing, I thought. If Lonny were here, he'd go fishing. If Lonny were here, he'd be sitting next to me now, happy to be in camp. And whether I felt frustrated with him or not, I'd also feel safe. And I'd have someone to talk to.

I made myself another drink and put my jacket back on. Why the hell had I wanted to come on this trip alone, anyway? Had I forgotten just what it felt like to be alone in the mountains as dark closed in?

I got up and got my gun out of my saddlebag. There was still enough light to see by. I checked to make sure there was no shell in the chamber, though I knew this was how I'd left the gun. Five bullets were what I had; I'd brought no spare ammunition. The pistol was for self-defense in an emergency, for scaring off bears in the unlikely event it was necessary, for shooting a horse in what I hoped was the extremely unlikely event of a broken leg. I sincerely believed I would get through the whole trip without using it.

Putting the gun back in its leather holster and snapping the safety strap over the hammer, I hung it on my belt and sat back down. The pistol was bulky and awkward there around my waist, but comforting, too.

I took a long swallow of my drink. Bright against the darkness, flames crackled in dry pine boughs. I could hear something moving in the trees and scrub, probably a deer.

What is it about sitting by a fire and hearing animal noises outside in the night? Despite the fact that I knew perfectly well that deer were the likeliest cause, I felt nervous. Fixing my eyes on the fire, I listened to the sounds of brush breaking and wondered what exactly was out there. Bears? Bigfoot?

I took another swallow of my drink. You knew this would happen, I reminded myself. You've been alone here before. Some kind of caveman instinct kicks in as it gets dark. The animal noises seemed to scare me almost automatically, a reaction as simple and primitive as hunger.

Time to go to bed. I put another log on the fire, wanting the companionship of its flickering light as I went to sleep. Roey looked up at me as I dug my flashlight out of my duffel bag, her first sign of life since we'd made camp.

"You can sleep with me," I told her.

Clicking the flashlight on, I followed its beam out to where the horses were tethered. They stood quietly, unperturbed by the deer or whatever it was. I ran the light over them. Plumber looked pretty ganted up, his flanks sucked in high and tight. Damn. This was not a good sign.

I checked him over closely, but he seemed okay otherwise, one foot cocked in a horse's typical resting pose. I'd just have to see how he was in the morning.

Back to the fire. I took off my jeans and boots, left my underwear and tank top on, made a pillow of my jacket, put the pistol under it, and crawled into the sleeping bag.

"Come on," I said to Roey.

She got up stiffly and picked her way over the ground toward me, looking pretty damn sore. I lifted her paws and checked them in the firelight; the pads were intact, no cuts or scrapes. She wagged her tail when I was done, stepped carefully into the tent, and curled up in a fold of my sleeping bag.

I left the tent door open, so I could look out at the night sky, and the fire made comforting orangy shadows on the nylon. The dog's warm weight pressed against my side and I snuggled deeper into the bag. In a rush as sudden as it had come, the fear went. I felt cozy and happy lying there alone, miles from any other human. The distant white sparkle of the stars seemed friendly. I dozed. Then I slept.

Sometime later I woke up. I didn't know how long I'd been asleep; it was still dark. I lay in my sleeping bag with the feeling that something was wrong.

The fire had died; I must have slept for a few hours, anyway. What had woken me?

Then I heard it. *Thump, thump, thump.* A familiar sound. The sound of a horse pawing the ground.

I scrambled out of the sack, fear twisting inside of me. Shoving my bare feet into my boots and grabbing the flashlight, I went to check the horses.

As I'd more than half suspected, it was Plumber. Pawing the ground and looking unhappy. Colicked.

Damn, damn, and damn. I had known this might be a problem. What Plumber probably had was a stress colic; I had seen it before with other young horses on their first pack trip. The long day and unaccustomed circumstances produced a mild bellyache.

Trouble was, in horses a mild bellyache could be life-threatening. The equine digestive system is constructed such that a horse can't vomit. Thus, upset stomachs could result in ruptured guts and death. Colic, a general term for any sort of intestinal disturbance, is a common and often serious problem that I frequently had to deal with in my role as a veterinarian.

But it was different when it was my own horse and we were twenty miles into the backcountry. The sort of help I would need with a severe colic—the ability to hook the horse up to an IV, a surgery center if need be—was simply not available. And Plumber was my friend. The distress in his eyes upset me in ways that overrode the detachment I'd cultivated in my veterinary career.

Still, I'd come prepared. Taking a deep breath to calm myself, I patted Plumber's neck and walked back to camp to get my vet kit.

In the kit was a bottle of banamine and a syringe and needles. Setting the flashlight down on a rock, I filled the syringe with eleven cc's, my hands shaking a little with chill and anxiety.

Back to Plumber, who was pawing the ground again. I took his pulse briefly and watched his respiration in the flashlight beam. Both were only slightly elevated, and he wasn't sweating. There was every chance in the world this shot of banamine would put him right.

I slipped the needle into his jugular vein, watched the blood well into the syringe, and injected the shot. Then I waited.

Plumber had accepted the pinprick of the needle quietly; now he watched me watch him. In a minute I could see a change in his expression. The worried look in his eyes vanished, and the normal curious brightness returned. He bumped me with his nose.

Good. The painkiller had kicked in. I studied the horse while I shivered in the night air. My bare legs were covered in goose bumps.

Should I turn him loose? The type of colic he had was probably due a great deal to stress and tension. Plumber was unaccustomed to being tied up all night, and this confinement could be contributing to his discomfort. If I turned him loose he could relax. Lie down, crop a little grass, move around when it suited him.

On the other hand, he could also run off. Or eat too much and make his digestive problems worse. Or, worst-case scenario, the pain could return and he might lie down and thrash. In which case it was possible his intestines would twist, like a hose with a kink, and he would die. I would never be able to get him to a surgery center in time to save him.

I stared at him and he tugged impatiently on his tether. He wanted to be turned loose. I made a decision and slipped his halter off. Without hesitation, he walked over to a nearby patch of grass and started eating. He felt fine, for the moment, anyway. Thank God for drugs.

Running the flashlight over Gunner, I ascertained that he looked okay. I gave him a pat on the neck and marched my by now thoroughly chilled body back to camp. I pulled off my boots, soaking wet from the dew-covered grass, and crawled back in the sleeping bag.

Roey grunted. She'd never even moved. I doubted that she'd even woken.

I, however, was now wide awake. I listened to the sound of Plumber munching grass and worried. Given that his colic was as mild as I supposed, the banamine should relieve his pain for at least six or eight hours. And, if I was right, when the drug wore off, the horse would be perfectly fine.

But if I was wrong and he was, or became, worse, the pain would come back and I would be forced to decide what to do. I would go out, I decided, lying in my sleeping bag and shivering. I would go right back out and try and save my horse.

I watched the dog snoring gently next to me and made another choice. I had planned to ride to Dorothy Lake, a mere five miles away, the next morning, but I would not. My dog was sore and tired, my horse was sick. I was pretty worn out myself. I would give us all a rest day. Make sure Plumber was completely okay before we moved on.

Choices made, I rolled over, hoping to doze before I got up to check the horse. It looked like I would be spending a little more time at Snow Lake.

TEN

Everything seemed better in the morning. I'd checked Plumber twice during the night and he appeared to be fine. The second time I'd tied him back up and turned Gunner loose. I woke several hours later to the soft gray light of dawn and a feeling of calm.

Little white mists rose off the silvery surface of the lake. The sky over Bonn Pass was a paler gray, announcing the approach of the sun. I could see Gunner, out in the meadow eating. Plumber stood quietly on the picket line. All was well.

I snuggled back down in my bag and waited for warmth. I am not one of those people who springs up early on camping trips, building a fire while fingers and toes grow numb. I like to luxuriate in the sleeping bag until the sun gets me up.

The lagoon camp was ideal for this, which was one of the reasons I liked it. When the sun rose over the ridge, rays streamed across the lake and hit my tent—pale yellow light as cheering as a fire at night.

Light and heat, how wonderful. I watched with satisfaction

as the sun rose, stronger and more golden every moment. And warmer. The lake gleamed; the sky went from gray to blue. Not a cloud in sight. A perfect Sierra morning.

I lay quietly and peacefully in the sleeping bag while the sunlight dappled the tent, content. When it grew warm enough to be encouraging, I got up and slipped my wet boots on, caught Gunner and tied him up, and turned Plumber loose.

The little brown horse looked absolutely normal; nickering at me as I walked toward him, eager to eat. This was good, but I wouldn't be sure he was all right until noon or so, when the last effects of the banamine would be out of his system.

Building a fire, I heated a pot of water and made cowboy coffee. Strong and rough, the coffee suited the place and my mood. I sat in my chair in the morning sunshine, wearing my tank top and underwear, and took hot, harsh sips from the insulated cup I'd brought.

Motion in the woods. Turning my head, I saw a buck step from the trees into the meadow. I froze. Moving only my eyes, I checked the dog. Still asleep in the tent. Oblivious.

I watched as the buck, a four-pointer, began to crop grass. Another stepped out of the trees. Six points. And another. Seven bucks in all emerged from the pines—one with an enormous twisted rack, like nothing I'd ever seen. I wondered how he managed to walk through the trees.

They grazed in the sunshine, apparently unworried by the horses or the fire. Park bucks, no doubt. The boundary of Yosemite National Park was right on top of the closest ridge, and hunting was not allowed in the park at any time. These bucks probably spent hunting season safely holed up—thus their indifference to my camp.

Seven big sandy-colored bucks, grazing by the shore of a bright lake in the early-morning light. I smiled and took a carefully unobtrusive sip of my coffee. Now this was living.

Ten minutes or so later, when they'd drifted off toward the

forest, I relaxed my muscles and stood up. I was hungry.

Putting a cast iron skillet on the fire, I got out a package of bacon and some scones. I laid the strips of bacon on the skillet one by one; they sputtered and hissed and steamed. The sweet, salty smell rose into the air, and the dog woke up.

She blinked at me from her position on the sleeping bag, ascertained that I really was frying bacon, and got to her feet. A long, stiff stretch, a big yawn, and a shake—then she walked toward me a little gingerly, wagging her tail.

I patted her wide, wedge-shaped head. ''Yes, you can have some.''

Taking the cooked strips out, I let the grease cool a minute, then poured it on the dry dog food Roey had ignored last night. She wagged her tail enthusiastically when I set the bowl in front of her. Now this, she seemed to say, is more like it.

The dog dug in; I munched strips of bacon and bites of cinnamon raisin scones, washing them down with hot coffee. There was some real strength in the sun now.

When I was done eating, I stripped off my clothes and boots, pulled on a bathing suit and some rubber and nylon water sandals, and prepared for a morning bath. Had the lake been a little more isolated, I wouldn't have bothered with the bathing suit, but just my luck, a whole party of good old boys would probably ride up as I dove in.

Not that I dove in immediately. First I walked down to a small pebbly beach and tried the water. Cool, not cold, as this lagoon had been the last time I camped here. So far, so good.

Spotting a good diving rock that I remembered, I walked over and stretched myself out on top of it, waiting for the sun to warm my skin. It took half an hour of concentrated sun bathing; I let my mind wander.

This was the thing about life in camp; this was the reason I'd come to these mountains alone. This sense of timelessness, this freedom from schedules and pressure, from other people's expectations. If I wanted, I could spend my whole two weeks at Snow Lake, dozing in the sun and swimming. No reason not to. No reason to do anything, except by my own inclination.

In the mornings I was always happy to be alone. The fear that came with darkness seemed inexplicable and slightly ridiculous in the morning light.

I rolled over, sunning my front side. The sky above me was a deep, pure cobalt blue. Turning my head, I could see the lake coming at me in gentle green swells rimmed with gold; the breeze had come up. I snuggled into my rock.

Being here, just being here, was what I wanted. Aware of myself as a still, solitary speck on the great rolling sweep of the globe. All my thoughts, all my worries reduced to insignificance.

The sun grew hotter on my skin. I turned over again, propped my chin on my hands, let my eyes drift over the granite slopes on the far side of the lake. Sometimes I felt like a small vulnerable animal up here, a house cat mistakenly lost in the wilderness.

When I was younger, I had come to these mountains with expectations, seeking a comfort that they would not give. In love with their beauty, I returned again and again, to see if in some way they would condescend to seem familiar.

I put my cheek against the rock. This is the intimacy you can find, I told myself. Just this. Alone with yourself in the present moment. Quiet in this austerely lovely place.

Now I was hot. I stood up, stretched, walked to the edge of the rock. The lake was blue-green, clear, deep. I could see the stones on the bottom. I put my hands over my head, chose my spot, and forced myself to spring off the bottoms of my feet and part the water with my hands.

My God, it was cold. Cold, green, silky, wet. I came up, gasped, and swam. Water clear and soft around me, clean as air. In a moment, it was cool, not cold.

I swam under the surface, stroking quietly through the underwater world. Green and shadowy, mysterious and dim, so different from the bright, sharp-edged land up above.

A few strokes later, I turned back. Never swim alone, they say. And particularly not miles away from any help, they would probably add. Whoever they were.

I swam back to shore, washed my face, armpits, crotch, and hair with the biodegradable soap I'd brought, dumped a pot of water over myself to rinse off, and swam again. Then I lay back down on my rock.

So, what about Lonny? Could I find some clarity in my aloneness here that would help me in my relationship? I loved Lonny in much the same way I loved Plumber and Gunner and Roey. He was part of my life. But were we really well suited as a couple?

Just what was it I wanted that he didn't give, I asked myself, staring at the big gray boulder in front of me.

Someone who was sensitive to who I was, who could make room for my way of being—that was the answer. I wanted a man for whom I would be more than a pleasant addition to a satisfactory life.

My skin and hair were drying rapidly. I sat up. Maybe there was no right man for me. I certainly didn't have another one in mind. I also doubted that Lonny would ever change much. He liked himself; he liked his life. He could, as he was proving, get along without me.

And me, I was lonely. In some ways, I was lonelier at home than I was here. I missed having a partner. I was thirty-five; there were lines around my eyes, some gray strands in my dark hair. I was past the point of being a cute young thing, if I'd ever been one. I had zero interest in checking out the dating game.

Maybe I needed to reacquaint myself with solitude. Maybe that was why I was here.

I was dry now. Getting up, I walked back to camp. Roey was asleep in the sunshine, full and content. I hoped she would rest all day and be able to travel tomorrow.

Plumber grazed in the meadow, looking fine. I caught him and tied him on the picket line and turned Gunner loose. Then I pulled off my wet swimsuit, hung it on a bush to dry, and put on some clean, dry underwear, shorts, and a tank top. Grabbing some dried fruit and nuts to nibble on, I sat down in the shade of a pine tree with a book.

Not just a book. With *Walden*. Henry David Thoreau's masterpiece was a tradition for me. When I'd first gone backpacking in the Sierras I'd brought *Walden* to read; in fact, it was *Walden* that inspired me to attempt some solitary camping in the woods. And on every trip thereafter, I brought it as some might bring the Bible. Brought it and read it.

"I went to the woods because I wished to live deliberately, to front only the essential facts of life, and see if I could not learn what it had to teach, and not, when I came to die, discover that I had not lived."

I put the book down. Here I was, alone in the woods, following in Henry David's footsteps. Looking up, I watched the white streak of a jet trail progress across the sky. Some things had changed, others were the same. People were crowded into the cabin of that jet, reading, writing, thinking, twenty thousand feet up in a little metal box. On their way to Chicago, maybe, or New York. And all the while I sat here by the side of my lake and built a fire to cook my breakfast.

I read some more. Ate a chunk of dried pineapple. Swatted at the pesky and persistent flies. A hummingbird zoomed into camp and swooped up to each red object she saw, exploring them for signs of nectar. Disappointed, she whirled away, in search of better feeding ground.

Thoreau was beginning to pall. I looked up, saw that Gunner had quit eating and was resting in the shade, idly swishing flies with his tail. He could just as well do that on the picket line.

I caught him and turned Plumber loose. By now all effects of the banamine would be gone—and Plumber looked fine. His flanks were no longer ganted up, his eye was bright, and his attitude seemed good. As soon as I unclipped his lead rope, he put his head down and started eating.

Sitting back down in my chair, I watched him meander around the meadow. He wasn't really hungry; he ate a bite, walked a few steps, took another bite. Then he walked down to the shore and had a long, leisurely drink.

Done with that, he looked around, took a step forward into the lake, splashed the water once with his foot, and lay down. I leaned forward in amazement as he rolled in two feet of lake water, putting his whole head and most of his body underwater and getting himself thoroughly wet. I laughed out loud.

"Haven't you ever seen a horse take a bath?"

The voice came from behind me; I jumped up with a lurch, heart thumping. Even as I whirled, I registered a familiar voice.

Ted. Ted sitting on Hank, in the woods behind my camp, watching me.

"How did you get here?" I demanded.

"Rode from Bigelow."

"Oh." The trail from Bigelow Lake, a mere mile away, came down the opposite slope from the trail I'd ridden in on.

"So what are you doing here?" I asked.

"I packed Dan Jacobi and his crew in there yesterday."

"I thought he was going to Huckleberry."

"He was. He changed his mind. He wanted to be somewhere less crowded. I told him Bigelow."

This made sense. Huckleberry Lake was big, with a few large islands, pretty campsites, and great fishing. Though a long ride in, it was very popular. Bigelow, smaller and much higher in elevation, was rocky and almost treeless, seldom visited. The fishing was equally good, though.

Ted smiled at me. "I thought if I took him to Bigelow I could come visit you."

I stared at him, wondering if he could possibly be as obtuse as that sounded. I hadn't ridden into the mountains alone in search of company.

"But I wasn't sure you'd still be here," Ted went on.

"I didn't mean to be. Plumber colicked last night. I thought I'd give him a layover day."

"He looks all right," Ted said.

We both watched the horse, who was eating grass, his back wet and shiny.

"I've never seen a horse roll in water like that," I commented.

Ted smiled. "They do that."

We were both quiet. Ted made no move to dismount, just sat on Hank and watched me. For my part, I did not invite him to sit down. I was feeling intruded upon and mildly resentful. Why in hell had Ted considered it his civic duty to come check on me?

Ted's eyes moved around my campsite and then back to me. "You look like you're doing okay."

"I'm fine." A thought struck me. "Lonny didn't send you to check on me, did he?"

Ted raised one hand. "Lonny has no idea I'm here." He met my eyes. "I didn't say a word to him."

I shrugged my shoulders, puzzled. "Well, when you get back to the pack station you can tell him everything's going well. Are you riding back out tomorrow?"

"Yep. I'm leaving Dan and his boys at Bigelow for a week. They're keeping their saddle horses and two pack mules, in case they want to make an overnight ride. The one kid knows enough to pack a horse."

"Uh-huh." I nodded, not much interested in any of this. I would avoid Bigelow Lake, and with any luck at all, would never run into Dan Jacobi and his crew, which included the obnoxious blond Steve.

"Well, I'd better get on back." Ted was still watching me. He seemed to be waiting, I didn't know what for. I was damned if I was going to invite him to sit down with me. I hadn't ridden all these miles to gossip with Ted.

"See you later, then," I told him.

"You bet." Ted turned Hank and looked back at me. "See you later."

Once he was gone, I got up and made myself a tortilla with peanut butter on it for lunch. It was too early for a drink. Or was it? The sun's over the yardarm somewhere, as my friend Lisa Bennet used to say. What the hell. I was on vacation.

I made a Jack Daniel's and water, weak, and sipped it with my impromptu peanut butter sandwich. I read some more of *Walden* and took another swim. Then I took a nap. Life in camp.

By the time late afternoon arrived, I could tell that all my animals were feeling rested and more chipper. Roey quit snoozing and found a pinecone to play with. Plumber trotted off across the meadow, looking like he wanted to go somewhere. I caught him and let Gunner loose.

Tonight, I thought, I'll make myself a proper dinner. Salad and steak and garlic bread.

I had these luxuries because I had packed a small cooler with a block of ice in it. It wouldn't last the whole trip, but for the first few days, anyway, I was traveling in style.

First I made myself a drink. Who can cook without a drink in hand? Then I built a fire, made a salad, buttered bread and wrapped it in foil, and marinated my strip of skirt steak in soy sauce and garlic.

All things prepared, I sat in the sun and sipped my drink and read *Walden* for an hour. Camp seemed peaceful; I was no longer worried about Plumber; dark was several hours away. Life was good. I felt all set to enjoy my solitary evening.

But it wasn't to be. Just as I got up to put another log on the fire and freshen my drink, Gunner nickered. Plumber echoed him. Roey barked. I looked up to see two horsemen picking their way down the trail from Bigelow Lake. Even at this distance I recognized Ted's big buckskin. The other horse was a gray. Looked like I was having company.

ELEVEN

Ted and Dan Jacobi rode up to my camp and dismounted while I was catching Gunner. By the time I had both my horses securely tethered to the picket line Hank and Dan's gray gelding were tied to nearby pine trees and Ted and Dan were sitting on convenient boulders near my fire. Roey sniffed them in turn and wagged her tail.

"We came to have a drink with you," Ted said.

"That's nice," I replied, doing my best to keep the chagrin out of my voice. "I'd ask you to stay to dinner, but I'm afraid there's only enough for one."

"We won't stay," Dan Jacobi said politely, rubbing Roey behind the ears.

"No, but we brought you a drink." Ted was carrying his saddlebags. He opened them up and produced a bottle of Stoly's, a bottle of tonic, three limes, and a plastic bag of ice. "Your favorite."

I had to smile. I might not welcome their company, but a vodka tonic on ice sounded just fine.

"Thanks," I said, as Ted made and handed me the drink.

He produced a small bottle of Jim Beam and proceeded to make whiskey and waters for himself and Dan. It took a minute, but finally it dawned on me that the elaborate vodka tonic preparations had been brought solely on my account. And they had to have been thought of and organized back at the pack station. Had Ted intended to come visit me all along? And if so, why?

This question occupied my mind while we all sat around quietly and sipped our drinks. I waited. Damned if I was going to make conversation. This whole visit was their idea; let them talk.

Ted tried a smile. "I told Dan he should stay in camp," he said. "When a man rides out to have a drink with a pretty lady, he wants to go alone. But Dan, here, he had to come with me."

Dan Jacobi smiled briefly. I had a moment's sense of his inner force, then his expression became even and unremarkable. An odd man, I thought. He wouldn't stand out in a crowd, really, but he seemed a good deal more intense than the average person when you paid attention to him.

"So how's it going?" Ted asked.

"Fine." I was still feeling uncooperative.

"How's your horse?"

"He's fine." I took a cold sip of my drink and sighed. What the hell did Ted want?

There was some more quiet.

"I been thinking," Ted said at last. "Thinking about Bill."

"Oh." Sad to say, I'd more or less forgotten about Bill Evans. His death had been striking and tragic, but I'd had more than enough on my mind for the last two days.

"I keep wondering why he did it." Ted took a swallow of his drink and stared at the fire. "He didn't say anything about me, did he, Gail?"

"No. He talked about colicked horses. Horses with fire in their bellies. Said he wanted to die. That was it."

"Nothing else?" Ted still watched the fire.

"Well, there was some more along those lines. Green fire, I think he said, and he couldn't save them. Something like that. It really didn't make any sense."

"But he didn't talk about me throwing him out of the bar or anything?" Ted was still off on his own track. "I been telling Dan, I'm worried about that. If I'd known he was thinking of killing himself, I never would have done that."

Dan gave Ted a level look. "What did I tell you? You heard what she said."

"Yeah." Ted drank some more whiskey. "Dan, here, he told me to ask you. I'm still worried it was on Bill's mind."

"Well, I can tell you he never said anything about it while I was there." I looked away.

I wasn't liking this conversation. Talking about Bill Evans was bringing the whole thing back to me, and I wanted to forget. The sight of that man, lying on his back, shot through the chest, waiting to die . . . I shivered. Wanting to die all alone, staring up at the distant stars. And I hadn't saved him.

It brought mortality, my own mortality, all too close. Those same indifferent stars would watch me die, if something went dramatically wrong up here. All alone.

We all took sips of our drinks. Dan Jacobi spoke. "It's a bad deal, but it's not your fault." He looked at Ted. "Let it go."

Ted said nothing.

I handed him my empty glass. "Since you're here, why don't you make me another. That ice will just melt."

Ted seemed to rouse himself with an effort. He smiled, a faint echo of his usual cocky grin, and took my glass. Slowly, carefully, he began to make the drink.

I turned my attention to Dan Jacobi. The man was beginning to interest me. I liked his quiet assumption of power, his apparent lack of the need to assert it. I watched his eyes as he watched the fire. It struck me that they were eyes that were accustomed to looking straight at problems, whether dissatisfied horse buyers or unruly colts. He had spoken firmly but not unkindly to Ted, whom he seemed to regard as just such a problem, at least for the moment.

Dan was aware of my eyes on him, I could tell, but he said nothing.

Ted handed me my drink, and poured a splash more whiskey in his own and Dan's. The sun had dropped behind the canyon rim, and dusk was beginning to gather. The flames of the fire were brighter. I was ready for these guys to go any time. I had no wish to cook and eat my dinner in the dark.

Ted didn't seem to be in a hurry. He squatted back down on his boulder and regarded the fire. After some seconds of this, he said, "Bill didn't say anything about Blue Winter, did he?"

"No," I said shortly. "I told you what he said, as well as I could remember. What have you got going about this guy, Blue?"

"Blue's a thief," Dan Jacobi said evenly.

"So you said. How did he happen to steal your horse?"

Dan shrugged. "Took him home and never paid for him."

I waited. The man said nothing more. I had the definite impression that the subject was off-limits.

Oh well. So what? I had only a passing interest in the whole thing anyway. If Dan Jacobi didn't want to talk about it, fine.

"You haven't seen Blue out here, have you?" Ted's voice held the familiar gossipy tone.

"No." I was really getting tired of this. I stood up. "I haven't seen anybody except you two. If you'll excuse me, I need to cook my dinner before it gets dark."

"Of course." Dan Jacobi stood up, too. "We'll be going."

"Thanks for the drink," I said, as he turned toward his horse.

"Any time." He tipped his white straw cowboy hat briefly. Ted followed him more slowly, stopping to look back at me.

"Sure you don't want some company tonight?" He grinned at me, his barroom grin, the little-boy smile that had won several dozen hearts. Or if not hearts, at least bed companions.

"I'm sure." I laid the skirt steak on the grill.

Dan was already mounted. I looked his gray gelding over curiously. He was, indeed, big and pretty. Too big and pretty for me. I don't like horses with that sort of heavy, massive muscling; I think they're prone to problems. And I've often thought that overly pretty horses are like overly pretty men— not as likely to be good ones as their plainer counterparts. To top it all off, I'm not crazy about dapple grays, everybody else's favorite color. They're more likely to get melanomas, for one thing. And they're just so obvious.

Still, I did the polite thing. "Nice-looking horse," I said to Dan Jacobi.

"Thank you."

Ted laughed. "I told him he shouldn't take that ten-thousand-dollar son of a bitch up here in these rocks. He should rent one from me."

Dan said nothing.

Ted was on Hank now. I heard him cluck, and the two horsemen moved off. I waved. "See you later," I said.

"You take care." Ted looked over his shoulder at me.

"Night." I could just hear Dan Jacobi's low voice.

Turning back to my fire, I got to work on dinner. But even as I warmed the bread and cooked the steak, I thought. What in the world was in Ted's head? Was he feeling that guilty over Bill Evans's death? Belatedly I wondered why, exactly, Ted had thrown Bill out of the bar. Could that have something to do with Ted's excessive and morbid-seeming curiosity?

Too late to ask him questions now. I wasn't sure I would have bothered, anyway. I wanted to forget the whole thing, not think about it more.

Try as I would, though, I found I couldn't. I thought about

Bill Evans's death as I made and ate my dinner, as I fed the dog and checked my horses, as I got ready for sleep. I thought about it to the exclusion of anything else, despite my intention to do otherwise.

Why had the man shot himself, really? Why was his death upsetting Ted so much? And what, if anything, did it have to do with me?

Naturally I had no answers to any of these questions, but that didn't stop them spinning uselessly around my mind. Along with unwanted images of Bill Evans's face, and bloody chest, and confusing words.

Damn. I didn't want this. I didn't want anything to do with it. Why in hell had I happened to find him?

The fire gave me back no reasons. It flickered and smoked. I stared at it from my sleeping bag, wishing I could drop the subject of the unfortunate man's suicide.

Roey snuggled up against me, and I reached down to stroke her head. "I can't even go to sleep," I told her pointlessly. "This is bad." Little did I know.

TWELVE

The next day, I saw Blue Winter. I'd saddled and packed up in the morning and was on my way to Wilma Lake. I met him in Grace Meadow.

I was in new territory now. Once I left Summit Meadow and crossed Bonn Pass, I was on trails I'd never seen, only traced on my map. Of course, I'd heard plenty of stories. All my years with Lonny had been filled with recounted pack-trip sagas and I knew many secondhand details about the trail to Wilma, and Jack Tone Canyon, and Benson Lake.

Still, everything I saw was new to me. Bonn Pass, the highest pass I'd cross on my trip, was less spectacular than I'd supposed. Dorothy Lake, which I passed en route, more severe and dramatic than I'd ever imagined. And, unlike my ride to Snow Lake, I had to stop and consult my map often.

Unfamiliar trails were challenging. I didn't know where the tricky spots were ahead of time; I found myself getting tense when I saw steep, rocky climbs or descents ahead of me. I never knew whether they would be easy or downright dangerous until I was right in the middle of them.

Experienced packers can tell slickrock at a glance, at least sometimes. Sometimes they can't, until a horse slips. Slickrock doesn't always look much different from less slippery granite. And though I knew the basics—enough not to let my horses step in V-shaped wedges, and to keep them off obviously loose stepping stones—I wasn't experienced enough to eyeball a section of rocky trail and know immediately where the worst sections were.

Thus, although I enjoyed the new scenery, I was pretty tense by the time we'd worked our way down Bonn Pass. So far, so good; no cuts or scrapes on either horse, and we were in level forest land, a ride in the park.

Grace Meadow appeared up ahead of us, a long, rambling grassland that followed Hetch Hetchy Creek down to Jack Tone Canyon. I rode until I found a pretty spot along the creek with a sandy bank and a convenient pine grove nearby. Lunch time.

Roey plopped herself down next to me when I sat. She'd traveled well today, neither wearing herself out with unnecessary excursions nor falling behind. She trotted patiently in Plumber's wake, conserving her strength. She was learning.

I took my boots off and soaked my feet in the truly bone-chilling water. It was snowmelt, and I could only bear it for a minute.

Burying my toes in the warm sand to thaw and dry them, I busied myself making a tortilla sandwich. Roey snoozed next to me; my horses dozed in the shade of the pines. None of them saw the approaching horseman. Only me.

Riding along the trail through Grace Meadow, going the same way I was going. At first he was just a distant rider; I watched him curiously. First person I'd seen today. The details began to sink in. A dun saddle horse, a smaller sorrel pack horse. A gray hat with a fedora slant. I could see a small white dog running alongside.

My immediate reaction was mixed. I'd liked this man when I met him, but Dan Jacobi's insistence that he was a thief, and Ted's obvious mistrust, had made me wonder. I could see his red hair under the gray hat now. I wonder if he knows about Bill Evans, I thought.

He had left the pack station the morning after we'd found Bill. I hadn't known, then, whether the man was dead or alive. I didn't know that Blue Winter even knew that Bill Evans had shot himself, though surely he couldn't have missed the chopper.

And Ted had said that Blue had lived with Bill's wife for a while. The solitary rider was close enough that I could see his face, as well as the red-brown freckles on the white dog. What should I say, or not say?

Blue Winter rode up the trail until he was fifty feet away from where I sat on the banks of the creek. Reining his horse to a halt, he watched impassively as his young dog raced up to me, wagged her tail in my direction, and sniffed noses with Roey. The two dogs began an elaborate greeting ritual, composed of much tail wagging, sniffing, and leaping about.

"Hello, Stormy," Blue Winter said.

I smiled. This man had that effect on me. Reminding myself that Dan Jacobi had said he was a thief, and I didn't know what, if anything, he might have had to do with Bill Evans's suicide, I let my smile die.

"Hi," I said.

We were both quiet for a moment. Normal backcountry etiquette called for a least a few words of pleasant conversation here. And normally, I would enjoy exchanging some polite talk with another traveler; it made a nice break from the solitude of my own thoughts. But I was wondering what in the hell I ought to say to Blue Winter.

For his part, the man seemed quite content to be quiet, a trait I'd noticed in the bar. He regarded me without a sign of impatience, seeming happy to sit on his horse in the sunshine and watch me.

His stolen horse, if Dan Jacobi was to be believed. The big blaze-faced dun gelding looked worth stealing. Unlike Dan Jacobi's gray, this horse had the sort of long, flat muscling that I liked, and he wasn't overly pretty. He looked to be in good flesh, too; traveling in the mountains didn't seem to have stressed him any. If Blue Winter had stolen him, at least he was taking care of him.

"So, how's it going?" I said at last.

"Good enough. How about you?"

As I'd remembered from our previous conversations, his face remained remote, giving no clues to his thoughts. If I had any curiosity at all about him, I was going to have to work at satisfying it.

"I'm doing okay," I told him. "I've been camped at Snow Lake the last two nights. How about you?"

"I'm going to Tilden," he said briefly.

Well, it was one piece of information. Tilden Lake was several miles from Wilma Lake, and a popular backcountry destination because of its large size and good fishing.

"Planning to catch some golden trout up at Mary?" I asked. Nearby Mary Lake had one of the few remaining populations of native California golden trout. Most of the other lakes had been overrun by imported rainbows and brookies.

Blue Winter smiled. "I'm not much of a fisherman."

We watched each other with what I thought was mutual curiosity. I had the idea we both wanted to ask, "So, what do you come here for?" but courtesy forbade it. There was no answer to the question, anyway, but the discussion would be interesting.

Instead, I said, "I ran into Dan Jacobi and Ted Reiter at Snow Lake."

If I'd been hoping for a reaction to this, I'd have been disappointed. As I expected, Blue Winter's face showed nothing. Since it wasn't a question, he made no answer. Just sat there on his horse, watching me.

Suddenly I felt self-conscious, sitting on my sandbank, barefoot and defenseless. I stood up, scanning the meadow for my dog. She was wrestling happily with Blue's dog, twenty yards away. My two horses were still safely tied to pine trees. I turned back to my visitor.

"They mentioned you," I said.

He continued to say nothing. He was a master at it.

Then to my surprise, he dismounted. Holding his reins in one hand, he said, "Mind if I have lunch with you?"

"No, of course not." I stumbled over the words, too startled to consider what to say. I wasn't sure if I minded or not. But Blue Winter was already tying his horses up. He returned and sat down on a log, a polite ten feet from the sandbank where I'd settled back down. He was carrying his saddlebags, and produced an apple and some beef jerky.

Eyeing my tortilla, cheese, and salami, he smiled. "I'll trade you some apple for some cheese."

"Deal," I said, smiling back. Damn, he had a nice smile.

We swapped food and munched. The apple was a fine complement to my sandwich. I was still wondering what, if anything, to say to him, when he spoke.

"Did Dan Jacobi tell you I stole the dun horse?"

"Uh, yeah, he did." I swallowed a mouthful of tortilla and regarded the man cautiously.

I should have guessed. His face remained quiet; he said nothing. Just ate a piece of cheese.

As a conversationalist, he was difficult. But I was genuinely curious now.

"So why did Dan say that?" I prompted.

"He thinks I did, I guess," was the reply.

"And did you?"

"We disagree about that." Blue Winter ate a piece of apple and watched me quietly. "I'll tell you the story, if you're interested."

"Yes, I'm interested."

"All right, then." He paused. "I've known Dan awhile, and he knows me. About a year ago a friend of mine wanted a rope horse. He had plenty of money, but not much knowledge. He came to me to help him." Once again Blue Winter smiled. "I'm the opposite. I've got some knowledge and no money to speak of.

"Anyway, I went with this guy to Dan's and helped him try horses, and eventually we settled on this one." He looked over at the dun.

"My friend took him home, pending a vet check." He looked at me and I nodded. I knew about buying horses with the caveat that they would pass a veterinarian's inspection. I was often the vet in question.

"Of course, you know all about that. Anyway, that night the horse colicked, bad." He looked at me, and I nodded again.

"My friend didn't even realize something was wrong until the horse was in pretty bad straits. He called me; I came out and had a look and called Bob." Once again, the look.

I nodded and said, "Uh-huh." Bob was Bob Barton—our main competition for the equine veterinary market in Santa Cruz County.

"Bob said the horse needed to be operated on right away. You know what that costs."

I nodded and said, "Uh-huh" again. I did.

"My friend didn't want to pay that kind of money to fix a horse he didn't own yet. I called Dan and explained things to him. Dan wasn't willing to pay for it either. 'Just keep treating him,' he said. 'He'll either die or live. I'm not paying five thousand dollars for surgery.'

''But Bob was sure the horse had a twist. He'd die.'' Blue Winter shook his head.

''I don't have a whole lot of money. But the horse was just five years old. And he was a real nice horse and a hell of a rope horse. I called Dan back and asked him if I could have the horse if I paid to have him operated on. He said, 'Take him. I don't care.' '' Blue shrugged.

''I didn't have five thousand dollars to spare. So I convinced Bob to do the operation at his place in Watsonville. He didn't want to, but it was either that or let the horse die. He has enough of a facility to do minor surgeries on horses, and I convinced him that I wouldn't blame him if the horse didn't make it.''

I nodded again. I knew that Bob, just like Jim and I, did not normally do colic surgeries. We all sent those off to the major surgery centers, where they did, indeed, cost five thousand dollars, minimum.

''Bob operated on the horse and fixed him. Cost me a thousand dollars.'' Blue Winter's face stayed quiet. ''That was all the money I could spare, period.

''Dan called and asked me what became of the horse a few weeks later. I told him, and said I was taking care of the horse and that in six months or so, I'd know if he'd really be all right.''

I nodded and said, ''Uh-huh,'' yet again. Colic surgeries have a long recovery period.

''So eventually I knew the horse was all right, and I took him to a couple of ropings. Dan rides up to me at one of them and says, 'You owe me six thousand.'

''And I said, 'Why is that?'

''And he tells me, 'That's a seven-thousand-dollar horse, and you paid one thousand for his vet bill, and you owe me the other six thousand.'

" 'Well,' I said, 'wait a minute, my understanding was that I could have him for the price of his vet bills.'

"And Dan, he said, 'That's not right. You owe me for what he's worth. For all I know, that horse would have been fine without the operation. You only paid a thousand dollars for him. You owe me six.' "

Blue looked at me. "You can see the position I was in. I couldn't afford to give Dan six thousand dollars, even if I thought he was right, which I didn't. I could give him the horse back, but I'd spent every spare cent I had to fix him, and I'd taken care of him and fed him for a year. As far as I was concerned, he was my horse.

"So I didn't say anything. I just rode off. I figured if he thought I'd stolen him he could take me to court."

"So, did anything come of it?" I asked.

"He rode up to me one other time and said he owned Dunny; he still had the papers and I had no bill of sale. The horse was his, he said.

"I told him it was true enough about the papers and that I had no bill of sale. But I told him he knew and I knew what had really happened. And Bob Barton knew. And my friend who had originally taken the horse knew."

"So, what did he say?"

"Not much. He just said it was his horse, and he wanted me to pay for him or give him back. I said I had done what I thought was right and left it at that. So far as I know, the only thing he's done about it is go around telling everyone I stole the horse."

"How does that make you feel?"

Blue Winter shrugged his shoulders. "People can think what they like."

The cowboy ethic in action. Still, there was one thing that puzzled me. "Why would Dan want to do something like that? He's got plenty of money, from all I hear."

Blue Winter shrugged again. "You'd better ask him. He didn't get to be rich by giving money away."

We were both quiet. I stared at the big dun gelding. He was standing quietly, one back foot cocked in a resting pose. Blue Winter's story made sense. There is a gray area when a horse is being "tried." The former owner has relinquished control of him, and the new owner isn't committed to buying him. Problems like this can result. But I wouldn't have thought it was in Dan Jacobi's best long-term interest to take this particular tack.

"Did you hear about Bill Evans?" I asked. As soon as the words were out of my mouth, I regretted them. Talking to Blue about the horse had caused me to drop my guard; I hadn't stopped to think what would follow from the question.

"No, what happened?" Blue's face was as unreadable as ever.

"He shot himself the night before you rode in. Didn't you hear the chopper come to take him out?"

"I heard the chopper. Didn't figure it was any of my business."

More quiet. I waited for him to ask a question.

"Is he dead?" he said at last.

"Yeah."

"That's too bad."

And that was it. Blue Winter nibbled his apple core and volunteered nothing more. I wondered if I wanted to ask him a question or two and decided I didn't. What was it going to achieve? If he knew something about Bill Evans and his suicide, he clearly wasn't going to tell me.

I could tell him the story of my finding the man, but again, why? And I could hardly haul off and ask him if he used to live with Bill Evans's wife.

108

I began putting my socks and boots on. Blue stood up, all six-and-a-half feet of him. He looked down at me.

"Thanks for listening to my story," he said. "I didn't want you to think I stole a horse from Dan."

"I understand. Have a good trip," I added.

"You, too. Maybe we'll run into each other again." Blue was tying his saddlebags back on the dun gelding.

I wondered if he knew more about Bill Evans's suicide than he was letting on. He'd dismissed the whole matter pretty abruptly. Surely that wasn't natural.

He was on his horse now, pack horse in tow. He whistled for his dog, who bounded up obediently. I stood by the side of the creek looking up at him.

He stared down at me for a moment, then touched the brim of his hat briefly. "It was good to see you. Bye, Stormy."

Before I could make any reply, he'd turned and ridden off.

Well, well, well. I watched him disappear down the trail, then set about organizing myself to go. As I tied my own saddlebags back on and tightened cinches, I wondered. I found I'd become very curious about Blue Winter.

THIRTEEN

I made camp at Wilma Lake in good time. It turned out to be a pretty lake, but there were two parties of people in, one group complete with teenagers, rubber rafts, and boom boxes. This, I supposed, was because Wilma, though two days' ride from Crazy Horse Creek, was a short day away from Hetch Hetchy Pack Station. Though I saw no horses in evidence, it was apparent from the amount of stuff both groups had with them that they had been packed in. No doubt the packers had ''dropped'' these parties and would be back to collect them later.

The worst part of all this was that Wilma was not a huge lake, and fully one half of the shore line consisted of vertical rock wall dropping into blue-green water. Pretty for sure, but providing no campsites. The other half of the lake was open enough, but the two biggest (and best) campsites had been taken by the large parties.

Had I been backpacking, I might have found an obscure ledge somewhere on which to pitch my tent, but my two horses required a patch of level ground and some grass. The only likely-looking spot I saw was right along the trail. A stone ring showed that it was used as a campsite, and there was a good-sized pocket of meadow and a nice rock wall against which to set the tent. But the trail ran right through it.

It isn't good manners to camp alongside a trail, nor did I like to do it; traffic through one's camp is disturbing. But I didn't see that I had much choice. It was either that or park myself cheek by jowl with one of the other groups, which was equally rude.

Reluctantly, I unsaddled and unpacked the horses at my chosen site, then put them both on a picket line out in the meadow. I wouldn't turn them loose, not with this many people around.

Chores done, I wandered about, finding that the river that departed the lake just beyond my camp featured a wonderful granite drop-off festooned with many small waterfalls and bathtub-sized cascading pools. Golden-orange leopard lilies overhung one of these in combination with nodding red and yellow columbines—a vignette more telling than any carefully arranged garden feature I'd yet encountered.

After a brief foray I returned to camp, unwilling to leave the horses for long. Once again I made a drink, collected the jar of peanuts and *Walden*, and parked my camp chair where the last rays of sunlight would hit me. For an hour I read, sipped, and munched, relatively undisturbed.

Every so often the teenagers in the next camp, who were engaged in water fights out on their rubber rafts, would emit particularly loud squeals and shouts, enough to cause me to look up. It was during one of these brief lifts of the head that I saw the two women.

They were coming toward me on the trail, from the direction of Hetch Hetchy. One tall, one short, both with backpacks on their backs, walking with end-of-the-day weariness. Hetch Hetchy might be an easy day's ride, but it was a good long slog of a hike, and all uphill.

These two hikers looked understandably beat. They also looked miffed as they surveyed the lake with its all-too-obvious complement of campers. I knew how they must feel. Despite the fact that we all know it's unreasonable, those of us who frequent the backcountry always hope to find our destinations of choice pristine and undisturbed. After a long day's journey through the wilderness, it's somewhat of an anticlimax to search for an empty campsite as though you were looking for a vacant space at an RV park.

After a minute the two women halted, not twenty feet from me, and surveyed the situation at Wilma Lake. I watched them idly, wondering where they would choose to camp. If it were me, I thought, I'd cross the creek and camp on the other side. The shorter woman said something to her companion.

I stared. The short women's face was turned directly toward me, with the setting sun full on it. It was Sara. Lonny's ex.

I recognized her with a jolt of emotional resonance all out of proportion to my actual acquaintance with her, which was virtually nil. I'd met her twice, and only briefly then. But she'd been a part of my life for many years, a shadowy, threatening presence, a woman I'd found myself almost fearing.

Sara had left Lonny two years before he and I had started dating, so I had never felt even peripherally responsible for the end of their marriage. Several years later, Sara had decided she wanted to move back in with the man who was still, technically, her husband, and she had been extremely angry when Lonny had chosen to continue his relationship with me. The ensuing fireworks had, more or less, precipitated their divorce. Thus Sara blamed me for, as she had once put it, ''coming between'' her and Lonny.

I thought this unreasonable, and I'd said so, which hadn't made her like me any better. In short, our one conversation had not been a friendly chat. I regarded her now with considerable apprehension.

112

How in the world had she happened to appear here and now, on the shore of Wilma Lake, in the Sonora wilderness, just when I happened to be camped here?

It was Sara; I was sure of it. The year since I'd seen her hadn't treated her kindly; she'd gained some weight, cut her hair short, and dyed it blond, none of which was flattering. But she was, quite recognizably, the woman who had worried me and haunted me for so long. Lonny's wife.

His ex-wife, I reminded myself. And the last time I saw her she was dating another man. Sara had no real reason to resent me.

I was still uncomfortable. For a second I contemplated getting up, turning my back, hiding by my horses . . . anything to avoid a confrontation.

But self-respect, and for that matter, curiosity won out. I stayed where I was, facing the trail, and waited.

In the quiet evening air, I could hear bits of their conversation. The unknown woman looked somewhat younger than Sara; a Viking of a human being, she was taller than I, perhaps about six-foot-even, with long brown-blond hair in a braid down her back and a strong Scandinavian face.

Sara was addressing her in querulous tones, and I caught the phrases ''nowhere to camp,'' ''too noisy,'' and ''too many people.''

Eventually the two moved forward again and stopped when they were ten feet from me, just where the trail ran past my camp.

''Hello,'' the tall woman said.

I looked up from my book. My eyes searched Sara's face. ''Hi,'' I said.

I saw Sara start. She knew me, just as I knew her. Perhaps she, too, had thought about me for years—the woman who had stolen Lonny's devotion away from her, as she would see it.

We stared at each other. On her face I saw a range of expressions—surprise, hostility, and yes, curiosity.

"It's Sara, isn't it?" I said.

She said nothing to me, just looked at her companion. "Lee," she said urgently, "that's Lonny's girlfriend."

The woman so addressed stared at me with equal curiosity, but a complete lack of hostility. She had pronounced smile lines around her eyes and a strong chin. Like Sara, she wore regulation walking shorts and hiking boots, topped with a fleece jacket for the cool evening air.

"Hi," I said again.

For a second it seemed we were at an impasse. Sara, stony-faced, wouldn't look at me. I had no idea what else to say. We all stared awkwardly.

The tall woman finally chipped in with, "I was just going to ask you if you knew of any other good campsites nearby, since this lake seems so crowded."

"It looked like there was a nice spot across the creek," I said.

I watched Sara as I spoke, finding myself fascinated. Perhaps all women who have shared a man have this odd connection. It isn't often friendly, but it's there. He who has loved me has also loved you. In a strange way, I almost felt as if Sara and I were related.

These thoughts raced through my mind in short order as Lee asked me how I'd gotten across the creek.

"I didn't," I said. "I just saw a nice spot over there. I guess you'd have to wade."

I didn't quite make it to the end of this statement before Sara interrupted me. "Come on, Lee," she said. "We don't want to talk to her."

Lee looked taken aback at this piece of overt rudeness; I wasn't terribly surprised. Sara had shown herself quite capable of being rude the last time we'd spoken.

To my amazement, I found myself speaking to her. "I didn't

take Lonny away from you, Sara. I had nothing to do with the failure of your marriage. You know that.''

Why in the world I said it, I had no idea. Perhaps because it had been on my mind for years. Whatever the reason, it just came out of my mouth as though it simply needed to be said.

As I might have expected if I'd thought about it, this direct form of address triggered all the anger that Sara had been somewhat unsuccessfully bottling up.

''How dare you say that to me? If it wasn't for you, Lonny and I might have gotten back together. He might have been willing to work on our marriage. You were the reason he wouldn't.'' The words came tumbling out of Sara with a force and velocity equal to my own.

Something raw leaped inside of me. I looked her right in the eyes. ''You know as well as I do that you left Lonny. You found a boyfriend. That was the reason your marriage ended. And I know just how unhappy it was for years before that. You blame me because you don't want to look at your own failure.''

Sara's eyes flashed hot sparks at that. ''Did you ever once think what a rotten, selfish thing you were doing?'' she demanded. ''Lonny and I had a long history together. Our marriage wasn't perfect, but we could have saved it if it weren't for you.''

Sara's chin tilted up as she said it. Taking a step toward me as if she would have liked to hit me, she stopped abruptly. ''Someday you're going to find out what it feels like.'' She enunciated the words clearly. ''You're going to be the one who suffers.''

Her fine-boned face looked almost contorted, the somewhat thin-lipped mouth twisted over her teeth. I held perfectly still and wished distinctly that I'd never provoked her.

Her companion seemed as aghast as I was. ''Come on, Sara,'' she muttered. ''Let's go.''

Without a word, Sara turned and marched down the trail in

the direction from which I'd originally come. The tall woman followed her, looking back once over her shoulder.

Whew. I took a swallow of my drink as I watched them disappear up Jack Tone Canyon. I couldn't imagine a stranger encounter. Although this was a popular hiking area and Sara could be expected to know it well, having spent many summers with Lonny at Crazy Horse Creek . . . still. What odd chance had brought us to this meeting?

For a second paranoia kicked in and I wondered if Sara might have found out somehow about my solitary pack trip. A moment's reflection ruled that delusion out. Sara had been as surprised to see me as I was to see her. It had been plain on her face.

The sun had now set. I got up and made another drink, grubbed some dried fruit and more peanuts out of the pack bags, and turned my camp chair so that it looked out over the darkening lake. This was not going to be a cooking night.

One of the advantages of traveling alone—it incommoded no one if I preferred simply to eat peanuts and drink.

Roey still snoozed by the pack bags; I didn't think she'd even been aware of the two hikers. I hadn't built a fire yet, and now I wondered if I would. My neighbors' fires glowed, bright orange torches in the evening air. I could hear occasional friendly shouts and bits of music; I certainly didn't need a campfire of my own to dispel the loneliness of solitude.

I sat and watched the dark water of the lake, thinking of Sara. I wondered if she knew Lonny had moved away. Wondered how she'd feel if she knew how much I was struggling in my relationship with him. Vindicated, probably. I was getting what I deserved in her opinion, no doubt.

Taking another swallow of Jack Daniel's and water, I wondered where Sara and her friend had camped. I couldn't see their fire.

It was getting well and truly dark now. I could hear the peaceful sound of my horses cropping grass in the meadow when the neighboring campers were quiet. I'd move them along their picket lines before I went to bed so that they'd each have a fresh patch of grass to graze on.

At the thought, I heard a voice. Low and soft, almost a whisper. "Fucking horses."

At least that's what I thought I heard. I leaped up and spun around to face the trail.

A figure stood there. In the dim light I could see that it carried a backpack, with what looked like various oddments tied on here and there. Short, square, apparently male. The figure turned toward me and I could see that he had a dark beard. He stood on the trail and stared at my camp.

"What are you doing?" I demanded.

"Nothing." The same soft, low tone. "Nothing to do with you."

For a second we stared at each other. I could see the gleam of his eyes in the dim light, but I couldn't make out his expression. But surely I had heard him cursing my horses?

"You shouldn't be camped so close to the trail." His teeth showed white in the dark beard when he spoke.

"I know," I said. "There are a lot of other people here. I couldn't find a better spot."

"None of you would be here if it weren't for the damn horses. None of you could make it in here with all that stuff. Fucking horses," he said again. "Ruining the mountains."

Oh no. A genuine tree hugger, as the cowboys were apt to put it. I knew that many hikers were resentful of horsemen, but I had never run into any who cursed me openly.

The man still stood on the trail, regarding me and my camp. Slowly I made out little details of his kit. Shorts with ragged edges, what looked like a canvas rucksack—sleeping bag and pots and pans tied all over it—a floppy hat on his head. He would have presented a rather engaging gnomelike appearance, if it weren't for the animosity in his voice.

"I'm sorry," I said at last. "I know my camp's in the way here. Have a good night."

Turning, I stepped back toward my saddlebags, where the pistol was. If, God forbid, this guy was really a nut, I wanted to be able to get it out fast.

His strange voice stopped me in mid-stride. "You'd be better off leaving your horses at home," he said. "Bad things can happen to them up here. The last bunch of horses I saw were at Deer Lake. They aren't there anymore."

"What do you mean?"

"I turned them loose. People left them tied to trees and went fishing. Fucking horses were pawing the ground, tearing up the trees' roots. I turned them all loose."

"That's wicked." I edged toward my saddlebags, not turning my back on the gnome. "It's wrong for people to leave their horses tied like that; it is bad for the trees. But those horses could be hurt or killed, running around loose."

I could see him shrug. "Leave them at home then. They don't belong here. This is the most beautiful spot on earth, and the fucking livestock is ruining it."

I took one more step toward my gun. Roey woke up at the motion, lifted her head, saw the man on the trail, and gave a startled woof.

"Stay," I told her.

She subsided; the man continued to watch me. I had no idea what to say, or do, next.

He spoke again. "You got anything to drink, or smoke?"

"No," I said shortly. This was a palpable lie; I held a mug of bourbon and water in my hand. But I was damned if I was going to share my precious store of liquor with this horse hater.

"I've been in for two months now." There was a faint whine in his voice.

"Is that right?"

"I just walk around, look at things. The more I see, the more I understand."

I was standing right next to my saddlebags now, fighting the urge to get the pistol out and wave it at this guy, yelling, "Go away!"

Instead, I said, "I'm sure that's true."

"We need to ban all livestock from these mountains and most of the people. That's what it will take to save this place."

"Uh-huh." How in the hell was I going to get rid of him?

"All I carry with me is beans and rice. That's all I need." He sounded plaintive again. "Sure you don't have anything to drink?"

"I'm sure," I said. "Good night."

After a minute more staring in my direction, he turned and moved off.

Jerking my pistol out of the saddlebag, I hung it on my belt and hustled over to check the horses. They were fine. I moved them to new spots on the picket line, and then put my tent as close to them as was practical. I turned the tent so that its open doorway faced the horses and climbed inside.

Stripping my boots, jeans, and jacket off, I wiggled into the sleeping bag, and put the pistol under my folded jacket.

Damn. What an evening for company. I definitely preferred being scared of dark solitude to being over-impacted by people.

Looking out of the tent, I watched the distant glitter of stars over Wilma Lake. An image of other nomads, in other times and places, looking out of other tent doorways at the selfsame stars came into my mind. That's what I was, for now, merely another nomad. And tomorrow, I thought, I'll move on.

FOURTEEN

I left Wilma Lake early the next morning, in search of more solitude. The plan called for me to go to Benson Lake next. It would be a long day, but I could just possibly do it. Or I could stop and camp somewhere in the middle. I thought I'd decide when the time came.

Riding toward Seavey Pass, I worried about how tough the trail was going to be. En route, I had passed the cutoff trail to Tilden Lake, and wondered briefly if Blue Winter was still there, or if he, like me, was moving on. No way of knowing.

I kept riding, casting occasional glances at the sky. Unlike the previous three days, big thunderheads were building up. I could be in for some weather.

This was not a surprise. Afternoon thunderstorms during the summer in the Sierras were more the rule than the exception. I had merely been lucky so far.

Well, I had rain gear in my saddlebags. I had a tent, and a couple of tarps to cover my stuff. I'd do fine.

Gunner plodded down the trail, half-asleep. A few days in the mountains had inured him to pine forests and granite boulders. It took something more dramatic to spark his interest. Maybe thunder and lightning would do it.

Damn. I cast another glance at the rapidly graying sky. Despite my preparations, I was not looking forward to a storm. I didn't much like lightning myself. Not to mention the granite got slipperier when it was wet.

Gunner plodded on through the pines, undeterred. Plumber followed, leaning back a little on the lead rope from time to time. Roey trotted behind Plumber, accustomed to the caravan life.

I began to think about alternative destinations as the sky grew darker. Red Can Lake was maybe two miles ahead and half a mile off the trail. I would reach it in an hour or so, all going well. The only trouble was, there was no trail to it.

Lonny had told me that Red Can was a wonderful little lake, one of his favorites. But the half mile between it and the main trail was unmarked except for a few ducks.

"Ducks?" I said.

"Yeah, ducks. You know."

"No, I don't know." I'd had an odd mental image of mallard ducks squatting at strategic spots, pointing the way.

"Ducks are little stacks of rocks. People mark routes with them."

"I thought they used blazes on the trees."

"Not anymore. Forest Service doesn't like it."

"So I look for little stacks of rocks?"

"That's right." Lonny had gone on to describe the route into Red Can Lake; I thought I could remember it well enough.

"All right, I'll go there," I said out loud.

Gunner cocked an ear back at me. I looked up at the darkening sky. The wind was starting to blow—an ominous sign. I could see the granite of a steep ridge up ahead. As I understood it, Seavey Pass was at the top of that ridge, and Red Can Lake was a little way down the other side.

Without warning, Gunner spooked—a sudden, violent sideways leap. I clutched at the saddle horn and clung with my legs and stayed on, barely. I could hear the scramble of Plumber's hooves behind me, even as another noise registered. A buzzing noise. Rattlesnake.

Gunner stood still and snorted, looking at the rock from which the buzzing emanated. I straightened myself in the saddle and looked at it, too.

No sign of the snake. The rock was (now) twenty feet away, a safe enough distance. And fortunately the forest I was riding through was open; detouring around the rock would be easy. Still, if Gunner hadn't jumped when he did . . .

I stared at the rock. It was right by the side of the trail. The snake had stopped his rattling. No doubt, though, that he was coiled under that rock. If Gunner had walked past, there was a distinct chance he would have been snakebit at this point.

It wouldn't kill him, I told myself. My knowledge of rattlesnake bites in horses was sketchy and secondhand. Where I practiced, on the coast of California, rattlesnakes were rare. I had never had occasion to treat a horse who had been bitten.

Rattlesnakes were fairly common in the Sierras, though. I knew something about them, mostly through Lonny. I knew, for instance, that they had two types of bite—a fear bite and a food bite. When they struck at a large object, such as a horse or a human marching down the trail, they attacked out of fear and did not inject much venom. Thus, rattlesnake bites were seldom fatal, especially not in animals as large as a horse. A dog now, would be another thing.

I looked back. Roey was lying down just behind Plumber, showing no inclination to investigate the snake. She'd learned to rest when she could.

The worst thing about a snakebite in a horse, Lonny'd told me, is the swelling. "The horse will swell up something terrible," he said. "It's a nuisance if it's in one leg, but if the snake bites the horse on the muzzle, it can kill him because he swells so much he can't breathe."

The other thing he'd warned me about was the food bite. "That's the most dangerous. If you're climbing through the rocks and you reach your hand up on a ledge and the snake sees something small he thinks he can eat, and strikes at you, that's bad. They inject a lot more venom in a food bite."

"So, what do I do?" I asked.

"Ride out, if you can. It still won't kill you, probably. But it'll make you damn sick."

"Great."

Thinking dismally about how it would feel to embark on a two-day ride while I was deathly sick from a rattlesnake bite, I guided my caravan on a wide detour around the snake's rock.

When we were once again moving down the trail, I found I was a hell of a lot more jumpy. The sky grew darker; the wind blew.

I could see jumbled rock and a steep climb up ahead; it looked like the storm would be upon me in an hour or so. Still, I could make it to Red Can Lake, if I hurried.

Or I thought I could make it to Red Can Lake. If Seavey Pass wasn't too tough. If there were no more rattlesnakes. If I didn't get hit by a bolt of lightning. If, if, if.

Get a grip, Gail, I admonished myself. A storm is not the end of the world. And Lonny said the trail over Seavey Pass was okay.

But my mind jittered. I didn't like lightning at the best of times, and alone on a high pass on top of a steel-shod horse was not the best of times. Not to mention Lonny's idea of an okay trail and my idea of an okay trail were apt to differ greatly. Lonny rode across country in the same style in which he team roped—balls to the wall. Many times he'd told me, "Come on, this is fine," and I'd found myself on some frigging cliff.

I could see Seavey Pass ahead of me now, and it did not look good. A steep tumbled slope of boulders, it had the appearance of a giant avalanche. And the trail ran right up through the middle of it.

Reining Gunner to a stop, I stared upward. Shit. The sky was a deep, blue-violet gray. There were distant rumbles in the general direction of Nevada. The storm would be here soon.

I clucked to Gunner and started up through the rocks, feeling distinctly nervous. The trail looked reasonably well made, but the country was ungodly rough.

Gunner picked his way slowly and cautiously, allowing me to guide him. He had a characteristic I found useful: he would let me change his intended footfall in mid-stride, just by the lightest indication of the reins. Thus I could select which rocks he put his weight on.

Plumber I couldn't help much. All I could do was be sure he had plenty of slack in the lead rope when he was crossing a tricky section.

We progressed. Slowly. The wind blew my shirt away from my body, and I wondered if I should have stopped to put my rain gear on before we began the ascent. There were no places to dismount here.

Just for a second I let my concentration wander, looking away from the granite slabs of the trail and scanning the steep jumbled slope around us, the wild gray windy sky above. My God, I thought, it's beautiful. And I am really out here.

The next second I heard a horrifically loud rumble crashing above me, and my mind spun. Thunder? No. Rockfall.

"Jesus." I had time only for the one word before I saw the rocks crashing down on the trail behind us, coming from somewhere up above.

The noise was terrifying; both my horses leaped forward. Too rapid for thought or fear . . . I corrected Gunner's tendency to plunge, did my best to hold him and Plumber steady and to the trail. Rock was still falling, landing, so far, behind us; I let the horse scramble forward, keeping everything controlled as well as I could.

No time to look for the dog. No time for anything but go, go as fast as I could. Rocks pinged and clanged behind me, not so loud now. The worst of it was over.

But rock was still falling. My heart thudded in great leaping bounds. I could feel Gunner's heart thumping between my legs. My God, my God.

We clambered up the trail at the long trot. I could see Roey's small foxlike shape right on Plumber's heels. I said a brief prayer of thanks.

The last of the rocks was rattling down the canyon. Taking a deep breath, I checked Gunner down to a slower pace. Keep moving, not so fast, no need to break a leg getting away.

Up and up we went, climbing an increasingly steep trail. I could see what I thought was the top of the pass. My heart thudded steadily. I wanted off this rock slope so bad I could taste it. I didn't think I'd ever been so frightened in my life.

Eventually we topped out. I stopped for a moment and dismounted, looked both horses over carefully. Plumber had a small scrape on his right front pastern, down near the hoof. Besides that everybody seemed fine, including Roey.

Hastily I put my slicker on, mounted, clucked to Gunner, and moved out. I was well and truly spooked. Thunder boomed above me; as soon as I could find a decent spot, I was making camp.

But a decent spot demanded that it have horse feed and water, and I couldn't find one. No convenient meadows appeared by the side of the trail. The map told me that Red Can Lake, a mere quarter of a mile away as the crow flew, was my closest campsite. Next was Wood Lake, a full five miles distant, but right on the main trail.

Drops of rain spattered around us; a cold wind blew out of the heavy gray sky. I was shivering with fear and chill. Casting my eyes over the countryside around me, I recognized the landmark Lonny had told me of. "A great big fallen pine by the side of the trail, just after you top Seavey Pass. Turn off there."

Here was the fallen pine. That was it. No trail, no sign, no ducks even. Should I?

I stared off through the trees and rocks. I could get myself in a pretty bad situation out there. But I really wanted to make camp before it started pouring, and Red Can Lake was close. I went for it.

Clucking to Gunner, I guided him around the log and down the gully Lonny had described. Sure enough, in fifty feet or so, I saw a duck.

"Follow the ducks until you come to the fern meadow," Lonny had said. "From there you can see the lake."

I followed the ducks. It was easier said than done. The wind blew in fitful gusts, whipping scattered drops of rain along. The horses were antsy and uncooperative, still upset, just as I was myself. Whenever I had to stop and reconnoiter, Gunner pranced and Plumber tugged on the lead rope.

At one point I found myself on what appeared to be a pathless field of granite, my way marked only by these obscure little rock stacks. I followed where they led, hoping some practical joker hadn't moved them all last week.

I heard a crack of lightning and the accompanying roll of thunder and shivered. The rain came down more heavily, dripping steadily off the hood of my slicker. Gunner's neck was wet. My jeans were starting to soak through where they stuck out beneath my slicker.

Damn. This whole day had gone so far wrong it would be laughable, if I weren't having to cope with it. Here I was, alone in a literally trackless wilderness with a storm about to break overhead. Having just escaped a rattlesnake and some major rockfall.

Lightning flashed again; thunder rumbled almost immediately. Rain cascaded out of the sky, as if someone had suddenly turned up the shower. Visibility was getting difficult. I parked Gunner under a pine tree and stared out at the uncompromising place I'd chosen for my vacation.

Another clash of light—a huge *ka-boom*. The storm was right above. Peering through the half dark, I tried to judge whether my pine tree was the tallest one around. It was providing us with a certain amount of shelter; big drops fell on us at intervals rather than a steady barrage of wind and rain, but this would not be a worthwhile trade for being struck by lightning.

Never stand under a tree in a lightning storm, they say. I wondered again who they were. This advice was ignored by virtually everyone I knew. Who wouldn't take shelter in a downpour?

The horses stood quietly now, heads down. Water ran off them. They lifted their heads sharply at each flash and drum roll, but seemed willing enough to wait out the deluge under the tree.

In the next second my hair stood up. Lightning again, a strange green light and an eerie crackling hiss. Instantaneously, a deafening crash.

Shit. "That was too close," I told the horses. "That hit right near us." They huddled together, their eyes big. Roey was curled in a small, shivering ball at the base of the pine.

I tried to decide whether I should leave the shelter of the tree. Rain poured down in sheets; I stayed put, shivering.

The next bolt of lightning was farther away. I kept thinking about one of Ted's favorite stories—the two cowboys who had been struck by lightning as they were crossing Emigrant

Meadow. "Both their horses killed dead under them." Ted would repeat it with apparent relish.

I trembled with cold and fear and wondered what in the hell I was doing here. What had made me think I could cope with all this alone, what stupid hubris had drawn me out into this godforsaken country to what looked to be my imminent demise.

The rain was abating a little, but I still huddled under my tree, feeling helpless. Jesus, it was all just too much. I didn't feel up to dealing with it. I wanted to crawl into my nice warm bed in my cozy little house. I wanted back to civilization, pronto. I'd had enough of the wilderness.

I stared down at my small red dog, who was shivering even more than I was. Tough luck, Gail, I told myself. You chose to be here, and you have to take care of these animals. They're counting on you; you can't let them down.

"Okay, okay," I said aloud. One thing about being alone in the mountains, you get to talking out loud. "I'll persevere."

The downpour had decreased to a sprinkle; it was time to ride on. I could hear intermittent thunder a ridge or two away, but the sky was steadily getting lighter where I was. I lifted the reins gently, clucked to the horses, and called Roey.

Wet and bedraggled, we moved out, aiming for the duck I could see up ahead. Three ducks later we were in the fern meadow. Through an opening in the trees, I could see the gray, restless water of Red Can Lake. Now all I had to do was get down to it.

Once again, easier said than done. Lonny had explained to me that this was the tricky part. "Follow the ledge to a crack that runs down the rock face. It's a pretty wide crack. Just stay in it. You'll be fine. The crack will take you right down to the lake."

Lonny's directions proved accurate, but, as usual, he'd way underestimated the scary factor. I felt completely exposed, riding a horse along a granite face that looked as if it should have been reserved for rock climbers.

Gunner picked his way obediently down the crack under my direction; I could only hope Plumber would do the same. My heart thumped steadily and I cursed my own foolhardiness. Why, why, why had I ever chosen to put myself and my horses in this much danger?

The lake was just ahead of us now. I could see what Lonny meant. Despite its storm-ruffled appearance, it was truly lovely. Smaller than Snow Lake or Wilma, Red Can nestled in a granite hollow on the rim of a huge canyon. The entire shoreline was granite, except for the small green jewel of a meadow we were descending into.

The meadow was ringed by rocky gray walls on three sides and by the lake on the fourth—a proper box canyon. I could turn both horses loose here.

There was one small grove of pine trees with a little-used fire ring in the middle. I rode the horses up to it and dismounted.

The rain was over; the sky had turned a pale, misty gray. I stared around at the most perfect campsite I'd ever seen and patted Gunner on the neck.

"We made it," I said.

FIFTEEN

The next morning dawned gray, but with no actual precipitation—yet. It hadn't rained all night, either, for which I was grateful. I spent a leisurely few hours in camp, taking my time over coffee while Gunner and Plumber grazed contentedly in the meadow. I figured I'd ride to Wood Lake in the afternoon and camp there. It hadn't been part of my original plan, but what the hell. Plans were for changing.

Eventually I got everything packed back up again—no small chore. The pale, evenly gray sky had resolved itself into a pile of heavy thunderheads over the peaks, and I thought it might rain again in the afternoon. I wanted to be snug in camp at Wood Lake when the storm broke.

Getting out of Red Can turned out to be trickier than getting in. I stared at the steep crack I'd descended the day before and wondered how in hell I'd get back up. Leaving my horses tied to trees, I investigated on foot.

A closer inspection was not encouraging. As Lonny had told me, a horse had to stay in the crack. The steep granite slope on either side was slickrock, and absolutely prohibitive. Any horse who tried to clamber along there was going to fall.

I tried to decide what to do. I could lead the horses up, one at a time, hoping they would stay in the crack behind me. But there were problems with this. I had less control when I was leading them rather than riding; I couldn't really stop them from moving off the dirt onto the rock. Also, they would be anxious, separated from one another, and this might cause them to hurry.

On the other hand, if I rode Gunner and led Plumber, I wouldn't really be able to control the pack horse at all. Odds were he'd follow the saddle horse, but I couldn't be sure. And if Gunner slipped and went down, I'd go with him. Scary thought.

I stared at the crack, my heart starting to pound. There was no other way out of here. I had to go up that thing unless I planned to spend the rest of my life at Red Can Lake.

''We went down it; we can go up it,'' I said out loud, though I knew this wasn't necessarily true. Horses tend to go very slowly and carefully down steep descents, and they have an equal impulse to hurry on climbs. Trying to get some momentum up, I supposed. Whatever their reasoning, it made going up tricky spots more dangerous than going down. Down felt scarier but was actually safer. All the major wrecks I'd seen on mountain trails involved a horse or mule scrambling while climbing up a tricky piece of rock.

I couldn't stand here all day staring at it. Walking back over to the horses, I untied them and mounted. For lack of a good reason to do otherwise, I was going to do this the cowboy way.

Clucking to Gunner, I pointed him in the right direction; he started up the crack. I tried to keep a steady, gentle guidance on the reins, checking him when he hurried, aiming him toward the dirt footfalls, not disturbing his concentration. I leaned slightly forward so my weight was over his withers where he could balance it best. I kept my eyes on the crack, my concentration straight ahead. I could hear Plumber behind us; there was slack in the lead rope. I didn't look back.

We almost made it. We were near the top of the crack, right where it merged into the ledge, when it happened. The first warning I had was the tension on the end of the lead rope. I looked over my shoulder to see that Plumber had balked, unwilling to make a steep step up that Gunner had taken in stride. I clucked and tugged firmly, trying to stay calm.

Plumber hesitated and then, to my dismay, he stepped to the right, out of the crack, trying to go around the step up. I tugged on the lead rope, said "Whoa," to no avail. The little brown horse took one step on the slickrock and slipped, going down to his knees.

I let go of the lead rope; no use pulling Gunner down, too. Plumber scrambled; his shoes clanged and crashed against the rock, throwing sparks. He was up; he went down again; I thought he would surely roll to the bottom of the slope.

"Please, God, please, God." The words were loud inside my head. Somehow the little horse came up again and stood, all four feet in the crack, shivering.

"Whoa," I said out loud, trying to sound calm. What in the hell am I supposed to do now, my mind shrieked. I didn't have hold of the lead rope; I couldn't dismount. After a moment the only possible answer presented itself. I had to ride Gunner out of here and take my chances on what Plumber would do.

I clucked to my saddle horse and put some slack in the reins. He stepped up the crack. Looking back over my shoulder, I could see that Plumber was following, dragging the lead rope. I prayed he wouldn't step on it and throw himself off balance.

He didn't. We made it onto the ledge, in one piece, more or less. I dismounted and looked Plumber over carefully. He had a few scrapes and he'd lost a shoe. The scrapes were mostly minor, though one on his left front cannon bone was bleeding pretty steadily. The lost shoe, however, was a problem.

I got on and rode off the ledge into the fern meadow. Here I tied both horses up and dug some antibiotic salve and an EZ Boot out of my saddlebags. I rubbed the salve on Plumber's scrapes, and pulled the EZ Boot, an adjustable plastic boot made for this purpose, over his bare left front hoof. Then I walked back down to the crack to look for the shoe.

I found it very near the spot where Plumber had fallen. It was bent; he'd clearly stepped on it with either a back foot or his other front foot when he was scrambling. I wasn't sure what good it was going to do me. I had some minimal shoeing gear stowed in my pack, but my skills weren't really up to straightening this shoe out and nailing it back on.

In the course of my work as a veterinarian, I'd learned to pull horseshoes off. This was a necessity; in order to take X rays of the feet, I needed to remove the metal shoes, and I could hardly demand that the client do it, or expect that a horseshoer would always be handy. But pulling a shoe off was a two-minute job, requiring only minimal skill and some familiarity with the operation. Nailing a shoe back on was a good deal more difficult, and I had never done it, though I had seen it done, often.

I walked back to the horses, carrying the shoe. Plumber could wear the EZ Boot for now. Maybe he could even wear it for the rest of the trip. It was a cinch he couldn't be barefoot in this rocky country. He'd get sore right away.

Stuffing the shoe in my saddlebag, I untied the horses and climbed back on Gunner. Onward.

We retraced our route to the main trail and began descending the other side of Seavey Pass. Big vistas of granite and sky opened up in front of us. Thunderheads were piled high above the ridges, their tumbled gray masses complementing the rough gray rock below.

Beautiful, and slightly ominous, the Sierras beckoned. A siren saying come hither. I smiled to myself. Here I was, hastening to follow the call. To what end?

We went on. Once we were off Seavey Pass and in woodland again, I started to relax. No more tricky trail, and the clouds looked as though they might be breaking up. Perhaps it wouldn't rain after all.

I began to fantasize about a warm, sunny afternoon in camp at the as-yet-unknown Wood Lake. I would take a swim. Two days of no bathing had left me feeling a little grungy. Time for a wash.

The trail continued gradually descending. Wood Lake was a few miles ahead—an hour's ride.

Looking back over my shoulder, I watched Plumber for a while. He was sound, at the walk anyway. Apparently, neither his scrapes nor the lack of a shoe was causing him much grief. The EZ Boot was doing its part and staying in place. If his leg swells, I thought, I'll stand him in the cold water of the lake for a while.

Pine trees and granite, pine trees and granite. Down the trail we went, in a steady procession, Roey trotting quietly behind Plumber. I was half asleep when Gunner jumped up in the air, nearly jarring me loose. I clutched the saddle horn with one hand and jerked on the reins with the other.

"Dammit," I swore. Gunner froze.

It took me a second, but I got it. Rope under his tail. I hadn't been paying attention, and the lead rope had slipped under Gunner's tail. Plumber must have leaned back on it a little and it had become wedged up high.

Gunner was still frozen in place. Thank God. I had seen an otherwise gentle rope horse buck furiously and violently until both its rider and the rope under its tail came loose. But many horses, and Gunner appeared to be one, tended to freeze up.

I got off slowly and carefully, talking soothingly. "Take it easy, buddy, just whoa, I'll get it out, no big deal."

Patting Gunner's rump, I reached for his tail and gently pried it up. Gunner trembled, but he allowed it. I eased the rope out. Gunner snorted. His eyes were big. I patted his shoulder and told him what a good horse he was as I climbed back on, reminding myself to be more careful. Lonny had broken his shoulder when a horse bucked him off in the rocks—all because of a rope under the tail.

Fortunately my horse was not inclined to bucking. Still, a rope under the tail was just cause, and I needed to prevent it from happening.

We rode on. I stared ahead through the seemingly endless forest, looking for the openness and light that would indicate a meadow or a lake. The ground grew wetter; a stream ran along the far side of the canyon, but the low ground we were traveling on was just plain muddy.

Both Gunner and Plumber snorted and hesitated each time we had to cross a mucky spot. Like most horses, they hated mud. I kept a careful eye on Plumber, hoping he wouldn't pull the EZ Boot off.

The canyon was narrowing and I could see light ahead. The trail was also growing wetter. We scrambled through some spots that were knee-deep, both horses floundering.

I was getting nervous; I didn't like mud either. Visions of quicksand rolled around my mind. At each wet spot I balked right along with the horses, trying to determine where the footing was firmest.

Damn. The trail passed between a rocky bank and a bit of thick forest, and the crossing looked like a tar pit. Thick, gooey, black mud—churned up from all the feet that had crossed it previously. Yesterday's rain hadn't helped it any.

The horses and I stared. I felt like snorting, too. It didn't look like there was any way around. Dubiously I selected the right-hand side as being the likeliest, and urged Gunner forward. He hesitated, then lunged.

Big mistake. He sank into the mud to his shoulder; the abrupt forward motion and sudden dive to ground level pitched me off. Fortunately it wasn't far to fall. I landed easily in wet black goo and floundered to a purchase on a log. Gunner and Plumber struggled and scrambled, bogging down and heaving themselves out, until they stood on the other side of the muddy crossing. Roey trotted over to me and licked my hand.

Damn, damn, damn. Ignoring the dog, I picked my way toward the horses. At least they stood. They stood on all four feet, black with mud, but apparently okay. I remembered Lonny telling me that he thought a bog was almost as great a danger as slickrock.

Thanking God that neither horse was inclined to run off, I caught them and inspected them closely.

Shit. Damn. Son of a bitch. I wished I knew some better cuss words. Plumber had lost the EZ Boot. It was no doubt at the bottom of that bog, and I knew right away that I'd never find it. I had one more in my saddlebag, and that was it.

Cursing steadily, I climbed back on. Plumber didn't need the boot on this soft ground, and I wasn't taking a chance on losing my last one. I'd put it on him when we got to some more rock.

Mud dripped off me as I rode on. I could see light up ahead but it wasn't cheering me much. Nothing seemed to be going right. I was virtually snarling as I rode out of the trees into a meadow that fringed the shore of a lake. Wood Lake, by my reckoning. And there, camped at the edge of the forest, was Dan Jacobi and his crew.

SIXTEEN

I pulled up. My thoughts were unprintable. These were the last people I wanted to see. And there was no getting out of it. There were three men in camp, and all were staring right at me. Dan, blond Steve, and a third, shorter man with brown hair, whom I didn't recognize.

I was covered in mud, I was in a foul mood, and now I had to deal with these guys. "Hi, Dan," I said, pretty damn ungraciously.

"Howdy, ma'am." He touched his hat. "Looks like you had a little trouble with that crossing."

"I did." I knew I sounded pissed as hell.

He ran a practiced eye over my horses. "They look okay."

"I think they're all right." At this point my brain kicked in, pushing my emotions out of the way. I might not be glad to see these guys, but they could be the solution to one of my problems. "The pack horse lost a shoe," I added diffidently.

Dan nodded. "Did you find the shoe?"

"Yeah, I did."

"Bring any shoeing equipment?"

"A little. Some nails. A hammer."

Dan smiled. "If you'd like, Jim here can nail it back on. He's a shoer."

Since this was just what I was hoping for, I accepted with alacrity. "Thanks. I'd appreciate that."

Patting myself on the back for having some vestiges of intelligence, anyway, I dismounted and tied my horses up. Fishing the shoe out of the saddlebag, I handed it over.

Roey walked up to Dan, sniffed his pants leg, and wagged her tail. He reached down and scratched her absently behind the ears. "I'll need to unpack the pack horse to get at the shoeing gear," I said.

The short, brown-haired man, who was apparently Jim, ducked his chin and smiled briefly. "Don't bother. I've got some nails and stuff handy here. I'll just pound this out flat and nail it back on. Won't take a minute."

"Thank you." I looked around their camp. Two small tents, a fire with a coffeepot chugging on top of it, fishing poles leaning against the trees. Five horses were picketed alongside. Three saddle horses and two pack horses.

"So, how do you guys happen to be here?" I asked Dan.

"Oh, we decided to wander through the mountains a bit, see some more lakes."

"Did Ted go back out?"

"No." Dan looked down. "He said he was going to ride to Buck Lakes, looking for some mule that got left there."

"Oh yeah." I knew about this. "That mule got hurt pretty bad on a pack trip earlier this summer. They said they left her in the meadow at Upper Buck Lake to heal up. Ted must think he can bring her back out now."

"That's right," Dan said. "He thought she might be healed up enough to travel."

I kept my eyes on Dan as we talked, but I was aware that

Steve was watching me with an expression somewhere between hostility and avarice. Not surprisingly, in view of my mud-covered clothes, he also looked amused. No doubt, I thought glumly, there was also mud in my hair and on my face.

Nothing I could do about it now. Pride forbade my scrubbing at myself with the tail of my shirt. I held my head up and looked Steve in the eye. I didn't give a fuck what he thought of me, anyway.

"You look like you could use some help," he said.

I heard the sneer in his voice and worked at remaining detached. "I'm doing all right," I told him.

"A woman doesn't belong out here all by herself."

I shrugged. Judging by his tone, no answer I could have made to this would sink in. I'd met men like Steve before. For some reason, the combination of my competence and lack of sexual interest in them was threatening. They always reacted with hostility, and they were always a pain in the butt.

Though I don't consider myself a feminist, I have a short fuse with the Steves of this world. I'm an individual; I don't feel any more invested in the fact that I'm female than in the fact that I'm a veterinarian, and own horses, and am tall. Whatever. I've never felt that being a woman held me back in any way, and I've dealt with a lot of good old boys.

In my opinion, good old boys mostly respected competence, and if I was competent with a horse and knew my medicine, they noticed it and figured I was all right. I'd heard some women say that "a woman shouldn't have to prove herself just because she's a woman," but I thought that was bullshit. When it comes to fields where there is some risk, where skill is necessary for survival, everybody has to prove themselves. The new guy and the new gal are regarded with almost equal suspicion.

And if the new gal was regarded with a little more suspicion, at least in my line of work, it mostly came down to a simple bottom line. Men are, generally speaking, physically stronger than women. And physical strength is a big asset when you're working with horses.

Fortunately, I'm pretty strong. And I didn't resent people's preference for a vet who could deal competently with all the physical stuff that came along. But once in a while I ran into a Steve. And they were different.

I looked at him now, while various thoughts floated through my mind. Blond, handsome, in his twenties, a white straw cowboy hat on his head, a small butt encased in blue denim, mean brown eyes. Had I flirted with him, he would have acted friendly toward me. But the meanness would still have been there. The Steves of this world just don't like women.

That didn't mean they didn't want to bed them. Guys like this seemed to regard women as prey, scoring them off as notches on the belt.

I stared at Steve's belt, adorned with a holster. This guy was carrying a pistol. I glanced around the camp. No other guns in evidence. Neither Dan nor Jim, who was bent over nailing the shoe on my horse, was wearing a holster.

I looked back at Dan curiously. If I were him, I wouldn't want any help as surly and insolent as Steve carrying a gun.

Dan met my eyes easily. He'd watched my brief interchange with Steve, and he'd seen me notice the gun. None of it seemed to bother him in the slightest.

The man intrigued me. "I ran into Blue Winter," I said.

"Is that right?" Dan appeared mildly interested.

I waited.

Dan smiled. "Don't tell me. He told you all about the dun horse and how he didn't really steal him."

"That's right." Dan said nothing.

After a minute, I asked him, "Do you think he owes you money?"

Dan Jacobi had a poker player's face. Or, for that matter, a horse trader's face. Nothing flickered, nothing changed. "You only know what Blue told you," he said.

I took that in. It was true enough.

"I wouldn't listen to Blue Winter, if I were you," he went on. "I'd be real careful about that guy. He tells you what he wants you to hear."

I stared at him. Two days of struggling through the mountains had pretty much driven everything else out of my mind. In a rush, I remembered all my speculations about Bill Evans.

"Are you telling me you think Blue Winter is dangerous?" I asked Dan.

He shrugged one shoulder. "I'm telling you I don't trust him."

The words had a note of finality. Dan Jacobi turned away from me and went over to inspect the job that Jim was doing on Plumber. This left me face to face with Steve.

Before I could move or flinch, Steve stepped forward until his face was two feet from mine. Reaching a hand out, he dragged a finger across my chin.

I leaped backward and Steve grinned. Holding his hand up so I could see it, he drawled, "Just wiping off a little mud."

Shit. This guy was really a loose cannon. I turned away without a word. I did not want to provoke Steve, not out here in the middle of nowhere.

Plumber's shoe was nailed back on, nice and neat. I thanked Jim and then thanked Dan as I untied my horses and mounted Gunner.

"So where are you off to?" Dan asked me.

"Oh, Buck Lakes, I guess." This was an outright lie. I'd never intended to go to Buck Lakes, and was even less inclined to do so now that I'd heard Ted was there. Some miles past

Wood Lake, the trail forked. Here I planned to take the trail to Benson Lake. But I saw no reason to tell Dan that.

He smiled at me. "Good luck, then."

"Thanks. And you, too."

I clucked to my horses and rode off, thinking with relief that the whole thing had not gone too badly. Steve was downright scary, but Plumber was shod again and I hadn't told anyone where I was headed.

Trouble was, I'd meant to camp at Wood Lake, but I did not want another visit from Dan Jacobi, or more particularly, from Steve. As soon as I was out of sight of their camp, I dug my map out of the saddlebag and looked at it.

As I'd remembered, Wood Lake was a very long, narrow lake—almost a mile long. It had two small, round bulbs at either end with a channel connecting them. Dan and crew were camped at one of the bulbs. If I rode all the way down to the other, I ought to be far enough away that they'd neither see nor hear me.

I rode. The trail followed the side of the lake. I could look down into the clear water and see big brookies swimming along.

Wood Lake was well named. It was in the woods, all right. Aside from the small meadow where Dan Jacobi had been camped the trees came right down to the lakeshore everywhere. I crossed my fingers that there would be a decent campsite down at the other end.

And there was. The far end of the lake, when I finally reached it, formed another circular bowl. The forest sloped down to it for about half its circumference; the other half was rocks and a brief spit of meadow. There was a fire ring in a flat area amongst the rocks and enough feed for one evening anyway. I tied my horses up and started making camp.

Owing to my leisurely morning, assorted wrecks, and bout of horseshoeing, it was now late afternoon. The clouds had disappeared and the sun poured into the far end of Wood Lake with a low golden slant; pine trees and cedars on the ridge stood erect, blue-green shoulders stiff and military, each needle outlined with light. Light sparks glittered on the water of the lake, and all in the world I wanted to do was peel my clothes off and go for a swim.

But camp needed to be built. Dutifully, I unsaddled the horses, put Gunner on a picket line and turned Plumber loose to graze, and began setting up my tent. One by one, I did the familiar chores. By the time I'd finished gathering firewood, building a fire, and pumping water, the sun was behind the ridge and the lake didn't look so inviting. What I needed, I decided, was a drink.

I made myself one and sat down in my chair to enjoy it. Putting my feet up on a rock, I sighed. The last two days had been difficult, to say the least. But we were in one piece, and it felt good to be in camp this evening. All in all, I wouldn't complain.

I made and drank another drink, then heated a can of chili for dinner. Two more logs on the fire, and I leaned back in my chair, alternately watching the flames and reading Thoreau. Slowly the light died out of the sky. I could barely see the print on the page.

Setting a manzanita root on the campfire, I stretched and sighed. Mosquitoes hummed fiercely around me as dark drew in. So far on this trip they hadn't been much of a problem, but the low, boggy country around Wood Lake appeared to be an ideal breeding ground.

I'd smeared mosquito repellent on my face, neck, and hands earlier; now I pulled the hood on my sweatshirt up over my head and tied it under my chin. I wasn't getting bitten much—the repellent kept the little buggers at bay—but the noise was starting to drive me crazy.

A high-pitched whine like an engine gone berserk, or a swarm of angry bees, the mosquito hum seemed to fill the evening. It was a nervous sort of sound and always made me antsy. The sweatshirt hood blocked a lot of it.

I stared out at the glossy, darkening lake, then back at the bright flames of my fire. Sweet manzanita smoke, like incense, filled the air. It was a warm night. Suddenly the water looked inviting again.

Why not? It was too dark for anybody—Steve, Dan, or whoever—to be stumbling around the mountains. I could count on being private here. I walked down to the lakeshore. Roey followed me.

Peeling off my boots, jeans, sweatshirt, tank top, and underwear, I waded in. The dog whined anxiously on the shore behind me.

Wood Lake was a warm lake, and the water seemed to be the same temperature as the night air. When I was waist-deep, I made a short, shallow dive and started swimming.

The water felt wonderful against my skin. Cool black silk, soft and shiny and unbelievably sensuous. I floated on my back for a moment, seeing the dark pine tree tops sketched against the deep midnight-blue of the sky—and one star. The evening star. Venus herself.

Mosquitoes buzzed around my ears and I rolled and dove, blocking out the world with cool water. After a few more leisurely strokes, I swam back to shore to pacify the dog, who was most unhappy. Roey swam when she thought it appropriate; apparently swimming in this lake at night didn't seem right to her.

Patting her head, I dripped my way back to camp and stood by the fire. As I dried myself gradually in its heat, swatting at mosquitoes meanwhile, a nearly full moon rose above the ridge, with a few pine boughs traced against it. Smoke curled up from my campfire and drifted across the moon. A witch's night.

I toweled the rest of the dampness off my body, checked the horses, and crawled into my sleeping bag. Looking at my fire and the moon over the lake, I felt content. It was the last peaceful night I would spend in the mountains.

SEVENTEEN

I left Wood Lake early the next morning, determined to put some distance between myself and Dan Jacobi's crew. If I never ran into Steve again, it would be just fine with me.

Cinching the pack rig down with numb hands, I swore under my breath. Leisurely mornings in camp were more my speed; I was no big fan of this move-out-early stuff. Still, I swung stiffly aboard Gunner and pointed my entourage down the trail just as the first pale gleams of sunlight filtered over the ridge.

Today, I thought, I'll make it to Benson. I'd heard about Benson Lake for years—the Riviera of the Sierras, one guide-book called it. It featured a long white sand beach, unusual for a High Sierra lake. I had every intention of taking a sunbath on that beach.

Dan Jacobi thought I was headed for Buck Lakes. Ted was at Buck Lakes. If I wanted to avoid company, I would just avoid Buck Lakes.

The trail to Benson was also the route to Upper and Lower Buck Lakes, for the first seven miles, anyway. However, whichever direction they were headed, I strongly suspected Dan Jacobi and his boys would not get an early start.

They were probably warm right now, though. I pulled some light polypropylene gloves out of the pocket of my jacket and worked my numb hands into them. The sun's coming up, I encouraged myself. In an hour or so, you'll take your jacket off.

I rode down the trail, letting my mind drift. According to the elevation lines on my map, this trail wound through relatively level forest land for several miles. Should be easy riding. Good for a pilot who was still half-asleep.

The banality of my thoughts always surprised me. Alone in the mountains, with the new sunlight poking encouragingly through the branches of the pines and cedars, my mind kept turning incessantly to my hair. Should I cut it? Would I look more attractive with some short, sleek style? I'd worn my hair long, mostly in a ponytail or braid, for years. Maybe I needed a change.

Don't be ridiculous, I chastised myself; think about Thoreau, for God's sake. Think about solitude. Don't think about your hair. Was I about to become one of those sad, desperate middle-aged women who persistently wear too much makeup and too-tight clothes and routinely change their hairstyle in order to appear sexually attractive to men? God, I hoped not.

So why, then, did my mind constantly want to dwell on whether I should try to lose ten pounds? What was going on somewhere deep in my psyche that these odd insecurities popped into my head whenever I wasn't actively engaged in thinking about something else?

Maybe the prospect of breaking up with Lonny. Once again I was surprised. Was I really thinking of breaking up with Lonny? I'd never allowed myself to voice those words before.

Was all this mental nattering about whether I was attractive to do with the fact that I wanted a new sexual partner?

The woods slipped by me unseen, as I tried to decide if this was true. Lonny was part of my life and I loved him, but I was aware that my frustration with him was growing.

I rode. Little puffs of dust rose under Gunner's feet; the air grew drier and warmer. I unzipped my coat and peeled the gloves back off and stuffed them in my pocket. We still had quite a ways to go before we hit the cutoff trail to Benson.

The forest was peaceful in the sunshine, the sturdy pillars of trees thick around us, the warming air filled with the sharp, resinous smell of pines softened by trail dust. Lulled by the stillness and my thoughts, I paid no attention to the warning.

Bees buzzing. I heard it, but it didn't register. In some faraway corner of my mind I filed the sound under honeybees-in-the-garden, a pleasant, innocuous noise. Forgetting that I was in the middle of a pine forest, not the ideal habitat for honeybees.

Suddenly Gunner jumped. I grabbed the saddle horn and looked quickly to see if the rope was under his tail. No. But there were a couple of bees buzzing around him.

Plumber snorted and lunged forward and the buzzing sound intensified. Bees everywhere. Shit. Yellow jackets, not honeybees, and I must have disturbed a nest.

''Damn!'' A red-hot stab in the neck as a wasp stung me. Clinging to the horn as Gunner plunged forward, I clucked to him and kicked his ribs, my one thought to get out of there.

We hit the high lope, Plumber in tow, buzzing yellow jackets swirling around us. I yelped as another sting nailed my wrist, and Gunner crow-hopped in the middle of a stride, pissed as hell.

Clinging to the horn, I thumped on his ribs with my heels. ''Don't buck, run,'' I urged him.

He lunged forward again, just as a wasp stung my forearm. I let go of Plumber's lead rope. The forest was thick around us, no possible escape route but the trail. A big tree leaned

148

across it just ahead. There was room to pass underneath, barely.

Another wasp stung me and I kicked Gunner fiercely, ducking my head as we scrambled under the tree, pushing through branches.

Whump—everything moved, earth shook—a branch cracked across my face like a whip. Dust rose in a cloud.

Disoriented by noise and violent motion, I pulled Gunner up sharply. The tree had dropped like a sledgehammer just behind us, missing Gunner and me by a foot, no more. My God, my God. Where was Plumber? Where was Roey?

My heart drummed frantically. A random wasp stung my arm; I barely felt it. I stared at the heavy trunk and tangle of branches blocking the trail, paralyzed with fear.

A shrill nicker. Plumber was alive, anyway. Was he down? Hurt? I couldn't see him.

I took a step toward the fallen tree and saw a small, neat brown head, ears up, eyes wide, peering at me over the foliage. Plumber. On all four legs and just fine.

"Roey," I called weakly.

The red dog scampered through the branches toward me, wagging her tail. I nearly fell off Gunner in a collapse, the relief was so great.

"Jesus," I said out loud.

What an incredible piece of luck. We had crossed under half-down trees many times on this trip; some of them had obviously bridged the trail for long years before we passed along the way. This tree looked like it had just tipped over. Had it not been for the yellow jackets, I might have inspected it more carefully before I pushed my way through. I might have noticed how unstable it was. On the other hand, had Gunner and I not been moving at the lope, the tree probably would have fallen squarely on us.

The thought caused a visceral shudder. We would be dead. Or very badly hurt, at the very least.

Don't go there, I urged myself. The problem is what to do now. Deal with it.

Thankfully the wasps had dispersed. Either the falling tree had upset them, too, or we were just far enough away from the nest we'd inadvertently disturbed.

"What I need to do now," I said out loud, "is catch Plumber and get him around this tree."

The sound of my own voice sounding calm and logical was reassuring. I climbed down off Gunner and tethered him to a pine branch, noticing that he had several welts on his shoulders and rump. God, I hoped he didn't start into an allergic reaction.

I walked back toward the tree and my other horse, Roey at my heels.

The pine lay squarely across the trail. It was about two feet in diameter—not an enormous tree, but plenty big enough to do some serious damage. Belatedly it occurred to me that had I not let go of the lead rope during our flight from the yellow jackets, Plumber would probably have been much closer on Gunner's heels. The tree would have landed on him.

And Roey had been saved because she'd developed the habit of tracking along right behind Plumber. Even in the confusion, she'd dutifully followed the pack horse. Thank God.

I stared at the tree, which now presented a fairly major obstacle. The trunk bridged the trail at about chest height on a horse—too high to jump or step over. And the thick tangle of stiff branches looked impenetrable. I walked toward the stump end, and stopped dead.

Someone had chopped this tree down. I could clearly see the marks of the ax. The butt end, rather than being ripped and splintered, as it would be if it had fallen naturally, showed the short, sharp indentations of an ax blade. I could smell fresh pine sap.

"What the hell?" Now why in God's name would someone choose to chop a pine down here and leave it. For firewood? I stared around at the forest. Ridiculous. There were downed branches everywhere, and no fire ring to mark a campsite. No obvious spot to camp, either.

I found a route around the fallen tree, and walked toward Plumber, who was nosing at the branches. Had the tree been partially down, and some traveler decided to cut it all the way down with the notion of making it safer? And if so, why leave it hanging precariously over the trail?

Cursing backpackers in general, perhaps unjustly, I caught my horse, who seemed perfectly fine. Leading him on a convoluted route between tree trunks, I guided us back to the trail and Gunner, staring at the downed pine malevolently the whole time.

It was pissing me off. What a stupid, stupid thing to do. Fear receded, anger pumped through my veins. I wanted to throttle the bastard who had almost killed me and my horses.

With a last glance at the tree, I mounted Gunner and started back down the trail. There was nothing I could do about it now.

I rode, looking around with considerably more attention than I had earlier. The hell with how attractive I was, or wasn't. I just wanted to survive.

Another mile of forest, with the trail ascending gradually, and I rode into a small, scrubby, much-eroded meadow that the map called Groundhog Meadow. I stared at the obscure little elevation lines on the paper. Just ahead was Cherry Creek Canyon, which looked big and steep. And after that, the cutoff trail to Benson.

I clucked to the horses and rode on, hoping the trail would be okay through Cherry Creek Canyon.

It wasn't bad. I emerged from a small stand of cedars out into rock with the full panorama of the canyon spread out in front of me.

Wow. Like a softer, more silvery version of the Grand Canyon, Cherry Creek Canyon cut a mile-wide swath through

151

rocky country—a great, deep gorge. I could see glimpses of Cherry Creek itself down in the bottom.

The view was incredible—also the exposure. But the trail seemed well made, blasted right into the rock in the tricky spots. Gunner and Plumber picked their way along, old hands at clambering down granite slopes. I tried to enjoy the scenery.

Wind blew along the slopes of the canyon, fingering the pine boughs with long sighs. The sky was a bright and cloudless blue. A vast emptiness seemed to radiate outward from a gray granite center.

On we went, one switchback at a time. The slope grew steeper. Looking straight down, I could see Cherry Creek, many distant feet away, immediately under my right stirrup. I could also see what looked like a bridge down there.

God, the exposure was severe. If my horse slipped here, he'd be dead for sure. And me, too, if I stayed with him. I took my feet out of the stirrups. If I had to jump off, I would.

We approached another hairpin turn, with a cliff beyond. The wind whistled in the rocks. Gunner moved carefully, one step at a time, seeming aware of the danger. I tried to keep my focus on the trail, not the drop.

Wind moved in a grove of pine saplings as we started into the turn. Gunner stepped down over a rock. With a *whoosh*, something yellow blew into his face. A slicker, for God sake.

For one heart-stopping moment I felt his body tense to spring and thought he would jump. I yelled, "Whoa!"

He trembled; a sapling waved wildly; the slicker landed on the ground at his feet. Gunner stared at it—ears pointed forward, eyes big. He snorted; I could feel his heart thumping. Mine, too.

A bright yellow slicker. Where the hell had it come from? I looked at the drop under my right foot, and said another silent prayer of thanks. Gunner had had enough faith in me to listen to my "whoa" in the face of this new danger. And/or enough sense not to jump when a jump would have killed us all.

The slicker lay next to his left foreleg. Gently I urged him past it, watching to see that Plumber followed. Two switchbacks down, the trail leveled out into a grove of pines. Finding a spot, I tied both horses and walked back up the hill to the slicker.

This isn't right. The words echoed in my mind as I approached the yellow object. A very ordinary rubber rain jacket. I picked it up. Yes, that was what I thought I'd seen. White string. The slicker had a piece of string attached to it. And the string ran up to the tip of one of the pine saplings and was tied there.

Bending down, I investigated further and found two small pieces of wood that looked like they'd been carved with a pocketknife. The trigger. This was, in fact, a snare.

A little more searching revealed the string that had been drawn across the trail. I stared down at it. Someone had rigged the slicker to be a horse-spooker. He had tied it to the sapling, bent the sapling back, and attached it to the carved hook of the trigger. The other string had also been attached to the trigger and then pulled tight across the trail. When Gunner broke it, the trigger flew loose, releasing the pine, which had flung the slicker in our direction.

I looked down at the drop. Someone had rigged this horse-spooking trap on perhaps the most dangerous corner on the entire descent. Someone had meant business.

But against whom? Anyone who passed along this trail was a possible victim. I wasn't necessarily the target.

Could it be some sort of bizarre joke? Or maybe . . . I froze. The fallen tree. I hadn't looked, hadn't considered. The same sort of trigger might have existed. When I brushed through the branches, I had set off a deadfall trap.

In that second I was sure of it. There was no other reason for that freshly chopped pine to be suspended so precariously across the trail. And now this.

These traps were both geared to horses. Oh my God. A crazed backpacker out here with an ecological bee in his bonnet. Rid the mountains of horses . . . now. And I had met the guy back at Wilma Lake. Was it possible?

Slowly I retraced my steps back to the horses, Roey trotting at my heels. If these traps were not the work of an irrational horse hater, then why?

I untied Gunner and climbed back on him, feeling confused, frightened, and undirected. The one thing I did not want to do was run into the author of these traps. But I had no idea if he, she, or they were ahead of me or behind me. Or if more booby traps were waiting.

Keeping my eyes on the trail, I rode on, scanning for string or twine, anything that looked unnatural. Periodically, I ran my eyes over the rocks, looking for color, listening for voices. Was someone out here, hunting me? And if so, why?

The whole thing was beyond belief. Like a bad dream, full of odd and frightening events with no reasonable explanation.

Gunner was walking down the trail, nearing the bottom of Cherry Creek Canyon, and I was looking for snipers. The chatter of the creek grew louder; I could see the white water flashing in the sun. And there was the bridge.

Not as high or long as the one near the pack station, it was still a scary proposition. Particularly in the mind-set I was in. I felt totally exposed and vulnerable as Gunner approached the landing.

He snorted, stopped, bowed his neck. I kicked him in the ribs. ''Come on, get on with it.''

Gunner lowered his head until his muzzle touched the wooden planks. He snorted again. I kicked harder. ''Come on.''

I could feel his body tense up. The harder I kicked, the firmer he felt. I thumped him a good one, and he took a step. Backward.

There he stood, planted rigidly. Nothing I could do, including whacking him with the end of the lead rope, budged him at all. Gunner, obedient throughout the trip, flatly refused to cross this bridge. Something was wrong.

EIGHTEEN

I wouldn't normally take a horse's refusal to cross an obstacle as anything other than disobedience arising out of natural fear. But I was spooked. I'd run into two booby traps this morning. What if this bridge were another?

Rather than slapping Gunner again with the rope, I sat frozen in the saddle, staring at the bridge with eyes as big as his. What if? What if something were wrong? Gunner had crossed bridges before, including the much scarier bridge over Deadman Creek. Of course, he'd never seen this particular bridge; he might be balking because of the novelty factor. But still.

I didn't hit him again. Instead, I rode him over to some trees by the side of the trail, and tied him and Plumber up. Taking a length of twine out of my saddlebag, I tied Roey nearby. I didn't want her following where I was going. Then I set out to explore the bridge.

Walking onto it was not an option. If something were really wrong, I couldn't take the chance. Gingerly, I worked my way down the bank, trying to see underneath the structure. The bank was no sheer cliff, but it was pretty damn steep. As soon as I lowered myself five or six feet down it, I regretted my choice.

I'm no rock climber. I have no innate ability to cling limpetlike to granite faces, teasing out delicate holds with my fingertips. The whole idea gave me vertigo. Scrambling down this bank, with a fifty-foot drop to the noisy creek below, was scaring me big-time.

Trying to keep my mind on the task at hand, I got a stable foothold on a large flat shelf, and clung with both hands to a couple of bombproof holds. Then I leaned out, peering up at the underside of the bridge structure.

Nothing. Beams and boards, arranged in an orderly fashion, just as one would expect. No loose ends dangling, no fresh saw marks. I stared at the bridge. It looked fine.

Maybe Gunner was full of shit. Maybe he just didn't like the look of this particular bridge. I gave the planks one more cursory evaluation, and started to haul myself up the rocks. I would get back on my horse and we would go across this damn bridge.

I was about to climb up onto the trail when something caught my eye. A different color. Right under my hand. A little patch of golden-pink dust.

I stared; I picked up a pinch of the stuff and smelled the unmistakable tang of fresh sawdust.

My eyes shot back to the bridge. Slowly, I lowered myself back down the bank where I could see beneath the structure. Still nothing obvious. But there was some mud on the two main supporting beams, near where they connected to the landing. Mud that looked fairly fresh.

How in the hell did that mud get there? Had someone sawed through those beams, filled the notches with mud so they wouldn't show, and climbed back up the bank, carrying some sawdust on their clothes or shoes? It was impossible for me to work my way over to the bridge without a rope; the bank was too steep. If someone had undermined the beams, they must have had a support rope to hang from.

Slowly I climbed back up to the trail. Now what? It was the flimsiest of speculations, and yet, I couldn't ignore it. A tree had fallen almost on top of me this morning. The horse-spooking slicker had definitely been a snare. I could not afford to assume this bridge was all right.

I walked back over to the horses. Plumber nickered at me. I patted him, and then Gunner. Gunner turned his head to look at me, and I rubbed his forehead. "You trusted me," I said out loud. "Now I'm gonna trust you."

Dragging my map out of the saddlebag, I studied it. I could still get to Benson Lake, but it was a long damn way around.

I looked back at the bridge. Maybe this was all a bunch of foolishness, but how could I know? The bridge looked solid and respectable in the midday sunshine. My eyes roved the landscape. No one in sight. Just trees and rocks.

Rocks. I laughed out loud. "That's it," I told the horses. "Rocks."

I picked up a handy boulder, lugged it over to the bridge, and pitched it on board. Fifty pounds, more or less. A couple of dozen of these and I'd have twelve hundred pounds on the structure—about what Gunner weighed. If the bridge would hold the rocks, it would hold us.

Carrying rocks was time-consuming and sweaty. I stripped down to my tank top and thought longingly of a swim in Benson Lake. The lake was only a couple of miles away, if I could get across this bridge.

Another rock. The granite was gritty and dusty and abraded my hands and wrists. I lugged another boulder over, and rolled it onto the bridge. I had quite a pile of them out there now. If I was right, the bridge was undermined right next to the bank that I stood on; the rocks were on top of the weak place.

Five more and I would reach my target number of twenty-four. I selected a particularly large boulder. Well over fifty pounds. My biceps ached as I toted it to the bridge. I half rolled it, half pitched it forward and started to turn away.

A long, moaning creak, and the rending shriek of wood tearing. I jerked around. As if in slow motion, the bridge ripped free from its moorings. With a crashing, echoing boom, it twisted and fell, slamming against the opposite bank, wood shards flying.

I stepped to the horses, grabbing their lead ropes. Both were snorting, eyes big. The bridge broke apart, shattering against rocks and bank. Dust rose, wood splintered, noise reverberated off the canyon walls. The whole structure collapsed into the gap it had once spanned.

I gazed disbelievingly at the wreckage. It couldn't be. But it was. The bridge had been booby-trapped.

Implications sank in, one by one. My heart raced at a steady pace as I dug my pistol out of my saddlebag and fastened the holster to my belt. I unsnapped the leather strap that held the hammer down and rested my hand on the butt for a second.

Some crazy lunatic was out here in these mountains. He had to have undermined the bridge from the bank I was on. Therefore if I retraced my route, I was riding right toward him.

There was no other choice. I untied the horses and the dog and mounted Gunner, keeping an eye on the cliff I was about to go back up. The saboteur was out there somewhere. But I had to get back to the ridge.

I clucked to my entourage and started up the trail, planning my new route as I went. I would head back toward the pack station by the shortest possible route. The dangers of the backcountry were one thing, booby-trapped trails were entirely different. I wanted out.

Trouble was, any way I figured it, the pack station was three days' hard ride from here. There weren't any shortcuts.

I scanned the steep walls of Cherry Creek Canyon, wondering who in hell could possibly be booby-trapping the trail, and why. For the first time in my life, I wished earnestly that a forest ranger would appear.

No such luck. The mountains remained ominously silent; the cry of a hawk circling in the blue was the only sound.

This can't be happening. My mind repeated the words uselessly and frantically. I tried to focus my attention in wide-ranging sweeps over the trail and surrounding rocks.

Twenty minutes later, I was most of the way to the ridge when I saw motion up above me on the trail. Gunner saw it, too. He lifted his head, ears straight forward, and neighed.

We both heard the answering neigh. I craned to get a glimpse of the horse and rider, torn between fear and hope.

A brief flash of tawny color behind a rock and then a gray hat and a blue denim shirt were visible. I stared. Blue Winter blocked the trail above me.

"Well, hi, Stormy," he said.

NINETEEN

My hand flew automatically to the butt of my gun. I looked at the man in front of me, saw his eyes follow the motion of my hand, saw them widen slightly. I said nothing. He said nothing.

I kept watching him, waiting for some sign that would indicate whether I was facing a friend or a foe. I could not imagine why Blue Winter would set booby traps for me, but let's face it, I barely knew the man. Dan Jacobi had told me not to trust him. And here he was, blocking my route away from the bridge.

"You look upset," he said at last.

I pondered my reply. "The bridge is out," I said finally.

"You're kidding."

"No, I'm not." I waited, not volunteering any information.

"Damn. Now why would it wash out at this time of year?"

I said nothing. If Blue Winter had set the trap, I was better off appearing ignorant. He would then have no reason to consider me a threat.

His eyes rested quietly on me. "It's a long way around."

"I was just figuring that out."

He glanced at the sky. "I'd say it was about three o'clock."

Sure enough, he wasn't wearing a wristwatch either.

He looked back at me, appearing to consider his next words. After a minute, he said, "Were you going to Benson?"

I said nothing. Once again, my mind was racing around in frantic circles, like a rabbit with a cat on its tail. What should I tell him? Why had he asked that?

Blue Winter shrugged. "You can get by me here, if you like."

"All right." I clucked to Gunner and started up the hill. As he'd said, there was room for the horses to pass each other where he stood.

I rode on until we were face to face. He looked at me; I stared right back at him. I was aware, as I had been before, of a sense of inner stillness. His eyes, steady and gray, stayed on my face without a flicker. I wished I could read his mind.

Carefully, I worked my little pack string by his, watching him meanwhile. He didn't move, merely sat like a statue. His dun horse sniffed noses briefly with Gunner; the freckled dog wagged her tail but remained lying down beside a rock, where he'd told her to stay.

I called Roey to heel as we passed, then looked back over my shoulder. Shit. He was turning his saddle horse around, obviously intending to follow me.

He met my eyes. "Looks like we're going the same way," he said.

Oh, great. Once again my hand went automatically to the gun on my belt, but I jerked it quickly away. It wouldn't do me any good, with this guy dead behind me. I would have to gut this out.

If Blue Winter was the lunatic who had set the traps, I would be safest if I seemed not to suspect him. In the interests of which, I ought to act friendlier. But I was finding it hard to do. Riding up Cherry Canyon with a potential killer on my heels was raising my anxiety level to new highs. Chatting seemed impossible.

He might have nothing to do with it, I reminded myself. He might simply have been riding from Tilden Lake to Benson Lake, a very typical route. Tilden and Benson were two of the biggest lakes in this part of the backcountry.

On the other hand, someone had definitely booby-trapped the bridge. And Blue Winter was the someone who was here. A worst-case scenario that kept intruding into my mind involved the notion that he knew perfectly well how I'd escaped going down with the bridge. He'd been sitting up on the ridge watching me through binoculars while I piled rocks. He'd come along prepared to silence me, and was just taking his time.

Damn, damn, and damn. Visions of violent death and nightmares of rape fled through my head; I tried to push them aside, tried to concentrate on the present moment. This man had never struck me as threatening, and usually, my intuition was good. I tried to believe he might be an innocent bystander.

But with each clink of shod hooves on stone, my fear grew. I wanted to get away from this guy. I felt trapped and scared and desperate with him riding behind me.

Risking a glance back over my shoulder, I saw that he was a polite twenty feet or so behind my pack horse. I could see no sign of a gun on him, but that didn't mean he didn't have one in his saddlebags.

I looked back up the trail. We were nearing the ridge. Not far ahead was Groundhog Meadow, where there was a branch trail. There was also a creek. I would stop in Groundhog Meadow, get off, water my horses, and wait until Blue Winter rode on, then I would take another direction. Any direction but the trail he took.

Blocking my mind to the fear that he wouldn't let me go, I

rode toward the grove of cedars on the rim of the canyon. Groundhog Meadow was just beyond.

Gunner's head bobbed gently in front of me with every stride; I could feel gentle tugs through the lead rope as Plumber trooped along behind. Business as usual. It was hard to believe there was some sort of crazed lunatic on my tail.

I was in the cedars now; I could see the light and openness ahead that was Groundhog Meadow. The creek was on the far side—a little trickle with numerous potholes. I would ride to it and stop. If need be, I'd just camp there. I'd run Blue Winter off with the gun, if I had to.

My heart thudded in a steady, frightened tattoo as I envisioned the scene that might be coming. But I was not, I was damned well not, going to keep riding with this man behind me.

We were in the meadow now, the trail dusty beneath Gunner's hooves. Without a word, I veered off the beaten track, headed for the creek. As we neared it, Gunner's ears went forward and he lengthened his stride; he was thirsty.

Roey scampered past me, the little freckled dog running along with her. Both dogs waded into the nearest pothole and paddled around, lapping water as they swam. I wished I could do the same.

I looked over my shoulder. Blue Winter was following me. Well, what did I expect? Maybe he only wanted to water his horses.

I rode Gunner into the creek and stopped. Plumber crowded alongside and I let both horses drink. Blue Winter went a few feet downstream and watered his livestock. Neither of us said a word.

When my horses were finished drinking, I rode them across the creek and over to a small grove of pines near the rocky edge of the meadow. It would be adequate as a campsite if I had to stay. I dismounted and tied the horses up.

Damn, damn, and damn. Blue Winter was following suit, dismounting and tying his stock. What in the hell was going on?

Once again, my hand went automatically to the butt of my gun, but I jerked it away. No use making trouble I didn't need to have. I started walking toward the creek.

Out of the corner of my eye, I could see him walking toward me and I stopped, facing him. Nothing in his body language or demeanor gave me a clue to his thoughts. He looked removed, aloof, and big, very big.

I tipped my chin up in order to meet his eyes as he neared me. Jesus, this guy was tall. Despite my resolution, something of the fear I felt must have shown on my face, because Blue Winter stopped dead. Eyes locked, we stood like statues.

"What's the matter with you?" He said it quietly.

I had no idea what to say. "I just want to be alone." Nothing like the truth.

"Fine, no problem. You'll be alone as soon as I have a drink."

We stood still, staring at each other. He took a step forward and I flinched.

"Jesus." He shook his head. "I'm just going to get a drink out of the creek, okay?"

He took another step and reached a hand toward my shoulder. I jerked sharply sideways, avoiding his grip. Instantaneously, I heard a loud crack.

For a split second nothing made sense. Blue and I stood frozen in place, while echoes bounced off the rocks. That was a shot, my brain chanted.

Crack!

"Shit!" Blue took three running steps and dove into the creek bed, yelling, "Get down, dammit! Somebody's shooting at us."

I scrambled after him, totally confused. Another loud crack

as I crouched behind a rock; I could hear the bullet ripping through pine boughs behind me.

"Knock it off, asshole!" Blue roared.

I huddled behind my boulder. Somebody was shooting at the two of us. Did this mean Blue was innocent, and the crazed hiker was out in the woods with a gun? Or was it some kind of elaborate ruse?

I looked over at Blue; he lay prone on the ground. One hand clutched the opposite bicep; I could see the wet red stain growing under his fingers. His eyes met mine briefly.

"They shot you," I said blankly.

"Looks like it. What in the hell is going on?"

"I don't know."

I started to move toward him, and he stopped me with a quick, "Stay put."

Another shot rang out. It clipped a rock nearby with a sharp ping; a shard of granite flew in the air.

"Knock it off, you bastard!" Blue shouted it at the top of his lungs.

He looked over at me. "You better goddamn well tell me what's going on here."

"I don't know," I repeated. "I think some crazy guy is out there."

Crack!

This time Blue didn't yell. "Get your gun out," he said quietly.

I pulled the pistol out of its holster, and told him evenly, "I only have five bullets and there's no more ammunition."

"All right. He's in the bunch of trees there." One finger pointed. "Can you shoot that thing?"

"Well enough. I doubt I can hit him from here, even if I could see him, which I can't."

"That's okay. Can you put a shot through that grove?"

"More or less."

166

"All right."

I sighted down the barrel of the .357, using one small pine as a target. Without stopping to consider the wisdom of this course, I took a deep breath, held it, and squeezed the trigger gently.

Ka-boom. My ears rang and my arm slammed back with the recoil.

I had no idea if I'd gotten anywhere near the target pine.

As the echoes died, Blue yelled again. "Get the hell out of here, you son of a bitch, or the next one's going right through you."

Quiet. No shooting. No reply.

Blue lay on the ground behind his rock, his eyes fixed on the pine grove. I watched it, too. I could see nothing.

"How did you know the shots came from there? Can you see him?"

"No. But I did a lot of shooting when I was young. That's where he is."

I crouched behind my rock and stared at the pines. No motion; no color that didn't belong. So where was the madman?

A sudden thought struck me and I looked wildly around for Roey. I couldn't see her. I raised my head to look over at the horses.

"Get down." Blue's voice was clipped.

I ducked. Still no shots.

"Your red dog's by the horses," Blue said. "She's hiding in some scrub."

"She's afraid of loud noises," I said. "She hates fireworks. I thought she might have run away."

"Both the dogs are with the horses. I can see the horses and everything's fine. He's shooting at us, not the animals."

Somewhat reassured, I glanced over at my companion. The stain on his arm was growing, and his words seemed to be coming through clenched teeth. He still held his bicep.

"I'd better have a look at your arm," I said.

"Not now."

My eyes went back to the pine grove. "So, if you can't see him and I can't see him, how do we know if and when he's gone?"

"We don't."

"Do we have a plan?"

"Wait."

I thought about it. Waiting made sense. The impatient itch in my muscles didn't. I wanted to be up and out of here. I considered the idea of another shot and rejected it. I had four bullets left. Who knew when I might need them? And I couldn't see the sniper.

Another thought occurred to me. "So, is there someone who has a reason to be after you?" I asked.

Blue turned his head toward me and I got a level look from the gray eyes. "Dan Jacobi," he said.

"He's not going to shoot you over a horse."

"I wouldn't think so."

"No one else?"

"Not that I know of."

We regarded each other, huddled behind our respective rocks. "I found three booby traps on the trail today," I said at last. "Any one of them could have killed me. The bridge over Cherry Creek collapsed because somebody sabotaged it. You were riding down that trail, too. Maybe the traps were meant for you."

Blue Winter took that in. His face stayed still. "I don't know who it would be," he said at last. "Bill Evans had a reason to hate me, but you say he shot himself. And you're right, Dan Jacobi wouldn't kill me over a horse. Bad for business." He gave a brief smile.

"Well, I don't know of anyone who has a reason to kill me either. The only thing I can think of is it's some crazy backpacker who hates horses. I met one like that at Wilma Lake."

Blue said nothing for a moment. Then, "That's why you were acting so strange, earlier. You thought I was your crazy man."

"Maybe."

"I'd have to be crazy, wouldn't I? To hurt you." He kept his eyes on the pine grove.

I stared into the trees and could see nothing. Only blue-green boughs, gray trunks, the soft red-brown duff of the dead needles that carpeted the ground. "So how long do we wait?" I asked.

"I don't know. I'll wave my hat, if you want."

"Forget it. It's what, four o'clock now?"

"More or less," Blue said.

"Let's just lay low till the light dies. That'll make shooting difficult. If your arm will wait." I looked at the spreading stain.

"It'll wait. Whoever he is, he's shooting with a pistol. And he can't shoot all that well."

"Okay. So we lie here and wait for dark."

"That's right." Blue turned his head and gave me that sudden smile. "You can tell me a story."

TWENTY

Dark took its sweet time in coming. I shifted my weight, tensed and relaxed my muscles in turn. Occasionally I considered creeping toward the horses, but gave it up as too risky. Once I eased my way down to the creek and took a long swallow of water.

Mostly I stayed behind my rock, waiting. I couldn't see the dogs, but Blue reiterated that they were fine, and with the horses. His face seemed to me to grow paler the longer we lay there, and the sleeve of his shirt was dark with blood. Yet each time I tried to move toward him to examine his arm, he told me to wait.

Eventually the sun dropped behind the ridge, outlining the pines and cedars on the western horizon. Then, as the sun sank further below the rim of the world, came the gentle blurring of edges. Dusk crept in.

One moment we lay there, waiting. The next, without a word, Blue took his hat off his head and waved it with his good arm. Nothing. Slowly he began getting to his feet.

I looked at him.

"Stay down," he said.

For a second I had the impulse to get to my own feet right along with him, but rejected it. What the hell. If this guy was so chivalrous as to want to get shot in my stead, I'd let him.

No shots came. Blue climbed awkwardly up the bank, cradling his right arm with his left. After a minute, I followed him.

No response of any kind came from the pine grove.

"They're gone, I guess," I said out loud.

"Looks like it."

We walked to our horses, and the two dogs came to greet us, stretching and wagging their tails. They seemed glad of the rest, anyway.

But Blue looked terrible. He sat down on a fallen tree with an abruptness that made me think the short walk was too much for him. His face was white; he gripped his arm and looked at the ground.

"You'd better let me have a look at that," I said.

"Okay." His response was barely audible.

I dug out my human first-aid kit (small), and my equine emergency kit (bigger). This was all the stuff I had. Bringing my water bottle with me, I approached Blue Winter.

"Let's get that shirt off," I said.

Obediently, he unbuttoned his shirt, and wincing, unstuck the wet red sleeve from his arm. Even as I focused on the wound, I noticed the long, hard muscles. He was built like a Thoroughbred, tall and lean.

The bullet had gone right into the bicep of his right arm; at a glance, I thought it must also have broken the humerus bone.

"Can you move your arm?" I asked him.

I could see him gather himself for the effort. His fingers curled, but the arm barely twitched.

"No," he said. "It must be broken."

"I think so," I said. "The wound looks fairly clean, but I ought to wash it and wrap it, and then splint that bone as well as I can and make a sling. All this is going to hurt. You'd better take some painkillers first."

I looked at him.

"I've got some codeine in my first-aid kit. I've also got some torbugesic. If I put it in IV, it would be a lot quicker," I told him.

"Torbugesic?"

"Yeah. It's a horse drug. I use it for severe colics. It's a great painkiller. It'll work on people, too."

"Are you sure?"

"Yeah, I'm sure." I smiled at him. "I had a friend in vet school who used to try all the drugs he gave the horses on himself. He gave me a full report."

"Better give me the torbu—whatever it is." Blue closed his eyes. "This hurts pretty bad."

I got out a syringe and filled it with one cc of torbugesic. By my reckoning, this was a light dose for such a big man. Still, though I'd tried to sound confident when talking to Blue, I was a long way from sure this was the right thing to do. What if he reacted negatively to the stuff?

I stared at the syringe in my hand. Light was evaporating like rainwater in the sun. In a little while it would be dark. I needed to work on this man's arm in the light.

"Okay," I said. "Here we go."

What I wanted, I thought, was the vein in his wrist. That was where nurses always gave the IV injections.

"Make a fist with your left hand," I told him.

Squinting in the faint light, I rolled the skin of his wrist under my fingers until I could feel and see the vein. "This will sting a little," I said.

Gently but definitely, I inserted the needle. I glanced at Blue. His face was impassive.

Attaching the syringe to the needle, I injected the shot. We both waited. In a minute I could see his face relax.

"That's better," he said.

I smiled. "Now for the hard part. I need to clean this, put some antibiotic salve on it, and wrap it. Then we've got to splint it and make you a sling."

"All right." Blue definitely sounded better.

"The bullet is probably still in there, from the looks of it, but I think we're better off just to leave it there for now. I want to get you fixed up to travel."

I paused in the act of swabbing the wound with water and Betadine scrub. "I guess we'd better head straight for the pack station."

"It's a three-day ride."

"I know. Have you got a better idea?"

Blue was quiet a minute. "How about we ride to Bridgeport?"

"Why Bridgeport?"

"It's closer, for one thing. We could make it in two days, if we pushed. And . . ." He stopped.

"And what?"

"Do people," he said carefully, "expect you to ride back out to Crazy Horse Creek?"

"I suppose so." I smeared antibiotic salve on his wound, put a telfa pad on it, and began to wrap it with Vet Wrap (horse Band-Aids). "Are you suggesting whoever is doing this crap is after me, and that it's someone who knows me?"

"I'm not suggesting anything." Blue's mouth was compressed. "I'm thinking out loud here. I don't know who this bastard is after; it's a cinch he shot me. But maybe I was just in the wrong place at the wrong time. Still, if this person is hunting either you or me particularly, for reasons we don't understand, we're both known to have ridden in from Crazy Horse Creek. My truck and trailer are parked there. Are yours?"

173

"Yeah, they are." I finished wrapping his arm with Vet Wrap and looked around for a suitable stick for a short splint.

"So, anyone who was halfway observant could know that we both planned to ride back out that way. Now that we're upset, it's a likely bet we'll head out. If this person is after one of us, wouldn't their likeliest move be to wait and sabotage us on the trail to Crazy Horse Creek?"

"It makes sense." I had an appropriate stick; I began ripping strips off Blue's bloody shirt.

He watched me blandly; the torbugesic seemed to be doing its job.

"So, they won't be prepared for us to ride to Bridgeport. And it's a shorter ride," he said.

"What's the most direct route?" I held his arm gently in place as I fashioned a rudimentary splint and sling to support his humerus bone.

"Over the bridge that's now gone." He winced as I wrapped the arm to the stick. "Otherwise we have to ride through Kerrick Meadow and down Buckeye Canyon. Right by Benson Lake."

"So you think we should go that way?" I tightened the sling.

"Yeah, I do. How much of that turbo stuff do you have, anyway?"

"About six more doses like the one you just had."

"We ought to make it, then." He looked over at the horses and stood up. "Let's go."

"Now? It's dark."

"Did you want to wait around here for whoever shot at us to come back?"

"I guess not." I stared at him in the dim light. "How bad's the trail going to be? It's not going to help us much if we escape being shot only to fall off a cliff in the dark."

"I agree. But the trail's not too bad—at least as far as Benson. And the moon will be up in another hour. If we start now, we can make Benson Lake by midnight and then maybe stop and sleep awhile.''

''All right,'' I said dubiously. What he was telling me made sense, and I didn't have any better ideas. Nor did I want to abandon Blue to his fate, or for that matter, go my own way to deal with a lunatic in the backcountry all by myself. No, I definitely wanted to stick with Blue, now that I was sure he wasn't a villain. And Blue seemed pretty clear on what he wanted to do.

He started toward the horses, a little stiffly, but looking a lot better than before the torbugesic. I watched him untie them with his left hand. The little freckled dog ran up to him and wagged her tail.

He turned to me. ''I might need help with this.''

''That's what I figured.'' I took the pack horse's lead rope. ''I'll hold her.''

Blue got his left foot in the stirrup, while I steadied the dun horse by the bridle reins. Gripping the saddle horn with his left hand, and protecting his right arm as well as he could, he swung his right leg over the saddle; I could see by his face that it cost him. When he was settled I handed the lead rope to him and went to get my own horses.

Roey gave an excited yip as I mounted, and dashed over to her new canine friend, wagging her tail wildly. The dogs were ready to roll.

I wasn't so sure about Blue. He'd dealt with being doctored, and he seemed determined to move on, but just getting aboard his horse had been difficult, I knew. He sat crookedly in his saddle, reins in his left hand, lead rope dallied around the saddle horn, head down.

''Let's go,'' he said quietly. Turning his saddle horse he headed back toward the trail.

''Do you know where we're going?'' I fell in behind him.

''Pretty much. We leave this little meadow where the trail

175

forks and the sign says Kerrick Meadow that way.''

I remembered the fork and the sign.

"Then the trail goes down into Cherry Creek Canyon and out the other side. Benson Lake is just before we get to Kerrick Meadow.''

We were riding through the near-dark; I saw Blue rein his horse left at the trail fork and followed him. My horses seemed to be moving confidently, undisturbed by the lack of light. I was worried, though.

"I'm not sure I like this riding in the dark,'' I said.

"No one can see to shoot us in the dark,'' came back Blue's reply.

They would have a hard time setting snares in the dark, too, I added to myself. And I knew perfectly well that horses have much better night vision than people. Still, I wished the moon would rise.

We were riding through level, fairly open country; the trail was mostly dirt. At the moment, the darkness did not present much threat. As far as I was concerned, it would be an entirely different deal when we were descending into Cherry Creek Canyon.

We rode. Blue's pack horse had a flaxen tail; the pale straw-yellow color showed up well in the semi-dark. I fixed my eyes on her tail, and tried to trust that Gunner would see and deal with the footing.

We rode. There was a glow on the eastern horizon; the moon would rise soon. Dusk had definitely verged into night; stars showed as pinpricks in the blue-black sky.

Steadily the glow intensified. I watched the mare's tail glow whiter in the silvery light. We rode out of a small grove of trees, and the moon was visible above the rim of Cherry Creek Canyon. A gibbous moon, big enough to shed some useful light.

The trail began descending through granite; I was torn between fear and awe.

Cherry Creek Canyon was a sight. Moonlight reflected on the tumbled granite slabs and scattered scree. Ridges stretched out in the distance, impossibly rich with light and shadow, intricate and mysterious as a Chinese wood-block print. All black, silver, and gray, and yet each nuance, each shade seemed to have meaning.

I stared. Moonglow lit a granite world; trees were black silhouettes. I forgot my fear, I forgot the sniper. The great canyon glowed, as it did every moonlit night. Shadows of pine boughs laid bars across the path.

This is always here, I thought. Eternally present. Always, in myriad forms, the natural world sends its message of beauty blooming; we so seldom hear it or see it. I felt almost thankful that danger had driven me into this canyon by moonlight.

Blue's voice broke the spell. "How are you doing?"

"Okay. How about you?"

"I'm hanging in there."

"Good. This is really something, isn't it?" The moment the words were out of my mouth, I regretted them. How inane could you get? That's the trouble with things like beauty and truth. They don't translate into words.

Blue seemed to understand, though. I heard his voice come floating back. "It sure is."

I sighed and looked out over the endless vistas of silver granite under the three-quarter moon and thought how lucky I was. I'd survived so far, and now I was here. Things could be worse.

Three hours later, I wasn't so sure. We'd traversed Cherry Creek Canyon and were traveling through some rocky country to the east. Blue had assured me that the cutoff trail to Benson would appear any minute—but so far it wasn't appearing.

I was tired, the horses were tired, the dogs were tired. Blue and I had quit talking. We just rode.

I could only guess at how much pain the man ahead of me might be in. He said nothing. I could see how crookedly he

177

slouched in his saddle, though, his whole body curved protectively around his right arm.

Suddenly he pulled his horse up. I saw him look down, saw him rein the horse to the right. In a minute, I knew why. The small wooden Forest Service sign indicating the cutoff trail was plain in the moonlight. We were on our way to Benson Lake.

I didn't ask how far it was; I just followed the pack mare's flaxen tail. On and on, down and down—the trail descending into a dense forest where the moonlight came in shafts. The trail wound between trees, crossed a creek, then followed its banks. More trees.

And then, without warning, the forest fell away. The trail led into a small meadow with the stream running through it and beyond . . . my God. Beyond stretched a half-mile crescent of shining white sand, ringing dark water. The moon lay a silver path down the middle of the water, bright as a fairy tale.

Blue pulled up and I rode alongside him. He turned his head to meet my eyes.

"So what do you think of Benson Lake?" he said.

TWENTY-ONE

We made camp on the beach. What camp we made, anyway. It was mostly a matter of unsaddling and unpacking the horses and putting them on run lines in the meadow. After that, both Blue and I threw our sleeping bags down on the sand.

"Do you want another shot of torbugesic?" I asked him. "It might help you sleep."

"Okay." He sat down on a fallen tree.

I got a syringe, needle, and the drug out of my saddlebags and filled the syringe by the light of the moon. Blue rolled the sleeve back on his left arm. His forearm was pale in the moonlight, the skin cool to the touch and yet warm, too, as I rolled it with the tips of my fingers.

How can skin be cool and warm at the same time, I thought distractedly as I found the vein and injected the shot. I held his arm with my left hand; I could feel the long bones and hard muscles cradled in my palm.

When I was done, we both waited. After a minute, Blue looked up at me and smiled. "That's better," he said.

I smiled back. "Good. Do you want something to eat?"

He shrugged his good shoulder. "I don't know. We'd better not build a fire."

"You think someone's followed us?"

"I don't know. If they have, they're pretty good. I haven't noticed anything, have you?"

"No."

"But lighting a fire would be stupid," he said. "Anyway, I'm so damn tired. I just want to go to sleep."

"How about a granola bar?" I had a couple of these stashed in my saddlebags for just such an emergency.

He shrugged again.

"Have one. You'll feel better in the morning."

"All right." He took the foil-wrapped bar I gave him and began munching steadily, as if eating it were a chore he had to complete.

I did the same. The granola bar didn't have much taste except sweetness, but I knew I should eat. As far as I could remember, I hadn't eaten a thing since the granola bar I'd had early this morning. It seemed like a lifetime ago.

When we were done chomping, Blue began taking off his boots. Or he tried to, anyway. Pulling off cowboy boots using just your left hand isn't easy. Especially when you're right-handed.

I watched him for a minute. He kept struggling.

"Let me help," I said.

"All right."

Taking hold of the heel of each boot in turn, I pulled them off his feet. It was an oddly intimate gesture and reminded me suddenly of the boyfriend I'd had in college.

I looked at Blue and our eyes met. His looked surprised, as near as I could tell in the moonlight.

"There," I said. "Good night."

"Thank you, ma'am." He got stiffly to his feet and walked over to his sleeping bag.

I unlaced my packer boots, which were a good deal easier to get off than Blue's traditionally styled cowboy boots, and crawled into my sleeping bag with relief. Roey curled up next to my body and I rubbed her head for a while.

Glancing over, I could see a small white shape curled up next to Blue Winter. Freckles slept with him, then, just as Roey did with me.

As if he could feel my eyes on him, I heard his voice come out of the night. "See you in the morning, Stormy. Thanks for everything."

"Right." I smiled to myself. By my reckoning, this was really a sweet man. What did he have to thank me for? A bullet in the arm, and the abrupt end of his planned vacation?

Or could this whole thing be about him? Was I the one who had been in the wrong place at the wrong time? Had the booby-trapped trail been prepared for Blue, and I happened to ride down it first?

And if so, my mind asked, did Blue really know what was going on here, and was he hiding it from me? Was that why he was so sure which way he wanted to ride out? Perhaps he knew just who the pursuit was, and where they were coming from.

On and on my mind went, inventing new and more complicated scenarios every moment. Just shut up, I told myself. Roey snuggled up to me.

My instincts said that Blue Winter was all right. If there were things he wasn't telling me, so be it. I was going to trust him and see where it got me. It was a cinch I didn't know what was going on, anyway, and I needed help. More than that, I wanted company.

The motionless shape in the sleeping bag ten feet away might not seem to be doing much for me, but he dispelled the frightening emptiness of the night in an amazing way. For a second I imagined myself lying here alone, not knowing who might be out in the dark, stalking me. I shook my head abruptly. No thanks.

Snuggling deeper into my bag, I tried to fall asleep. Maybe it had all been some isolated craziness, as I had first thought. Maybe that loony from Wilma Lake was camped along the trail to Cherry Creek Canyon. Maybe we had left the whole thing behind us. On that comforting thought I fell asleep.

I awoke to sunshine. On my face, on the aspen in the meadow, on the white sand of the beach. Turning my head away from the light, I closed my eyes. It was comfortable here in the sleeping bag, curled into the forgiving sand. I didn't want to get up.

I could see the horses looking impatient out on their run lines; they'd eaten all the grass within reach. Reluctantly I struggled out of my bag and pulled my boots on.

Glancing over at Blue's prostrate form, I ascertained that he was still asleep and decided to let him be. I walked out into the meadow, Roey following me. Freckles stayed with her master, though she flattened her ears and wagged her tail when I looked at her.

Gunner and Plumber nickered when I approached them; Blue's two horses followed suit. I studied the situation for a moment. Then I untied Gunner, an easygoing horse who could be trusted to get along with the others and stay out of trouble. Plumber was a little feistier, apt to pick fights with other horses.

Moving Plumber along the picket line so that he could reach more grass, I approached Blue's two horses. The small sorrel mare pinned her ears. The big dun gelding regarded me with wide, alert eyes. I moved the gelding down the line and retied him, then walked cautiously toward the mare. In general, I mistrusted cranky mares. I'd been kicked good and hard by a few of these.

This mare made a ferocious face at me, but when I took hold of her lead rope her ears came up and she made no attempt to bite or kick. I retied her where she could reach a new patch of grass and left all four horses happily munching.

Walking back to camp, I turned to watch the livestock grazing, their red, brown, and gold coats bright in the sunshine. It was a peaceful sight; yesterday's adventure seemed like a bad dream.

A little breeze rustled through the aspen trees that dotted the meadow, and I smiled. I loved aspens. Of all the mountain trees, they were my favorites. Always flickering, always talking, their green and silver leaves a glittering kaleidoscope against the sky.

"Pretty, isn't it?" came a voice from behind me.

Blue was awake. I turned to look at him, and beyond him at the white sand beach and the water of the lake—bright blue-green in the morning light.

"It's great," I said. "How do you feel?"

"I hurt." He smiled briefly.

I studied him. "Do you want me to give you another shot? I've got five doses left."

Blue lay on his back, staring up at the sky. "What's the plan?" he said, after a moment.

I stared back at him. "We ride out, I guess."

"The horses need to eat."

"I know," I agreed. "So do we."

"We'll spend a few hours here, then."

"Yeah, I guess so."

"Better give me some codeine, and save the shots for when we travel."

"All right." I got the small vial of codeine tablets out of my saddlebag. Six tablets—stashed for emergencies.

"This is going to make you drowsy," I said.

He gave me half a smile. "I better stay in bed."

"You do that," I said, as he swallowed a tablet. "Do you think we can risk a fire?"

We both glanced around. The rocky walls that ringed Benson Lake on all sides were quiet in the sunlight, the little meadow and the beach empty except for us. It all looked perfectly safe. Snipers seemed ridiculous.

"Sure, why not? They can see us in the daylight, if they're looking. A fire won't change anything."

"Okay. I'll make coffee."

Once the fire was made and the coffeepot was on, I poured some dog food for Roey. The little freckled dog wagged her tail and looked at me in a shy and ingratiating way. I laughed out loud.

"Can I feed her, too?" I asked Blue.

"Sure. There's some dog food in my pack."

"Okay." I got the dog food and poured some on the ground. "Here, Freckles," I said.

She walked up to me and lifted her head for a pat, which I gave her, then dipped her whiskered muzzle to the food. I laughed again.

"What are you laughing at?" Blue asked me.

"Your dog."

"Poor Freckles. Everybody thinks she's funny-looking."

"It's the blue eyes. Or maybe that terrier muzzle. I don't know. She's pretty cute. Do you want me to turn your horses loose?"

"You can turn the gelding loose if you want. He won't fight with the other horses and he won't leave the mare."

"Okay. What are their names?" I smiled. I had a thing about that. I always liked to know the names of the horses I handled.

"The gelding's Dunny," Blue said.

It figured. Cowboys often called horses by their colors. Bays

184

were Bay, sorrels Sorrelly, buckskins Bucky, blacks Blacky . . . et cetera. Naturally the big dun horse was Dunny.

"I call the mare Little Witch," Blue went on.

I laughed again. "That fits."

He smiled over at me. "She just likes to act cross. She's really pretty sweet. She's just a three-year-old."

I grinned at him. "I used to ride a horse like that. He pinned his ears all the time, and acted like he wanted to eat you, but he'd do anything for you." This was Burt, Lonny's head horse.

"Yeah. This filly's like that. I owned her mother, and I've raised this one since she was born. She acts ornery, but she's not, really. She's been easy to train. Better not turn her loose, through. The geldings might fight."

I nodded. In my experience this was true. Mares were a problem, even if they were sweet-tempered themselves. All the geldings fell in love with them and fought for their favors. It didn't seem to matter that the relationship was necessarily going to be platonic; the geldings got pretty damn devoted. This was a major nuisance and one of the reasons I refused to own a mare.

I turned Dunny loose and watched as he sniffed noses with Gunner. No squeals, no strikes. Gunner pinned his ears in a mild way, stating that he intended to be dominant, and Dunny moved off submissively and began eating grass. No problem.

I walked back to camp and poured coffee. Blue propped himself against a log and took the cup I handed him. Sitting down on a rock, I took the first hot sip.

Our eyes met. He smiled. "Ahh," he said.

"It sure tastes good," I agreed.

I stretched my back, feeling the warmth of the sun through my tank top. Sipped some more coffee and stared at the lake.

"There's an island right in the middle," I said.

"Yeah. I swam out there once. It's pretty big for an island in a Sierra lake. Almost half an acre, I'd say. Mostly rocks.

185

There's a couple of trees and a little flat spot where it looks like somebody camped once.''

"That must have been interesting." I could see a couple of pines and a rocky outcropping from where I sat. Looked like it would be a decent swim. If this were still a vacation, I'd be thinking of swimming out there in the afternoon.

My eyes went back to the man beside me. He raised his coffee cup to his lips with his left hand; I could see the faint wince of pain at the movement. Sitting here in the sunshine, everything seemed peaceful and relaxing, but there was no getting around it, Blue had been shot.

We needed to get him to a doctor, and more than that, we needed to get out of the backcountry, on the chance that whoever had shot him was after us. But I still sat, feeling the sun on my back, idly watching my companion.

He raised his cup again and I saw the long muscles in his arm tighten; the light sparkled on the red-gold hairs of his forearm as on fine copper wires. I allowed the thought to cross my mind: This was really an attractive man.

For a moment I stopped to wonder what attraction is composed of, anyway. Would another woman think Blue Winter was attractive? I didn't know. All I knew was that his long, lean body, red-gold hair and quiet gray eyes were speaking to my physical self in a constant, powerful way.

Then I shrugged. He probably had a girlfriend. I had a boyfriend. For all I knew, he didn't find me physically attractive at all. Not to mention, his mind was hardly likely to be on such matters, not with a bullet in his arm.

"How about a granola bar for breakfast?" I asked.

"All right." He said it without enthusiasm.

"I know. But it's quick and we should probably get organized to go. How long a ride is it to Bridgeport?"

"A solid eight hours."

"We'd better leave in an hour or so."

"You're right."

We regarded each other morosely. Packing up seemed like a big chore. Better than getting shot, though.

I handed Blue two granola bars. "Eat these," I said. "You'll feel better."

"Okay."

We munched; I watched the horses graze. The dogs snoozed in the sunshine; the remains of my morning fire flickered. It was all so damn tranquil.

"I'd like to have a quick wash before we pack up to go," I said, as I stood up.

"Go right ahead." Blue looked rueful. "I'd like one, too, but I don't think I can manage it." He smiled up at me. "I don't think I'm going to be much help saddling and packing the horses, either."

"That's okay. I can do it. Is there anything you want before I go down to the lake?"

"No. I'll be fine."

"Okay." I took my boots off, got a towel and some soap, and started off across the sand. Benson Lake glittered ahead of me; the beach was warm and soft under my feet. I stared up at the towering rock walls that surrounded the water. This was really a unique spot.

The lake sat in the bottom of what was more or less a thimble. The canyon we'd ridden down was the only way in, the half mile of beach with the small meadow beyond it the only level ground along the shoreline. By the looks of it, it would be absolutely impossible to ride around this lake, and damn difficult to walk.

I was nearing the water; it was an odd feeling to be standing on a white sand beach lapped with little waves in the middle of the Sierras. Granite cliffs glowed in the sunshine. Suddenly, to my amazement, I heard a coyote howl. The sound echoed off the rocks and seemed to float upward—sweet, eerie, me-

187

lodious—uncanny in the bright light of morning.

I stood still. Another coyote answered the first, and then another. The cliffs carried the sound. Many voices now, as the howls rose to a long keening and then a crescendo of sharp *ki-yi-yi*'s, bouncing off the walls, seeming to come from all directions.

Mesmerized, I stood like a statue, as the strange serenade filled the bowl of Benson Lake. I had never heard coyotes sing like this in broad daylight. What could it mean? Perhaps there was a den in these rocks.

The sound died. One last voice rose in a solitary, mournful howl. Then all was quiet. After a minute I walked forward and stepped into the lake.

Icy water lapped my ankle; I jerked my foot sharply out and whistled. This lake was cold. For a minute I rethought my bathing plans. Maybe I'd just stay dirty.

You'll feel better if you wash, I told myself. You've got a long ride ahead of you. But I damn well wasn't going swimming.

I splashed water on my face and hands, washed my armpits briefly, and brushed my teeth. Then I toweled off, feeling a little cleaner and a lot wider awake.

I could see Gunner and Dunny, a little ways down the beach, drinking out of the lake. I needed to take Plumber and Little Witch down for a drink before I packed them, I reminded myself.

Gunner lifted his head, ears up, staring out over the lake. Suddenly with a snort, he whirled and ran, Dunny following him. For a second they thundered toward me along the beach, running free, manes and tails flying, a poster come to life. I watched them with a wide grin as they swerved off across the sand and galloped back to the meadow and their companions. Those two were feeling fresh enough to travel, anyway.

Making my own, much slower, way back to camp, I untied Plumber and the mare and led them down to the lake, taking care to keep them well separated so they didn't fuss. No use getting a horse kicked if I could help it.

188

Bringing them back, I tied them to trees near the gear and caught Gunner and Dunny. Blue watched me without a word. It didn't look like he'd moved all morning. I was beginning to worry about how he would deal with the traveling. Maybe another shot would do the trick.

The brightness seemed to have gone out of the morning; as I brushed the two saddle horses and put pads and blankets on their backs, I could see a haze in the air.

I heaved the saddles up and cinched them lightly, tied the saddlebags in place, and looked at Blue. He sat on the other side of the fire pit, half propped against his log, staring out across the meadow. I could smell the acrid tang of wood smoke, mingling with the clear, piney mountain smell. Camp smells of wood smoke, always.

I started to brush Plumber and looked back at Blue. His face had a fixed expression. I turned around to look where he was looking. For a second I saw nothing, just the meadow under the hazy sky. Just the smell of smoke.

Then I got it.

"My God," I said. "There's a fire."

TWENTY-TWO

U p the canyon,'' Blue affirmed. I couldn't read either his expression or his tone.

"Jesus, what do we do?"

"It depends," he said.

Smoke was growing thicker in the air every moment; panic grew inside of me.

"Depends on what?" I knew my voice was shrill.

"Get the binoculars out of my saddlebag."

I got them and went to his side. He raised them to his eyes with his good hand and pointed them up the canyon. There was a long moment of silence, then he lowered them.

"See for yourself."

I looked. For a second everything was a blur; I adjusted the spacing—instant sharpness. It didn't tell me much. Heavy clouds of smoke billowing into the air at the head of the canyon, that was it.

"So what do you see?" I demanded.

"The fire's in the canyon and the wind's blowing this way," he said.

I looked at the aspen trees in the meadow. Sure enough, the ever-present Sierra wind pulled their feathery tops in the direction of the lake.

"So the fire will burn toward us," I said.

"That's right."

"So, what do we do?" I could hear my voice rising.

"We've got a couple of choices," he said. "I don't think riding up the canyon is a good one; fires are unpredictable, and that wind is rising. We could get ourselves in real trouble."

I listened to him, trying to keep my chattering nerves on hold.

"We could wait it out, on the beach," he said. His laconic tone was getting to me.

"Is that going to work?" I demanded.

"Probably."

I stared at him. His face was quiet and he seemed in no hurry to do anything.

"What are our other options, in your opinion?" I asked him.

"I guess the safest thing we could do is hike around the lake to the far end. It's all rock; the fire won't get there. We'd be perfectly safe."

"And leave the horses here?"

"We can't take them around the lake; it's impossible. I've hiked down to the far end before." He gave me a brief smile. "You'd probably have to leave me, too. I don't think I could make it with this arm."

I looked at him, then looked out over the lake; smoke haze, gray as fog, filled the air of the bowl. Without a word, I walked to Gunner and got the torbugesic and the syringe out of my saddlebags.

"I'm giving you a shot," I said to Blue.

"All right." He rolled his sleeve back. "You want to try hiking, then?"

I met his eyes. "And leave the horses?"

"We'd have to."

"Is that what you want to do?" I asked him.

"No. I'd wait it out on the beach, and stay with them."

"Would we be okay, do you think? On the beach. Holding the horses." I injected the shot into his vein.

"Probably. Depends on the wind. And how panicked the horses got. I'm not sure we could hold them."

I watched for the slight relaxation of his facial muscles, heard the tiny sigh as the drug kicked in. Then I looked up the canyon. Smoke billowed fiercely; the haze in the air was getting thicker every minute.

I looked back out over the lake. Then I looked at Blue.

"How about we swim to the island?" I said.

His eyes moved sharply to mine and I could feel the quick calculations in his head. "We could," he said. "Swim the horses, you mean."

"Yeah. And the dogs."

"We could do it. There's a sort of rocky beach on the far side. And there's room to camp once we get there."

"We'd be safe," I said.

"If we made it."

"They can swim that far. So can we. So can the dogs."

Blue got slowly and stiffly to his feet. "That's true," he said. "I once scared up a fawn on the shore of this lake. It could only have been a few days old. It swam out to the island and made it. I watched."

I looked back up the canyon. Heavy clouds of smoke seemed to pour toward us; the fire was definitely moving our way.

"Let's do it," I said. "We can't just stand here talking. Can you handle it, with your arm?"

192

"Sure. I grew up on a lake. I could swim out there with one arm, if I had to."

"What about the horses? How should we take them, do you think?"

Our four equines stood quietly, unperturbed. The fire wasn't yet close enough to alarm them. Smoke in the air didn't register as a threat.

"We'll ride the saddle horses and lead the pack horses. We'd better leave the packs and the gear on the beach. Those loads would make it tough on the horses to swim."

"Okay." I started hauling my pack bags toward the lake. "Should we leave the saddles on?" I said over my shoulder.

Blue took hold of one of his own pack bags with his good arm and dragged it after me. "The saddles should be fine," he grunted.

Even as I toted my gear, my mind dithered. Was I doing the right thing here? What was the best choice, for me, for my animals? For Blue, as far as that went. He seemed oddly detached about the danger we were in; I could only assume that the pain in his arm was overriding all other worries.

Try as I might, I could think of no better plan. I knew little or nothing about wildfires and how they behaved. The notion of standing on the beach while flames torched the forest in front of me did not appeal to me one little bit. I had read that big fires sucked up oxygen in incredible ways; I had heard how unpredictable they could be. I knew horses were terrified of fires. I wanted away from this one.

Dragging the rest of my pack gear down to the lake, I asked Blue, "Can you get on your horse?"

"I think so. You might have to help me."

He was towing his second pack bag; I forbore to tell him that I could do it.

When the gear was in a pile on the beach, we went back to

the horses. I could see an occasional flash of orangy flame through the smoke; it scared me.

"Come on," I urged Blue. "Let's go."

The dogs wagged their tails as we untied the horses. They didn't know we were in danger; they thought we were moving on in the normal way.

Let's go, let's go, the words rattled in my brain. Blue stared at Dunny as if the effort of getting on him was too much. How in the hell was he going to swim across the lake if he had to?

I stepped to his side and bent over, lacing my two hands together in a cup. "I'll give you a leg up."

Blue didn't say anything, but obediently lifted his left leg and set his toe into the step I'd created. Like everyone who's spent time with horses, he knew about getting a leg up.

"One, two, three," I said. I lifted, he pulled with his left arm and swung his right leg over Dunny's back. Thank God the gelding stood still. Blue was on, looking a little unsteady, but there.

I handed him Little Witch's lead rope and climbed on Gunner. We both called our dogs and headed off across the beach. I coughed. The smoke grew thicker every moment.

"Have you ever swum your horses before?" Blue asked.

"No. Not these. I used to swim the horse I had when I was a teenager, though. Bareback in the San Lorenzo River."

Blue smiled—a motion that came and went in an instant. "Then you know never to get in front of a swimming horse. They'll try to climb on you."

"Yeah," I said.

"They reach out in front of themselves with their front feet," he went on, "but they don't reach behind. You're perfectly safe right behind your horse. In fact, if he's having trouble swimming, it's best to slip off the back and hang on to his tail."

"Can't all horses swim?" I asked.

"Not necessarily. I had a big palomino gelding when I was

a kid who couldn't. I went camping with some friends by a lake and we all decided to swim our horses. This horse went in just fine; the lake was one of those with a shore that shelved down and then dropped off. This horse stepped off that drop and went straight to the bottom.''

''You're kidding.''

''Nope. Down he went all the way underwater. Me, too. The waters just closed over my head; I didn't know what would happen.''

''So, what did happen?''

''He went all the way to the bottom and then shot straight up and out of the water, like a dolphin. Then down to the bottom and then straight up again. It was a wild ride, I can tell you.''

''Great. Jeez, I hope neither one of my horses do that.''

Blue laughed. ''They probably won't. I never knew another one that did. Just don't let go of your horse, whatever you do. Because if you're swimming out there and he sees you, he's going to figure you're something he could stand on.''

''Great.''

We were on the shore now. Fire behind us, water before us. I looked back over my shoulder. Smoke was gray everywhere. A fine dusting of ash covered my arms and Gunner's mane. I coughed again.

Digging into my saddlebag, I found the gun and got it out. ''Heel,'' I said firmly to Roey. Then I looked at Blue. ''Are you ready?''

''I'm ready.'' He tipped his fedora down a little further over his eyes.

I clucked to Gunner and kicked his ribs and he stepped into the lake. He waded to his knees with no resistance, Plumber following. Roey followed Plumber, looking nervous.

Gunner moved forward; my boots were in the water. It was cold, damn cold. We were committed now.

195

Deeper and deeper. Icy water over my thighs. I could feel the horse begin to grow weightless, to float. Water to my waist, water all around me. I held the gun over my head with my left hand and clung to Gunner's mane and the reins with my right. I barely felt the cold, so much adrenaline was pumping in me.

Gunner swam; I could feel the long strokes of his legs under me, see his head in front of me, nose determinedly lifted out of the water. I could only guess at his expression.

I looked back. Plumber swam, head up, eyes wide, nostrils flaring. Roey paddled behind him.

Next to me, Blue clung to the swimming Dunny. I looked over my shoulder; Freckles was still on the shore, dashing back and forth and uttering frantic yips.

"Your dog!" I yelled to Blue.

He turned and called. We both watched the little dog race back and forth, back and forth, crying.

"Come on, Freckles. Here, girl," Blue called again, his voice calm.

I looked at the billowing smoke filling the sky and felt anything but calm.

"Will she come?" I asked him.

"She doesn't like to swim. But she'll come."

Once again he called her; I could see her put both front feet in the water, hesitate, and then plunge forward. Then she was swimming, a ways behind us, but following. We were all afloat.

I looked ahead. The island seemed a long way away. But it was clearly visible with its trees and clumps of rocks. I guided Gunner straight toward it, prayed he'd make it.

I looked back at Plumber and Roey. Freckles was just visible, a tiny white dot in the water. Beyond that was the sand of the beach, a pale crescent beneath an angry blanket of roiling smoke. I could see an occasional flash of flame as trees in the little wood beside the lake torched alight.

Once again, I glanced at Blue. His face was steady and impassive, his eyes straight ahead. I couldn't imagine a man who was any calmer under pressure than this one.

The island was closer now, but I thought Gunner was tiring. He seemed to struggle more to keep his nose up; his swimming felt more frantic.

"How does my horse look?" I called anxiously to Blue.

His eyes moved to Gunner. "He's doing okay," he said. "We'll get to the island. Don't worry."

I let my feet slip out of the stirrups and my legs float to the surface, clinging to Gunner by his mane.

"Don't let go," Blue warned.

"I won't."

The island was distinctly closer. We'll make it, I told myself. "Come on, boy," I urged Gunner.

I doubt he heard me. The splashing hooves and the now-audible roar of the fire drowned out all but yells.

"The beach is on the far side," Blue shouted.

I could see only rocks, steep and precipitous, but I obediently steered Gunner to the left, following Blue's lead. In a moment, a small shelving, pebbly bank came into view. Must be what he meant.

Aiming for the so-called beach, I prayed silently that we would make it, we would all be okay. The two dogs still followed, Freckles swimming steadily at the rear.

The beach was close now. Suddenly I could feel Gunner's hooves touching bottom, the lift of his body under me as he picked up his own weight again. I reached my legs down his sides and clung with my knees and calves as he heaved himself out of the water, as anxious to be on solid ground as I was.

I could see Dunny scrambling ashore next to me, the two pack horses following in our wake. I looked back just as Roey made a landing; a minute later Freckles touched ground, looking scared, but all in one piece.

Suddenly Gunner shook himself, a vigorous, rattling motion

that made me gasp and grab his mane. I could feel Blue looking at me.

When I met his eyes, he smiled. "I hate it when they do that," he said. "I once fell off a horse when I was a little kid because he shook like that. I've never forgotten."

"Uh-huh." I said it absently; I was staring back at the fire. The little forest by the meadow was alight and burning, by the look of it. It was hard to tell because of the smoke.

I turned back to Blue. He was slowly lowering himself off Dunny, protecting his right arm as much as possible. Despite the pain he was undoubtedly in, not to mention our current predicament, his face remained detached. I was beginning to wonder if there was anything that could rattle this guy.

Dismounting, I looked around for a place to tie my horses. Choices were few. Half a dozen small pines formed a grove near the pebbly beach. Beside them was a fire ring—which looked as if it had only been used once or twice. As for feed, there were enough scrubby tufts of grass to give each horse a few mouthfuls, that was it.

Thanking God they'd filled up this morning, I tied Gunner and Plumber to the pines and walked over to a large rock that faced back toward the beach and our former campsite.

I sat down, soaking wet and beginning to shiver. Smoke filled the air, thick and smoggy as L.A. on a bad day. I couldn't even see the mountains that ringed the lake. All the beauty of the Sierras disappeared in an ugly haze.

Roey sat down next to me and I hugged her wet body to my side, feeling forlorn.

Oppressive and ominous, the smoke made me claustrophobic, even though I supposed we were perfectly safe here. But I was trapped, stuck on an island in the middle of Benson Lake, a long day's ride from any help.

Not for the first time, I wondered what in the hell I was doing here. Smoke seemed to press down on me like a gigantic hand. Life had never seemed grimmer. Some vacation.

TWENTY-THREE

Blue came and sat beside me. Seeming to guess at my thoughts, he put his good arm around my shoulders. "We'll be okay," he said.

"Will we?" I knew I sounded pathetic.

"Sure we will. We'll spend the night out here. By tomorrow that fire will have spent itself. The meadow's too wet to burn anyway. We'll swim back across, let the horses eat, and have a look around, see what's what."

"See what's what?" I asked him.

He turned his head away. "Find the best route out, I guess," he said noncommittally.

"What do you mean?"

He looked back at me for a long second, as if weighing what to say.

"What are you thinking?" I demanded.

More silence on Blue's part.

"Come on."

"Do you think this fire just happened by accident?" he said at last.

I gazed at the shore of Benson Lake, almost hidden now by a heavy curtain of smoke.

"Do you think it was set deliberately?" I asked him.

"I wonder. It's too early in the year and we're too high up for a fire to be very likely. There hasn't been any lightning. If it was a runaway campfire, where were they camped? There aren't any good campsites in that canyon."

"Oh."

More silence while I took this in, wondering how it all fit into the complex and disjointed sequence of current events.

"You think whoever shot at us and booby-trapped the trail tracked us here and set that fire, hoping to kill us," I said at last. "You think whoever it is is after us specifically. Or you. Or me specifically."

Blue considered this statement. "Yes, I guess I do. That fire is just too unlikely."

"I see." He still had his arm around me, and I leaned into him as the breeze riffled sharply across the lake, causing me to shiver. "Do you have any ideas who's after us, or which one of us they're after?"

Silence again. I waited. I was learning that this man didn't care for ill-considered replies.

"No, I guess not," he said finally.

"You're wondering about something, though."

"Well, it's also a question of who *could* have done it. Who's in the mountains right now. Who has a reason to know where either one of us is."

"Dan Jacobi," I said. "But why?"

I could feel his body shrug. "I don't know. Like you said, he's not going to kill me over a horse."

"And he's got no reason at all to kill me."

We were both quiet. I stared through the smoke haze glumly.

200

This whole deal was a miserable, surreal farce. What possible reason could Dan Jacobi have to stalk either one of us through the mountains?

And then I remembered the dead man in Deadman Meadow. Once again, he'd slipped my mind, a seemingly unimportant detail in this cascade of unlikely catastrophes. But surely he was the wild card—the unexplained and unexpected event that might have precipitated the chain. But how and why?

I looked over at Blue's remote face. I was growing used to his expression—reserved, aloof, still. It no longer connoted unfriendliness to me. But I still wasn't sure where I was permitted to tread.

"Bill Evans killed himself the night before you rode in," I said. "Maybe that was the trigger." I hesitated. "Ted said you used to live with Bill's wife."

Silence and smoke in the air. I coughed. Blue let his arm drop from around me. I could feel my shirt drying rapidly in the breeze.

"Is there anything about Bill Evans or his ex that could be causing . . . all this?" I waved a hand at the smoke-filled sky.

As I expected, a long pause. Then, "I wouldn't know what it would be."

"Whatever happened to her? Ted said her name, but I can't remember it."

"Katie." Blue smiled quietly. "Ted spent a little time with her, too. I bet he didn't mention that."

"No. He sure didn't."

"Katie was on the rebound, I guess. She wanted away from Bill and his drinking. I should have known better. I ran into her up at Crazy Horse Creek—it must be three summers ago. She was a pretty thing."

"Ted told me she lived with you awhile and then went back to Bill," I said diffidently.

More quiet. I was beginning to think Blue wouldn't reply to

this sally when he seemed to rouse himself. "She left me; I don't think she stayed with me longer than six months. She got bored of me, I guess. I don't make a lot of money, unlike her veterinarian husband. I couldn't keep her entertained."

"So she went back to Bill."

"I don't think she had any idea where else to go. She left him again pretty fast. And that time she spent a little while with Ted."

"You're right about Ted not mentioning that." But somehow I wasn't surprised. If Katie was "a pretty thing," it would have been like Ted to try and get her into bed.

"Did Bill Evans know about Katie and Ted?" I asked Blue.

"He must have. Everybody knew. But by all accounts, he didn't hold it against Ted the way he did against me. I didn't know the man, but a couple of guys told me he'd threatened to come kill me."

Well. If Bill Evans were only alive, we'd have a motive. But he wasn't. Once again, I wondered what Bill and Ted had really had words about the night before Bill shot himself. Had they talked about Katie? Was that why Ted had been so anxious to know what Bill had said to me?

Or . . . and then a very bad thought struck me. I held it in my mind, turning it this way and that, almost afraid to speak it out loud.

The silence grew and Blue turned his head to face me. "What are you thinking?" he asked.

I still didn't want to say it.

"Come on. We need to pool our resources here."

I stared at his face, but I wasn't seeing him. "I heard that Ted threw Bill out of the bar the night before Bill shot himself," I said. "And Ted was really anxious to find out what Bill said to me before he died. What if . . ." I could hardly bring myself to say it. It was ridiculous, I told myself.

"Go on," Blue said.

"What if they were fighting about Katie? What if . . ." Another thought, more fantastic than the last, struck me. "Whatever happened to Katie?" I asked him.

"I don't know. She disappeared. I never heard where she went to."

"She just disappeared, huh?"

Blue stared at me. "What are you thinking?" he said again.

"I don't like to say it," I told him. "It sounds ridiculous and I can't believe it myself."

"Go ahead."

I coughed and brushed ashes off my arm. "It's just that Ted was so anxious to know what Bill said."

"Wait a minute," Blue interrupted. "What do you mean, 'what Bill said'?"

"Oh. I guess you don't know. I found Bill Evans out in Deadman Meadow. He'd shot himself in the chest, but he was still alive. He told me he wanted to die . . . stuff like that. By the time Lonny and Ted and the rest of them got there, he was unconscious, and he died on the way to the hospital."

"So you're the only one who knows what he said."

We looked at each other.

"Yeah," I said. "And Ted was really anxious to find out what it was. And he'd gotten in a fight with Bill the night before. I keep wondering if it could be possible that they fought about Katie, say. And," I looked over at him, "I know this sounds unbelievable, but what if Ted shot Bill?"

"Why would he?"

"Over Katie."

"But she's long gone."

"I know. Where did she go? What if Ted, say, killed her, for reasons that we don't know, and Bill found out about it. Maybe Bill threatened to turn Ted in."

Blue took this all in and shook his head. "Then why didn't Bill Evans tell you that Ted shot him?"

"I don't know. Covering up for some reason. But the thing is," I looked at Blue again, "Ted's in the mountains, too. Right now."

"He is?"

"Yes, he is. Dan Jacobi told me. Looking for a crippled mule. At least that's what he said. But there's a way that Ted, unlike Dan, could know which way I'm going. Lonny knew, and I'm sure he would have told Ted if Ted asked."

Blue looked out over the lake and appeared to ponder.

I watched him and another thought came. Insidious as smoke, doubt crept into my mind once again. The motive I'd assigned to Ted could be Blue's motive, too. What if Blue had killed Katie, and killed Bill Evans because he found out? Suddenly I did not want to be stuck on this island with this man.

I stood and he looked up at me. His eyes, for all their stillness, had an earnest quality to them, reminding me of a young boy anxious to do the right thing. I simply had a hard time thinking evil of him.

And again, I told myself, why would Bill Evans cover up for Blue Winter, or for that matter, for Ted Reiter or anyone else? Knowing he was dying, or believing so, anyway, why on earth would he shield his murderer? It didn't make sense.

Surely Bill Evans had shot himself, just as he said. I only wished I knew why. I had the stubborn conviction that his suicide and my current predicament were somehow connected, but I sure as hell didn't know how.

"I'm going to unsaddle the horses," I told Blue.

"All right."

He remained seated as I took the gear off the saddle horses and turned Dunny loose. I left the others tied up, more out of a disinclination to deal with the confusion of four loose horses in such a small space than for any other reason.

"I'll let them all loose one at a time, so they can have a bite and get a drink," I offered.

"That's fine." Blue remained seated, staring in the direction of the beach, not that the beach was visible anymore. Heavy smoke obscured everything but the lake immediately surrounding us. Fortunately we were far enough away from the fire that no large sparks carried our way. Just a steady dusting of ash.

I began gathering firewood, more out of a need for something to do than any real reason. By my reckoning it was now mid-afternoon. If we were spending the night here, we might as well have a fire.

We wouldn't be having much to eat. I had a few more granola bars and some hard candy in my saddlebags. That was it. That and the gun, my veterinary and medical kits, my rain gear, my map, a water bottle, and one EZ Boot. I wondered what Blue had in his.

What else did I have? In my pockets were the waterproof container of matches, my knife, and the little flashlight, which probably wouldn't work after its soaking. Camp was going to be pretty sparse tonight.

Blue still sat and stared; I had no idea what was going through his mind. Belatedly it occurred to me that his arm might be starting to ache again; the shot would be wearing off. I had hoped we would get out today. At this rate, I would run out of shots to give him.

"How about a codeine tablet?" I asked him.

"I think I'd rather have a drink." He turned his head my way and smiled.

"Sounds good. Where are we gonna get it?"

"Out of my saddlebags."

I walked over and picked them up and brought them to him. He fished a tequila bottle out of the right-hand bag with his good arm.

"Tequila?" I said.

"My favorite. Care for a drink?" He produced a lime and a salt shaker out of the saddlebag.

I laughed. "Not yet. You go right ahead." I hesitated. The island was small enough that privacy would be difficult. "I'd like to get these wet jeans off and hang them up so they dry before dark, if you don't mind."

"I don't mind at all." Blue tipped the tequila bottle back and took a long swallow.

"Okay." It was easier to say than do, though. I felt uncomfortable undressing in front of a stranger. But my heavy jeans were damp and clammy. What the hell.

I walked around a rock, sat down and took off my boots, then stepped out of my jeans. My underwear was more discreet than most bikinis, I told myself. Plain red cotton underwear—no lace, no thong.

Draping my jeans, long-sleeved shirt, and socks over a rock to dry, I walked down to the shore of the island wearing my tank top and panties. I sat on a log and wrapped my arms around my knees. Blue could see me from where he was, but at least I wasn't right in his face.

I stared out at the pall of smoke and thought about the things we'd said. Nothing really connected, and yet I sensed the connection was there, somewhere.

Two hours later, the sun was starting to lower itself toward the western ridge, and I was no closer to an answer. I'd turned each horse loose to pick at grass for a while and get a drink, then tied them each back up. The pickings were pretty slim on this little rock outcropping. The horses would be hungry in the morning.

Us, too. My jeans and shirt were reasonably dry and I put them back on. Dug around in my saddlebags for the last couple of granola bars.

Blue lay on his back, head propped on the seat of his saddle, hat tipped over his eyes. I had no idea how much tequila he'd consumed.

"Hungry?" I asked.

"A little." He didn't move.

"We've got a couple of granola bars."

"Oh boy."

"Better than nothing. Did you save any tequila for me?"

"Yes, ma'am, I sure did." Blue pushed his hat back and sat up, very slowly and stiffly. "How about another shot of that torbu stuff?" he asked.

"We've got three more left," I said.

"I'd better have one."

"Okay." I got the syringe and torbugesic out of my saddle-bags and filled the shot. Blue rolled his sleeve back.

Once again I took hold of his forearm and felt for the vein. His skin was freckled with red-gold flecks. My eyes moved to his face. Mustache, eyelashes—all that fiery shade.

Blue raised his eyes to meet my gaze as I injected the shot. For a long moment we stared at each other. What in the world did I look like, I wondered. Best not to think about it.

Once again I saw the tiny relaxation of Blue's facial muscles, the curve of his mouth into the start of a smile. Torbugesic was doing its job.

"Thanks, Florence," Blue said.

"Any time. Feel better?"

"Yes, ma'am. How about we get a fire going before the sun goes down and then I'll make you a drink before dinner."

"Before my granola bar, you mean." I smiled at him.

"Right." Blue got to his feet and smiled back down at me. "Let's build a fire," he said.

TWENTY-FOUR

I put everything on hold. All my suspicions, all my ideas, all my worries. I didn't think about them. Instead, I drank tequila.

I will admit that initially the thought crossed my mind: Is this wise? But it went away after a couple of shots. As if we had made an agreement, Blue and I tacitly avoided all mention of the fire, of Bill Evans, of saboteurs and snipers. We talked of horses and dogs and our lives back in Santa Cruz County.

The fire flickered; darkness hid the smoky sky. Orange glows along the shore of Benson Lake marked smoldering trees. Our dogs lay close to us, and we all moved closer to the campfire as the night grew colder.

I took another small swig of tequila and a squeeze of lime. "So just what do you do for a living?" I asked Blue.

"I'm a greenhouse manager and a plant breeder. I grow roses."

"Roses?" I'm not sure why I was surprised.

"Roses, you know. Old garden roses."

"Really." I stared at the fire. "I like old-fashioned roses."

"I work for Brewer's Roses, in Watsonville," Blue said. "We've got a display garden you can come look at, if you're interested."

"I'll do that." Inwardly I was trying to put it all together, paint a mental picture of the man beside me. He seemed to be such an interesting juxtaposition of contrasts. Team roper, solitary mountain man, plant breeder. I wouldn't have thought it a likely combination, but there you are. Like his hat, which somehow managed to connote both a cowboy hat and a sophisticated fedora straight out of a forties movie, Blue Winter was hard to categorize.

He was quiet now, seeming content to stare at the fire and take occasional sips from the bottle. I liked the way his face looked in the firelight, still and intense at the same time. I liked his strong chin and the shape of his mouth.

Reaching for the bottle, I took another sip. The tequila was going to my head; I could feel it. I wasn't sure I cared. I wanted to touch Blue Winter's skin.

Roey pressed against me and curled up a little more comfortably. I looked down at her and thought of Lonny. Lonny playing with my puppy. What about Lonny?

I should be loyal to Lonny, as Lonny was, I believed, loyal to me. Nothing that had happened, including my frustration with Lonny or this unexpected proximity to Blue, was a good reason for cheating on my boyfriend.

Even supposing this man had any interest in me. Snap out of it, Gail, I told myself firmly. Quit being an idiot. And no more tequila.

I sat up a little straighter, feeling uncomfortable with myself. I needed to break this strange mood.

"So what's your real name, if you don't mind me asking?" I said.

Blue smiled at the fire. "I don't mind. Robert. When I was a kid, they called me Rob."

"And you got named Blue in Australia."

"That's right. I traveled for a while when I was in my twenties. How about you? Have you done any traveling?"

I shook my head. "No. I'm kind of ashamed to admit it, but I've never been out of California, except for going up to Tahoe. I was born and raised in Santa Cruz County, and my parents died when I was in my last year of high school. I spent my twenties putting myself through college and veterinary school, and then I went into practice."

That was a nice, short, neat summary of my life, I reflected. No pathos, no mention of what a struggle it had all been. No, I hadn't had time or money for traveling. It was only recently that I'd started to feel financially secure.

"So, where do you live?" I asked Blue, wanting to keep the conversation going.

"On the rose farm." He smiled at me. "In a trailer. One of the reasons Katie didn't care for me, I think. It isn't too upscale."

I took that in. "And you keep your horses there, too?"

"That's right. It suits me," he said quietly. "I'm not ambitious. I don't need a lot of money, or a big house. I like where I live."

It was the most personally revealing statement he'd made yet, and I added another facet to my mental image. No doubt about it, this man interested me.

Too much, I told myself. Too much. I stood up.

"I think it's time for me to get some sleep. I'm going to drag the saddle pads over near the fire. I'll bring you a few."

"Thanks." Blue remained sitting; I was glad he seemed willing to accept my help when it came to small chores. He needed to conserve his strength for the ride out.

I started to lay the pads near the fire; as I walked by Blue he reached up and brushed my arm. "My rain jacket's in my saddlebags," he said. "We could lay it over us for a blanket."

Us? What did he have in mind?

My thought must have shown on my face. Blue smiled at me. "We'll be warmer if we lie next to each other."

"Uh-huh." I got our respective rain gear out of the saddle-bags and brought it over.

Blue patted the pads next to him. "Just lie down here and put the raincoats over us. I'll keep you warm."

I regarded him steadily. "What do you want?" I asked.

"To keep you warm." He met my eyes. "I know you have a boyfriend."

"And you?" I found I really wanted to know the answer to this question.

"No one. I'm a solitary wanderer." He smiled again, but I had the impression the smile concealed some sadness.

I sat on the pads next to him and then lowered myself down on my side. Leaning my head on my hand, I looked at the fire, feeling unsure and uncomfortable. What did I want here?

I could feel him moving, laying raincoats over the two of us with his good arm. "Just relax, Stormy," he said. "I won't bite. Put your head down."

So enjoined, I rested my head on a saddle blanket, which smelled strongly of horse, and closed my eyes. Very gently his hand touched my back, caressing me in long strokes, as one might pet a cat. In another minute he turned, and I felt the warmth of his long, strong back pressed against mine.

"Good night, Stormy," he said.

"Good night."

I wasn't sure if I was disappointed or relieved. Both, I guess. I lay there and listened to Blue Winter breathe and restrained myself forcibly from rolling over and putting my arms around him.

Leave it be, I told myself. If this is meant to happen, it'll happen in its own time, and when it's right.

So I lay against his back, with the fire's warmth on my face, and waited. Some time later, I fell asleep.

Waking up wasn't easy. Not just because of the tequila, though I'm sure it was a factor. Dawn was faint in the sky when I opened my eyes. Immediately I shut them again. I didn't want to wake up.

My head hurt, and the day loomed in front of me like an insurmountable mountain. Besides, it was cold. The fire had gone out during the night.

Blue lay on his back next to me, with his good arm thrown across me like a blanket. I snuggled into the warmth of his body, forgetting all possible reservations. At least he was warm.

Still asleep, too, or so it appeared. He breathed gently and quietly and molded his body against mine.

I wondered what the day would bring, and had an even stronger inclination to keep my eyes shut. Why couldn't I just lie here next to this man, content with the feel of his long, strong body and the peaceful sense I had of him?

But my mind, the incessant chatterer, wouldn't let me alone. The horses are hungry, it said. And what about that fire? Who set it; who's out there? And what are you going to do?

Damned if I knew. Maybe Blue had an idea.

"Are you awake?" I asked.

"No." Blue didn't open his eyes or move.

I started to get up, and felt his arm pinning me down. "Just lie here," he said. "Just for a minute."

I subsided, and looked over at him. Slowly, very slowly, he turned his head so we were face to face. Then he opened his eyes and looked into mine.

"I was wondering if you'd care to give me a kiss," he said. "Just one. Just a token."

Despite everything, I had to smile. I leaned toward him so our lips touched; damn, I'd wanted to do this. He kissed me as gently as he'd touched me last night, and yet firmly, too, with a sense of something more, waiting.

When our lips parted, I kissed him again, with longing and curiosity. It felt good.

This time Blue smiled when I moved away. "That was nice," he said.

"Uh-huh." Now is not the time, I told myself. "We'd better get up and get going," I said out loud.

Blue moved slightly and winced. "You'd better give me another shot of that stuff."

I hesitated. "There's only two doses left."

"I know. But if I'm going to get up and get on that horse, I need something. I can always take codeine to keep going. With any luck, we'll get out to Bridgeport today."

"With any luck." I echoed his words. With luck, and no snipers. But I kept that last bit to myself. What was the point of saying it? We both knew.

"So, do you have a plan?" I asked him as I began filling the syringe.

"Sort of." He gazed up at the sky as I injected the shot. "If the smoke's cleared enough, I thought I'd try to get an idea through the binoculars where they're camped."

"You think they're out there, then?"

"Sure. They must wonder what happened to us. That smoke was too thick yesterday for them to see us swim out to the island. At a guess, they're camped at this end of Kerrick Meadow, which is right about there." He pointed a finger in the general direction of the trail that led up the canyon. I could see nothing.

"We really can't get out of here without riding up that canyon," he went on, "and they must know that. What they might not know is that there's a little plateau about halfway up the canyon which will give us a good view of their camp, if they're where I think they are."

"Then what?" I asked.

"Then we make a plan. If we're careful, we can get the advantage on them. Or him. Whoever it is."

We were both quiet. "All right," I said. "Do you figure we'll just shoot whoever it is?"

"I don't know," Blue said. "We'll have to see what's what."

"All right." This didn't sound like a hell of a plan to me, but I acknowledged that it was impossible to know what to do until we understood the situation. We would just have to play it by ear.

Slowly, with numb fingers, I began assembling the gear and saddling the horses. Everybody was impatient, moving about, tossing their heads, stomping their feet. They were hungry.

I was clumsy and short-tempered. Gunner stepped away from me for the third time and I whacked him hard with the end of the lead rope. "Dammit, stand still!"

I could feel Blue's eyes on me, but he said nothing.

Eventually the saddles and what little gear we had was aboard the horses. Blue got stiffly to his feet, and with my help, climbed on Dunny. The sun wasn't yet showing over the eastern ridge when we stood facing the cold water of the lake.

Once again I got my pistol out of the saddlebag. Holding it in my left hand, I gripped the reins and a chunk of Gunner's mane in my right. My heart pounded steadily as the horses waded in. I knew how icy it would feel. I was scared and excited and just plain shivering with cold, all at once.

My feet were brushing the surface of the water now; cold wetness crept up my calves and my thighs, which were tingling with shock. I clung to Gunner's mane and fixed my eyes on the white beach. I just had to hang on till we got there.

Gunner was swimming now; I looked back to see Plumber swimming, too, Roey just behind him. Blue and his two horses were afloat, and Freckles, I was glad to see, had gone right in this time. Maybe she was getting used to swimming.

Once again I looked ahead. To the beach, to the eastern ridge, with the sun about to peek over. Some faint smoke haze still hung in the sky, but nothing like yesterday. I looked over at Blue on the swimming Dunny, his hat tipped forward over his eyes. For just a moment, I saw it all as a picture—cowboys, horses, and dogs, swimming a lake at dawn, under a pale, metallic sky. Something out of a Charles Russell painting.

Then it was back to the present. Freezing cold water lapping at my waist and the horse swimming underneath me, the beach still a long ways off.

We would make it, I told myself. We'd all swum across successfully once before.

Slowly, we drew closer to the beach. I could see the meadow clearly now. It looked empty, and the grass was still green, although some of the aspen were scorched. The forest was pretty black.

We probably would have been okay on the beach, I thought. But the island had felt a lot safer. If only I could get out of this frigging icy water, I'd think we made the right choice.

My legs had gone from tingling to numb to a slow, steady ache. I wondered exactly how cold Benson Lake was.

The beach was close now. I could see our packs on the shore. Not burnt, thank God, or disturbed. There would be dry clothes and food in those packs.

What seemed an eternity, but was probably only a minute or so later, the horses scrambled up on the beach. I heaved a deep sigh of relief and climbed off Gunner.

Then it was back to work—unsaddling the horses and turning them loose to graze, unpacking the packs and searching for food and dry clothes. Feeling considerably less shy, I stepped behind a bush and stripped down to my clammy skin, not particularly worried about whether Blue watched or not. I was too damn cold.

Dry clothes felt good. I stepped back out into the open to see Blue sitting on a log. His shirt was off, but he still wore his dripping jeans and boots.

Belatedly it occurred to me that he might be having a hard time getting them off.

"Do you need help?" I asked.

"I guess so." He sounded sheepish.

"I can help," I said.

"If you could just help me get my boots off," he said.

"Sure."

I bent to the task for the second time, aware as I did so how silly I must appear. The left boot came free; I set it on the ground and looked up at Blue. He was smiling.

I shook my head at him. "So you like having a valet?"

"I don't mind at all. You make a pretty cute valet."

I smiled. In general, I'm not crazy about being called cute, but somehow when Blue said it, I kind of liked it.

I pulled off the right boot, set it on the ground, and straightened up. "So what's the plan?"

"The plan is, I put on some dry clothes and we walk up the canyon with the binoculars and see who, if anyone, is camped at the end of Kerrick Meadow."

"Should we leave the horses here?"

"I think so. They need to eat, and they're hungry enough not to wander. If you want to string a run line and put the mare on it, we can be sure they'll stay put."

"Okay." I agreed with Blue. Tying Little Witch up would safeguard us against losing the horses in the event something startled them. After spending several days together, our four equines considered themselves a herd, and the geldings would certainly be unwilling to leave the mare.

I strung a picket line and put Little Witch on it, making sure she could reach plenty of grass. By the time I was done, Blue

216

had changed into dry clothes. Like me, he wore nylon and rubber sandals suitable for walking or swimming. I smiled again.

"You don't look much like a cowboy in those," I said.

He glanced down at his feet, which were as long and slender as his hands, and pretty much snow-white. "I don't know," he said. "Cowboys all have white feet."

"True enough."

We grinned at each other companionably. Despite the problems ahead, I had a faintly euphoric feeling—perhaps the successful swim, perhaps just this man's presence.

Blue seemed to feel the same. Swinging his binoculars by the strap, he gestured at the canyon.

"Lead on," he said.

I led. We walked up the trail, out of the meadow, through the blackened forest, avoiding smoldering tree skeletons. The fire was pretty much out, except for the occasional stump. Soon we were clear of the forest and headed up the canyon. Vegetation diminished.

Blue stopped. "Here's where this fire was set." He pointed to various spots. "Here and here and here and here. It looks to me like whoever it was had a hard time getting it going."

"Whoever it was." I said it softly and Blue looked my way. "Come on," I said. "Let's go."

Reaching down, I touched the butt of my gun. It sat in its holster on my belt and made me feel safer. What good it would actually do me if whoever it was appeared, I didn't know, but it sure was better than nothing.

Blue led me off the trail and up a side canyon. We were scrambling through the rocks now, but I felt better as soon as we got off the main trail. Whoever it was would have no reason to be up here.

Up and up we went. My hands and nose were cold, but in

general, the exercise was keeping me warm. Shafts of early sunlight lit the granite here and there. Blue picked our way slowly, trying to protect his arm.

Suddenly and without preamble we stepped into a pocket meadow high on the canyon's side. I could see Benson Lake below us in its thimble-like hollow. Blue stopped, took a deep breath, and raised the binoculars to his eyes.

I looked where he pointed them, on the opposite ridge, where the main canyon topped out. I could see a flat spot and some trees, that was it.

For a moment Blue was quiet, staring, his face as unreadable as ever. He adjusted the binoculars, moved them slightly. A more pronounced stillness seemed to come over his features.

"There he is," he said quietly.

TWENTY-FIVE

Who is it?''

"See for yourself." Blue handed me the binoculars.

I looked where he pointed and saw only a blur. Fiddling with the adjustment blurred things more rather than less. Suddenly pine trees swam into focus. I saw a tent. And then I saw a man.

Dan Jacobi. Engaged in the prosaic task of building a fire.

I lowered the binoculars. "Do you really think he did all this?"

"Who else?" Blue said. "I don't believe it's a coincidence he's camped here."

I picked up the binoculars again and scanned. No sign of Steve or Jim. I could see a couple of horses picketed in the meadow. Dan continued to crouch over the fire.

Once again I put the binoculars down. "But why?"

I was trying to put it all together in my mind. The snares along the trail, the shooting, the fire. I could picture blond Steve doing those things. Suddenly it bothered me that I couldn't see Steve.

"Let's get back to the horses," I said.

"All right." Blue seemed as eager as I to see the stock. We scrambled down the canyon as fast as he could do it, the dogs trotting happily with us. They were glad we'd gone for a walk.

Once we were on the main trail, I kept my eyes open while thoughts sailed in and out of my brain like kites.

"Do we have to ride by them to get out?" I asked Blue.

"Yes. Unless you want to head back toward Crazy Horse Creek. But that's more than three days' ride. And Bridgeport's about eight hours away. But we have to go through Kerrick Meadow."

"What's the trail like on the other side?"

"Right as you come out of the meadow there's a tough spot. It's called The Roughs. It's tricky, but it's short. After that it's all easy riding down Buckeye Canyon to town."

"Are there any really dangerous spots in The Roughs?" I asked him.

"There's a place called Dead Horse Corner. It's not that bad if you stay to the inside. But the rock slopes out and down, and it's slickrock. You can see the bones of a horse or two down below."

"That ought to work," I said.

"What do you mean?" Blue stopped in his tracks.

"Come on," I said. "I'll tell you while I'm packing up to go."

We were in the meadow now; despite my racing heart, I took a moment's comfort in the sight of our placidly grazing horses, their backs shiny in the early sunlight. But I kept moving.

I caught horses and began saddling and packing. Blue helped me as much as he could. And while I packed, I talked.

I told Blue about the snares along the trail to Cherry Creek Canyon, told him in detail this time. Particularly about the slicker.

"Could you," I asked him, "rig a horse-spooker like that?"

"Sure. I used to make snares for rabbits when I was a kid. I know how to carve the trigger."

I nodded in satisfaction. "And we've got a raincoat and some twine."

"So, what do you want to do, Gail?" Blue stared at me, holding a bridle in his good hand.

"Trap them with their own trap," I said. "It looks like they're barely awake; their horses are still out in the meadow. They know we have to ride by them to get out, so they figure they're sitting pretty. They're not afraid of us."

"True enough." Blue sounded puzzled.

"So, let's say we go galloping right through their camp, flat out. We'd catch them by surprise, wouldn't you think?"

"Sure."

"So, what do you think they'd do?"

"Saddle the horses and go after us, I guess," Blue said.

"That's what I think, too. But they'll be a ways behind us. And if we can get up into The Roughs and rig a horse-spooker at Dead Horse Corner, we might catch them by surprise again."

Blue took this in and then grinned. "You want to set them up?"

"That's right. Look at it this way; if they're innocent, they won't chase us, and if they do chase us, they're the ones who've been trying to kill us."

Blue's grin grew wider. "How many bullets do you have left?"

"Four," I said.

"All right."

Neither of us extrapolated on this. The horses were packed and saddled.

"Let's get you on," I told Blue. "We don't have any time to waste. I want to catch them while they're still in the sack."

Once again we went through the ritual of boosting Blue onto

Dunny. Then, pack horses and dogs in tow, we headed out of the meadow.

My heart was really thumping now. Like a rope horse about to make a run, I could feel adrenaline surging into my system. Fight or flight—the old message. Live or die.

I knew that I could be killed. They had shot at us once; they could shoot again. There was no knowing. My heart pounded furiously.

I thought of the horses, and the dogs. We would all have to take our chances. I prayed that we'd survive, that we'd all come out unscathed.

We were out of the meadow now, on rock, climbing the trail that led up the canyon. Blue was in the lead; once again I followed Little Witch's flaxen tail.

On and on, up and up. Past the marker that pointed to Benson Lake, back on the main trail, up toward Kerrick Meadow. Not too far now, by my reckoning.

Blue pulled his horse up at a flat spot. I rode alongside him.

''That's Ranchero Creek,'' he said, indicating a small, clear stream to our right. ''When we round the next bend, we'll be in the lower end of Kerrick Meadow. They're camped to the right of the trail, along the creek, where the meadow narrows.''

We both stared at the trail ahead. Innocuous in the morning sunlight, it looked pleasant and inviting. Level trail, leading to a meadow. With an enemy guarding it.

''Should we start moving here, or when we round the corner?'' I asked Blue.

''Let's kick the horses up to a trot here,'' he said in even tones, as though he'd been thinking about it. ''That way we'll all have some momentum going. As soon as we round that bend we'll see their camp. Beyond that the trail runs on level ground through the meadow for at least a mile. We can cover the whole thing at the lope. Then there's another mile uphill through forest before we hit The Roughs.''

"Okay," I said. "Are you ready?"

"I'm ready."

Both of us clucked to our horses and leaned forward in our saddles. Gunner picked up the trot easily. I dallied the lead rope around the saddle horn and pulled Plumber out of the walk and into the trot.

"Heel," I told Roey, probably unnecessarily. She was following right in Plumber's wake.

The bend was coming up; I clucked again as I saw Dunny and Little Witch break into a lope. The pine trees rushed by me as Gunner picked up the gait.

Then we were around the turn, the meadow ahead of us. My eyes shot to the right. Tents, still quiet. No sign of humans. I kicked Gunner in the ribs.

Hooves pounded, saddles squeaked. We thundered down the trail past the campsite. A horse neighed out in the meadow and Plumber answered shrilly back. A man's voice, loud and surprised, "What the fuck?" Steve's voice.

Motion around the tents, I thought, but I kept my eyes straight ahead. My body rocked to the rhythm of Gunner's long stride; I could feel Plumber galloping alongside, leading like a well-trained dog on a leash.

We were past their camp. More neighs from horses in the meadow. Yells behind us. Then the sharp crack of a shot. I ducked lower over Gunner's neck, my heart pounding.

Gunner galloped on without a check, as did Plumber. I could see Blue and his horses and dog. I looked back over my shoulder. Roey was there.

There was a man standing in front of the tents. Steve. He pointed a pistol at us and shot again. I ducked and hustled my horse, but I knew we were out of pistol range. Thank God, he didn't have a rifle.

In another minute we would be out of sight of their camp. Kerrick Meadow opened up around us, green and sunny. We raced headlong down the trail, horses and dogs and all.

At a guess, Dan and crew would now be scrambling to catch horses and saddle up. We would have at least ten minutes' head start on them. We needed to use it.

Moving at the high lope, Kerrick Meadow sped by. Sharp, silvery, saw-toothed peaks rose on the skyline; we were on the eastern side of the Sierras now, everything steeper and more abrupt. The meadow was a green plateau in a vertically thrusting rock landscape.

Gunner stretched out eagerly underneath me, trying to stay ahead of Plumber. The competitive instinct seems to be bone-deep; horses don't need to be taught to race.

Even though I knew the hunters were behind us somewhere, my heart lifted at the rhythm of the gait and the wind on my face. To be galloping across a sunny mountain meadow in a charging pack of horses and dogs—some atavistic gene, some ancestral hunting instinct, spoke to me in an exhilarating voice.

On we galloped, the trail following the creek, more or less. Level and sandy, it wound in gentle serpentine curves through the grass, leading us toward a forested ridge.

Gradually the land began to rise. We drew closer to the ridge. Gunner was tiring. I could see the damp sweat on his neck, feel his inclination to slow. I let him drop to the trot.

Plumber fell in behind him. Blue looked back and checked Dunny. "We'll be in The Roughs in about a mile," he yelled.

"Let's see if we can cover it at the long trot," I called back.

"All right."

Blue's two horses lined out along the trail; I followed Little Witch. The dogs were staying with us, but their tongues were hanging out.

Trees around us now, but the ground was still sandy. Growing steeper all the time, with occasional rocky outcroppings.

Off to our left, the little creek poured over one such spur, cascading in a white waterfall to a good-sized pool with a beach beside it.

"Wow," I said out loud. Now there was a campsite. I earmarked it for a return journey.

If I survived this one. We kept trotting through the woods; the trail growing progressively steeper. Occasionally I looked back over my shoulder, but there was no one there.

I didn't see how there could be. Even if Dan and crew were willing to ride bareback, which I doubted, they would still have to catch and mount their horses. At the very least, we had to be five minutes ahead of them.

The trail was getting rocky. Over a small ridge and then down into deep forest. Loam and ferns under the trees—a mix of cottonwoods and pines.

The trail crossed the creek, and Blue stopped to let the horses drink. I did the same. Only half a minute, then we tugged their heads up and moved on.

The trail rose rapidly out of the woods, ascending toward a dramatically steep granite ridge. In a minute or two we were on a ledge where the route had clearly been dynamited.

Blue led at the walk. "We're in The Roughs now," he called back over his shoulder.

Up and up, steeper and steeper, rock all around us. My heart, which had slowed down, pounded faster.

I could see a sharp notch above us, looking like the spot where the trail topped the ridge.

"So where's this Dead Horse Corner?" I yelled to Blue.

"Just over the top," he said. "You'll see."

I concentrated on helping Gunner pick his way. This bit of trail was as steep and tricky as any I'd been on yet. The horses seemed to be handling it, though.

We were nearing the notch; I watched Dunny scramble a little as Blue was silhouetted on the skyline. Then they were over, Little Witch following smoothly.

The V-shaped notch was tricky for sure, slanted rock on both sides. Gunner and Plumber negotiated their way up it and we stepped through the gap.

I looked up, for a second, away from the trail, and gasped. Before us, a steep cliff and then a long canyon winding off into the misty distance, into the high desert of Nevada. We had crossed the mountains.

Twenty feet below the pass, Blue pulled his horses off the trail into a small level hollow. I rode alongside him.

"That corner is just ahead," he said. "What I think we need to do is have you hide the horses and the dogs while I set the trap."

"All right," I said.

Blue dismounted awkwardly and tied Dunny and Little Witch to pine trees.

"Just follow the trail," he said briefly. "Be careful and stay to the inside of the bad corner. Not too far, and you'll come to a grove of willows. You could tie your horses and dog in there and then come back for mine."

"All right," I said again. I didn't ask him any questions; there wasn't time. If we were to get this done, I had to trust that we would both do our parts.

I rode Gunner out of the hollow and headed down the trail, Plumber and Roey following me. Sure enough, immediately ahead was a straight drop down to the creek, many feet below. The trail had been blasted into the cliff, and to the inside, where the rock was rough, it looked perfectly safe. But as Blue had said, the trail sloped out and down; I could see how dangerous it would be to get caught on the outside.

Hurry, hurry. The voice in my head said we would run out of time. I hushed it. Tried to sit relaxed in my saddle. Let Gunner and Plumber pick their way over the rock slowly and carefully. Not a footfall slipped. I kept my eyes averted from the drop.

Now we were around the corner, negotiating our way down the slope. Some loose rock, much rough trail. No place for hurrying, though hurry, hurry said my mind.

It seemed like forever until we were in the willow grove. I found a place and tied the horses, got twine from the saddlebags and tied Roey, too. I could hear her whining after me as I jogged back up the trail.

I was gasping for breath as I got back to Dead Horse Corner. Blue's voice came from up above. "I'm getting this thing rigged. I've got the trigger carved now. When you come back, keep your eye on the trail, so you don't trip the trap. And bring the gun back with you."

"All right," I panted.

Clambering up the last stretch, I forced myself to slow to a walk as I approached Blue's horses. Hurry, hurry. They would be coming.

I gave a moment's thought to raising Blue's stirrups to fit me, but rejected the notion. I untied Dunny and climbed on, my feet dangling freely, praying he would be as gentle and trustworthy as he had appeared. Not to mention surefooted.

Leading Little Witch, I called to Freckles, who was lying obediently with the horses. She looked at me doubtfully, but she came.

Off we went, to the incessant ticking of the timer in my head. By my reckoning, they might be here in five more minutes. Hurry, hurry.

I took a deep breath. Purposefully relaxed all my muscles. Tried to send Dunny a positive, confident message. He felt entirely different from Gunner. Taller, wider, and much heavier-moving. Like riding a draft horse.

He picked his way over the rock with the same care, though, and I could feel his intelligence and willingness in his body. We rounded Dead Horse Corner and Freckles looked up toward where I knew Blue was.

"Come on, girl," I encouraged her and she followed the horses, looking back over her shoulder.

Now we were going down, drawing closer to the willows. Dunny stumbled once in the scree, bringing my heart rate sky-high, but he recovered and kept going.

I could hear Plumber's shrill nicker as we approached the spot where the horses were tied. I rode Dunny into the willows and found a place near my two horses. Working carefully and methodically, trying not to fumble or waste motion, I tied Dunny and Little Witch up, found another piece of twine in my saddlebag, and tied Freckles. Then I got the gun.

One more glance over the horses and dogs to make sure everybody looked safe, and I was running again, holstered gun clutched in my hand. Hurry, hurry.

Back to Dead Horse Corner. I stopped abruptly. I could see nothing on the trail, but Blue had said to be careful.

In a second I heard his voice. "Come on up here, Gail, I need your help."

"All right."

"Climb up here," he said. "Just to your right. The trip line's about ten feet ahead of you, across the trail. I rigged it with fishing line."

I couldn't see it. Obediently I clambered up a cleft in the rock; in a minute I could see Blue, though he was completely hidden from the trail.

He gestured back over his right shoulder with his chin. "Take that sapling and bend it down to the ground as far as you can."

I could see the sapling he meant. I pulled it downward with all my strength. I could hear the small sounds of Blue working behind me, a muttered "damn."

Then, "All right, you can let go of it—real gently."

I eased the pressure off the tree. It stayed bent. Blue gave a small grunt of satisfaction, then pointed to a flat rock. "If we sit here, we get a good view of the trail. They won't be able to see us." He looked at the gun, still clutched in my left hand. "We'll have the advantage."

"So you think we should shoot them?" I said evenly.

"We can't count on the trap working, and we definitely can't count on it taking out all three of them," Blue said.

"Do you think they'll all come?"

"They might."

I looked at him. "There are four bullets left. I don't shoot all that well. Do you want the pistol?"

"I'm righthanded." Blue said. "You've probably got a better chance. But I'll take it if you want."

Thoughts spun through my brain. Useless, disconnected. I didn't want to kill anyone. It was my gun, my responsibility. I didn't want them to kill me or Blue. I didn't want our horses and dogs abandoned up here.

That last thought decided me. "I'll carry the gun," I said. "But I'm really not a very good shot. And I haven't practiced in years."

"I'll help you." Blue crouched behind the rock and indicated a place for me next to him. "Rest the barrel on this rock so it stays steady," he said. "Sight down it, until you're aiming at the spot by that pine sapling next to the trail. Imagine there's a man there. Aim for the middle of his body. Okay?"

"I don't know," I said.

"It'll be okay. I'll tell you when to fire." Blue's voice was calm.

I was far from calm. My heart thumped steadily and my hands were shaking. I rested the barrel of the pistol on the rock and took a deep breath. Hold it together, Gail.

We waited. Nothing but quiet and the small sounds of the mountains. Wind in the pines, the distant murmur of the creek far below. We're ready, I thought. Blue turned his head sharply.

"I heard a voice," he said.

Ready or not, they were coming.

TWENTY-SIX

I couldn't see them, but I could hear them. Or rather, I could hear Steve.

His light tenor voice, carrying through the rocks to our hiding place. "Those stupid bastards can't be far ahead, Uncle Dan."

Uncle Dan? I wondered for a second if it was a Godfather-like term of respect, or if Steve was really Dan's nephew. Then my mind snapped back to the present.

They were coming up the slope. They would appear in the notch soon.

"What's the plan here?" I whispered to Blue.

He looked over at me. "Take them out, I guess."

We stared at each other.

"We can't count on being able to hide from them, or get away from them," he said quietly. "Just remember what I told you about aiming the gun. I'll tell you when to fire."

I didn't say anything. I simply could not believe the mess I was in. People were hunting us through the mountains, trying to kill us, for no reason that I knew. And I was trying to kill them in return. Believe it or not, Gail, I urged myself, just keep your mind on the job. Focus.

I narrowed my vision to the spot where the trail appeared through the notch. Waited.

Steve's voice again. "Once we get through these rocks, there's a big valley. We'll catch them there. We can move a lot faster than they can with those pack horses."

A low reply. I couldn't hear the words, but I recognized the deeper baritone of Dan Jacobi's voice.

And then Steve appeared in the notch. Riding a sorrel horse, wearing a straw cowboy hat, pistol prominent on his belt. The sorrel slipped and scrambled a little in the V-shaped cleft, and Steve cursed him.

"You dumb son of a bitch. Keep your feet under you." He gave the horse a sharp jab with his spur.

The sorrel lunged forward, slipping again, but managed to stay upright.

"Stupid bastard." Steve jabbed the horse one more time.

Now the big gray gelding was silhouetted in the gap—Dan Jacobi, following Steve. My heart pounded. Steve was coming toward us, toward the trap, toward Dead Horse Corner. On they came, looking ahead, down Buckeye Canyon.

"I can't see them." Steve sounded disappointed.

I could feel Blue's body tense next to me. Almost there. Steve would never see the fishing line.

The sorrel horse took another step. And things started happening so fast I couldn't follow them. With a *woosh*, the pine sapling cut loose and Blue's raincoat flew into the face of the sorrel.

The animal shied violently; his foot came down on the steep, sloping slickrock, he slipped, came up, scrambled, slipped again. Steve yelled, a short, startled bark of anger and fear.

Then the horse was down, his hooves crashing and clashing, fighting for purchase as he slid over the bank.

"Shit!" Steve was off, struggling to get away from the frantic horse, and the horse was going over.

Whump. Whump. Whump.

I gasped at the sound, horrible beyond belief, of the horse's heavy body hitting and falling and hitting and falling again.

"Damn." Dan Jacobi's voice. The gray horse had spooked back and slipped—all this registered in the periphery of my vision—gone down, and got up. Dan Jacob was off, lying on the ground. The gray horse trotted away, going toward our horses, apparently unharmed.

Steve stood, his hand on the butt of his pistol; Dan Jacobi lay by the trail. I could see no sign of Jim.

Steve looked around, his face and body rigid.

"Those bastards," he said furiously to Dan.

Dan said nothing.

Steve was scanning the rocks above the trail. He drew his gun. He walked toward us.

My heart thudded. He understood the horse-spooker trap; he had rigged one himself. He was looking for our hiding place.

The gun trembled as I did. Blue put his left hand over the barrel and looked me in the eye. His lips formed the word. "Wait."

I waited, resting the pistol on the rock, sighting down the barrel, watching Steve walk in our direction.

Closer he came, and closer. I took a deep breath.

Blue's hand moved to my wrist; his eyes cautioned me.

Steve was twenty feet away now, looking up in the rocks. He stared at the sapling.

"You bastards," he said again. And pointed his pistol and fired.

Crack! The shot was aimed in our general direction, but I didn't think he could see us.

He took another step forward and pointed the gun right at us.

"Now," Blue said urgently.

I pulled the trigger.

Ka-boom. The .357 went off in a deep-voiced explosion. Echoes bounced, my hand jerked back. For a second I saw Steve's face—amazed, furious—as the force of the bullet shoved him backward. He fell, rolled, and went over the bank, leaving only the rattle of falling scree behind him.

I looked at Blue. His face registered nothing. He watched the cliff where Steve had disappeared.

I looked over to where Dan Jacobi lay on the ground. He, too, watched the spot where Steve had fallen.

It seemed for a moment that we all held our breath. No noise, nothing. Just the sound of the creek in the canyon.

Dan's face turned in our direction. "I haven't got a gun," he said clearly. "I think my leg's broken."

Blue and I glanced at each other. "What do you think?" I whispered.

"Be careful," he said.

"Put both your hands where I can see them," I called to Dan, training the pistol on his body.

Slowly he raised both empty hands in the air.

"Where's Jim?" I yelled.

"Back in camp."

Once again, Blue and I looked at each other. "Let's go," I said. "Let's get out of here."

He took this in and stood up. Slowly we clambered back down to the trail. I didn't look at the cliff, tried not to think about Steve or the horse. I kept my eyes on Dan, kept the pistol pointed at him.

He lay on the ground, hands raised. He neither moved nor spoke until we stood on the trail.

"Don't leave me here," he said evenly.

I stared at him. By the angle at which it lay, I could see that his leg was broken—a compound fracture, probably. I knew the kind of pain he would be in. His face was quiet; his eyes watched us.

I felt no sympathy for him. I felt no anger either. I felt detached. There he lay in front of me, suffering, and I felt no more pity than a rabbit who is suddenly empowered to kill the bobcat. Let him suffer, I thought.

Dan showed no sign of the pain. His face stayed quiet, composed even. A little tightness in the way he held his mouth, that was all.

He met my eyes. "Help me," he said.

"Why?" I pointed the gun at his face. "Why did you do all this?"

For a long moment those hard, dark eyes looked right at the end of the gun. "I can show you," he said at last.

His hand moved and my own hand jerked in response.

"I don't have a gun," he said again, holding still. "I want to get something out of my pocket."

I stared at him. "If you pull a gun, I will kill you," I said steadily.

"I know that. I don't have a gun. Can I show you?"

I wavered. What in the hell? "Move very slow," I warned him.

His hand went slowly to the pocket of his shirt. He unbuttoned the flap, reached in, fumbled a minute, brought his hand out, fist closed.

"See," he said. And he opened his hand.

For a moment I didn't understand what I was seeing. Small, shiny pieces of glass, little clear stones that glittered in the sunlight. I peered forward, keeping the pistol on Dan's face.

They were jewels, I realized. Loose, not set. Cut, faceted gemstones, clear and shiny, green in color. Emeralds? If they were emeralds, they looked strangely pale and washed out, there in the palm of Dan's hand, in the clear, pure Sierra sunlight. Like chips of glass, lacking any of the green fire in their hearts that the word emerald brings to mind.

"Green fire," I said out loud.

"That's right." Dan looked mildly pleased. "I knew you'd see it, sooner or later. One way or another."

My mind was adding things now, coming up with a new equation. "Green fire in their bellies," I said. "That's what Bill Evans meant."

Dan nodded ever so slightly. I looked over at Blue, who was watching us silently.

"That's what all this was about. I heard Bill Evans say 'green fire in their bellies.' I never thought twice about it. I thought he was talking about colic. But he meant horses with smuggled emeralds in their guts. That's why they colicked, probably."

"That's right," Dan Jacobi said. "We brought Peruvian Pasos in from South America. Juan used a balling gun to give them the emeralds down at the other end. Sometimes they colicked; a couple of them died. Bill was my vet. He knew all about what we were doing; it was impossible to hide it from him when he was dealing with the colicked horses. I gave him a cut, but he was never happy about it."

"When he said 'green fire,' he meant the smuggled emeralds," I said again, still taking it all in.

Dan watched me quietly.

"But I had no idea what it meant," I said. "I never would have guessed."

Dan nodded slightly. "In the end you would have repeated it to someone, though. And 'green fire' has a real specific meaning to anyone in the trade. Those cops were already asking me questions about my relationship with Bill. They've been trying to catch me for years.''

"They knew you were smuggling emeralds?''

For a brief second Dan almost smiled. "Nah. They thought I was smuggling cocaine. Every time I'd bring in a load of horses from South America they were worried. They even brought their sniffing dogs out to my place once. But there wasn't anything to sniff. These don't smell.'' He rolled the stones in his palm.

I stared at the shiny bits. "You didn't smuggle cocaine?'' I asked him, curious despite everything.

"Nah,'' he said again. "I don't like the business. And I don't care for the people you have to deal with. These,'' he rolled the jewels again, "you deal with a different bunch. A better class of crooks.'' His lips twitched.

I stared at him. "You were crazy to try to kill me,'' I said at last. "It was an off chance that I'd ever repeat that phrase or anyone would ever understand what it meant. You're in a lot worse trouble now.''

"You're right.'' For a second Dan glanced at the cliff. "Steve convinced me we could get rid of you and no one would ever know. Just a minor problem solved.''

"That rockfall,'' my mind was jumping back, "that was what he tried first, didn't he?''

Dan wouldn't meet my eyes. "I just wanted to talk to you, find out how much you knew,'' he said finally. "I got Ted to take me to your camp. But I made the mistake of telling Steve. He's worked for me since he was a kid. He's my sister's son. She never could deal with him. He knew all about the jewel business; he handled the horses at this end and got a cut. He wanted to get rid of you.''

Dan looked into my face again. "I'm not a killer,'' he said. "I'm a horse trader. And I'm not above smuggling a few emeralds. But I've never killed anyone in my life. Steve just left camp one morning and said he was going to take care of my problem. I let him go.''

"You knew," I said. "You knew what he meant to do."

"Maybe," he conceded. "But I didn't ask him. When he didn't get it done the first time, he got more determined. And when he came back the second time, he said we had to kill both of you because you would figure out who was after you."

"So you set the fire." I said.

"Steve did." Dan shook his head, almost imperceptibly.

"You could have stopped him." Suddenly I was angry. I turned toward Blue. "Let's go," I said. "Let the son of a bitch lie."

"Take me with you." Dan said it quietly; it was as close to begging as he would get.

I ignored him and spoke to Blue. "We can't. We'd never get him on a horse with that leg. And I don't trust him."

Blue looked at Dan, then at me. "What do you want to do?" he asked me.

"Leave him here. We'll send the paramedics, and the sheriffs, after him when we get to Bridgeport."

Blue watched Dan, who stared at us, saying nothing. "Let's give him a shot of that stuff," Blue said.

"We've only got one shot left. Don't you think you might want it?"

Blue twitched his right shoulder and winced. "Give it to him. I'll take a codeine. Give him what's left of the codeine, too."

I was quiet. I looked at Blue, then looked at Dan. A dozen thoughts came into my mind. I looked at Blue again. "All right. If that's what you want. I'll go get the stuff. You hold the gun on him. I don't trust him."

When I returned, Blue was leaning against a rock, the pistol idly pointed in Dan's direction. Both men were quiet.

I approached Dan, holding the syringe in my hand. "Keep the gun on him," I said to Blue.

To Dan I said, "If you do one thing that even vaguely alarms me I will tell him to shoot you. Believe me. You owe this painkiller to Blue, not me."

Dan nodded slightly. He set the handful of emeralds on the ground beside him. "Take these," he said.

I felt slightly sick. The pale green stones gleamed against the rough gray granite. Little bits of glass—oddly out of place. "I don't want them," I said. "You?" I looked at Blue.

"Not me."

"Give me your arm," I told Dan. I injected the shot as quickly and competently as I knew how, closing my mind to everything but doing a job. "Keep your emeralds," I said when I was done.

He picked one up and looked at it. "Pretty things," he said. "Must be the gypsy in me. Steve was like that, too. He loved them."

Automatically, it seemed, we all looked at the cliff. I didn't want to think about it.

I tossed the codeine vial at Dan. "Keep what's left of these. Codeine," I said briefly. I set a water bottle on the ground near him. "We'll send the paramedics after you. Just remember one thing. I am going to tell the sheriffs in Bridgeport every single thing you told me as soon as we get there. There isn't going to be any reason to go after me anymore. The cops will know everything I know."

"I understand." Dan showed no more sign of the relief of his pain than he had of the pain itself.

"All right?" I asked Blue.

Without a word, he turned and walked down the trail, pistol in his good hand.

We untied the dogs and the horses, and I helped him on Dunny, stowing the pistol back in my saddlebag. For a second we both looked in the direction where Dan lay.

"It's all right," Blue said. "Come on. Let's go."

I turned toward the man on the lion-colored horse and followed him, not looking back.

TWENTY-SEVEN

W e rode into Bridgeport that day. Through The Roughs and down Buckeye Canyon, right to the main street of the little town. Bridgeport sits where the sharp spires of the eastern Sierra Nevada meet the plains of the high desert, as dramatically beautiful a spot as you'll find. It seemed surreal to be there on such strange business.

It was surreal enough just to be in the midst of civilization again. We clopped down the road in the late afternoon, and I stared at houses and cars as if I'd never seen them before.

Blue guided us to the Bridgeport Inn, which actually had a hitching rail in its dirt parking lot. We tied the horses up, and the dogs. The four horses stood quietly, heads down, close to each other, back feet cocked. The dogs lay down, side by side.

Blue looked at me and caught my weary expression. He smiled. "Can I buy you a drink?" he said.

"I guess so." I gave him a weak smile in return, thinking of investigations, and probably, inquests.

We walked toward the Bridgeport Inn; I stumbled, climbing

the wooden steps, and Blue took my elbow with his one good arm.

So it ended. In a bar in Bridgeport, appropriately enough. Blue Winter and I sat side by side on bar stools in the Bridgeport Inn, having called sheriffs, paramedics . . . et cetera. They were coming, they said; we would wait.

I stared at our reflections in the mirror behind the bar. My dark brown hair waved in messy rivulets around my dirt-smudged face; Blue's fedora was dusty and limp. Even his red-gold curls looked limp.

The dead man in Deadman Meadow had brought another dead man in his wake. He lay at the bottom of The Roughs, waiting. As Dan Jacobi lay waiting.

As for me, I sat by the side of this tall, red-headed stranger and wondered what I was here for. Perhaps I was waiting, too. Waiting for the change that would unmake my life.

I should call Lonny, I thought. But he seemed distant, unconnected to my present reality. Trouble was, I wasn't even sure what that reality was. Something had shifted during the last few days, and I had a sense that the change was only just beginning. Who knew where it would end?

I met Blue's eyes in the mirror. He looked at me, then down at his margarita. Raising the glass in his left hand, he turned his head and met my eyes directly.

"Here's to you," he said.

I raised my own margarita and clinked it gently against his glass. "Here's to us," I said.

MW00754847

STILL WATERS

STILL WATERS

Nigel McCrery

PANTHEON BOOKS, NEW YORK

Copyright © 2007 by Nigel McCrery

All rights reserved. Published in the United States by Pantheon Books, a division of Random House, Inc., New York. Originally published in Great Britain by Quercus, London, in 2007.

Pantheon Books and colophon are registered trademarks of Random House, Inc.

ISBN 978-0-307-37703-6
Printed in the United States of America

For Nelly with all my love

ACKNOWLEDGEMENTS

With grateful thanks to: Andrew Lane, for help and assistance; John Catherall, for allowing me to borrow some of his physical characteristics; Robert Kirby, for brokering a deal so tirelessly; Nic Cheetham, for having faith in me; the irrepressible Gillian Holmes, my long-suffering editor; plus Sylvia Clarke, Eve Wilson and Iris Cannon, who taught me in various ways how to write and, more importantly, how not to write.

STILL WATERS

PROLOGUE

Summer, 1944

'Granny, what are these?' shouted Kate.

Iris Poel sighed. The sun was a white-hot eye in the centre of a bright blue sky, staring at the back of her neck. Her head felt leaden, and it hurt when she moved. The prickling of sweat on her arms and back made her feel as if ants were crawling all over her skin.

'What are what, darling?' she said for the hundredth time that morning. Putting her secateurs down, she turned away from the rose bush that she was pruning and looked over to where her granddaughter was supposed to be playing with her brothers and sisters.

'These.' Kate was standing over by a shrub on the other side of the garden. It was covered in glossy leaves and small red berries. Kate was cradling a cluster of the berries in her hand.

'Leave those berries alone,' Iris said sharply. 'They're poisonous.'

'I know that, but what *is* it?' Kate repeated.

'It's called a daphne,' Iris snapped, feeling spikes of pain lance through her temples with each word. 'Now leave the berries alone and go back to your game.'

'That game is boring,' Kate proclaimed with the weariness that only a six-year-old child can manage. She turned away and ran across the garden to where Iris had set out a low table for the children, covered with a white cloth. An entire toy tea set was arranged on the table, along with plates of cakes and biscuits.

Nobody was sitting at the table. Three of them were

3

kneeling on the grass playing with Kate's dolls. Two more were running around a small tree that Iris had planted in the middle of the garden the previous spring. The rest were probably in the house – Iris's daughter-in-law's house. Or rather, her son's house, but Frank was in Africa, fighting for his King and his country, and Judith went to work in a factory every day, making parts for aircraft. And Iris was left to look after the children. Every day. Every single day that God sent to try her.

Iris sighed, and turned back to the rose bush. There were dark splodges on a couple of the leaves. She snipped them off. It looked like blackspot, and there was no point taking chances.

'Are these blackberries?'

Iris jerked her head around. 'Kate, I thought you were supposed to be having a tea party with your friends?'

'That tea tastes funny,' Kate said. 'Are these blackberries, Granny?' She was closer to Iris now, gazing up at a yew tree that cast a little shade across the lawn.

'No, they're not. Leave them alone.' The pain in her head intensified. 'That tea, as you call it, is sarsaparilla. You *like* sarsaparilla.'

'I don't like *that* sarsaparilla.'

Iris's hand was shaking, holding the secateurs. She closed her eyes. She had spent all morning making those cakes and biscuits. She had put the best tablecloth on the table as well, just to make it look nice, and the girl was ruining it.

Iris looked over at the table, and the food that was going to waste. Wasps were crawling on the jam tarts.

Iris closed her eyes, but she could still feel the sun glaring down on her. The pounding in her head was making her sick. It felt as if something was coiling and uncoiling in her stomach. She couldn't keep still; her fingers were twitching and her head kept flicking left or right, like she had seen something out of the corner of her eye.

She took a deep breath, and opened her eyes again. The

garden was too bright; the incandescently blazing sunshine made her eyes ache.

She reached out with the secateurs for another leaf that was showing signs of blackspot.

'Granny!' Kate yelled.

Iris's hand jerked, and the secateurs cut through the stem of the rose. The plant toppled into Iris's face. A thorn caught her cheek as she turned her head, catching the skin just below her eye and ripping a long graze.

The pain seemed to rip through her soul.

'You stupid child!' Iris shouted. Kate stepped backwards in shock. 'Look what you've done!'

Iris lashed out and caught Kate's shoulder with her hand, dragging her closer. 'Do you know how long I spent making those cakes, you ungrateful little bitch? I'll teach you to wander around the garden touching stuff you shouldn't when you ought to be having a tea party.'

The words were spilling uncontrollably from her mouth like a stream of vomit, and she couldn't stop herself. She didn't know where it was all coming from. All of the boys and girls were staring solemnly at her. Her head was pounding, and the shimmering heat in the garden was making her disoriented and nauseous.

'You want to disobey me? I'll show you what happens when you disobey me.'

Before she knew what was happening, Iris had closed the secateurs on the thumb of Kate's right hand. The child screamed, eyes distended with horror. She tried to pull herself away, but Iris's grip was too strong.

The handles of the secateurs were held apart by a powerful spring, and Iris had to put all her effort into forcing them together. The blades sliced through Kate's thumb like they had through the rose stem. The thumb fell away. Bright blood spurted across the glossy green leaves.

The pitch of Kate's screams went up and up. Her eyes rolled back in her head and she started jerking.

Iris closed the secateurs on the girl's index finger, and brought the sharp blades together. The finger swung down, but a flap of skin still held it on to the palm. Iris cut again and the finger vanished.

The next three fingers were easier. Kate's hand looked so small when she had finished.

Iris turned around. The other children were rooted to the spot. Their gaze was fixed on Iris as if they couldn't believe what they had seen, and they were waiting to see how the trick had been done.

Iris straightened up and concentrated on the nearest girl. Her name was Madeline.

'Come here, Madeline,' she said calmly, although the inside of her head was a raging torrent of incoherent thoughts. 'Come here now, or I will come and get you …'

CHAPTER ONE

The sky was a misty grey-blue, a wash of unbroken colour from one end of the street to the other. Hidden behind the half-cloud, the sun was just a brighter patch in an already bright sky. No shadows darkened the pavement or the road. Something about the diffuse light made the cars, houses and lamp posts seem as if they had been cut out and placed onto a perfect picture of the street, barely connected to reality, able to be repositioned at will.

The delicate, almost translucent quality of the sky put Violet in mind of the duck eggs she used to collect as a child: a colour so unusual, so textured, that it almost seemed like the product of a deliberate act, rather than the randomness of nature.

Now where had that thought come from? She remembered the duck eggs perfectly – the weight of them in her hand, heavier than chicken eggs, and she also recalled the way tiny scraps of feather would still be stuck to their shells – but she couldn't quite place when or where. The detail was there, but the background was absent.

She tucked the thought away. There were more important things to worry about today. She had a job to do.

As she toiled along the street from where she had parked her car, pushing her wheeled shopping bag ahead of her, she kept casting glances up into the sky. No aeroplanes, no helicopters – just a deep, translucent blue. For a moment the world was timeless. With a small effort she felt as if she could be six again, or sixteen, rather than sixty.

But the effort would have been too much. That's what happened when you got old. Things that were easy were suddenly hard. Energy that had once seemed boundless was something to conserve in miserly fashion.

With relief she realised that she had arrived at the front door of number 26. She stopped for a moment to gather her breath. There was a chill in the air, but the long walk from where she had parked her car had left her feeling hot and flustered.

She glanced at the front of the house. The paint was cracked in a pattern of small scales across the top half of the door, where the sun caught it every morning. Scratches marred the surface around the keyhole. The letterbox had been repaired with sticky tape on more than one occasion. The bricks were a faded red, pitted with small holes and scabbed areas, and the mortar holding them together was powdery.

Her gaze wandered to the small front garden, barely large enough to accommodate the dustbin and a few tired geraniums in pots. Weeds had found their way through the paving slabs and around the circular metal cover that led down to the coal cellar. The bottom few bricks of the garden wall were half-hidden by dusty cobwebs and old snail shells layered one upon another like an outbreak of boils.

It really was time to move on.

The seaside, perhaps. She could do with some fresh air, and a change of scenery.

One of the geraniums was badly overgrown and dehydrated. A few of its leaves were brown and wilted, giving up their life so that the other leaves could soldier on. Violet reached into her shopping bag and removed the small pair of secateurs she always carried with her. Taking one of the dying leaves, dry and papery, in her hand, she snipped it off close to the stem, then repeated the pruning with the others. There, wasn't that better?

Making a mental note to bring a jug of water out later to moisten the soil, she pushed the wheeled shopping bag up to the front door and delved into her handbag for the key to the door. Slotting it into the lock she forced the stiff mechanism round and pushed the door open.

Darkness, and the smell of old lavender and boiled vegetables, reached out to embrace her.

'Dear – I'm back!' she called.

No answer. She moved into the house and shut the door behind her. 'Daisy? I said I'm back!'

The small hall was carpeted in linoleum patterned with small diamonds. Stairs to the left led up to the bathroom and the bedrooms, while the walls were papered in a floral pattern that looked almost as tired as the geraniums outside. A barometer hung opposite the stairs, massive and pendulous. According to the indicator there was a change ahead.

The house had an air of neglect, of something that was sagging into dust and decay. Violet could tell the first time she walked in that nobody visited any more. That nobody cared any more.

She pushed the shopping bag ahead of her, past the parlour and the dining room, and opened the door to the kitchen. Bordered by slide-door cupboards and melamine-covered work surfaces, it was more like a split-off section of the hall than a room in its own right. Tucked to one side by the cooker, just next to a china teapot, was the kitchen's sole concession to the modern age – a cordless electric kettle. A small refrigerator wheezed asthmatically in one corner, next to the door that led out into the conservatory. It gave the impression that it was about to fall over and die at any moment, but it had been working away for the nine months that she had been visiting the house, and for many years beforehand. It would almost certainly outlast Daisy Wilson.

Placing her handbag on the corner of the kitchen counter, she folded the handle of the shopping bag down and unzipped it. She hadn't picked up much shopping – the important items she had collected from her own flat that morning – but Daisy didn't seem to need much to keep going. In her experience, older people could subsist perfectly well on cups of tea, slices of bread, boiled carrots and the occasional biscuit.

Slipping on a pair of thin cotton gloves that she always kept in her coat pocket, she unpacked the bag. Bread, butter, bleach, rubber gloves, tea towels and a caddy of tea leaves that rustled as she put it down on the counter.

She reached across, switched the kettle on at the mains and clicked the button down to boil the water. The initial *whoosh* settled down into a steady murmuring as the water heated up. She opened the top of the tea caddy and let the smell of the leaves drift up to her nose. She closed her eyes and mouth, and breathed in. Dry, slightly spicy, and overlaid with the delicate floral notes of the Christmas rose petals and leaves that had been mixed in with the Darjeeling. Perfect.

The fragrance was mesmerising. For a long moment, she wasn't in the kitchen at all. She was standing in her own garden – her private, secret garden, not the one belonging to the ground-floor flat she rented – breathing in the mixed scents of the foxgloves, the delphiniums and the corn cockles.

No. That thought needed to be tucked away as well. She had a job to do. Once today was over, she could relax for a while. Go away. Move away. By the sea. A change was as good as a rest, they said.

While the kettle was talking to itself she walked back into the hall and took her coat off. Before placing it on one of the hooks just behind the door – so reminiscent, she always thought, of a row of butchers' hooks waiting for the meat to be hung from them – she took a look around the hall, committing it to memory. The lino. The wallpaper. The stairs. The whole thing so rooted in the 1950s, when the street had been built to replace ones lost to Hitler's bombs, that it was almost possible to hear the laughing voices of *Children's Hour* drifting on a wave of static from the speaker of a Bakelite radio set.

She shook herself. Stay in the present, Violet, she told herself. Stay focussed.

She pushed open the door of the parlour. The curtains were half-closed, and in the turquoise light the room could have been underwater. The fireplace dominated the room on one side: cold now, as it had been for some years, and flanked by two metal andirons. A massive bureau dominated the other side of the room: the marquetry almost invisible in the dim, aquatic light. Over in the window recess a television set stood mute.

Daisy was sitting in the armchair with the curved wings, grey hair still curled from her last visit to her hairdresser. Her eyes, nestled in puffy, criss-crossed flesh, were closed. She didn't seem to be breathing.

'Daisy?' Violet reached forward to shake her parchment hand. 'Daisy?'

Daisy jerked awake with a cry. She flinched away from Violet like a dog expecting to be struck.

'It's only me. I'm back from the shops.'

Daisy was still twisted in her chair. She gazed suspiciously up at Violet. Slowly the suspicion receded, and she smiled. 'I was only resting my eyes,' she muttered.

'You dropped off,' Violet said, moving across to the window, beside the television, and pushing the curtains open.

'I was thinking. Remembering.'

'I'm making a cup of tea.' Violet turned and smiled at Daisy. 'I was remembering too, walking up the road. Duck eggs. Do you remember duck eggs?'

Daisy laughed. 'I haven't had a duck egg in an age. Not since the War. Used to have them all the time, then. Blue, they were. Tasty as well.'

'They're coming back in the shops now,' Violet said. 'Speciality items, they're called. Did you want a cup of tea?'

'Speciality items,' Daisy said scornfully. 'That's supermarkets for you. Make you pay more for food that tastes the way food is meant to taste anyway. I remember when ordinary eggs weren't just eggs, they were Norfolk Greys, or German Longshanks, or Dorkings. All different sizes and colours.

Some of them with freckles and some plain, some rough and some smooth. Not like now. They're all plain and brown and the same size now.' She suddenly caught up with what Violet had been saying. 'Tea would be nice, ta.'

Violet went out into the kitchen. The kettle had just boiled, and the air was heavy with steam. She poured a little water into the teapot and sloshed it around, warming the china, then she poured it out in the sink and scooped two spoonfuls of tea from the caddy into the pot. She poured water from the kettle carefully, watching it froth as it hit the leaves. The smell wafted up to her nose again: that wonderful aroma of spice and roses. She closed her eyes and luxuriated in it, feeling the steam turning to moisture on her cheeks and forehead.

'I'll tell you another thing I remember,' Daisy called from the parlour. 'The coal man, making deliveries, wearing that cap with the leather back on it, reaching down his neck. Black with the coal dust, he was. Three sacks of anthracite every Tuesday fortnight, poured right down into the cellar.' She paused. 'He always had a smile for me, he did. Called me his little flower.'

Violet slid open one of the cupboards and retrieved two cups and two saucers. Placing them on the counter, she turned to the wheezing fridge and got the milk from the shelf in the door. A splash in each cup, and she returned the bottle to its place.

'Did you ever get the scissor-man coming around?' she called.

'The scissor-man? With his bicycle and his grindstone attached to the back?' Daisy chuckled. 'Haven't thought about him in a while. Whatever happened to the scissor-men? Don't scissors or knives need sharpening any more?'

'I think people just buy new ones nowadays,' Violet said absently as she poured the tea into the cups, one after the other.

'Wasteful,' muttered Daisy. 'That's why there's so much

clutter. Too much stuff being made, not enough stuff being kept.'

Violet reached down to where a tray was resting on its edge against the side of the fridge. She carefully lifted the cups and saucers onto the tray and carried it into the parlour.

'Here's your tea,' she said as she placed the tray carefully on the side table beside Daisy. Daisy glanced down at it, then up at Violet.

'Thank you, dear,' she said with sudden hesitation.

Violet crossed to the window again and gazed out. The skin on her cheeks and forehead was prickling from the steam, and she could feel a slight pressure in her throat. No matter. Every road had its potholes. Hadn't someone told her that once?

The street outside was peaceful. Most of the houses were unoccupied during the day. Husbands worked and wives worked too: Violet still found that a little disturbing, but she supposed the world changed and people changed with it. Wives so rarely stayed at home, these days. It was term-time, as well, and the children were still safely at school. The best thing about the street as far as Violet was concerned was that it didn't lead anywhere. People or cars never cut through on their way to somewhere else. If you were in the street then you were visiting one of the houses, and during weekdays that was rare.

From behind she heard a slurp as Daisy drank her tea. She smiled.

'I picked up your pension from the bank,' she said, the thought just popping randomly into her head. When Daisy failed to reply, she turned around. Daisy was staring at her, eyes defensive, teacup poised in her hand.

'You don't have to do that for me,' Daisy said. 'I used to be able to pop down to the post office myself, when I still had a pension book. The bank's not that much further.' She paused, judging Violet's reaction. 'In fact, I was thinking a walk wouldn't do me any harm. Might be nice to get out into the fresh air ...'

Violet let Daisy's words hang for a moment. She deliberately kept her face impassive. They'd had this discussion about once a week for the past two months, and there was no point getting angry. The decision was made and the river that was life was already flowing on, except that Daisy hadn't quite realised yet. Or still had some hope of reversing the current and taking back some small measure of independence.

'Not with your leg,' Violet said. She knew Daisy couldn't see her expression, with the light from the window behind her, but she kept her expression neutral. 'Those ulcers still need dressing every day. You don't want to make them any worse.'

'Maybe I should make an appointment down the doctor's,' Daisy wheedled. 'The ulcers don't seem to be clearing up, and Doctor Ganz was always so good about looking after me.' She sighed. 'I used to be a dancer, you know? Now look at me. Can't even walk down the shops.'

'I told you,' Violet said, 'I talked to the chemist. The cream will clear up the ulcers if we keep using it. What you need is rest. I can get all your shopping and your prescriptions, and now you've written to the bank I can make sure your pension is drawn out on time as well. Now, don't let your tea get cold.'

'I'm very grateful to you, m'dear.' Daisy took a noisy sip of tea, spilling some into her saucer. 'You look after me properly. Don't know what I'd do without you.'

'Everyone should look after their friends and neighbours.' Violet grimaced. The skin on her forehead was feeling tight and warm. 'There's not enough of that around, these days.'

'You know what I really miss?'

Violet wasn't sure whether Daisy was going to keep on about her lost independence or go back to duck eggs and anthracite, so she just said: 'What's that, then?'

'Whist drives down at the church hall. Once a week, Friday mornings. Used to see all me friends, have a chat and a cup of tea and some biscuits. Used to look forward to it, I did.'

'I'm not sure they do whist drives any more.'

'They do – I'm sure I saw it in the local paper.'

'Well, you don't want to strain your eyes. You've got to be careful at your age.'

'I can read the paper all right.'

'Daisy!' Violet let a tart edge slide into her voice. She was getting tired of this bickering. 'I'm only trying to help out. If you don't want me to do things for you – if you don't want me to get your shopping, and your prescriptions, and whatever else – then just say so and I'll leave you to it. I'm sure there are lots of other ladies your age who'd be grateful for the help.'

'I'm sorry, Violet, I didn't mean – '

'That's okay.' Soothing. 'Least said, soonest mended. Now did you want a refill?'

Daisy looked down into the dregs of her cup. 'Don't mind if I do,' she said. 'That was a nice cup of tea.' She swilled the cup around in her hand, staring intently at the tea leaves as if she was trying to see the shape of her future in them. 'What's these white bits?'

Violet took the cup from her hand and walked back into the kitchen. 'I took some Christmas rose petals from my garden and sprinkled them in with the tea,' she replied as she sloshed the remaining tea into the sink. 'I always think it gives it a nice, flowery taste. And it's meant to be good for you.' She paused for a moment. 'Who knows – if you drink enough of it, maybe you'll be able to *run* down to the shops and the bank!'

Daisy laughed, and Violet felt herself relax slightly. Crisis over.

She poured another cup for Daisy, and brought it back into the parlour, placing it carefully down on the tray next to her own cup. Daisy had drifted off again, and Violet sat quietly watching her breathe and thinking about her garden. Her beautiful, bountiful garden, filled with the most marvellous flowers. She didn't visit it as often as she should, but she knew she would be making another trip very soon.

After a while, Daisy stirred. She blinked a few times, then smiled hesitantly at Violet.

'Your tea's still warm,' Violet prompted.

Daisy smiled her appreciation, and reached for the cup. As she glanced down to see where it was, she noticed Violet's still full cup beside her own. 'Don't you want your tea, dear?'

'I'll wait for a while. I'm still out of breath from going to the shops. The pot's still hot: I can get another cup if that one goes cold.'

Daisy nodded, and sipped at her tea.

'Can you play whist?' she asked eventually. 'I really fancy a game, right now. Make a change from the telly, and the local paper.'

The question caught Violet by surprise. 'I'm ... not sure,' she said eventually. 'I *think* I can.' She tried to remember. There were flashes of memory, like images cut from photographs, of her hands holding cards, but there was no context, no background. The memories were isolated, barely connected to reality and able to be moved around at will throughout what little she could recall of her life.

And there was another memory, another image. A table. A long table, set for tea in a darkened room.

Push that memory away. Push it away *fast*.

'I'm sure there's a pack of cards somewhere,' Daisy said, gesturing vaguely to the bureau. 'Perhaps we could have a game later. Just a short one.' She smiled hesitantly.

'Perhaps,' Violet said, still feeling unsteady after the intrusion of that unwelcome memory.

'And then I could –'

Daisy stopped. Spittle flew from her lips, spraying the air. Her lower lip suddenly glistened as saliva spilled across her dentures and down her chin. 'Violet –!!' Another explosion of spittle as she coughed. 'What's happening to me?'

Violet backed away, her heart fluttering lightly but rapidly. The world seemed suddenly bright and pin-sharp. She could see red streaks in the saliva as a thick glistening string of it dribbled out of Daisy's mouth.

'Not to worry,' she heard herself saying. 'It'll all be over soon.'

Daisy's hands clutched at her throat, clawing the sagging parchment skin. Her lips were crimson, puffy. A deep flush spread across her throat and thick, guttural noises emerged from her mouth with every burst of spittle. 'Gra – geh – helgh –!'

'You know, I'm amazed how quickly the blistering has come on,' Violet said, taking a deep breath to calm herself down. She backed away from Daisy and perched herself on the edge of the sofa. 'I had expected it to take a lot longer. I wasn't sure of the dose, of course, so I probably erred on the side of extravagance.'

She leaned forward and looked into Daisy's eyes. Normally the whites were yellowed and the irises were a faded porcelain blue, but now they were heavily bloodshot and weeping profusely, the tears rolling down her cheeks to join the red river of saliva streaming from the gaping cave of her mouth.

'I realise it must be alarming,' Violet murmured as Daisy fell back into her armchair and her eyes rolled up in her head, 'but it will all be over soon, I promise.' She leaned forward and patted Daisy's hand, which was clawing at the arm of the chair. One of Daisy's eyes fixed on Violet with desperation. The other seemed to have taken on an independent life, and was pointed away toward the ceiling. She broke wind: a long, wet sound that seemed to last forever.

'You're probably wondering what has caused this,' Violet went on. 'Christmas rose sounds so charming, doesn't it? Or winter rose, which it's also referred to as in the gardening books. Black hellebore sounds much more forbidding, but I don't suppose you would have drunk so much of the tea if I told you that it had black hellebore in it. Not just the flowers, but powdered root and bark as well. Funny, the different names that people give to the same things.'

Rolling over the lavender and boiled vegetable smell of the house came a darker, nastier smell. A smell of faecal matter, cloying with foul sickness. Violet winced and turned away on the sofa. It'll all be over soon, she told herself. All over soon.

Daisy was sitting in a spreading pool of her own watery, blood-soaked faeces now. Violet was going to have to burn that chair in the back garden later, along with Daisy's clothes and a lot of garden waste to cover the smell. And the remaining tea leaves, of course. She couldn't leave those lying around. What if she forgot, and made herself another cup of tea while she was cleaning up!

Violet giggled to herself, covering her mouth politely with a delicate hand. Despite the mess, she really did enjoy this part of the game.

'There are all kinds of horrible things in the Christmas rose,' she said, watching to see whether Daisy could still hear her. 'Helleborin and hellebrin are both like digitalis, which I've also used before, but there's saporin and protoanemonin as well. It's a very nasty cocktail.'

Daisy's hands were both clutching at the armchair now, levering her body forward as if she was going to stagger upright and totter over to where Violet was sitting. Violet raised a hand to ward her off, but Daisy convulsed, falling backwards into the chair again as a thin waterfall of muddy vomit cascaded from her mouth and into her lap. Some of it splattered onto the floor. That, Violet thought ruefully, would be difficult to get out.

She decided not to use the Christmas rose again. It was certainly quick, and definitely easy to prepare, but it was too messy for her purposes. Cleaning up was bad enough without all those bodily fluids to worry about. Foxglove, perhaps, or bryony. Or perhaps oleander. She liked the smell of oleander.

Daisy's arms were flapping around now. The end was very close. Very close indeed.

'Your throat will have closed up almost completely by now,' Violet murmured, 'and your heart will have slowed down quite dramatically. I don't know whether you will suffocate before your heart actually stops beating of its own accord, but either way you will be dead within a minute or two. I don't even know if you can still hear me, but if you can I'd like to tell you that you are a selfish, stupid old woman, and I've hated every single moment of the time I've spent with you. Apart, of course, from the last few minutes. Those I have enjoyed very much.'

Daisy was silent and motionless. Her eyes were dull and sunken, and the saliva dripped slowly from her slack mouth.

Violet leaned forward, trying to see whether her heart still fluttered in her chest, whether the blood still pumped sluggishly around her veins, but she couldn't tell. She would come back later and check Daisy's pulse, she decided. After she tidied up. And if Daisy wasn't dead now, well, she would be very soon.

It was going to be a long afternoon, and Violet found that she couldn't immediately raise the energy to get off the sofa. The light streaming through the window seemed to have a weight all its own. It held her down, sapping her strength and sending waves of languor flowing over her body. From where she sat she could see a slice of the smoky blue-grey sky imprisoned between the top of the window frame and the roofs of the terraced houses across the street. The sight didn't quite provoke an image in her mind of a slate-grey sea eternally lapping at a stone causeway, but it provided an avenue through which the image could creep into her thoughts. Wave after wave after wave, battering against the stone, wearing it down a minuscule amount at a time.

Violet shook herself. If she wasn't careful she would fall asleep, and she might lose half the afternoon that way. The seaside could wait: tidying came first.

Despite the fact that she had been visiting the house – often every day – for months now, Violet had a very good idea of what she had touched over the course of that time. The kitchen and bathroom would have to be scrubbed with bleach, of course, to remove any fingerprints or whatever else might give her presence away. The parlour and the dining room were less problematic: Violet had been careful about what she touched, and had often wiped down a handle or a surface while Daisy wasn't paying attention. If she had noticed at all, she had just thought that Violet was helping keep the house tidy. Daisy's bedroom and the spare bedroom – used for storage for the past thirty-odd years – had nothing of Violet in them. No, removing traces of her passage through the house would be easy.

Cleaning up after Daisy's messy death would take longer, and would be less pleasant, but there Violet didn't have to be perfect. Old people were often incontinent, in her experience, and as long as all the obvious signs of diarrhoea and sickness were removed then the odd stain and the odd lingering smell would not be too disastrous. And besides, modern cleaning technology was marvellous.

Violet stood up and made her way into the hall. Her legs were unsteady – the relief of having got Daisy's death out of the way, she assumed – and she leaned against the wall for a moment before pushing open the door to the dining room.

Daisy had always kept the dining room immaculate, in case she ever had to entertain, which meant that it had been used perhaps twice in the past ten years. The centrepiece of the room was a solid mahogany table with legs turned in spirals. Three silver candlesticks sat on the table, and prints of hunting scenes were spaced around the walls.

A folded wheelchair leaned incongruously against the far chimney breast. Behind it, a large sheet of grey plastic was folded on the carpet.

Violet had brought the wheelchair and the plastic sheet into the house a few days ago, whilst Daisy was snuffling and murmuring in her sleep. Now she carried the sheet back into the parlour and looked around. Not the floor – she was going to have to scrub and hoover that pretty thoroughly. Perhaps the sofa.

Yes. She unfolded the plastic and draped it over the sofa until it was just a grey lump, like a shiny outcrop of stone. She could lift Daisy's body – light as it was – onto the sofa, then take the chair out to the garden and clean the carpet thoroughly. Once she had done that she could undress Daisy, wash her down with flannels and towels which she could also take out into the garden, and then re-dress Daisy in some of her other clothes from upstairs. Then Daisy could be lifted into the wheelchair, covered with a blanket and wheeled out of the house and down the street: just another old lady out for a breath of fresh air, fast asleep and dreaming of the past.

Violet glanced over at Daisy. In the time since she had last looked, something mysterious and irrevocable had happened to the woman she had once called 'dear'. What had once been loose flesh and jowls was now just a covering laid on top of an ancient skull. What had once been eyes that had looked out on eighty-odd years of history were now just dull buttons upon which dust was already beginning to settle. There was nothing there any more. The miracle had occurred once again: what had once been a woman named Daisy who had loved and lost and lived was now just ... just nothing. Skin and bone and a hank of hair. And everything that she had owned now belonged to Violet. Soon it would just be money.

It would have to be done carefully, of course. One step at a time. Nothing to cause suspicion. But given a few months, it would all be hers.

Once she had cleaned the house.

Because every journey started with a first step.

CHAPTER TWO

When Mark Lapslie's mobile phone bleeped, the sound tasted to him like chocolate. Dark chocolate, bitter on his tongue and gritty between his teeth and on the inside of his cheeks.

It was still dark outside his bedroom window, but birds were beginning to chirp and there was a freshness to the air that told him it was almost dawn. He had been drifting for some time, dreaming of the days when his house had been full of life and laughter, so the shock of the sudden noise – and the sudden flood of flavour in his mouth – hadn't disturbed him too much. Part of him had been expecting a call. He'd been tasting strawberries very faintly all day – a sign that something unplanned was about to happen.

The bleep was telling him that he had a message, rather than an actual incoming call. If it was a call the ring tone was an extract from Bruch's 1st violin concerto and tasted more like mocha coffee. He gave himself a few minutes to wake up fully before he reached across and picked the mobile up from the bedside table.

Pls call DS Bradbury, it said, followed by a mobile number.

Before dialling Detective Sergeant Bradbury, whoever he was, Lapslie padded into the bathroom and turned the shower on full. Catching sight of himself in the mirror above the sink, he winced. In his mind, he was twenty-five years younger, his hair wasn't grey and his stomach didn't bulge. Reflections kept catching him by surprise; the only reason he didn't take a screwdriver to the mirror and remove it for good was that shaving would be almost impossible.

'Hello?' The voice was female, tainted with lemon and lime, the accent pure Estuary.

'DS Bradbury? This is DCI Lapslie.' He walked back into the bedroom so the cauliflower hiss of the shower didn't drown out her voice. 'What can I do for you?'

'Car crash, sir,' she said succinctly.

'Car crash?' He took a breath. 'Sergeant, I'm on indefinite sick leave. I don't get called out on investigations any more.'

The voice was wary. 'Understood, sir, but there's something about the scene of the crash that, when it got called in, made your name jump up on the computer. When I tried to get a number for you I was told that you were on gardening leave, but it didn't say why, and when I put a call in to Chief Superintendent Rouse, he gave me permission to ring you.'

'Okay, what was it about the crash that made my name jump up on the computer?'

'I'd rather not say, sir. It's just ... special.'

'Give me a clue, at least.'

'There was one person in the car, sir – the driver – and there was no other vehicle involved, but when the first responders got to the scene they found two bodies. One of them was the driver's. The other had been there for some time.'

Interesting. That was almost worth being woken up for. 'And?'

'And there's something about the state of the second body that apparently links to some old case you were involved in.'

'An old case of mine?' He cast his mind back quickly, thinking of anything odd, anything out of the ordinary in his career, but he could come up with nothing. No serial killers still on the loose, no bizarre cults, nothing. 'What was strange?'

'Sir, I'd really rather not say. It would be easier if you came on down.'

'Where are you?'

There was a pause. Steam was drifting in from the bath-room, and Lapslie imagined the DS looking around her in the dark, trying to work out the local geography.

'Out along the B1018, heading from Witham to Braintree, there's a side road that cuts across to Faulkbourne – you know it?'

'Cuts across the river?' He cast his mind back to the last time he'd driven up that way, for a dinner date that had ended in an argument and yet another night sleeping alone, longer ago than he really cared to remember. 'Near the Moorhen pub?'

'That's the one. We're about five miles down the road from the pub.'

'I'll be there within the hour,' he said.

'You won't have any problem spotting us,' she replied. 'Look for the chunk of metal that used to be a Porsche.' And, Lapslie thought, there was genuine sadness in her voice at the thought of a deceased high-performance car.

He showered quickly, his brain picking over the bones of his career, but finding nothing of any relevance. By the time he was dressed the sky was tinged with pink and the birds had gained confidence. He was in his car and pulling out of his drive barely twenty-five minutes from the time the message arrived.

His car was almost silent as it slipped through the narrow country lanes that led away from his isolated cottage near Saffron Walden, guided by the satnav system toward Witham and an event that was already over apart from the inevitable clean-up. He didn't bother putting on the radio, or a CD. He could never listen to music when he drove: there was no knowing what tastes and, occasionally, smells might suddenly distract him if a particular track was played. Before his medical condition had been diagnosed, back in the time when he thought *everyone* could taste sounds rather than just him and a handful of others in the entire world, he had once been almost fatally distracted whilst driving when a Beatles song suddenly flooded his mouth with rotting meat.

Life was just a rollercoaster of unexpected sensations when you had synaesthesia.

The sun rose above the horizon, casting long shadows across the fields. He drove fast but carefully, pacing himself on the long stretches of road that cut through town so that the traffic lights were all green when he reached them, then accelerating on the bypasses and ring roads to make up time. The minutes slid away, one after the other, as the houses fell away behind him and were replaced with woodland. He drifted into a trance as he drove, deliberately trying not to speculate about what awaited him at the scene of the crash.

The fact that he'd been called in the first place was strange. Lapslie had been on special medical leave from the Essex Police for the past six months – ever since his synaesthesia had suddenly escalated and his wife and children had been forced to move out of the house because the constant noise was driving him insane. They still kept in contact, but Lapslie was becoming slowly used to the fact that they would never be a proper family again. He was between posts, in a kind of limbo, reading reports and keeping himself current on the ever-changing world of police practice, writing the occasional report or think-piece for the police hierarchy, popping into the Headquarters in Chelmsford every now and then but never actually attending a crime scene or leading an investigation. Until now.

The case – whatever it was – obviously had something to do with his previous career, but what it was he couldn't tell. Looking back, there was nothing that particularly stood out. Nothing that might have tied him in with any unsolved case more important than assault and battery, or low-level burglary.

Shortly after crossing the Brain, and about an hour after leaving his cottage, Lapslie turned onto the road where the crash had apparently occurred. Trees laced their fingers together above the car, and the rising sun behind him cast a deep shadow along the road.

Striped barriers blocked his way a hundred yards or so before a lazy curve in the road. Bright white light spilled through the trees. A uniformed constable with a clipboard self-consciously straightened up and walked towards him, silhouetted by the false white dawn, already shaking his head. Lapslie brought his car to a halt and rolled his window down.

'DCI Lapslie,' he said, holding his warrant card out.

The policeman looked at the card and then back at Lapslie. He frowned. 'You might want to get this renewed, sir,' he said. 'The photograph's a bit ... out of date.'

Lapslie glanced down at the card in his hand. Okay, his hair wasn't brown any more, and there was a little more of it in the photo than in real life, but apart from the size of the collar on his shirt he didn't think he looked *that* different.

But it had probably been taken while the policeman standing beside his car was running happily around a playground somewhere.

'Happy the way it is,' he said tersely.

The policeman noted his name and car registration on the clipboard as he spoke. 'Shall I move the barrier for you?'

'Don't bother. I'll leave the car off the road and walk.'

It wasn't difficult to spot the crash site, just around the curve. The Crime Scene Investigators had set up arc-lamps on poles which bathed the scene with a harsh, unforgiving light, despite the encroaching day. Lapslie paused for a moment, taking in the sight.

The smell of petrol and burnt rubber still hung in the air. Twin skid marks intertwined with each other along the road surface, showing where the car had braked, skidded and spun like some demented fairground ride. He could only imagine the horror in the driver's mind, twisting the wheel back and forth in the sure and certain knowledge that it wasn't going to do any good and he was probably going to die. Judging by the marks, the car had been hurtling along the country road before suddenly seeing the curve ahead. What had happened? Had the driver's attention been distracted by a boiled sweet or a phone call? Had his headlights been dipped so that he couldn't see the curve until it was too late? Or had he just been drunk? That was for forensics to determine, but Lapslie couldn't help speculating. Alive one moment, dead the next. The facts could be explained, but the driver's state of mind? That could only ever be guessed at.

He'd made the mistake of saying to a colleague at another crash scene some time ago, 'I wonder what the last thing that went through the driver's mind was.' The man had just looked at him blankly. 'The windscreen,' he had muttered, and walked off.

The melted rubber marks ended at the point where the road curved away. A stone kerb marked the point where tarmac gave way to uneven ground covered in leaves, tiny fretted ferns and bushes. The car had obviously hit the kerb side-on and the impact had flipped it into the air, spinning again but now around its longest axis so that when it struck the trees it was almost exactly upside down. Two trunks had been splintered at a point some ten feet off the ground. The car – or what remained of it – sat beneath them, crumpled like a discarded chocolate wrapper.

Another barrier had been set up fifty or so yards down the road. An ambulance was parked by it, beside a police Peugeot 406 – painted in the yellow and blue squares that had jokingly become known to police across the country as the Battenburg colour scheme – a dusty Mondeo and a van which had probably brought the CSI team to the area. Two paramedics were chatting to a uniformed policeman, their casual demeanour indicating that their work was done, if indeed they'd had any work in the first place apart from pronouncing the driver of the car dead at the scene.

A plastic marquee had been set up just off the road, a few feet from the remains of the car. The arc-lamps behind it made it glow. Grotesque shadows of the people inside it were cast against its walls: bent figures with distended hands, moving together and apart again in some strange ritual dance.

It was all so familiar and yet, after his time away from work, so alien. So strange.

He pulled his mobile from his jacket pocket and, after a moment's thought, dialled a number that he didn't think he would remember.

'Essex Constabulary, can I help you?'

'Superintendent Rouse, please,' he said.

'Putting you through now.'

Moments later, a new voice said: 'Detective Chief Superintendent Rouse's office.'

'This is DCI Lapslie. Would it be possible to speak to the Superintendent?'

'He's not arrived yet. Can I ask what it's about?'

'I've apparently been pulled off leave of absence on the Superintendent's orders. I was wondering why.'

The voice on the other end of the line went muffled for a moment, as if Rouse's PA had put her hand over the receiver while she sought instructions. After a few seconds, she was back. 'I can get the Superintendent to call you later. Does he have your number?'

'I wouldn't be surprised,' Lapslie said grumpily, and broke the connection.

Slipping the mobile back into his jacket, Lapslie headed for the marquee and pulled the entrance flap open. The interior was large enough to host a wedding reception. The CSI team – figures clad in papery yellow coveralls – were gathered in two groups, taking photographs and examining the ground for evidence. A woman was with them, chatting. Her hair was short and spiky; her make-up highlighted her sharp cheekbones. Her breath appeared like cigarette smoke in the cold morning air. When she saw Lapslie she broke away and walked towards him.

'DS Bradbury?' he asked.

'Morning, sir,' she said. Lemon, as on the mobile, but with a hint of grapefruit now. Her suit was a designer special, but it looked like she'd been sleeping in it when the call came in about the crash. 'Sorry to get you out of bed this early.'

'Not a problem. I'm just glad to be back in the saddle. Gardening leave gets very tedious after a while.'

Bradbury was obviously dying to ask him why he was on gardening leave – that wonderful catch-all term that meant someone was being paid to sit around the house all day – but she was too polite, or too political, to try. Covering the momentary lapse in conversation, and remembering Bradbury's comment on the mobile about the wreck of the performance car, Lapslie nodded back to where the car was located, outside the tent. 'Sorry to hear about your loss,' he joked.

She sighed. 'Porsche. Lovely machine. Complete bloody write-off. What a tosser.'

'I presume from the tyre tracks that he lost control coming into the curve. Hitting the kerb knocked the car into the air and hitting the trees totalled the car.'

'That's the way I read it. Nothing to indicate that any other vehicles were involved. The car'll be checked out, of course, but there's no reason yet to assume mechanical failure.' She shook her head sadly. 'Some people just don't deserve to have nice cars.'

Lapslie glanced across to where the CSIs were gathered in their two groups. 'What happened to the driver?'

'Pulled himself out of the near-side window and crawled into the trees, which is where we found him.'

'Dead?'

'As a Dover sole on a fishmonger's slab.'

'What happened?'

Emma Bradbury smiled, revealing small white teeth. 'He must be the unluckiest sod in history. Even at the speed he was going, his seatbelt and airbag should have saved his life, but a short branch on one of the trees punched through the driver's-side window and went right through his neck. He bled out while he was crawling.' She indicated the left-hand group of CSIs. 'That's him over there. We're waiting for the forensic pathologist to turn up. Apparently she's been delayed.'

'Do we know who he was?'

Emma fished in her pockets and pulled out a transparent evidence bag with a wallet inside. 'Name of Sutherland. Businessman, apparently. Mid-forties, lives just outside Chelmsford. Looks like he might have been on his way home after a late meeting, or something. I've sent someone to notify his wife.'

A late meeting. A snatched dinner at a Little Chef or a Beefeater before the long drive home, dazzled by oncoming headlights. Lapslie remembered it well. Once upon a time, there had been someone curled up in front of the TV in their dressing gown, waiting for him to turn up. Someone who would have cared if he'd been involved in a car accident.

He looked around. 'If there was no other car involved, who called the police?'

Emma grinned. 'A couple who were parked up and at it like rabbits just down the road heard the impact and the sound of glass breaking.'

'So the earth really did move for them,' Lapslie murmured.

'They motored down – after adjusting their clothing, of course – and when they saw what had happened they called it in. Uniform took statements and let them get back to their respective partners.'

Lapslie turned his attention to the other group of CSIs, clustered around something on the ground. 'And the real reason you woke me up and dragged me all the way here? The reason my name flagged up on the computer?'

'The other body Uniform found near the driver when they were checking to see whether he was still alive.'

'You said on the phone that there was something about the state of it?'

'I think we're dealing with *Dawn of the Living Dead.*'

He nodded. 'Well, let's see.'

The two of them moved towards the group. Small twigs and branches snapped underfoot, and Lapslie wasn't sure whether the sour smell in his nostrils was due to the sounds or the crash or both. Dawn had turned into morning now, and the scrap of sky that he could see through the tent flap was clear and blue. All around him he could taste birds and animals moving around.

They walked past the first group of CSIs, and Lapslie couldn't help glancing across at the figure on the ground: a man, crumpled up like his car, wearing a dark suit that was glossy with congealing fluid. A bloody write-off, to use Emma's phrase.

The second group was clustered around something on the ground, no more than ten feet or so away from the first body. As Lapslie approached they seemed to tense, possessive of their find.

'DCI Lapslie,' he said firmly. 'What have you got?'

The Crime Scene Manager stood, brushing his gloved hands on his coveralls. Lapslie had seen him at other crime scenes, years ago: a small man, mid-fifties, with a paunch pushing out the fabric of his coveralls and a quiff of white hair standing straight up from his head.

'We appear to have a dead body,' he said in a disconcertingly thick Irish accent, the final words sounding to Lapslie almost like 'deed baady'. His voice tasted the way Lapslie imagined blackberry wine would taste: musty and thin.

'Not connected to the crash?'

'Connected, but not in the way you mean. Take a look.'

There, rearing up from a pile of earth, ferns and leaves, was a corpse. And this *was* a corpse, more like a skeleton to which things had been added rather than a body from which things had been subtracted. The face was all sharp cheekbones and hollow eye sockets, the head twisted to one side and the jawbone gaping open as if in some terrible, silent agony. Whatever skin remained was as dull and as grey as the hair that was spread out around the skull. Its arms were stretched out behind it, as thin and as dry as the twigs that surrounded them. What Lapslie could see of the fingers clutched in vain at the loam of the forest.

And most bizarrely of all, the body was surrounded by dirt-encrusted plastic sheeting, bunched to form two huge wings, one at each shoulder.

Half-aware of the banter between the CSI team members, Lapslie knelt down by the body, checking first that he wasn't disturbing anything that hadn't already been disturbed. All corpses looked old, of course, but this one looked like it was actually the corpse of someone old. The bottom half was still buried in the ground, the plastic tightly wrapped around hips and legs, but the torso was slanted up at an angle of about thirty degrees. The arms looked as if they were supporting the weight of the body, but that was just an illusion caused by the fact that they were hanging down, the bony knuckles resting on the ground. Although the material of the clothes had been stiffened and faded by the passing of the seasons, it seemed as if the corpse had been wearing a blouse, a cardigan and a pair of slacks in some dark material.

He leant forward to check around the back of the skull. Difficult to be sure without touching it, but there looked to be some evidence of damage. It might have been caused by predators, but it might also have been caused by an act of violence. Whatever the cause, this was certainly a suspicious death. People, in Lapslie's experience, did not wrap themselves in plastic before calmly lying down to die.

Without disturbing the twigs or the dirty plastic sheeting around the body, Lapslie made a close examination of the area around where the hands rested. The body was actually half-buried in a trench of some kind. Somehow, the trench had been disturbed – the ground around it was churned up and the ferns partially ripped out – and the body had been pushed up and out like a moth from a chrysalis. The fingers were half-buried in the loam, and –

Wait. Lapslie leant closer. The scent of damp and decay filled his nostrils, but bizarrely he could taste something decadently fragrant in his mouth, like lychees.

The fingers weren't complete. The ends were missing from about the second knuckle onwards. Although it looked at first sight as if the rest of the fingers were embedded in the earth, he could see that the ends rested *on* the leaves, rather than poking *through* them.

Somewhere in the back of his mind a memory that had been asleep for a long time began to stir. Hadn't he talked to someone about a case like this once? Hadn't he written something about it? Not a case he was working on as a policeman, he was sure, but something else. Something that was almost a sideline.

'Is this why you called me?' he asked DS Bradbury, who was standing behind him. 'The fingers? They look as if they've been removed.'

'I noticed them when I first saw the body,' she said. 'When I radioed the details in, the Duty Officer typed them into the computer system. As soon as he typed the stuff in, a message flashed up with your name attached. Apparently you've seen this kind of thing before – a body with missing fingers.'

'Not as far as I can remember. Not a body, at any rate ...' And yet, there was something. The taste of lychees, and a vague memory of someone telling him about missing fingers.

He could worry about that later. For now he was back at work, for the first time in a long time, and he had a body in the here-and-now to worry about, not something vague in the past. A body that was pushing itself out of the ground as if possessed by some restless spirit.

But what had disturbed it? What had forced the earth to give birth to its dead?

Lapslie's head turned toward where the wreck of the car sat, outside the marquee.

He rocked back on his heels. 'You've got to be joking,' he muttered to himself.

'We never joke,' the Crime Scene Manager said, coming over towards him.

'Are you seriously telling me that the body was buried here in plastic sheets for some ungodly length of time, undisturbed by anything, before that car came along and just scooped it up out of the ground?'

'I'm not telling you anything, serious or otherwise, until we've collated all the evidence, photographed the entire scene and assessed it all back at the lab.' He shook his head, lips twisted into a grimace. 'But if I were a betting man, which I am, I'd put a pony on that being the final conclusion. Bizarre as it may seem, I think that car crash managed to excavate a murder victim.'

Which might, Lapslie thought, explain the damage he thought he'd spotted to the back of the skull.

He glanced over his shoulder to where the other group of CSIs were attempting to slide the dead businessman into a large vinyl body bag without disturbing it too much. 'We owe you a vote of thanks,' he said to the body, a kind of final valediction as 'he' turned to 'it', a person becoming a thing to be moved around, cut up and pored over. 'If it hadn't been for you, we might never have found her. Whoever she is.'

He straightened up and turned to the CSM. 'And you are?'

'Burrows,' he said. 'Sean Burrows.'

'Well, Sean, I think you've got a busy day ahead of you. I'll make sure to get a supply of bacon rolls and coffee sent up.'

'That,' the CSM said with a heartfelt sigh, 'would be most welcome.'

Emma Bradbury was standing over to one side. Glancing between Lapslie and Burrows, she smiled. 'What now?' she asked.

'Now we talk to the first responders,' he replied.

The two of them exited the marquee and walked back towards the road in silence. As they emerged from the tree line, Emma glanced down at the skid marks left by the car.

'Look at that,' she said, pointing. 'See the darker and lighter stripes in the rubber?'

Lapslie looked closer. She was right, there were indeed streaks where the rubber appeared to be embossed into the road's surface, and areas between them where the fine structure of the road could be seen. 'What's the cause of that?'

'ABS,' she said gloomily. 'Anti-lock Brake System – pulses the brakes automatically to maintain grip on the road. That car had everything, and the bastard trashed it.'

Walking on, they found the uniformed policeman still talking to the paramedics. 'Excuse me, sir,' he said as the paramedics melted backwards, 'but can we shift the car and open up the road yet? It doesn't get particularly busy, this time of day, but there's no easy alternative route.'

Lapslie considered for a moment. The crash was just a red herring as far as he was concerned. The old woman's body intrigued him more. 'Get the car out of here and shipped back to the garage so they can test the brakes and whatever. When it's gone, get the local authority to cordon off about fifty feet of one side of the road next to the trees and set up temporary traffic lights for traffic on the other side.'

'You sure that's necessary, sir?' Emma said from beside him.

'No,' he replied firmly. 'As my old Superintendent said, when in doubt – cover it.' He turned his attention to the policeman: a young man in a cap that kept threatening to slide forward over his head. 'You are?'

'Henson,' muttered Emma from beside him. 'I've already talked to him.'

'Were you first on the scene, Henson?' he said, ignoring Emma.

'I was,' he said. 'Me and PC Rhodes. He's manning the other barrier. The one you came in through.'

'What about this road, then? Does it see many accidents?'

He shrugged. 'It's not a blackspot, but the corner can come

35

up on you fast if you're not paying attention. We get called out here a couple of times a year.' He thought for a moment. 'Last time was probably before Christmas – maybe five or six months back. Maybe a little bit more.'

'When you were here last, did you see any churned-up areas of earth? Anything that looked as if something had been buried?'

Henson shook his head. 'Nothing like that, I'm sure.'

'Thanks,' Lapslie said. 'We may be in touch later.'

The PC turned away to rejoin the paramedics. Lapslie looked up and down the road. From where he stood, in the centre of the curve, he could see in both directions: long stretches of trees on either side forming a tunnel with their interlaced branches.

Not a bad sight, if it was your last.

Emma glanced down the road towards where she had left her car. 'Well, if that's all, boss …'

'We need to establish who she is, as a matter of priority,' Lapslie mused, only half-hearing his sergeant. 'We can come at it from two directions. A search of the body might throw up a purse, a receipt, a scrap of paper, a bus pass or something with her name and address on it. I didn't see a handbag anywhere around the body, but the search might turn it up somewhere in the long grass. I'll keep in touch with the CSIs and the pathologist, but you can cover the other direction. Once we've got an approximate age and a likely range of dates for the death, I want you to check through the missing persons records and pull out anything that fits. With luck, we can narrow it down. And then, when we know how she died, we can start pulling everything together.'

'Wouldn't it be nice,' Emma muttered. 'Look, sir, I'd like to make a move, if you don't mind. I've been here since about three a.m., and I could do with a shower and a change of clothes.'

'Okay,' Lapslie conceded, 'you crack on. I'll hang around

and wait for the pathologist to turn up. He should have been here by now.'

' "She", sir. Apparently the local pathologist is a Doctor Jane Catherall. I've called her twice, but no response. CSI claim she's always turning up late to crime scenes.'

'I'll get the number off them and try again. You can go. Check in with me later.'

Emma nodded gratefully, and walked off. Lapslie watched her go, the material across the seat of her designer trousers pulling diagonally in one direction and then the other as she walked. Women in the police force had a rough time of it: most of the time they were forced to come across as more laddish than the lads, protective coloration in the tight-knit boys' club of the police. Emma was no exception, but Lapslie suspected that underneath was a schoolgirl vulnerability. Perhaps he ought to reach out: make sure she understood that he was not taking her at face value. And he probably owed her an explanation of his time away from the police; a period that had so abruptly come to an end with her call.

He found himself following Emma before he had even made a conscious decision to move. Perhaps now was a good time to start building bridges.

She reached her Mondeo a few seconds before he did. As he approached, formulating the words of praise in his mind, he could hear her talking. He assumed for a moment that she was making a call on her mobile, but then she moved to one side and he realised that she was speaking to someone sitting in the passenger seat of the car, someone who was rubbing their eyes as if they'd just woken up.

'I can have you back in – ' she was saying, and then she saw Lapslie. The skin around her eyes tightened, and her gaze flickered from side to side as if she was automatically looking for a way out.

'Sir – was there something else?' she asked, sliding sideways to block Lapslie's view of her passenger.

Lapslie stepped sideways, but Emma's companion had turned his head away so that all Lapslie could see through the open passenger window was an ear with a small gold earring and a tousled mane of hair.

'Can I have a word?' Lapslie snapped, all the praise he had been about to deliver sliding out of his mind like rain off a windowpane.

Emma stepped away from the car, walking around Lapslie so he had no choice but to turn away from the car.

'You brought someone with you tonight,' he said, stating rather than asking.

'Sir.' Not giving anything away.

'This is a crime scene. We're professionals, doing a job. You don't just bring spectators along. What's going on?'

'Difficult to explain, sir.' Her gaze slipped away from him. 'Although not as difficult as explaining it to his wife,' she muttered. 'I'm sorry, sir. It won't happen again.'

'Emma – talk to me. Tell me what's going on.'

She sighed, and looked away. 'I was … with a friend when the call came in about the body. The extra body. We were in a hotel. His car was back in a car park near the club where we met. I wanted him to take a cab, but he wanted to … well, to come along with me. I honestly thought there wouldn't be much to see, just a pile of clothes or a tramp who'd had a heart attack. I thought we'd be clear inside an hour. Didn't plan on this turning into a crime scene.' Her gaze switched back to meet Lapslie's. 'He never got out of the car, boss. I promise you that.'

Lapslie took a deep breath. These things happened. Sometimes it was difficult to disentangle personal from professional. God knew, he'd had enough experience of that himself over the years.

'Okay. We'll leave it there. Get your boyfriend home, get a bacon sandwich and a cup of coffee inside you and I'll see you back at the office later.'

'Thanks, boss.' She nodded, waiting until Lapslie had

started to move away before she moved back towards her car. Lapslie took a few steps more, until he heard the *clunk* of her car door closing, then he turned and watched as she gunned the car to life and pulled away. He stood for a couple of seconds, watching it go, wondering whether to take things any further or just forget about it.

And just as he realised that there was another car, a black Lexus with a tinted windscreen, parked in the trees a hundred yards or so down the road, it too gunned its engine to life, quietly pulled out of the tree line and drove away after DS Bradbury.

CHAPTER THREE

It was dark by the time Violet returned to the house that had once belonged to Daisy but now belonged to her. The thin wash of cloud that had given the sky its texture and depth during the day now gave the night an oppressive closeness, like sheets of sackcloth pinned from one side of the street to the other and sagging in the middle under their own weight.

She turned the ignition key and let the Volvo's engine die away. Something inside the bonnet whirred for a few seconds more, then it, too, gave way to the silence of the night. Violet just sat there, sinking back into the seat and letting the nervous tension drain out of her body.

Lights were on all the way down the street. Behind those lit windows, families were boiling pasta and heating up sauce, watching TV, telling stories to excitable children or sitting quietly and reading a book. Life went on – if repeating the same old routine, night after night, was life.

Tiredness had wormed its way into Violet's joints. Every time she turned her head slightly she could feel the tendons and muscles pulling tight across her neck.

Come on, Violet, she thought, *focus. You still have a job to do. This was only the first step.*

She climbed out of the car, locked the door and took a look around her. Nobody was watching. No curtains were twitching. She was safe.

Violet had parked a few hundred yards down the street from her new house, of course – just opposite a patch of waste ground where children played football at the weekends – and now she walked slowly along the pavement to that familiar front door, with its crazy-paving paint and its tape-bandaged letter box. She paused for a moment, gazing at the drooping geraniums. Those would have to go, she thought. Too dreary. Too drab. Too meaningless.

Perhaps she could plant a nice Christmas rose before she left. In memory of Daisy.

Smiling, she inserted her key into her lock and walked into her house.

The smell hit her as soon as she entered. Older now, and fouler, undercut by the acridity of bleach and overlaid by Daisy's favourite lavender perfume, but still lurking there like some old, mangy dog. Air fresheners and pot-pourri could only do so much, but there was obviously more cleaning required. Quickly, Violet walked along the hall – slipping her thin cotton gloves on as she did so – then through the tiny kitchen and out into the conservatory. She flicked the latches on the back door, top and bottom, and opened it as far as it would go.

The fresh air was a sudden relief, and she took a couple of deep breaths, gazing out into the dark, shadowy back garden as she did so. From a patio of pebbled concrete, criss-crossed with silvery snail tracks, a tongue of paving stones wound its way through big, unkempt bushes of various kinds. Tall fences on either side separated the house from its neighbours, and the far end of the garden gave on to a ten-foot brick wall, almost invisible in the murk at the bottom of the garden. Daisy had never been sure what was beyond that wall, even though she had lived there for over fifty years.

A metal dustbin sat in the centre of the concrete patio, its sides streaked red with rust that had leaked from the rivets and welds of its construction. Inside the bin were Daisy's stained clothes, along with the cushion that she had been sitting on and the doilies that had been draped over the arms of her chair. The chair itself stood next to the bin, looking smaller in the open air than it had done in the dark parlour.

Tomorrow she would set the clothes in the bin on fire, accelerated by a splash of lighter fluid. The chair she would have to think about. She could either burn it where it stood, and risk leaving scorch marks on the concrete, or she could attempt to take it apart with a screwdriver and a small saw to a point where she could get the various parts into the burning bin. That might work.

The deliciously cool, fresh air reminded her that she needed a through draught to get the house to a state where she could work in it, so she turned around and walked back through the house and into the parlour. The smell was worse there, and Violet held her breath until she could undo the catch on the central sash window and push it up six inches or so. The sudden breeze through the house, from back to front, quickly cleared the air, and for a moment Violet had a strong image of the house itself slumping with relief as it exhaled a stale, rank breath.

Turning away from the window, Violet's gaze was caught, as it often had been while listening to Daisy's interminable rambling stories, by the bureau opposite the fireplace. She had carried an image of that bureau around in her mind for months. Whenever she got the chance she had checked books on antiques in the local library, or browsed through them while standing by the shelves in the nearest bookshop. She was fairly sure it was mid-eighteenth century, and in very good condition. If she was careful, it could perhaps realise ten thousand pounds at auction. The barometer in the hall was almost certainly French, dating from the early nineteenth century. That could net something approaching two thousand pounds. The andirons on either side of the fire could fetch between three and five thousand pounds, depending on whether they were originals or merely good reproductions. And there was other stuff in the house, such as the dining room table, the silver candlesticks and a complete set of pristine Spode china that Daisy had shown her once, wrapped in newspaper and kept in a Queen Anne chest upstairs 'for best', as Daisy had put it.

All in all, Violet thought that there was about twenty-five

thousand pounds' worth of furniture and nick-nacks in this house. They had all been in the family since before Daisy was born, bought by her father, her grandfather, his father and so on when they weren't antiques but just ordinary items. Daisy had been widowed young, with no children, and so there was nowhere for them to go. And here they had stayed. To Daisy they were just a part of the house, but to Violet they were something else entirely. They were assets to be realised as cash as soon as possible.

And that was before she stripped Daisy's estate of the small amount of pension that had accrued over the years, the various bonds and shares that she might have collected and, most important of all, the house. That wonderful unmortgaged 1950s house, in a quiet part of the city, ideal for commuters who wanted to be near work and yet isolated from it. Worth, according to an estate agent with whom Violet had once had an interesting chat, something in excess of a quarter of a million pounds.

Not that she would sell it straight away. No, that would raise too many questions. Although it had only taken a couple of glasses of brandy to persuade Daisy to sign power of attorney over to her, some months ago now, Violet was a little wary of exerting too much authority too soon. More haste, less speed, as they said. Best to wait until the dust had settled a bit.

Although it was late, she had an important job to do before she could slide between the sheets of her bed and gaze up at the ceiling of her room with calm satisfaction. She had to clean the parlour.

Violet went into the kitchen and retrieved the plastic bag of cleaning utensils from the counter. Looking along the shelves in the shop, she had been bewildered by the sheer range of things that people used to clean their houses. How could anyone use that many products? And how was it that houses these days were so much dirtier and dustier than they were when Violet was a child, when all they had was beeswax polish and soapstone and coal tar soap?

And, of course, soda crystals.

She pulled the blue, rather plain box proudly from the bag. At least someone still made soda crystals.

Using hot water from the tap, she made up a strong solution of washing soda in a bucket from the conservatory, and set to work with a pair of rubber gloves and a brush, working the liquid into the parlour carpet and soaking up the brown residue – the remnants of Daisy's blood and faeces – with a series of tea towels. The area where the chair had sat was almost unaffected, apart from splashes and drips that had found their way down through the upholstery. After half an hour the carpet around the edges was almost indistinguishable from the carpet in the centre, and the smell had transferred itself to the growing pile of tea towels. Carefully, she carried the towels out into the garden, threw them into the metal bin and sprinkled bleach over the top. Then she threw the rubber gloves in after them. They almost certainly wouldn't melt properly in the fire, but at least any last trace of Daisy would be burned off them.

According to the clock in the parlour – reproduction ormolu, unfortunately, dating from the 1950s and worth less than ten pounds – it was almost midnight. The muffled sounds of the TV set from next door had vanished some time before. There was no sound now, apart from the slow creaks that resulted from any old house settling itself down for the night. Violet desperately craved sleep, but there was one more thing she had to do before she could surrender herself to the darkness. One last act to make the house hers.

Methodically, room by room, Violet collected up all the photographs of Daisy. There was one in a frame in the dining room, set high on the bookshelf: an old black-and-white picture with creased corners of a young woman with a beehive hairdo posing against a railing with a beach behind her. On the back, in spidery brown writing, were the words 'Camber Sands, July, 1953'. It didn't look much like the shrunken woman with the liver-spotted arms and baggy medical stockings that she had become, but then, it looked even less like Violet, so it couldn't stay.

Violet held it for a moment, reluctant to let go. Camber Sands, July, 1953. The photograph had been taken by the young man Daisy had been seeing at the time. He had worked in a bank. They had seen each other for two years – 'walked out', Daisy had called it – until he was called up for National Service. He had promised to write, but he never did.

Another photograph rested on a small table in the hall: a colour picture of a group of four middle-aged ladies laughing in front of a hotel entrance. It had been taken in Mallorca some time in the 1980s; Daisy hadn't been too sure of the year. Susan, Janice and Patricia. They'd worked together on the checkouts in a supermarket on the edge of town for a while, and all decided to go on holiday together. Patricia had met a widower and ended up spending most of her days and all of her nights with him. Daisy had been bitterly jealous.

And there was the wedding photograph, set on the white melamine bedside table where it would have been the first thing Daisy saw when she woke up and the last thing she saw at night. Black and white again, two people, formally posed. Daisy in a huge white Bo Peep dress foaming with lace, a wide-brimmed hat on her head, and beside her a taller man with short hair and a moustache, stiff in a formal morning suit. His name had been Peter, and Daisy hadn't been able to talk about him without a tremor in her voice and tears forming in her watery eyes. He had been the love of her life, and he had died of an aneurysm in 1979 after twenty-one years of marriage.

They were all that was left of Daisy's life, and so, despite the memories that sprang up whenever Violet looked at them – memories that weren't hers but were *becoming* hers – the photographs went in the bin in the back garden. For burning.

The frames she kept, of course. They might bring in a few extra pounds.

After a quick bath to wash the remains of the day from her body, Violet changed Daisy's bedding for a fresh set of sheets and blankets and slid naked into the bed. She lay there, staring at the ceiling, allowing the pillows and the mattress to gradually adjust themselves to the shape of her body. Or perhaps to allow her body to adjust itself to the indentation left by Daisy Wilson after however many years she had slept there.

The street lamp outside cast an orange glow across the ceiling. The alarm clock on the bedside table tocked loudly, regularly. Somewhere outside, a cat yowled, and then it was quiet apart from the normal background rumble of distant traffic that nobody in the city could ever get away from.

As Violet felt her body gradually grow limp, and as her thoughts flitted from image to image, never settling for long enough to feed, she realised that she could hear the soft hiss of blood in her ears, a susurration like waves lapping gently against a shingle beach. The cat yowled again, but this time it sounded more to her like the cry of a seagull as it floated above the waves the way she was floating *on* them. The room itself grew dim around her, and the cold orange glow of the street lamp became the warm light of the sun setting behind a watery horizon, casting a glittering path across the sea towards her floating body. She drifted there, alone and unafraid, letting the tide take her further and further out to sea, washing her clean of everything she had done, absolving her sins as it washed the dirt from her body. The light faded as the sun dipped further and further beneath the horizon. Darkness spread in from the edges of her vision, and she was asleep without knowing she was asleep.

For the next few hours Violet was lost in a slow kaleidoscope of dreams, sometimes surfacing enough to be aware of where she was, sometimes submerged in the moments and the memories, attempting to make some sense of their fragmentary chaos.

Rising from depths of sleep where she had been lost and stumbling in an art gallery full of portraits of people she did not know, she found herself on a beach of pebbles in various shades of grey and ochre. Somewhere out in the darkness, waves crashed on shingle, rattling as they withdrew and then crashing again, relentlessly, mindlessly, over and over again.

Tock.

Startled, she turned around. Nothing was moving. The pebbles ranged away from her in all directions. Somewhere over to her left there was a sketchy indication of a breakwater, but that was the only thing to stand out in this otherwise featureless place.

Tock.

She turned again, in a full circle. There was nothing to see but pebbles and darkness, nothing to hear now but the waves.

Tock.

That had come from the ground, by her feet. Glancing down, she was shocked to see a pebble move. Rounded by the sea, dark red in colour, it suddenly lurched towards her on tiny feet. Violet backed away rapidly, faster than the pebble could move. It had tiny claws which it waved at her, and she could almost swear that it had a tiny face between the claws, a wizened little face with two eyes buried in puffy, criss-crossed flesh.

Tock. Tock-tock.

Behind her now. She turned again, heels catching in the shingle. Two more pebbles were scuttling towards her, waving their minuscule claws. One had a little curl of grey hair hanging between its eyes.

Terrified, she edged backwards.

Something moved beneath her heels.

Tock-tock. Tock.

The shingle heaved beneath her. She felt herself tumbling, screaming as she fell into their claws, into their tiny, tiny claws –

Violet jerked awake, heart racing, breath rasping in her throat. The bedroom was black, washed with amber from the street lamp. *Tock, tock, tock,* went the alarm clock, one *tock* for every two thumps of her heart. She lay there, gradually relaxing back into the bed, until sleep claimed her once again. Deep, dreamless, anonymous sleep.

She woke, as she usually did, at half past seven in the

morning. The street outside was as busy as she had ever seen it. Every few minutes a front door closed behind someone in a suit or smart clothes, heading for the bus stop or the station. She stood in the window, one of Daisy's dressing gowns wrapped around her. She loved watching people. Their unconscious grimaces and their little sideways glances when they thought nobody was looking fascinated her. They always had, ever since she was a child.

A man, still half asleep, yawned as he locked his front door behind him, covering his mouth with the back of his left hand while he manipulated his keys with his right. Violet raised her own left hand to her mouth, touching her lips against the skin on the back in the same way he did, counting the seconds silently, feeling her breath tickle the fine hairs on her skin, until he lowered his hand and turned to leave. A woman on one side of the street carrying a thin briefcase on a strap over her shoulder cast sideways glances at the door of a house on the other side, hoping someone was going to come out. Violet practised those same darting looks under half-closed eyelids, knowing and yet not knowing that she was doing it.

Yes, she loved watching people. But even more than that, she loved *being* them.

Breakfast was a slice of toast with butter and a smear of marmalade along with a cup of tea – made with Daisy's teabags, not the tea leaves she had brought with her the day before. After breakfast she set a match to the items in the metal bin in the back garden and, while they burned, set to work searching the house.

She started at the bottom – literally. The cellar hadn't seen light for many years. The cobwebs hanging from the crude wooden rafters were so burdened with dust they looked like grey chiffon scarves. Apart from a patina of coal dust that glittered in the light from the naked bulb there was nothing for Violet in that dark, dead place. She didn't even go all the way down the stairs. At the back of her mind there was a nagging fear that her feet might sink into the coal dust up to the ankles, and all she would hear would be the dry rustling of thousands of insect carcasses crushed beneath her soles.

The parlour was old, familiar territory, but she searched it anyway, just in case she had missed something along the way. The bureau was stacked with crockery, cutlery, glassware, old music manuscripts and cuttings from newspapers dating back twenty years or more. The newspaper cuttings she threw on the bonfire; the rest of it looked worthless, but might fetch a few pounds somewhere. If not, she could always donate it to charity. One had to do one's part, but charity did begin at home.

The kitchen yielded nothing unexpected. Violet had spent so many hours in there, boiling the kettle for one of Daisy's endless cups of tea, retrieving biscuits from the cupboard ('Arrowroot, m'dear – helps my digestion!') and grilling the occasional fish finger or, if it was a special occasion, piece of cod, that she knew the contents of every cupboard and drawer like she knew the pattern of freckles on her arm. There were a couple of Apostle teaspoons that bore further investigation, to judge by their hallmarks, but nothing else. Nothing that would give her purchase on Daisy's bank accounts or other financial assets.

The dining room was just that: it contained the dining table and a rosewood cabinet in which the china and silverware were stored. There was nowhere for any paperwork to be kept, but Violet paused in the doorway, wanting to leave but unable. The dining table pulled her back. The black dining table.

Violet shook her head convulsively. No time for dilly-dallying. 'Take time by the forelock', as the old adage went.

She quickly headed up the stairs and gave the bathroom and the front bedroom – her bedroom – a thorough going over. The bathroom didn't take long, but the bedside cabinets contained piles of letters and postcards that Daisy had, presumably, lain in bed reading. These Violet put to one side. She already knew everything that was in them from the endless monologues that she had encouraged with brandy and the occasional weak infusion of flowers from her garden – the names and addresses of old friends, the background details of Daisy's previous life that could be dropped in conversation or used to deflect questions – but it was worth going through them, just in case. One could never be too careful.

Finally, Violet turned her attention to the back room. The storage room. Previously, when Daisy was alive, she had only been able to stand in the doorway and look around, but she was pretty sure that most of Daisy's paperwork was kept there. What little paperwork Daisy had, anyway. That's why she had left it until last.

There was a truckle bed against one wall, and bookcases flanking the door, but Violet's attention was fixed immediately on the desk that sat beneath the window. The chair in front of it was, disconcertingly, a 1970s-vintage secretary's swivel chair with upholstery patterned in a psychedelic swirl of green and blue. Heaven alone knew where Daisy had got it from – or indeed why. With some qualms, Violet sat in the chair and methodically went through the desk drawers.

And it was all there. Building society statements, showing that Daisy was in the black to the tune of several thousand pounds. Mortgage details – and it turned out to be the case, as Violet had strongly suspected but needed to confirm – that the mortgage was freehold and had been paid off many years before. The deeds on the house. An insurance policy on thick parchment that had been taken out in the 1930s and would, presumably, pay out a pretty penny now, if Violet wasn't intending to keep Daisy alive – at least, as far as the rest of the world was concerned. Some premium bonds that might be worth investigating, and perhaps cashing in. Some certificates almost certainly inherited or acquired by Daisy's deceased husband that gave Daisy shares in companies that, to judge by their names (Amalgamated Nickel Engineering, Imperial Celluloid), had probably gone to the wall many years beforehand. Still, she put them to one side. Best to be sure. For all she knew, Amalgamated Engineering might have changed its name to British Steel and the shares could be worth millions now.

She leaned back in her chair and gazed out of the window. From this perspective she could see the entire length of the garden: unkempt, overgrown but potentially quite attractive. She might spend some time out there later on, trimming the bushes with her secateurs. Perhaps plant a few nice flowers in the borders as well. And while she was at it, there were people who would come in and spring-clean the house. The wallpaper and paintwork were old-fashioned, to be sure, and the kitchen could certainly do with bringing into the twenty-first century with a new cooker, new refrigerator and new cupboards and work surfaces, but those were big jobs that would require careful planning. And they might not be necessary.

Once she had finished searching the house – and it suddenly occurred to her that she needed to take a quick look in the attic, just to be absolutely sure she hadn't missed anything – Violet decided that she would take a wander down to the High Street. She could treat herself to a cup of tea and a steak pie and some new potatoes in one of the department stores, and then take a slow walk along the row of estate agents. What she needed was one slightly down at heel, one that specialised in lets and sub-lets rather than actual sales. And – although this might require some careful observation from a seat in a coffee shop – one that dealt more with what Violet thought of as the lower end of the social spectrum. Immigrants. Students, perhaps. If the rent was set low enough – and Violet wasn't greedy, far from it – then she was sure that tenants wouldn't mind an old-fashioned kitchen and some faded wallpaper. It was probably better than they were used to.

The best thing was, the estate agents would make all the arrangements, choose the tenants, collect the rent and just forward it to wherever she wanted, after taking their cut, of course. And Violet didn't begrudge them their cut, considering the load they were taking off her shoulders.

Streamers of smoke drifted up past the window. Somewhere down below, on the concrete patio, Daisy's clothes were burning away to ashes. Violet didn't like using the word 'evidence' – it sounded so harsh – but she was comforted to think that soon the events of the previous day would have vanished into the air.

And soon, after the house had been sorted out and whatever assets were in the house had been converted to cash, so would Violet.

The drifting smoke drew her gaze up into the sky: a deep cloudless azure that seemed to go on for ever and ever. She wished that, when she brought her gaze back down again, instead of overgrown bushes and thin trees she might see a glorious stretch of turquoise water, with the wind blowing spume off the crests of the waves and distant container ships breaking the straight line of the horizon.

And she decided there and then that she'd had enough of the small towns she had been hiding in for so long. She longed for the seaside, and that's where she would go next.

As she was descending the stairs, the telephone rang. Without even thinking, she picked it up off the table in the hall and said, brightly, 'Hello. Daisy Wilson speaking.'

CHAPTER FOUR

The mortuary was located between a park and a fire station on the outskirts of Braintree: a nondescript two-storey building that looked as if it had originally been intended as a temporary measure but now just sat there, set back from the road, fading further and further from people's minds. It was, Detective Chief Inspector Mark Lapslie decided as he pulled off the road and parked in one of the designated spaces, the closest thing to an architectural blind spot it was possible to get.

He wasn't in the best of moods. The morning before, after Emma Bradbury had driven off from the forest where the body had been discovered, Lapslie had hung around, waiting for the forensic pathologist to arrive. The press had turned up in the early afternoon, just before Jane Catherall, tipped off, he suspected, by one of the paramedics. By the time he had dealt with them and spent half an hour on the phone to the Crime Scene Manager she had already departed with the bodies, leaving him furious. Some mix-up in the admin had resulted in most of the uniformed police being pulled away from the crime scene in order to cover a local football match. And Superintendent Rouse had not called back. All in all, it had been a frustrating day.

Emma's Mondeo was two spaces across from his car. This time, it was empty. No strange men in the passenger seat, waiting for her to return and whisk them away.

The front door had a push-button combination lock. He'd known the combination once, but he'd forgotten it several times over the years, so he did what he usually did: buzzed the intercom. It was a good minute before anyone answered.

'Detective Chief Inspector Mark Lapslie,' he said, bending down to the level of the intercom. Why was it they were always installed by dwarves? Or did the installers expect lots of school parties to visit the mortuary unaccompanied?

The door buzzed, and he pushed it open.

Despite the summer sun outside, the building was pleasantly cool. The hallway was carpeted with tiles that had, over the course of the years, picked up so many coffee stains they were piebald. The walls were plastered and painted in a muted shade of blue. A young man wearing a white coat over jeans and a T-shirt was waiting for him.

'DCI Lapslie?'

He handed his warrant card across. The man inspected it carefully, although Lapslie was pretty sure he wouldn't have been able to tell the difference between a proper warrant card and a Scotland Yard gym membership.

'This way, please.'

He led Lapslie down a corridor and gestured for him to go ahead through a set of double doors. The temperature dropped appreciably as Lapslie pushed the doors open, and he became aware of a strong smell, like bleach that had been poured down a blocked drain. The smell was so strong, so cloying that he could taste it at the back of his throat. His synaesthesia momentarily went into reverse; the taste of the disinfectant, or cleaner, or whatever it was, overlaid on the smell of decay filled his head with deep, sonorous chimes. It didn't happen very often, and he staggered slightly, one hand to his forehead, disoriented.

'Are you all right?' asked an unfamiliar voice.

'Fine. Fine. The smell just got to me for a moment.' He blinked a couple of times, forcing the sound of church bells to the back of his mind.

The room he had entered was large, and tiled in white from top to bottom. Several large ventilation units had been fixed to the ceiling, positioned above stainless-steel tables that stood in the centre of the room. Each table had a raised lip around the edge and a tap with an attached hosepipe and shower head, also in stainless steel, at one end. Two of the tables had shrouded bodies on them; one much larger and more irregular than the other.

The woman standing between the tables was smaller than him, with a stomach so pronounced and so rounded that it was almost as if she had thrust a basketball under her white coat, and bulbous blue eyes that gazed at Lapslie with disconcerting mildness. She smiled, and Lapslie thought that he had never seen such a sweet smile on a woman.

'Polio,' she said, her voice tasting of brandy and soda.

'Pardon?'

'I noticed you looking over at me yesterday, when I finally arrived at the scene of the crime. You were probably wondering what caused me to look like this. The answer is polio. I contracted it as a child. I was probably one of the last children in England to catch it.'

'I'm – sorry.' He wasn't sure what she wanted him to say.

'Six months flat out in a hospital bed, and several operations to fuse my spine together. It could have been worse. Of course, if I'd been born a year or two later, it could have been a lot better. Such is the uncertainty of life. We've not met. Doctor Jane Catherall. Pleased to meet you.'

She walked towards Lapslie with jerky steps and held out her hand. He shook it, noticing as he did so that she had double cuffs on her shirt, pinned together with delicate gold chains. A woman who cared about her appearance. 'DCI Lapslie,' he said.

'I've been expecting you. Your colleague is already here.' She kept hold of his hand, and Lapslie had the absurd impression that she was expecting him to bend down and kiss it. 'I wouldn't want you to think I always greet everyone with the unfortunate story of my health,' she added. 'I wanted to make the point that our bodies are a permanent record of everything that happens to us. Broken bones, illnesses, diseases ... they're all there, preserved in the flesh. And if all we have to work with is the flesh, then we can work backwards and re-create the person from the list of things that happened to them.'

'Thank you for the lecture.' He could feel her charm beguiling him, but he wasn't going to succumb. 'We didn't get a chance to talk yesterday,' he said tersely. 'I was too busy dealing with the press when they turned up to deal with you when *you* finally turned up.'

Dr Catherall looked away. 'I apologise for arriving so late. Alas, one of the physical effects of the polio is a weakness in the intercostal muscles. I have to wear a face mask connected to a respirator when I sleep. It maintains a positive pressure in order to ensure that I keep breathing but it does lead to a very disturbed night's sleep, and I find it difficult to wake up in the mornings. I missed the first four calls on my mobile.'

'Then buy a louder mobile,' Lapslie said unsympathetically.

Dr Catherall gazed up at him with those disquietingly mild eyes. 'The victim had been there for many months,' she said. 'Two more hours was not going to compromise any evidence on the body, and it ensured that when I did arrive I was not making any mistakes through lack of sleep. Let me do my job, Detective Chief Inspector, and I will provide you with everything you need to do yours.'

The long silence that grew between them was broken by the doors to the mortuary opening and Emma Bradbury entering the room. The mortuary assistant who had let Lapslie in was following her.

'Boss,' Emma acknowledged.

'Sergeant. Been here long?'

'Half an hour or so. Dr Catherall let me use her office to make a few calls.'

Lapslie nodded. 'Well, shall we get on with it?'

Dr Catherall led Lapslie and Emma over to the first table and nodded towards the shrouded body. 'Your crash victim,' she said. 'I took the liberty of conducting the post-mortem this morning, before you arrived.' She glanced sideways at Lapslie. 'As I understand it, he was the victim of a car crash, rather than of a suspected murderer. It occurred to me that you would not want to be stood around waiting while I fiddled about in his innards.'

'Correct. Was there anything unusual about the body?'

'Nothing that caused me concern. Bruises and abrasions caused by the crash, some burning from the airbag, and a massive trauma to his neck, cutting through his carotid artery. All consistent with what was found at the scene. I have, of course, sent blood samples off for testing. We may get traces of alcohol, or drugs. Happy?'

'Ecstatic. What about the other one?'

With a flourish, she pulled the white cloth off the bulky, irregular shape on the second table. 'Et voila!'

Seeing the corpse in the forest, a natural thing nestled amongst other natural things, had seemed almost normal. Seeing her here, laid out naked on harsh metal, surrounded by the plastic sheets that had been disinterred with her and crusted with dirt, Lapslie was struck by a sense of wrongness. Nobody deserved to be left like this. Death should have some dignity, surely.

What remained of her was mottled grey, and dry. Her hips and shoulders made tent shapes under her skin, and her stomach had decayed away, or perhaps been eaten away, to reveal the lumpy shape of her spine. Her face was dominated by the rictus-like grimace of her mouth, where the skin had pulled back to reveal black gums.

Framed in the plastic sheets, she seemed smaller than she had in the forest.

'Well,' Dr Catherall said quietly as her assistant wheeled a stand supporting a tray of surgical instruments across to her. 'With no further ado, let us commence.'

For the next hour, Lapslie and DS Bradbury watched from the sidelines as Dr Catherall painstakingly unwrapped the sheets and cut her way through the old woman's cadaver, taking samples as she went and talking quietly into a minidisc recorder while her assistant took occasional photographs. Her work was meticulous and detailed, and her manner was more like a woman doing a difficult crossword puzzle than a medical expert slicing up a body.

Lapslie felt himself falling into an almost hypnotic trance as he watched, lulled by Dr Catherall's effortless technique. He had expected her hands to be clumsy, based on her shape and her medical history, but her movements were precise to the point of minimalism. Every gesture was exactly what was needed, no more and no less.

Emma Bradbury, on the other hand, fidgeted endlessly. After a few minutes she found a laboratory stool and perched on it, but she couldn't seem to get comfortable. Every now and then she would shift position, scratch her head, tug at her ear or search her pockets for something that she never seemed to find. She was plainly bored, and not very good at disguising it.

As Dr Catherall had penetrated to the last layer of plastic sheet around the body, she suddenly stood back. 'Good Lord,' she murmured. She leaned closer to examine something within the sheets. 'Good Lord,' she said again, and gestured for her assistant to move closer. He started taking photographs as Dr Catherall carefully removed a number of objects from between the plastic sheets and the corpse and transferred them to the third post-mortem table.

'You might want to take a look at this,' she said, turning to Lapslie. He moved to join her, but before he could get to the table his mobile rang. Dr Catherall cast a dark glance at him.

'DCI Lapslie,' he said.

'Lapslie?' The voice was familiar: dry, like grass cuttings, and slightly tinny, which probably meant that he had Lapslie on speakerphone. 'Alan Rouse. You called yesterday.'

Dr Catherall gestured abruptly towards the door.

'Sorry, sir – could you hang on for a moment. I'm in the

middle of a post-mortem.' He strode towards the door and out into the corridor. 'That's better,' he said as the doors swung shut behind him. 'Sir – it's been a long time.'

'Too long.' Lapslie could imagine Rouse leaning back in his chair in his white, glass-walled office. 'How's Sonia?'

A stab of unexpected pain; an icy knife in his heart. Lapslie's breath caught in his throat. 'She's – okay.'

'And the kids?'

'Fine. Thanks for asking.'

'And what about your ... ah, medical condition?'

'Unchanged – which is why I was startled when I got a call from a young copper attending a car crash.'

'Ah yes. She called me when your name popped out of the computer.'

'That's one of the things I wanted to ask you about. Why was my name in the computer in the first place?'

There was a pause on the other end of the line: the aural equivalent of a shrug. 'I'm not entirely sure,' Rouse said eventually. Lapslie found that his tongue was tingling, as if he'd dipped it in something mildly spiced, but he wasn't sure what that meant. 'Presumably something about the case resonates with some previous investigation you've been involved with. Some unsolved murder, or suchlike.'

'I can't say I can hear the sound of bells ringing.'

'Perhaps it's a glitch. Computers are the bane of a policeman's life, these days.'

Another momentary silence, but this time Lapslie had the impression that Superintendent Rouse was waiting for him to make some comment. 'I was under the impression that I was on indefinite sick leave,' he said eventually. 'You know that my synaesthesia makes it difficult for me to work in an office environment.'

'I know that's what we talked about, Mark, but you understand that we can't have you off sick indefinitely. We've been looking for some kind of job you can do without being in the office, but it's not been easy. I know you've written a couple of reports for the Chief Constable, but there's pressure from the Home Secretary to get as many people back in work as we can. So when your name was flagged up as someone who might be able to contribute to this case, well, I took it to be a sign. A sign that it was time you came back to us. I've arranged a desk for you here in Chelmsford, and you'll have access to a Quiet Room if you need it. We'll sort out something for you once this case is over.'

'And until then I'm the investigating officer?'

'Correct.'

'As DCI? Isn't that over-egging the pudding a bit?'

'Look on it as a way of easing yourself back into harness.'

'Nice talking to you, sir.'

'Pop in, when you're in the office. Let's have a chat.'

Lapslie slid the mobile back into his pocket and took a deep breath. It looked like he was back on the job. Not entirely unexpected – he'd been waiting for something like this to happen – but not entirely welcome either.

Sighing, he entered the pathology lab again.

Laid out on the stainless-steel table were the objects that Dr Catherall had removed from the stomach of the dead body: five desiccated corpses of what were either field mice or voles, along with two rats and something larger that Lapslie assumed was a polecat, or a ferret, or something along those lines. The smaller animals looked to Lapslie like no more than matchstick bones in twists of matted fur.

'Apparently we're looking for a serial killer, sir,' said DS Bradbury dryly.

Dr Catherall favoured her with a level glance. 'These animals had managed to worm their way through gaps in the sheeting and get to the old woman's body,' she said. 'I found them clustered around the stomach area, where they had started eating their way through. And they all died before they could do much damage.'

'Died how?' Lapslie asked.

'That,' Dr Catherall said, 'we will determine in due course. For now, I have a post-mortem to complete. It is not the kind of thing that you can come back to later.'

She worked in a logical progression, starting at the crown of the corpse's head and finishing at the soles of its feet. Half way through the process, the cadaver was splayed open, with Dr Catherall wrist-deep in its dry innards examining whatever remained of the organs, but by the time she had finished, the corpse was very nearly back to the condition in which it had started the post-mortem, albeit with a massive Y-shaped incision, stitched up with thick black thread, marring the body from groin to chest, where it split and continued up to either shoulder, passing above the flaps of its breasts.

As Dr Catherall finished with the body, Lapslie thought that she looked smaller: drained by the process. It seemed to him as if she didn't have much in the way of stamina within that diminutive frame of hers.

'What can you tell me about her?' Lapslie asked, as Dr Catherall washed her hands thoroughly and wearily.

'Let us start with the state of decomposition,' she replied. 'The body is in remarkably good condition, considering where it was found. The plastic sheeting in which she was wrapped would have provided something approaching an anaerobic environment, which would have slowed decomposition down and deterred all but the most determined or' – she indicated the small corpses on the next table – 'smallest predators. Given the condition of the skin and the flesh, and taking account of the effects of the environment, I would estimate that she has been dead for between seven and ten months.'

'Which is about what we thought,' Emma said.

Dr Catherall sniffed. 'Sometimes pathology is about confirming the obvious, rather than bringing rabbits out of hats. Judging by bone density and porosity I would put her towards the end of her natural life, somewhere between seventy and eighty years of age. The progression of arthritis in her joints confirms this. Her lungs had been damaged by childhood rheumatic fever, and she had suffered from numerous other diseases during the course of her life – rickets, some small skin melanomas and so on – but none of them carried her off. She had also been suffering from low-level malnutrition for some years, I would estimate, but that did not carry her off either.'

'Then what did?' asked Lapslie.

'I'll come to that in a moment.' She leaned forward and indicated a puckered scar on the corpse's neck, sitting in the notch of the breastbone. 'This scar indicates the insertion of a breathing tube at some stage early on in her life. Without seeing her medical records it is difficult to be sure, but I would lay odds that it is the result of childhood diphtheria.' She paused for a moment, considering the body. 'The hips are worn, but they are hers, rather than replacements. Apart from the normal signs of extreme ageing, there are no indications of any age-related issues that might have caused her death – no tumours, no evidence of a stroke. And, as far as I can tell this far after death, she had a heart like a horse. In fact, if I were her doctor, and if she were still alive, I would say she had several years left in her yet. She did not die of the set of symptoms we collect together under the aegis of "old age".'

'Then –'

'I am getting there.' Dr Catherall rubbed a hand across her chin thoughtfully. 'Exposure cannot be entirely ruled out. The degeneration of tissue means that I cannot definitively test for shock or circulatory collapse, but for reasons I will explain in a moment I do not believe that exposure is probable – at least, as a primary cause of death. It may, of course, have been contributory.'

'Of course,' Lapslie murmured. Dr Catherall gave the impression that she had either been rehearsing her little speech all the way through the post-mortem or that she carefully structured her thoughts down to subordinate clauses and subjunctive moods even as she spoke.

'To cut a long story short,' she said, seeing the look in Lapslie's eyes, 'you probably noticed yourself when you examined the body yesterday that there was some damage to the back of the skull. This was not accidental. I would estimate that she was battered once or twice, shortly before death, with a blunt object.'

'Nothing was found at the scene,' Emma murmured from beside Lapslie.

'Any other damage to the body?' Lapslie asked.

'No stab wounds, no fractures, if that's what you mean.'

Lapslie frowned. 'I was thinking more of the fingers.'

Dr Catherall nodded slowly. 'A strange one, that. The fingers on the right hand appear to have been removed by some sharp object. I'll have to do further tests in order to determine whether they were sawn off, cut off or bitten off, but they're certainly missing and I'm reasonably sure it was done after death. They certainly weren't removed surgically – there was no attempt to close up the wounds.'

'And the left hand?'

'Intact,' Dr Catherall said. 'Which is, of course, a little odd.'

'Does that mean anything to you yet?' DS Bradbury asked.

Lapslie thought for a moment. Apart from that maddening faint taste of lychees, caused more, he suspected, by the memory of a sound than by the sound itself, there was nothing more than a nagging familiarity. He'd talked to someone about missing fingers before, but where? When?

Silence filled the room. Lapslie eventually broke it by tapping the metal lip on the autopsy table with his hand. 'Do you have any idea whether the place where we found her was the actual scene of the crime? Did she die there, or did she die elsewhere and was moved there afterwards?'

'That's more a question for the CSIs to answer,' Catherall said judiciously.

'Doctor Catherall – Jane – I get the feeling that you've never stinted from venturing an opinion, especially when you have evidence backing it up.'

'Ah, how well you know me after such a short acquaintance. There were traces of earth and vegetation beneath the nails of her left hand, which indicates to me that she was alive when she arrived in the forest. More than that, I cannot say.'

'We still need to establish the identity of the victim. Did you find any clues on the body or in the clothing?'

'Her clothes were badly affected by the time she had spent in the forest,' Dr Catherall said. 'I will send them to the forensic team, of course, but I would be surprised if there was any usable evidence on them. The labels indicate that they came from a range of department stores, although the general style and colour, as well as the patterns of wear and the repairs that had been carried out on them, suggest that they had all been worn for a number of years.' She paused for a moment. 'I realise that it is not my area, but I did notice cotton threads hanging from a button here, or a zip there. I suspect you may find that many of the clothes were bought second hand, perhaps from charity shops, and the threads were the remnants of the labels. Just a suspicion of mine: Forensics will have more to say.'

'Doctor Catherall, I can't imagine *anyone* having more to say than you,' Lapslie said, smiling.

'You're too kind,' she murmured.

'So, we're no closer to discovering her identity.'

'That is not entirely the case.' She turned away. 'Dan, could you bring me the evidence box over by the fume cupboard?'

Lapslie looked over his shoulder. The young technician was busy putting the surgical instruments into an autoclave for sterilisation. At Dr Catherall's request he walked across to a large glass-fronted box on one side of the room and retrieved a plastic box with a standard CJA label stuck to the top.

'Take a look at the victim's mouth,' Dr Catherall said to Lapslie. 'What do you see? Or, rather, what do you *not* see?'

Lapslie bent closer to the skull-like head, catching a whiff of something unpleasant as he did so. 'I don't see any teeth,' he said.

'Indeed.' Dr Catherall opened the plastic box with a flourish. 'She had lost all of her teeth somewhere along the way, and replaced them with these!'

In the box Lapslie could see a set of dentures: bright and sparkling. Bizarrely, he wanted to laugh. They looked more like something from a joke-shop than something a person would put in their mouth.

'And these help us how?'

Dr Catherall carefully picked the dentures out of the box and turned them over. 'Because they have a serial number,' she said, indicating what looked to Lapslie more like a set of small scratches than anything meaningful. 'And that special ortho-dontic design serial number, which is unique to these dentures, will allow us to trace them back to the dental technician who made them. And that will allow us to identify the body.' She smiled that sweet smile up at him. 'And when I say "will", what I mean is "already has". Young Dan over there made some phone calls earlier on, and we now know who this lady is.'

'Doctor Catherall, I am amazed. Truly amazed. All you have to do is tell me who killed her and we'll have solved the entire case without leaving the room.'

'In true Nero Wolfe style,' she said, blushing at Lapslie's praise. 'Sadly I cannot help with identifying her murderer, but at least I can provide some of the information you need. Her name was Violet Chambers. She was seventy-nine years old, and she lived in Ipswich. That is all the information I have: I did not want to trespass too much on your undoubted area of expertise.'

'Doctor Catherall, you are truly amazing.'

'Please, call me Jane.'

'Even more amazing is the fact that you knew who she was and what killed her before I even walked into the room, and you still gave me the entire performance.'

She shrugged: a contorted movement of her shoulders. 'It is

so rare that I get an appreciative audience. I have to take advantage where I can.'

'Jane, it's been a privilege being taken advantage of by you.'

'Then perhaps I could lure you into my office, where I could offer you a cup of coffee and show you what little information young Dan here has been able to unearth about Violet Chambers.'

'Are you propositioning me, Doctor Catherall?'

'Oh, I was taught never to end a sentence with a proposition,' she said, smiling.

Lapslie turned to where his DS sat. 'Emma, head over to Forensics. Find out whether they discovered any skeletons of animals around the crash site.'

Emma nodded and left, obviously grateful for the chance to actually do something, rather than just sit there watching someone else doing something.

'Dan,' Dr Catherall said to her assistant, 'could you organise two coffees for me? Cream and sugar to the side. We'll be in my office.'

She gestured to Lapslie to precede him. For a moment, Lapslie thought she wanted him to take her arm. He still wasn't sure quite how seriously Dr Catherall took herself, but he suspected he might wound her pride if he laughed.

Pushing the double doors open, he walked out of the post-mortem room and turned instinctively to his right, where a side corridor ran off the main spine of the building. As Dr Catherall let the doors close softly behind her, he moved along the corridor – slowly, so that she could keep up.

The doors he passed were closed, labelled 'Laboratory', 'Stores' and 'Evidence'. At the far end, a fire-door with a push-bar across it gave access to, presumably, the rear of the building. Just before the fire-door, to his left, was a door that had been left a few inches ajar. The sign said, 'Dr J. Catherall, Senior Forensic Pathologist'. He waited for her to join him and, when she gestured for him to enter the office, he pushed the door open and walked inside.

Based on his short experience of Dr Catherall, Lapslie had expected papers and books to be scattered all over the desk, the bookshelves, the filing cabinets and the floor. Instead, he was pleasantly surprised to find it was almost bare. A bookcase held copies of medical journals and some reference works, but apart from that there was nothing but plain work surfaces and a Dell computer sitting on the desk, its screensaver running.

No, that wasn't quite all. On top of the bookcase, next to the computer's printer, was a framed photograph of a young man with black hair. He was smiling at whoever had taken the photograph. Something was written across the bottom, but Lapslie didn't like to look more closely. It would have seemed too intrusive for such a short acquaintance.

Dr Catherall gestured to a chair and said, 'Please, take a seat. I will just be a moment.'

He did so. Dr Catherall pulled open a drawer and rummaged around inside, and Lapslie was irresistibly reminded of how, less than an hour before, she had been doing much the same thing inside a dead human body. Eventually she pulled out a thin folder.

'Here – this is what Dan discovered about her identity, along with a list of the clothes and possessions we found,' she said, handing it over. 'I'll print another copy off for you to take away.'

Lapslie opened the folder and leafed through the pages. Some had obviously been typed up – probably by Dan, the Doctor's assistant – but others were copies of e-mails. He started to read, then looked up, aware that the atmosphere in the office had changed in some subtle way.

Dr Catherall was staring at the computer.

'Anything wrong?' he asked.

'I have not used the computer this morning,' she said. 'I did not even switch it on when I arrived.' She nudged the mouse, and the screen flickered to life.

There, on the screen, was an open word-processing program, with the file that Lapslie was reading prominently displayed.

'Someone has been playing around with my computer,' Dr Catherall snapped, her mild demeanour changing suddenly to something much darker. 'Dan!'

Footsteps in the corridor, and the Doctor's assistant arrived carrying a tray with two cups and saucers, plus a sugar bowl and a jug of cream. 'Yes, Doctor?'

'Have you turned my computer on today?'

Dan shook his head. 'Definitely not.'

'Do you know who did?'

'There's only been you and me in this morning. And the Detective Sergeant, of course, but she spent most of her time in here reading the paper, as far as I could tell. The computer was off when I last checked.'

'Well it's on now.' She turned her gaze towards the book-shelf. 'And the printer has been turned on as well. Someone has been in here and printed off a copy of the information we discovered about Violet Chambers!'

'That's impossible,' Dan blurted, putting the tray down on the desk. 'What would they want to do that for?'

'And why leave the computer on?' Lapslie asked, frowning. 'Why leave the file up on screen?'

'Perhaps whoever it was got disturbed when Dan brought your DS in here,' Dr Catherall said. 'Perhaps they had to get out in a hurry and did not have time to close the computer down. They could have got away through the fire-door outside. If they'd parked their car in the car park they could have been back to it in a handful of seconds.'

Lapslie looked from the computer to the printer and then to the file he held in his hands. It didn't make any sense. An elderly murder victim buried in the woods, *that* he could understand. It was the kind of thing that had happened before. A break-in at a pathology laboratory in order to copy a file, that he could understand as well, albeit at a stretch. There had been cases – usually gang-related murders – where there had been pretty sophisticated attempts to tamper with the evidence, including in one instance, he recalled, someone setting fire to the laboratory where the post-mortem was taking place. No, it was the combination of the two that was throwing him.

He looked at Dr Catherall, whose face was contorted into a thunderous scowl. 'I'm having a hard time believing this,' he said. 'Are you sure you didn't leave your computer on last night when you left?'

Dr Catherall said something scathing in reply, but Lapslie didn't catch it. Something she had said earlier was biting at the back of his mind. Something about whoever had gained access to the office and turned the computer on – if indeed she hadn't forgotten to turn it off the night before, or Emma Bradbury hadn't turned it on herself for some unknown reason – parking their car in the car park outside.

And then he realised what it was. When he visualised that car, he imagined it as being a black Lexus with a shaded windscreen.

Just like the one that had been parked near the place in the forest where Violet Chambers' body had been discovered. The one that had driven off before he could find out who was inside.

CHAPTER FIVE

Daisy Wilson left her car – or *Violet*'s car, as she was already thinking of it with a mixture of nostalgia and distaste – in a side-street in Colchester. She could have driven it all the way, but something made her stop twenty or so miles short of her eventual destination and complete her journey by train. Partly it was the usual caution that had served her so well for so long. There was something about leaving her car where it might be connected to her that made her feel itchy and vulnerable, despite the anonymity that her new identity afforded her. Mainly, however, it was the fact that driving made her nervous, while trains calmed her down. If she was going to live in this area for a while, she wanted her first impressions to be happy ones.

Leaving the relative anonymity of the A12 dual carriageway she drove cautiously through the outskirts of town, looking for the nearest station. She had a pretty good idea that the trains to Leyston-by-Naze stopped at Colchester on their way, although she wasn't entirely sure how she knew. The problem was, Colchester seemed to have three different stations, and she didn't want to end up too far away from the right one. Eventually, after driving past Colchester Station and North Station, and having detoured around the plain architecture of the Dutch Quarter and the contrasting ornate Gothic monstrosity that was the Abbeygate arch, she ended up at Colchester Town, chosen by the simple expedient that it was the closest station to the road signs that pointed to Leyston-by-Naze.

She left her car parked in a disabled spot outside a quiet row of shops with two storeys of flats above them, taking with her only a small suitcase and her handbag. She had a disabled badge for the car, although she wasn't actually disabled, and she left it on the dashboard before wiping over the places she had touched with a damp cloth soaked in sugar soap and locking the car up. She glanced around, as if looking for a particular shop front: florists, second-hand bookshop, laundrette, bookmakers, small supermarket. Nobody was watching. Nobody would be able to describe her later. Despite its closeness to the station it was a quiet location, out of the main flow of traffic. The car should be safe there for a few days before anyone became suspicious, and she fully intended to be back to collect it before then.

Daisy patted the roof of the car absently with a gloved hand. An F-registration Volvo 740 in a dull shade of bronze – 'Champagne', she believed it was called – she had obtained it at some stage in her travels and kept it because it was so completely undistinguished. Nobody would give it a second glance. And nobody was likely to steal it. For a start, it didn't even have a working radio, let alone anything more modern.

Then again, if someone did steal the car it might actually help. Loath as she was to find a new one, Daisy was becoming increasingly aware that the Volvo was a link to Violet Chambers – a link she really should consider breaking. It wasn't as if she was emotionally attached to the car – Daisy knew, without any great upheaval of the heart, that she wasn't emotionally attached to anything in the way that she supposed other people to be. It was more that the car was the perfect blend of blandness and reliability. It was also an automatic, which made her feel a lot more comfortable when she drove.

Locking the car, she walked briskly away towards the station, suitcase swinging from her left hand. Time and tide waited for no woman, and she was impatient to see the sea.

According to the notice boards in an anonymously modern station – all girders and columns and glass – she had a half-hour wait before the next train, so she bought her ticket with cash and had a bland, milky cup of tea in the station café. The place smelled of strong coffee and hot pastry. Nobody gave her a second glance: a small woman in a tweedy jacket and hat sitting by herself, sipping at her cup. She was well aware of the impression she gave – or failed to give. It was something she consciously cultivated.

For some reason Daisy had expected an old 1950s vintage British Rail diesel pulling four dusty blue coaches, but the train she boarded was a bland, white, modern train with electric doors covered in graffiti. Regardless, the sight of the train pulling into the curve of the station filled Daisy with nostalgic longing, although she was disturbed to realise that she wasn't sure exactly what she was being nostalgic about. Perhaps it was just for the past itself.

Daisy settled herself down into an empty second-class compartment. A small mist of dust and stuffing rose from the upholstery as she sat, the strangely familiar smell suddenly provoking a memory of ... of what? Her, sitting on a train, looking out at an ocean of red poppies. How old was she? *Where* was she?

She closed her eyes. No time for memories now.

The train started with a jerk, and Daisy felt her breath quicken with anticipation as her carriage pulled out of the shadow of the station and coasted gently through the outskirts of the town before accelerating into the countryside. For the next half hour or so she gazed raptly out at rolling fields and hills, haystacks and barns, and at small towns with evocative, perfectly British names like Wivenhoe, Alresford, Great Bentley, Weely and Kirby Cross.

She saw her first seagulls just as the line split, the right-hand arc heading off towards Clacton, the left-hand arc towards Frinton-on-Sea, Walton and Leyston-by-Naze. They sat in groups on the roofs of houses and wheeled slowly above the Essex marshes, great grey and white birds with tiny black pearls for eyes, and beaks hooked cruelly, like fish-knives.

By the time the train stopped at Frinton she could smell the sea itself prickling her nostrils, salty and cool, a smell like nothing else on earth. A smell that hadn't changed since a time before houses, farms and people, before cars and tractors and trains. Perhaps the only original smell left on the face of the planet.

The door to the carriage slid open and an elderly woman stepped in. Despite the thinness of her arms her skin sagged beneath the bones, and the veins on the backs of her hands were knotted and twisted like the roots of a storm-weathered tree. Beneath the hand-knitted hat that covered her hair, her eyes and face seemed carved into a perpetual smile.

'Good afternoon,' she said. 'May I join you?'

'Please do,' Daisy said automatically, although she could feel disappointment seeping through her body and souring her mood. 'I was feeling quite lonely, sitting here.'

The woman smiled and sat down opposite Daisy. Without thinking, Daisy arranged her hands in her lap in the same way as her new travelling companion.

A whistle blew somewhere down the platform, and the train began to pull away.

'On holiday?' the woman asked, glancing at Daisy's suitcase.

'My cousin has been taken ill,' Daisy replied. It was her standard cover story. She tapped her chest vaguely. 'It's her ... you know. She's in and out of hospital, and I thought I'd pop down and make sure she was all right.'

The woman nodded. 'Terrible,' she said, nodding. 'Still, it's amazing what the doctors can do these days.' She leaned forward, extending one of her gnarled hands. 'My name is Eve,' she said. 'Eve Baker.'

'Daisy Wilson – pleased to meet you.' Daisy shook the offered hand, feeling the way the papery skin moved against the bones. She could take Eve's wrist in her left hand and push those fingers back until they snapped, one by one, leaving Eve breathless with pain and shock. If she wanted. The feeling excited her.

'And what about you?' she asked instead. 'Are you on holiday as well?'

If she was, Daisy had no use for her. Although she usually waited until she had got her bearings and somewhere to stay before she started looking around for her next victim, there was no point in passing up a perfectly good opportunity if it presented itself. All is fish that comes to the net, as they said.

'Oh my, no.' Eve laughed. 'I live in Leyston. I've lived there since I was a child.'

'Really?' Daisy allowed her face to adopt an encouraging expression.

'Oh yes.' Eve leant forward confidingly. 'I was evacuated here during the war, you see, and while I was here my home in London was bombed during the blitz. My family was killed, so I stayed with the family I had been placed with.'

'I'm sorry to hear that.'

'Oh, it was all such a long time ago, now. I was educated here, I married here and I brought up three children here.'

The little spark of interest that had begun to flicker in Daisy's breast guttered in a discouraging wind.

'You have three children?'

'Oh yes. They've all moved away, of course, but they still visit every week or so. One of them works in a bank, one works in computers and one is a school secretary. And they've given me so many lovely grandchildren.'

'That's wonderful,' Daisy murmured, letting her gaze slide away from her travelling companion and alight again on the flat, green countryside that was rolling past the window. Children and grandchildren. Family. People who would notice if she vanished. People who would care.

'Where does your cousin live?' Eve asked brightly.

Daisy paused for a moment before replying, just long enough to give the impression that she had thought the conversation was over. 'Near the church,' she replied vaguely. There was bound to be a church in Leyston.

'Which church?'

'The Methodist one, I believe.' That should still be safe. How many Methodist churches were there likely to be?

'Ah. I see.' Eve subsided back into her seat, looking disappointed that her new friend didn't want to continue their conversation.

The train began to slow, and Daisy's heart began to beat faster. It was always like this, coming into a new town, a new home, for the first time, but there was something else as well, a feeling that this time she really *was* coming home. It was something to do with the briny smell of the sea, the plaintive cries of the seagulls, the feeling of almost infinite space just beyond the bushes that lined the track. And then they were pulling into the tiny station, just two tracks separated by a platform between them.

The train lurched to a halt, and Daisy was surprised, looking away from the window, to see the little old lady still sitting opposite her. She had almost dismissed her from her mind.

'Nice to meet you,' she said.

'And you. I hope your cousin ... you know.'

'Thank you.'

Daisy allowed the old woman to disembark first, then, as the woman scurried towards the metal and glass ticket barrier, so different from the solid red-brick one she had expected, she busied herself for a few moments with her suitcase, allowing some distance to grow between them before she moved off.

Daisy walked out into the sunshine, and stopped to drink in the view. To her left, a row of three-storey houses with tall windows curved leisurely out of sight. To her right, a public house named, of course, The Station Hotel. And ahead of her, across a triangular green fringed with bushes, lay the North Sea, heaving and billowing like a grey-blue sheet rippling in the wind. She walked toward the seafront, entranced. How long had it been since she had seen the sea? She couldn't even remember. All the places, all the names and the faces were blended together in her mind. She knew she must have been to the seaside at some stage in her life, but she couldn't remember when.

Daisy took a look over her shoulder, a valedictory farewell to the life she was leaving behind, and found her vision filled with a block of flats in Victorian design: red brick, tall windows and a massive front door. She had walked around it to get from the modern glass ticket office to the green, but it looked so much like the older ticket office she had been expecting that she had to blink and look again, just to check she wasn't imagining things. And then, noting the location of the flats in relation to the building, she realised what must have happened. The building had once actually been the ticket office, but it had been closed up and converted into flats. Presumably it was worth more that way. Now the way into the station was through an anonymous building built from a kit, and the people who lived in the old ticket office now had no idea about the history they were walking amongst.

The short walk from the station brought her out on the esplanade. Directly ahead of her was the pier: a long wooden road leading out into the sea, supported on an elaborate truss-work of poles and struts. To her left was a row of hotels and guest houses, receding into the distance. To her right was what looked at first glance like a whole pile of children's building blocks in bright colours, piled higgledy-piggledy, one on top of the other. It took Daisy a few moments before she realised that they were beach huts: simple wooden sheds painted in reds and greens and yellows, set into a sloping hillside and separated from one another by concrete walkways.

But it was the sea that kept pulling at her attention. The rest-less sea, a thousand shades of blue and grey, all blurring together as the waves crashed onto the sand and ebbed back again, only to gather their strength for another assault. She could feel the sea-spray in the air, pricking at her skin. So chaotic, so relentless and so endlessly fascinating. She could watch it for hours.

But she still had to find somewhere to stay. The drive from the London suburbs to Colchester followed by the train journey had taken it out of her, and she craved nothing more than a long, hot bath and a long, dreamless sleep.

The best thing she could do, she decided, was to find a nice hotel for a few nights. That would allow her to take her time looking for something more permanent – a flat, perhaps, on the ground floor of an old house somewhere within walking distance of the beach. As long as she had a kitchen where she could cook and a bed where she could sleep, she would be happy. A lair, from which she could emerge to hunt. First, as the old proverb had it, catch your hare.

A garden would be nice, but not essential. After all, the trunk of her car, still back in Colchester, was filled with various twigs, leaves, flowers and roots that she had picked from her *real* garden, her *proper* garden. That should be enough to keep her going.

Slowly, and with increasing tiredness, Daisy turned and wandered along the line of hotels and guest houses. The first few looked as if they were designed to catch the first people off the train: bland, plastic affairs with no character and nothing to recommend them apart from their proximity to the station and the beach. The next one was a large public house with rooms above the bar: too noisy, she decided. And then, a little way on, she discovered a small Edwardian frontage, four storeys high, which advertised itself as The Leyston Arms Hotel. She stood for a few moments, looking it over. The windows were clean, and the front steps were spotless.

Someone in there knew about soda crystals, she thought.

Decision made, she walked purposefully up the steps and into the foyer. The carpet had been freshly vacuumed, and she could smell furniture polish in the air. These were all good signs. The man behind the front desk was impeccably dressed in dark trousers, white shirt and maroon tie. The twin folds down the front of his shirt indicated that either this was the first time he had worn it or he had his cleaning and ironing done professionally, but she could forgive him that by the way he smiled at her.

'Good afternoon, madam. Can I help you?'

'Do you, by any chance, have a room?' she said, smiling back.

'We do,' he said. 'How many nights will you be staying?'

She thought for a moment. 'It might be up to a week. Would that be all right?'

'Let me check.' He looked down and consulted what Daisy suspected was a computer screen hidden below the level of the desk. Computers were everywhere, these days. How had the world managed to function without them?

'We have a room overlooking the beach, or one at the back of the hotel,' he said eventually. 'They're both the same price.' His eyes flickered to a velvet-covered pegboard, the same colour as his tie, which hung to one side. On it were displayed the prices for single rooms, twin rooms, double rooms, family rooms and for breakfast. Daisy took the information in for a moment, suspecting that the man was already wondering, based on her age and her clothes, whether she had enough money to pay for the room.

'Is there any difference between them?' she asked.

'The one at the back of the hotel gets less traffic noise, especially in the mornings, but it doesn't have quite the same view,' he said, smiling again.

'Then I'll take the room at the front.'

He nodded. 'May I take a credit card?'

'Oh,' she said, 'I don't have a credit card.' Forestalling his surprised reaction, she quickly added, 'I don't like them. I've never needed one, and I don't see why I should start now.'

He was momentarily nonplussed. 'We normally require some form of … surety,' he said eventually.

'Could I pay for two days in advance?'

He thought for a moment. 'That will be fine,' he said. 'If you could fill out this form for us …' He reached down under the counter and retrieved a clipboard with several pre-printed forms attached to it. Sliding it around so that she could see it properly, he added, 'Just put down your name and address – I'll do the rest.'

A pen was attached to the top of the clipboard by a length of chain. Taking it gingerly, Daisy placed the tip of the pen against the paper and started to write her name.

And realised with horror that she couldn't remember what it was.

Who was this woman, standing in the hotel foyer? Daisy Wilson? Violet Chambers? Jane Winterbottom? Alice Connell? How did she sign her name: simply, ornately or in copperplate handwriting? Her mind whirled with the flotsam and jetsam of too many abandoned lives. She was paralysed with indecision. Her hand trembled, making small patterns on the form.

'Is everything all right, madam?'

She took a deep breath. 'I'm sorry – it's been a long day.'

Work backwards. Where had she driven from? What did the house look like? What did the street look like? *Who was she?*

'Daisy Wilson,' she said firmly, grasping onto the nearest, the most recent memory as it floated past. 'My name is Daisy Wilson.' Quickly she filled out her name and, with some misgivings, Daisy's address. It was a trail, of sorts, but it couldn't be helped. After all, she was going to be playing Daisy for a while yet.

'Thank you,' he said as she slid the form back and delved into her handbag for her purse. 'I've taken the liberty of putting you in room 241. The bar is to your left, the dining room is to your right. Will you be requiring dinner tonight?'

She thought for a moment. It had been a long drive, and she didn't particularly want to wander out looking for a civilised restaurant. 'Yes, that would be lovely. About half an hour?'

'I'll make sure a table is available,' he said. 'I hope you enjoy your stay.'

Daisy took her suitcase up to her room. It contained a bed, a desk and chair and a small armchair, all arranged in the smallest possible space without actually looking cramped.

Another hotel. Another town. Another identity.

A wave of ... something ... rose up unexpectedly and crashed around her. It wasn't quite grief, or sadness, or regret, or anything in particular. It was more as if a low-key version of each of those emotions had been blended together to form something new, something with no name: a general feeling of sad disconnection from the world. For a moment she was lost and drifting. For a moment.

'Focus,' she murmured. 'Focus.'

She washed quickly and, taking a pen, notebook and a pile of plain stationery from her suitcase, she headed down to the dining room.

Dinner was two lamb chops with asparagus spears and potatoes dauphinois, simply prepared but very pleasant. She followed it with a trifle – something she hadn't had for years. It was what she considered to be 'nursery food' – plain but comforting – and none the worse for that. The portions were small, but enough was as good as a feast, as she always said.

While she ate, she started on the next phase of her task. Before leaving the house in London in the tender care of the estate agents, she had carefully combed through Daisy's letters for the names of friends with whom she was in intermittent contact. Some of her correspondents had drifted away or died over the course of the years, but Daisy was still receiving Christmas cards and the occasional round-robin letter from seven people – old friends or work colleagues with whom she had shared some part of her life. Taking several sheets of stationery, Daisy carefully wrote the same message to each person or family in the almost perfect copy of Daisy's scrawled handwriting that she had worked on whilst dancing attendance on the old bitch.

I'm sorry that I haven't been in touch for some time, but life has been rather complicated. I don't know if you remember my cousin Heather, but she has recently been taken ill. She is currently recuperating at home, and she asked me to come down and look after her and her cats. I don't know how long I will be away, but I suspect it might be some time. I have let the house out while I'm gone – I was worried that it would be empty, but at least this way I know it will be looked after, and I'll get some (much needed!) income.

I'll let you know when I have more information – in the

mean time, if you get around to writing to me then please use the address above.

On each letter, Daisy added in the names and some personal details and questions she had gleaned from the letters, in an attempt to make them all seem more personal. She left the tops of the letters blank. When she had settled down somewhere local then she could fill the return address in. Or, if she wanted to really play it safe, she could use a PO box number.

She read through the letters again. She wasn't sure if they were too formal, too carefully worded. Daisy had been quite demotic in her speech, but what little writing of hers that Daisy had seen betrayed a sharper mind and a trained writing style. Having been through the house and seen Daisy's choice in books, Daisy had revised her opinions of the woman. Daisy, she believed, had been putting it on a little.

After dinner she dropped the letters off in her room and walked through into the hall, intending to go for a quiet stroll around the town. The sun had gone down since she had arrived, and the indigo sky of sunset that had acted as backdrop to the drama of the sea was now a black curtain against which the glowing bulbs of the esplanade's lights were displayed. The bar, however, was just to her right, and she decided that she deserved a drink before setting out. The day had gone pretty well, all things considered.

The room itself was furnished with cane chairs and low glass tables. It wasn't quite her 'scene', but she persevered, walking steadily up to the long bar and asking the barman – a lanky youth who was probably a third of her age – for a small dry sherry.

His thick brows contracted into a single line. 'Don't think we do sherry,' he said without even looking at the bottles.

Daisy was not going to be put off. 'Then I will have a Dubonnet with lemonade, please.'

He poured it with bad grace, and she took her drink to a

table over in one corner from where she could see the entire bar area. It was pretty empty – most people had probably gone out on the town – but one or two of the tables were occupied. A middle-aged woman in a shawl was sipping on a gin and tonic at one table. Her husband, dressed rather uncomfortably in a suit, was sitting across the other side of the table. Neither of them was talking. The woman was staring at her glass as if it contained the secrets of the universe, and her husband fidgeted as if he was constantly on the verge of saying something just in order to break the silence and then reconsidering at the last moment when he realised how banal it would sound.

Daisy found herself holding her Dubonnet like the woman at the table was holding her gin, and she forced herself to stop. She'd already had one moment of slippage. She had to keep a grip on who she was, lest it all slide away from her, leaving her with no character at all. Or a faceless stranger, perpetually reflecting every character she came across.

At another table a lone man sat, nursing a pint of dark liquid. He was burly, florid, with more hair on his knuckles than on his head. A flat cap sat on the table beside him. There was an air about him that made Daisy think he was drinking something old-fashioned and manly, like mild and bitter, or brown ale. She wondered briefly whether she should engage him in conversation, but she decided against it. She never stalked men: it was almost impossible to strike up a friendship without the sexual element creeping in, and there was always that ever-present worry that they were stronger than her should her little poisons not work quickly enough. And, of course, taking on their identities directly was almost impossible: she would have to find some sideways approach to realising their assets when they were gone, and that itself was adding an extra risk to the proceedings. No, best not.

Delicately she drained the last drops of her rather tart Dubonnet and gathered her handbag and coat together. A little walk around town and then bed, she decided.

The air outside was cold. Across the road she could see the metal railings of the esplanade but behind that, where earlier there had been the beach and the sea and the sky, there was nothing. A black void, immense and empty. It was as if the world ended at those railings, and an unwary pedestrian might stumble and fall, pinwheeling for ever through space until the end of time.

Daisy shook herself. Really, the thoughts that were entering her head. It wouldn't do. It really wouldn't do.

She let her feet guide her, not planning where she was going. A side street led away from the esplanade and deeper into town. She crossed what she assumed was the High Street – occupied mainly by teenagers who appeared to be migrating from pub to club and back again – and found another side street that was lined with antiques and curio shops. Something was pulling her on, some deep, primal attraction towards something sensed but as yet unseen. She stumbled on, letting the shop fronts and the lights all blur together.

Until she found herself in front of a gaudily lit frontage, all blue neon and yellow letters. It looked as if it had once been a cinema, but now it was used for another kind of entertainment.

Bingo.

A session had obviously just finished, and a crowd of women was descending the steps. Some were wearing wraps, some coats, some just low-cut silvery tops and skirts. They were laughing coarsely. *Secretaries,* Daisy thought, dismissively. Behind them came a gaggle of older women in long coats and woollen hats, walking in ones and twos, and suddenly Daisy's senses came alert. Her mouth went dry, and every detail stood out as if spotlit. She could *smell* the lavender perfume, lovingly dabbed on from bottles bought twenty years beforehand. She could *feel* their rough, hand-knitted cardigans and scarves. She could *see* the surreptitious gleam of their scalps through their carefully coiffured hair. As they went their separate ways, with goodbyes and waves and little pecks on the cheek, Daisy noted which streets they went down, which directions they left in, who leant on a cane for support and who didn't, who left in company and who left alone.

These were her natural prey.

And tomorrow, the hunt would begin again.

CHAPTER SIX

It was several weeks after the autopsy that Mark Lapslie and Emma Bradbury drove up to Ipswich together in Emma's Mondeo. Technically, Ipswich was outside their manor, falling within the boundaries of Suffolk Constabulary, but Lapslie had made some phone calls before setting out and they'd been given permission to continue with their inquiries. The roads were busy, but Emma managed to weave her way through the mass of other cars, overtaking where necessary and under-taking where she had to, in order to get them there in good time. Lapslie just let himself sink back in the passenger seat, eyes closed, the roar of her engine sending pulses of marmalade through his mouth and provoking his salivary glands into spasm. He was so used to the sound of his own car engine that he couldn't taste it any more, but he hadn't spent long enough in Emma's car to get used to the noise, or to be able to screen it out. He'd wanted to drive up himself, but it made no sense for them to take two cars on the journey, and police etiquette demanded that a DS drove a DCI, not the other way around.

Once she reached out to switch the radio on. Firmly, he switched it off again. She glanced uncertainly across at him, but said nothing.

After a series of turns separated by shorter and shorter distances, Lapslie opened his eyes to find Emma slowing down to look for a parking space. They were in a wide road lined with a mixture of silver birch and lime trees and, behind the trees, semi-detached houses built some time around the 1970s. Most front gardens had bikes, or scooters, or wheeled toys shaped like small tractors or lorries abandoned on them. The area gave off a welcome sense of prosperity and supportiveness. Not like some of the sink-hole estates that Lapslie had visited over the years. That was the trouble with being a policeman. You ended up getting a distorted view of the world.

Emma parked in a space under a lime tree. As she and Lapslie got out, Lapslie glanced behind them. There were no other cars driving along the road. He wondered what exactly he had been looking for. A black Lexus perhaps? He turned back to Emma. He was beginning to take this conspiracy thing a bit too seriously.

Emma cast a dark glance at the overhanging branches. 'This tree's going to drip sap all over my car,' she muttered. 'I know it is. Sticky sap. It's a bugger to get off, but it stains the wax if you don't.'

'It's okay,' Lapslie said soothingly. 'We'll stop off at a car wash on the way back.'

She frowned. 'This car's never seen the inside of a car wash, and I'm not about to start now. Do you know what those rotating brushes do to your paintwork? I might as well take a scouring pad to it.'

The nearest house had a plate attached to the gatepost with the number '58' attached. A metal climbing frame sat on the recently cut front lawn: fronds of longer grass and a handful of daisies poking up around the frame where it touched the ground. 'That's Violet Chambers' last known address,' Emma continued. 'Doesn't look abandoned. Also doesn't look as if an old woman lived there.'

'If she lived with her family then someone should have reported her missing some time ago,' Lapslie said.

'Which they didn't, according to the records.'

Lapslie walked up towards the house. A bedroom window was open, and a maroon Toyota Camry estate sat on the drive. The rear section contained two backwards-facing seats just large enough for two six-year-olds.

The warm taste of vanilla flooded his mouth, and for a

moment Lapslie wasn't sure why. Then he heard the sounds of children shouting from the back of the house. The sound and the taste and the memories they evoked made him suddenly dizzy: he reached out to hold on to the frame of the swing to steady himself.

'Are you okay, sir?'

'Fine.' He straightened up. 'Let's get on with it.'

Emma rang the bell, and they waited for a few moments. There were sounds of movement inside the house, then the door opened. A woman in her thirties looked at them curiously. Her brown hair was tied back into a pony-tail, and she wore a flowered silk blouse, tied loosely beneath her breasts, and cord culottes. Her feet were bare. 'Hello?' she said cautiously.

'Detective Chief Inspector Lapslie, Essex Constabulary,' he said, holding out his warrant card. She glanced at it blankly. 'And this is Detective Sergeant Bradbury. Sorry to bother you, but we were looking for the house of Violet Chambers.'

The woman shook her head. 'I know most of the families around here,' she said. 'And I've never heard of a Violet Chambers.'

'She was an elderly lady. In her seventies.'

'We've got mostly families around here. There's an elderly couple across the road – number sixty-seven. They might know her.'

Emma stepped forward, tossing her hair back with a flick of her head. 'How long have you been living in the area, Miss –?'

'Wetherall. Mrs Suzy Wetherall.' She smiled at Emma, and Emma smiled back. 'We moved here six months ago. We're renting, but we love it here so much that we're hoping to buy a house in the road if any come up for sale.'

'What made you move here?' Emma asked.

'My partner's job relocated from London. We thought we'd take the chance to find somewhere nicer to live.' She made a vague gesture towards the garden. 'And we succeeded.'

Lapslie smiled in response. 'Who are you renting the house from?' he asked.

'An estate agents near the station. I can't remember the name.'

'Do you know who was in the house before you?'

She shook her head. 'No, but they left it absolutely spotless.'

'And what about the owners of the house?'

'I assumed the estate agents owned it.' She shrugged. 'We just pay them every month.'

'And you've never heard of Violet Chambers?' Lapslie asked again, just in case the conversation had dislodged a random fragment of memory from the woman's mind. He'd known it to happen before.

'Never. But ask David and Jean over at number sixty-seven. They might be able to help.'

'Thank you for your help,' he said, smiling.

Emma extended her hand towards Mrs Wetherall. 'Thanks,' she added, squeezing the woman's own hand.

They turned to leave. As the door closed behind them, Lapslie said: 'Instinct?'

'She's telling the truth. We can check it with the estate agents –'

'And we will.'

'– but I don't think she's stringing us along. Looks like the family moved in a couple of months after Violet Chambers died, assuming the post-mortem results are accurate. So – what's the next step, boss?'

'We talk to the neighbours over at number sixty-seven to see whether they remember Violet, and then we drive down to the nearest station and check with the estate agents to find out who is renting the house out.'

Vanilla suddenly exploded across his tongue as if someone had squashed an ice cream cornet into his mouth. On the back of the explosion came the sound of shouting from the garden: a sudden argument, a fight, or just a moment of triumph in a game. The shock made him stumble: he caught his stride again but his ankle turned slightly and he staggered sideways, into the grass, before he could catch himself.

Emma was at his side in a moment, holding his arm.

'Sir – are you all right?'

He felt his face warm up as he blushed. He hated showing weakness. But he probably owed her an explanation, especially if it stopped rumours spreading that he might be alcoholic, or mentally unstable.

'Let's get to the car.'

Leaning with his back against Emma's Mondeo, the heat of the sun-warmed metal comforting through his suit jacket, he took a deep breath. How best to start?

'Look, sir,' she said, standing with her hands on her hips and staring out along the road, 'if you want to talk about it, that's fine. If you don't, that's fine too. Either way, it goes no further.'

He nodded, and took a deep breath. 'I've had it for as long as I can remember,' he said quietly. 'For a long time I assumed everyone was the same as me, but when the kids at school started teasing me, and saying I was crazy, I stopped talking about it. "Crazy bonkers", they used to say. "Mark's gone crazy bonkers".'

'And the Force know about it? Whatever it is?'

He nodded. 'Don't worry – it's not depression, or psychosis, or anything like that. I'm not going to suddenly sit in a corner and sob for hours on end. My doctor's aware, but there's nothing he can do. Nothing anyone can do. It's not life-threatening, or even life-changing, or anything that would make them do anything about it. It's just ... part of me. Part of who I am.'

Emma nodded, but she looked like she wanted to shake her head instead. 'So – what exactly is it then?'

'It's called synaesthesia. Nobody knows quite what causes it, but it's as if the nerves in the brain have got short-circuited somehow. Signals going in on one route get rerouted to somewhere else. The best theory is that it all starts in infancy. Babies perceive the world in a mish-mash of sensory impressions, because their brains are not completely developed and they can't separate out smell, taste, touch and so on – they're all mixed up. As the brain develops, the senses start to separate from one another. For people like me this separation may not take place for reasons we don't understand. Some people see different colours when they listen to music. There was a Russian composer called Alexander Scriabin, for instance – he could tie particular notes and chords to different shades of colour, and composed his music not just to sound good, but to *look* good as well – at least, to him. Others can actually feel tastes. Roast chicken might be sharp spikes on the palms of their hands. Orange juice might cause the feeling of soft balls rolling on their scalp.'

'You mean –' She paused, grasping for the right words. 'You mean like some people say that something's making them feel blue? Like that?'

'Not like that. That's just people using examples. Blue just means depressed. These are real feelings.'

'Hallucinations?' Emma asked, frowning. 'Surely it must just be hallucinations?'

'If so, they're consistent. The same things always provoke the same responses.'

'And what is it with you? Lights or feelings on your hands?'

He laughed, bitterly. 'Those I might be able to ignore. No, with me, certain sounds translate into tastes. If I ever hear "Ticket To Ride" by the Beatles, it's like I've just taken a bite out of a rancid chunk of pork.'

Emma ventured a smile. 'I thought everyone reacted that way to Paul McCartney.'

'Yeah, but when my cell-phone rings it tastes like I'm drinking a mocha coffee.' He nodded towards the house. 'And the sound of children playing always makes me taste vanilla. Sometimes it just takes me by surprise, that's all. Overwhelms me.'

Emma glanced at him. 'And there's nothing that can be done?'

'Nothing. It's not going to kill me, and it's not stopping me from working. My doctor's suggested acupuncture, which shows how desperate he is, and the neurology department of the local hospital are more interested in studying my brain than they are in finding a treatment. So I just keep on going. Most of the time it doesn't change anything. I can still work. It's just that ... every now and then, it's like I get ambushed.'

'Ambushed by a taste?'

He glanced over at her. 'Ever bitten into an apple and found it had gone rotten inside? Ever taken a bite of a chocolate and found it was coffee flavour rather than strawberry? Sometimes, flavours can surprise you. Sometimes, they can shock. That's why I had to take time off work – go on gardening leave. Things at home weren't going well, and my synaesthesia took a turn for the worse. I couldn't stand to be in an office, *tasting* everyone else's chatter, banter, lies and deceits. I was overwhelmed. The Chief Super signed me off for a few weeks. A few weeks turned into six months. I've been doing little odd-jobs for the Chief Super ever since – writing reports and conducting studies into how we can do policing better – but this is the first time I've been on active duty for a while.'

'And the family, sir? You said things weren't going very well.'

'They got worse,' he said shortly. 'The synaesthesia got to the point where I couldn't even bear to hear my kids playing in the garden any more. I couldn't listen to their voices without wanting to throw up. It was ... difficult.'

An understatement. It had nearly driven him to suicide. And it had driven him and his wife apart.

Emma shrugged. 'Well, thanks for telling me. I won't mention it to anyone.' She ran a finger across the roof of her car, rubbed her fingers together, and grimaced. 'Bloody sap. Careful of your jacket – dry cleaning won't get this stuff out. Shall we get on with talking to the old couple across the road? If you're all right, that is?'

'I'm fine.' He straightened up. 'Thanks.'

'No problem.' She hesitated. 'Do I taste of anything?' She suddenly blushed. 'I mean –'

'I know what you mean. Lemon, most of the time. Lemon and grapefruit if you're in a good mood; lemon and lime if you're not.'

She looked strangely pleased. 'Could be worse,' she said. 'You know what they say: if little girls are made of sugar and spice and all things nice, then why do women taste of –'

'Anchovies. Yes, I know.'

They walked across to number sixty-seven. The lawn was so close-cropped that it might have been cut with nail scissors. There were no toys in the front garden; instead, a cast-iron bird bath took pride of place. The curtains twitched as they approached.

'Detective Chief Inspector Lapslie,' he introduced himself to the tall, white-haired man who opened the door. 'And this is Detective Sergeant Bradbury.'

The man nodded. He was dressed in pressed slacks and a blue shirt. The skin around his neck had sagged into set folds. 'Is this about the Neighbourhood Watch? It's taken you long enough.'

'No sir, it's not about the Neighbourhood Watch. We're making inquiries about Violet Chambers. Did you know her?'

'Violet?' He looked surprised. 'Yes, of course. She lived opposite.' He glanced back over his shoulder. 'Jean, put the kettle on, will you? We've got visitors.' Turning back, he added, 'Would you care for a cup of tea? Or coffee? I know you're on duty, so I won't offer you a sherry. Name's Halloran. David Halloran.'

'A cup of tea would be most welcome.' Lapslie followed Halloran into the hall, wondering if anybody under the age of seventy still drank sherry. Emma followed them both.

Mrs Halloran was standing in the living room, which ran through the house from the bay windows at the front to a conservatory at the back. A backless set of shelves extended half way across the room, dividing it roughly in two. A sofa and two armchairs covered in flowery material sat in an L-shape facing a rather old television set. The walls were decorated with Regimental badges and pictures of men in uniform. 'Did I hear you say you were with the police?' she asked.

'Asking after Violet,' her husband said. 'Violet Chambers.'

'Poor Violet,' Mrs Halloran said enigmatically, and vanished into the kitchen.

Mr Halloran gestured for them to sit on the sofa. He sank into one of the armchairs. 'Army days,' he said, nodding at the photographs. 'Everything from Korea through to Northern Ireland. Spend my time worrying about the little bastards playing hide-and-seek in my hedge now. Funny old thing, life.'

'About Violet Chambers...?' Lapslie prompted.

'She was here when we moved in, twenty years or so ago. Her and her husband – Jack. He died a few years later. Heart attack, the doctors said. Went quick, whatever it was. One moment he was weeding the garden, next he keeled over like he'd been shot.'

'And Mrs Chambers?'

'She stayed on in the house. Mortgage was paid off. I suppose she could have moved away, but they had no children. She seemed to manage okay. Pottered down to the shops once a week. We offered to help, but she was a bit stand-offish. Didn't like to socialise. I think she thought she'd married beneath her when she married Jack. I don't think we ever saw inside the house. Not once, in twenty years. That's why it seemed so odd.'

Emma leaned forward. 'What seemed odd?'

Mrs Halloran arrived from the kitchen with a tray which she put down on a small table between the armchairs. 'Well, one day she popped a note through our door saying she'd had to go away,' Mrs Halloran said. 'Which was unusual, as she'd never bothered telling us about anything like that before. Apparently her cousin had been taken ill. We didn't even know she had a cousin. She said she was going to look after her. We never saw her again – not that we ever saw her much when she was there. But the next thing we knew, someone else was moving into the house.' She looked up, eyes meeting Lapslie's as she poured the tea. 'We presumed she died.'

'She did,' Lapslie confirmed.

'And what about the cousin?'

'I really don't know.' Lapslie glanced across at Emma, hoping she could pick up the story. Mrs Halloran's face, so close to his, was mildly off-putting.

'There's some question about the estate,' Emma took over smoothly. 'We're just making routine inquiries. You say she kept herself to herself, and you very rarely saw her. Did she have any visitors that you noticed?'

Mrs Halloran handed Lapslie a cup of tea. 'I can't really say.'

'There was someone,' Mr Halloran said suddenly.

His wife eyed him. 'Was there?'

'A woman. Saw her a couple of times leaving the house. Thought she was a home help or something, although come to think of it she was a bit old to be a home help.'

Mrs Halloran frowned as she handed Emma her cup of tea. Emma looked at it as if she had never seen one before. Perhaps it was the bone china that was putting her off. 'Now you come to mention it, I think I might have seen her once. She was carrying something out of the house. I assumed she was from the social services.'

'Did you know her name?' Lapslie asked.

'Oh no. We never got to talk to her.'

Lapslie slurped his tea back quickly. 'Thanks for your help. If you remember anything else ...' He made to get up, but something in Mr Halloran's eyes kept him sitting.

'Didn't we get a Christmas card?' he asked his wife.

'You're right,' she said. 'I think I still have it.' She headed for the back half of the room. 'Give me a moment and I'll find it.'

'She keeps everything,' Mr Halloran confided. 'We've got Christmas and birthday cards dating back to when we were married.'

'And the card – that was sent *this* Christmas?' Emma asked.

'That's right.'

Emma glanced over at Lapslie. He knew what she was thinking. Violet Chambers had died somewhere in the region of nine months before. When people had been cheerily singing Christmas carols and exchanging presents, when they had been watching the Queen's Speech or sleeping off a surfeit of turkey, Violet Chambers' body had been slowly decomposing, and small animals had been burrowing through her innards.

So who had sent the card?

After a few moments rummaging in a cardboard box, Mrs Halloran returned triumphantly, holding not only a Christmas card but a postcard as well. 'I'd forgotten this,' she said, waving it in her husband's face. 'It arrived a week or so after she left.'

Lapslie looked at the Christmas card first. Mass produced for some charity, the picture on the front was so generically festive as to be laughable. Some people, he reflected, went through years studying graphic arts at college with high hopes of working in advertising or magazine design, only to end up churning out endless paintings of robins and snowmen and snow-laden branches. Probably in July, so the cards could be ready in time. What happened to these people? Did they eventually die of a broken heart, their dreams of a high-profile career dashed, or did they end up committing suicide, depressed by all the production-line festivity they had to create? He'd have to ask Dr Catherall whether she had a glut of dead graphic artists in her mortuary come the autumn.

Thinking of Dr Catherall made him realise that he needed to talk to her about the results of the tests she had ordered on the samples from Violet Chambers' body.

All that was written in the interior of the Christmas card was a signature, appended to the usual meaningless printed message. The writing was cursive, rounded, done with a fountain pen. The postcard had, to all appearances, been written with the same fountain pen. It was a plain, white card with no picture on it. The Hallorans' address was written on one side, and the message on the other simply said: 'Dear David and Jean. I don't know how long I will be away, but I suspect it might be some time. I have let the house out while I'm gone – I was worried that it would be empty, but at least this way I know it will be looked after, and I'll get some (much needed!) income. Take care, Violet.' The stamp on the front was a standard first-class stamp, and the postmark was blurred into incoherence.

'And this is the only communication you've had since she left?'

'That's right,' Mrs Halloran said.

'What about the writing? Is it Violet Chambers'?'

'I really wouldn't know. I don't think she ever wrote to us when she was here.'

Lapslie passed the two items to Emma. As she examined them, Lapslie asked: 'I don't suppose you kept the envelope the Christmas card came in, by any chance?'

'Why would we?' Mr Halloran replied, genuinely surprised.

'No reason,' Lapslie sighed. 'No reason at all.' He made as if to get up. 'Well, we won't take up any more of your time. Thanks for the tea.'

'A couple more questions, if I might,' Emma said, still sitting. Lapslie sank down heavily in his chair again. 'Do you have any photographs of Violet Chambers?'

Mrs Halloran shook her head. 'No, my dear. I can't think of any reason why we might.'

Emma nodded. 'What about her appearance, then? Was there anything out of the ordinary about her? Any distinguishing features?'

As both the Hallorans considered, Lapslie nodded at Emma. Good question.

'There was a scar,' Mrs Halloran said eventually.

'On her neck,' Mr Halloran confirmed. He tapped his own neck, just below the Adam's apple. 'Just here.'

'Thanks,' Lapslie said again. He glanced over at Emma. 'If there's nothing else…?'

She shook her head, and they left, taking some time to disengage themselves from the Hallorans' hospitality. For one horrible moment Lapslie thought they were going to be invited to stay for lunch, but fortunately it didn't happen.

Walking back to Emma's car, Lapslie said, 'That was good thinking about the distinguishing features. I'd forgotten about the scar on the corpse's neck. Diphtheria, wasn't it?'

'Breathing tube inserted when she was young,' Emma confirmed. 'At least, according to the pathologist. It gives us some additional faith that the body is Violet Chambers.'

'Were we in any doubt?'

'Well, all we had were the dentures.' Stopping to unlock her car, she said: 'Where do we go from here, sir?'

Lapslie looked up and down the road, thinking. 'The estate agents near the station – the ones that have been renting Violet's house to the Wetheralls since she disappeared. At the very least, they can tell us where the rent is being paid to.' He sighed. 'I feel as if we're getting more and more information without making any progress. We know that Violet Chambers died in the middle of a forest. Someone must have left her there, even if they weren't responsible for her death – and we still don't know how she died. We can assume that the same person sent the postcard and the Christmas card to the Hallorans. There might be more cards floating around as well, if she had other friends. Either way, it looks as if someone is trying to keep Violet Chambers alive, at least in people's minds. Why? What's in it for them? I can't imagine that the rent coming in from the house is enough to justify the risk, no matter how nice this area is.'

'Then how do we proceed, sir?'

'That, Detective Sergeant Bradbury, depends on two things: what we find out from the estate agents, and whether the good Doctor Catherall has managed to establish a cause of death yet.'

They found the nearest station within ten minutes. It was just off a crossroads of shops, wine bars and restaurants. There were three estate agents' premises within a short walk of one another, and Lapslie and Emma had to check all three before they struck lucky. Lucky, Lapslie reflected, was a relative term. According to the girl they talked to, the house had been put up for rent less than a year before. She hadn't been working there when the house had come onto their books, but according to the computer files – which she consulted with rather bad grace after repeated prompting from Lapslie – the owner, a Mrs Violet Chambers, had completed most of the paperwork by post. The rent money – minus the standard cut taken by the estate agents – was paid regularly into a building society account. And that was that.

They drove back in silence from Ipswich, each concerned with their own thoughts. As they hit the motorway, Lapslie's mobile bleeped. The taste of mocha in his mouth made him realise that they hadn't eaten lunch yet.

The message on the mobile's screen said: *You may wish to revisit the mortuary. I believe I have established the cause of Violet Chambers' death. It is not –*

The message stopped there. Trust Dr Catherall to avoid the contractions and short cuts of texting and over-run the number of characters allowed in a message. A few seconds later, with another beep, a second message – or, rather, the continuation of the first – appeared.

– exactly what I had been expecting. I will be working late. Arrive whenever convenient. Jane Catherall.

'Head back to Braintree,' he said, deleting the messages. 'Doctor Catherall's found something. And if you know of any decent pubs on the way, stop off. I could do with a bite to eat.'

Following a quick cheese and ham baguette at a white-washed pub just off the A12, they made good time. Emma brought the Mondeo to a halt in the mortuary's car park just short of three in the afternoon.

'Do you want me to come in, sir?'

Lapslie considered for a moment. Emma didn't particularly like standing around listening to technical talk: that had become clear last time. 'No,' he said finally. 'Check the building society account the rent is paid into. I want to know who's spending that money. I'll get a car from the station to pick me up.'

Dan, the mortuary attendant, let him in when he buzzed. Lapslie strode ahead and pushed his way through the double doors.

The mortuary tables were empty. Dr Catherall was over by a small autoclave, leafing through a sheaf of pink paper, her polio-ravaged body dwarfed by the size of the tables, the cabinets that lined the room, the air-conditioning pipes in the ceiling. The ever-present background smell, cloying and faecal, made his throat tighten. He forced the reaction down. How did she ever get used to it?

'Doctor Catherall?'

She looked up from the papers she was reading. He had forgotten how mild and blue her eyes were. 'Ah, Detective Chief Inspector.'

'Mark.'

'Mark it is, then.'

'You texted me.'

'I did. A hateful thing, texting. It encourages lazy writing and imprecision of thought. It is, however, too useful to lose.'

Impatiently, he cut through her stream of consciousness. 'What else have you found?'

'You will remember,' she started, placing the papers down on top of a cabinet, 'that the body had been subject to slow, anaerobic decomposition and to a certain amount of animal activity. This made the examination problematic, to say the least. There were, however, no immediate signs of heart attack, stroke or exposure as far as I could tell. Given the fact that the body was found in a shallow grave in the middle of a forest, with no obvious means of transport around, wrapped tightly in plastic sheeting and with the fingers on the right hand removed by a pair of sharp, opposed blades, like a pair of chef's shears, I am inclined to rule out natural causes.'

She smiled. Lapslie just sighed quietly to himself.

'Now, apart from the damage to the back of the skull, which could have resulted from the car crash that excavated her body, there are no signs of pre-mortem attack – no fractures, no stab wounds, nothing that would account for a sudden collapse.'

'Doctor, you've spent the past few minutes listing every possible thing that *didn't* kill her, with the exception of a freak meteor shower. If I don't find out soon what actually did the job then I'm going to strap you to one of those spare tables and prod you with your own surgical instruments until you tell me.'

She had the good grace to laugh. 'Very well. You will recall that we found the corpses of several small animals nestled within her chest cavity. This started me thinking. What could have caused them to die, and die so quickly that they could not escape? To cut to the chase, I tested the poor lady's stomach contents – at least, what remained of them – for toxins. And I found some.'

'*Poison!*' That was the last thing Lapslie was expecting.

'Indeed. To be more precise, her stomach lining, liver and kidneys were saturated with colchicine – a drug used in small doses to treat gout.'

Lapslie shook his head slowly. 'So she accidentally overdosed on her own medicine? In the middle of a forest?'

'I have no idea how she got into the middle of a forest,' Dr Catherall replied with asperity, 'but she certainly did not overdose on her medicine. Firstly, she was not suffering from gout, nor was there any evidence she had ever done so. Secondly, her stomach contents indicate that the poison was not administered in the form of tablets, which is how colchicine is most often given, but in what I can only describe as its raw form.'

Lapslie was beginning to feel like the straight man in a double act, feeding Dr Catherall lines so she could get to a punch-line. 'You're going to have to explain that, as well.'

'Colchicine is derived from the seeds of a plant known as the meadow saffron, otherwise known as the autumn crocus, although, strangely enough, it is not actually a crocus. Despite the passage of time, there are still traces of seeds in the stomach. My best guess – and it really is a guess – is that she somehow ingested enough meadow saffron to provide a lethal dose of colchicine.'

'Accidentally?'

She shook her head. 'I really cannot see how. For a start, meadow saffron does not grow anywhere within fifty miles of where she was found. And besides, there were enough traces of other substances in the stomach contents that I can be reasonably certain that the plant was administered in the form of a cake.'

It took a few moments for Lapslie to fully understand what he was being told. He understood the individual words, but putting them all together in the form of a sentence, even one as convoluted as Dr Catherall preferred, took him to a place he really didn't want to go. Despite the coldness of the room he could feel a prickly kind of heat across his neck and upper arms. This was deliberate. Worse than that, this was planned as some kind of domestic *event*.

'Let's be clear, Doctor,' he said finally. 'You know what you're saying?'

'I do,' she said. 'Colchicine overdoses of the size I believe occurred here are particularly painful and protracted. If done deliberately, it verges on torture, I would say.'

Silence filled the room.

'This now becomes a murder investigation,' Lapslie said.

CHAPTER SEVEN

As Daisy Wilson awoke from a deep sleep, troubled by dreams of a long dining table around which faceless figures sat in uneasy silence, she rose through a series of previous identities like a balloon floating up through layers of cloud.

For a while she was Alice Connell, a former librarian in Epping, living alone but for a white cat in a small house near a canal. She liked walking along the canal in the afternoons just to be able to see other people and to smile at them. Sometimes the cat would walk along with her. Then Alice was left behind and she was Jane Winterbottom, an obsessive collector of Victorian hairbrushes who kept her collection in her flat on the bottom floor of a Victorian block in Chelmsford and who had nobody to whom she could show it. Jane, too, receded into the distance, and she was Violet Chambers, a widowed old lady living in a house too big for her, too proud to make friends with her neighbours, sitting at her living room window and watching the world pass her by. And then Violet was falling away.

With the cocoons of her previous existences sloughing away from her, she dimly remembered that there had been others as well, others before Alice Connell. The names were vague now, but she could just make out the dim outlines of stolen memories: an old, cobbled street somewhere in south London with rusted tram lines running down the centre; a familiar seat in a public house with a half pint of Irish stout set on the table; a grey room with a grey metal bed; a powder-blue eiderdown coat; a tortoiseshell comb; an Aga. No faces, no names, just snatches of things seen and half-remembered. Fragments of too many lives; a pile of different jigsaw puzzles, fallen to the floor and mixed together, never to be undone.

And behind all of those, a long dining table, set with bone china cups, and those silent figures. Those silent, waiting figures.

She lay there for a while, the sunlight playing on the ceiling of her room, letting her mind idly sort through the fragments until she could reassemble herself. Daisy Wilson. She was Daisy Wilson, and she was establishing a new life in a small seaside town named Leyston-by-Naze, on the east coast. She needed a place to live, she needed to make some friends, and she needed some money. Those were the priorities of the day.

Eventually, she got up out of bed and gazed out of the window of her hotel room. It was still early. There was barely any differentiation between the water and the clouds; one blended into the other in a continuous sheet of grey. Only a large container ship, crawling infinitesimally right to left, marked the location of the horizon.

Daisy washed, dressed, left her room and headed down to the restaurant where she had eaten on the previous night. The tables had been stripped and reset for breakfast, with small pots of jam, saucers of butter and steel cutlery stark against white linen. The ghosts of old coffee rings were still visible on the linen. Small signs marked which tables were reserved for which rooms. She located the table for room 241 – set for one – and sat down. Within a few moments, a tired-looking young girl in a black skirt and white blouse came over to her.

'Good morning, ma'am. Would you like tea or coffee?'

Daisy considered for a moment. Was she a tea or a coffee person? 'Tea, please,' she said eventually.

'And would you be wanting a cooked breakfast?'

Less of a hesitation this time. 'No, thank you. Just toast, please.'

'Fruit juice?'

'Yes please – grapefruit, if you have it.'

'If you want cereal, it's on the table over by the window.'

'Thank you, m'dear.'

The waitress left. As Daisy waited for the toast to arrive, she glanced around at the other hotel patrons. The couple from the night before – the man in the suit and the woman in the shawl – were just finishing their breakfasts. They were still failing to find any topics of conversation. The florid man with the flat cap was absent, but a family of four – mother, father and two children, both girls – were making a big production number over swapping knives, buttering toast and cutting up fried breakfasts so that the children could eat them. The girls were dressed in identical outfits: white cloth patterned with green leaves and vines, like something one might use as a curtain. Daisy wondered if their mother had made the clothes herself.

'Your toast, ma'am. Tea's on the way.'

The waitress had reappeared by Daisy's side. She placed the toast on the table, then headed over to help the family sort out the mess they were making.

Daisy felt a prickle on the back of her neck. Turning casually, she saw an elderly woman enter the restaurant. She was elegant, with a long green dress cinched in at the waist and covered with a long cardigan made of wool. The necklace circling the corrugated skin of her neck might have been pearl. Daisy would have to get closer to be able to tell for sure.

Daisy tracked her progress across the room. Knowing in her heart that the woman was probably on holiday, which more or less ruled her out as a prospect, Daisy was nevertheless unable to stop herself. It was like those lions one saw on wildlife documentaries: an antelope walks past and the lions look up, watching the animal move, calculating the line of least effort between them and their prey. It doesn't matter that they aren't hungry, it just matters that they are lions and the thing going past is an antelope. Instinct overrules everything.

Her heart beat a little faster as the woman seemed to be heading for a table with a single setting, but slowed as she bypassed it in favour of a table set for two. The woman sat down, and a few moments later a man in a cream-coloured jacket, walking with a cane, entered the room and followed her.

Probably for the best. One should never foul one's own nest, isn't that what they said?

The tea arrived and she poured herself a cup, breathing in the rich, aromatic steam. It was a blended tea, half Ceylon and half Darjeeling, as far as Daisy could tell. She was good with tea.

Daisy spread a thin layer of butter over the toast and took a delicate bite while she considered her options. At some stage she would have to visit an estate agents and arrange to rent a property in the area. After all, she couldn't live at the hotel for ever. A predator needed a trap, and the hotel was too public, too exposed. The problem was that she knew little about the town: where the best areas for retired folk were, which were the noisy public houses and which were the quiet ones, and so on. Her usual tactic was to buy as many local papers as the area could support and read through them a few times, getting a feel for wherever she had ended up. She had found, through long experience, that the classified advertisements and the announcements provided a lot of useful background informa-tion, not the least of which was the section devoted to forthcoming funerals or the anniversaries of deaths. After all, one had to start somewhere, and widows were easy prey.

Finishing her toast, Daisy got up to leave. Nobody in the restaurant bothered watching her go, and that was the way she liked it.

Outside the hotel, the weather was warm despite the grey, cloudy sky. The tide was on its way in, creeping slowly up the sandy shoreline. Off to her right, the pier jutted out into the water; a bridge heading into nowhere. Pulling her cardigan closer about her, she turned left and walked along the sea front. Ahead of her the esplanade curved away to the left, hiding all but the next row of houses, bars and hotels and making it appear as if the sea lapped directly against the buildings. Far away in the distance the shore curved back into sight again, rising into a knob of land that towered above the town – the Naze itself, named, she assumed, from the French *nez*, meaning 'nose', which is what it actually resembled.

As she walked, she realised that she had turned left with deliberate purpose, as if she was heading for somewhere in particular, but when she examined her motives she realised that she didn't really know where she was going. She had approached the hotel from the other direction the day before, and when she had gone for her evening walk she had turned right, back towards the station. Now, heading in an unknown direction, she had the distinct feeling that there was something familiar around the curve of the road: something that she wanted to see, if only she knew what it was.

A few steps, and she could see further around the bend. And there was a public garden: a small walled area on the corner between the esplanade and what she thought might be the High Street. As she approached, she saw that it had benches around the edge, and was planted with rows of brightly coloured flowers. It was a small oasis of calm amid the seaside bustle.

Rather than keep on going around the corner and into the High Street, Daisy cut through the garden. With practised eye, she identified the plants that she passed. Over by the brick wall of the next building, pennyroyal plants were reaching upward, their little bursts of pink and white blossom separated by stretches of stem. Next to them, Daisy spotted the dark red, five-petalled flowers of a row of delphiniums reaching towards her. Both of them were poisonous, although the essential oil would have to be extracted from the pennyroyal first: a fussy process that Daisy would rather not have to do again. There were other plants in the garden as well, but she had less interest in those. They might have looked nice, they might even have smelled nice, but they had no practical purpose. They couldn't be used to kill anyone.

It reminded her of her own garden. She smiled for a moment, recalling the dark scents and the glistening flowers that she had left behind. When she had taken Dais – no, *she* was Daisy – when she had taken the *body* away and left it where nobody would find it, she had taken the opportunity to tend her garden, to remove some of the weeds that were growing up around the mulch and to cut back some of the more extravagant growths. It made her feel calm. It made her feel centred, somehow.

Leaving the garden behind her, she turned into the far end of the High Street.

The road was long, and lined with shops of various kinds. Every second one appeared to be selling something to do with the beach: swimwear, sticks of rock, inflatable rings and mattresses, towels – all the paraphernalia of a day by the sea. In between these holiday-specific shops were the ones she would expect to find in any small town: newsagents and banks, florists and shoe shops, bakeries and butchers: the kinds of shops that, in some bigger towns, had been rendered obsolete by hypermarkets and telephone banking, but managed to survive in places such as this like barnacles clinging to rocks.

She popped into the first newsagents she came to and bought one of the three local papers that were sitting on the lowest shelf. A few yards along the High Street she found another newsagents, and she bought the second of the local papers. Buying three local papers in one shop probably didn't count as suspicious behaviour, but she didn't like leaving a trail, even if that trail was only one of memories. Daisy far preferred to slip unnoticed through people's minds; just one more little old lady living her life one day at a time.

A little further along the road, she found a W. H. Smith. There she bought the third local paper, and managed to get a plastic bag to go along with it. Now, with all three in her possession, she needed to find somewhere to sit down and read them. For a moment she hovered on the verge of turning around and heading back to the public garden, but she knew the intoxicating smell of the pennyroyal and the delphiniums would just distract her. A café would do just as well.

Walking further along the High Street, Daisy found herself turning left into a shop doorway before she knew what she was doing. It was only when the burnt sugar smell of candy floss hit her that she looked up and realised she was in a gift shop. What had made her think this was a café? Smiling vaguely, she backed out and kept walking, looking around more carefully this time.

She almost missed the place across the road. It was part of a building that extended from one street corner to another, built out of the same red brick and with the same buff adornments on the corners. The building had once been a large post office: it still was, at one end, but the other end had been converted into a genteel coffee shop advertising gateaux and pastries, espresso and cappuccino on a chalk board pinned to the red brick wall.

She entered the coffee shop and looked around. It had the same kind of dated feel as her hotel: backward looking, rather than forward, with lace doilies on the tables and sepia-tinged photographs in frames on the wall. A perfect place to sit and read. She found an empty table and perched herself on a chair. Having established from the plastic-covered menu on the table that she could, in fact, order tea as well as coffee, she asked the waitress for a pot and then spread the first local paper, the *Tendring Gazette*, over the table.

Dismissing the headlines, which involved accusations of fraud in the Council and blocked inquiries into the sale of school fields in the vicinity, she concentrated on the later pages. The local stuff. There were small news paragraphs of course. One of them, headlined 'Milk and Beer Taken', reported on how thieves had broken into a local garage and stolen a bottle of beer and a bottle of milk from a fridge, drunk them both, and then smashed the milk bottle, which Daisy decided summed up perfectly the parochial approach of local newspapers to events.

The world might be heading for ecological disaster, nations might be at war, but as long as one local journalist was on the job, no case involving a stolen milk bottle would go unreported. Another paragraph reassured readers that a horse that had been stuck in mud had been freed by fire-fighters. It wasn't until page twenty-two that Daisy found a section headed 'Neighbourhood News', which listed the activities of various local organisations such as the Fuchsia Club, the Bridge Club and, of most interest to her, the Widows' Friendship Club. Anyone who was a member of a club, of course, was, by definition, bound to know people there, but Daisy knew that she could quite easily befriend one of the widows, separate her from the flock and gradually take over her life. The other widows might wonder from time to time what had become of their friend, but they would probably only make cursory attempts to check she was all right. Once a couple of telephone calls had been missed, once a few knocks on the door had gone unanswered, they would give up. It was human nature.

The next page listed local churches and services, and Daisy made a mental note of their locations and the types of activity they undertook. She didn't want to stumble into anything evangelical, after all. Still, she was pleased to see that there were plenty of Methodist churches. Her spur-of-the-moment story on the train the day before was safe.

Three pages of death notices followed, and Daisy read through them all in detail. The words were much the same, as if they all followed a small number of templates, and she sneered to herself at all the various euphemisms employed. 'Died peacefully.' 'Passed away unexpectedly.' 'Taken from us in the prime of life.' All ridiculous. How many of the notices covered up days of messy, agonised and undignified writhing on the part of the dear departed? How many of the fond remembrances covered up neglect, abuse, even murder?

Her tea arrived, late, and Daisy poured a cup, added milk and took a sip. It was stewed. The girl had obviously left it somewhere and forgotten about it. What was the world coming to? If she was that careless, perhaps Daisy should come back one day and slip something into one or two sugar bowls whilst nobody was watching: a fine sprinkling of white powder that would be undetectable when it dissolved in tea or coffee, but which would cause agonising convulsions hours later.

She wouldn't, of course. That would draw too much attention. But it was nice to dream.

Towards the back of the paper, the *Gazette* had ten pages of property adverts. The first eight pages were houses and flats for sale, but the last two covered rental properties. She scanned them with as much care, and as much emotion, as she had read the death notices. The going rate seemed to be between five hundred and seven hundred pounds per month: not a rate she wished to sustain, but something she could manage while looking for a proper house that she could slide into. An occupied house. A house that would soon be hers.

Finally, Daisy came to the classified ads. She loved looking through these sections. It was like getting a small glimpse through the curtains and into somebody's life. Just a small glimpse, open to all sorts of interpretation, as you were walking past. What to make of: 'Family-tree historian seeks f, to form a new branch and dig up some roots together'? Would he ever get his wish? Was the 'Tall, medium-built postman, cat owner, seeks compatible female' giving away too much information?

And then there was 'Happy, lively lady, 50s, seeks male companion and escort for boot fairs, garden centres, etc.' That one looked promising. If she was advertising in the newspaper then it implied she had given up on clubs, or church, or any of the other ways mature women made friends. And that meant she was likely to be isolated. Daisy made a careful mental note of the response number at the bottom of the ad. She was familiar with the process: it varied little from town to town. The number would be a message line run by a company on behalf of the newspaper. Verbal messages could be left, or text messages could be sent. The text messages were preferable as far as Daisy was concerned: if she wanted to lure this woman out into the open and befriend her, she would have to identify her. And that meant she would have to arrange a date at some convenient location, and observe from afar when the woman turned up and waited in vain for her erstwhile paramour to arrive.

Erstwhile paramour. The words made her smile. She'd never had a paramour, erstwhile or otherwise, and had no intention of ever acquiring one, but she knew enough about the relationship between men and women to send a convincing text message.

The remaining two papers – the *Leyston Recorder* and the *Walton and Leyston Post* – were much of a muchness with the *Tendring Gazette*. The story of the horse stuck in mud appeared in both of them, while the one about the stolen bottles of milk and beer was in the *Recorder* but not the *Post*. Of the three, Daisy decided that the *Tendring Gazette* probably had the most to offer. Already it had yielded several leads.

She left enough money on the table to cover the cost of the tea, but without leaving more than a few pence as a tip. Waitressing of that low quality did not deserve a reward.

Leaving the coffee shop, Daisy continued right along the High Street, as much to reconnoitre the area as for any other reason. Across the other side she could see, in the distance, the Bingo Hall where, the night before, she had caught her first scent of prey. The type of shop between her and the Bingo Hall was shifted slightly away from the holidaymakers and towards the more utilitarian: a hairdressers, an ironmongers, and so on. Coming up to a corner with a florists on one side and a Visitor Information kiosk on the other, she paused. The road off to the right led away from the High Street, away from the sea front and from Daisy's hotel, but she decided on a whim to take a wander and see what was down there.

The road curved away to the right, and all Daisy could see for the first few minutes as she walked along were detached and weatherworn houses on either side. The gaps between the paving stones were caked with sand, brought in from the beach by wind and by storm, she presumed.

After a few hundred yards, the houses on the right-hand side gave way to an earth bank, taller than she was and covered with grass and more sand. Every so often, concrete steps led up the side of the bank, vanishing into mystery at the top.

Ahead, the road came to an abrupt stop at a wire-mesh gate. A sign hanging from it read, 'Leyston Yacht Club' in large letters, and then in smaller letters underneath, 'Members Only'.

Daisy took a few more steps towards the gate. A yacht club might be a useful thing to know about. At the very least, it would give her an immediate social veneer. She knew little about boats, but she was sure she could learn. A few hours in the company of a yachtswoman, or even a few hours spent in the same room, and she would be moving and talking as if she had been on boats all her life.

Daisy turned away from the Yacht Club, and gazed absorbedly at the grass bank to her right. It lay there, the faint wind-stirred movements of grass on its flanks like the slow, deep breaths of some recumbent beast. From somewhere beyond the bank she could hear the screeching of gulls, like screaming children. The sound made her unaccountably nervous: she had never had children, never even felt the touch of a man's hand, but something about that sound made her want to scream.

The nearest set of steps was only a few yards away, and with mounting nervousness she walked up them, taking small bird-steps.

As her head rose above the top of the bank, the first thing she saw was a line of houses, far in the distance, and then, as she reached the top, her breath suddenly fluttered within her chest as she saw the stretch of calm water that lay between her and them. The bank dropped down on the other side to a concrete dock, and the water stretched from the dock all the way across to the far side, a misty grey-blue surface, a wash of colour.

It was a marina, a place for boats to tie up, and there were hundreds of them there, hulls painted white and bows sharp and somehow cruel to Daisy's eyes. Somewhere nearby there must have been a channel or a river that led to the North Sea, allowing the boats access. Now they sat still, watchful, waiting for their owners to come and untie them and take them out into the rough ocean.

Daisy walked down the steps on the other side and up to the edge of the dock: slow, unwilling steps, as if something were pulling her forward against her will, or something were pushing her back from a long-sought goal.

Bending down, she could see her reflection in the water: a figure, outlined by blue sky, one hand resting on the dock, the other reaching out to touch the water.

But it wasn't her.

The figure looking up at her from the water of the marina was a young girl with red hair, tied back in a pony tail. She was wearing a checked dress. There was something covering the front of the dress: a stain, like jam, or fruit juice.

Or blood.

Daisy staggered to her feet, backing away from the edge of the concrete. Whatever she had seen in the water was wrong. So very wrong. And it had perverted everything around her as well. She hadn't noticed before, but it was obvious to Daisy now that the concrete had crumbled in places and cracked in others, and the various chains and rings that had been set into the concrete were leaking orange rust. The boats looked sorry for themselves; behind the cruelly curved bows their hulls were dirty and their ropes hung limp.

Above the boats, and between them, seagulls either hung precariously upon the breeze or bobbed on the water, hoping for a morsel of food to float past. Their cries were making Daisy panicky, and she turned away and ran up the concrete stairs of the bank as fast as she could.

Catching her breath at the bottom of the bank, she composed herself and walked back the few hundred yards to the High Street. Somehow, it felt as if she had crossed between two worlds.

Daisy was keeping her eye out for a library, and found one a little further down the High Street. It was a single-storey building, built out of a sandy stone. Once her breathing had returned to normal, she went inside.

The library was bright and airy, built on two levels with a ramp in between. Daisy spent ten minutes or so wandering around, familiarising herself with the layout. Fiction at one end, non-fiction at the other, with a space in the middle for the sadly omnipresent Internet terminals and DVDs. Books seemed almost to be a secondary concern for libraries, these days.

A door leading out of the library led not, as she might have expected, back to the street but to a courtyard nestled between the library and the building behind it. Roses had been planted in pots, and benches artfully positioned around. A few people were sitting out there, reading books they had brought out of the building.

Within moments, Daisy had identified three women over sixty sitting alone, reading.

With studied indifference, she went back into the library and wandered along the shelves until she found a book entitled *Leyston-by-Naze: A Personal History*. Always good to know something about the place you were going to be living in. Daisy had lived in some anonymous towns in her time, and she was quite looking forward to somewhere that actually did have a history. She took the book outside, found a bench with nobody sitting on it and started to read, making sure that she was scrunched up enough at one end that someone could sit comfortably at the other. If she was lucky, they could strike up a conversation. If she was really lucky, the other person would be an elderly widow with no friends and no social life.

For the first ten minutes or so, Daisy paid little attention to the book. She was more concerned with the comings and goings within the courtyard; the little courtesies, the way small customs appeared to have sprung up amongst the regulars. But after a while, as nobody came to sit with her, she began to get absorbed into the book.

It had been written by a local historian, and privately printed as far as she could tell. There was certainly something less than professional about the typeface and the way the pages were cut. The author knew his subject, however, and he could turn a good phrase. Daisy actually found herself becoming interested in the details of how the beaches of Leyston had become a key source of hardcore aggregate for the building industry, and how the local station had been a marshalling yard for transporting the broken rocks into London. Who would have guessed?

Other chapters dealt with Leyston during the war, and then the expansion of Leyston as part of the Tendring Hundreds area. History seemed to have pretty much bypassed the town for a long time; small events took on a greater significance, just because there was so little else that happened. Daisy already knew that, of course – any town where the theft of a milk bottle and a beer bottle made headlines in the local paper was not making its mark on history – but the book's author had to scrape the bottom of the barrel in order to come up with interesting stories.

At least, that was what Daisy thought until she turned a page to find a chapter about sensational crimes in the Tendring Hundreds area. To illustrate it, there was a photographic reprint of the front page of a newspaper dating from the 1940s. The headline said, simply, 'Local Woman in Murder Tragedy'.

And beneath the headline was a black-and-white photograph of the girl whose reflection she had seen in the water of the marina.

CHAPTER EIGHT

Before he had made Detective Chief Inspector, Mark Lapslie's office had been a small, rectangular room in a monolithic 1950s building on the outskirts of Chelmsford, with a grim view across the police station car park and plasterboard walls that showed signs of continual overpainting in a variety of colours. Triangular pieces of sticky tape, yellowing with age, had adorned the walls, though the posters and photographs they had secured had long since been removed. Angular metal conduits, studded with rivets, had been fixed along the skirting board at some stage in the past to take electrical cables and sockets; more conduits had been added at waist height at a later date to take computer network cables. The building had no air conditioning, but the policemen and women who had worked there had quickly learned which windows to open and which to leave shut in order to create a continual cool flow of air through the corridors. In winter, Lapslie had kept cartons of milk out on the window ledge. A lady with a trolley used to come through, once at eleven o'clock and once again at three, selling sticky buns and stewed tea. Another lady with a trolley would come through half an hour later to empty the out-trays on the desks and deliver any new post.

Now, Lapslie had a desk on the eleventh floor of an open-plan office in an architecturally award-winning office block built only a few years before in the redeveloped town centre. Incoming post was scanned in and delivered electronically to the computers on every desk. Outgoing mail had been replaced with outgoing email. The windows were coated with metallic film, for security and energy efficiency, and they couldn't be opened. Nobody was allowed to stick anything to the walls, and the notice boards were pruned once a month for offensive or out-of-date items. All of the electrical and ethernet cabling ran under the raised floor. So did the ventilation: small, circular vents every few yards provided an almost unnoticeable flow of fresh air. The chairs were state-of-the-art, like black sculptures: plastic mesh on a metal frame, promoting comfort and coolness. A cafeteria in the basement sold *venti lattes* and almond croissants at grossly inflated prices. A chalkboard sign on one wall compared their grossly inflated prices with those of other coffee bars in the locality and came to the conclusion that the coffee there was just cheap enough that it made no sense to go out for one, unless you just wanted a walk. They had a gymnasium, a dry-cleaners and a hairdressers actually on the premises.

And Lapslie hated it. He hated it with a passion beyond telling. The noise of thirty or so officers and civilians of various ranks, all talking to one another, talking to themselves or talking on the telephone was distracting beyond measure. To Lapslie it had been like having the taste of blood in his mouth for the entire working day. Following a letter from his doctor to the Assistant Chief Constable, Lapslie had been allowed to use one of the Quiet Rooms – usually set aside for confidential discussions – as a surrogate office if he needed a break. The rest of the time, he wore earplugs.

Still, there were some consolations. Shortly after the force had moved in, some of the lower-ranking officers had discovered that if they covered the floor-based ventilation grilles in a line at the same time, leaving the last one uncovered, then the resulting air pressure out of that vent could quite easily lift a skirt high above the waist on any passing woman. That had kept them amused for a while, until a circular came round forbidding the practice.

Now he sat in the Quiet Room, reading through Dr Catherall's final autopsy report. He'd spent several weeks chasing her to get it finished.

There was no doubt – Violet Chambers had been murdered. The cause of death was uncertain – she had certainly been poisoned, but she also appeared to have been struck on the back of the head. Either could have been the fatal occurrence, although the dirt under her fingernails matched the ground in the vicinity, meaning that she had still been alive when she had been dumped in the forest. The fingers on the right hand had been removed by a sharp, bladed object like a pair of scissors, but that had been done at some stage after Violet Chambers had died, and so blood loss could be ruled out.

Lapslie put down the autopsy report and picked up the report on the area where the body had been found. Tests on the plastic in which she had been wrapped were inconclusive: it was a standard make, available from any large DIY store, and both time and weather had erased any fingerprints that might have been there. And, based on some complicated calculations involving insect pupae and moss, it had been definitively established that her body had lain there for more than eight but fewer than ten months before having been so rudely excavated by a crashing car.

Which still left the two big questions: who had killed her, and why?

Something moved in his peripheral vision, and he twisted around. Emma Bradbury was standing just outside the glass door to the Quiet Room, waving at him. She was wearing a pinstripe trouser-suit offset by an orange sash tied around her waist. He gestured her to enter. She pushed the door open, and Lapslie could immediately taste blood as the susurration of the open-plan office washed over him, as if he'd suddenly bitten his tongue.

'What's up, Emma?'

'Message from the Super, sir. Could you give him an update on the case? Apparently his PA has been trying to get hold of you, but you haven't been at your desk.' The saltiness of the blood receded, replaced by lemon and grapefruit. For a moment the two tastes combined in his mouth: something exotic, like lemongrass, only deeper and more intense. Emma closed the door behind her.

'An update on this case? The Violet Chambers one?'

'Yes, sir.'

'Bit beneath his level of interest, surely?'

Emma shrugged. 'Not for me to judge. Oh, you asked me to trace where the rent from Violet's house was going, sir. Turns out it's going into an account opened some years ago in the name of J. Chambers.'

'Jack Chambers?' He remembered the name from the interview with the elderly couple living opposite what had been Violet's house. 'Violet Chambers' husband?'

'That's right. According to the bank, when he died, back in 1984, she had the account transferred across into her name. And she used it intermittently right up until we know she died, ten months ago. And, bizarrely, she's been using it since as well.'

'Someone's been taking money out of the account? That would certainly track with theft being a motive, but I can't imagine it's a whole load of money. What is it – a few hundred pounds a week?'

Emma nodded. 'Something like that, sir. I've known murders happen for less.'

'In the heat of the moment, yes, but this has the hallmarks of something longer term. Something premeditated. I can't see anyone taking a risk like that for a few hundred pounds a week. How has the money been taken out? Cashpoint, debit card or cheque?'

Emma consulted a sheet of paper in her hand. 'All of the amounts taken out have been cashpoint withdrawals from a variety of banks scattered around London, Essex, Norfolk and Hertfordshire. No cashpoint machine was ever used more than once, as far as I can tell.'

Lapslie leaned back in his chair and ran a hand through his hair. 'All right, let's summarise where we've got to. The crime scene where we discovered the body is a bust – the evidence has just been washed, carried or blown away over the past ten months. The body is a bust – we can't say for sure how she died, and there's no trace evidence. The victim's background is a bust – there's nothing there that could give any cause for murder, apart from this trickle of rent. The only thing we've got is this woman who may have been seen going in and out of Violet Chambers' house before she died, and that may be completely innocent. We could spend the next few months tracking down a chiropodist, if we're not careful. So what's left? Where do we go from here?'

'The nature of the crime itself. Poison is generally a woman's weapon, and the fact that it may have been administered in the form of food indicates a domestic setting – something casual. The murderer was known to the victim, and trusted enough for her to take a slice of cake or whatever it was that the murderer had baked.'

'Okay – it's something to be going on with. Set up a house-to-house in the neighbourhood around Violet Chambers' place. Ask anyone if they remember Violet having any regular visitors in the month or so before she disappeared. Check local shops to see if they recall any women who appeared around that time and then vanished again. Pharmacies and off-licences might be a good place to start. Check with the local surgery as well – whoever this woman was, if there was a woman, she might have taken Violet to an appointment at some stage. Or made one herself.'

'Will do. Anything else?'

Lapslie thought for a moment. 'Yes – run a check into unsolved poisonings. See if this ... colchicine ... has been used before. It's a long shot, but we might strike lucky. I can't imagine it's a common poison, all things considered.'

Emma nodded, and headed off. The door swung shut behind her, and Lapslie was cut off from the noise of the office. Cut off from all noise apart from the sound of his own breathing and the rustle of his clothes as he moved. And if he kept very still, then even that was hushed to the point of silence.

Silence. The blessed state that he craved above all else, and so very rarely achieved.

When Lapslie explained his synaesthesia to most people, they either didn't believe it or they were fascinated. They asked him questions about how it felt, and they sympathised – as much as they could – but they never really understood. Not even the doctors and the psychiatrists, who spent their time reading textbooks and devising experiments to help them understand what synaesthesia implied about the way the brain worked. They never appreciated how it felt to be constantly battered by sensations you weren't expecting. Constantly ambushed by unplanned floods of flavour – some pleasant, some sickening, but all of them unwelcome.

How could you explain that you could never listen to the radio? Never watch the television? Never attend a sporting event or a concert, for fear that a stray taste provoked by an unexpected sound could make you throw up? How could you tell them that you couldn't spend your evenings in the pub with the lads because the raucous atmosphere was like a stream of rancid fat in your mouth, masking the taste of the beer, the whisky or whatever else you tried to use to cover it up with? He'd got a reputation in the force for stand-offishness, for being remote and aloof. The truth was, he just couldn't do it. He couldn't join in. He felt as if he was slowly going mad.

Even eating out was difficult. When they first started seeing each other, he and Sonia had tried to go out for the occasional meal, but they'd had to look for restaurants with no background music. Even then the murmur of other people's conversations underpinned the whole meal, from starter to coffee, with the flatness of blood. No matter what main course he ordered, the meat always tasted raw. After a while, they stopped going out entirely, apart from on Sonia's birthday, when Lapslie steeled himself for an unpleasant evening. And, frankly, that just wasn't fair on her.

It wasn't only one way, either. Over the years, Lapslie had found himself eating blander and blander food, if only because his working life was a morass of clashing flavours. Sitting in a silent house, eating rice or pasta, was the ultimate in luxury for him.

A quiet house. A house without a wife, without children.

Sonia had tried to understand. Not one for going out much herself – her job as a nurse took up most of her time, and resting took much of the remainder – she valued the peace they had together. They went for long walks in the woods. He read, sitting quietly in an armchair, while she did needlepoint and crosswords.

A little island of peace and contentment, which had lasted until precisely the moment when Sonia unexpectedly fell pregnant. With twins.

Lapslie loved his children desperately. He also hated them; or, rather, he hated the constant noise, the squalling when they were young and the shouting and arguing when they were older. Earplugs helped; working late in the office and going out for long walks alone helped even more, but that just put more strain on Sonia, who had to look after the children and the house by herself. And slowly he found himself losing touch with them. Watching from a distance as they got on with life without him.

He couldn't now remember whether it was he or Sonia who had suggested splitting up. They had obviously both been thinking about it for some time, and when one of them broached the subject, almost in passing, the other leaped on it. 'A trial separation', they had called it. And, as with many of the trials that Lapslie had been involved with over the years, it was getting increasingly rancorous and there seemed to be no sign of it ever ending. They were still in contact, but they were drifting apart. Through no fault of his, and no fault of hers, they were just drifting apart.

But there was no such thing as complete silence.

Even after his wife had moved out with their two children, even after he'd had the house recarpeted in thick shagpile and made sure he walked round without his shoes on, even after all of the sash windows had been replaced with double glazing that didn't go with the exterior stonework but kept the noise from the street outside from getting in, Mark Lapslie found that sounds still intruded on him.

Sometimes, if he turned a tap off too quickly, the pipes would bang and clatter as if someone was hammering them with an iron bar. For an hour or so after the central heating came on the house would creak as the joists expanded slightly. The wind blowing around the walls caused the air vent in the bathroom to vibrate if it caught them at the wrong angle. And sometimes there were noises behind the walls or in the ceiling that might have been mice scurrying past or might just have been fragments of plaster falling down gaps between the bricks.

The sounds caused a continual and unpleasant background taste in his mouth when he was in the house; a strange combination of lime juice and walnuts that had been allowed to rot. To avoid it, he tried wearing the earplugs whenever he was alone; these were form-fitting foam rubber ones that were meant to seal out any noise, but all that did was force him to concentrate on the sounds of his own body: the regular thudding of his heart, the occasional wheeze in his chest, the rush of blood through the arteries of his neck and the squeak of shifting mucus in his nose. And they tasted worse.

His doctor again advised him to take long walks in the countryside to get away from the sound of cars and people, but the first time he had tried that without Sonia had also been the last. He once thought the countryside was quiet, but it wasn't. What with birds singing, dogs barking, foxes screaming and the sudden hum of an insect investigating him, he found he was better off indoors.

With no television, radio or stereo, Lapslie spent a lot of time reading when he was alone, but even then the rustle of the pages as he turned them made him taste hot pilchards in tomato sauce on toast. To avoid that, he had to place the books flat on a table and lift the pages carefully when he turned them, but he found that the unnatural position caused spasms in his back after a while. Other times he just sat in an armchair, drifting, trying not to shift his position in case the chair creaked or the stuffing in the cushions shifted.

He felt sometimes as if he was spending his time sitting perfectly still, perfectly quiet, while life slid past him like water past a rock. Other people could enjoy themselves in bars and pubs, restaurants and cinemas, but he was condemned to a monastic life of near-silence and contemplation. There were times when he wished he could just ask a surgeon to slice through the nerves that transmitted sensation from his mouth to his brain, but even then he thought he would probably still experience the unwanted tastes. After all, they weren't real – merely phantoms of sensation originating somewhere in his brain. He knew that because, in the early days of the synaesthesia, he had sometimes tried to numb his taste buds, either with an oral anaesthetic gel that he had found in a pharmacy or, in desperation, with the hottest murgh phall curry that he could order in the takeaway nearest his cottage. Neither option worked. With the oral anaesthetic he found he could still experience sounds as tastes, although they were unpleasantly muted and distorted, while the phall just gave him heartburn for two days.

He sighed. Better go and see what the Superintendent wanted.

He chose a route to his office – one of the few actual offices in the entire building – that minimised the number of people he had to pass on the way. 'Office' was a bit of a misnomer – in fact, it was just a section of the office 'floorplate', as they called it, separated off by frosted glass panels – but at least it was something. When he arrived outside, the Super's personal assistant glanced up at him from her desk. She was frowning. 'I've been trying to get hold of you,' she said.

'Sorry,' he murmured. 'I was caught up.'

'He's got someone with him, but he'll be free in a moment.'

Lapslie stepped away from the desk and over to a nearby notice board. While he waited, he let his gaze flicker across union notices, fire alarm reminders and cards offering rooms to rent and laundry services. So much information, these days, he thought. So many signs everywhere to read. How do we keep all this information in our heads without going mad?

A sudden increase in noise made him turn his head. Superintendent Rouse stood in the doorway of his office, saying goodbye to two men. They were both in their late thirties, short-haired, and wearing black suits with a subtle pinstripe. The Superintendent was, as usual, in full uniform.

The two men moved away, and the Superintendent bent to have a quick word with his PA. As the men passed Lapslie one of them turned his head slightly. Lapslie glanced sideways, and the two gazes met with a noticeable jolt. The man raised his eyebrows slightly, involuntarily, as if he recognised Lapslie. Then he was gone, and Lapslie was left with his interest heading one way and his body heading another.

When he turned his attention back towards the way his body was moving, the Superintendent had re-entered his office. His PA gestured Lapslie in. 'Ten minutes, then he has to leave for another meeting.'

He knocked and entered. The Superintendent had sat behind his desk and was rearranging a sheaf of paper. The desk was placed so that the office's window was to his right, and the light cast one side of his face into a flattering glow and the other into sharp and craggy relief. His face had once been memorably, if uncharitably, described by a young DS as looking like a bag full of spanners. He was older than Lapslie by a few years, a battle-scarred veteran of police politics and in-fighting who had worked his way up the ranks, regardless of prejudice and the old-boy system, to a position of relative authority. Despite the fact that he was Lapslie's boss, and obviously had one eye on the next job in line, Lapslie liked him.

'Mark, thanks for popping along.'

'I understand you wanted an update on the Violet Chambers case, sir?'

Rouse's gaze flickered down to the sheaf of notes in front of him. They were hand-written. Lapslie had often seen Rouse make similar notes in meetings, a contemporaneous record of what was being said to remind him later, something between a set of personal minutes and a stream of consciousness. Had he made the notes during the meeting that had just finished? And, if so, why was he consulting them now?

'That's the woman whose body was found in the woods? Quite decayed?'

'That's the one.'

'Has the coroner been able to establish a cause of death?'

'It's a toss-up,' Lapslie replied, moving across to the window and gazing out at the surrounding landscape of office blocks and, off to one side, an elevated slice of road visible between two buildings. 'She was poisoned, but she was also bludgeoned on the back of the head. It's going to be impossible to determine which one caused her death.'

'But it's murder?'

'Either that or the most elaborate suicide I've ever seen.'

His gaze dropped to the car park below. He could see his own car, parked off to one side. There were too many Mondeos for him to be able to tell where Emma had parked. He could hear the Superintendent making notes as they talked.

'Any suspects?'

'Not as yet. We've finished processing the crime scene – or at least, the location where the body was found. The dirt under her fingernails would indicate she was killed there. We're currently checking into Violet Chambers' background, in case there's something in her past that would explain her murder.'

Two figures had just left the building, far below. They were heading for the spaces reserved for visitors.

'Do you think there's a realistic chance that you can catch whoever is responsible?'

He shrugged. 'Too early to tell, sir. We've not run out of leads yet, if that's what you mean. Not quite.'

The two figures down in the car park had separated now, and were moving either side of a black car. It was difficult to tell from where Lapslie was standing, but it might have been a Lexus.

The scratching of the pen stopped for a moment. 'I was wondering whether the relatively low chances of success in this particular case mean that you should scale down the investigation. Concentrate on something else, where you're more likely to make an arrest.'

As the car below them started off and drove out of the car park, Lapslie turned to meet Superintendent Rouse's gaze. 'Are you suggesting that I should let the case drop, sir?'

'I would never suggest we let a case drop, Mark. I'm merely asking whether our priorities are arranged correctly.'

'I think it's too early to tell,' he said, knowing Rouse was prevaricating. There was a strange flavour in his mouth: something like nutmeg, although he couldn't quite place it. He'd tasted that flavour before. Usually it was during an interrogation, when some toerag was lying to him about their whereabouts, or trying to convince him that the top-of-the-range BMW they'd been trying to get into at three in the morning had been loaned to them by a friend whose name they had temporarily forgotten. It was the taste of lies; or, at the very least, it was the flavour of evasion. Of someone saying one thing to avoid saying another. But why would Superintendent Rouse be evading his question?

'I can let you know in a few days whether I think there's any realistic prospect of a conviction,' he said.

Rouse nodded. 'I think we may be devoting too many resources to this problem,' he said, pursing his lips. 'It's an old case, and there's precious little evidence. Perhaps we should scale down the team.'

'The *team*,' Lapslie said levelly, 'is one Detective Chief Inspector who's been pulled back from sick leave and one Detective Sergeant who has an attitude problem. Unless you want to swap Emma Bradbury for Mary from the canteen, it's hard to see how much less effective the team could be.'

'Very well,' Rouse said, avoiding Lapslie's gaze. 'We'll keep things the way they are. For the moment.' Putting his pen down, he leaned back in his state-of-the-art chair and gazed at Lapslie, smiling slightly. 'We've both come a long way, haven't we, Mark?'

'Since Kilburn CID, back in the eighties? Since those nights we spent arresting crack dealers and Yardies and breaking up three-day-long raves? It's like another world now.'

'I'm surprised you keep going – especially with your problems. Have you thought about taking early retirement?'

He shrugged. 'Who hasn't at our age? Watching the sun rise from your desk for the tenth time in a month? Finding out that an overtime ban means that all the hours you've been putting in are for free? And knowing that my particular ... problems ... aren't enough to get me pensioned off, but they are enough to stop me getting promoted again? The thought has crossed my mind more than once.'

'Then why stay around?'

Sighing, Lapslie turned to gaze out of the window again, not at the car park this time but out past the elevated section of road, towards the nearest thing to a horizon one could see from this office. 'Where would I go?' he asked, more to himself than to Rouse. 'What exactly would I do? I'd be yet another retired cop in a land full of them. I just haven't got the energy to set myself up in business as a security consultant, or head up the investigation branch at one of the big banks. I'm a cop, sir. That's what I do. That's all I can do.'

'What about –'

'Sonia? She's not coming back. Neither are the kids.' And this time it wasn't a sound, but the memory of a sound, that filled his mouth with the taste of vanilla. The memory of his children playing in the back garden, calling each other silly names, screaming as they chased each other around the car. The memory of them calling to him as they ran through the woods, their voices hanging directionless on the wind. The memory of them crying as they fell over and grazed a knee, and laughing as they tried to catch birds on the lawn. Odd how time could freeze around a few moments, projecting them backwards and forwards through his memories. For Lapslie, his children were always the age they were when they left. He couldn't really remember how they had looked when they were born, or when they were crawling around the house. And, despite the occasional visits and the photographs that Sonia sent through, he found it hard to keep a grip of what they looked like now. It was their faces on those last few days, playing in the garden, running through the woods, that he would always remember.

'It's a shame.'

'That it is,' he said heavily. 'That it is.'

'If there's anything I can do to help ...'

He nodded. 'Thanks for the offer,' he said. 'But what about you? Is your star still in the ascendant? Are you still managing to keep your grip on the greasy pole?'

Rouse smiled, and for a moment the years dropped away and he looked much like he had back in Kilburn, all those years ago. 'I'm considering my options,' he said judiciously. 'There's an offer on the table from the Serious Organised Crime Agency for me to take over their counter-terrorist section. And I've heard that there's a team being put together to look at the security implications of the London Olympics. Either of those would suit me.'

'On promotion, of course.'

'Of course. There's only two directions to go on the greasy pole – up or down. Staying still isn't an option.' Rouse gazed up at him, and his eyes crinkled in what might have been the beginnings of a smile, or the beginnings of a worried frown. 'Let's do lunch soon. We should talk about the future. *Your* future. I'll get my PA to arrange it.'

He turned his eyes back to the notes in front of him and started writing. It was a dismissal. Lapslie glanced once more out of the window and then left the office, closing the door behind him. He felt slightly floaty, slightly disconnected from the world.

Outside, he paused by the PA's desk.

'Those two men who left just before I went in,' he said. 'I

could have sworn I recognised one of them. I think we were on a course together at Sandridge. Who were they?'

The PA consulted her computer. 'They were visitors from the Department of Justice,' she said. 'Mr Geherty and Mr Wilmington. Which one was your friend?'

'Oh, I didn't say he was my friend,' Lapslie said quietly. 'Thanks for your help.'

Geherty. There couldn't be too many people with a name like that working for the Department of Justice – assuming that's where they actually came from.

Returning to his desk, grimacing at the salty wash of blood in his mouth from the general hubbub of conversation, he looked up the switchboard number for the Department of Justice's new offices in London on his own computer, then dialled it.

'Good morning,' he said, when the call was answered, 'Could you put me through to Mr Geherty, please?'

There was silence for a few moments as the receptionist presumably checked her screen for details. Lapslie wondered idly whether she was actually in the Department of Justice building, or whether she was based in a call centre in Mumbai, perhaps, or New Delhi, and spent her lunch hours laughing about the strange names of people in England.

'I'm afraid I'm getting no answer,' the receptionist's voice said. 'Shall I put you through to Mr Geherty's voicemail, or would you like to speak to someone else?'

'Actually,' Lapslie said, 'I need to put something in the post to him. Can you confirm his title and department for me?'

'Yes, of course. It's Martin Geherty, Assistant Director, PRU. Do you need the full address?'

'That's okay,' Lapslie said, 'I know where he is.'

PRU? What did that mean? Assuming that the black Lexus in the car park and the black Lexus that he had seen back at the place Violet Chambers' body had been discovered were the same – an assumption that would need to be proven – and assuming that the two men coming out of Superintendent

Rouse's office were the ones who had got into the Lexus in the car park – again, something he could work with but which would require evidence backing it up – then it looked as if there was some kind of parallel investigation going on. But what interest could the Department of Justice – and in particular the PRU, whatever that was – have in the murder of an old lady? And why had Superintendent Rouse been trying to subtly manoeuvre him off the case, first by asking whether he had too much work on to undertake the investigation properly, and then by suggesting early retirement to him and trying to get Emma Bradbury reassigned? If Rouse wanted things dropped, why not just order him off?

Presumably, because he would have to give reasons.

And he couldn't.

The noise was getting too much for him, and Lapslie headed back to the Quiet Room, hoping that nobody had nipped in for a quick snooze whilst he'd been gone. Friday afternoons were particularly bad: once he'd found three officers sleeping off a lunchtime drinking session: one in the chair, one flat on his back on the desk and one curled up underneath it.

Fortunately, he was in luck. The room was still empty.

He shut the door and leaned back in the chair, letting the silence slide over him. Slowly his breath, which he hadn't even realised was tight, relaxed.

He found his thoughts turning back to the mortuary, and the question of whether there had been an intruder going through Dr Catherall's files. He hadn't mentioned it to Emma Bradbury. Although she had been alone in Catherall's office for a while and, by any theoretical analysis of the situation, was a potential suspect, Lapslie had discounted her immediately because she was a police officer, because he knew her and because she had no apparent motive. Now, suspecting that his own immediate superior knew more about the case than he should and could therefore have asked his Detective Sergeant to do some undercover work for him, Lapslie paradoxically trusted Emma even more. If Superintendent Rouse was involved then so were the two strangers from the Department of Justice, and it made more sense that they had been going through the files than that she had. After all, it looked as if they had been present at the scene where the body had been discovered.

A disquieting thought occurred to him. Had they been there *when* the body had been discovered? But that was impossible, surely. It was more likely that they had somehow picked up the news from the local police or the journalists at the scene. But in that case, what exactly was it that had triggered their arrival? Did they turn up to every car crash that occurred in the area?

Or did they just turn up every time the body of an elderly woman was discovered?

He thought about letting Emma in on what had been happening, on the basis that she could turn up something about these mysterious strangers, but something stopped him. He needed information, but he had a strong feeling that it needed to be outside normal channels. Retrieving his mobile from his pocket, he scrolled through the list of contacts until he found a name and a number that he thought he'd never have to use again, but had avoided deleting just in case.

'Dom McGinley,' said a voice that triggered an inappropriate but familiar taste across his tongue, like salmon-flavoured bubblegum.

'McGinley? Mark Lapslie.'

'Mr Lapslie. It's been a long time.'

'It's been fifteen years. I probably look now the way you did back then.'

McGinley laughed; a noise that at one time could have cleared a bar. 'I usually only accept calls from coppers when I have something on them,' he said. 'I seem to recall that you and I parted on even terms.'

'Then this is your lucky day,' Lapslie said. 'I need a favour. Can we meet up?'

'Ah, I thought this day would never come. Wednesday – the usual boozer on the Thames. You remember.'

'I try to forget, but I can't. All right – Wednesday it is.'

The phone went dead, and Lapslie stared at it for a moment. A voice from the past, indeed. Dominic McGinley had been a legend in North London, back in the 1970s. He ran most of the drugs, most of the protection rackets and all of the prostitution between the North Circular and the City of Westminster, bounded on the left by the A5 and on the right by the A10. Lapslie had been only one of many policemen to try and get something on him, but McGinley was always several steps removed from the crimes. Tracing anything back to him was impossible.

And now Lapslie needed his help. Funny, the way things turned out.

CHAPTER NINE

Something Daisy Wilson had missed, reading through the local papers covering the Tendring Hundreds area, was the arts pages. It was only later that afternoon, sitting on the esplanade and gazing out across the grey waves, trying to recall where she had seen the face of that girl in the library book before, that she remembered. Delving into her bag, she recovered the *Gazette* and flicked through the pages until she found what she was looking for. Yes! Apart from the usual end-of-pier shows – faded TV entertainers who would attract the wrong type of target entirely – there was a theatre in nearby Clacton which appeared to show real plays. Cultured entertainment. If her previous experience, several victims ago, admittedly, was anything to go by then the pickings at a theatre should be pretty good. Even if she avoided the couples and the coach parties then she should be left with a fair selection of women who had enough money to afford a theatre ticket but nobody to share their evenings with. Perfect!

According to the timetable she had picked up from the Visitor Information kiosk, there was a bus leaving Leyston at six o'clock in the evening that would get her to Clacton in good time for the performance. And fortunately she had packed some clothes that were formal enough to go to the theatre in but casual enough that she wouldn't have any problems catching a bus in a seaside town late at night.

Returning to her hotel, she showered and put on some make-up: not enough to be obtrusive, but just enough to help support the story she would be selling: that she was refined without being posh, that she had money but no friends. The mirror image of the person she would be looking for. People were often, she had noticed, attracted to their own reflections.

The dress she pulled out of her suitcase was black, but not funereal. With a belt, a pair of tights and an overcoat, it would be perfectly acceptable. She cast her mind back, trying to remember where she had obtained it. She certainly hadn't bought it – Daisy tried not to buy anything, if she could possibly help it. Had it belonged to Alice Connell? Jane Winterbottom? Daisy tried to remember their faces, but all she could recall was their clothes with her own features on top, looking back at her. No, Alice had been taller than her, and Jane a lot wider. Was it someone earlier than Alice? She had a vague memory of a woman in Leeds who had died slowly after Daisy had grated yew tree bark into her food over the course of several weeks. She had seemed absolutely fine, to the point where Daisy was about to switch to a different plant, and then she had suddenly dropped dead, apparently of a heart attack. Daisy hoped her heart had been weakened by the yew bark. It would have been a waste of time and effort if she had died of natural causes.

Now what had that woman's name been? Was it another Jane? She really couldn't remember.

No matter. To go with the dress, Daisy chose a rather nice necklace that she remembered had belonged to Violet Chambers, once upon a time. It set the dress off nicely. By the time she had finished dressing, it was almost time to go.

It was nearly night by the time she left the hotel. The pier was coming to life: what had been tawdry paint and worn woodwork in daylight was now hidden by the glare of the light bulbs which surrounded the entrance and were strung along the dark bulk of the pier like sparkling drops of water on cobweb threads. Daisy could hear music too: a regular, hypnotic pounding that echoed back in strange counterpoint from the houses. How could people live here, night after night, with that racket going on?

The bus was on time, and the journey along winding country lanes and through nameless villages was long enough for Violet to fall into a daze. The bus was half full, and the passengers were evenly divided between teenagers and older people, some of whom were probably on their way to Clacton for the play. Daisy deliberately didn't take note of any of them. There would be time enough for that later.

Every so often Daisy would glance out of the window, but the encroaching darkness meant that more often than not she just saw her own reflection. And, as she slipped deeper and deeper into a reverie, her reflection sometimes became that of someone else. Once, when she looked over, the woman looking back was thinner than her, and wore glasses. Deirdre – Deirdre something? Another time, it was the former Daisy Wilson who turned to meet her gaze, her eyes deeply sunk in puffy flesh, her white hair piled high on her head in a sad remnant of the beehive hairdo she had once sported so proudly.

And once, when Daisy opened her eyes and looked into the dark mirror of the window, a young girl was staring back at her. A red-haired girl in a flowery dress, stained down the front with something dark and wet and terrible.

With a jerk, Daisy woke up. Her heart was pounding fit to break. She took a deep breath, having to fight to get it past the lump in her throat. Gradually, her heart eased itself back into its normal rhythm.

Daisy knew that girl. She knew that face, she even knew that dress, but there was something about the girl that she didn't want to think about. When she saw the girl's photograph at the library she had slammed the book shut and left. Now she deliberately focused on the lights outside the window, trying to wipe all trace of the girl from her mind.

The bus was pulling into Clacton now. The lights were brighter than Leyston, the music was louder and everything was more intense. If Leyston was the shy, retiring brother then Clacton was the older, outgoing and rather blowsy sister.

Taking her cue from some of the other older passengers, Daisy left the bus and found herself just a short walk from the theatre. Looking up at the frontage, she realised that she hadn't even checked what play was being performed that night. Now, gazing up at the title, a giggle escaped her lips.

Arsenic and Old Lace.

How apt. How perfectly apt.

The audience heading into the theatre seemed to be mainly people around her own age, and her dress and overcoat did not mark her out from the rest of the crowd. She headed towards the box office and managed to secure a ticket in the balcony. A better class of person went in the balcony, she had found.

Sitting in her seat, with just a few minutes to go before the curtain rose, she gazed around. The theatre was about half full, and she could already see a few good prospects in her vicinity. Best to wait until the interval and see what transpired.

The play was well performed and the set was a convincing reproduction of a down-at-heel boarding house in the 1950s, but Daisy felt her attention wander after a while. She didn't recognise any of the actors – no doubt they were well known from television soap operas or something of the sort, but she rarely watched television. They rushed around the stage, keeping the audience laughing with the story of two old ladies who were killing off the single male guests in their house and burying them in the cellar, but Daisy found it all too frantic and too unbelievable.

There was a woman sitting two rows ahead of her, and just to the left. She was white-haired, and quite stocky. The seat to her left was empty; the one to her right was occupied by a man, but he was younger than her and his head was turned towards the person on his other side. She wore a silk scarf tied around her neck. She was absorbed in the play, and Daisy became more and more absorbed with her as the play went on. She kept glancing at her, taking in the curve of her neck, the shape of her ear, the way the earring she wore sparkled in the light. Daisy felt her pulse quicken: this was the kind of drama she liked.

Come the interval, Daisy quickly manoeuvred out of her aisle and made sure she was slightly ahead of the other woman in the queue for the bar. She wanted to make sure that she had been seen. It was always best if the first move came from the prey, rather than the predator.

Daisy bought herself a small gin and tonic at an extortionate price, then went to sit by the nearest window, making sure there was a second chair at her table. The bar was too warm for comfort, but a cooling breeze came in from outside, flavoured slightly with candy floss and hot oil from the nearby sea front. She composed her expression into one of quiet resignation, and gazed blankly out of the window.

'Excuse me, is this seat taken?'

She turned her head. The woman she had targeted was standing beside the empty chair.

'No, I'm – no. Please, feel free.'

The woman sat down. She was holding a glass of white wine. Daisy could just make out her perfume above the smell from outside. 'My name is Sylvia – Sylvia McDonald. Are you enjoying the play?'

'It's very good. Yes, *very* good,' Daisy replied. 'I don't get to go out much, and I do so enjoy the theatre.'

'So do I. I thought the actors were terribly good.'

'It's such a lovely theatre, too.'

'It is. And so convenient.'

'Do you live nearby?' Daisy asked.

'I live in Leyston,' the woman said. 'I drove in this evening. I'm parked just down the road.'

'Daisy. Daisy Wilson.'

They raised their glasses at each other, and smiled.

'My husband used to love the theatre,' Sylvia said after a few moments.

Daisy looked around. 'Is he –'

'I lost him, nine years ago last month.'

'I'm terribly sorry.'

'And you?'

'Oh,' Daisy said, 'I never married. There was a man, once,

but ...' She trailed off, leaving Sylvia to fill in the rest of the story. 'I've just moved into Leyston myself,' she added. 'It's such a quiet place.'

'And it can be quite beautiful,' Sylvia added.

The bell rang for the second act. Daisy realised she only had a few seconds to make her move. 'It can also be so lonely,' she said. 'If you don't know anyone in the area ...' She gazed out of the window, leaving the thought hanging.

'Perhaps you'd like to meet for a cup of tea,' Sylvia offered. 'Let's organise something after the play finishes. Perhaps I could offer you a lift back?'

Daisy finished her drink, aware that the glass was trembling slightly in her hand. And so it began: the long dance of friendship, dependence and ultimately death. She felt as if she was poised on the brink of a long slope. One step, one small step, and she would be committed.

'That would be lovely,' she said.

Daisy hardly noticed the rest of the play. She was too busy rehearsing her own production in her head: practising her lines until the words and the mood were perfect; choosing various locations for the scenes until she found the ones that best conjured up the mood she wanted to create. Following the final curtain, the two of them nattered while walking to Sylvia's car, and nattered more as they drove. And by the time they arrived outside the station, where Daisy had asked to be dropped off, they had arranged to meet the next day at the coffee shop by the post office – the only one that Daisy knew, although she wasn't going to admit that. She went to sleep that night exultant, and she slept the sleep of the dead.

The next morning, Daisy awoke early. She had a lot to do. After a quick breakfast, she made her way through the town until she found an estate agents that met her criteria: not the flashiest, but not the most down at heel either. One tucked away in a side street that catered to local people, not holidaymakers wishing to rent a flat for the summer.

Daisy knew her requirements, and politely rejected everything she was shown until the young man helping her showed her a photograph of a house a little way out of town, close to the cliff. Old in style, with a small garden at the back and a passion-fruit climber wrapped around the porch and trailing up to the first-floor window, it was just what she was looking for. The first floor was already let to a foreign girl studying at the local college. The ground floor was available for immediate letting. It was, Daisy decided as she looked at the photograph, the perfect web in which to trap the fly she sought. Using bills addressed to Daisy Wilson's old address as proof of identity, she obtained a set of keys and went to view the flat by herself, although the young man offered to drive her. It hardly mattered.

The flat was a little small for her purposes, with a living room at the front, a bedroom at the rear and a combined kitchen and dining room off to one side. At least it had a small conservatory, which made it slightly less pokey. Knowing she wouldn't be living there for long, assuming everything went to plan, Daisy went straight back to the estate agents and put down a deposit. She still had a week or more left at the hotel, which gave her time to obtain some furniture and make the place look as if she had been there for a while. Until then, she would have to make sure that she was invited to Sylvia's place, not the other way around.

Walking away from the estate agents, Daisy identified three shops in the back streets that sold second-hand furniture, and would deliver. She needed things that looked used. Things that she might well have brought with her from somewhere else.

Daisy and Sylvia met for coffee that afternoon. They talked for an hour and a half about inconsequential things: the play the night before, the weather, how lovely the town was. Towards the end, Sylvia told Daisy about her husband, and how he had been a part of the volunteer lifeboat crew for fifteen years until cancer took him away. Her eyes were bright with unshed tears. Daisy risked patting her hand gently and offering her a tissue. Daisy, in turn, explained how she had been a nurse for almost three decades, and how the demands of duty meant that she had never managed to find anyone to settle down with. Using elements of the story that had brought her to Leyston in the first place, she told Sylvia that her cousin had been taken ill and that she had moved in with her to nurse her through her final days. It was a calculated risk, and Sylvia did ask what Daisy's cousin's name was, but Daisy explained that her cousin had been disabled for many years and rarely left the house. Sylvia seemed satisfied with the explanation.

Sylvia insisted on paying for the coffee and the cakes. She used a debit card, which pleased Daisy no end. It meant she was solvent. It meant that she was even more of an attractive prospect than Daisy had originally thought. They parted on friendly terms, having exchanged addresses, and after Sylvia had invited Daisy round for tea the afternoon after next.

Back at the hotel, she sat at the writing table over by the window. From her pocket, she produced the copy of the debit card slip that she had so carefully taken from Sylvia's handbag when Sylvia had visited the ladies' room, just before they left. Using a plain sheet of paper, she copied Sylvia's signature again and again, first slowly and then getting faster and faster, until she could reproduce it perfectly.

Daisy felt like celebrating, that night. Instead of eating in the hotel, she wandered out into the town and found a small restaurant that advertised locally caught seafood. Daisy had scampi and chips, and thoroughly enjoyed it. Even more, she enjoyed the fact that she wasn't watching the people around her, just in case a likely prospect came in. She had found her prospect. Now she just had to follow through.

The next morning, she told the desk clerk at the hotel that she would be leaving at the end of the week. For the rest of that day she visited various second-hand shops along the

High Street, ordering furniture to be delivered and buying bits of bric-a-brac, old books, cutlery, plates, dishes and cups, which she ferried back to her new flat on the bus in a wheeled shopping bag that she picked up for five pounds in a charity shop.

Come the evening, Daisy was hungry, but instead of looking for somewhere to eat she found her footsteps turning towards the marina again. Something about the stillness of the water had soothed her, the day before, and she wanted to recapture that feeling. It only took her a few minutes to find the road again, and to walk along it until she found the bank of earth and the gate to the Yacht Club. Slowly she climbed up the shallow concrete steps, feeling the effort more then than she had the day before. At the top, she raised her eyes to take in the expanse of water.

It wasn't there. Instead, Daisy was confronted with a corrugated expanse of greenish-grey mud. She descended the steps on the other side of the bank, trying to work out what had happened. Had the tide gone out? It seemed too dramatic a change to have occurred in so short a time, but she supposed it was the only explanation.

The boats that had sat so calmly in the water the day before were now canted drunkenly on the mud, their masts pointed at crazy angles. Seagulls stalked amid them, pecking at the oozing surface. Daisy could suddenly smell a rank, fish odour that made her nose wrinkle involuntarily.

She walked to the edge of the concrete jetty and looked over into the mud. The sun had baked parts of it to a hard crust, riven by cracks through which glinted an unpleasant wetness. Rusty cans, bottles, pipes and unidentifiable but sharp-edged objects emerged from the mud as if they were part of something larger, buried underneath, that was attempting to pull itself back to land. Small insects skittered across the wet surface, searching for somewhere to lay their eggs. It was hard to believe that something so unpleasant could have been concealed by something so beautiful; that something looking and smelling so disgusting could lurk beneath the pure and glittering surface of the water.

Daisy turned to go. She felt soiled. She would make sure that she never came back to the marina unless it was high tide.

That night, Daisy dreamed of the red-haired girl again. She had been sleeping uneasily since she had gone to bed, repeatedly jerked to the edge of wakefulness by the distant electrical clash of bumper cars on the pier and the sounds of teenagers singing and shouting as they made their way along the esplanade. As time went on, as the pubs and clubs shut their doors and the pier emptied of people, her room grew quieter and she slipped deeper into unconsciousness like a rusty tin can sinking into mud. By midnight, she was oblivious to everything.

In her dream, Daisy was in a dining room dominated by a large mahogany table. Place mats had been set out in front of each of the chairs: cork-backed, with laminated pictures of plants on the front. The room itself was dark, apart from candelabra on the table itself, but Daisy got the impression of curtains in the darkness; soft, velvety curtains, dropping in swoops and furls to the floor, muffling all noise.

Daisy was sitting at one end of the table. The picture on her place mat was of a rhododendron bush. Looking to her left, with the slow, underwater motions of a dream, she could see that the place mat there had a picture of an azalea bush. The one on her right was a mountain laurel.

'Did you know,' said a girlish voice from the other end of the table, 'that honey made by bees who have collected pollen from rhododendron bushes is actually poisonous? I read that in a book, I think.'

Daisy looked up. A girl was sitting opposite her. She was about eight years old, and she had red hair and wore a flowery dress. She seemed dwarfed by the heavy mahogany chair she was perched on.

'What's your name?' said Daisy.

'I don't remember,' the girl replied. 'What's yours?'

Daisy shook her head. 'I don't remember either. Where are we?'

'In my secret place. Do you like it?'

'I don't know, m'dear. I can't really see it that well. What are we doing here?'

'We're having a tea party. We always have tea parties here.'

With no particular surprise, Daisy saw that the place mat in front of the little girl now held a tea pot and two cups on saucers: small cups, small saucers, more fit for dolls' houses than for people. With exaggerated care, the girl filled the two cups with steaming brown liquid, then slipped from her chair, picked one cup up by the saucer and carried it around the table to where Daisy was sitting.

'It's lovely,' she said as she placed the cup down. 'I made it myself.'

'And what did you make it out of, m'dear?' Daisy asked as the girl returned to her chair.

'Sugar and spice and all things nice,' the girl said. 'Like I always do. You have to drink it.'

'I'm not really thirsty.'

'But you have to.' It was less of a command; more a statement of fact.

Daisy found her hand reaching out for the cup. She tried to pull it back, but her fingers closed around the warm china and she lifted it up towards her mouth. 'I really don't think –'

'But you *have* to. It's the game.'

Daisy felt the steam from the tea turn into moisture on her upper lip. She could smell something bitter and unpleasant. 'What *is* this?'

'Don't you know?' The girl smirked.

She could feel the cup in her fingers, feel the increasing heat transferring through to her skin. 'It smells ... familiar.'

'It used to grow in your garden. It used to grow all over your garden. You made a drink from the berries. Don't you remember? The gardener called it "belladonna".'

The cup tipped back, and the liquid trickled into Daisy's mouth. She tried to spit it out, but whatever was controlling her hand made her swallow, and swallow again.

'Rabbits can eat it,' the girl said primly, 'and it doesn't affect them. But if you eat the rabbits, you can be poisoned.'

Daisy could feel a burning in her mouth, although the tea wasn't that hot. Blisters were coming up on her tongue and lips, and her forehead was suddenly damp with sweat.

'Apparently, witches used to use belladonna when they were dancing together at night. It made them think they were flying. My mummy says that witches aren't real, but I know they are.'

Daisy's hands put the cup down on the table and folded themselves neatly in her lap, but the fingers were tingling and the palms were wet.

'Roman ladies used belladonna in make-up, to make their skin look really white.' The girl was leaning forward in her chair, her hands clenched on the arms, watching Daisy intently. '*Your* skin looks really white now, but I don't think that's make-up. I think that's the belladonna working.'

Her hands were completely numb, and the room was getting blurry and white. She could just see the girl's outline, but the blurriness turned her fine features into a skull, a red-haired skull, grinning insanely at Daisy.

'How does it feel?' the girl screamed. 'How does it *feel*?'

Daisy shot upright in bed. For a moment she could still feel the blisters in her mouth and the growing burning in her throat, but the sheets were cool beneath her clutching hands and somewhere outside the window she could hear waves on sand.

The next morning, Daisy took longer than usual to get ready. She was feeling old and tired. Something about this town was sapping her strength; it was as if arriving here had awakened old ghosts and she had to try and lay them to rest if she was going to make any progress with Sylvia.

She spent the morning pottering around the hotel and the

town, and after lunch she took a taxi to Sylvia's house. She had already checked where it was on a map of the town she had obtained from the Visitor Information kiosk, which was proving increasingly useful to her, and she knew that she could get a bus that would drop her off ten minutes' walk away, but she wanted to arrive fresh. And besides, it gave the impression that she was used to travelling in some comfort, which would probably go down well with Sylvia.

The house was high up, near the top of the knob of land that pushed out into the sea, north of the town, part of an estate that Daisy estimated had been built in the 1930s. It was well-proportioned and wide, built of red brick, with a garage and a small round window over the front door. It was detached from its neighbours, and set back from the road. As Daisy got out of the taxi and paid the driver, she could hardly take her eyes off it. Of all the houses she had ever lived in, or ever intended to, this was the best. She would enjoy living there, once she had got Sylvia out of the way.

Sylvia was waiting by the front door. 'A taxi,' she said. 'How extravagant.'

'I couldn't face the bus,' Daisy replied, following Sylvia into the house. 'What a lovely place you have here.'

'Would you like a tour?'

Sylvia showed Daisy around with pride. The house was immaculately kept, and there were obviously rooms that Sylvia just didn't go into any more. The kitchen was huge, with wood-panelled cupboards, and the master bedroom had a view between the houses opposite to the sea. It was perfect.

Well, not quite perfect. None of the fixtures or fittings would fetch more than a few thousand pounds, at best. Still, the house itself would be worth quite a bundle when Daisy finally got tired of it.

The weather was warm enough that they took tea in the back garden. Sylvia kept it beautifully tidy, and they spent some time talking about the various flowers. Daisy commented particularly on the well-kept privet hedges, and the morning-glory vine that trailed up the rear of the house.

Sitting in chairs out in the back garden, Daisy said, apropos of nothing: 'It seems awfully quiet here. You must have good neighbours.'

'I don't really see that much of them,' Sylvia admitted. 'There's a family on one side: they go out a lot, and we rarely talk. The man on the other side is a bus driver. He's very quiet.'

'What about the others? The other side of the road?'

'Quite a few of them are new, over the past few years. It's happening everywhere nowadays. It used to be that people would be in and out of each other's houses, offering a hand, having cups of tea, borrowing sugar or milk. Now, people keep themselves to themselves. It's a shame.'

'It is,' said Daisy. 'Everyone needs friends. Life can be so terribly lonely otherwise.'

They talked for a while about the changes they had seen during their lives, and how people today seemed less caring than they had twenty or thirty years ago. The nature of society had shifted, and they felt left behind. Part of the past.

The talk turned to other things. Daisy ventured a comment about her own varicose veins, and how they made walking difficult sometimes.

'I know,' Sylvia said. 'I had one hip replaced, ten years ago, and the other hip done a year after that. I swear that the surgeons put one in shorter than the other, but they won't listen to me. "I'm the one who has to walk on it," I told them, "and some days I feel like I'm walking in circles", but they didn't want to know. Told me it was impossible.' Her face fell. 'Sometimes I just can't get comfortable at night, with these hips. I don't think I've had a good night's sleep since they put them in.'

'You should take something for it,' Daisy said, sensing an opening the way a cat can sometimes sense a mouse without even seeing it.

'Oh,' Sylvia said, 'I don't like the thought of sedatives.'

'I was thinking more of something herbal,' Daisy said casually. 'A herbal tea, perhaps. I could make you some up. If you would like.'

'Oh Daisy,' Sylvia said gratefully, 'you're just killing me with kindness.'

CHAPTER TEN

There was a poem that Mark Lapslie had read once, while searching online for other people's experiences of synaesthesia. It was on a website that noted, with some pride, that there were many artists, poets and musicians who were synaesthetic, although it then went on to admit that this might be because they were more likely to notice and even take advantage of their symptoms. The poem was by a nineteenth-century French writer named Baudelaire, and it stuck in Lapslie's memory. It captured in a handful of words something that he wished he could achieve in his own life – a sense of the beauty and the majesty that synaesthesia could apparently provide.

> *There are perfumes fresh like the skin of infants*
> *Sweet like oboes, green like prairies,*
> *– And others corrupted, rich and triumphant*
> *That have the expanse of infinite things,*
> *Like ambergris, musk, balsam and incense,*
> *Which sing the ecstasies of the mind and senses.*

He remembered the poem again as he made the long drive, under a grey early-morning sky, from his cottage in Saffron Walden to the hospital outside Braintree where he was under the occasional care of the consultant neurologist. *The ecstasies of the mind and senses.* If only that were as true for him as it apparently was for Baudelaire.

Still, Baudelaire had been a syphilitic opium addict with a

drink problem, so Lapslie felt justified in not taking his pronouncements too seriously.

He parked his car near the hospital and walked through the main entrance. Rather than wear a suit, he had chosen chinos, a plain shirt and a moleskin jacket. He'd booked a day's leave for the appointment, and to meet an old friend later on.

The central atrium was tall and airy, surrounded by planters of ferns, with fountains plashing gently in the centre and stone benches all around. Walking through a set of double doors to one side of the atrium, he quickly found himself in the hospital proper: a maze of square corridors that smelled of disinfectant, their walls and linoleum scuffed and scarred by decades of hospital trolleys. The original, 1950s vintage, hospital was hidden behind the impressive new façade in the same way that the ladies of Baudelaire's time used to hide their pox-ridden faces behind caked layers of make-up.

A handful of people sat around, waiting for the neurology outpatients clinic. Lapslie waited with them for his appointment, trying not to make judgements about them. After all, he was on leave, not on duty.

He had timed his arrival perfectly, and within five minutes his name was being called. The consulting room was small, anonymous, with white walls, a hospital trolley, a desk with a computer on it and a couple of chairs. It could have been any consulting room in any hospital or clinic, anywhere in the country.

The young man sitting at the desk was new to Lapslie. He was reading information off the computer screen as Lapslie entered, and he stuck out his hand without taking his eyes off the screen. 'Hello. I'm Doctor Considine. I don't think I've seen you before, have I?'

'Mark Lapslie.' He shook the doctor's hand and sat down. 'I've been seeing Doctor Lombardy for the past ten years or so.'

'Doctor Lombardy retired about six months ago. A very clever man. Great loss to the hospital.' He consulted the computer again. 'I see you're a synaesthete. We don't get to see many synaesthetes here – estimates of its occurrence vary between six people in a million and three in a hundred, depending on how wide you want to draw the boundaries, but most of them either don't know they have it or assume that everyone does. You, it appears, are in that small subsection for whom the effect of synaesthesia is strong enough to cause problems in your day-to-day life. When was the last time you were seen here?'

'A year ago.'

'And has your condition changed in that time – got worse or got better?'

'It's stayed at the same level.'

'Hmm.' He tapped his fingers on the desk. 'I presume that Doctor Lombardy told you there is no treatment and no cure for synaesthesia? It's something you just have to live with.'

Lapslie nodded. 'He did tell me that. We decided that it was worth me coming back once a year or so to check whether there had been any major advances in the research.'

Dr Considine shook his head. 'Not to my knowledge. It's still pretty much a puzzle. We know from magnetic resonance imaging of the brain, for instance, that synaesthetes such as yourself show patterns of activity that are different from people who are normal – for want of a better word – but we are still trying to work out what that difference means. It's still a puzzle.'

'One that's affecting my career and my personal life,' Lapslie said bitterly. 'It's easy to say there's no treatment, but you don't have to live with it. My career has stalled because I can't socialise the way the others do. I've separated from my family because I can't bear the continual taste in my mouth when they're around. And I can't watch television, or go to see a film or a concert, for fear of suddenly throwing up. Runny egg yolks and chalky antacid tablets are bad enough, but a sudden rush of raw sewage or vomit down your throat can spoil your entire evening.'

'I see.' The doctor wrote a few notes on a pad in front of him. 'And forgive me for asking this, but is there an up-side? Does the synaesthesia bring any benefits with it?'

'I have a very good memory for people – I suspect that's because I can associate their voices with particular flavours.'

'Which makes me wonder – does my voice have a flavour to it?'

Lapslie laughed. 'You'd be surprised how many people ask me that question, when they hear about my problem. No – not all sounds trigger flavours. I don't know if it's to do with pitch, or timbre, or what. Some voices do, but yours doesn't. Sorry.'

'Anything else? Any more benefits?'

Lapslie considered for a few seconds. 'Strangely,' he said, 'I can usually tell when people are lying to me. It's an unusual taste. Dry and spicy, but not in a curry way. More like nutmeg. It's helped me investigating crimes before.' To Considine's raised eyebrow, he added: 'I'm in the police.'

Considine frowned. 'I can just about understand how sounds can be mistranslated into flavours somewhere in the brain,' he said, 'but lying isn't a *sound*, it's got to do with the content, the meaning of what's being said. That's a bit of a stretch.'

'The way I rationalise it,' Lapslie said, 'when people lie, there's a certain amount of stress in their voice, changing the way it sounds in subtle ways. Somehow, I'm picking up on that stress and tasting it.'

'I presume you've been asked to take part in research projects? There are labs all over the country becoming interested in synaesthesia.'

'I've been asked, and I've occasionally taken part in experiments, but it usually turns out that I'm just some glorified lab rat. I want to understand and control my problem, but the trouble is that most researchers want something else. They want to use the synaesthesia as a window into the way the brain operates.'

Considine nodded. 'I can sympathise. There are psychiatric

techniques you could use to try and help control the flood of sensations you are getting. Cognitive behaviour therapy, for instance, could help you weaken the connections between stimuli such as particular sounds and your habitual reactions to them. The tastes might stay, but your reactions could be modified. If you want, I can recommend you to a therapist.'

Therapy. Lapslie shook his head. It wasn't for him.

'Thanks,' he said, 'but I think the problem is more deeply rooted than that. Changing the way I think won't affect it.'

'Then you're just going to have to live with it.'

'Thanks for your time.'

'Come back in another year,' Dr Considine said as Lapslie stood up to leave. 'Who knows? By then we might actually know what synaesthesia is and how to suppress it.'

'Who knows?' Lapslie said as he left.

It had rained whilst he was in the hospital. Pools of water congregated along kerbs and in dips in the road. Driving out of the hospital grounds, he headed for the A120, but a small voice in the back of his mind told him that he wasn't too far away from where Violet Chambers' body had been discovered in the forest outside Faulkbourne. Abruptly he turned right instead of left at a roundabout and quickly typed a new destination into his satnav system. He wasn't sure why, but he wanted to take another look at the area. Get a feel for it during the daytime, rather than the early morning. See it when nobody else was there, rather than having it filled with policemen and Crime Scene Investigators.

Accelerating along the road, he let his mind drift, trying to analyse why he wanted to spend what remained of his day off investigating a murder. There was something unsatisfying about the crime. Something slightly out of the ordinary. He had investigated so many murders over the years that he was inured to them, to the sights and the smells, the reasons and the rationales, but this one didn't seem to fit into the usual channels. Partly it was too mannered, too organised. Poisoning was not a crime of passion, but one of meticulous planning. But then there was the blow to the back of the head and the dumping of the body, apparently still alive, in the forest. That spoke of haste, of the murderer panicking and leaving the body behind. The two just didn't go together.

Unless ...

Unless the murderer had been interrupted on their way to dump the body. Perhaps they had chosen a site where they could abandon it with no fear of detection, but something had happened on the way. The poison hadn't worked properly: the supposed body had come back to life again. The thoughts all tumbled together in his mind. The murderer – or, rather, the attacker at this point – pulls over on a deserted road to finish the job with a quick blow to the back of the skull with a handy tool – a spanner, or a wrench, or something – but why not keep on going once the victim was dead? Why dump the body there?

Was there an interruption? Did someone see the car, parked by the side of the road, and pull over to see whether the murderer needed any help? Did the murderer have to leave the body where it was in order to deal with this interruption?

The rain-laden clouds were dark overhead but there was blue sky off to one side. The sun shone diagonally across the landscape, lighting it with a strange golden glow against the dark backdrop. It looked more like a stage set than a real place. Lapslie pushed the problem back in his mind, where his subconscious could chew on it, and set about enjoying the quietness of the drive.

Within half an hour he was heading along the same tree-lined road that he'd been on just a few weeks before. The rain had sluiced the air of dust, and the leaves seemed to glow with a preternatural light as the sun caught them. Shafts of brightness lanced through gaps in the trees, picked out by the moisture in the air. He slowed as he approached the bend in the road where the crash had occurred, pulled over and parked under the trees, his tyres biting deep into the loam.

Lapslie got out of the car and stood for a moment, breathing in the earthy dampness of the air. The CSI team had cleared up and left. Nothing remained of their presence apart from a churned-up area of ground where their tent had been, and some small scraps of yellow tape.

Turning, Lapslie gazed back along the length of the road he had just driven along. If he was right – and it was less of a theory, more of a hypothesis at the moment – the murderer had been driving along that road on their way to dump the body of their victim somewhere. For some reason they had stopped and their victim – who was not quite dead – had taken the opportunity to attempt an escape. A quick tap to the back of the head, and the victim really was dead. The murderer wrapped her in plastic and left her there, rather than drive on to the spot where they actually wanted to leave the body.

First question – why did the murderer stop the car? Three immediate possibilities occurred to him – either the victim had shown signs of life and had to be dealt with immediately, or there had been something at the scene already that had forced the murderer to stop, or the car had developed a fault. Now, which of those possibilities was the most likely? If the victim had shown signs of life while the murderer was driving the car then they might have stopped and hit them hard enough to finish the job, but why dump the body there? Why not keep on driving to the place they had originally intended to dump it? Scratch that idea. If there had been something on the road – a car in trouble perhaps – then why stop? Or, if the murderer had been forced to stop – by a police presence clearing the scene, perhaps – then why dump the body in a place where there were people around? Again, why not just keep going? No, the more Lapslie thought about it, the more he believed that the murderer's car had developed a fault.

In his mind's eye, he could see it happening, playing out against the picturesque setting of the misty road. A lone car, driving carefully, trying not to attract attention. A puncture, perhaps, or steam coming out of the radiator. The car draws quickly to a halt. The driver – a shadowy figure – gets out and checks the tyre, the bonnet, wherever the problem is. Unseen, the back door opens and a form crawls out, heading into the safety of the trees. The driver sees it, follows it across the bracken. A branch is picked up and descends abruptly: once, twice. The driver returns to the car and reluctantly makes a call to the emergency services. Before they can arrive, the driver takes a roll of plastic out of the back of the car and wraps the body up, piling bracken and earth on top to the best of their ability in order to keep it from being discovered. And then they wait for the AA, or the RAC, or whoever to arrive.

It made sense. It was only a possibility, of course, but it made sense. Which meant that the question was: what evidence might there be confirming or denying it?

Lapslie took his mobile from his jacket and held down the button that allowed him to voice-dial. 'Emma Bradbury,' he said, and the phone ransacked its memory for her number. Within a few moments, she answered.

'Sir? I thought it was your day off?'

'It is. I got bored. Emma, I need you to do something for me. I'm at the site where the body was found. I want you to check whether any recovery services or mechanics were called out to a broken-down car on this spot between, say, nine and eleven months ago. Check the police as well: they may have a record of something having happened. Give me a ring back when you have it.'

'Will do. What's this all –'

He cut her off abruptly, not wanting to talk, concerned somehow that if he was to explain his theory – his *hypothesis* – then it would all crumble to dust and Emma would laugh at him. He would wait until she called back with actual evidence – one way or the other – before he told her what he thought. And while he waited, he decided to take a walk in the woods.

The leaf mulch gave spongily beneath his feet as he walked. All around there was a slight crackle of vegetation drying out after the rain, and the occasional flurry of activity as a bird or a fox moved in the underbrush, but the smell of damp leaves rising from the ground covered any other taste that might have been triggered in Lapslie's mouth. There were no trails, no paths through the bushes to follow. He found himself having to step carefully over fallen trees and skirt around hawthorn bushes in order to make any progress.

Within a few moments he couldn't see the road, or his car. He might just as well have been in the middle of the forest as at its edge, and if he wasn't careful he might just keep walking until he *was* in the middle. There was no way to check direction, and although he tried to catalogue the shapes of trees that he passed, he found they all ended up looking the same.

People talked about cities having personalities, and in his time stationed in London as a Detective Sergeant he had come to know the comfortable excesses of the capital – a raddled old whore who still managed to attract clients – but there was a different kind of personality here in the woods. Something timeless and dark. Whatever it was, it had seen the murder of Violet Chambers and it didn't care, just as it hadn't cared about any of the hundreds, thousands, millions of deaths it had witnessed over the millennia.

Turning back, with some effort, Lapslie retraced his steps as best he could. And within ten minutes, he was back at his car again, and it was as if the forest had been a dream.

His mobile rang: Bruch's First Violin Concerto, and a burst of chocolate.

'Sir? Emma. I've phoned all the recovery and car mechanics firms covering the area. It's something of a blackspot, that curve. Quite a few cars end up coming off it in the wet or if it's icy.'

'How many?'

'In the timeframe in question, there were' – she paused, consulting whatever notes she had made – 'five incidents where someone was called out to repair or recover a car. Three of them involved families, so I think we can rule them out. One was breathalysed at the scene by police and taken into custody. His car was impounded. I guess we can forget that one as well.' There was something creeping into Emma's voice that made Lapslie pay attention. It wasn't quite nutmeg, but there was something definitely odd about it. She was holding something back. 'The last one was a lady. No age given. Volvo 740, bronze, it says here. Car was repaired, and she went on her way.'

Lapslie thought for a moment. More poisoners turned out to be women than men, and the people living opposite Violet Chambers' house had mentioned seeing a woman going in and out shortly before she left – or disappeared. It was worth following up. 'Did they get a name?' he asked.

'You're going to like this, sir. The woman gave her name as Violet Chambers.'

And that was it. His hunch had paid off. 'Right. It's too much of a coincidence that the real Violet Chambers broke down here shortly before her body was discovered. It's much more likely that whoever dumped her body used her name as well. Get copies of their report form, check the registration number of the car and trace the owner. And, just in case, check whether the real Violet Chambers owned a car.'

'Will do. Anything else?'

'Yes. Put out a general request for assistance. I want to know where that car is now. I'll ring you later.'

He rang off, then pressed the redial button as something else occurred to him. Emma answered, sounding surprised. 'Boss? Something else?'

'Yes. Phone around as many garages and mechanics as you can find within a fifty-mile radius of this forest. I want to know if anyone else has ever been called out to that car, and where it was at the time. If we get lucky, we might be able to tie it down to wherever our murderer lives. Or lived.'

'But there must be hundreds of car mechanics in the area, if not thousands. That's going to take –'

'A significant slice of your time, I know. Just think of the overtime.'

'Any chance you can get a constable assigned to this case, sir?' she said sourly. 'I could use the help.'

'I'll see what I can do,' Lapslie said, ringing off.

The sky was getting darker again, and there was a chill in the air that suggested more rain was on its way. He needed to get away: he had an appointment in London to go to. But for the moment, he found he could not leave. There was something about the spot where he was standing. A person had died there, and yet there was no acknowledgement. No sign. Nothing to mark the passing.

Perhaps that was the state of the world, and the human need to place crosses and markers was just a futile attempt to battle against the tide. The woodlands had been there for hundreds, perhaps thousands of years. Possibly they had been there before human beings had moved into the area. If every person's death that had occurred in those woods over the past two thousand years or more was marked by a red spot, would there be any greenery left?

Morbid thoughts. He climbed into his car and drove away, leaving the woodlands and their ghosts behind him.

He left his car at Audley End station, then caught a train to London, grabbing a quick sandwich on the way. The journey took less than an hour, and during the time he looked out of the window at the passing fields and factories and let his thoughts drift. Earplugs cut out the noise of the people talking around him, replacing them with blessed silence. Every time he found his thoughts turning toward Sonia and his children, he stopped and deliberately thought about something else. The pain of that scar throbbed enough; there was no point picking at it any more.

He called DCS Rouse's office from the train. The DCS wasn't available, so he left a message with his PA asking for some extra resources to help Emma Bradbury with her inquiries. He didn't hold out much hope – the top brass didn't seem to want to provide any more resources, despite the interest that DCS Rouse was showing in it – but he had to try.

The train left him at Liverpool Street, and he used the Underground to get across the river to Rotherhide. The earplugs were less effective at blocking out the constant rattling and roaring of the train through the tunnels, and he had to keep swallowing to wash the taste of gorgonzola away. Eventually he slipped a mint into his mouth, just to cover it up with something else.

At Rotherhide he left the station and made his way through cobbled back streets to an old, familiar public house perched on the edge of the Thames. The Golden Hind was tall and thin, slightly lopsided, constructed from blackened timbers and white-plastered brickwork. It looked at first glance like any one of a thousand faux-Tudor inns scattered about England, until you realised that it really did date from Tudor days. Things had been added and subtracted since that time, but it gave off an air of permanence at odds with the buildings around it.

He entered through a narrow doorway and looked around. The interior resembled a collision between three or four rooms of different sizes on different levels. Dom McGinley was sitting in a corner, a half-finished pint of Guinness in front of him. He raised his glass to Lapslie and took a swig.

'A pint of Guinness and a pint of lager,' Lapslie said to the barman. When he turned back with the drinks, McGinley was heading away from the door, towards a small exit at the back of the pub. Lapslie followed on, and found himself on a short pier extending out twenty feet or so into the Thames. Wooden benches were scattered around. There was nobody else out there.

McGinley slumped heavily into a seat. Lapslie put the pints down on the table in front of him, sat on the hard wooden bench and took a sip of his lager. It was largely tasteless, which was why he liked it.

'They found Dave Finnistaire tied to the piles beneath here,'

McGinley said eventually. Lapslie felt his mouth prickle with gherkins, pickled onions and piccalilli, and quickly took another sip of his lager to cover the taste. 'Fifteen years back. After your time. The tide doesn't come in too high on a normal day. They reckon he was tied there as a warning. Problem was, there was a surge tide and he drowned. They reckon he might have been hanging there a week before it happened.'

'Didn't he call out?'

McGinley shook his head. 'He probably tried, but after what they did to his tongue he wasn't going to have much luck. Happy days.' He took a swig of his Guinness.

'Happy days.'

Lapslie glanced out into the gathering darkness. The sun was going down, somewhere over the centre of London, and the sky was a glorious set of terraces laid out in scarlet, orange and maroon. The light reflected off the small gold stud that McGinley had in his left ear lobe. For a moment, Lapslie wondered about other synaesthetes, the ones whose senses were cross-connected in a different way from his and who saw colours instead of tasting flavours. Was this the kind of thing they experienced? Was this what *the ecstasies of the mind and senses* meant?

'I was surprised when you called,' McGinley said. 'After all, it's been a good few years since you left Kilburn, and we were never really what you'd call mates then.'

'Strangely, you were the closest thing I had,' Lapslie murmured.

'That's right – you didn't get on with the blokes in the nick, did you? Never went out drinking with them.'

'Not like you did. You were always buying drinks for the coppers. And the occasional car. Favours received, I guess.'

To either side of the pier, old warehouses and new apartment blocks jostled uneasily together, silhouetted against the pastel sky. A tug ploughed gracelessly down river, hooting mournfully. Seagulls rode the waves, their beaks hooked and cruel, their eyes glinting.

'Harsh, Mr Lapslie. Harsh. I've still got a reputation up Kilburn way.'

'But I understand that, what with the Yardies, then the Turks, then the Albanians moving in, then the Turks and the Yardies working together, then the Albanians getting together with the old Maltese gangs in Soho, things have got a little confused since I left. You might have a bit of a reputation, but you haven't got much of a manor any more. What is it down to now – two streets and a stretch of waste ground?'

'Albanians? You're a little behind the times. There's over four hundred different gangs in London and the South East now, all fighting for a little bit of turf and a little bit of respect. In the old days there was maybe four or five main groups. Now you need a computer just to keep up.'

'Makes you nostalgic for the Krays, doesn't it?'

'You can laugh. Latest ones are the Muslim Boys – they claim they're part of Al-Qaeda, but they're just trading on fear. And they're dangerous. Time was when you had to work to get some respect. Now all you need is a knife or a gun, and the willingness to kill someone you've never met and know nothing about.'

'I feel for you, McGinley. I really do.'

'You said you needed a favour. What can I do?'

'What do I have to do in return?'

McGinley gazed at Lapslie over the top of his glass. 'I might need a favour back, some day.'

Lapslie nodded. 'Okay – the PRU. It's a department in the Department of Justice. Know of it?'

'Can't say I do.'

'There's a man works there named Geherty. He's turned up on my patch, and it looks like he might be interfering with a murder case I've got on. I want to know more about him.'

McGinley took another long drink from his pint glass. 'I'll ask around. Give me a day or two.'

Lapslie sank his pint and stood up. 'Phone me from a

pay phone,' he said. 'There's a rumour around that you're acting as a mediator between some of the main gangs in the capital. Branching out into criminal diplomacy. I wouldn't be surprised if your mobile is being listened to.'

McGinley nodded. 'Why are you telling me that now?'

'Because that,' Lapslie said, 'is the favour returned. I don't like the thought of you holding something over me.' He walked over to the entrance back into the bar, then turned and gazed out over the Thames. It rolled past like a ribbon of tar in the encroaching darkness. 'I heard that it was you that tied Dave Finnistaire to the piles beneath this pier,' he said. 'Any truth in that?'

'No, Mr Lapslie,' said McGinley. 'But I did carve his tongue into strips beforehand. Safe journey now.'

CHAPTER ELEVEN

Over the course of the next week, Daisy and Sylvia met up twice for lunch, and once for a drive out to a garden centre near Frinton so that Sylvia could pick up some plants for her borders. The sun shone down out of a cloudless blue sky as Sylvia drove carefully through the back lanes in her small, but well serviced, Fiat. Daisy gazed out at the fields as they passed. The tall yellow flowers that seemed to be all that was cultivated around here swayed under the breeze. An over-poweringly floral scent seeping in through the windows made Daisy feel dizzy.

Being in the car reminded Daisy of her own Volvo, sitting quietly in a back street in Colchester. She had been neglecting it, and by now it may already have attracted parking tickets, perhaps even been clamped. Retrieving it would be risky, and given that Sylvia had her own car, pointless. Soon this car would be hers, and she could leave the Volvo to rust in peace.

Sylvia parked carefully beneath the shade of a large tree outside the garden centre. They went in together, and while Sylvia pottered around looking for something suitable for a herbaceous border, Daisy wandered over to the area set aside for small trees. An entire row was dedicated to yew trees, and Daisy spent an enjoyable half hour wandering along it, noting the differences between the English, Canadian and Japanese varieties, running her hands through the needle-like leaves and across the reddish-brown, scaly bark. Such a versatile tree. So sturdy, so appealing, so deadly if used in the right ways thanks to the high dose of taxine in the bark, leaves and seeds.

Turning her head, she could see Sylvia pushing a trolley along, stacked up with small pots of various types. She let herself daydream for a moment, imagining how she could feed the yew to Sylvia. The needles alone could cause what she believed was termed anaphylactic shock, if chewed as part of a strongly flavoured dinner. On the other hand, a gradual introduction of powdered bark into Sylvia's food could weaken the heart to the point where it would stop. How delicious.

Growing tired of the yew trees after a while, Daisy went looking for Sylvia. She found her bending over a display of chamomile, trying to select the healthiest specimens.

'Don't they smell gorgeous?' she asked. 'I do so love the idea of a chamomile lawn. They thrive by being trodden on, you know.'

And some people are the same, Daisy thought to herself, anticipating the day when she would be in charge in the house and Sylvia would dance to her tune. A month? Three at the outside, if she didn't rush things. 'Don't you find the smell a little sickening?' she asked. 'I don't think it's quite the right thing for your garden. Let's look for something else.'

'If you really think so ...' Sylvia looked slightly hurt by Daisy's reaction.

'I do. You'll thank me for it.' Turning to the trolley, she noticed the large number of plants that Sylvia had collected. 'Are you sure you can afford all this?' she asked.

'Oh yes,' Sylvia smiled, her momentary hurt forgotten. 'My husband left me very well provided for. The widow's pension I get every month is more than I used to earn when I was working. I don't know what to do with all that money.'

And that, Daisy reflected, was the best news she'd had all week.

While Sylvia pottered about looking at more herbaceous plants, Daisy wandered across to where a fine display of rhubarb was spreading its leaves and nodding gently in the sun. Such a neglected plant. Who, these days, ever cooked rhubarb pie or stewed rhubarb? And did anyone still remember that while the stalks were delicious, the leaves were highly poisonous, if cooked along with them? Oxalic acid, she believed.

Turning away from the rhubarb, Daisy found Sylvia talking to a gentleman in a blazer and sharply creased trousers. They were debating the various merits of bugle and cranesbill as a ground cover plant, and there was an expression on Sylvia's face that Daisy didn't like at all. She was smiling. More than that, she was *radiant*.

'Oh, Daisy,' she said, flustered, as Daisy approached, 'this is Kenneth. He used to work with my husband, years ago. We just bumped into one another, would you believe it?'

'What a lovely coincidence,' Daisy said brightly as Kenneth took her hand. She couldn't help noticing that his gaze only strayed briefly from Sylvia's face. 'My dear, we should really be going if we want to make it back in good time.'

'I thought we might have a cup of tea first.' Sylvia's hand reached out to touch Kenneth's sleeve briefly. 'Kenneth and I have such a lot to catch up on. We haven't seen each other for *years.*'

Reluctantly, Daisy found herself pulled along to the garden centre's café, where she had to endure what at times seemed to her like a long-delayed and very polite courtship. Kenneth was charming, there was no doubt of that, and Sylvia was suitably charmed. Over tea and scones, which Kenneth paid for, Daisy saw her plans begin to erode. By the time the last cup of tea had been poured and the last spoonful of cream had been applied to the last crumbs of scone, Kenneth and Sylvia had arranged to go to the theatre together the following week. Daisy was invited as well, of course, and she accepted in order not to look petty – something might still be retrieved from the situation – but she knew in her heart of hearts that Sylvia was now lost to her. She had another friend now, and that would make isolating her from the flow of the world and making her dependent on Daisy all the more difficult. Perhaps even impossible.

A part of her wanted to cook Sylvia and Kenneth a wonderful rhubarb pie, just to show there were no hard feelings, but there was no point in letting her frustration get in the way of her long-term plans. She would just have to start again.

After they had finished their tea and scones, the three of them parted: Kenneth to hunt down some slug repellent and Sylvia and Daisy to the Fiat, and then back to Leyston-by-Naze. The journey back was rather more strained than the journey there. At one point, Sylvia turned to Daisy and said, 'Are you feeling all right? You're very quiet.'

'I'm just tired,' Daisy said, and she wasn't sure whether she was talking about the day or her life in total.

Sylvia dropped Daisy off just down from the station, after Daisy broke another long silence by saying that she wanted to do some shopping in the High Street. For reasons she couldn't quite explain, Daisy had been reluctant to let Sylvia see where she lived. Now she was grateful for her caution. If she was going to have to break things off and start again, it was best there was no connection between one potential victim and the next – even if that connection was Daisy's rented accommodation. As the small Fiat drove slowly away, Daisy watched it go with mixed feelings. On the one hand, there was the aching loss of the house, the car and the wonderful pension. On the other hand, Sylvia had been quite strong willed. Dominating her would have taken time and energy, and Daisy had the feeling that both of those were in increasingly short supply. Something was pressing her on, forcing her to leave shorter and shorter periods between her murders. Sylvia would no doubt wonder where her new friend had gone, but she would recover – with Kenneth's help. And she would never know what a lucky reprieve she had been given.

Instead of heading down towards the High Street, Daisy found her footsteps leading in a different direction – towards the other side of the pier, where row upon row of beach huts sat, waiting until the holiday season when they would open up like flowers, shutters and doors flung wide to catch the warmth of the sun.

From the road above the beach huts, Daisy stared down at the brightly painted roofs – red, blue, green and yellow. Concrete paths wound between the rows, while concrete steps with steel pipe handrails connected them to the beach below. It all looked rather drab and sad now, but in the height of the summer the whole place would be heaving with children and parents, and smelling to high heaven of suntan lotion.

Carefully, Daisy walked down the nearest stairway towards the beach. Sea grasses were growing up along the edges of the stairs and in between the treads: hardy survivors that would flourish even in the harshest of conditions. Sand had drifted into every crack and every crevice. The doors of one or two of the beach huts had been smashed in by teenagers looking for somewhere to shelter, to smoke their cigarettes and paw their unwilling girlfriends. As she reached the last set of steps, and carefully climbed down to the damp sand below, she could feel the weight of the beach huts at her back, like a hundred staring eyes.

The tide was in the process of going out, and her footsteps squeezed water from the beach as she walked. The receding water had carved the sand into tiny ripples. Small tubes of sand lay curled up every few yards: casts left behind by lugworms searching for scraps of food. Somewhere below the sandcastles and tide pools of the beach there was an entire world of blind, thoughtless life, writhing and squirming away, and yet nobody ever thought about it when they were lying in the sun trying to get a tan, or running around playing volleyball, or throwing themselves into the waves. They weren't aware of the horrors that lay just beneath the surface.

To her right, the dark bulk of the pier dominated the sky: blocking her view of the side of Leyston that she had come to know so well over the past weeks. On a whim, Daisy began to walk across to the massive wooden supports that held the pier up. She could walk beneath it, then find a way up to the esplanade on the other side. From there she could catch a bus back to her flat.

The wooden pilings were each set in a water-filled depression, carved out by the retreating waves as they swirled around the posts. The wood itself was covered, to a height of six feet or so, by seaweed: bladderwrack and various other kinds. Moss-covered rocks littered the waterlogged sand, and Daisy's nose was assaulted by the overpowering aroma of decaying vegetation. She kept walking, avoiding the pools of still water and the stumps of rotted wood that poked out of the muddy sand, holding her breath until she reached the other side.

There, the panorama of the sky and of the esplanade calmed her down somewhat, and she even ventured to walk out towards the retreating tide. A small, still voice in her head suggested that she take off her shoes and paddle in the water for a while, but she knew that she would have looked ridiculous. She kept walking along the beach, the massive promontory of the Naze up ahead of her. Other people were also on the beach, alone or in pairs, walking dogs or just wandering along by themselves. She felt isolated, vulnerable, and yet also somehow anonymous. To anyone on the esplanade she was just another figure walking along the sand.

Daisy reviewed her options. The theatre, she reluctantly decided, was not on the cards, if only for the fact that Sylvia and Kenneth looked like they might be confirmed theatre-goers, and Daisy didn't want any well-meaning interference in her stalking. Perhaps the Widows' Friendship Club might be worth investigating. Alternatively, she could always try popping along to one of the local churches on a Sunday evening. Morning services, she found, attracted too big a crowd. Worse, they all tended to know one another and socialise together. Sunday evening services tended to be more for the loners, the people who wanted to worship by themselves, rather than in company. She should be able to find a decent victim there. The problem was that the kind of women who tended to go to worship on a Sunday night were as poor as church mice, pardon the pun. Worse, she would almost certainly be noticed and approached by the vicar, and the last thing she wanted was a well-meaning cleric on her doorstep.

There ought to be a bowls club in the vicinity, Daisy decided. She was pretty sure she'd seen a bowling green from the bus on the way to her flat. Perhaps she should join.

The afternoon sun behind her cast her shadow out across the sand, and suddenly it was joined by another one. She turned her head warily. A small bundle of hair and teeth rushed past her feet and up to the water, backing up suddenly and then rushing towards the waves again, barking.

'Terribly sorry,' said a voice behind her. 'He's always like that. Always racing off, chasing his own shadow. I hope he didn't frighten you.'

Daisy turned. The woman behind her was wearing the oddest assortment of clothes: legwarmers, a billowing skirt, a velvet waistcoat over a denim shirt, and a voluminous coat over the entire ensemble. Her hair, or what could be seen poking out from beneath a shapeless hat, was quite wild, turned gold by the rays of sunshine that spread low across the skyline. Her face, shadowed as it was by the sun behind her, was creased, rather than lined, and her eyes were a faded blue. She might have been ten years younger than Daisy, or ten years older: she had one of those faces that was difficult to put an age on. In one hand she clutched a plastic bag, and in the other a dog lead.

'I said, I hope he didn't frighten you.'

'I'm quite unfrightenable,' Daisy said, staring at this apparition as if it had arisen from the sand in answer to her unspoken prayers.

'Good for you,' the woman said. 'I'm Eunice. Eunice Coleman.'

'Daisy Wilson.'

'And are you a visitor to this benighted town, or do you have the misfortune to live here?'

Daisy couldn't help smiling at the woman's forthright manner. 'I moved here recently.'

'Then you have my condolences.'

The small bundle of fur and teeth that had rushed past earlier suddenly rushed past again, heading across the sand at breakneck speed in pursuit of the shadow of one of the gulls that hung in the air above them.

'That's Jasper,' said Eunice. 'Named for Jasper Johns, the artist.'

'Is he famous?' Daisy asked. 'I've never heard of him.'

The woman looked at her strangely. 'You've never heard of Jasper Johns?'

'No.'

'You'll be telling me you've never heard of Jackson Pollock.'

'I never have.'

'Joan Miró?'

'Her neither.'

'Joan Miró was a him, not a her.' Eunice shook her head grimly. 'What is the world coming to?'

'Are you an artist?' Daisy asked, feeling as if she'd been drawn into a conversation that was spiralling out of her control.

'I run an art gallery and craft centre,' Eunice said, as if that were the same thing. 'Not that people around here are that interested in arts. Keeps me occupied. Stops me from going doolally.'

'What kind of arts and crafts do you have?'

Eunice shrugged. 'Paintings I've picked up along the way. Some pottery. A couple of wall hangings. Nothing as tedious as embroidery. That's not art, that's just fiddling about. I do classes as well, or I would if anyone cared enough to come along. Coffee and cakes. All sorts. I've got a converted barn just out of town, next to the house. Off the beaten track, though. Not on the main tourist routes.'

'It sounds rather fun,' Daisy said with as much conviction as she could pull together. 'You must tell me where it is.'

'I've got a map. Somewhere.' Eunice rummaged around in her bag and pulled out a handful of leaflets. 'Printed them myself.'

And Daisy could tell. They had been put together on a computer of some kind, but there were too many different fonts crammed too close together. 'It's ... very impressive,' she said finally.

'No it's not. That's the problem. I can do art, I can do craft, but I can't do advertising. I don't know how people think. No head for business. Accounts just leave me cold. Don't understand cashflow; don't understand the lingo.'

'You need someone to help you out.'

Eunice shrugged. 'I used to have someone to do that, but they left. I have a tendency to speak my mind, you know. Some people respond badly to that. Good riddance to them, I say. Problem is, I seem to have burned my bridges. Nobody here wants to help out any more.'

If Daisy had believed in God, she would have put this meeting down to divine providence. As it was, she could only think that when one door closed, another door opened. 'I was looking for something to do in my spare time,' she said without even thinking. 'Perhaps I could help you out. Design some proper leaflets, get some advertising put up around town, that sort of thing.'

'Are you sure?' Eunice looked doubtful. 'Why on earth would you want to?'

'It'll stop me getting bored.' She looked at the leaflet. 'Should I pop in tomorrow? We could talk it over.'

A smile broke out on Eunice's face. Suddenly she looked ten years younger. 'That would be wonderful. There'll be coffee and cake waiting. There's always coffee and cake, just in case. Mostly it just goes to the birds. The cake, that is. Not the coffee. Ta-ta.' She stomped off, her dog following on behind. Beneath the fringed hem of her skirt and the legwarmers it looked as if she were wearing what Daisy could only describe as 'pixie boots'.

What a strange woman. And yet, what an interesting

prospect. Her stream-of-consciousness way of talking would probably drive Daisy to distraction after a short time, but perhaps a short time was all she needed. If she didn't have much of a grasp of business then she would probably welcome Daisy taking control of that side of things, and if she didn't have any friends in the town then she wouldn't be missed if she disappeared. And a barn! Daisy didn't want to get her hopes up – it was probably rat-infested and falling down – but that kind of property was always in demand for conversion into luxury apartments. If nothing else, there was the land.

Feeling a lot happier than she had when she first set foot on the beach, Daisy set off for a celebratory cup of coffee. Not at the post office café, however. Too much chance of seeing Sylvia there now. No, she would have to find somewhere else.

The next day, after a dreamless night, Daisy checked the location of Eunice's arts and crafts barn on her local map. The bus to Clacton went close by, and Daisy set off. It would have been more convenient with a car, of course. Having more or less consigned her Volvo to the past, and having now lost the chance of Sylvia's Fiat, Daisy decided as a matter of some priority to find a car she could use – one with no history that could tie it back to her in the event that anything went wrong. Perhaps Eunice had a car.

The bus journey took half an hour or so, and left Daisy with a ten-minute walk along a rutted country lane. A hand-lettered sign advertising, rather grandly, *Arts and Crafts Centre* had come loose from its fixings, and now pointed vaguely up to the clouds. But it was a glorious day, and Daisy could still smell the sea. She had a good feeling about this.

At the end of the track was a rather grand house, probably dating from the last century: five bedrooms at least, possibly more. Daisy gazed up at it, enraptured. What a prospect for developing into a bed and breakfast establishment. Not hers, of course. That would mean settling down and putting her name on paper in too many places. But someone with vision would pay a lot of money for that house.

Beside the house was a barn: large, long, with a slate roof. The entrance had been closed off with a new addition: a glass and wood double door, open now to provide ventilation to the inside. Daisy approached gingerly and put her head around the jamb. 'Hello?'

'Hello? Who's that?'

Daisy entered the barn. Inside it was surprisingly light and airy. Some considerable effort had been put into painting it and separating areas with partitions on which were hung paintings in various styles. Pots and sculptures sat on pedestals around the space. The floor was covered in cork tiles. Eunice Coleman was sitting behind an L-shaped bench by the door. To her right was a till. In front of her was an open book of black-and-white photographs which she had been leafing through.

'It's Daisy. Daisy Wilson.'

Eunice's face lit up with recognition. Whatever happened, Daisy reflected as she entered, she would never have any problem in telling what Eunice felt. Every emotion seemed to hit her face and her voice before it actually crossed her mind.

'The woman from the beach! I was worried you might have been being polite, and you weren't going to come.'

'I would never do that,' Daisy said virtuously. 'If I say I will do something then I will do it, come hell or high water.'

'Would you like a coffee?'

Eunice busied herself at a small area at the back of the barn, where four round tables and a handful of chairs were clustered near a serving hatch, behind which Daisy could just make out an urn of hot water and some cakes under transparent perspex domes. Daisy looked around while Eunice prepared the coffee. Appearances had been deceiving: the paintings were badly hung, and the sculptures were covered in dust. There were also piles of newspaper and boxes of odds and ends stacked up in the corners. Eunice was apparently one of those people who

considered clearing up to be not only hard work but also difficult as well, in the same way that a crossword puzzle is
difficult.

The two of them sat down at one of the tables and talked.
Or, rather, Eunice talked and Daisy alternately listened and let
her mind drift.

It seemed that Eunice had led quite a free and easy life. The
daughter of a well-off family in the Home Counties, she had
studied at St Martin's College of Art in London when she was
younger, and had lived in various communes and communities
for the following twenty years or so, drifting into and out of
relationships with both men and women, acting as muse for
some artists and model for others, taking soft drugs and generally living the kind of vacuous and unproductive life that Daisy
thoroughly disapproved of, although she didn't tell Eunice this.
On the death of her father, Eunice had inherited quite a lot of
money, and rather than move back to the family home (or
'mansion' as she inadvertently referred to it at one stage) she
had arranged for it to be sold, then bought a house close to the
sea in the Tendring area with one of her many lovers, with a
view to settling into a bucolic farming lifestyle. Farming turned
out to be hard work, however; her lover left and she had
stayed. Men had come and gone over the intervening time, and
those of a practical bent had helped her get the house and barn
into some kind of order, turning it into an arts and crafts centre
that she was certain would attract patrons and become, in the
fullness of time, a mirror image of the artistic communities she
had been a part of when she was much younger and much
more beautiful. And now she was alone, apart from the occasional passing tourist.

By the time Daisy left she had offered to help Eunice turn the
Arts and Crafts Centre into a going concern. She had also
developed a venomous hatred for Jasper the dog, who seemed
to have as little brain as his mistress without her appealing
flashes of sentiment.

Daisy returned the next day and started on clearing the rubbish out of the barn. Most of the boxes were filled with packing material or odd things that Eunice had picked up over the years. These she threw straight out. The newspapers were also old: both local and national papers dating back several months or, in the case of one pile hidden at the back, several years. Daisy could tell how old they were just by the colour and the texture of the paper: in the conditions of the barn, anything dating back more than a few weeks was yellow and stiff.

It was while she was clearing a pile of newspapers near the till that Daisy caught sight of a headline that almost made her heart stop.

BODY OF PENSIONER FOUND IN FOREST

Daisy bent closer to the newspaper and read quickly through the article.

The body of a 79-year-old woman was discovered yesterday in a forest near Ipswich. The corpse had been wrapped in plastic sheets and buried in a shallow grave.

According to police, pensioner Violet Chambers was discovered by accident when a car came off the road near where she had been buried. The driver was pronounced dead at the scene of the crash.

Violet Chambers had not been reported missing, and police are still investigating why her disappearance had not been noticed before. Sources in the forensic team have said that the body looked as if it had been in the forest for many months.

The words on the newspaper seemed to dance in front of Daisy's eyes.

Violet Chambers. They had found Violet Chambers.

It was the first of her victims to be found. The first link in a long chain of evidence.

One mistake. Just one mistake, and it could ruin everything.

She glanced up at Eunice. She would have to move quickly. She needed to get herself established, burrow in and disappear. She needed to take on a cloak of respectability.

'Is everything all right?' Eunice asked, startling Daisy. 'You look as if you've swallowed something nasty.'

'Not me,' Daisy said. 'Not yet.'

CHAPTER TWELVE

The trouble with maps, Mark Lapslie decided, was that they demystified everything.

He was sitting in the Quiet Room, back in the police HQ in Chelmsford. He had an Ordnance Survey map of the forest where Violet Chambers' body had been found spread over the desk, and he was attempting to trace where the car that dumped her body might have been heading.

The forest had seemed so daunting when he was walking through it, waiting for Emma Bradbury to phone back. He'd had the impression that it might have gone on for miles, rolling across the English countryside like a dark stain, ancient and unyielding. There might have been patches of ground in there upon which man had never trod. There might have been monsters. Now, looking at it on the map, he could see that it only covered a few square miles and was bounded on each side by roads, caged in by progress. Somehow, splayed out on paper for all to see, it had lost its enchantment. 'Here there be dragons', the old maps used to say, but the whole point of maps was that they removed all the places the dragons were hiding, making them accessible to any fool with a car and a pair of walking boots.

Jesus, he was feeling cynical. Perhaps it was the effects of meeting up with Dom McGinley. The man hadn't phoned back yet, and Lapslie wasn't even sure he would. The two of them had a certain amount of respect for one another, the same kind of respect that the last two dinosaurs to die probably had, but that didn't mean McGinley would actually do him any favours. It was a long shot, but long shots sometimes worked.

Which was why Lapslie was bent over the Ordnance Survey

map, tracing his finger along the road where Violet Chambers' body had been found. The interesting thing was that the road cut through the centre of the forest. Anyone going to any of the big towns in the vicinity would almost certainly have taken the major roads on either side. They were better lit and they were faster. The road through the forest didn't really go anywhere apart from a small set of villages.

A knock on the door of the Quiet Room sent the taste of bacon trickling through his mouth. He looked up. Emma Bradbury was standing outside, holding a piece of paper. He gestured to her to enter.

'Boss, we've got a break,' she said as the door swung open, her words undercut by the sound of chattering from the open-plan office outside. The smoky taste of the bacon hadn't quite faded from Lapslie's mouth before it was joined by lemon from Bradbury's voice and dried blood from the raised level of conversation. And there was strawberry mixed in there as well: a bizarre mélange of flavours that could only have been matched in real life by a child mixing their dinner and dessert up on the same plate.

'Great,' he said, wincing and swallowing to try and get rid of the incompatible tastes. 'What's happened? And close the door for God's sake – I'm virtually having a four-course meal in here.'

'Sorry.' She entered the room and shut the door behind her. 'The car that had a flat tyre – the one we thought might have been carrying the body of Violet Chambers ...'

'What about it?'

'We've found it. Well, a copper in Colchester. It had been parked up near the station for quite a while – legally, but nobody had moved it, and it was looking like it had been abandoned. The council were about to tow it away, but this copper who was passing checked it against that call you put out. When he realised that we were looking for the car, he called it in.'

'Good man.' Lapslie leaned back in his chair. 'Colchester's, what, twenty miles away? Okay – I want a full CSI team down there. I want every inch of that car examined *in situ*.'

Bradbury looked sceptical. 'I know you've been out of the loop for a while, boss, but it's more usual to move suspect vehicles to a CSI garage so they can be taken apart under controlled conditions.'

'Thanks for reminding me of standard procedure, but the evidence might be more to do with the place it's parked than the car itself. I know it's been there a while, but there could be a footprint in dried mud, or something fallen out of the car when the driver got out. We can get it to a garage later, but for now I want the whole place treated as a crime scene – car and parking space and all.'

'Okay.' She nodded. 'You want to head out there and see it?'

'Yes.'

Bradbury looked at her watch. 'Almost lunchtime. We could stop for something on the way.'

The abstract mix of flavours was still lingering in Lapslie's mouth, dominated by the taste of Bradbury's voice. 'Thanks,' he said sourly, 'but I've already eaten.'

Lapslie insisted that they take his car rather than Bradbury's. The last thing he wanted at that time was marmalade from her Mondeo's engine purr added to the stuff already in his mouth. Surprised, she agreed.

While they were driving, Bradbury was on her mobile getting the CSI team arranged. It took her five separate calls, plus the possibly empty threat of Lapslie phoning the Detective Chief Superintendent's office and getting him to reprioritise their work, to move his case up their list. At one point Lapslie could taste blackberry wine, very faintly, across the back of his tongue, and he guessed that Bradbury was talking to Sean Burrows, the Crime Scene Manager who had previously been called out to the forest where Violet Chambers' body had been found. He was concentrating on driving, so he didn't catch everything that Bradbury said, but judging by the harsh tone of voice she used she was pressing the point home quite heavily that this was an important case.

Eventually she put the mobile back in her pocket. 'I've been asked to tell you,' she said, 'that by prioritising this case above the rest of CSI's workload you've potentially threatened the investigation into two other suspicious deaths, and you can expect calls from the DCS within the next hour.'

'Life's like that,' Lapslie said. 'A series of choices, each of which has unfortunate consequences. You just have to do what seems best at the time. When will CSI get to the car?'

'They were already on the road to another crime scene. They're turning round and heading for Colchester now. That little Irish git says they'll be there within the hour, which is probably about as long as it'll take for us to get there.'

The roads were relatively clear, Emma Bradbury didn't seem inclined to talk, and Lapslie found his thoughts wandering as he drove. He was working on the assumption that someone – yet to be identified – had killed Violet Chambers and taken on her identity, writing postcards and Christmas cards to make people think that Violet was still alive while he, or she, presumably, plundered whatever money Violet had and rented her house out via an estate agent. According to Bradbury's investigations, the money collected by the estate agents was paid into a separate account in Violet's name from which occasional withdrawals were made in different locations. But as far as Lapslie could see, the money wasn't enough to make it worthwhile killing Violet Chambers for. Perhaps as a crime of passion, a killing on the spur of the moment, but this had all the hallmarks of careful planning and execution. So why go to all that trouble just for a trickle of money?

Lapslie shivered. He had the distinct impression that the body in the forest, the house that had been rented out and the abandoned car were just the tip of the iceberg. There was a lot more of this case hidden below the surface. And, like an iceberg, it was going to be cold and hard and very unpleasant.

They arrived in Colchester less than an hour after they had set out. Bradbury guided Lapslie in through narrow streets with high stone walls alternating with wider, more modern roads flanked with warehouse-style superstores until they came to the street where the car had been abandoned.

The CSI team had got there before them. Their van was parked near the Volvo and they were already deploying the yellow plastic tent that would keep their work isolated, although Lapslie was aware that the amount of time that had passed since the car had been abandoned meant that most of the evidence would have been blown away by the wind or washed away by rain.

He glanced around, trying to get a sense of the place. They were in a wide street which curved away in either direction. On one side was a row of shops: a florists, a laundrette, a bookies and a couple of unidentifiable frontages that were closed or boarded up. A couple of the shops were selling things that were completely at variance with the signs above them. It was obviously the kind of place where property changed hands faster than the signs could keep up, if anyone bothered changing the signs in the first place. Above the shops were two storeys of flats: windows curtained even in the middle of the morning and grimy with dust and pollution. Overflow pipes projected from the flats like regularly spaced industrial gargoyles. The bricks beneath most of the pipes were green with moss in a sharp triangle, showing where water had dripped or poured on a regular basis over the years. Sheets of newspaper, yellow and crinkled, blew along the pavement and collected in corners. There was nobody about, and a deadness to the air, as if any sound was instantly swallowed up before it could go too far from its source. Even the light seemed grey and tired. The place felt like the end of the world had come early, and it had ended not with a bang but with a whimper.

' "And what rough beast, its hour come round at last, slouches towards Bethlehem to be born?" ' Lapslie murmured as he got out of the car.

'Sorry, boss?' Bradbury said, getting out of the passenger side.

'W. B. Yeats. It seemed apt. I was just wondering what kind of person we're going to find at the end of all this.'

Bradbury gave him a strange look, but said nothing. Together they walked across to where the tent was being erected around the boxy shape of a car.

Sean Burrows was waiting for them. He was dressed in ordinary clothes, but he was holding the papery overalls that all the CSIs wore when they were carrying out their investigations. 'You are aware,' he said with painful sarcasm, 'that we prioritise our work strictly on the basis of importance. An abandoned car that may or may not be connected to a nine-month-old death does not come high up that list.'

'Not your call to make,' Lapslie said. 'Let me give you a couple of reasons why you should do this job as top priority. First: I outrank the investigating officers of all the other cases you have on your list. Second: I can get Chief Superintendent Rouse to give you a call and reprioritise your workload until your ears bleed. And third: I'm the only investigating officer who provides you with bacon rolls while you're working.'

Burrows stared at him for a few moments. 'Sold to the man with the attitude,' he said finally. 'And can we have some sausage rolls mixed in this time? One of the guys is Jewish. Had to eat the roll and leave the bacon last time.'

'Doesn't he know what's in the sausages?' Bradbury asked.

'He won't ask and we won't say,' Burrows answered. 'Trouble is that he can't turn a blind eye to bacon.'

'Can you find a local café and arrange for a regular delivery of rolls and tea?' Lapslie asked Bradbury. She nodded, and walked away.

The tent was up by this time, and Lapslie entered. The dull light from outside was enlivened by its translucent yellow walls, casting a macabre light over the dusty bronze car that sat in the centre. Three of Burrows' people were starting work on the car: one taking photographs and measurements on the inside, one opening the boot while the third opened the bonnet and checked for the serial number inscribed on the engine.

'Any clues as to what we're looking for?' Burrows asked.

'Whatever we can find that will lead us to the driver,' Lapslie answered.

'You think this is the car that old lady's body was dumped from?'

'It's the only candidate so far. And I have a suspicion that the old lady that was found in the forest isn't the only body this car has seen.'

Burrows nodded. 'Volvos, you see. Lots of boot space, nobody ever pays attention to them and they're very reliable. If you're carting dead bodies around, a Volvo's what you want.'

'I sometimes worry,' Lapslie said, 'about what might happen if you guys ever decided to go freelance.'

'We do talk about setting up a murder consultancy,' Burrows admitted. 'But we'd have to register for VAT and everything, and it's just too much trouble.'

The person who had opened the boot was gesturing to her colleague with the camera. He joined her and took photographs of whatever they had found, flooding the tent with the light from the flashgun. Burrows frowned, and walked across to join them. He glanced into the boot, then gestured Lapslie to join him.

'What do you think – a body?' Burrows asked.

'That's all I need right now,' Lapslie said as he walked over towards the car: 'one more body and no more murderers.'

As he got closer to the car he could make out a faint smell of flowers and earth. For a moment he thought it was his synaesthesia reaction to a low-level sound somewhere outside, but when he reached Burrows' side he realised that the smell was a real smell, and it was coming from the boot of the Volvo. The large space was filled with twigs, leaves and colourful petals, all carefully held together with twists of gardening wire.

'Not exactly what I was expecting,' Burrows said. 'I'll have them bagged up and identified.'

Lapslie watched for a while as Burrows' team painstakingly examined the Volvo. They fingerprinted the inside, and picked up samples of hair and lint from the seats. They were, Lapslie thought, like beetles crawling over the carcass of a dead animal, stripping it of whatever flesh it had left. It must have been his imagination, but the car seemed to shrink as they worked, as if the mystery it contained had bulked it out. It occurred to him that Violet Chambers' body must have gone through a process very much like that: plump and fleshy when she was first dumped in the forest beneath a few inches of earth, then progressively stripped of everything that made her human until she was just a collection of bones, tendons and mummified skin, at which time the various scavengers moved on to the next thing on their priority list.

'Apart from the boot, which is covered with a layer of dirt, the car's surprisingly clean,' Burrows said. 'It looks like it's been vacuumed on a regular basis: possibly put through a valet service as well. There's no fingerprints on the steering wheel: my guess is that whoever left it gave it a quick once-over with a J-cloth before they walked away. The outside's been scoured by the elements as well. No chance of getting anything off the door handles.'

'Good work,' Lapslie said. 'Keep going, and if you find anything, give me a ring.'

'Sure,' the CSM said. 'It's not as if I had anything else to do with my day.'

Emma Bradbury was talking on her mobile when Lapslie walked out of the tent. She waved him over, flipping the phone shut as he arrived.

'What's up?' he asked.

'I managed to get a Special Constable to do some legwork on the question you asked me,' she said. 'The one about whether any car mechanic or garage within fifty miles of the forest where Violet Chambers' body was discovered had been called out to look at a Volvo with this licence plate.'

'How did you manage that? I thought there was some unspoken moratorium on getting any help on this investigation.'

'I just didn't tell anyone,' she said. 'Anyway, it turns out that a garage in Malden was called out three years ago to an isolated house in the countryside. This car was there, and it wouldn't start. Turned out that the owner had left the interior lights on by mistake and the battery had run flat. All the mechanic had to do was jump-start it and it was okay.'

'Who was the driver?'

'The name on the form is smudged. He can't make it out. He remembers that she was a woman in her sixties, though.'

Lapslie thought for a moment. 'That address might well be where whoever murdered Violet Chambers is living. We need to proceed carefully. Notify Control that we're on our way.' He paused for a moment. 'We're potentially dealing with a murderer here. I think we might need an Armed Response Team.'

Outside, the local police had cordoned off the tent with incident tape, looped around trees and lamp posts and attached to drainpipes. A small collection of people who lived, worked or shopped in the area had gathered, pressing themselves against the tape so they could get a better look at whatever was going on, which was presumably more interesting than anything else they had to do that day.

Lapslie took a deep breath. The air itself seemed listless and insipid. Small flurries of wind, caught in shop doorways, drew up the dust into spirals. They were the most animated things about the scene.

Emma was arguing into her mobile as they walked. Lapslie caught the occasional terse word and suppressed curse. Eventually she flipped it shut and turned to him. 'It's no-go on the firearms team,' she said, face thunderous. 'Apparently they're unavailable. Some kind of counter-terrorism thing in Dagenham. Control reckons that it'll be a day or so before they're free, and even then there's no guarantee that we can have them. Do you want to wait?'

Lapslie shook his head. 'Has it occurred to you,' he asked, 'that we've had to fight for resources at every step of the way in this case? DCS Rouse tried to take you off the case, the uniforms at the crime scene were pulled away to cover a football match, of all things, the autopsy records were interfered with, and any request I make for additional manpower is turned down flat. Something's going on in the background that I'm not privy to, and I don't like it.' He scowled. 'No, I'm going to head over to that address, and I'm going to do it without armed backup. I won't order you to come along, but I could do with the company.'

She nodded. 'Count me in,' she said.

Bradbury was about to say something else when her mobile rang. She turned away to talk, and Lapslie took the opportunity to phone DCS Rouse on his own mobile. Rouse's PA answered, and Lapslie said: 'This is DCI Lapslie. I need to talk to the boss.'

'He's ... out at a meeting,' the PA said, with only a momentary hesitation, but her voice was shaded with dry spice. She was lying. Lapslie had a sudden intuition that Mr Geherty from the Department of Justice was standing over her, listening in. He rang off without saying goodbye.

'I've had Control check the address out,' Bradbury said, flipping her own phone closed. 'It's listed as belonging to a Rhona McIntyre. No records of any incidents related to the address, and she's clear as far as the system can tell. Council Tax is paid off every year, no outstanding mortgage. I've got someone back in the office trying to get a search warrant arranged, but'– she shrugged –'I can't help feeling there'll be an unexpected delay.'

'Just long enough for someone else to get there first,' Lapslie said. 'Okay – let's go. We're half way there already. And if we think there's a crime about to be committed, we can go in without a warrant and explain ourselves afterwards.'

They drove off in silence.

The drive to the farmhouse took just over an hour, and Lapslie noticed as he drove that a number of road signs were pointing back towards the forest where Violet Chambers' body had been discovered. Depending on where one was coming from, the road through the forest would be an obvious route to take if you were heading for the house. As, he suspected, the murderer was.

There were two possibilities, as far as Lapslie could see. The first was that the murderer lived in the house and was returning there with the body for some reason. The other was that the murderer didn't live there, but wanted to leave the body there anyway. The third possibility was that the house had nothing to do with the murder of Violet Chambers, but Lapslie didn't want to think about that, partly because he desperately wanted there to be a break in the case but mostly because he could taste strawberries, even though the radio was off and Emma Bradbury wasn't saying anything. He was in for a surprise, but whether it was going to be pleasant or unpleasant was still uncertain.

Emma's phone rang. After a few seconds of 'Yes,' and 'Uh-huh,' she disconnected the call and turned to Lapslie. 'Surprise,' she said. 'The search warrant's been turned down.'

'Someone's got it in for us,' Lapslie said bitterly.

The last few hundred yards were along a dirt track that showed little sign of ever having been maintained. Hawthorn hedges flashed past on either side. Through gaps in the hawthorn, Lapslie could see fields that had returned to nature: weeds and grasses predominating over whatever had once been planted there. If there was anyone still at the house, they weren't farming any more. If they ever had.

They found the house around a turn in the track. It was set

in the middle of an overgrown grass lawn and was built of red brick, two storeys high, with tall windows and a large portico topped with a pointed wooden roof. The windows were all curtained.

The car stopped in front of the house, on a mossy stone drive through which hardy weeds sprouted. Lapslie approached the portico. Two steps led up to the front door, vertical cracks running through the stone like frozen trickles of black water. Emma Bradbury was just behind him, and she touched his shoulder before he could lift the doorknocker.

'Boss,' she said, 'look over there.'

He followed the direction she was pointing. Off to one side of the house, shielded by a low fence, was a garden. Unlike the drive and the surrounding fields, it appeared to be beautifully kept. Scarlet and mauve flowers burst open against a background of vivid green leaves. Lapslie could see berries of various kinds – red, blue, purple, black – hanging heavily from nodding stems.

'Someone's been here,' Emma warned. 'That garden has been maintained, and recently.'

'Okay, let's get on with it.'

The door had been painted green at some time in the past, but sunlight and rain had faded it to the point where it was difficult to make out what shade it might originally have been. The wood of the door frame was crumbling along its sharp edges. A window, a few feet to the right of the door, was white with cobwebs, both inside and out. One of the panes of glass was cracked.

He knocked once, twice; the echoes rolling thunderously through the house in search of anyone who might answer. There was no movement, no sound, nothing. Lapslie knocked again. The sounds joined the previous set of echoes, bouncing back and forth, rolling from room to room and from downstairs to upstairs and back. Still nothing.

Stepping back, Lapslie twisted his body and swung a foot up

at the door, his heel hitting it a foot or so below the lock. The wooden door frame splintered. He kicked again, and the door flew open, knocking a pile of letters against the wall. They scattered like snow.

'Police!' he called. 'Come out where we can see you!'

No movement, and no sound. Together, Lapslie and Bradbury entered the house.

An old, dead smell hung in the air, and Lapslie had to fight the urge to brush it aside as he moved. The hall was dark; a faded carpet running its length. Various doors led off the hall. They were all shut.

He approached the closest room – the one whose window he had noticed to the right of the front door – and pushed it open. It whispered against carpet as it swung back. The smell of something deeply unpleasant suddenly intensified.

Light from the cobwebbed window filtered into the room, illuminating a long dining table set for dinner. Fine porcelain tea cups were placed at every setting. A matching tea pot sat in the centre.

Twelve people sat quietly at the table. They didn't react to Lapslie's entrance: no turning heads, no expressions of surprise, nothing.

'Police,' Lapslie repeated. 'DCI Lapslie. Who owns this house?'

Nobody moved.

Emma Bradbury strode across to the window and opened the curtains. Light flooded in.

Lapslie took a step back. Emma gasped. 'Oh good Christ,' she said flatly.

The twelve people sat around the table were all women, and they were all dead. They had been placed in order of death. The body closest to Emma was the freshest, but even so, its raddled flesh had sagged away from the bones, bloated and fly-blown, green and purple and grey. Her eyelids had shrivelled back against empty sockets. The body closest to Lapslie was the oldest: no more than a skeleton whose flesh had gradually desiccated. All of them were ruined things that once may have been beautiful.

'What the hell are we dealing with?' Emma whispered.

' "Why this *is* Hell," ' Lapslie murmured softly, ' "nor are we out of it." '

CHAPTER THIRTEEN

That night, her ceiling dappled with moonlight reflected off the sea, Daisy lay awake. Her sheets were clammy beneath her, and she could feel every fold in the cotton against her old, wrinkled skin. No matter what position she curled into, she could not find that elusive door to sleep.

It was the newspaper report that was bothering her. The report of the discovery of Violet Chambers' body. The first mistake she had ever made, and it was going to come back to haunt her. She knew it would.

And in her mind, the wet *smack* of the branch as it hit Violet's head, caving the bone in. The blood, matting the grey hair. The long gasp as she exhaled her last breath.

And as she relived the memories, as she went back to the time before the branch hit Violet's skull, when she was driving along that country road with Violet Chambers slumped in the passenger seat, she slipped slowly and inadvertently into the long dark tunnel of sleep and the memories turned surreptitiously into dreams.

The sun shining through the leaves made patterns like black lace on the road. She maintained a steady forty-five miles an hour in her Volvo – not fast enough to attract anyone's attention; not slow enough to annoy people sufficiently that they would remember her, and the car, for more than the few moments that it took for them to overtake her.

She had carefully manoeuvred Violet's dead body into the car before dawn that morning, using the wheelchair she had brought in specifically for that purpose. Fortunately the driveway led all the way up to the front door, so she didn't have to wheel the body down to the road, as she occasionally had before. The tricky bit, as always, had been the moment when she had to slide the body from the wheelchair into the passenger seat, but the arm on the wheelchair folded down and the application of a little strength, and the passing of a noisy refuse lorry, had made the job easier.

A tartan blanket over Violet's lap completed the illusion that she was merely asleep. Her eyes were closed, and a little tape laid sticky side out across her gums ensured that her mouth wouldn't gape open at an inopportune moment, such as when they were parked at traffic lights. A thin length of white cotton hidden in the folds of her neck and knotted behind the head rest stopped her head from lolling in an ungainly fashion onto her chest. All in all, Daisy thought as she gazed sideways at Violet from the driver's seat, she looked better now than she had in real life. She certainly didn't look like someone who had ingested a fatal dose of meadow saffron only twelve hours before.

Half an hour after eating the cake into which Daisy had carefully grated several meadow saffron roots, Violet had suffered a series of convulsions while she was sitting in the back garden. Daisy had watched with pleasure as white foam had trickled from Violet's mouth and her lips and skin turned blue. Sweat trickled along the prominent folds in her skin that gave her such a disapproving look all the time. Her hands clutched at the arms of her deck chair, locking on with such force that Daisy had to later use a kitchen knife to prise them off. And then, after a sudden and violent arching of the back, she had subsided, head slumped forward and eyes hooded, breathing her last, few, shallow breaths.

'Of all the women I have ever poisoned,' Daisy had said to her, 'you have been the most arrogant, the most insensitive and the most stand-offish. You seem to believe that you can look down at everyone else because your father had a big house and didn't have to work for a living. In fact, you are a sad, deluded old woman who is dying alone and unmourned. Nobody will know, or care, that you have gone.'

Perhaps her eyelids flickered. Daisy would never know for sure, but she liked to believe that Violet had heard that last valediction, and seen the essential truth in it, before she died. Befriending Violet had been one of the most difficult jobs Daisy had ever done – although she was calling herself Annie then. Annie Moberley. Violet had been suspicious, and it was only because Daisy – Annie – hated to break off half way through that she had persevered. She had first met Violet in the local supermarket, where it was obvious that Violet was shopping for one, and wasn't buying the cheapest cuts of meat and the 'reduced items' that pensioners, in Annie's experience, usually selected. They got chatting on the third or fourth occasion that they bumped into each other, and soon she was popping around for coffee. Soon after that, she was collecting Violet's prescriptions for anti-inflammatories from the local surgery.

Violet had been an odd mix. She desperately wanted some human contact, but at the same time she wanted to be able to look down on whoever she was with. For Annie, who automatically looked down on all her victims, the next few months had been amongst the most tiring she could recall, as the two of them vied for dominance without Violet ever consciously realising that a battle was going on.

In the hours that Annie spent driving Violet's body through the early morning she daydreamed about the next few months; of how she was going to progressively strip the house of any expensive items it contained, and raid Violet's building society account of whatever money it contained. And, from small clues that Violet had let slip, she suspected it contained rather a lot. She would take on Violet's identity, like slipping on an old overcoat, letting her current one fall away, and become lost in the past. And then, when she grew tired, she would move on, looking for another victim. Although perhaps one less supercilious this time. Annie had felt for a while that Violet was treating her more as an unpaid companion than a friend, and towards the end more as an unpaid servant than a companion.

The car slipped through forests and past industrial estates as the darkness gave way to daylight. After some unquantifiable time, Annie knew that she was nearing her destination: the place where all of her friends eventually came to visit, and did not leave.

A sudden *bang* from beneath the car startled Annie from her dreams. The steering wheel jerked in her hands, and the car began to drag itself towards the trees just as they were coming up to a bend. Panicking, she slammed her foot on the brakes, and the Volvo slewed violently to a halt, half on the road and half on the grassy verge.

Annie turned the ignition key with a shaking hand. The engine died away. Silence filled the forest.

Eventually, when she could breathe again, when the fluttering of the blood in her neck and her temples had faded, she got out of the car. The front tyre on the side where Violet was sitting was deflated and forlorn, appearing half-melted on the road. She felt panic wash through her. What did one do with a flat tyre? She supposed one had to change it, but how was she supposed to get it off? And where was the spare tyre kept? Was there even a spare tyre in the car? Any tools?

She looked along the road ahead of the car, as it bent to the right, and then back along the direction she had come. There was nobody in sight. No other cars; no other people. She was alone.

What to do? Annie slumped against the side of the car, hearing the clicking and ticking of the engine as the hot metal cooled. Nothing like this had ever happened to her before. So near to her goal, the safe refuge where all her friends sat waiting.

In part of her mind Annie knew that she could walk for help, but she couldn't remember seeing any houses for the last few miles she had driven, and she had no idea how far ahead the next set of houses might be. She was old and tired: she could hardly make more than a few hundred yards before she would have to take a rest. The next best thing would be to flag someone down, but that could take all morning. And whether she went for help or waited there for it to arrive, the people who helped her would see Violet sitting in the passenger seat. They would ask if she was all right. They might offer her a drink of water. And they would realise, sooner rather than later, that she was dead.

And then it would all start to unravel. Every carefully woven thread of Annie's life.

Whatever she did, she would have to get rid of Violet's body first. For a moment she wondered whether she could manhandle the body into the boot of the car, but she rejected that thought. The spare tyre was probably somewhere in there, and if not the spare tyre then probably some tools or something else that would be needed. No, the boot was too much of a risk. She would have to get the body into the woods somehow, perhaps bury it beneath some bracken, and then come back later to collect it. And all that without making herself look as if she had been dragged through a hedge backwards.

Annie nodded to herself. Hide the body, flag someone down, get them to change the tyre for her, then, when they had gone, retrieve the body and continue on her way. It was a plan.

She pushed herself away from the car and walked around the bonnet. The open passenger door registered in her mind for a good few seconds before she realised the significance of what it meant. Then she noticed the empty passenger seat.

Violet's body had gone. *Violet* had gone.

Annie looked wildly around. She was still alone. For a long moment she was convinced that she had left Violet's body back at the house and somehow imagined that it had been sitting beside her for the past few hours; then she was sure that someone had come and taken the body from the car while she was distracted. It took a few moments before the truth sank in. Her cake had been a failure. Violet had still been alive when

Annie put her in the car, albeit in something so close to a coma that Annie had been fooled into thinking she was dead. Somehow she had come back to consciousness, and escaped. Did she realise what had happened to her, or was she operating on instinct, just heading somewhere, anywhere, away from the unfamiliar confines of Annie's Volvo?

Did it matter? Annie had to find her again. Find her, and kill her for sure.

And whatever happened, she was never using meadow saffron again.

A faint trail of bent grass led away from the car and into the dank green depths of the forest. Annie checked the road, forward and back, once more, just in case someone was approaching. The road was clear. She set off in pursuit of Violet.

The floor of the forest was covered in twigs and low shrubs which Annie couldn't identify. The occasional fallen tree made barriers she had to manoeuvre around, but crushed flowers and disturbed patches of ground indicated to her where Violet had scrambled her way across the ground. Buttery light slanted down through the tops of the trees, and everywhere was hushed. Annie could hear her own footsteps shushing through the leaves, sounding almost as if she were making her way through thick snow. She could smell the deep, intoxicating scent of old wood and foliage, the world's oldest and most profound perfume. The occasional insect buzzed past her, and a sudden flurry of activity in a bush showed where a small animal had suddenly heard her approach and made its escape.

She wasn't looking for small animals. Her prey was much larger.

Annie stopped in a small clearing, listening. Somewhere across the other side she could hear a crashing sound, as if something was pushing its way heedless through bushes and shrubs.

Her breath was rasping in her throat now, and her legs were weak, but she kept on going. Low branches reached for her face, while roots clutched desperately at her ankles, trying to trip her up. Every so often she reached out to steady herself on a tree trunk, but the rough bark burned the palms of her hands.

Through a gap in the trees she caught sight of a flash of artificial colour, stark against the natural greens and browns of the forest. A bright red: the same colour as the cardigan that Violet had been wearing when Annie thought she killed her. And when she came back to life again. Annie slowed down, taking her time as she approached, shielding herself behind a large bush.

Violet was bent on all fours by a large oak tree. A string of saliva dropped from her mouth. She was panting: a harsh, almost mechanical sound. The skin on her hands and knees was muddy with dirt and blood from the numerous small scratches she had sustained as she fled. But now she was here; out of breath, out of time, out of options.

Annie crouched and picked up a fallen branch from the forest floor. She hefted it in her hand: it felt almost industrial in its density, like a crowbar, or a tyre iron. Her hand fitted perfectly around it, and for a moment she wondered why she kept going back to poison when physical violence could be so seductive. And then she envisaged the dining room table, and the silent faces around it, and she remembered.

Violet reached out a hand towards the oak tree, supporting her weight so she could stand. Concerned that she might try to get away again, Annie took a step forward from behind the bush.

She must have made a noise, because Violet turned her head and caught her in a wild-eyed stare. Her teeth were bared wildly.

Annie took another step, and swung the branch loosely by her side, ready to use it.

'Why...?' Violet mouthed, her eyes seeming to lose focus and then regain it again. 'Why did you *do* this?'

'Because I could,' Annie said. 'Because I have before and will again. Because it gets me what I want. And, above all else, because I just got tired of your constant complaining, your continual sneering at your neighbours, your old friends and me.'

She took two steps forward and raised the branch up above her.

Violet turned away, ready to scuttle to safety, but Annie brought the branch crashing down on the back of her head. She didn't know what she expected – a dramatic gout of blood perhaps, the skull crumbling beneath the branch like a snail stepped on in the garden, revealing the soft, grey, oozing flesh within, but there was none of that. Violet's head merely changed shape, a depression appearing beneath the sparse grey hair. Annie was reminded of the duck eggs she had eaten as a child, boiled hard, their shells crushed in by a spoon. And Violet slumped gracelessly to the floor of the forest with a soft sigh, the air leaving her lungs for the last time, free of that old body forever.

Annie sat down beside her for a moment and rested, letting the muted sounds of the forest – the soft susurration of the wind in the leaves and the calls of the birds – drain the tension and the tiredness from her bones. After a while, she reached across and checked Violet's pulse, both in her stick-thin wrist and also in the leathery wattles of her neck, but there was nothing. The blood was still within those prominent purple veins.

Annie walked unsteadily back to the car, partly to retrieve the plastic sheet that she had brought with her from the house – the one she had laid Violet's body on when she cleaned it – and partly to check whether anyone had stopped for the car. The road was clear, and might have been that way ever since her burst tyre had occurred. She popped the boot of the car, and pulled out the grey plastic sheet, then paused. What was she going to do? Walk back into the forest, wrap Violet's body up and bury it as best she could? But the ground was hard, and difficult to dig without a shovel, and if she wanted to come back later to retrieve the body, how would she find it? At least the corner where she had stopped was reasonably memorable. Perhaps she could pull Violet's body most of the way back and bury her just off the road. That way, locating her again would be easier. It also meant that she would be able to hear if someone stopped to help her.

Looking around, Annie saw a rotted tree trunk, lying half-buried in the soil, victim of some long-passed storm. Walking over to it, she reached out and gave one of the branches an experimental tug. The trunk rolled over slightly, revealing moist ground, depressed where the trunk had lain, and pale white shoots beneath. She thought for a moment. If she could move this trunk out of the way then it would leave behind something similar to a half-dug grave. She could wrap Violet's body in the plastic sheet, drag it back, lay it in the grave, then cover it over with leaves and earth. It would do, until she could come back again for it. It would do.

It took her ten minutes to move the rotten trunk out of the way and make it look as if it had always been where she put it. Rolling Violet's body in the sheet, dragging her back to the side of the road and laying her in the scar took another five, as did the task of kicking twigs and loam and leaves over the top of the sheet.

Half way through, when the plastic-wrapped corpse was lying in the depression in the forest floor, but before she could cover it over, Annie heard the sound of a car engine, far away. She stopped. Of all the times to be offered help, this was the worst. Quickly she stepped back into the darkness of the forest. The car drew closer. She glanced out at her Volvo, checking that the doors were closed and the emergency lights were not flashing. Reassured, she moved further back into the forest, trying to become as one with the trees. The sound of the car engine changed as it approached the bend. For a moment she was terrified that it was about to stop, that the driver had seen her car and was going to park and see if anyone needed help, but whoever was in the car was just changing down gears as they approached the bend. The car swept past, the driver just a blurred figure, then the engine noise changed again and the car accelerated away.

When she was sure that Violet's body was completely covered, Annie stepped back to examine her handiwork. Apart from a bump in the forest floor, no different from so many others she could see around her, there was no sign that a human being rested there.

Annie returned to her car and sat quietly in the driver's seat, letting the world pass her by. She kept casting glances over at the mound where Violet lay, half wondering whether she might see the ground move slightly, or a hand push itself out of the earth like a fat pink spider, but there was nothing. Nothing at all.

After a while she reached out and switched on the emergency lights. The clicking seemed incredibly loud to her, after so long sitting in the quiet. Perhaps someone would stop for her now.

Rooting around in her handbag, she brought out a mobile phone. She had bought it some years back from a branch of W. H. Smith in Brent Cross, having carefully established from the sales assistant that it worked on a 'pre-pay' basis, and she could charge it up with credit at most supermarkets or petrol stations. She had forgotten which of her many identities had bought it, but as far as she knew there was no way it could be traced back to her. And she only used it sparingly.

She dialled a number for Directory Inquiries.

'Good morning,' Annie – Violet – said primly, 'I would like a garage somewhere near the Thetford Forest. I've broken down, you see.'

'I have three garages nearby,' the voice on the other end of the phone said, 'or I could put you through to the AA or the RAC.'

'Could you put me through to the first local garage you have?' Violet said.

Within a minute she had talked to a mechanic, told him where she was, told him what had happened and arranged for him to come and get her back on the road.

The mechanic turned up half an hour later in a big truck. He was a rather common man, of the kind that Violet had always preferred not to deal with, and he kept up a constant stream of chatter whilst he changed her tyre for her. Noticing the dirt on her hands, he asked her jokingly what she'd been doing. 'I fell over,' she said sharply.

She paid by cheque – using the chequebook and cheque card that she had found in the handbag, of course, and signing with Violet Chambers' rather flowery signature. He waited until she had got in her car and driven off, just to check that the tyre held up, and she had to decide whether to keep on going to where she had originally been heading – her special place, where all her friends waited for her – or to start the long drive back. She wasn't going to disinter the body – the nameless body, as she was already thinking of it – while the mechanic was watching her, and she didn't want to drive off, turn around, come back and do it all then. And without the body there was precious little point in heading to her special place. Reluctantly, she decided to go home. She could always come back another time for the body.

The journey took several hours, and although the tyre held up perfectly she was exhausted when she got back to the house. Violet's house. *Her* house. She toasted some bread, ate it without butter or margarine, and went to bed. She was asleep within moments, and her last thought was that the body was spoiled now. Broken. It would not fit with the others at the tea party. She would leave it where it was.

And as the night moved on, and the shadows crawled across the ceiling, Violet slept.

And Daisy woke up.

The smell of the seaside drifted in through her window: salt, candy floss and decay. The flat tyre, the burial in the forest, the drive back to Violet's house – that had all happened nearly a year ago now. She had been Violet for nine months, while she found and befriended Daisy Wilson. Now she was Daisy Wilson. Soon she would be Eunice Coleman.

And there would be more people than ever at the tea party.

CHAPTER FOURTEEN

After four hours in the house, Mark Lapslie couldn't take any more. He walked outside, legs feeling as weak as if he'd run a cross-country race. He couldn't even think straight. Those faces – those ruined, rotted faces – would haunt his thoughts forever.

Four local police cars and a CSI van were parked outside the farmhouse. The van didn't belong to Sean Burrows' team; they were still working on the Volvo. Lapslie had, however, rung Burrows on his mobile to tell him that it wasn't just one murder they were working on now but thirteen, and the Volvo was now the most important evidence they had, as it may well have been used to move the bodies from wherever they had been killed to where they had been fated to spend the rest of their time.

Looking back up at the red brick of the farmhouse, he could see a resemblance to a skull that he hadn't remarked on before. The upper windows were like dark, vacant sockets; the portico was the hollow nasal passage; the cracked steps were the top and bottom rows of teeth; and the crumbling brickwork was the bone itself, worn down by the passing of the years. It was pure fancy, of course – after four hours in that house, with the twelve bodies sat around the table, frozen into their perpetual tea party, everything he saw was going to remind him of skulls, skeletons and dry, rotting flesh.

Emma Bradbury was resting on the bonnet of his car, one booted foot up on the front bumper. She was smoking a cigarette.

'If I did that to your car,' he said, 'you'd deck me.'

'Sorry, boss.' She straightened up and threw her cigarette on the ground, stubbing it out with her toe. 'It's just –'

'Yeah. I know.'

The wind was cool on his face after the stuffiness of the house, and he breathed deeply, taking it into his lungs and flushing as much of the moribund air of the house as he could. That air had been laden with particles that had drifted from the corpses as they slowly slumped into deliquescence. Knowing that something of them remained within his mouth, his nose, his lungs, that it coated his suit as well, made Lapslie feel soiled.

'I need a shower,' Emma said, mirroring his thoughts.

'I feel the same way, but we've got to stay here and focus the investigation. The entire house needs to be examined. We're going to need to pull Sean Burrows' team in to cover it once they've finished with the Volvo. And frankly I don't see Jane Catherall managing all those autopsies this side of Christmas. She's going to need extra help.'

Emma turned to look at the house. 'I still can't believe it,' she said. 'From the outside there's no sign of what we found. With crack houses, or brothels, there's something about the outside that gives them away, if you know what you're looking for, but this … You'd expect something that looked like a haunted house, all leaning sideways with stuff growing up the walls, but this place just looks old. It looks like my gran's place.'

'Still waters run deep,' Lapslie said, looking back at the house. Somehow the fresh air and the sunshine had blown away that resemblance to a skull that he had noticed. It was just a house again. Just an ordinary farmhouse.

'They're going to be like Violet Chambers, aren't they?' Emma asked. 'When we discover their identities we're going to find that they're not listed as being missing. As far as Social Services, and the Inland Revenue, and the Department of Health and everyone else is concerned, they're not dead. Somewhere in England, they're still walking around, claiming benefits and taking the income from whatever properties they own. Someone out there is pretending to be them.'

'They're just puppets,' Lapslie agreed. 'Manipulated by their murderer. But isn't that the cleverest thing of all? If the thing that trips most murderers up is disposing of the body, then why increase the risk by scattering your bodies around? Why not keep them all together, somewhere isolated, where nobody will ever go, and then make sure that they won't be looked for by keeping their identities alive? Like Violet Chambers, I guarantee they'll all have no families and no close friends. They'll have been living solitary lives, alone and unremarked, until someone came along. Someone who befriended them and wriggled into their lives, then killed them and took on their identities.' He shook his head. 'So many identities, and whoever it is has to keep them all alive, because the income is still coming in. The pensions, the rents, the investments – everything. So much to juggle.'

'Where do we start?' Emma said simply.

Lapslie thought for a while. 'The Volvo will be a bust,' he said eventually. 'It led us here, and there may be evidence inside it linking it to some of the bodies, but it's still listed as being owned by Violet Chambers. I think our murderer just adopted it. Spoils of war. They probably do this with every victim: strip them of what's useful, then sell the rest. Unless there's some trace of the murderer in the car – and I think they're too clever for that – then it's a dead end.'

'The house?' Emma said, indicating it with her head.

'Similar. It will belong to one of those corpses. Probably the one that's been there the longest. What was the name – Rhona McIntyre? She'll be the one at the head of the table. The mortgage is paid off on the house, and our murderer makes sure the Council Tax is paid every year. Flawless.'

'Can't we trace the payment on the Council Tax?'

Lapslie shrugged. 'We can and we will, but I guarantee it'll have been paid from the account of one of the other women around that table. It's an unbreakable circle. The murderer is using each of the accounts to pay bills on the other ones, and taking cash out when she needs it. She never pays for anything herself. There's no trail back to her.'

'Are you sure they're all women, boss? Some of those bodies are so decayed it's difficult to tell from just looking at them.'

'So far it's all to do with women: Violet Chambers, Rhona McIntyre, the woman who was seen leaving Violet's house, the more identifiable of those bodies.' He sighed. 'Don't you feel it? The poison, the precision, the planning ... and the choice of victims ... I guarantee the murderer's a woman as well.'

Emma gazed around. 'So what now?'

'Now we leave the CSIs to do their stuff here. I'll make some calls and arrange to get as many spare pathologists drafted in to help as we can.' He frowned. 'What *is* the collective noun for a group of pathologists, I wonder? We can't call them "a murder of pathologists". That's already been taken for crows. "An incision of pathologists"?' He shook his head. 'Never mind. I want you to check into the background of this house. Find out when Rhona McIntyre was last seen, what her background was, what happened to her and especially whether anyone else was seen with her just before she was last seen. Talk to anyone who lives nearby. Go into the nearest village and talk to the publicans. Local stores. Anyone. Just get me some background on Rhona McIntyre.'

'And when I've finished with that, some time next week?'

'Then you can have a rest.'

Emma looked around. 'I haven't got a car.'

'Get one of the local constables to drive you around. It'll make them feel useful, and who knows? They may have some information about the house, or the owner.'

'Actually,' she said, 'I've got a friend in the area. I'll give him a ring.'

Emma walked off, pulling her mobile from her pocket, and Lapslie just stood there for a while, looking away from the house. It was located in a valley: the ground rose gradually up, dark and imposing, on two sides, making the place feel claustrophobic. Behind him was the dirt track he had driven in on, and in front of him was ... the garden.

He walked over to the gap in the fence that gave access. The fence was well maintained, compared to the rest of the farm, and the plants, as far as he could see, weren't anywhere near as overgrown as the fields he had passed on the way. It looked as if whoever was visiting the house wasn't just planting corpses.

He walked through the gate, and it was as if he had walked through some kind of invisible curtain. The scents of the plants hit him like a rich and heady perfume. He felt giddy, but he breathed it in gladly, replacing the stench of old, dead flesh with the mixed aroma of pennyroyal, delphiniums, foxglove, corn cockle and countless others that he remembered from childhood, or from Sonia's attempts at growing borders in their back garden. Hydrangea and hyacinth, rhododendron and tansy: the garden was a riot of smells and colours. There were shrubs and trees as well: yew and peach, privet and eucalyptus. Small blue flowers hung beside large red ones, bell-shaped yellow flowers drooped over flat pink ones. It was chaos, and yet Lapslie could almost see some kind of plan to it. There was logic there, but not the kind of logic he could understand. Or wanted to.

He stood for a moment with his eyes closed, letting the scents rather than the sights guide him. For him it was the aromatic equivalent of standing in the middle of a factory, with the clashing of machines, and the shouting, and the tannoys and whatever else causing his olfactory senses to overload with synaesthesic signals. If he turned his head he could almost make out a pattern. The plants to the right of the gate were more floral; the plants to the left spicier, earthier, richer in tone. Ahead of him were more medicinal scents. It wasn't a random selection: these plants had been carefully chosen to tell some kind of story.

He opened his eyes and looked around. Selecting a low bush, he knelt and examined it. Some of the lower branches had been pruned back: the marks of the shears were still visible. The roots of the plants had been bedded in compost as well.

Yes, the garden was maintained, looked after on a regular basis.

On a whim, he walked along the rows. When Dr Catherall had mentioned that Violet Chambers had been poisoned with colchicine, which was derived from a plant known as the meadow saffron, he had looked it up in a gardening book that Sonia had left behind when she moved out. A single stem splitting into three or four foot-long leaves that canted up at a sharp angle. Pink or white or purple flowers appearing in autumn. All parts of the plant poisonous. And there it was, nestled between two plants he couldn't identify: a whole row of meadow saffron.

He looked around with fresh eyes, and a cold feeling in his stomach. Twelve dead bodies in the house, plus one found in the woods, and at least one poisoning. Was it too much to suspect that they had *all* been poisoned? And what were the odds that they had all been poisoned with toxins extracted from plants in this garden?

What the hell was he up against here? What kind of person could take it upon themselves to cultivate an entire garden of poisonous plants? It had yet to be proved, of course, but Lapslie knew he was right.

' "The strongest poison ever known, came from Caesar's laurel crown",' he quoted softly, and shook his head.

Emerging from the garden and heading towards his car, he noticed that the vans had arrived to take the bodies away to the pathology lab. One of the bodies was being carried down the steps of the house as he watched, swathed in green polythene sheeting. Presumably it was so fragile that trying to get it into a body bag would have risked breaking it in half.

A red Jaguar was just pulling away from the house. From his position Lapslie could see Emma Bradbury in the passenger seat, but he couldn't make out the driver's face. Maybe it was whoever she'd had in her car when they'd first found Violet Chambers' body in the forest.

Lapslie followed the pathology van along winding country

roads until it joined the B101. Within half an hour they were on the motorway, heading for Jane Catherall's mortuary. The van drove sedately: not as slow as a funeral procession, but not pushing the speed limit either. It was as if the driver was acknowledging, even in passing, that death could not be hurried. Or perhaps he was frightened that the bodies might disintegrate if he hit a bump too fast.

Lapslie kept pace with the van for its entire journey. He could have accelerated past it and got to the mortuary with half an hour or more to spare, but it would have accomplished nothing, and he felt, as the driver presumably did, that the corpses in the back of the van deserved some kind of respect. Or an escort, at the very least.

Eventually they were driving along Braintree's familiar streets. Lapslie slowed as the van pulled off the road and into an unremarkable tarmac drive that led around the back of the mortuary. He parked in what he now thought of as his usual place.

Before he could buzz the door, his mobile rang.

'Lapslie.'

'Mr Lapslie! Nice to hear your voice!'

He tasted mustard and vinegar across the back of his tongue. 'McGinley? I was beginning to think you were never going to get back to me.'

He imagined Dom McGinley the way he'd last seen the man: sprawled behind a table in a pub, his stomach pushing his polo shirt out into a smooth curve, a pint of Guinness in front of him, and chuckling.

'You asked a favour, and then did me a favour in return before I could say anything. I owed you one, and I don't like owing people anything. I try and clear my debts as quickly as possible.'

'Very laudable,' Lapslie said. 'So what have you got for me?'

'You were asking about a man named Geherty, at the Department of Justice.'

'Yeah.' Lapslie thought back to the black Lexus that had

turned up in the forest where Violet Chambers' body had been discovered, and again outside his police station. He thought back to the two men who had walked out of Chief Superintendent Rouse's office as he was walking in, and had glanced at him as if they recognised him. And he remembered the way that Jane Catherall's office had been searched, and files copied from her hard disk. 'Yeah,' he repeated, 'I was, wasn't I? What have you found?'

'I put out some feelers, and asked some friends of mine who work for the Department of Justice who he is. It wasn't easy – the bloke keeps his head down, but I eventually struck lucky. He's Assistant Director of the PRU.'

'I knew that. What else have you got?'

'PRU stands for Prisoner Rehabilitation Unit. It's a department that looks after long-term inmates in Her Majesty's prisons who, for whatever reason, need careful rehabilitation into society when they get released.'

'I've never heard of them.'

'I'm not surprised. They're a close-knit bunch. They don't advertise themselves. Myra Hindley was one of theirs, before she died of a chest infection. Apparently they were preparing her for release when she died, despite the number of legal appeals that she'd lost. Ian Huntley's on the list – the bloke who killed those two girls in Soham. So are Ian Brady and Rosemary West. All the jailbirds who keep getting mentioned in the papers are theirs. It's the PRU's job to make sure that when they eventually get out of jail they can reintegrate into society without having the *Sun* or the *Mirror* camped on their doorsteps within ten minutes of them getting out.'

'Lovely,' Lapslie said. 'I wonder if anyone ever leaves school thinking, "I know what I want to do – I want to prepare serial killers for release into a society that hates their guts".'

'Hey, we don't all end up doing what we wanted, you know? I was going to be a car mechanic.'

'I'm touched. I really am. What else did you find out about the PRU?'

'They also spend a year or so before the release training their "customers" up so they know who's Prime Minister and how much a loaf of bread costs. They were the ones who apparently found Maxine Carr a place to live and got her a new identity. And a new boyfriend, from what I hear. You remember her, she was Ian Huntley's girlfriend, but she got out way before he ever will. And Dennis Nilsen – he was the one who killed fifteen male lovers, boiled some of them up and then forced their remains down the drain. He's on their books. He'll be eligible for parole in a year or two: they must be getting him ready now, I would have thought.'

'I hate to say it, McGinley, but you've excelled yourself.'

'Yeah, but does it help?'

Lapslie thought for a moment. 'I can't say it does,' he said.

'Then let me add something else. While I was asking around, I picked up a rumour or two. No corroboration, but it's whispered that Myra Hindley didn't die of a chest infection at all.'

'What, she killed herself? Not much of a story there, McGinley.'

'No, the rumour is that she's still alive, and she was released from prison under a false name. Rumour is that she's living somewhere in Wales, under constant observation. Costs the PRU a shed-load of money, but it was some kind of deal between the Home Secretary and the judiciary. There was no legal reason to keep her in jail any more, but the public outcry if she was released would have been immense.'

'The slate's clear, McGinley. I don't owe you anything and you don't owe me anything. Understand?'

'The ironic thing,' McGinley said, 'is that if things had gone slightly differently, if you had ever got the goods on me, then I might be a customer of the PRU myself.'

'A touching thought, and I suspect the closest thing to a confession I'll ever get.'

'Stay in touch, Mr Lapslie. There's precious few of us left, you know.'

And with that, the mobile went dead.

Lapslie stood for a moment, the mobile still in his hand. He knew more than he had before, but he didn't have a clue what it all meant. If the PRU were involved it meant that his case had something to do with a long-term prisoner who was either about to be released or, more probably, had already been released, but did that mean his murderer was their 'customer'? And if so, why were they allowing her to wander around committing murder?

' "Where is the wisdom we have lost in knowledge?" ' he said softly, quoting T. S. Eliot. ' "Where is the knowledge we have lost in information?" '

Jane Catherall was in the large autopsy room, supervising the placing of the corpses. One was being unwrapped on the furthest metal table. Three more were being lined up on gurneys on the far side of the room.

'How many more of these poor creatures can I expect?' Dr Catherall said, gazing at Lapslie from beneath lowered eyebrows.

'Another two vans' worth is my estimate,' he said. 'Assuming four bodies per vanload.'

'Twelve bodies? Apart from coach crashes and fires in night clubs, I can't think of many circumstances that produce so many bodies in here at the same time, and in both of those instances the cause of death is pretty well established before I start. I am going to have to conduct each autopsy here from first principles.'

'I think I know what you're going to find.'

She raised an eyebrow. 'Please – no clues. It spoils the fun.'

Lapslie looked at the body on the metal table. Unlike poor Violet Chambers, whose body had been wrapped in plastic and had withered and dried rather than decayed, this one was mostly eaten away by bacteria and by bugs, leaving behind a stained skeleton to which leathery flesh still adhered. The eyes had vanished, and the skull was covered by a thin, dry coating of skin that had drawn back from the discoloured teeth, making the corpse look as though it was perpetually screaming.

'Are they all like this?' Dr Catherall asked.

'If you lined them up in the right order,' Lapslie told her, 'you could take a photograph and use it to illustrate the process of decomposition from beginning to end.'

'The deaths occurred at different times then? Over the course of several years, perhaps?' Her faced creased into a smile. 'I'm actually looking forward to this.'

Lapslie looked at her diminutive, twisted frame. 'Can you cope?'

She looked perversely mutinous for a moment. 'I'm going to have to, aren't I?'

Lapslie frowned. 'I tried to get some of the bodies diverted to other mortuaries, but I was told nobody else was available.'

Dr Catherall smiled, and turned away. For the next few hours she examined the arriving bodies, one after the other, with the same concentration and dedication that she had displayed when she examined that of Violet Chambers. Samples from the bodies were placed in plastic jars, sealed into transparent envelopes and sent away for testing. Photographs were taken, sketches made and notes dictated. It all began to feel like a dream to Lapslie as he sat, watching her work; a never-ending, recurring dream in which the same words were spoken, the same incisions made and the same samples taken, with only the state of decomposition of the body changing. There were moments when Lapslie's concentration slipped, or he fell asleep for a while, that made him think that Dr Catherall was carrying out the same long autopsy but that the body on the table was more and more decayed each time he looked.

Eventually she consigned the last body to be taken away, and walked slowly across to Lapslie. She looked exhausted. No, he thought; she actually looked ill.

'I find that my body tires so much quicker than my mind,

these days,' she said, weariness evident in her voice. 'So many autopsies on the trot has not been a pleasant experience.'

'"Ah, but a man's reach should exceed his grasp, or what's a heaven for?"' Lapslie asked.

Dr Catherall smiled through her tiredness. 'Robert Browning. How nice.'

'Is there anything you can tell me?'

'There is much I can tell you, most of which you won't be interested in. The key things you want to hear about are approximate time of death and likely cause of death, and on both of those issues I am sadly bereft of much useful information. The approximate time of death will be plus or minus several months in each case. I will need to make some calculations. What I can tell you, however, is that the deaths were not equally spaced apart.'

He frowned. 'What do you mean?'

'I mean that there appears to be over a year between the times of death of the oldest bodies, but there's only a few months between the times of death of the freshest ones. Your killer, whoever it is, is striking more and more frequently. Whatever their reason is for killing, it's not giving them the same satisfaction now that it used to. They're speeding up.'

'Satisfaction?' Lapslie asked.

Dr Catherall looked up at him. 'Oh yes. You don't kill twelve women over the course of many years in a fit of rage. You do it because you want to. Because it fills some sick need.' She looked back at the bodies. 'The cause of death in each case is not immediately obvious, although I have sent samples away for toxicological testing, for obvious reasons.'

'Obvious reasons?' Lapslie asked.

She looked askance at him. 'You failed to mention it, but these deaths are connected to that of Violet Chambers, are they not?'

'I believe so,' he said. 'What makes you think so?'

'They are all elderly women, for a start, and the lack of a

distinguishing cause of death suggests that poisoning is a possibility worth investigating. And, of course, there's the fingers.'

'The fingers?'

'You didn't see?' Dr Catherall shook her head. 'How careless of you. As with poor Violet Chambers, the fingers on the right hand of each of the victims had been cut off, all the way down to the knuckles.'

CHAPTER FIFTEEN

Daisy spent most of every day for the next five days with Eunice at the Arts and Crafts Centre, helping get the meagre accounts in order, and in all that time she could only remember a handful of people actually coming inside. One of them had been a local artist, thin and grey-haired, clad in black corduroy, hoping to have his wares exhibited by Eunice. He was doomed to disappointment: Eunice held one of his paintings in front of her, turning it this way and that, squinting as if the sunset over seascape that the artist had tried so hard to emulate was actually putting out fierce rays of light.

'Oh no,' she had said. 'Oh no, no, no. These waves are all too similar. Waves should be majestically chaotic. No two alike, you see? And they should blend together indiscernibly. These ones look like you've painted them separately, cut them out and stuck them over one another.' She paused, making a gradual left-hand turn with the painting. 'The framing is quite good though.'

Two of the remaining visitors had been local people who had been sorting through the effects of recently deceased loved ones and found what looked to Daisy like a piece of gimcrack china and a dusty and over-varnished painting. Eunice had surprised Daisy by buying both pieces; one for fifteen pounds, the other for thirty-five. After they had left, clutching their cash, Daisy had quietly asked Eunice what she had seen in the pieces. The replies had surprised her.

Of the china piece, which resembled nothing so much as a seagull with an unnaturally large and removable head, the whole thing coloured with a lurid yellow wash, Eunice had said: 'This is a Martin Brothers bird, I believe. Made around 1901 in Southall. The Martin brothers were well known for their grotesque animals and fish. This base is ebony, if I'm not mistaken.'

'And you intend exhibiting it?'

'No, I intend selling it.' Eunice sniffed. 'At auction, this little piece will fetch over five thousand pounds.'

'And that woman who sold it to you – she had no idea?'

'Caveat emptor works both ways, my dear. If they don't do their research, I cannot be held responsible. Not in law.'

Concerning the painting – a hunting scene with fat horses tottering on matchstick legs across a brook, the whole thing browned and glossy with old varnish – Eunice had told the seller that it was a mass-produced Victorian item of little or no value. When the man had gone, she had placed it reverentially on the counter in front of her and sat, head in hands, gazing at it.

'It's very badly done,' Daisy had said. 'Those horses are exceedingly top-heavy.'

'It was the style of the time,' Eunice had sighed. 'Don't let the varnish deceive you: underneath the surface is something rather surprising. This is an original Henry Alkin. I've seen prints taken from it, but I never thought I would see the original.'

'And you intend selling it at auction?'

'After a while,' Eunice had said dreamily. 'After a while.'

'For how much?'

'In excess of ten thousand pounds, I would imagine.' Eunice had glanced up at Daisy, who had put what she had hoped was a disapproving expression on her face. 'You don't imagine I earn enough from *this* place to make a living, do you?'

The remaining visitors had been holidaymakers, breaking their car journeys for a cup of tea and a slice of cake, or sheltering from the rain when they were out walking. They had spent an hour or so in the barn, looking around in a desultory manner, and then vanished, taking with them a few token postcards and leaving behind a faint smell of damp clothes and cigarette smoke.

And each of the five days that Daisy had spent at the Arts and Crafts Centre had seen her hating Jasper more than the last.

Jasper was Eunice's pride and joy. He was a small, snappy dog of indeterminate breed, and he hated Daisy. He growled at her constantly and followed her around the barn, his overly large black eyes glinting malevolently at her; and he smelled like old washing. His expression seemed to say: 'I know who you are, old woman. You can fool her, but you can't fool me.'

Daisy determined to do away with Jasper as soon as she possibly could. Eunice could wait – Daisy needed to squeeze her of as much information about her past life as possible – but the dog had to go. Regard it as a dry run, she told herself. A chance to test out a poison she had never used before, but had been meaning to for some time.

Every day that week that she had spent at the Arts and Crafts Centre, Daisy had brought in a bag of apricots for her and Eunice to eat. With the excuse of tidying up, she had collected all the apricot stones once the fruit had been eaten and taken them home with her each night, drying them out on her kitchen windowsill. On the fifth evening, using a cheese grater bought on the way home from a small kitchen store in Leyston, she had carefully rasped at the kernel of the stones until she had a pile of grey powder on a piece of kitchen towel. If she was right then the grey powder contained a lethal dose of hydrocyanic acid, but she had never used apricot kernels before, and she was worried that she might have misjudged the dose. Perhaps the apricots needed to have achieved a certain ripeness before the poison could be extracted. Or maybe the kernels needed to be heated first before being grated. Fortunately, Jasper would act as her test case. She could sprinkle a little on his food every day and monitor what his reaction was. And when he died, *if* he died, then all Daisy had to do was to multiply up the amount she had used to take

Eunice's weight into account, and then bake it into a shepherd's pie or something similar. Perhaps an apricot crumble. After all, it seemed a shame to waste the fruit she would be buying.

On the sixth day, Daisy rested. She needed to give some thought to her next steps, but more than that, she needed Eunice to realise how empty her life was when Daisy wasn't there. Using the excuse that she needed to do some work on the designs for the Arts and Crafts Centre leaflets, she stayed at home. But before she left the barn, she turned the ringer volume on Eunice's telephone down to zero. Eunice would be able to make outgoing calls with no problems, but if anyone tried to ring in then Eunice wouldn't be able to hear the phone. It was crude, but it would help to make her feel even more isolated from her few remaining contacts. And after a couple of weeks of Eunice failing to answer her phone, people would stop calling. It was so simple, it was perfect.

The next day, Daisy returned to the barn. Eunice was pathetically glad to see her.

'My dear,' she said, 'you have no idea how boring it is here. I've been going gaga. Thank heavens I've had Jasper to keep me company.'

'Actually,' Daisy said, 'I brought some food in for Jasper. I cooked some chicken yesterday for my dinner, and I thought he might fancy the leftovers. Would that be all right?'

'You are so very thoughtful,' Eunice said. Jasper just eyed her warily from his position by his mistress's side. 'Jasper really appreciates the way you look after him.'

Daisy took her bag into the kitchen area at the back of the barn and put the chicken on a saucer. A translucent jelly had congealed around the pieces, making them glossy and brown. Looking around to check that Eunice wasn't watching, she took a Tupperware container from her bag and, pulling the lid off, sprinkled a teaspoon of the grey powder on top and then mixed it in with the jelly. With luck, Jasper would not suspect a thing.

Returning to the barn, she set the saucer down by the side of the counter. The dog trotted across to sniff at it. He looked up at Daisy, then back at the food. He sniffed again. Bending his head, he snuffled the chunks of meat and jelly and poison up into his wrinkled little mouth.

'There's a good dog,' said Daisy.

At lunchtime, Daisy made a cup of tea. Eunice took a packet of pills from her bag and, as she had done every lunchtime that Daisy had been there, pushed a small blue and red torpedo-shaped pill from its blister pack and popped it in her mouth, swigging it down with a mouthful of tea. The blister pack looked like it was mostly used up.

'I hope you don't mind me asking,' Daisy said, 'but are they vitamin pills?'

'I'm afraid not,' Eunice said. 'Atorvastatin, I think it's called. It lowers cholesterol. Prescription drug, from my doctor.'

'It must be awful, going into town all the time to get new prescriptions.'

'The damn surgery won't let me just phone up and order the tablets,' Eunice said with some bitterness. 'I have to drop the repeat prescription in to them with forty-eight hours' notice. Apparently it's all to do with that doctor who killed hundreds of his patients. The one with the beard and the glasses. Shipwell? Shipston? Can't remember his name. Anyway, it's such a pain.'

'Perhaps I could help,' Daisy said casually, as if she had not been planning this all the time. 'I have to go past the surgery and the chemists when I go home. Would you like me to drop your repeat prescription in and then pick the tablets up when they are ready?'

'I couldn't ask you to do that,' Eunice said.

'It's no trouble. It would make me happy if I could help in any way.'

Eunice gazed at Daisy for a few moments, then rummaged in her bag. 'I'm nearly out,' she said, pulling a green repeat prescription form out and ticking a box with a pen that lay beside the till. 'Would you be a dear, and drop this in for me?'

'Nothing would give me more pleasure,' said Daisy, and she meant it. Another small takeover of Eunice's life had occurred.

Jasper was wandering round the barn in some confusion. He was coughing, as if trying to retch something up, and going around in circles. Daisy made a mental note to double the amount of powder she used the next time she fed him. She wanted a quick reaction when she tried it on Eunice; not a slow, drawn-out death. She'd had enough of those.

'Do you think he's all right?' Eunice asked, gazing at Jasper with some worry. 'He looks like he's swallowed something he shouldn't have.'

'Probably just a hairball,' Daisy said vaguely. 'He'll be all right in the morning.'

Eunice looked sorrowfully at the telephone beside the till. 'It's been very quiet,' she said. 'I can't remember any calls for an age. Should I get the engineers to take a look at the line?'

'Things go up and down,' Daisy said. 'There might be a glut of calls next week. Leave it until then: see what happens.'

'You're a brick,' Eunice said. 'I know I get paranoid sometimes, but you're always there to bring me back to earth. I'm so glad you're here.'

'I'll always be here,' said Daisy. She gazed at the dog, who was still wandering around the barn as if he had lost something. 'This place has become a second home to me. I feel as if I really belong.'

Daisy sipped her tea, and gazed at Eunice. She despised the woman more now than she had when she first met her. The six days the two of them had spent together had been nothing but a long monologue from Eunice concerning her past life, her friends, her lovers, her various accidental pregnancies, which had either ended naturally or been terminated unnaturally, and her relationship with her family. Daisy had volunteered very little information about herself, and Eunice had hardly noticed.

Even when she had asked Daisy a question about where she had lived and what she had done in her life, she invariably ended up talking about herself. The up side of this was that Daisy had quickly gained a solid appreciation of Eunice's life – the names, the dates, the significant moments. The down side was that, of all the women whose lives Daisy had taken over, Eunice's was the one furthest from her own experience. Becoming Eunice was going to take a major effort.

Ah, but when it happened ... when Eunice was dead, and had taken her place in Daisy's tea party ... that would be a moment to savour. Daisy let her mind wander, imagining Eunice's form not as it was now, fleshy and sagging, but sitting proudly at the table with the others, reduced down to its essentials; the skin removed by nature to reveal the purity of what lay beneath. That would be a sight for sore eyes.

A tiny moth of worry began to eat away at the fabric of Daisy's self-confidence. Violet Chambers' body had been found, in its unmarked grave out in the forest. She had been on her way to the tea party with Violet when her tyre had burst. The thing that was bothering her was, did the police have any clever way of tracing her car, and working out where she had been going? She rarely watched television, and never watched crime dramas, but Daisy had some vague understanding that the police had access to all kinds of scientific techniques that hadn't existed in the past. Things that seemed more fantasy than reality. Could they discover her little hideaway, her paradise, her refuge? The thought made her feel uncomfortable. She shivered and scratched herself.

'Are you okay?' Eunice asked. 'If you're not feeling well, you should go home. I don't want to catch anything!'

Forthright to the point of rudeness, that was Eunice. 'I suddenly felt as if someone had just walked over my grave,' Daisy murmured.

The thought nagged at her for the rest of the afternoon. Policemen, rummaging through everything that she held dear:

the one thing that was constant through all the changing identities and the new homes. Her core. Her centre.

She couldn't remember where the house had originally come from. The identity of the owner was buried back in the mists of Daisy's past – and the owner was, Daisy dimly recalled, still sitting at the head of the dinner table. All she knew was that she had inherited the house from somewhere, and there was no mortgage outstanding on it. For as long as she paid the Council Tax on it – and she visited every month or so in order to pick up the letter from the local Council telling her how much to pay – she had assumed that it would remain safe. Undisturbed. She had deliberately switched the gas and electricity supplier several times, ensuring that the last time she closed the accounts without starting new ones up. That way there would be no reason for a computer glitch, or a gas leak, to start accruing costs on her account and eventually for bailiffs to get called in. That would have been a disaster. In fact, the last few times she had been at the house – the last time being six months before, with the body of the original Daisy Wilson – there had only been a few letters waiting for her. Long periods in which nothing happened at the house seemed to have caused the address to have dropped off even the most tenacious of postal marketing firms. Even the *Reader's Digest* didn't send letters there any more. Only that one occasion when she had, reluctantly, had to arrange for a mechanic to visit to start her Volvo had marred the isolation.

But now ... Daisy couldn't focus her thoughts on the accounts in front of her. The possibility that her guests might be disturbed, might even be *removed,* was making her tense and irritable. Twice she snapped at Jasper as he stopped near her and coughed.

Did she dare make a return visit? That was the question. When Eunice finally succumbed to the apricot kernels – assuming they worked their magic on Jasper first – then Daisy would have to dispose of the body somewhere. She quailed at the idea of just dumping it in a quarry or a wood, or throwing it off the Naze. That was not only clumsy and messy; it was also risky. Bodies disposed of like that were bound to surface, literally or metaphorically. A bad penny always turns up again; that was what they said. No, it was far safer to place bodies in a controlled environment, where the chances of passers-by finding them were so remote as to be discarded. And besides, Daisy had always taken great comfort in the notion that all of her victims – with the exception of poor Violet – were keeping each other company.

Despite her concerns, Daisy didn't want to risk making a visit now. Going to the house to see whether the police had found it was like wandering around with a lighted match looking for a gas leak: the consequences of discovering the worst were likely to be worse still. No, she would wait until Eunice was safely dead, and then make a decision based on what had appeared in the newspapers, and what her intuition was telling her.

'Do you want to go for a walk?' Eunice asked. 'Get some fresh air? You're looking a bit peaky.'

'That would be nice,' Daisy said. She had got about as far with the accounts as it was possible to go; not only sorting out for Eunice where all her money was going but also ensuring that Daisy herself had a list of account numbers and knew where all the relevant paperwork was kept. She would need that knowledge later.

'Jasper!' Eunice called. 'Come on, you slugabed. Walkies!'

Jasper had retired to a corner of the barn where, at some stage in the past, a tartan blanket had been thrown down for him. Now it was matted and twisted into a mirror image of his shape, and he was nestled into it, tongue hanging out, panting for breath.

'He's looking a bit peaky too,' Eunice said, concerned. 'I hope he's not coming down with something. He's quite deli- cate, you know. Quite artistic, in his personality.'

'I'm sure it's nothing,' Daisy said reassuringly. She thought she could see a trace of blue around the inside of the dog's mouth as it panted. Perhaps she had overestimated the amount of grated apricot kernel necessary to kill an elderly dog, in which case she probably had enough left to kill Eunice several times over. 'He's probably tired out from rushing around.' As if Jasper ever did anything as undignified as rushing around. 'We should leave him here and check on him later.'

Together they set out, walking first along the lane towards the road where the bus dropped Daisy off every morning and picked her up every night, and then striking out along an established track that ran between fields. The sky was bright blue, and what little cloud existed was being pulled in different directions, combining and drifting apart as it moved. Daisy could smell the pungent aroma of the flowers that lined the fields on either side of them; bright gold, spindly, and nodding in the same faint breeze that pushed the clouds around.

Eunice strode ahead, swinging a walking stick manfully. Daisy found it a chore to keep up, but the exercise cleared her mind of her worries concerning the house.

'I know all the walks around here,' Eunice confided over her shoulder. 'Some of them have remained unchanged for centuries, perhaps millennia. They say that some of these tracks follow the paths of ley lines, you know? One can imagine Roman soldiers walking across these very fields. Or Druids, perhaps.'

Daisy was spending more time imagining Eunice twisted in agony and turning blue as the hydrocyanic acid burned its way through her body, but she merely said, 'Yes, indeed,' as they walked. Her shoes weren't really ideal for this kind of thing.

They were walking up a slight incline, and at the top Eunice stopped and gazed, entranced, ahead. Daisy struggled to catch up. When she too crested the ridge at the top of the incline, she felt what little breath she had catch in her throat.

Ahead of them lay a church. An old church, made of grey stone, with a squat tower in its middle and an older structure, made of wood, attached to the end furthest from the large double doors that gave entry to the inside. It sat in the midst of a graveyard, separated from the surrounding fields by a dry-stone wall. A track led away towards some distant buildings.

'St Alkmund's Church,' Eunice said. 'No vicar, not since the 1970s. There's a padre who cycles round every four weeks, as part of a rota of local old churches without their own vicars, but the attendance is small and it's going down as people die off. Lovely architecture, though. Mainly Norman influence. Be a shame to lose it. Look at that wooden hut thing on the end: I remember reading somewhere that it dates from a previous church on the same site. Anglo-Saxon. Built without nails. Held together with wooden pegs, apparently. Let's go closer.'

'I'd rather not,' Daisy said, but Eunice was striding off ahead.

Daisy glanced again at the church. Something about the way it squatted, alone but unrepentant, in the middle of the fields made her uneasy. It was as if it had been waiting for her. Waiting all these years for her to return, with dark thoughts mouldering in its heart.

Eunice had reached the dry-stone wall now, and was walking around to the lych gate entrance. Daisy followed, knowing that something was not right.

The graveyard was long overgrown with weeds and flowers. The gravestones had been eroded by the salt air and colonised by moss to the point where they were almost as rounded as boulders. Whatever writing had been carved onto them was nothing but depressions in the granite, like memories that had faded until there was nothing left but the faint recollection that something had once been there and was now lost forever.

Eunice ran her hands across a gravestone that was tilting at an angle. 'Imagine,' she said, 'the history of this place. The way it has stayed the same while everything around it – the countryside, the country, the world – has changed.'

But Daisy wasn't listening. Around the corner of the church

she had spotted a gravestone that had been set flat in the ground. She walked closer, feet unwilling to move but unable to stop. Protected, perhaps, by the bulk of the church, the letters carved into the slab were almost readable.

Madeline Poel, it said, but that was impossible.

Because before she had been Daisy Wilson, before she had been Violet Chambers, before she had been anyone, she knew that she had been Madeline Poel.

CHAPTER SIXTEEN

Find one old lady dead, Mark Lapslie thought sourly, and you get a desk and a Detective Sergeant; find thirteen of them and you get an entire incident room and so many staff it's hard to remember their names. Even the DCS hadn't been able to stop the investigation from ramping up, although the rumour was that he had tried several times. Apparently Rouse had attempted to claim that until the deaths were attributable to foul play then he couldn't approve a murder investigation, but the fact that the Volvo 740 could now be used to link the corpse in the forest – which had undoubtedly been murdered – with the ones in the farmhouse meant that his objections were half-hearted and easily overcome by someone who still had a few friends at Scotland Yard.

Half of the room in the Chelmsford HQ was filled with desks, each loaded up with its own telephone and computer, each telephone connected to a headset with attached microphone, each computer networked into the police system. The other half was dominated by two Perspex boards. The first one had photographs of the victims blu-tacked all over it, along with notes written in wipeable pen. On any normal incident board there would be lines drawn between the photographs indicating connections: unbroken lines for the known connections and dotted lines for the ones where there was an indication but no corroborating evidence. On this board, there were no lines. Despite all of the constables manning the phones and the computers, nobody had yet established a connection between any of the victims. None of them had been to school together, none of them had lived in the same towns or villages, none of them had shared the same hobbies or subscribed to the same magazines. The only things they had in common were their sex – they were all female – their age – they were all over sixty – and their general geographical location – they all lived in the South or West of England. And, of course, the fact that they had all been murdered and mutilated.

Lapslie stood by the victims board, ignoring the flood of rust and salt and coconut that filled his mouth each time he came into the incident room and heard the chatter of people talking on telephones, talking to each other and typing away at keyboards. He kept shoving breath fresheners under his tongue to cover the mélange of tastes, but it didn't work. The problem was psychological, not physical. He tried to spend as much time as he could in the Quiet Room, but he had to show his face to his staff, listen to their problems, brief them on new aspects of the case and generally be there as a figurehead. Emma Bradbury was doing the best she could to take the pressure off his shoulders, but he'd had a persistent headache for several days now and he was finding it difficult to eat. When he'd had a mouth full of conflicting flavours all day, the last thing he wanted was to add more to them.

It was driving him mad. This was why he'd taken leave of absence from the police in the first place; this, and having to split from Sonia and the kids.

He let his gaze scan across the photographs on the board. He'd never really thought about it before, but in the same way that all babies share similar features so all elderly people do as well. It was as if everyone is born the same and dies the same, and the bit in between is where we have the chance to distinguish ourselves from the rest. The correspondences were more marked than the differences: white hair, liver spots on the hands, skin that had sagged into set folds beneath the chin, eyebrows that had been pencilled in, bags beneath the eyes, faded, cloudy irises. Something told Lapslie that if he ever managed to catch his killer, he could put her photograph up there and it would just blend in with the rest.

Some of the photographs had names written in beneath them: Violet Chambers, of course; Daisy Wilson; Deirdre Fincham; Alice Connell; Rhona McIntyre; Kim Stothard; Wendy Maltravers – identified by a combination of medical records, dental records and clues found about their bodies. Not missing persons records, of course – although that was a key factor in identifying most murder victims, it was no help here. Each of the dead women was actually still out there as far as the system was concerned. They were all still claiming benefits, paying their Council Tax, receiving rent from the properties they had moved out of, filling out their tax returns and sending the occasional postcard or Christmas card to the neighbours they had left behind.

'Everybody is dead who should be alive,' he murmured to himself.

Where the first Perspex board had no lines linking the photographs, the second one had nothing but lines drawn all over it, with cryptic notes written alongside the lines. It was a map of the financial arrangements: direct debits and standing orders, payments in and out. Each node on the board was an account in a bank or a building society, and each line showed money being transferred. And there was nothing, in that complex web of finance, to identify the spider in the middle. There was no central account to which the others drained their money. Every so often there was a dotted line leading away from the web, like an anchor line, marking where cash had been taken out of one or other of the accounts – hundreds of pounds in most cases, sometimes thousands – but it was never in the same place.

On the other side of the board, a map of the Essex area had been blu-tacked in place. Red stickers marked where cashpoints had been used to remove money from the accounts. There were clusters of stickers, but nothing that would indicate that their killer lived in a particular place.

Lapslie caught the eye of one of the passing constables. 'Who's responsible for updating this board?' he asked.

'PC Swinerd, sir,' the girl said in a smoke-filled voice.

'Can you send them over?' Lapslie asked. He wasn't entirely sure he could remember who PC Swinerd was.

He turned out to be a blond lad with a receding hairline. 'Sir?' he said as he approached. His voice was gooseberries and cream.

'These stickers – they're not ordered in any particular way?' He frowned. 'Sir?'

'There's no numbering on them to indicate which ones were the earliest transactions and which were the latest ones.'

'Trouble was, sir, I was putting the stickers on while the information was still trickling in. The banks haven't been very co-operative, and we're having to keep getting warrants signed off for each victim's accounts as they're identified. Until all the transactions are shown we don't know what the very first or very last transactions are, and so we can't number the ones in between.'

'And there are still six victims not identified?'

'That's right, sir.'

Lapslie thought for a moment. 'We might never identify them, that's the problem. Can you write numbers on these stickers – "1" for the first, and whatever the highest number is for the most recent. We can always change the numbers later, if more information comes in.'

'Sir,' the PC said. He looked sceptical, probably at the amount of work he was being asked to do, but he walked away without argument.

'One more thing,' Lapslie called after him. 'Put green stickers on to mark where the victims' houses were.'

'Yes, sir,' PC Swinerd called back.

Emma Bradbury walked in as PC Swinerd walked away. She caught Lapslie's eye, and came over.

'Boss, we've got preliminary autopsy results in from Doctor Catherall. She's really pulled the stops out. Apart from the disfiguration on the right hand of all the victims, there's no signs of violence, but the toxicology reports suggest that poison was involved in at least five of the deaths.'

'Only five?'

'The other bodies are too decayed. The reports point out that some poisons degrade over time to the point where they can't be detected.'

'So – what poisons did they detect?' he asked.

Emma consulted her list. 'Pyrrolizidine alkaloid,' she read, stumbling over the words, 'andromedotoxin, taxine, cyanogenic glucoside, a complex terpene that can't be properly identified. And colchicine, of course, from Violet Chambers.'

'No strychnine? No cyanide? No warfarin?'

'Not so far. None of the classics.'

Lapslie thought for a moment, remembering back to the garden next to the house where all the bodies had been discovered. The Garden of Death, as he thought of it.

'Get back to Doctor Catherall,' he said. 'I want to know if any of those toxins can be obtained from common or garden plants. Remember that colchicine comes from the meadow saffron.'

'Yes, boss. How could I forget?'

Lapslie looked around the incident room again as she walked off. Everyone seemed to be busily engaged in urgent activity. He left before the chatter and the clatter overcame him.

Sitting in the Quiet Room with the door closed, he gradually let himself relax. In his mind, a picture of the killer kept forming; vague, blurred, but definitely there. She was almost obsessively methodical, for instance. The way she had arranged the finances of her victims indicated that she could keep a complex series of facts in her head at one time, and the way she sent postcards and Christmas cards after the event suggested that she kept detailed records. She didn't just kill and move on. No, she kept the plates spinning, kept all of her victims alive. Did she, in some sense, believe that if she kept them alive then they weren't really dead?

Bacon trickled across his tongue before he registered the knock on the door. He turned his head. Emma Bradbury was standing there. He gestured to her to enter.

'Doctor Catherall says that all of the poisons can be easily made up from sufficient quantities of plants. She kept talking, and I couldn't make notes fast enough, but I got the impression that some of the plants were common or garden – as it were – and others were rather more obscure. Specialist items, as it were.'

'That house where the bodies were found is our killer's base of operations, then,' Lapslie said grimly. 'She keeps going back there, not only to drop off fresh bodies but also to obtain her raw materials. I think that garden is our murder weapon.'

'The garden?'

'Get one of the constables to get in touch with a botanist. I want them to go through that garden and work out which plants are poisonous, which *part* is poisonous and what the poison is.'

Emma looked baffled. 'Where do we get a botanist from?'

Lapslie shrugged. 'A university or a garden centre, wherever. Get hold of Alan Titchmarsh, for all I care. Just get an expert in that garden. And make sure someone is keeping watch on that house. I want everyone who visits it checked out, postmen and door-to-door salesmen included.'

'Yes, boss. Oh, and PC Swinerd was looking for you. He says he's finished with the map.'

As Emma left, Lapslie took a deep breath and slipped another breath tablet into his mouth before leaving the Quiet Room and heading back to the incident room.

The Perspex board with the financial spider's web was still rotated so that the map showed, but there were green stickers amongst the red ones now, and the red stickers had numbers on them. Lapslie stood a little way away and just tried to take the information in. It hadn't been obvious before, but now he could see there were clumps of red stickers around where the green ones were. It made sense: the killer got rid of a victim and moved into their house for a while, taking on their iden-tity, and while she was there she had to take money out of whatever accounts she controlled. She may have used different cashpoints for safety, but she obviously didn't want to travel too far. Or perhaps she couldn't travel too far. Whatever the reason, she stayed within a few tens of miles of what was, for a while, home.

There was one cluster that didn't have a green sticker as its centre.

Lapslie moved closer, feeling excitement stirring within him. If the killer used her latest victim's house as a base, then a cluster of red stickers with no green sticker might indicate where the latest victim was.

Or would be.

Squinting, he checked the numbers written on the red stickers in that clump. They were all high numbers. Quickly, he scanned the rest of the board. There were no higher numbers anywhere else. Those transactions were the most recent ones.

She was there! He'd located his killer.

He focused on the map behind the dots. East and north of London. The area that used to be known as the Tendring Hundreds – a name that lingered on in the name of the local council and the local newspapers. Clustered around the coast: Clacton, Frinton, Walton and Leyston.

He had her. Or, at least, he knew where she was.

He turned around to face the incident room. 'All right – pay attention!' he yelled, cutting across the general commotion and, for the first time in a long time, causing a flare in his mouth that didn't correlate to any known fruit, vegetable or meat. The taste of his own voice, shouting. 'There's a good chance our killer is located on the east coast, somewhere in Essex. That's where all the most recent financial transactions have taken place, but none of the victims so far identified have had houses there. I want a list of all hotels and guest houses along that stretch of coast, running back, oh, twenty miles inland, and I want to know if they have rented rooms for more than two weeks to a lone woman over sixty. I want every estate agent in that area contacted and I want a list of all flats or houses that have been rented out in the past six months to a lone woman over sixty. And I want it *now*. Remember, this woman is probably stalking her next victim while you're working. She's getting to know her, taking over her life, finding out everything she can before she poisons her. She might be slipping that poison into a cup of tea right now. We don't have any time to waste. Get on with it!'

Emma Bradbury had come in while he was shouting. Now, as the noise in the incident room suddenly ramped up, she crossed the room to where he was standing.

'There's always the chance that one of the unidentified victims has a house in that area,' she said. 'The murder might already have happened.'

'And a meteorite might suddenly wipe out this police station in a freak accident,' he riposted. 'But we still come in every day. We live our lives regardless. We can't plan for what might or might not happen. If we're lucky, we'll find her. If we're not, we won't. That's how it goes.'

She looked at him appraisingly. 'He said you never give up,' she said softly, as if vocalising some internal thought.

'Who said?'

Emma's face suddenly tightened. 'Nobody,' she said. 'Just a conversation I was having. Canteen talk.'

Lapslie stared at her for a few moments more, aware that something was going on but unsure what it was. 'Okay,' he said. 'Let's crack on. Keep the team on their toes – I want updates every hour on how that list is going.'

Emma nodded, and walked away. Before Lapslie could move, one of the PCs in his team – Swinerd, he thought – approached.

'Message from the Chief Superintendent,' he said. 'Could you pop up to his office?'

Acting on a sudden impulse, Lapslie walked across to the

window. The incident room was on the fifth floor, and he could see down into the car park. It was filled with the kinds of cars that police officers drove when they were off-duty; sporty cars: Ford Mondeos, Peugeot 406s and Saab 95s, all in nondescript colours. No Volkswagens, no Skodas, no Minis, and definitely no Volvos, which policemen generally referred to as Belgranos. It was similar to the auto factory car parks one could see from the train sometimes; row upon row of similar vehicles extending to the horizon.

And a black Lexus, parked at the end of one row. Its engine was idling; Lapslie could see vapour drifting up from the exhaust.

He looked around the incident room. Everyone was working hard, heads down, headsets on, lips moving as they spoke into the microphones. Nobody was looking at him.

He walked out of the room, unnoticed.

The lift up to the floor where Rouse's office was located seemed to take an age to arrive. When the doors opened, it was empty. He was glad. The last thing he wanted was to make small talk when he was on his way to something that felt like it might be his execution.

Part of him wanted to press the button for the ground floor, walk out of the lift, through the security door that led into the car park and just keep on going, walking away, leaving it all behind, but he couldn't do that. He needed to know what was going on. As Emma had said, he never gave up.

Rouse's PA told him he could go straight in, but his gaze was fixed on the man who was standing by Rouse's desk. Alone. The DCS was notable by his absence.

'Detective Chief Inspector Lapslie?' said the man. 'Please come in.' His voice was like disturbed earth, or leaf mould. He was still wearing that black suit with the subtle pinstripe. His hair was sandy, brushed straight back off his forehead. The bare scalp that was revealed was covered with small freckles.

Lapslie leaned over the PA. 'Is there a key to this office?' he asked. 'We might need to leave some sensitive stuff on the desk and pop out for a while.'

'Er ... yes,' she said, reaching into a drawer and bringing out a Yale key. She held it out uncertainly towards him.

'Thanks.' He took the key from her. 'I'll bring it back later, I promise.' Turning to the office, he said: 'Mr Geherty, of the Department of Justice's Prisoner Rehabilitation Unit, I presume?'

Geherty had the grace to look a little abashed. 'You've been doing your homework.'

'I don't like being followed around. And I don't like thieves.'

'We haven't been following you, Mr Lapslie, we've been following your investigation. It's been an education for us all. Shame it's got to stop.'

'It stops when we catch the murderer,' Lapslie said.

'It stops when our Minister says it stops,' Geherty responded. 'And we're not thieves, by the way.'

'You broke into Doctor Catherall's mortuary and you took the information off her computer.'

'We're Civil Servants, and the mortuary belongs to the Civil Service. No problems there, surely? And I think you'll find that there's no information missing from Doctor Catherall's computer. We merely copied it and left. We just want to be kept apprised of your progress.'

'I'm intrigued. Your department deals with integrating serial killers and other undesirables into society when they've served their sentences. Does that mean the killer of these women is one of yours? Did you give her a new identity and a new place to live, only to find that she's returned to her old habits?'

'Old habits die hard, and you can't teach a dog new tricks. Clichés, all of them, but there's a grain of truth in there.' Geherty shrugged. 'These people spend most of their lives in prison, but when their time is up they have to be reintegrated. We prepare them. We teach them how to survive in a world that's moved on in the ten, or twenty, or thirty years that have passed since they were incarcerated. We get them houses and we get them jobs as waiters, or travel agents, or on the perfume counter in Debenhams. And we evaluate them, trying to determine whether they have actually changed, or whether there's still a core of evil within them. Sometimes we get it right and sometimes we get it wrong. That's the way it goes. When it goes wrong, we have to clear up the mess.'

'"A core of evil",' Lapslie said. 'You don't blame society or upbringing, then?'

Geherty shook his head. 'Oh, I've looked into the eyes of men who have killed more people than I've ever known. I've looked into the eyes of women who have banged nine-inch nails into the skulls of their victims with hammers. I have seen evil, Mr Lapslie. Society isn't blameless, and neither is upbringing, but in the end they are catalysts. If the evil isn't there to begin with, they have nothing to work with.'

'What I don't understand,' Lapslie said, 'is why you can't just arrest them, put them on trial and bang them up when they're found guilty. Why all the Secret Squirrel palaver?'

'Because some of them aren't even supposed to have been released,' Geherty said, checking his watch. 'You know what it's like in prison. They say we're almost up to capacity; in fact, we passed capacity years ago. For every person who's sent to jail, one has to be released. Sometimes we do it by commuting sentences, or arranging for criminals to get parole when they technically shouldn't, but that's only nibbling at the problem. The real issue is the lifers cluttering up the system. The murderers who can't be released, either because there would be a public outcry or because some judge somewhere has said that life means life, and the Minister either can't or won't interfere.'

Something that Dom McGinley had told him suddenly echoed in Lapslie's head. Something about the child-killer, Myra Hindley, not having died of a chest infection at all, but living her life under a new identity somewhere in Wales.

'So you release them anyway,' he said bitterly.

'We have to. We take all the precautions we can, but life is life. Things go wrong.'

'And my killer?'

Geherty looked at his watch again. 'Time ticks away,' he said.

'Satisfy my curiosity. Who is she?'

'You've met her. Don't you remember? You were assigned to ACPO, profiling major criminals. Actually, we were considering offering you a job, but that medical condition of yours stopped us. You interviewed a number of lifers, looking to see if there was any psychological test that could be applied to tell whether someone was likely to become a killer or not. And you interviewed her.'

The taste of lychees, almost impossibly sweet and decadent in his mouth, like something rotting in treacle. 'Madeline … Poel?'

'Madeline Poel,' Geherty confirmed.

'Broadmoor. What – twenty years ago.' He remembered a middle-aged woman, small and bird-like. She had been very polite, very old-fashioned, and her voice had tasted of lychees. 'It was back towards the end of the Second World War. Her grandmother had gone mad and killed all of Madeline's sisters and brothers in the back garden of their house, snipping their fingers off with a pair of garden secateurs and watching them bleed to death. Madeline only survived because her mother came back from the local factory where she was working. The police were called, and while they were making their way over, Madeline made a drink for her grandmother out of some of the berries in the garden. She told her grandmother that it was sarsaparilla, but it was something toxic. Her grandmother died before the police could take her away. Everyone thought it was an accident, just Madeline trying to be helpful, but over the next few years Madeline started acting stranger and stranger and ten or twelve old ladies in the village died in exactly the same way. It was as if she'd decided that all old ladies were dangerous, and she had to get rid of them. The logic of a girl who'd been driven insane by watching her family killed in the most horrific way by the woman who was meant to be protecting them. After a while someone cottoned on, and she was sent away. Committed to Broadmoor.' His mouth was flooding with that dry, metallic taste as his voice got louder. 'She died fifteen years ago of a heart attack – at least, that's what the newspapers said – but she never died at all! Is that what you're telling me? You actually *released* her into society?'

'Because we didn't think she posed a threat any more. And because we needed the space.' Geherty suddenly looked tired. 'It was before my time.'

'That's no excuse.'

'That's not an excuse – that's an explanation. Her death was faked – we even made up a tombstone at a church near where she grew up – and a new identity was created for her. We got her a job waitressing in Ipswich, and a nice flat. And we watched her – extensively for three months, then intermittently after that. And then, when she thought we weren't watching carefully enough, she vanished. Turns out she'd spent several months crafting a new identity, and she just slipped out of the one we'd created for her and into the one she'd created for herself. We've been looking for her ever since.'

'And I'm looking for her now. We should work together.'

Geherty shook his head. 'The only reason you're looking for her is because we asked Chief Superintendent Rouse to bring you in on the case. You'd known her. You'd talked to her. If anyone had an insight into how her mind worked, it was you.'

'So let me catch her.'

'You've located her. That's all we need. If you arrest her now, she goes to court and it all spills out. If we catch her, she vanishes. Forever.'

'That's not justice.'

'No, but it's *just*.'

Lapslie gazed at Geherty. 'I can't let that happen,' he said.

Geherty nodded. 'I'm not asking you to,' he said. 'I'm telling you. Or rather, Detective Chief Superintendent Rouse is currently taking a call from my Minister telling him to put a stop to this case. It's over. We'll take it from here.'

'Over my dead body,' Lapslie snapped.

'No – over your dead career,' Geherty said, and smiled.

CHAPTER SEVENTEEN

'Are you feeling better?' Eunice's voice boomed from the kitchen.

Sitting in Eunice's sparse front room with a cup of tea clutched in her hands, Daisy's stomach was churning. All she could see in her mind was the graveyard.

The churchyard and the gravestone.

The gravestone with the name on it: Madeline Poel.

'I'm ... not sure,' Daisy said. It sounded to her as if her voice was coming from a long way away. Or perhaps a long time ago. Something was wrong with her ears: everything sounded muffled, distant, unimportant. Her hands were trembling.

'Perhaps I should call the doctor?'

'No.' She swallowed, trying to ease the feeling in her ears, but it would not shift. 'No, I'll be fine. I think it was just the sun.'

Daisy did not want to think about Madeline Poel, but now that she had seen the name on the gravestone she found that she could not stop. She felt dizzy and breathless, the way she imagined Eunice's dog, Jasper, was feeling now, with his food dosed with poison. Unbidden, unwelcome, faces were appearing in her mind. Faces and names.

So many names.

Before Daisy Wilson there had been Violet Chambers, and before Violet Chambers there had been Annie Moberley, and before Annie Moberley there had been Alice Connell, and before Alice Connell there had been Jane Winterbottom, and before Jane Winterbottom there had been Deirdre Fincham, and before

Deirdre Fincham there had been Elise Wildersten, and before Elise Wildersten there had been Rhona McIntyre, and before Rhona McIntyre there had been someone whose name was now lost to the past, and another before her, and another before her, all just shadows in the darkness now, but before all of them, at the very beginning of it all, there had been Madeline Poel.

Daisy sat in the chair in Eunice's front room, rocking gently to and fro. Tea slopped from the cup into the saucer, and from the saucer onto the floor, but she didn't notice. The past, long denied, had her in its grip.

'Daisy?' Eunice was standing beside her. 'Daisy, my dear, whatever is wrong?' She took the cup and saucer from Daisy's hands and placed them on a nearby table.

'I used to live here,' Daisy said quietly. 'I had quite forgotten, but I used to live here when I was a child. My father had a house near the Naze, and I used to go to school in the town. I thought there was something strange when I came back. I still recognised some of the buildings, and the streets, and the pier, and the church. But a lot of things have changed. It is as if I can see the town the way it was, and the way it is, both at the same time. If I tilt my head, or narrow my eyes, I can even see them both at once. Isn't that strange?'

'Daisy, I think you need to lie down. Come on, let's take you up to the spare room. You can stay here tonight.'

Eunice led Daisy upstairs and eased her down on a single bed with white sheets and a pale blue duvet. Daisy was disoriented enough that she failed to take in anything of what she saw. Eunice took Daisy's shoes off and swung her legs onto the bed. 'Sleep for a while,' she said. 'You'll feel better when you wake up.'

'My handbag ...' Daisy murmured.

'I'll get it.' Eunice went downstairs and returned, a few moments later, with Daisy's bag. She put it on a chair beside the bed, closed the curtains and left.

Daisy reached out and grabbed the handbag from the chair. Opening it up, she fished around inside until she found what she was looking for. And then, holding the secateurs close to her chest, she laid her head back on the pillow and slept.

And she dreamed about Madeline Poel and a garden in summertime, long, long ago ...

The green lawn was still dappled with shadows of rust-coloured blood, although Madeline's brothers and sisters had been taken away some time before. Carried away, limp and helpless, hands trailing down. Hands that seemed strangely deformed.

She knew that she wouldn't be seeing them again. Even though they had looked like they were sleeping, their eyes were open, staring up at the bright, bright sun. And their eyes were dry. Dry and wide.

The blades of grass were stuck together in clumps by the blood. It reminded Madeline of the way her hair went sometimes when she'd got sap in it from the trees in the garden: matted and gummy and impossible to brush out. She didn't know how they were going to clear up the garden. Perhaps they were going to wait until the rain came. Nobody seemed worried about the garden. Instead they were clustering around her mother and her grandmother, or just standing around saying nothing.

Madeline stood in the shade of a bush, fingering the ripe red berries. The poisonous berries. Every so often she glanced over at where her mother was sobbing in the arms of a neighbour. People were standing around the garden as if they didn't quite know what they were doing there. And none of them were paying any attention to her.

Off to one side her grandmother was sitting in a cane chair by the table. A policeman was sitting with her and another one was standing behind her. The policeman sitting with her was asking her questions, but she wasn't replying. She was just twisting her fingers in the material of her cardigan, making tight little spirals of cloth, her face an impassive mask hiding something feral underneath.

Her grandmother had done something bad. Madeline

knew that, although she didn't understand exactly what the bad thing was. Her grandmother often did bad things. She hit Madeline and her brothers and sisters when her mother was working. She pretended to Madeline's mother that she didn't, but she lied. Sometimes she twisted their arms behind their backs, or hit them with branches, and then screamed at them that if they told their mother she would hurt them even more. And now she had, even though they never told a living soul.

Madeline took a handful of berries from the bush and crushed them slowly in her hand. The juice ran out between her fingers, red and slow, falling to the ground where it stuck the blades of grass together.

Madeline glanced over to where the tea party had been set up and then forgotten. The cups sat, ignored and forlorn, on the crisp white tablecloth.

She glanced down at her stained hands.

Perhaps her grandmother would like a drink, she thought.

Day turned into night, and dreams slipped past each other like deep-sea fish, stirring up sediment from the bottom of the ocean as they went. But as the night wore on the sediment settled and the fish hid themselves amongst rocks and strands of seaweed. By the time the sun rose and poked intrusive fingers through the gap between the curtains, Daisy Wilson had forgotten who she had been, and remembered only who she was now.

Eunice brought her a cup of tea while she was still in bed.

'How are you feeling?' she asked.

'I'm as weak as a kitten. What happened?'

'You had some kind of a fit. I think it must have been the exertion of the walk to the church, and the sun. You overdid it. Poor thing.'

'I suppose you must be right.' Daisy tried to remember what had happened the day before, but the attempt made her uneasy.

'Could you manage some breakfast?' Eunice asked.

'Feed a cold and starve a fever,' Daisy replied. 'Perhaps

just a cup of tea and a slice of dry toast. I'm sorry to be a burden.'

'No burden,' Eunice said, as she headed for the door. 'It's nice to have someone around the place. I do get lonely.' She stopped and looked back. 'I'll leave the Arts and Crafts Centre closed today. I think you need to rest.'

'Nonsense,' Daisy said. 'God tempers the wind to the shorn lamb. I'm sure it will be a quiet day, and pottering around will give me time to recover.' She paused momentarily. 'Perhaps I could lie here for a while this morning and then join you later in the barn. I am still feeling a little unsteady.'

After breakfast, Eunice opened up the Arts and Crafts Centre and Daisy, having first made sure that Eunice was out of the way, spent her time making an inventory of the items in Eunice's bedroom and the spare room. She had long suspected that Eunice was a diary keeper – all artistic people kept diaries, in her experience – and she found it within a few minutes, in a drawer of the bedside cabinet. Found *them*, in fact, for there were multiple volumes going back years. Flicking through the most recent one, Daisy realised that this was all she really needed, apart from the financial records in the barn. Everything Eunice thought, believed or experienced was in there. Every memory was preserved like a flower pressed between the pages of a book. She didn't need to spend time pumping Eunice for information now – she had it all. Everything that was Eunice was now accessible to Daisy.

Which meant that there was really no reason to keep Eunice alive any more.

Determinedly, Daisy set out from Eunice's house – soon to be her house – for the barn which housed the Arts and Crafts Centre just across the way. She still felt light-headed, but she had work to do and there was no point moping around in bed. She had to up the dose of grated apricot kernels that she was putting in Jasper's food and see how long it took him to die. That way, she could calculate the precise dose needed to kill Eunice.

In fact, Jasper died three days later.

He had been breathless and twitchy for two of those days, during which Daisy progressively increased the dose of grated apricot kernels that she was sprinkling over his food. On the morning of the third day he lay in his basket in the back of the barn, unwilling or unable to move his hind legs.

'Poor angel,' Eunice murmured, bending down to stroke his head. 'Poor, poor angel. We shall call the vet, yes we shall.'

'Let me,' Daisy said. She went to the phone and made a great play of pressing the buttons with one hand whilst her other hand unplugged the cable from beneath the phone. 'Hello?' she said to dead air. 'Is that the Tendring Veterinary Surgery? I need an urgent appointment for a dog that's having difficulty breathing.' She paused for effect. 'It *is* an emergency, yes. Nothing until tomorrow? Nothing at all?' She sighed. 'Very well. We'll bring him then. The name is Jasper. Sorry – yes, I see. The owner's name is Eunice Coleman. C-O-L-E-M-A-N. Yes, thank you.' She turned to Eunice with a mournful face as she put the phone down. 'They don't have any appointments until tomorrow afternoon. They suggest keeping Jasper warm and letting him have plenty of fluids.'

Eunice's eyes were heavy with tears. 'I don't know what I would do without Jasper. He's my constant companion. He's everything to me.'

'There is a time for every purpose under heaven,' Daisy said. 'If it is Jasper's time, then we can do nothing but make him comfortable, and be with him. And when he is gone, then *I* will be your constant companion.' *Until you in turn die, breathless and paralysed,* thought Daisy, but she kept the thought to herself.

Jasper's breath came slower and slower. At some stage during the morning, while Eunice was fussing about, finding blankets to put over him, he breathed no more.

Daisy, in contrast, breathed a sigh of relief. She had hated that little monster. Every dog had its day, that's what they said, and this particular dog's day had passed. And now Daisy had a good idea how much of the grated apricot kernels she needed in order to kill Eunice. It also looked as if the death would be mess-free, based on the way that Jasper had just slipped away. No vomiting, no diarrhoea, nothing to clean up. After the problems she'd had last time, Daisy was grateful.

Eunice sobbed inconsolably over Jasper's body. As Daisy had hoped, the dog's death had sent her into a spiral of grief which, if Daisy was any judge, would leave her even more dependent on the only person she had left.

Daisy took Jasper's body outside in a wooden box left over from a delivery some time in the past. She promised Eunice that she would take the body to the vets, and ensure that he had a decent burial. In fact, Daisy intended only to throw the box over the nearest wall when she left. She wanted as little to do with the dog now that it was dead as she had when it was alive.

Eunice spent the rest of the day lying down in her house, behind the barn. Daisy closed the Arts Centre down and joined Eunice in the house. While Eunice was sleeping, Daisy spent her time going through drawers and looking at photographs. All grist to the mill.

Later she checked in on Eunice. The woman was still asleep, snoring with a sound like bubbles forcing their way through mud. Daisy sat down on a chair beside the bed for a while, watching Eunice's face: absorbing every wrinkle and pore, every stray hair and mole. In sleep, Eunice's muscles slackened, gravity pulling the soft tissue downwards so that it seemed as if her flesh were slowly sliding off the skull beneath and pooling on the pillow. Her complexion was dry and over-powdered. The skin around her rouged lips was marked with thousands and thousands of hair-fine vertical chasms, like minuscule razor cuts. The signs of old age. The signs that the flesh was beginning to give way.

Daisy spent some time trying to twist her lips into the same shape as Eunice's; lower lip thrust forward, ends turned down, slightly parted. It wasn't that she had any delusion that she would gradually start looking like Eunice once she had taken on her identity; it was more that she wanted to fix the woman's face in her mind now, while she still could. When she was *being* Eunice, when she *was* Eunice, she wanted to be different from Daisy, from Violet and from all the ones that came before. And the best way to do that, she had found, was to hold the face in the memory, and never to look in mirrors.

Later, she rose from the chair and went downstairs to the kitchen. The percolator sitting fiercely on the marble surface frightened her, but she needed to master it. She suspected that the grated apricot kernels had a bitter taste, and she needed to mask it somehow. Strong coffee seemed like a good idea.

Girding her courage, she approached the device and tentatively pulled the glass jug out from where it sat on a circular metal hot plate. It came out surprisingly easily. Emboldened, Daisy examined the funnel-like arrangement that sat above where the jug went. There was a flap in the top which, when opened, revealed an opening where water probably went. Below that was a curved section that swung out when Daisy pulled on a projecting handle, revealing a plastic mesh filter, still damp from the last time Eunice had washed it. So – water in the top, coffee grounds in the filter, and jug underneath.

Chirpier, now she had worked out how the percolator functioned, Daisy filled the jug with water and poured it into the top of the machine. Opening a few cupboard doors, she eventually found a Portmeirion-design porcelain jar with a cork lid that proved to contain ground coffee and a plastic spoon. Before she put the coffee in the filter she reached into her handbag and retrieved the Tupperware container she had brought with her. A spoonful of coffee, then a spoonful of ground apricot kernels, then a spoonful of coffee, then a spoonful of ground apricot kernels. The filter was half-full, and as Daisy was uncertain how much coffee to put in for a strong cup, she spooned in another measure of each, just for good luck. Pushing the filter holder back into the machine, she hunted around for a moment before finding a switch on the base of the percolator. When she pressed it, the switch lit up amber. Within moments she could hear the swooshing of steam from somewhere inside, followed by a reassuring *plup plup plup*. Coffee trickled into the jug in a thin stream. Coffee, and something else.

The kitchen began to fill with the rich, spiky aroma of fresh coffee, undercut with something drier and more bitter. Daisy sniffed, then quickly backed away. It hadn't occurred to her, but what if the fumes from the apricot kernels were fatal? That would be the ultimate irony – to be killed by her own poison!

Daisy stayed in the front room for ten minutes, until the sounds of coffee percolating had ceased. When she was sure that there was nothing else coming out of the machine she went back into the kitchen, holding her breath all the while, and opened the window behind the sink. A few minutes should blow any fumes safely away.

Daisy removed the jug from the hot plate, dislodging a final drip of coffee from the filter arrangement above. It fell onto the hot plate, hissing for a moment or two as it boiled away, leaving a faint trace of dry residue behind.

An oily film covered the surface of the coffee, reflecting the sunlight from the kitchen window in murky rainbows. Daisy swirled the jug around, hoping to mix it in, but the oil just circulated like something alive.

Daisy poured a mug of coffee for Eunice – a mug rather than a cup because she wanted the dose to be as high as possible. She debated putting milk in the mug, but she didn't want to dilute the poison any further. Eunice alternated in the way she took her coffee; sometimes with milk, sometimes without, depending on how she was feeling. She always took it with sugar, however, so Daisy carefully stirred two large spoonfuls into the drink.

Placing the mug of coffee on a tray, Daisy was just about to take it upstairs when a thought struck her. Biscuits! If Eunice had a biscuit with her coffee, it might mask whatever aftertaste was left by the apricot kernels.

When she got to the bedroom, Eunice was sitting upright. She was looking brighter than she had before.

'You're a marvel,' she said to Daisy. 'I really don't know what I would do without you. Now that poor Jasper is gone, I'm not sure how I'll survive. He gave me the strength to keep going.'

'Leave everything to me,' Daisy said. 'Let me be your strength. Now, drink your coffee and sleep for a while. I'll check on you later.'

Daisy watched for a while, but Eunice just rested her head back against the headboard and closed her eyes. Daisy didn't want to push her into drinking the coffee; knowing Eunice as she now did she knew that the woman just got more and more stubborn if she felt she was being ordered around. She had to want to drink the coffee herself.

Daisy left her alone, and wandered along to the back bedroom, where Eunice kept her clothes on a long metal rail that she had painted, at some earlier time, in a Gypsy-like pattern of red and yellow flowers on a glossy black background. A full-length mirror had been propped against one wall. Daisy ran her hands along the clothes: frilled blouses, long skirts, kaftans and all kinds of what Daisy considered to be 'artistic' clothes. She would have to get used to them, though. When she became Eunice Coleman, she would have to wear clothes like that. Not because anyone would mistake her for Eunice, but because she was going to *become* Eunice and Eunice wore different clothes from Daisy, just as she moved differently and talked differently. It was as simple as that.

After half an hour, Daisy went to check on Eunice. The woman was asleep again, breathing heavily through her mouth. The coffee mug was empty.

On a whim, Daisy returned to the back bedroom. Selecting some clothes from the rack that she thought might just fit her, she held them up against her body and looked at herself in the mirror.

She glanced at the door. It was a risk, but she wanted to see what she looked like. She wanted to practise being Eunice.

She stripped quickly and dressed herself in the new clothes.

They were on the large side, but she could take them in. And besides, artistic people wore baggy clothes, did they not?

Daisy felt edgy in Eunice's clothes while the woman was still in the house. She moved quietly along the landing and peered around the bedroom door, just to check on the progress of the poison.

The bed was empty.

Daisy rushed into the room, checking the other side of the bed just in case Eunice had fallen out and was lying hidden, but there was nobody there. Eunice had vanished.

Downstairs, the doorbell rang.

CHAPTER EIGHTEEN

Standing in Detective Chief Superintendent Rouse's office, Mark Lapslie gazed into the mild brown eyes of Martin Geherty. The expression on Geherty's face was calm, almost clinical, as he stared back at Lapslie.

Lapslie wondered where DCS Rouse had gone. Geherty was inhabiting Rouse's office as if he owned it. Perhaps, given his senior position in the Department of Justice, he did. But whatever the reason, Rouse wasn't around to support his subordinate. He'd obviously made his choice on how best to climb the slippery pole of promotion. And, not for the first time in his career, Lapslie was on his own.

'We're not giving you a choice, DCI Lapslie,' Geherty said with surprising gentleness. 'You can drop the investigation now, of your own volition, or you can have it dropped for you, but either way we are taking over, and we are going to recover Madeline Poel ourselves.'

'And what makes you think you can have my investigation dropped?' Lapslie said, although he already knew the answer.

'You've already got a reputation for instability, thanks to this neurological condition of yours. We can have you removed on medical grounds. Any evidence you've amassed will just … go missing. Misfiled somewhere. It happens all the time.'

Lapslie walked across to the window and gazed out. Far below, the black Lexus was still idling impatiently. 'You arranged things that I'd get picked for this case from the start, didn't you?'

He saw Geherty nod, reflected in the glass of Rouse's office window. 'We did. Our psychologists put together a list of key elements of any crime that Madeline Poel was likely to commit. Based on her history and her mental state, they felt that she would be likely to murder elderly ladies who reminded her of her abusive grandmother, probably poisoning them using something natural, like berries or mushrooms, given that's the way she killed her grandmother in the first place. They also felt that she was likely to mutilate them in some way, probably by cutting their fingers off – visiting upon them the same mutilation her grandmother carried out on her brothers and sisters. There was a strong chance that she would keep changing identities – running further and further away from the child who had seen those terrible things, and running also from the knowledge that she was, in some horrible way, repeating the crimes of her grandmother. Based on that profile, we arranged for the police computer to throw your name up if any crime that met at least one of those criteria was reported. We wanted you to be put in charge of the investigation.'

'Why? Just so you could take it away from me at the last moment?'

'No – because you had the best chance of finding her for us. You had actually met Madeline Poel. You had talked to her.'

'So had your psychologists.'

Geherty shrugged. 'But they couldn't take part in an investigation without giving the game away. You were the only person who could look for Madeline Poel without *knowing* he was looking for her.'

'And yet you kept trying to stop me – taking away my resources, making things as difficult as you could. Either you wanted me to find her or you didn't.'

'We wanted you to find her, but only you. We didn't want the full force of the law descending on wherever she's hiding. You had to be made to walk a fine line – just enough resources to find her, but not to get to her before us.'

'That's madness,' Lapslie said levelly.

'Welcome to my world.'

Lapslie turned away from the window to face Geherty. 'It's

a slippery slope, isn't it? You start off by covertly preparing murderers for release into an unsuspecting society, then you have to cover up their crimes when they fall back on their natures, and then ... what, exactly? You've already faked their deaths and constructed new identities for them, so you can't just rearrest them and try them again. That would give the whole game away. Do you end up having to kill *them* as well, just so the knowledge about this whole prisoner rehabilitation programme doesn't get out? Is that *right*? Is that *just*?'

Geherty shrugged. 'Fortunately it's never gone that far. There are places we can put them, if they slip back to their old ways. The U.S. Government are happy to let us add one or two people to the roster at one of the para-legal detention centres they run, for instance, so long as we turn a blind eye to whatever extraordinary rendition flights touch down for refuelling at our airports. It's ... convenient.'

'And it's evil.'

'No,' he said patiently. 'What *they* do is evil. What *we* do is pragmatic. If it becomes known that we deliberately release murderers into society under new identities having faked their deaths, it would bring the Government down. The Minister now, and Home Secretaries for the past twenty years, would be called to account for their actions in the Old Bailey. You cannot imagine the fallout, both politically and socially. It must not be allowed to happen.'

' "Let justice prevail, though the heavens fall",' Lapslie quoted softly.

Geherty's lips pursed: the first sign of strong emotion that Lapslie had noticed. 'I studied Classics at Oxford, DCI Lapslie. I can find a quote to match any occasion or opinion as well. And you're wasting time that I could be spending recovering Madeline Poel.'

'What about the thirteen women she's already killed? And what about the woman she's probably stalking now? Don't they deserve anything?'

Geherty flicked his head, as though dislodging a fly. 'They are dead, and they had no family or close friends. There's nobody left to get closure, and Madeline Poel will be punished by us for what she has done. What else is there?'

'The fact that you're even asking the question is proof that you're not qualified to answer it,' Lapslie said.

Geherty slipped his hand in his jacket pocket and removed a sheet of paper which had been folded, twice, into a long rectangle. 'This is a letter from DCS Rouse to you, relieving you of your responsibility for this case.' He held it out to Lapslie.

'It doesn't take force until I read it,' Lapslie said, and turned to walk out of the office.

'Don't be stupid,' Geherty snapped. 'If I have to follow you out there are a dozen witnesses out there who will see me handing this letter over.'

'The first step is always the hardest,' Lapslie said, and shut the door behind him as he exited the office. Turning, he quickly locked the door using the key he had taken from Rouse's PA earlier.

The door handle twisted as Geherty tried to open the door, then twisted again, more violently. Lapslie could hear the lock straining as Geherty threw his weight against it. He wasn't cursing or shouting, just calmly putting all his energy into trying to break the lock.

DCS Rouse's PA was watching, open-mouthed, from her desk.

'I don't know how he got into the building,' Lapslie said to her earnestly, 'but we need to keep him there until the psychiatric nurses arrive.' He leant across, lifted the receiver from her phone and pressed the button that he knew would connect it to the one in Rouse's office. Behind the locked door, which was shaking furiously, a phone began to ring. 'Keep it ringing until he answers,' Lapslie continued, 'and then leave the phone off the hook. I want to block the line.' Seeing the look in the PA's eyes, he added, 'He's known for making obscene calls from the phones of important people. Try not to listen – it'll just upset you. I'll go for help.'

He moved quickly away, taking the key with him.

As he got to the lobby, Emma Bradbury was emerging from a lift.

'Boss, I was just looking for you.'

'What's up?'

'The lists of lone elderly women in the Essex coast area that you requested have been coming in from all the hotels and estate agents and whatever that we've been calling. They're arriving by fax and email and just dictated over the phone. I've had one of the constables cross-check the list as it's been growing with the names of the dead bodies. One of them sprung straight out – Daisy Wilson. She apparently rented a flat in Leyston-by-Naze two months ago, even though she's lying dead on a slab in Doctor Catherall's mortuary.'

Lapslie nodded. 'It's where she was brought up. It's where all this started. What drove her to go back?'

Emma looked like he'd just pulled a rabbit out of a hat. 'How do you know that's where she was brought up?'

'No time to explain. I'll drive down there now. Text me the address, then clear up the loose ends here and meet me in Leyston-by-Naze. And don't tell anyone else where I'm going, or why.'

As Emma Bradbury walked away Lapslie headed out of the building and straight for his car. He reckoned he had no more than five minutes to get out of the car park before Geherty managed to get out of Rouse's office or Rouse returned and ordered the door broken down. Reaching his car, he tossed the key to Rouse's office away, gunned the engine to life and swept out of the car park, programming the satnav for Leyston-by-Naze with one hand as he steered with the other. His mobile rang eight or nine times in the next fifteen minutes, but he ignored it. Eventually, when he was on the A12 and heading east, it bleeped to indicate an incoming text message, and he tasted bitter chocolate. That would be Emma Bradbury texting

Daisy Wilson's address through to him. Or DCS Rouse suspending him. Either way, he kept driving. Time to check the message later, when he was closer to his goal. While he still had a career, he needed to find Madeline Poel.

He kept checking his rear view mirror as he drove, half-expecting to see a black Lexus keeping pace with him, but the cars behind him were anonymous and amorphous, blurred together into a general haze. His mind kept skipping between two poles; the one being Martin Geherty, hopefully still locked in DCS Rouse's office, the other being the one interview he'd had with Madeline Poel long ago.

He could hardly remember her now. He'd been working on his Masters Degree in Criminal Psychology, having been given time off from the police. His thesis was that there were certain key traits of a criminal personality that could be detected by a simple questionnaire, and he was talking to as many criminals as he could in order to try and determine what they were. His synaesthesia was helping, although he would never admit that in his final dissertation; there were certain key flavours that kept coming up when he heard criminals' voices, like base notes in perfume.

Madeline Poel had been small and polite, he remembered, but she hadn't liked to talk about what had happened that day at the tea party. She had been diagnosed as borderline psycho-pathic, with a score of thirty-two on the revised Hare's Psychopathy Checklist. She had actually offered him tea, he remembered, although there was nothing on the table in the interview room. When he said yes, just to see what happened, she poured him an invisible cup of tea from an invisible pot, then added invisible milk and invisible sugar. All the time he watched her, waiting for her to realise what she was doing, but she continued the charade, even asking him why he wasn't drinking.

When he had read in the newspapers that she had died of a heart attack he had felt relieved and sad at the same time. Relieved, because he had felt when he talked to her that she would never be able to function normally in society. Sad, because underneath it all she had been friendly and talkative. And because she had offered him tea.

'Everybody is dead who should be alive,' he whispered, 'and those who are alive *should* be dead.'

Colchester came and went, and the car drove on. Signs for Clacton and Frinton passed by. The car screamed across roundabouts with as minimal deviation from a straight line as Lapslie could manage. The landscape was flat and coloured in great swathes: the brown of ploughed earth, the green of fields that had been left to recover naturally and the eye-aching yellow of flowering rape plants. The sky near the horizon was a deeper blue, reflecting the unseen ocean. He passed tractors, overtaking them on straight stretches of road when there was nothing ahead. Signs for Walton-on-the-Naze flashed past, advertising the sports centre, the pier, the sea front. And then there was only Leyston ahead: the end of the land, the end of the trail.

Lapslie stopped in a lay-by and checked his mobile. There were several voicemails waiting for him, but he ignored them in favour of the one text, from Emma. It was an address in Leyston-by-Naze, followed by a simple message: *World is ending here – don't answer phone.*

The satnav guided him past the station and down a hill towards the centre of town. Suddenly there was nothing on his right apart from a low stone wall and the implacable sea, but then houses intervened again and he was dropping down into the town, past a tea room, a bingo hall and a seafood restaurant, and along the High Street with its collection of butchers and bakers and newsagents alternating with tattoo parlours and shops selling inflatable rings, beach balls and candy floss. He braked to a halt at a set of traffic lights, and heard sand crunch beneath his tyres.

The High Street petered out in a rash of fish-and-chip shops and pubs, and he found himself emerging into the other side of Leyston-by-Naze: past a long recreation ground and signs for the marina. The road was on a level with the esplanade now, running parallel to it and towards the looming mass of the Naze itself, the gnarled cliff face that towered above the town. This area, leading away from the town centre, was more residential, with detached and weather-beaten houses set back from the road in gardens filled with hardy, cactus-like plants that could stand the salt and the storms, and inhabited by retired and weather-beaten residents who revelled in their semi-isolation.

The satnav directed him to a road that lay in the shadow of the Naze, curled back on itself and falling gently back towards the town. A cool breeze blew off the sea, taking the edge off the warmth of the afternoon. He parked just down the street. The house was on a corner: a white-washed two-storey building with leaded glass windows and ivy trailing up the sides. He approached on foot, aware that he should be accompanied by Emma Bradbury at the very least, and a full Armed Response Team at best, but also aware that the option was no longer open to him. He was on his own.

As far as he could tell from the two front doors, nestled side by side, the house had been divided into flats: one upstairs, one down. The bell for the upstairs flat was labelled with a name he didn't recognise. That left the downstairs flat as belonging to Madeline Poel, masquerading as Daisy Wilson.

He rang the bell, and waited.

When there was no response he took a small tool from his pocket, a kind of Swiss Army knife called a Leatherman that had been recommended to him years ago by Dom McGinley, looked around to check that nobody was watching from the street, and used its folding knife attachment to force his way into the downstairs flat. It was, he decided, just the icing on the cake as far as his career was concerned. And, if push came to shove, he could always claim that he thought a crime was in progress – which it probably was. Somewhere.

He could tell from the deadening silence in the hall that the flat was unoccupied. He walked into the front room. There were possessions scattered around – a cardigan, a bowl of petals, a pile of local papers – but something about it made him think of a theatrical stage set, waiting for the actors to arrive. Whatever was there was a prop, ready to support a performance. It wasn't real.

Having quickly checked the flat over to make sure that Madeline Poel wasn't asleep in the bedroom or out in the garden, Lapslie quickly searched the place without disturbing anything. Although he found some post addressed to Daisy Wilson he found nothing that mentioned Madeline Poel, and nothing that mentioned any of the previous victims. If Madeline – or Daisy, as she now was – kept trophies, or even just the kind of details she would need in order to keep twelve previous victims apparently alive, as far as the rest of the world was concerned, then she must have it all stashed away somewhere else. It certainly wasn't in the flat.

But he did find a pile of pamphlets advertising an arts and crafts centre on the outskirts of Leyston run by someone named Eunice Coleman. For some reason, Daisy Wilson was interested in it, and that gave him one more place to try if he wanted to locate her. Perhaps Eunice Coleman was her next victim. Perhaps, by now, Eunice Coleman was her.

The arts and crafts centre was probably twenty minutes away, according to the satnav in his car. He pulled away from his parking spot and accelerated on down the road, back towards Leyston town centre.

He found it along a muddy track. There were two buildings in sight: a sad, barn-like structure that was probably the centre itself and an impressive farmhouse built of red brick sat a hundred yards or so beyond.

Lapslie turned his ignition off and got out of the car. The fan in the engine ran on for a few seconds, disturbing the silence of the countryside, then it fell silent. The only sounds were the ticks of his cooling engine and the singing of the birds.

Eunice Coleman deserved to know that she was in danger, and she might know where Madeline Poel – now calling herself

Daisy Wilson, of course – could be found. Daisy might even be there, and Lapslie was unable to think of any circumstances in which he couldn't manage to arrest her without help. She was only an old woman, when all was said and done.

He walked over to the barn. Mid-afternoon, and the arts and crafts centre should have been open, according to the times displayed on the door, but it was locked. He banged on the door, just in case, and peered through the smeared glass, but there was nobody about. He headed across to the house.

Lapslie rang the doorbell, and waited. Just as he was about to ring it again, the door opened. A woman looked at him enquiringly. She was wearing a velvet waistcoat over a frilled blouse, and a purple skirt with a fringed hem that brushed the floor.

'Mrs Coleman? Mrs Eunice Coleman?'

She nodded. 'None other,' she said. 'Can I help you?'

He waited for the taste of lychees, but there was nothing save a hint, perhaps just his imagination at work. Was this the same woman who had poured an invisible cup of tea for him in an interview room in Broadmoor? She had aged, and her hair was different. It might have been her, but it might also have been Eunice Coleman. He wasn't sure.

'Detective Chief Inspector Mark Lapslie,' he said. 'I need to talk to you. I'm looking for a woman named Daisy Wilson.'

She smiled. 'Daisy's not here right now,' she said. 'I suppose you'd better come in. I've made a pot of coffee – would you like some?'

Lapslie stepped inside the house. Shadows enfolded him. There was a smell of sickness wafting through the hall, but he didn't know where it emanated from. Perhaps Eunice was lying upstairs, dying. Perhaps this was Eunice walking down the hall in front of him. He just didn't know.

She led him into a cluttered room in which sofas and armchairs fought for space with low tables and potted plants. 'Make yourself comfortable,' she said. 'I'll just be a minute. Sorry if I'm a bit dozy, by the way – I had a strange nap this afternoon.'

She vanished off towards what he assumed was the kitchen. He listened out for movements elsewhere in the house, but there was nothing. He still wasn't sure, and he couldn't afford to get this wrong.

The woman calling herself Eunice Coleman came back into the room with a coffee jug and two cups on a tray. She seemed surprised to find him still standing. 'You're making me nervous,' she said, putting the tray onto a side table and gesturing towards the sofa. He sat, and while she poured two cups of coffee he looked around the room. There were paintings of various kinds on the walls – some landscapes, some portraits and some abstracts – and all of the chairs were covered with embroidered throws. Obviously Eunice Coleman brought her work home with her.

'Milk?' Still, that maddening uncertainty. Did her voice taste of lychees, or was he hoping too hard that it would?

'Please.'

'Help yourself to sugar.' She put the cup on another table within his reach, then sat down in one of the armchairs holding her own cup. 'So, what can I do for you, Detective Chief Inspector Lapslie?' she asked.

'About Daisy Wilson ...' he said, watching the cup in her hands. It didn't tremble.

'Mad as a box of frogs, the dear thing,' she said. 'Yes, she's been helping me out at the crafts centre. I think she's gone to the pharmacy. What did you want her for?'

'I need to ask her some questions.' He raised his cup to his lips, then paused as he watched her face.

'What kinds of questions?'

'Questions about some women she might know.'

'Perhaps I could help. Daisy doesn't talk about her friends much, but she might have mentioned their names.'

'Has she ever referred to Wendy Maltravers?'

'No.'

'Violet Chambers?'

'I don't think so. Don't let your coffee get cold, by the way.'

'Alice Connell, Rhona McIntyre, Deirdre Fincham, Kim Stothard ...?'

'I'm sure I would have remembered. They are very distinctive names.'

He raised the cup to his mouth. The steam prickled against his skin. There was something spicy about it. His lips felt hot and swollen.

Eunice Coleman was watching him intently. She hadn't drunk any of her own coffee either.

'And what about Madeline Poel?' he said carefully, and watched as her hand twitched, sending coffee splashing across her lap.

CHAPTER NINETEEN

The sudden flush of heat on Daisy's leg shocked her, making her twitch again. The cup clattered in the saucer. 'Oh dear,' she said automatically, 'Many a slip 'twixt cup and lip, as they say. I'll just go and get a tea towel. I won't be a moment.'

She stood up, hesitating for a moment, then placed her cup and saucer down on the tray and walked off into the kitchen. 'I don't believe Daisy ever mentioned Madeline Poel,' she called back to the police officer who was sitting in Eunice's living room. 'No, I don't believe she mentioned her at all. Were they friends?'

Once in the kitchen she leaned on one of the work surfaces for a few moments, trying to regain her composure. Whoever this policeman was – and he looked strangely familiar to her, as if they had met before under different circumstances – he knew too much. He knew names that Daisy herself thought she had forgotten.

Including that of Madeline Poel.

Patting herself down with a cloth, Daisy's mind was frantically going over what he had said, looking for some explanation of how he had found her. The only possible way was if he'd discovered the pamphlets advertising the Arts and Crafts Centre in her flat, and that meant she had nowhere to retreat to. Her safe haven was compromised, contaminated. She could never go back there again. The only thing that was saving her from arrest now was that the policeman thought she was Eunice Coleman. Or perhaps he wasn't sure whether she was Eunice or not and was trying to find out. Either way, she had to play along, and get out of Eunice's house as soon as she possibly could.

But where would she go? Even her special place was lost to her now; her garden, with its beautiful scents and flowers. She had to assume the police knew about it, although she couldn't think of any way they could have found out. And that meant they had also found her little tea party.

All lost. All gone.

Black despair threatened to engulf her. She leaned against the refrigerator as her legs threatened to give way. Her heart was racing, and she could feel her breath rasping in her chest. The complex web of bank accounts and building society accounts was of no use to her any more. All that money, all that security, all those identities were lost now, washed away by the tide of circumstance.

She had to be strong. She had to move forward. She couldn't have expected her luck to last forever: the pitcher goes so often to the well that it is broken at last, wasn't that what they said? She'd started with nothing before; she could do it again. She would have to cut her coat according to her cloth; things would be hard for a while, but she would survive. After all, after a storm comes a calm.

Concentrating on those old, familiar proverbs, Daisy felt her heart slow and her breathing return to something approaching normal. The policeman wouldn't be a problem for long: the moment he had mentioned her name – well, Daisy Wilson's name – she knew that she had to get him inside the house and get him to drink some of the coffee that she had so carefully prepared for Eunice. With luck, he would be comatose before he finished the cup and dead within the hour.

Which reminded her – where was Eunice? Despite the way Daisy had dosed her with cyanide she wasn't in the bedroom upstairs any more. When Daisy heard the doorbell ring she had been terrified that Eunice had staggered downstairs and was going to open the door in some kind of delirium, but there was no sign of her. Where could she have got to?

That could wait. First things first: she had to rid herself of this policeman.

Pulling open the cutlery drawer, she retrieved a butcher's knife from the plastic tray where it sat: a grey triangle of metal that came to a razor-sharp point. She didn't like the idea of using a knife, but it was a useful backup. Just in case.

She emerged from the kitchen holding a tea towel behind which the knife sat, comfortable in her hand. 'Clumsy of me,' she said. 'I do apologise.'

The policeman was holding an empty cup. He looked at her with a slight frown, twin wrinkles forming between his eyebrows.

'Oh, my dear,' she said with exaggerated concern, 'you do drink quickly. Would you like another cup?'

'No ... no thank you,' he said. She noticed with pleasure that his hand was trembling slightly, and there was a mist of perspiration across his forehead. 'The coffee's a little ... a little strong for me. I'm fine with just the one cup.'

'As you wish,' she said, sitting. One cup should be enough. She had proved that with Jasper the dog, and then again with Eunice – wherever she was. A man was a slightly unknown quantity – she had never poisoned anyone apart from women before – but she didn't think the difference in size or sex would delay things by more than a few minutes. And if it did, well, there was always the knife.

The policeman put his cup down on the table beside him. He misjudged the distance and fumbled slightly, banging the saucer hard on the varnished surface. 'I think I should be ... going ...' he said. 'Perhaps I could come back when Daisy Wilson is here.' He tried to stand, but he couldn't seem to co-ordinate his movements. His hands slipped off the arms of the chair, pitching him sideways, and he straightened up slowly. 'What's happening?' he said vaguely.

'You are probably feeling your stomach twisting,' Daisy said. She leaned back in her chair, resting the towel-wrapped knife on her lap. 'That will be your digestive system hydrolysing the cyanogenic glycosides from the apricot kernels into hydrocyanic acid. Or cyanide, if you prefer. You will start to feel increasingly tired as the cyanide is carried through your body, and you may start to vomit, although I really hope not. It's such a tedious business, clearing it up. That's the trouble with poison, though – the body always seems to want to expel it, although it's usually too late.'

'Apricots?' the policeman said.

'Apricot *kernels*,' she corrected. 'I grated them up and mixed the powder with the ground coffee. I hoped that the bitterness of the coffee would cover any taste. *Could* you taste anything? I really would like to know. I may want to use this method again, at some stage. On another old woman.'

He lurched forward in his chair, and Daisy allowed the tea towel to drop away to let the policeman see that she was holding the knife. The blade gleamed in the light. 'I suggest you stay where you are while the poison gets to work. If you try to get up, I will have to stab you, and that would be a shame.'

'Madeline,' he said. 'Madeline Poel.'

'No.' She shook her head firmly. 'There is no Madeline Poel. I am Daisy Wilson now, just as I was Violet Chambers before and I will be Eunice Coleman next. Madeline is long gone.'

'You become these people. You take on their identities.'

'I have always had a knack for imitation. I enjoy watching people, working out their little foibles and habits. And it has paid me dividends over the years.'

'But you don't do it for the money, do you?'

'The money helps,' she said, almost unwillingly. 'It makes me comfortable.' She leaned forward. 'How are you feeling, by the way? Are your joints tingling yet? Can you feel the dryness in your mouth?'

'But you aren't rich, and you never will be. You choose old ladies who won't be missed, but you also choose ones who have a small amount of money. Nothing too obvious.'

'I so dislike ostentation,' she said. 'You must be feeling the discomfort in your bowels now. That will get worse. Much worse. Again, the clearing up will be wearisome, but it will be worth it for the effect.'

'But the money isn't that important,' he pressed. 'You do it for the comfort, of course, but you could have stopped at any stage. You could have stopped when you were Rhona, or Deirdre, or Kim, or Violet, or Daisy. What was it that kept you moving?'

Daisy glanced away from him. His questions were disturbing her. She would much rather he died in silence, or at most with some groaning and gasping.

'Habit, I suppose,' she said eventually. 'Your head will be throbbing, I think. I will enjoy watching you die.'

'What were you running from?'

'Nothing. I just wanted to be safe.' She raised the knife and pointed it at him. 'We have met before, haven't we? A long time ago. I offered you tea then.'

'*What were you running from?*'

She suddenly flung her arm out, knocking the small table over with the knife and sending her forgotten coffee splashing across the room. 'My *grandmother*!' she screamed, the words tumbling out of her in a rush, almost colliding with each other. 'I was running from my *grandmother,* and what she did to me, and what she did to my sisters and my brothers, but she kept following me. Whenever I thought I'd got away from her I would turn around and see her reflection, or catch sight of her from the corner of my eye. I had to keep on running. I had to get away from her and what she did!'

'And what you did,' the policeman said. 'You killed her. You poisoned her.'

'She deserved it. She kept hurting us. And then ... and then ...' Tears were suddenly coursing down her cheeks as she remembered back to the garden, and the heat, and the way little Kate screamed and screamed as the blades of the secateurs came together and her thumb fell away, trailing a ribbon of blood behind it.

'And you ended up here. In Leyston, where it all started. Where Madeline was born.'

'What goes around, comes around,' she said slowly. 'That's what they say, isn't it? I never really understood that before, but it's true.'

'And Eunice? The real Eunice Coleman? Did you kill her as well? Did you take out on her this bizarre retribution you've been carrying out on your dead grandmother for all these years?'

'She is upstairs somewhere: comatose, as you will be. She managed to stagger out of the bedroom. I assume she is in the bathroom, or the spare room. When I have finished with you I will go and check on her.'

The policeman straightened in his chair. His face lost its slackness, its vacancy. 'We found your house,' he said. 'We're digging up your garden. The people at your tea party have all gone home, I'm afraid. It's over, Madeline. And you are under arrest for the murders of Daisy Wilson, Wendy Maltravers, Rhona McIntyre, Violet Chambers, Alice Connell, Kim Stothard, Deirdre Fincham and six other as yet unidentified women, as well as the attempted murder of Eunice Coleman.'

Daisy just gaped at the policeman. 'But – the coffee? You drank it!'

'I poured it away,' he said impatiently, 'into one of your potted plants. One of *Eunice's* potted plants.'

'No!' she screamed, and leaped at him, knife raised. He caught her arm as her body crashed against him and pushed her backwards, holding on to the knife. She staggered back, the seat of the armchair catching her beneath her knees and forcing her to sit down suddenly. 'No!' she said again, the anger replaced with denial.

'We're going upstairs,' he said. 'Eunice Coleman might still be alive up there.'

Grabbing her wrists, he hauled her up from the chair and pushed her ahead of him up the stairs to the first floor. She squirmed in his grip, but she had no strength left. She could feel her bones grinding together beneath his fingers. His rough masculinity overpowered her, rendering her helpless as he took the knife away from her and threw it across the hall. Everything she had, she had invested in other identities. There was nothing left to fight with.

The policeman moved towards the front of the house, to the master bedroom where Daisy had left Eunice, dying. He pulled Daisy along behind him. Pushing open the door, he glanced around the room, but she already knew that he would find nothing.

He pulled her after him to the next room, the spare bedroom, but it was empty as well. The bathroom was at the end of the hall, and he pushed the door open with one hand while keeping Daisy's wrist pinioned with the other. The moment the door opened, Daisy could smell the sour smell of fresh vomit.

Eunice was lying twisted in the bath. Her face was glossy with sweat. Blood was trickling from her lips where she had bitten through them. Daisy could almost see the miasma of decay and death rising up from every pore and every orifice of her body.

The policeman pushed Daisy down on the toilet seat. With a tight grip on Daisy's arm, he moved to check Eunice's pulse. He dropped Daisy's arm and quickly turned Eunice into the recovery position so that if she threw up again she wouldn't choke. Not that it would do any good. Daisy had watched enough old women die to know that Eunice was beyond all help now. The journey into death, once begun, could not be reversed.

The policeman had taken a mobile phone out of his jacket and was calling for an ambulance, and for extra police. While he was distracted, Daisy slipped quietly out of the bathroom and into the hall.

There was no escape for her now.

No, she was wrong. There was one avenue left, if she dared take it.

Moving quietly but rapidly, Daisy descended the stairs to the hall. She cast a longing glance at the front door, but where would she go? She had no car, and the police would hardly have to exert themselves to find her waiting for the bus at the bottom of the road. No, she would not demean herself by running away like that.

Instead, Daisy turned and headed toward the kitchen.

The coffee pot was still where she had left it, sitting on the hot plate, half-full of black and steaming liquid. She reached out for it and picked it up by the handle. The weight of the jug almost overbalanced her, and she had to put out her other hand and hold the worktop to prevent herself falling.

For a moment she debated pouring the coffee into a cup, placing a splash of milk and a spoonful of sugar in it, just the way she liked it, and then drinking it slowly, in a civilised manner, but she thought she could hear the sound of footsteps pounding on the stairs, so she brought the glass jug to her lips and gulped the coffee down, tipping the jug further and further back. Steam wreathed her head, bringing beads of perspiration out on her forehead. The glass burned her lips and the liquid scalded her throat, but she kept on going. She could feel a growing heat in her stomach, spreading through her abdomen. Her mouth was raw, blistered, the coffee searing her throat like acid as it poured into her body.

Someone knocked the jug from her hands, and somewhere in the distance Daisy heard it smash against the wall, but her world was consumed by the fire in her stomach now. She fell forward, trying to stop herself from retching, but the heat of the coffee had made her throat close up and she could hardly take a breath.

Hands caught her from behind and lowered her to the kitchen floor. Tears blurred her eyes. Someone was talking urgently but the words slipped past her.

She seemed to have been lying down for a long time, although she had little sense of time passing. Pain creased across her stomach and sent tendrils along her arms and legs. Shivers racked her body. Snatches of meaningless conversation drifted past her – 'The woman upstairs is dead, boss', 'Where the hell's that ambulance?', 'DCS Rouse is having kittens back at the HQ!' – but it was all remote, abstract.

What was real was the gateway ahead of her. A hedge led off to either side, but through the gap she could see flowers of every hue. Entranced, she moved towards the gateway, and was not surprised when it swung open at her approach.

A path led through the garden, and she followed it eagerly. On her left was a bed of bright blue Cuban lilies virtually dripping with poisonous glycosides; on her right a clutch of Star-of-Bethlehem plants reached their little white hands up to heaven, filled with lethal convallatoxin and convalloside. Beyond them, on both sides of the path, Daisy could make out a profusion of water arum, with its bright red berries and its roots laden with deadly calcium oxalate raphides. And around them all, the oval green leaves of ipecacuanha plants, source of the drug emetine which could take weeks to kill if enough was given, and years to recover from if too little was used.

'I *will* escape her,' she said firmly. 'I *will,*' and as her legs gave way, dropping her to the floor amongst the plants, the beautiful, beautiful plants, they reached out to enfold her with their tender stems and cover her mortal body with their eternal leaves and petals. And finally, nestled in the bosom of her beloved plants, she found the peace she had craved all those long years.

CHAPTER TWENTY

Mark Lapslie watched as Madeline Poel slowly died there on the kitchen tiles.

He watched her as the front door was smashed open behind him.

He watched her as Emma Bradbury and the local police poured into the house, surrounding him in the kitchen and also rushing upstairs.

He watched her as Eunice Coleman was brought downstairs on a stretcher attended by paramedics.

He watched until she was dead, and only then did he let Emma Bradbury lead him away, out into the open air, where the wind could finally blow the hatred and the futility and the taste of lychees and of madness away from him, leaving only the faint tang of the sea in his mouth.